EMPIRES OF THE MONSOON

RICHARD HALL has travelled throughout the Indian Ocean region as an historical writer and journalist. Born in 1925, he spent part of his boyhood in Australia, was educated at Hastings Grammar School, served in a destroyer in the Royal Navy and then went to Oxford University. After working in London on the *Daily Mail*, he lived for thirteen years in Africa where he was editor of the *Times of Zambia*. He later became the Commonwealth correspondent of the *Observer* and a columnist on the *Financial Times*. In 1986 he founded the financial and political bulletin *Africa Analysis*. He has written biographies of the Victorian explorers Sam and Florence Baker and Henry Stanley, and of the modern merchant-adventurer Tiny Rowland. He lives in Oxfordshire.

EMPIRES OF
THE MONSOON

*A History of the Indian Ocean
and its Invaders*

RICHARD HALL

HarperCollins*Publishers*

HarperCollins*Publishers*
77–85 Fulham Palace Road,
Hammersmith, London W6 8JB

www.**fire**and**water**.com

This paperback edition 1998
5   7   9   8   6   4

First published in Great Britain by
HarperCollins*Publishers* 1996
Reprinted once

ISBN 0 00 638083 2

Maps by Leslie Robinson

Part title decoration from 'The Fleet of Vasco da Gama'
illustrated in *The Portuguese in India*, Vol. 1,
by Frederick Danvers

Set in Postscript Monotype Bembo by
Rowland Phototypesetting Ltd,
Bury St Edmunds, Suffolk

Printed and bound in Great Britain by
Omnia Books Ltd, Glasgow

Dedicated to the memory of
Harry A. Logan Jr
of Warren, Pennsylvania

CONTENTS

PART THREE: An Enforced Tutelage

Contents

LIST OF ILLUSTRATIONS

Muslim merchants sail to India (from the Schefer Maqamat in the Bibliothèque Nationale, Paris, and reproduced in *Livre des merveilles de l'Inde* by Captain Bozorg fils de Chahriyar de Ramhormoz, 1883, reproduced courtesy of the Bodleian Library, Oxford)

Ivory statuette of the Indian goddess Lakshmi

Statuette of the Greek god Poseidon uncovered at the site of a 2,000-year-old trading centre in western India

Small craft in Madagascar (Rupert Parker)

Marco Polo sets out from Venice for Cathay (Hulton Getty Picture Collection)

Fantastic creatures depicted in a sixteenth-century Spanish version of *Mandeville's Travels* (Houghton Library, Harvard University)

Kubilai Khan (from *The Book of Sir Marco Polo* by Sir Henry Yule, 1903)

The Chinese Admiral Zheng He 1405–1433 (16th-century Chinese woodcut from *The Western Sea Cruises of Eunuch San Pao* by Mou-Teng)

The giraffe transported by Zheng He from Malindi to China (*The Tribute Giraffe with Attendant* by Shen Tu 1357–1434, ink and colours on silk. Philadelphia Museum of Art: given by John T. Dorrance)

The gigantic Peng or Rukh (from *Lane's Arabian Nights* vol. 3, 1863, based on a Persian original)

The fictitious Christian emperor Prestor John (from *Marco Polo: Travels* by L. F. Benedetto, 1931)

Great Zimbabwe (National Archives of Zimbabwe)

The fourteenth century ruins of Vijayanagara, the 'City of Victory' in southern India (Hutchison Library/Isabella Tree)

A colossal monolith of Narasingha, image of the Hindu god Vishnu, at Vijayanagara (Hutchison Library/Isabella Tree)

An heroic representation of Henry the Navigator (Hulton Getty Picture Collection)

Caravels and carracks sailing in the East from an early engraving (Hulton Getty Picture Collection)

The great 'pepper port' of Calicut (Mary Evans Picture Library)

The ruins of a mosque in Kilwa, on the East African coast (© John Sutton)

Afonso de Albuquerque, founder of Goa (from *Lendas da India* by Gaspar Correa, 1526)

Emperor Susenyos welcomes the Patriarch Mendes in 1626 (from Jerónimo Lobo's *Voyage Historique d'Abissine*, 1728/photo courtesy of Philip Caraman)

Fort Jesus (British Library from *Livro do Estado da India Oriental* by Pedro Barretto de Resende, 1646/British Library Sloane mss. 197.f.104)

Fort Jesus (Hutchison Library/Isabella Tree)

Tipu Sultan (© Board of the Trustees of the Victoria & Albert Museum)

A life-size model of a tiger devouring a British soldier once owned by Tipu Sultan (© board of the Trustees of the Victoria & Albert Museum)

Table Bay settlement, founded by the Dutch East India Company in 1652 (William Fehr Collection, Cape Town)

Hugh Cleghorn, Scottish professor and resolute spy (St Andrew's University Library)

German missionary Ludwig Krapf (from *Travels and Missionary Labours in East Africa* by Ludwig Krapf, 1860)

John Hanning Speke (from *Journal of the Discovery of the Nile* by John Hanning Speke, 1863)

James Grant dances with an African Queen (from *Journal of the Discovery of the Nile* by John Hanning Speke, 1863)

The Sultan of Zanzibar, Seyyid Said, in a portrait by Lt. Henry Blosse Lynch R.N. (Peabody Essex Museum, Salem)

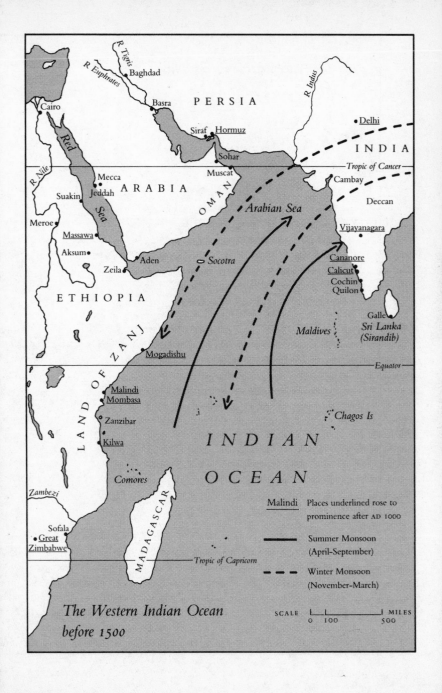

The Western Indian Ocean before 1500

SCALE

0   100   500   MILES

<u>Malindi</u> Places underlined rose to prominence after AD 1000

—————— Summer Monsoon (April–September)

– – – – – Winter Monsoon (November–March)

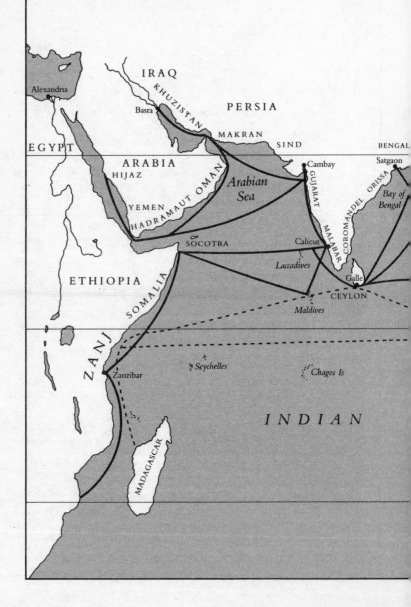

The Patterns of Eastern Seafaring

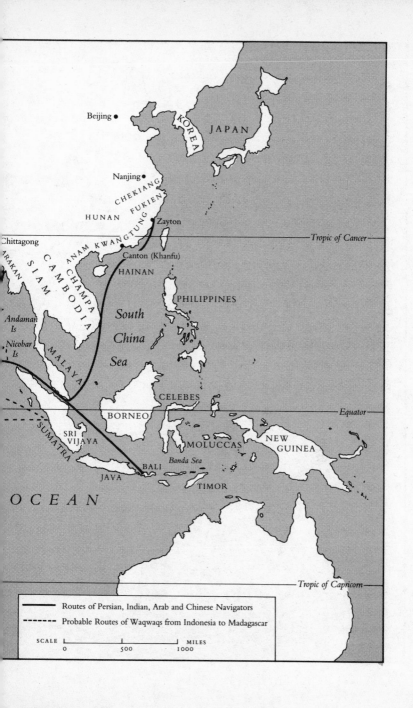

Beijing

Nanjing

CHEKIANG

HUNAN FUKIEN

Chittagong

ARAKAN

ANAM KWANGTUNG

SIAM

CAMBODIA

CHAMPA

MALAYA

Andaman
Is

Nicobar
Is

Zayton

Canton (Khanfu)

HAINAN

PHILIPPINES

South

China

Sea

KOREA

JAPAN

Tropic of Cancer

SUMATRA

SRI
VIJAYA

JAVA

BALI

BORNEO

CELEBES

MOLUCCAS

Banda Sea

TIMOR

NEW
GUINEA

Equator

OCEAN

Tropic of Capricorn

Routes of Persian, Indian, Arab and Chinese Navigators
Probable Routes of Waqwaqs from Indonesia to Madagascar

SCALE ┗━━━━━━━━━━┻━━━━━━━━━━┛ MILES
       0   500   1000

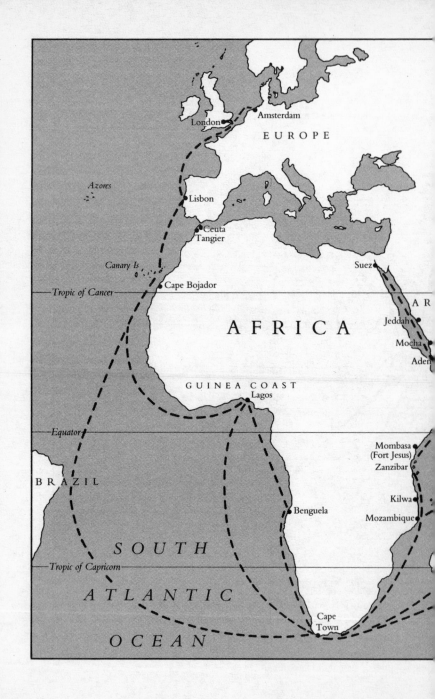

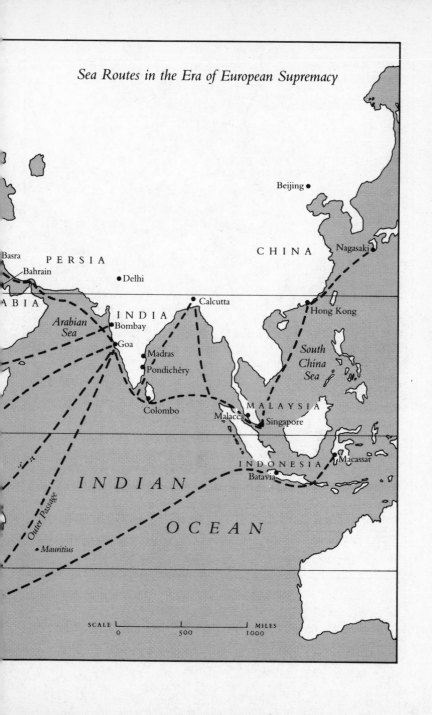

Sea Routes in the Era of European Supremacy

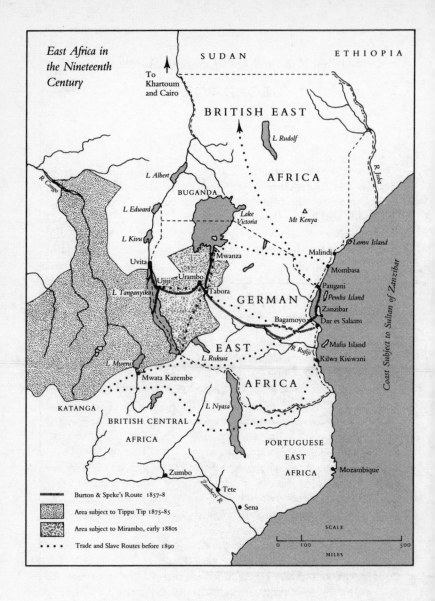

East Africa in
the Nineteenth
Century

To
Khartoum
and Cairo

SUDAN   ETHIOPIA

BRITISH EAST

L Rudolf

R Congo

L Albert

BUGANDA   AFRICA

L Edward

Lake
Victoria   Mt Kenya

L Kivu

R Juba

Uvita   Lamu Island

Mwanza   Malindi

Ujiji Urambo   Mombasa

L Tanganyika   Tabora   GERMAN   Pangani

Pemba Island

Zanzibar

Bagamoyo   Dar es Salaam

EAST   R Rufiji   Mafia Island

L Rukwa   Kilwa Kisiwani

L Mweru

AFRICA

Mwata Kazembe

KATANGA   L Nyasa

BRITISH CENTRAL

AFRICA   PORTUGUESE

EAST

Zumbo   AFRICA   Mozambique

Zambezi R Tete

Sena

Coast Subject to Sultan of Zanzibar

▦▦▦▦▦ Burton & Speke's Route 1857-8

▦ Area subject to Tippu Tip 1875-85

▦ Area subject to Mirambo, early 1880s

• • • • Trade and Slave Routes before 1890

SCALE

0   100   500

MILES

FOREWORD

Turn a map of the world upside down and the Indian Ocean can be seen as a vast, irregularly-shaped bowl, bounded by the shorelines of Africa and Asia, the islands of Indonesia, and the coast of Western Australia.[1] Unlike the Atlantic and Pacific, merging at their extremes into the polar seas, this is an entirely tropical ocean; to mention it calls up a vision of palm-fringed islands and lagoons where rainbow-hued fish dart amid the coral. That is the tourist-brochure image, but behind it lies the Indian Ocean of history – a centre of human progress, a great arena in which many races have mingled, fought and traded for thousands of years.

The earliest civilizations, in Egypt and the valley of the Tigris and Euphrates, had direct access to the Indian Ocean by way of the Red Sea and the Persian Gulf. At the hub, stretching towards the equator, lay the Indian sub-continent, itself the site of ancient cultures in the Indus valley. Since long before the time of Alexander the Great, travellers had brought back tales of the rich and voluptuous East. The emperor Trajan, arriving triumphantly at the Persian Gulf in A.D. 116, and watching mariners set sail for India, had mourned that he was too old to make the voyage and gaze upon its wonders.[2]

For almost a thousand years after the fall of the Roman empire the western side of the Indian Ocean, the focus of this book, was as much an entity as the Mediterranean, surpassing it in wealth and power. The arts and scholarship flourished there, in cities to which merchants came from all corners of the known world. There was also much turmoil, as conquering armies spawned in the remote parts of Asia swept down to overthrow old empires and impose new dynasties.

The lives of ordinary people, however, were always ruled more by nature than by great events, by the perpetual monsoons rather than by ephemeral monarchies. The word 'monsoon' comes from the Arabic *mawsim*, 'season', and ever since sailors had dared to venture on voyages across the open seas these seasonal winds had borne their ships between India and its distant neighbours. For six months they blow one way, then in the reverse direction during the other half of the year. The summer monsoon, coming from East Africa and the southern seas, is pulled eastwards by the rotation of the earth after passing the equator, so that it sweeps across India and up through the Bay of Bengal. Winds are fiercest between June and August.

The sea-captains of old might not understand why the monsoons happened (how colder air was being sucked northwards over the ocean in summer towards the hot lands of Asia, then southwards from the Himalayas and the Indian plains in winter); for them it was sufficient that the winds came on time, year in and year out, to fill their sails. For the farmers of India it was likewise enough to know that the summer monsoon would bring them rain.[3] However, on sea and land, the monsoon was always feared in its times of fury, when no vessel dared set out, when floods swept away villages, and cyclones left devastation.

It might be argued that the inescapable rhythm of this climate induced a certain fatalism among the Indian Ocean peoples. Yet the monsoon has also long been recognized as one of nature's most benign phenomena – 'a subject worthy of the thoughts of the greatest philosophers', in the words of John Ray, a seventeenth-century English scientist.[4]

Until the 'Age of Discovery', there had been a thousand years of almost total ignorance in Europe about the Indian Ocean and the lands encompassing it. Once, during the heyday of the Roman empire, a flourishing trade had existed with the East, conducted mainly by Greek mariners who had learned how to use the monsoons.[5] They brought back jewels, cinnamon, perfumes and incense, as well as silks and diaphanous Indian cloth much sought after by the women of Rome. But with the collapse of classical civilization in Europe, all the knowledge acquired by the Greeks was lost to Europeans.[6]

When medieval Europe started looking for a new route to India, to outflank Islam's barrier across the Middle East, its navigators were long thwarted by the great bulk of Africa, until the Portuguese finally rounded the Cape of Good Hope. Vasco da Gama's voyage to India and back in 1497–99 was by far the longest sea journey ever undertaken by Europeans.

This book shows how the European presence from the sixteenth century onwards changed Indian Ocean life irrevocably. Thriving kingdoms were subdued and former relationships between religions and races thrown into disarray. With the advent of western capitalism, ancient patterns of trade soon became as extinct as the dodo (which Dutch sailors had unceremoniously wiped out on the island of Mauritius). Yet although the guns of Europe could create new empires in the East, the populations there were too great to be held down permanently. What happened in the Americas was never going to be repeated in Asia. The record of European intervention and the response to it is made up of violence, depravity and courage.

Through thousands of years of change in the Indian Ocean arena, the African giant forming its long western flank was rarely anything other than a mute bystander. Its interior was *terra incognita*, its peoples excluded from fruitful dealings with the rest of the world. Since the eighth century, Africa's contact with the Indian Ocean had come under the sway of scores of Arab-ruled trading ports, strung along two thousand miles of coastline from Somalia to beyond the Zambezi river delta. These settlements looked to the sea; the interior of the continent interested them only as a source of ivory, gold, leopard-skins and slaves. For three hundred years after the arrival of the Europeans, little happened to alter that pattern.

But Africa south of the equator has been twice liberated since the mid-nineteenth century: first from its isolation, then from a colonialism which, although short-lived, seemed to have forged unbreakable bonds with the North, with Europe. Now the monsoons of history are blowing afresh, as the balance of world power swings back to the East. The start of the twenty-first century is seen as ushering in a new 'Age of Asia', in which the natural unity of the Indian Ocean can once more assert itself. This is the arena where the full potential of the peoples of sub-Saharan Africa will be put to the test.

A NOTE ON SPELLINGS

Where versions of names converted from non-roman scripts are widely recognized, they are adhered to: for instance, the spelling Mecca is used rather than Makkah, even though the latter is more exact. Likewise, the renowned sultan of Zanzibar in the second half of the nineteenth century should strictly be entitled al-Sayyid Sa'id, but his name was always 'Europeanised' as Seyyid Said. For other transliterations from Arabic the *Encyclopaedia of Islam* is generally followed, but without diacritical marks. With Chinese names the modern *pinyin* romanization has been adopted – so that the admiral formerly known in English as Cheng Ho appears as Zheng He. Most prefixes to root words in African languages are omitted for simplicity's sake.

Portuguese monarchs and princes are, in the main, referred to by the familiar anglicized versions of their names. Lesser beings are left in the original.

Geographical terms accord as far as possible with those in use at the times being written about. Thus Ceylon describes the island which became Sri Lanka in 1972. There is often a wide divergence between early European attempts at Indian names and those employed today; an example is Calicut, the once renowned port which appears on modern maps as Kozhikode.

PART ONE

A World Apart

ONE

Wonders of India, Treasures of China

Unmindful of the dangers of ambition and worldly greed, I resolved to set out on another voyage. I provided myself with a great store of goods and, after taking them down the Tigris, set out from Basra, with a band of honest merchants.
— Sinbad, starting his third journey, in *The Thousand and One Nights*

A THOUSAND YEARS AGO, a Persian sea-captain retired to write his memoirs. They made him famous in his day, although only a single copy of the text now survives, in a mosque in Istanbul. Captain Buzurg ibn Shahriyar called his book *The Wonders of India*, yet he did not limit himself to describing the civilization of the Hindus. Buzurg presented his readers with a kaleidoscope of life all round the shores of the tropical ocean across which he had sailed throughout his career. His spontaneity brings back to life the people of his time far better than any scholarly reconstruction could achieve: passengers terrified in a storm-tossed ship, merchants angry at being cheated, young men in love, proud monarchs staring down from bejewelled thrones.

He included, for amusement's sake, many fantastical anecdotes about mermaids, giant snakes which swallowed elephants, two-headed snakes whose bite killed so quickly 'there is not even time to wink', and women of immense sexual prowess. 'Buzurg' was just a nickname, meaning 'big', and he might well have earned it through his love of tall stories, rather than by being large in physique. However, his avowed aim was to take his audience on a tour – entertaining yet instructive – through many lands. Despite similarities between *The Wonders of India* and *The Thousand and One Nights*, the distinction is that Sinbad was a fictional hero, while much that Buzurg wrote stands up to historical scrutiny.

References to known characters and recorded events show that he was working on his memoirs in about the year 950 (A.H. 341 by his own Islamic calendar). He lived in the port of Siraf, at the southern end of the Persian Gulf, from whose narrow straits the Indian Ocean opened out like a fan. Just as the Romans had called the Mediterranean *mare nostrum* ('our sea') so the Indian Ocean was for Buzurg and his contemporaries an extension of the *Bilad al-Islam*, the World of Islam.

Siraf had 300,000 inhabitants, but was hemmed in by mountains. The city became like a cauldron in the summer months, and one of Buzurg's contemporaries called it the hottest place in Persia. It was also one of the richest. Fountains played constantly in the courtyards of the wealthier merchant families, and after dark the light from scented oil, burning in gilded chandeliers, shone down on divans draped with silk and velvet. Walls of the tall houses were panelled with teak from India, and mangrove poles from Africa supported the flat roofs. The biggest buildings in Siraf were the governor's palace and the great mosque. Ships in the harbour brought cargoes from many lands, including China; smaller craft took goods further up the Gulf to Basra, where ocean-going vessels often could not unload because of the silt brought down by the Tigris river.[1]

Even Siraf could not pretend to compete in luxury or grandeur with Basra – still less with Baghdad, capital of the caliphs. The colossal palaces beside the Tigris, their domes supported on columns of transluscent alabaster, were the wonder of the Arab world. The historian al-Muqaddasi, a contemporary of Buzurg, extolled its splendour: 'Baghdad, in the heart of Islam, is the city of well-being; in it are the talents of which men speak, and elegance and courtesy. Its winds are balmy and its science penetrating. In it are to be found the best of everything and all that is beautiful . . . All hearts belong to it, and all wars are against it.'

Although the power of the caliphs, the Commanders of the Faithful, had been fractured by dynastic rivalries, Baghdad still controlled an empire stretching from India to Egypt. Three centuries after its founding, the faith of Islam embraced many more people and far greater territories than Christianity, which was already near the end of its first thousand years. Buzurg's writings open a window on to this moment, at the ushering in of a new millennium during which the two religions were to be in almost ceaseless conflict.

The cities of Iraq, Persia and India would have astounded the impoverished peoples in the West, had they been aware of them; but Europe's horizons still scarcely reached beyond the uncertain boundaries of its semi-literate warlords. Western Europe lay on the outer fringes of world civilization, whereas Baghdad could boast of being at its centre, with Constantinople the only rival. The unifying concepts of 'Europe' and 'Christendom' had yet to take root. Half-pagan, half-Christian raiders from Scandinavia were still able to cause havoc almost everywhere.

Some remnants of classical learning had survived within the walls of European monasteries, but these could not compare with the libraries of Arab scholars, who by now had almost all the great works of ancient Greece available to them in translation. These writings would have been more readily available to Buzurg, a sea-captain in Persia, than to the most learned of Christian bishops in Europe.

Outside the boundaries of Islam, which extended along the coast of North Africa and into Spain, direct contacts between East and West were few. Almost the only European Christians who travelled further than Italy were traders going surreptitiously to Alexandria, pilgrims striving to reach Jerusalem, and young girls and boys sold into slavery. The girls were destined to serve in the Arab harems, in company with female slaves from Ethiopia and the remote African lands south of the Red Sea. The boys were eunuchs, castrated at a notorious assembly point at Verdun in France, taken over the Pyrenees into Spain, and shipped from there to the Indian Ocean countries in the charge of Jewish merchants known as the *Radhaniyya* ('those who know the route').

However, there had been a brief time, at the start of the ninth century, when a positive understanding between Christian Europe and Islam seemed possible. Despite their remoteness from one another, the caliph Harun al-Rashid and Charlemagne, Holy Roman Emperor, several times exchanged ambassadors, bearing messages about a never-fulfilled Arab plan for a concerted war to capture Constantinople, the capital of Byzantium. (The exchange of envoys is mentioned only by Charlemagne's scribes; Islamic chroniclers probably thought it unworthy of note, since Harun received ambassadors in Baghdad from so many lands and despatched his own in every direction.) In his youth Harun had besieged Constantinople, and now wanted to exploit the divisions between the Catholics and the eastern Christians. He only took this course after vainly despatching envoys to the Byzantine emperor, Constantine VI, urging him to convert to Islam.

The caliph made no such suggestion to Charlemagne, but sent him extravagant presents: jewels, ivory chessmen, embroidered silken gowns,

a water clock and a tame white elephant called Abu al-Abbas. Named
after the first caliph of the Abbasid dynasty, the animal had once been
the property of an Indian rajah. The man who successfully led it home
from the Euphrates to the Mediterranean was a Jew named Isaac, sole
survivor of a three-man mission to Baghdad. After a hazardous sea
crossing to Italy, the elephant was led over the Alps and finally plodded
into Charlemagne's palace in Aix-la-Chapelle on 20 July 802. The
emperor soon became devoted to Abu al-Abbas, who withstood the
European climate for eight years, until Charlemagne rashly took him
to the bleak Luneberg Heath in northern Germany, to intimidate some
marauding Danes.[2]

These contacts between the caliph of Baghdad and the 'philosopher-
king' of the Franks had proved to be only a brief flicker of light across the
religious and cultural divide. Charlemagne had arranged, with Harun's
approval, for the founding of a Christian hostelry in Jerusalem, and this
was the basis of a medieval legend that he had been the first crusader,
leading a pilgrim army to the Holy Land. However, the Crusades were
launched later – by Pope Urban II in 1095 – and the Arabs were then
to be stunned by the uncouth ferocity of their religious foes.

Whereas Christian Europe was confined and cut off from Asia, the
non-Christian Europeans – the Arabs settled in Spain and the Mediterranean islands – were free to wander across all the known world, even
as far as China. It meant travelling first through Egypt and Arabia to
reach some port such as Siraf, from where the 'China ships' set out on
what was then the longest voyage known to mankind. In one of Buzurg's
stories there is a passing mention of a man originally from Cadiz who
had been bold enough to stow away on a ship bound for China. This
man had crossed the divide between two contrasting maritime traditions.
The twisting, creaking vessel destined for China would have been totally
unlike the heavy, broad-bottomed craft, held together with massive
nails, which he would have remembered seeing in the harbours of Spain.

The use of coconut-fibre cording to sew the timbers of the Indian
Ocean ships was often explained away by the myth of the 'Magnetic
Mountain'; that ships built with nails were doomed if they sailed near
the mountain, since every scrap of metal in their hulls flew out towards
it. In one of the Sinbad tales, a captain 'hurls his turban on the deck
and tears his beard' when the Magnetic Mountain looms up in front of
his ship, for he knows he is doomed: 'The nails flew from the ship and

shot off towards the mountain. The vessel fell to pieces and we were all flung into the raging sea. Most of us were drowned outright.'[3]

The mundane truth, however, was that Arabia suffered from a short-age of iron, and its swordsmiths always had first call on metal imported from such places as Ceylon and East Africa. On the other hand, it was some consolation that if a 'sewn' ship had to be beached for repairs the raw materials were usually to hand, since coconut palms grew almost everywhere beside the Indian Ocean. The ocean also supplied materials for preserving ships' hulls, which were thickly smeared with oil from the carcasses of sharks and whales (as a ship-building port, Siraf had a factory for treating blubber); the aim was to protect timbers from rotting and keep them flexible, so that ships were less likely to be holed should they strike a coral reef.

These 'sewn boats' of the Indian Ocean have a long history. The earliest reference to them is in a nautical guide written by a Greek voyager in about A.D. 50. Known as the *Periplus [Circuit] of the Erythrean Sea*, this survey describes in a practical style the Indian Ocean's trading conditions and the people to be met with round its shores. It speaks of an East African port named Rhapta (whose site is yet to be discovered) where much ivory and tortoiseshell could be bought and the 'sewn boats' were built.[4]

Ships bound from Arabia to China sailed southwards along the coast of India to Ceylon (known as Sirandib, the Isle of Rubies), eastwards to Sumatra, through the Malacca straits at the southernmost tip of Asia, then north into the China Sea. The round voyage took a year and a half. The captains of such vessels often chose to travel in convoys, to be less at the mercy of pirates who were numerous off western India. Sometimes the pirates stationed themselves at intervals across a regular trading route to catch any lone vessel, then extorted goods or money before letting it pass; the overlord of a coastline where the pirates had their havens might even take a share of such proceeds.

However, the lure of China was irresistible, even though the risks of the voyage were so great. Its products were unequalled, its prowess awesome. About China, anything was believed possible.[5] Buzurg never claims to have sailed there, but relates without a hint of scepticism several pieces of information passed on to him by friends: one describes how a high imperial functionary had made a state entry into Khanfu (Canton) with an escort of 100,000 horsemen; another told Buzurg that a Chinese ruler, giving an audience to an Arab merchant, had been accompanied by some 500 female slaves of all colours, wearing different silks and jewels. While allowance must be made for the exaggerations of travellers' tales, it is true that the cavalry in oriental armies was numbered in tens of thousands, and that despotic rulers always took pride in their numbers of concubines.

Arabia became entranced by the magnificence of goods from China (porcelain is called 'Chinese' in Arabic to this day). Even the Red Sea had been called the 'Sea of China', because it was from there in the earliest times that ships began their voyages with cargoes of ivory, incense and gold, to barter for luxuries in that country the Romans, following the Greeks, had called Seres, the 'land of silk'.

The great Sassanian empire of pre-Islamic Persia had despatched missions to China. Although Persia's ancient civilization itself had much to offer – the Chinese were happy to imitate its techniques in silverware and blown glass – the rulers of China always took it for granted that every other nation must acknowledge their superiority and come to them; no other race has maintained this trait so rigidly. Although one Chinese scholar is known to have visited Baghdad in the tenth century, Buzurg never mentions any journeys by Chinese merchants to the western side of the Indian Ocean. When monarchs of distant countries sent gifts to the emperor, who was known to Arabs as the *Sahib al Sin*, these were loftily accepted as tribute, signs of obeisance. In return, Chinese titles were bestowed on the donors.

Despite the perils of ocean travel – or perhaps because of them – voyaging to faraway lands was a prospect that stirred the enthusiasm of the young: expressions of that spirit endure in the outlines of sailing ships, with their crews aboard, scratched into the plaster of excavated houses in ancient Indian Ocean cities. Yet there is no doubt that disasters were frequent. A Chinese official writing in the ninth century noted that 'white pigeons to act as signals' were carried by ships coming from the Indian Ocean: 'Should a ship sink, the pigeons will fly home, even for several thousand miles.' For sailors, land birds could also be good news, because after weeks on the open sea the first sighting of them confirmed that land must be near. Before the age of charts or precise instruments, a captain had to rely on such signs: a change in the colour of the water or current, drifting debris, even the amount of phosphorescence on the waves at night.

A famous captain who had made the voyage to China seven times is portrayed by Buzurg as a hero; in the end he goes down with his ship.

The Indian Ocean vessels, built to carry at most a hundred tons of cargo, and fifty or sixty people, always feared storms, but being becalmed was just as dangerous. Drinking water might run out, or diseases spread from the rat-infested holds. Sometimes the torments of heat and stench drove passengers off their heads. Those who kept their sanity spent much of their time reading holy books, searching through them for auguries of a safe arrival. Everyone yearned for the first cry from the lookout, *al-fanjari*, standing in the bows, that land was at last in sight.

Often the tales in *The Wonders of India* display an ironic humour in evoking life at sea. They can also be poignant. When Buzurg writes about how people behave in times of crisis, the intervening centuries suddenly vanish away. He tells of a shipwreck after which the survivors drift for days off the coast of India in a small boat. Among them is a boy whose father had been drowned when the ship went down. Hunger drives the survivors to think of cannibalism, and they decide to kill and eat the boy. 'He guessed our intentions, and I saw him looking at the sky, and screwing up his eyes and lips in silent prayer. As luck had it, at that moment we saw the first signs of land.'

Not surprisingly, many wandering merchants chose to stay in whichever port most took their fancy, rather than risk a return journey. If there was business to be done, a mosque to pray in, and slaves and concubines to satisfy physical needs, there was little more to be desired. In particular, travellers who reached China safely were often loath to come back. Two centuries before Buzurg was writing, Persians and Arab merchants in the East were already numerous enough to launch a seaborne raid on Canton, presumably to avenge some mistreatment.

One traveller who in Buzurg's manuscript does return from China is a Jew named Ishaq bin Yahuda. He had begun life in poverty in Sohar, the main port of Oman at the entrance to the Persian Gulf, but after a quarrel with a Jewish colleague decided to seek his fortune abroad. Taking with him his entire wealth, 200 gold dinars, Ishaq goes first to India and later travels on to China.

Only a few years before Ishaq arrived in China there had been upheavals during which more than 100,000 foreign traders and their families were massacred; but he stays and prospers. After thirty years the townspeople of Sohar are astounded to see him come home again, in the year 912. He is no longer travelling as a humble passenger, but in his own ship, packed with treasures such as silk, porcelain, musk, jewels and other precious stones.

Buzurg blandly tells how Ishaq reaches an understanding with the emir of Oman, one Ahmad bin Hilal. 'To avoid customs and the tax of one-tenth', they make an 'arrangement' worth a million of the silver coins called dirhams. Ishaq also cements their friendship by giving the emir a wonderful gift, a black porcelain vase with a golden lid.

'What is inside the vase?' asks the emir.

'Some fish I cooked for you in China,' replies the merchant.

'Fish cooked in China! Two years ago! What a state it must be in!'

The emir lifts the ornate lid and peers inside. The vase contains a golden fish, surrounded by sweet-smelling musk. The fish has eyes made of rubies and the contents of the vase are judged to be worth 50,000 gold dinars.[6]

With his immense wealth Ishaq soon becomes an object of envy. One man who had tried in vain to buy some of his merchandise resolves to seek revenge in Baghdad – a journey of more than 300 parasangs (1,000 miles) from Sohar. Eventually this jealous enemy gains an audience with the caliph al-Muqtadir, and tells him how the Jew has done a secret deal with the emir to avoid paying customs and taxes. He also excites the caliph's greed with a description of the wonderful goods Ishaq has brought back from China, his silks, porcelains and precious stones. Moreover, the Jew is childless, so if he dies there will be no one to inherit all his property. On hearing this, the caliph calls aside one of his aides, a negro eunuch named Fulful ('black pepper'), and tells him to go down to Oman with thirty men. Ishaq must be seized at once, and brought to Baghdad. (The subsequent behaviour of the eunuch Fulful would have seemed entirely in character to a tenth-century Muslim audience. Eunuchs were regarded as villainous and slippery, but in the service of powerful men they often rose high.)

When the emir in Sohar hears about the caliph's order, he has the Jew arrested, but lets him know that a substantial bribe can win his freedom. The emir then takes another step to keep his rich prisoner out of the caliph's clutches, and to guard his own position. He spreads the news of what has happened and warns all the other merchants in town that if Ishaq is carried off to Baghdad, none of them will in future be safe from similar treatment. The merchants respond as he has expected, first shutting down the market, then signing petitions, then rioting in the streets. They warn that they will all leave, and tell other merchants to keep away from the coasts of Arabia, where a man's property is no longer safe.

The emir writes a letter to the caliph, recounting what the merchants have said: 'We shall be deprived of our living, when ships no longer come here, because Sohar is a town where men get everything from the sea. If small men among us are treated like this, it will be worse for the great. A sultan is like a fire, devouring everything it touches. Since we cannot resist such power, it is better to leave now.' To drive their message home, the merchants line up their ships at the quayside and prepare them for sailing. Affairs grow so out of hand that the eunuch Fulful and his men decide to flee back to Baghdad. As a parting gesture they seize 2,000 gold dinars belonging to the imprisoned Jew.

After they have gone, Ishaq is freed, but is so possessed by rage that he decides to leave Arabia for ever and settle permanently in China. A ship fitted out, all his possessions are loaded into it, and he sails away. But he never reaches China. When his ship nears Sumatra, on the far side of the Indian Ocean, the ruler of a port there demands a huge sum in transit dues, before allowing him to sail on. When Ishaq refuses to pay, men come at night and murder him. The ruler takes the ship and everything in it.

Without offering any judgements, Buzurg allows the reader to deduce a lot from this story, which he clearly intended to be more than fiction, since historical figures occur in the narrative. Above all, it expounds the unwritten law by which trade was conducted throughout the Indian Ocean: whatever their race or faith, merchants should have the freedom of the seas and be given fair and equal treatment in every port of call. As a shipmaster, Buzurg understood exactly how the merchants shunned places where this rule might be broken. It was later claimed for the port of Hormuz, at the mouth of the Gulf, that it welcomed merchants from all the regions of the world: 'They bring to Hormuz everything most rare and valuable. There are many people of all religions in this city, and nobody is allowed to insult their religions. That is why this city is called the citadel of security.'

Readers of *The Wonders of India* would also have discerned a far more personal message in this story. The caliph and his Omani emir were Arabs, but Buzurg and his immediate audience were Persians. Although the Persians had been forcibly Islamicized for more than two centuries (Buzurg wrote in Arabic and prefaced his book with all the correct Muslim sentiments), there were many of his compatriots who looked back nostalgically to the glories of their vanquished empire and even clung to its ancient Zoroastrian religion.[7] They recalled how their Sassanid cities had been razed, how the Arab conquerors, once the despised nomads of the desert, had set up victory platforms on mounds of Persian dead. The last Sassanid monarch had even sent emissaries to the Chinese to plead for military help, but all in vain.

However, there was no route back to that proud past. While Islam was destined to come under pressure on its western flank from militant Christianity, throughout the Indian Ocean its influence still grew – within India itself, and beyond to Indonesia. Already Islam had taken control of the eastern shores of Africa, to which it looked to meet a perpetual need for human labour.

TWO

Lure of
the African Shore

I am being led in Damascus without honour,
as though I am a slave from Zenj.
— from a poem by the historian Abu Makhuaf (d. 774)

EAST AFRICA had been called Azania by the Greeks, but was now known as the Land of Zanj: the Land of the Negroes. The word *Zanj* (or *Zenj*) was originally Persian, but had been adopted by other languages. Once simply used to denote colour, the epithet was later applied in particular to Africans or black slaves – almost always one and the same thing if they were unfortunate enough to find themselves on foreign soil.

The prosperous island of Zanzibar took its name from the word *Zanj*, and was the usual destination of Arab and Persian captains sailing to Africa on the winter monsoon.[1] This voyage meant going beyond the equator, to latitudes where the guiding stars of the northern hemisphere were no longer visible, yet some captains ventured even further south. They went to the very limits of the monsoon, past the mouth of a great river which, it was said, joined up with the Nile in the centre of Africa. Several days sailing beyond the river they reached Sofala, the last big port on the Zanj coast.[2]

One lure of this remote region was gold, mined somewhere inland by Africans and brought down to Sofala to be bartered for cloth and beads. The gold was taken back to Arabia, where the risks of the long journey to Sofala were well rewarded, because a constant supply of the metal was needed for the minting of dinars, the currency used throughout the Islamic world. (Temples of the conquered religions had long since been stripped of their gold, and so had all the ancient tombs which could be uncovered.)

The Land of Zanj was not for the faint-hearted. Apart from lurid stories of cannibalism, of African warriors whose greatest delight lay in collecting the testicles of unsuspecting travellers, and the tales of tribes who lived on a mixture of milk and blood – drinking blood was most strictly forbidden by the Qu'rān – it was also rumoured that anyone who went to live in Zanj might find all the skin peeling from his body.

Yet what made Zanj distinct from other centres of trade around the Indian Ocean was its principal role as an exporter of pagan (*kafir*) slaves. Merchants travelled to India to buy embroidered muslins and jewellery, to China for silks and ornate dishes. But anyone sailing to the Land of Zanj would always expect to buy some young and healthy blacks. These slaves earned good prices in the lands along the northern shores of the Indian Ocean: a male labourer purchased with a few lengths of cloth could be sold for thirty gold dinars. If transported as far as the Mediterranean these human chattels brought even more handsome profits; a white slave or a horse would fetch less than thirty gold dinars, but the shortage of black slaves made them worth up to 160 dinars each. Some rulers took pride in having a personal guard of black warriors.[3]

Another prolific source of slaves was the mountainous country known as Abyssinia, reached from the western side of the Red Sea. This name derives from *Habash*, the Arabic word for the region. In time, anyone who was black tended to be called an 'Abyssinian'. Al-Muqaddasi, who had been so lyrical about Baghdad, was more mundane when he listed the goods imported through Aden: 'leather bucklers, Abyssinian slaves, eunuchs, tiger-skins and other articles.'[4]

Aden stood at the mouth of the Red Sea, so it was well placed to receive captives from raids on the Abyssinians. The Qur'ān was emphatic that Muslims should never be enslaved (although slaves might become believers); however, the Abyssinians were fair game because they were Christians, an offshoot of Byzantium dating back to the fourth century. Legend says that a Christian philosopher from the Levant was shipwrecked in the Red Sea and drowned, but his two pupils, Frumentius and Aedesius, survived and were found by local people, sitting under a tree, studying the Bible. They sowed the seeds of Christianity in the powerful state of Aksum, which had been in contact with the Mediterranean world since classical times and had supplied the Roman empire with ivory. Whatever the truth of the tale of Frumentius and Aedesius, by the fifth century there were certainly Christian missionaries from Syria active in what became known as Abyssinia.

The Abyssinians were also closely related to the people of Aden and its hinterland. Their forebears had crossed over the Red Sea in pre-Christian times, bringing with them from South Arabia an ancient written language they called *Ge'ez*, meaning 'traveller'. (With the triumph of Islam that language had been replaced in its homeland by Arabic, just as the old religion – the worship of the sun, the moon and their divine son – had been obliterated.) There was a time when the Christian Abyssinians even invaded South Arabia, to punish the persecution of their co-religionists there; now they were on the defensive, retreating higher into the mountains to avoid the slave-raiders.

In their centuries of expansion the Arabs had needed vast amounts of slave labour to build their cities, tend their plantations, work in mines and dig canals. It was not a system of their own devising, for the economies of Greece and Rome had also relied upon slavery, and the use of forced African labour has a history going back 5,000 years. The first hieroglyphic account of contact between the Egyptians and their black Nubian neighbours beside the Upper Nile was inscribed on a rock by King Zer of Egypt's first dynasty (before 3000 B.C.). Vividly illustrated, this shows a captive Nubian chief lashed to the prow of an Egyptian ship and the corpses of his defeated followers floating in the river. Five centuries later, the fourth-dynasty king Sneferu recorded that he had raided Nubia and brought back 7,000 blacks and 200,000 head of cattle. Slaves were used to help build the Pyramids.

In his time the Prophet Muhammad had laid down precise rules about the ownership of unbelievers, but the Qur'ān does not explicitly forbid it. The most common fate for the captive Zanj and Abyssinians was transportation across the Indian Ocean to the Persian Gulf and Basra, where they were brought ashore to be sold as labourers. After their long sea journey, during which they were manacled and subdued with whips, they were led from the waterfront between tall houses, past mosques where all men were equal, through streets crowded with donkeys, pack-horses and camels, to the slave market, the *suq al-raqiq*.

According to the African regions from which they came, the slaves were given group names, mostly no longer identifiable: Kunbula, Landjawiyya, Naml, Kilab. Those who managed to survive longest learned some Arabic, acquired Arab names, and acted as interpreters, passing on orders to their compatriots. More fortunate were the ones bought to become personal servants, for there was the chance that a kind master might one day make them free. Then colour ceased to matter and they became part of the great community of Islam.

Most pampered of all African slaves were the eunuchs named by al-Muqaddasi as being one of Aden's main imports. At the time he was writing there were 11,000 eunuchs in Baghdad, 7,000 of whom were Africans. A century earlier the caliph al-Amin had a vast corps of eunuchs; some white, whom he called his 'locusts', and some black, whom he called his 'ravens'. Those who especially gratified the caliphs rose to gain immense power, and the Spanish-born traveller Ibn Jubayr was disgusted when he visited Baghdad to find the army controlled by a young black eunuch named Khalis: 'We saw him one day going forth, preceded and followed by officers of the army, Turkish, Persians and others, and surrounded by about fifty drawn swords in the hands of the men about him ... He has palaces and belvederes beside the Tigris.' In other ways liberal-minded, Ibn Jubayr despised the blacks, observing: 'They are a breed of no regard and it is no sin to pour maledictions upon them.'

In his memoirs the Persian sea-captain Buzurg ibn Shahriyar turns repeatedly to tales of adventure in the Land of Zanj (with many hints that he writes from personal experience), and slavery is the subject of the most telling of all his stories. Behind its improbabilities lies a realism which vividly evokes the world in which he lived, and he shows a remarkable sympathy towards the principal character, an African chief. The narrator is a wealthy shipowner called Ismailawayh, who has sailed to every part of the Indian Ocean, but knows Africa especially well. In the year 922 he is on a voyage to Qanbalu (the main town on Pemba island, just north of Zanzibar), but storms drive his ship far to the south, towards Sofala. It is swept on to a notorious stretch of coast where the crew fear they are going to be captured and killed or, worst of all, eaten.[5]

On shore, the reception given to the strangers proves far better than Ismailawayh had dared to hope. The chief of the region, 'a young negro, handsome and well made', questions them, and says bluntly that he knows they are lying when they claim it had always been their intention to visit his country. But he promises them that they can trade freely, and will not be harmed. After doing good business the shipowner and his crew return to their vessel; the friendly chief, with several of his men, even comes on board to see them off. At this point Ismailawayh reveals his scheme: he will kidnap the unsuspecting blacks, carry them back to Oman, then sell them into slavery.

So as the ship begins to move and the puzzled chief and his men vainly try to get back into their canoes secured alongside, the Arab traders tell them what their fate is going to be. The chief replies with dignity: 'Strangers, when you fell upon our beaches, my people wished to eat you and pillage your goods, as they had already done to others like you. But I protected you, and asked nothing from you. As a token of my goodwill I even came down to bid you farewell in your own ship. Treat me as justice demands, and let me return to my own land.'

His pleas are ignored and he is pushed down into the hold of the ship with other prisoners: 'Then night enfolded us in its shrouds and we reached the open sea.' During the journey northwards, across the equator and into the Arabian Sea, the kidnapped chief never speaks a word, and behaves as if his captors are totally unknown to him. When the ship reaches port he is led away into a slave market and sold, together with his companions.

That seems like the end of a profitable piece of business for Ismaila-wayh. But some years later he is once again sailing down the Zanj coast with his regular crew and another storm drives them on to the same stretch of shoreline. The ship is quickly surrounded and the crew are marched away to be paraded before the local chief. To their horrified astonishment, the very man they had sold into slavery long ago is seated there once more on the chief's chair.

'Ah!' he says, 'here are my old friends.'

Ismailawayh and his sailors throw themselves on the floor, and are afraid to look up. 'But he showed himself gentle and gracious until we had all lifted up our heads, but without daring to look him in the face, so much were we moved by remorse and fear.' The chief tells them a remarkable story, of how he had been taken as a slave to Basra, then to Baghdad. From there he had escaped from his Arab master, had gone to Mecca, and finally arrived in Cairo. Seeing the Nile, the chief had asked where it flowed from, and was told: the Land of Zanj. He decides to follow its course, in the hope of reaching his homeland. After many adventures in the interior of Africa he succeeds. The first person he meets is an old woman, who does not recognize him but says the witch-doctors have divined that the country's lost chief is still alive and in the land of the Arabs. At that the wanderer goes joyfully back and reclaims his throne.

The chief tells his former captors that during his years as a slave he became converted to Islam. That is why he has decided to show magnanimity towards them; indeed, thanking them for being the cause of his conversion. But when they start preparing for their voyage back to Arabia, he lets them know that he cannot trust them too far, even though he is now a fellow-Muslim.

'As for accompanying you to your ship,' he says, 'I have my reasons for not doing that.'

With its pointed ironies, the tale of the black king and his white captives would have amused an Islamic audience. The closing message of brotherly reconciliation fitted well with a popular defence of slavery: that Africans so respected their masters that they bore them no grudges. In reality, however, slaves did not always submit quietly to being dragged from their tribes, their villages and the sheltering African forest. There was an Arabic saying: 'If you starve a Zanj he steals, if you feed him he becomes violent.' It reflected the fear that slaves would always seek a chance for revenge.

History reveals that they often did. As early as A.D. 689, less than sixty years after the death of Muhammad, there was an uprising by slaves working in the swamps near Basra, at the mouth of the Tigris and Euphrates rivers. It did not last long, and the bodies of the rebels were left hanging from their gallows as a warning. Five years later the slaves rose up again, led by an African called Riyah, 'The Lion of the Zanj'. This time the defiance was better organized and was not put down until 4,000 troops, also black, were let loose in a campaign of extermination. Ten thousand slaves, including women and children, were massacred.

In the middle of the ninth century a still more ferocious event took place: the third 'Revolt of the Zanj'. This happened during a period of widespread disorder, when there was a host of military and religious challenges to Islam.

A constant threat came from the radical Shi'ite movement, one of the two great contending forces of Islam. The Abbasid dynasty had chosen the other, the Sunni orthodoxy. The Shi'ites, who had helped to put the Abbasids in power, now felt rejected. They were also hostile to the luxurious habits of the caliphs. Power was fragmented, with the law in the hands of the Arabs and the Persians controlling the administration. The army was run by Turks, who were always prone to mutiny.

In the confusion leading up to the third 'Revolt of the Zanj' it was

a Shi'ite who took advantage of the revolutionary possibilities.[6] He was
a visionary zealot named Ali bin Muhammad – a Persian, but partly of
Indian extraction. As a young man he had led an uncertain life, writing
poetry and wandering through the deserts with nomadic tribes. Clearly,
he had messianic instincts, probably stimulated by his fanatical father,
who is reputed to have had a dream, when Ali was still a child, that his
son would grow up to destroy Basra, their home-town. As an adult,
Ali made it known that he could see writing done by an invisible hand,
and could read the thoughts of his enemies. These claims, similar to
those being made by 'holy men' elsewhere during this time of fanaticism,
brought round him a clique of dedicated followers; they included some
petty businessmen, including a miller and a lemonade seller.

His verses, of which more than a hundred survive, express his contempt for the self-indulgent rulers of Islam.

> How my soul grieves over our palaces in Baghdad and who
>   they contain – every kind of sinner –
> And for wines openly drunk there, and for men lusting
>   after sins.

He did not conceal the way his thoughts were moving:

> Submissively to adopt a moderate stance is humiliation for
>   God's servant.
> When the spark will not catch, I will fan it;
> When some leave the sharp blade in its sheath on the day
>   of battle, others will draw theirs.

Shortly before the Zanj slaves rose in revolt, Ali had been in Bahrain.
When he went home to Basra he was, unsurprisingly, viewed by the
authorities as a potential troublemaker; although he escaped into hiding
in Baghdad, his wife and children were jailed. In August 869, Ali's
moment arrived. There was near-anarchy in Basra, the governor had
fled, and prisoners had been freed from the jails.

He returned to Basra and made his way to the workshops where
masons prepared materials for restoring and enlarging the canals, and to
the sugar plantations in the surrounding marshes. Before him was carried
a banner, embroidered with a Qur'ānic verse, calling on the faithful to
'fight on the road of Allah'. He proclaimed a 'war to the knife'. His
first recruits were 15,000 slave labourers, men condemned to work in

heat and dust until death, flogged at the whim of their masters. They had little to lose.

Their new leader boldly went around the camps, ordering the black slaves to rise and beat their masters. They obeyed, giving them 500 lashes each. The Arab historian al-Tabari, living at the time of the revolt, even names some of the black lieutenants gathered around Ali, whom he piously vilifies as the 'Wicked One': al-Bulaliya, Abu Hudayd, Zurayq, Abu al-Layth. The greatest of the Zanj commanders was Mohallabi, who would fight to the very end.

For some years the uprising was to threaten the very heartland of Islamic power and ranks as one of the greatest slave uprisings in history, comparable with that led by Spartacus against imperial Rome. Today the event can only be re-created from obscure Arabic chronicles, but parts of it have a remarkably familiar ring after more than ten centuries, for at the same time as rebellion broke out in the marshes around the mouth of the Tigris river, the Kurds were also waging war.

Battle was soon joined by the makeshift army of slaves, against government troops equipped with swords, bows and arrows, and lances. No quarter was given on either side, all captives being put to death. The slaves' leader himself was a prime executioner, setting the example by decapitating one man just as he was pleading for mercy. The heads of the defeated were borne as trophies from the battlefield on the backs of mules. Once a whole boatload of heads was floated down the river to Basra.

As the slaves advanced through the swamps towards the great city, Ali maintained the trappings of a holy man. He rode a horse with palm leaves as a saddle and a piece of cord as a bridle. Before the battles he made stirring speeches to the Zanj, urging them on to victory. They put their faith in his magical powers.

There were setbacks: after one battle, Ali was forced to flee into the swamps and found himself with only 1,000 remaining followers, men and women. Although this might have seemed like the end of the revolt, the rebels were to win their next fight, with only stones as their weapons. Ali declared that supernatural powers had saved them, and recruits flowed in once more to sustain the revolt. Soon the slave armies became irresistible, spreading out through the whole region at the mouth of the Gulf. They pillaged the homes of the rich, auctioned off thousands of high-born Arab and Persian women as concubines, and cut all links between Baghdad and the Indian Ocean.

Leaders of the ruling Abbasid dynasty now saw that the black Zanj might represent a direct threat to Islam, because they were gathering support from other dissident groups, including Persians, Jews and Christians. It was fortunate for the caliphs that the rebels never formed any effective military alliance with the Kurds or the heretical Carmathians, but by the year 871 the Zanj were strong enough on their own to mount a direct assault on Basra, obeying Ali's plan for a three-pronged attack. It was led by the general Mohallabi. Two years earlier the citizens had beaten back the Zanj, but now the city was overrun and everybody unable to escape was killed. Some leading citizens were put to the sword as they prayed in the main mosque.

The caliph at Mu'tadid sent south a more powerful army than had ever been assembled, with the aim of dealing out merciless punishment to the Zanj. But once again Ali was victorious. His followers paraded before him, each one holding in his teeth, by the hair, the head of a victim. The slaves had now decisively turned the tables on their masters in Baghdad and Samarra, a new capital higher up the Tigris.

After this, the defeated Arabs decided that for the time being they had had enough. They withdrew northwards, making it their aim to contain the rebels within the two provinces encompassing the marshes and canals. It was the signal for Ali to create his own administration, to build himself a capital and – the ultimate show of treason in Islam – to mint his own coinage. Already famous as the 'Lord of the Zanj' or 'Prince of the Negroes', he now went on to declare himself to be the Mahdi, the new leader sent by Allah. He became known as al-Burku, the 'Veiled One'. For ten years he ran his kingdom unchecked, even spreading his revolutionary message right across Arabia to Mecca. In 880 a detachment of Zanj briefly seized control of the holy city. A year earlier they had been within seventy miles of Baghdad.

Then the tide of the revolution began to ebb. After three years of preparation an army of overwhelming strength was despatched from Baghdad under the leadership of the regent al-Muwaffaq. The Zanj were smashed in battle after battle, until at last they retreated into Ali's capital of al-Mukhtara, 'city of the elect', north of Basra. From one town abandoned by the rebels 5,000 women were freed and sent home to their families.

All prisoners taken by the government army were decapitated, just as the rebels' captives had been. One day, the heads of Zanj captives were paraded in boats in front of the besieged citadel. When Ali insisted that the heads were not real, but only the product of witchcraft, the general commanding the army ordered that the heads should be cata-pulted into the citadel by night. One black leader, cryptically described in contemporary accounts as 'the son of the king of the Zanj', was put to death by Ali after rumours that he planned to defect to the enemy.

In the end, in 883, the great slave uprising was finally crushed, although the most resolute of the Zanj fought to the last. Ali had refused an absolute pardon, probably doubting that the promises made to him would be honoured. His head was borne on a flagstaff back to Baghdad by the son of al-Muwaffaq, who had vanquished the Zanj. It became the centrepiece of celebrations. Two years later, when the slaves tried to rise again, five of their leaders held in prison were instantly beheaded.

One consequence of the revolt was an upsurge of fear and anger against the Zanj among the people of Baghdad. During a time of tumult the Arab cavalry in the army took the opportunity to massacre the caliph's black spear-carriers and bowmen, with the help of the citizens. However, it was not merely hatred of Africans which led to a fall in the numbers of black slaves being transported across the Indian Ocean; the decline of Baghdad and other Iraqi cities meant there was less need for labour to work on grandiose building projects.

After about A.D. 1000, Africa's ivory and gold became more sought-after than its people. Prisoners taken in wars with the Christians of Abyssinia met most of the needs of the slave trade. Nevertheless, the continent was still cast in a subservient role. The interior remained sealed off, dealing with the outside world through the Muslim intermediaries. Africans came to the coast, to live in the towns or to cross the ocean, usually against their will. They did not go back, to take inland the ideas which could have stimulated change.

The clearest contrast was with India, where coastal cities gave allegi-ance to powerful inland states whose culture and religion they shared. Watered by the monsoon rains, India grew enough crops on its fertile lands to feed a vast population as well as spices for export and cotton to be made into cloth. Its manufactures were sold throughout the Indian Ocean and beyond, just as the tales from its literature were translated and adapted all across the known world.

THREE

The Mystery of
the Waqwaqs

In the same way that the Sea of China ends with the land of
Japan, the Sea of Zanj ends with the land of Sofala and the
Waqwaq, which produces gold and many other wonderful things.
It has a warm climate and is fertile.

—Al-Mas'udi (893–957), *The Meadows of Gold*

AS OLD AS the monsoon trade between Arabia and East Africa, the
contacts across the eastern expanse of the Indian Ocean date back to
the time when Buddhism held sway over much of Asia. Two thousand
years ago ships were taking merchandise from the powerful Satavahana
kingdom of southern India to Sumatra, Java and Bali. It was a two-way
trade, with bronze ware from Indonesia being exported to India. These
contacts had been known to the Romans on one side of the world and
to the Chinese on the other. A much-travelled historian and diplomat,
Kang Tai, writing 1,700 years ago, told of ships from a Sumatran kingdom he called Geying sailing 8,000 *li* (about 2,500 miles) to a busy
Indian port where 'people came from all quarters'.

Indian monks spread Buddhism to the Indonesian islands; it was
traders who brought Hinduism. In later centuries, Hinduism was to
advance well beyond the Indian Ocean, extending northwards through
the China Sea to what is now Kampuchea. The surviving monuments
to this expansion are great temples and palaces overgrown by jungle,
the best-known being Angkor Wat.

Relations between India and its trading settlements across the ocean
to the south-east were not always friendly. Hindu armies were active
in Indonesia during the tenth century, and later a warlike Sumatran
state, Sri Vijaya, sent its fleets northwards to attack Ceylon. Such events
belong to the complex, interwoven history of the Indian Ocean spreading over several thousand years, and it is only in this context, of the sea

as a cultural and geographic entity, that the Waqwaq migrations westwards from Indonesia become credible. Even so, the French historian Hubert Deschamps has called them 'one of the greatest mysteries of mankind', and only fragments of the story have so far been assembled from archaeology, linguistics and anthropology.

Why the Indonesian seafarers known as Waqwaqs acquired such a curious name is, like much else about them, obscure; it may simply have been a mocking imitation by their enemies of the sound of their speech. More probably the source is *waka*, the name given in parts of Indonesia to the type of outrigger canoe the Waqwaqs used. The one indisputable fact is that they voyaged 3,500 miles from their homeland to discover and settle in Madagascar, off the coast of Africa.

Their migration to what would prove to be one of the world's biggest islands, a semi-continent, never until then inhabited by humans, is an astonishing chapter in the annals of ocean travel. The date when the first wave of Waqwaq migrants reached Madagascar is a matter of controversy; one clue is in the language they brought with them (and which still makes up more than nine-tenths of the Malagasy vocabulary, a bond across the ocean). It includes many Sanskrit loan words, and Sanskrit influence was at its strongest in Indonesia in about A.D. 400.[1]

The Waqwaqs were setting foot in a land where the animal life had developed in almost total isolation for 150 million years. There were no elephants, giraffes or lions, as on the African mainland 300 miles further west; but species which existed in Africa before Madagascar 'broke away' had lived on undisturbed, including the agile, wide-eyed lemurs, from the same stock as apes and humans. There are hundreds of varieties of insects found nowhere else in the world. In the deep seas near Madagascar lives the coelacanth, another survivor from the remote evolutionary past, a clumsy fish with huge scales and fins resembling legs.

Perhaps most remarkable of all the animals there when the Waqwaqs arrived was the *Aepyornis maximus*, a flightless bird which stood ten feet high and laid eggs more than a foot long. It probably gave rise to the persistent myth of a monstrous eagle, variously called a *rukh, peng* or gryphon, living in the Indian Ocean and believed capable of picking up an elephant, bearing it to the heavens, dropping it to earth, then devouring it. The Chinese were especially devoted to this fantasy, and described the bird as being able to fly 19,000 *li* before needing a meal. It must surely be more than a coincidence that the *Aepyornis maximus* became extinct around the time that the first Waqwaqs reached Madagascar. These awkward, inoffensive creatures would have been easy prey for humans equipped with bows and arrows; tales spread by the Waqwaqs of a bird which laid a huge egg may well have grown into something far more extravagant in the course of a few retellings.

The Waqwaqs' original landfall was almost certainly the African mainland, rather than Madagascar. They were eventually driven out by the local inhabitants, but left on the coast as reminders of their stay some Indonesian words and maritime techniques, such as outriggers to stabilize canoes. The intrepid newcomers set off again, travelling south for another 1,000 miles before sighting Madagascar. This time, there was nobody to challenge them: it was a long journey's end. In many places they found the coastline hostile, with sand bars or coral barriers, and parts of the island were dry and infertile; but there were also rich volcanic soils.

Most of the Indonesian boats were probably small and simple – little more than canoes, each carrying five or six men and women – with square sails and the outriggers to help them keep upright during storms. These small vessels may, however, have acted as escorts to larger ships, called *kunlun bo* by the Chinese. (The ancestors of the Maoris were to migrate to New Zealand in such vessels.) A Chinese account from the third century A.D. claims that these boats, which were also used to take Buddhist pilgrims from Sumatra to India, were large enough to carry hundreds of people and heavy cargoes. They had four sails, so skilfully rigged that the ships could set their course 'without avoiding strong winds and dashing waves, by the aid of which they can make great speed'.[2]

The Indonesian fleets undoubtedly travelled fast: from Sumatra, their most likely starting-point, it would have taken little more than a month to Madagascar in the May–October period, when the equatorial trade winds blow towards Africa. The strong east–west Malabar current would also have helped the travellers, carrying them first towards the 1,100 Maldive islands or, on the most direct route, to an uninhabited scattering of fifty coral atolls now called the Chagos archipelago, exactly halfway between Sumatra and Madagascar. Together these two island chains extend more than 1,500 miles from north to south.

The Indonesian voyagers would have found drinking water, to replenish their supplies, by digging shallow trenches on the islands. On beaches lined with coconut palms, *takamaka* trees, and other Asiatic plants –

progeny of seeds borne for vast distances on the ocean current – they could mend the hulls and sails of their boats. When they set off again, out of the lagoons and through the reefs surrounding these lonely islands, navigating was simple: the rising sun was always on their backs, the setting sun in their eyes.

There were other places to pause and hunt for food on this bold journey, for the Indian Ocean is dotted with coral atolls, specks of greenery in an amaranthine sea. Most have never been inhabited by humans, but are alive with animals. Turtles drag themselves on land to breed and giant tortoises march ponderously through the undergrowth. The brightly-coloured birds, unused to being hunted, could also be caught for the pot.

For their great trans-ocean venture the Waqwaqs had unique advantages. They were islanders, seafarers from childhood, and their needs afloat were few. Many Pacific islands were to be populated by similar long-distance voyages into the unknown. The boats carried baskets of rice, dried fruits wrapped in banana leaves, animal skins to hold drinking water, spears and lines for fishing, and live chickens for slaughtering *en route*. Rice was essential for survival on such voyages, because it did not go rotten; and if food ran out, aromatic leaves were chewed to fend off hunger-pangs.[3] How many of the migrants died on their way can not even be guessed at.

At the time when the first Indonesians set off across the Indian Ocean they lacked a written language, so there is no record of why or precisely when their great journeys were undertaken. They appear to have spoken a tongue now long forgotten in Indonesia, known as Old Javanese; it is likened to the language of the Batak people of northern Sumatra.[4] Some of Madagascar's religious rituals still retain vestiges of Hinduism, so it is likely that there were later migrations, over several centuries, by communities escaping from wars between rival Indonesian states.

The Indonesians who settled later in Madagascar – some after A.D. 1000 – probably did so because they discovered that people with origins like their own had survived and settled peacefully in a new island home. Such information may have come from China, that great storehouse of knowledge. References to the western flank of the Indian Ocean occur at various places in the records of the Tang dynasty (A.D. 619–906); in 863 the scholar Duan Chengshi was able to describe the Somali people. They were, he said, feuding pastoralists, living on a diet of blood and milk and 'drawing fresh blood from the veins of their cattle with a needle'. This was an exact description of the habits of the Galla (or Oromo), who inhabited the Somali hinterland at that time. Duan went on to say that the women were 'clear-skinned and well-behaved'; the people of Africa did not hesitate to 'make their own countrymen prisoners and sell them to foreigners at prices many times more than they would fetch at home'. The Spanish-born historian Ibn Sa'id, who worked in the thirteenth century for the Mongol warlord Hulagu Khan, knew of Madagascar; he had been told that some Khmer people, driven by the Chinese out of what became Cambodia, managed to find their way to the island.

However, what the faraway Chinese knew could only have been a fraction of the information available in countries to which the Indonesians had sailed for centuries. In India there must have been an awareness of the existence of Madagascar, which the Arabs called al-Qumr. Indian merchants dealt directly with the African mainland, and the glass beads they used for barter can be found in the sites of Zimbabwean villages, among debris dating to A.D. 500. By this date there was a flow of ivory to India, whose own elephants were too valuable to slaughter for their tusks, since they could be tamed and used for work and warfare. African ivory was also more desirable, since the tusks were larger and softer for carving. The herds were so vast that they could be hunted virtually on the seashore.

The Waqwaqs on Madagascar were well placed to compete with Arab traders for the ivory of the mainland, and for its gold. The gold-bearing veins were reached by sinking deep trenches and shafts. The rock was made hot by lighting fires beneath it, then cracked from the top by flinging on cold water. Children carried the baskets of ore to the surface, because they could squeeze more easily through the narrow spaces in the workings. The rock was then ground and washed to extract the metal.

However, the Africans cared little for gold themselves, and the fine dust was poured into porcupine quills for safe-keeping before it was carried down to the coast. As contact with the outside world grew, the African rulers took control, distributing Indian cloth and beads to their subjects as rewards for bringing them gold-dust and elephant tusks, which were passed to the waiting traders.

The Waqwaqs were disliked by other merchants in East Africa. The Arabs resented their piratical ways, while respecting their seamanship. These rivals from the 'Zabaj islands' were reputed to have among them 'men who look like Turks'; they may have been mercenaries from countries close to China, or the Khmer (Qumr) driven from Cambodia.

In A.D. 945 an armada of Waqwaq ships appeared off the East African coast and besieged the town of Qanbalu, on the island of Pemba. Before the newcomers' warlike aims became clear, the townspeople had asked them what they wanted. The reply was frank: they were after 'ivory, tortoiseshell, panther-skins and ambergris' – trade goods needed in their own homeland, and in China. More than that, they wanted to capture Zanj people, 'for they were strong and easily endured slavery'. By their own admission, the besiegers had been raiding towns and villages up and down the African coast. They were less successful when they tried to subdue Qanbalu, because it was heavily fortified; in the end they were repulsed and sailed away.

Essentially, the Indonesians and the Arabs shared a similar attitude towards the African mainland – one which was predatory. The Waqwaqs brought slaves back to Madagascar to look after domesticated animals and labour in their terraced ricefields (which were built in a style identical to that found as far east as the Philippines).

In time, however, the Waqwaq impact proved beneficial in many ways: the crops they had transported from Asia included rice, bananas, yams, sugar cane, breadfruit, mangoes, lentils and spices.[5] These food plants enhanced the lives of Africans right across the continent as they spread inland from community to community, starting at the coast around the Zambezi delta, which directly faced the early Waqwaq settlements on the western side of Madagascar. It is possible to re-create some of the routes by which these new crops advanced into Africa: what has been nicknamed the 'Banana Corridor' takes in a great swathe of land right up to the equator from near the mouth of the Zambezi. Bananas ultimately became the staple diet in Uganda, among peoples who knew nothing about the Indian Ocean or the origins of this new type of food.

The Waqwaq influence can also be traced in African musical instruments such as the xylophone,[6] as well as in fishing and farming methods; a mounted file used in Madagascar for opening coconuts, as well as a double-valved bellows for blowing life into fires, are both unmistakably Indonesian.

Although they brought much to Africa that was new, the Waqwaqs became indifferent to their own past. As generations passed, the truth about their origins became merged into mythology and they grew ever more remote from the culture of Indonesia, clinging only to their language and their obsession with death and burial customs; one of these involves digging up corpses after seven years and carrying them in procession through the community, the 'return of the dead'. As the population in the coastal regions of Madagascar became predominantly African, the Waqwaqs moved further into the mountainous interior of the great island. In the manner of colonizers elsewhere, they abandoned a skill they no longer needed, the ability to cross the open seas. Although they still buried their rulers in silver canoes, they could never go home again.

FOUR

Islam Rules
in the Land of Zanj

> The Zanj have no ships in which they can voyage, but boats land
> in their country from Oman, as do others that are going to Zabaj
> [Indonesia] . . . The inhabitants of Zabaj call at Zanj in both large
> and small ships and trade their merchandise with them, as they
> understand each other's language.
>
> —Al-Idrisi (1110–65), *A Book of Entertainment for One Desirous to go
> Round the World*

UNLIKE THE INDONESIANS, who forgot their original homeland after
migrating to Madagascar, the Arab and Persian settlers on the East
African coast always looked back to the great cities of the Middle
East. They looked back quite literally, bowing towards Mecca in their
mosques, where they heard the sermons of imams who read the Qur'ān
and sustained their faith. The dhows sailing south to Africa on the
winter monsoon brought goods which sustained their cultural links with
Islam.

The earliest settlements, dating to A.D. 750 or earlier, had been rudimentary, laid out in an African style, with protective wooden palisades.
Such places were too remote to make use of artisans who built in stone
in the Arabic manner. Sites of the first mosques are revealed by traces
of wooden post-holes in the earth, and these show a curious error: the
alignment is not directly towards Mecca, as the Prophet had ruled. This
suggests that the newcomers were simple traders who could not 'read'
the night sky correctly, since their only way of finding a precise bearing
was from the stars.

The logical first step for Arab newcomers was simply to install themselves in an established African fishing village, near a bay where boats
could be safely run up on the beach at high tide for unloading and
loading. In such places, nameless and ungoverned, life was ruthless. As
well as the threats from within an encampment, there was always the

danger – with nobody to call upon for help – of surprise attacks by seaborne raiders. One settlement in the Comoro islands, far to the south, was built on top of a cliff, through fear of the Waqwaqs from nearby Madagascar.

It was not only to protect themselves from one another that the rival settlers tended to live on islands. They had good reason to maintain a safe distance from the Africans of the mainland. Several early communities chose islands more than a day's sailing out in the ocean, such as Zanzibar, Pembra and Mafia, all big enough to be self-supporting in times of war. African dugout canoes, used for fishing inside the coral reefs, could not reach such islands to retrieve captives, and there was no risk that newly-acquired domestic slaves might try swimming back to shore.

Safe on their islands, the Arabs never wished to venture into Africa. They merely waited for the products of the interior to come to them. At their backs the mainland was a brooding and hostile giant, whom none cared to challenge. Local women taken as wives or concubines, and the slaves working in the gardens, were converted to Islam.[1] But there was no attempt to spread the faith within Africa – its people remained *kafirs*.

After a few generations the settlements grew more prosperous and secure. Bigger mosques were built, and although still of wood they were now on a true alignment to Mecca. When trading ships came over the horizon from the Gulf and the Red Sea, the settlers could afford to barter for many luxuries. By the ninth century they were eating off Chinese floral-pattern plates, as well as oriental stoneware and opaque white porcelain. These outposts could tap into trade routes reaching all the way, through cities such as Siraf, to the great ports of Tang China.

The settlers also possessed pottery and glass goblets from Persia, phials containing attar of roses, many household ornaments, and brass oil-lamps. Their combs were made of tortoiseshell, cosmetics were kept in carved copper bowls. They stored their water in tall pottery jars, originally used to transport oil and wine from the Persian Gulf.

In exchange for these reminders of a distant splendour, the settlers had more than gold, ivory and slaves to offer. There were leopard-skins used on saddles, rhinoceros horns for making medicines, and the buoyant pale blue ambergris – as valuable, weight for weight, as gold – which the winds and currents swept up on to the sandy beaches. The ambergris was used to 'fix' perfumes, and for scenting the oil in lamps: a tenth-century poet writes of the way 'gilded lamps, fed with ambergris, shine like pearls'.

The Chinese in particular valued this mysterious substance which, apart from its other qualities, was vaunted as an aphrodisiac; yet they did not know exactly where the ambergris came from, and named it 'dragon's spittle'. (The Zanj people simply called it 'treasure of the sea'.) In fact, it was an excretion of solidified fluids, sometimes as big as an ostrich egg, from the stomachs of the sperm whales which in those times abounded in the Indian Ocean.

As the Muslim pioneers grew even richer they began building with coral stone and bricks carried from Persia as ballast. Orange and lemon orchards and vegetable gardens were planted round their homes. The animal enclosures contained sheep, goats and even camels.

The sea itself was a ready supplier of food, although some species were gradually hunted into oblivion along the East African coast. An early victim was the dugong, a large harmless mammal living on sea plants. It was often to be seen basking on coral rocks, and from a distance could look almost human, so that it became the source of many Arabic tales about mermaids. By A.D. 1000 the dugong had vanished for ever from the western side of the Indian Ocean.

Other sea creatures to suffer at the hands of the newcomers were giant tortoises and turtles, valuable for their shells. According to Muslim law, the eating of tortoises was forbidden, and this should have been obeyed not only by the faithful, but also the *kafirs* working for them as slaves. However, there is evidence from ancient rubbish dumps that tortoises were consumed with gusto in some early settlements. Far in the south, in the Comoro islands, there was an equal readiness to eat lemurs, which would certainly have been prohibited fare for devout Muslims, since these animals live in trees and have monkey-like bodies.

This may suggest that some early settlers on the East African coast were fugitives or outcasts from the Arab world. In their isolation on the remote African shore they would be beyond the reach of enemies, and may have ignored some more inconvenient religious rules. It is hard to be sure, however, because legends about the identity of the Arabs who migrated to the Land of Zanj often contradict one another.

One popular account tells how Abd-al-Malik, an early caliph, gave orders that all of Oman's independent chiefs should be deposed. This was harsh treatment, for Oman had accepted Islam as early as A.D. 630, during Muhammad's lifetime. So two brothers, Sulaiman and Sa'id, organized the defence of Oman and drove back a land and sea attack by 40,000 men. Finally, 5,000 cavalry were sent in and the brothers could resist no longer. They decided to flee to Africa, taking with them their families and followers. The date, it is said, was around A.D. 700.

Other events in the expansion of Islam may also have sparked off migrations to East Africa. Most crucial was the overthrow of the original dynasty, the Umayyads, in 750, by the caliph Abu-al-Abbas, the 'Shedder of Blood'. He had defeated and executed his predecessor, then organized a banquet of conciliation for the dignitaries of the former regime. The guests arrived, sat down to eat, then were murdered to a man before they could start. A carpet of leather was thrown over the bodies, then the host and his followers sat down on it to enjoy a hearty meal. Supporters of the Umayyad dynasty – which re-established itself in Spain – would have been understandably keen to put some distance between themselves and Abu-al-Abbas; an expanse of Indian Ocean might have seemed appropriate.

Some newcomers ventured into little-known waters, far to the south. The Chibuene settlement was several days' sailing beyond Sofala towards the Cape of Good Hope, and its merchants traded inland along the Limpopo and Sabe river valleys. An eighth-century Islamic burial site has been found at Chibuene, and the town may even have been founded in pre-Islamic times.

When later communities arrived in Zanj, their leaders were quick to assert independence. Each proudly called himself a sultan and some claimed as their ancestor, real or symbolic, a famous trader named Ahmed bin Isa, who had left Basra for Arabia in the year 930. More importantly, these new rulers were all *sharifs*, meaning that they claimed descent from the Prophet. Their arrival in East Africa, towards the end of the eleventh century, marked the start of a visibly different era.[2] New towns, with mosques and palaces built of coral blocks, were established on offshore islands or mainland strongpoints. Soon there was rivalry between the towns over the size of their mosques and palaces and the elegance of their architecture.

The self-confidence of these new rulers was symbolized by the large-scale minting of coins. Although in earlier centuries some simple copper currency had been produced in the Land of Zanj, coins were now also cast in silver, and a few even in gold. They all bore a Qur'ānic inscription on one side and the name of a sultan on the other. The tiny copper coins, made from metal smelted in the African interior, were for buying goods in the local markets; they were intended to replace cowrie shells, the traditional form of currency brought from the Maldive islands.[3] The gold was likewise African, but the silver had to be imported – usually in the form of coins, which were then melted down. Foreign money, mainly Arab and Egyptian dinars, was also used. Traders brought home Indian and Chinese coins, but these were merely souvenirs. A pit at the site of one coastal town has yielded up an eleventh-century Hindu statuette; it possibly served as a trader's weight.[4]

Among the ruling families, at least on the male side, there was a high degree of literacy. This is reflected in the stylized script known as *kufic*, carved on coral slabs in the mosques and on tombstones; brought to perfection in Siraf, the floriate *kufic* was admired as far away as Spain. The flat-roofed stone houses of the wealthiest families displayed a regard for orderly comfort not witnessed before in Zanj: they had bathrooms and plumbing, glazed windows and plastered walls. Some buildings were three storeys high, with carved and brass-studded front doors, behind which entrance halls led into receiving rooms. The designs on the Persian carpets spread over the floors and hanging on the walls symbolized Arab society: the centrepiece represented the sultan, with his courtiers surrounding him, and the outer parts of the patterns stood for the villagers, artisans and slaves.

Although the new rulers, as well as their law-makers and courtiers, were certainly literate in Arabic, no contemporary accounts of how these dynasties established themselves have survived. A fragmentary chronicle, written at least four centuries later, tells the history of the island city-state of Kilwa, founded by a Persian named Ali bin al-Hasan. The name Kilwa means 'fishing place' and the chronicle says the island was bought from an African chief with enough cloth to stretch right round the island (a distance of about fifteen miles); in truth, the chief was probably given only a few bales.

Kilwa was to grow into the wealthiest city on the entire coast, able to control a nearby part of the mainland known as Muli, where rice and other crops were grown. It had the advantage of being several days' journey south of Zanzibar, and thus was strategically placed to exact tolls from ships travelling to and from the gold port of Sofala. Although Kilwa was remote, an experienced captain who knew exactly when to set out could sail there from India or Arabia in one monsoon season. It was a terminus of the ocean trade with Africa.

*　　　*　　　*

A few of the visitors to the coast took a perceptive interest in the mainland Africans. One was Abu'l Hasan 'Ali al-Mas'udi, an Arab writer who first sailed to Zanj from Siraf in A.D. 916, when he was in his early twenties. He was the type of traveller, always asking questions, whose enthusiasm never waned. Born in Baghdad, he made journeys to India, Persia, Armenia, the Caspian Sea, Syria and Egypt. While in East Africa he stayed mainly at Qanbalu, whose population he describes as a 'mixture of Muslims and Zanj infidels', speaking the 'Zanjiyya language'. The language was elegant, and the Zanj preachers would often gather a crowd and exhort them to 'please God in their lives and be obedient to him'. The crowd would then be told to remember their ancestors and ancient kings. Al-Mas'udi's account goes on: 'These people have no religious law ... every man worships what he pleases, be it a plant, an animal, or a mineral.' This is the earliest description of the local Swahili (coastal) people of East Africa, and shows that some, at least, still clung to their African religions.[5] Plainly, the towns had a ruling élite and a black population with which the Arab settlers were more or less integrated.

The villages of the Zanj, according to al-Mas'udi, stretched for 700 parasangs (2,500 miles) along the coast; an accurate estimate of the distance from the entrance of the Red Sea to the mainland facing southern Madagascar. Although he twice visited East Africa, he does not say if he travelled as far south as Sofala, but is quite definite that a king of the Africans ruled in that distant region, and had many lesser chiefs subject to him. This matches what is known from archaeology, that embryonic African states were taking shape at that time in the hinterlands of Mozambique and Zimbabwe. Since merchants travelled regularly up and down the coast, it would have been easy, even in Qanbalu, to learn about the cattle-keeping kingdoms of the distant south.

Horses and camels were unknown there, writes al-Mas'udi, but the people owned great numbers of cattle, which were used as beasts of burden. The king had '300,000 horsemen'; this is an odd statement, set alongside his assertion that horses were unknown, until it is recalled that the warriors of southern Africa were the guardians of great herds of cattle, and rode on oxen.

The king of the Zanj, he says in a summary of knowledge on Africa, is called the Waflimi. This is his version of Wafulme, the plural of an African name for a paramount chief. The king is descended from a

'Great God' named Mulkendjulu (*Mukulunkulu*). He asserts that some Africans were cannibals, who filed their teeth to points. The interior of the continent is 'cut up into valleys, mountains and stony deserts'.

The most common creature of all on the mainland was the giraffe, but the animal most hunted was the elephant. One way of catching elephants, says al Mas'udi, is by laying a bait of leaves containing a poison that completely paralyses them. He drily remarks that most tusks were sold in India, which he had visited, and China. That was why ivory was so scarce in Arabia. The Zanj were also good hunters on the ocean, and he vividly relates how they chased whales and harpooned them.

But voyaging to Africa was perilous. 'I have sailed on many seas, but I do not know of one more dangerous than that of Zanj.' He lists the captains with whom he has travelled. All had been drowned, paying the ultimate price for venturing to Africa.[6] Every successful journey in the flimsy craft of the Indian Ocean (called the Abyssinian Sea by al-Mas'udi) was a gift from God.

Qanbalu was a thriving place which minted its own coinage, although the Arab gold dinar was the main currency used in the Indian Ocean ports. Al-Mas'udi tells of sailing there with a number of Omani ship-owners from Sohar. Traders also sailed to Qanbalu from Siraf, home of the story-writer Captain Buzurg. Al Mas'udi knew of Buzurg's work – they were contemporaries, and had both grown up in or near Basra.

However, al-Mas'udi was to spend his later years in Cairo, a tolerant city where he probably felt safer, since his religious opinions were unorthodox. Only one work survives out of the thirty volumes he is known to have written on geography, medicine and natural history. His world encyclopaedia, *Murnj al dhahab*, (*The Meadows of Gold*), exists in a draft form, and his knowledge was at times flimsy: when he describes the Atlantic Ocean he says that 'Britanya' is towards its northern end and consists of twelve islands. On the other hand, he is the first Muslim writer to identify Paris, which he called Barisa, as the capital of the 'Franks', and is able to assemble an accurate list of French kings. (At that time, in the mid-tenth century, nobody in western Europe could have been remotely as well informed about Arabia or India. When medieval Christian scholars did begin describing the world, they clung to the belief that the three continents were a trinity, with the Holy City in the centre; they knew nothing of China, but said the East was where four great rivers flowed from an Earthly Paradise.)

While al-Mas'udi is the solitary eye-witness of life in the tenth-century Zanj, several of his contemporaries collected what facts they could about it.[7] The information available to a renowned geographer, Ibn Hawqal, was scanty. The Africans, he had learned, were 'not much inclined to the cultivation of the arts and sciences'. But also living in 'Zingbar' were white people 'who bring from other places articles of food and clothing' (undoubtedly a reference to Arab merchants from the Gulf). The anonymous Persian geography, *Hudud al-Alam* (*Regions of the World*), written towards the end of the tenth century, could only say that the 'country of Zangistan' was opposite India, and full of gold-mines. For the rest, the author relied on hearsay and prejudice. The Zanj people were 'full-faced, with large bones and curly hair', and extremely black. The people of Abyssinia were lazy, but obedient to their king.

At the time these accounts were being written, the merchants of southern Arabia were also establishing settlements on the south-west coast of India, which they called Malabar, the Land of Mountains, since the hills rose steeply behind the coastal plains. They were also starting to control the cinnamon exports of Ceylon. Many similarities were to be found between the Muslim communities of East Africa and Malabar, including the creation of a unique locally-based language, written in Arabic. Both traded widely throughout the densely-populated regions of the Indian Ocean, their ships going regularly to China.

Most intriguing of all the Islamic geographers is al-Biruni (sometimes written Alberuni), a learned Persian born in 973 near the Aral Sea. Known as 'The Master', he was also a mathematician and astronomer. One of his achievements was to calculate the earth's circumference with greater accuracy than had ever been achieved before; he was only 70 miles out. Taken to Afghanistan as a prisoner, he spent much of his life there and in the Punjab, compiled a *Chronology of Ancient Nations*, and travelled through India, of which he wrote a history, *Tahqiq al-Hind* (*An Inquiry into India*). Typically, al-Biruni has little favourable to say of the Africans: 'The Zanj are so uncivilized that they have no notion of a natural death. If a man dies a natural death, they think he was poisoned. Every death is suspicious to them, if a man has not been killed by a weapon.'

Turning to geography he is bold enough to criticize Ptolemy (whose work he had before him in translation) and offers his own assessment of Africa's shape and size. Looking at the continent from a northern perspective, he had decided that it protruded 'far into the ocean', passing beyond the equator and the 'plains of the negroes in the west'. It went much further than the Mountains of the Moon and the sources of the Nile – 'in fact, into regions which we do not exactly know', where winter prevailed during summer in the northern hemisphere. The sea beyond 'Sofala of the Zanj' was impossible to navigate, and no ship which ventured there had ever returned to give an account of what it had seen. Elsewhere he seems to contradict himself. 'This southern ocean is navigable. It does not form the utmost southern limit of the inhabitable world. On the contrary, the latter stretches still more southward.'

One ultimate geographical puzzle – where Africa ended – intrigued al-Biruni. He was not content with the Ptolemaic convention that it swung to the east, joining up with a long sliver of land along the southern limits of the Indian Ocean which eventually reached all the way to China. Instead, he believed there was a sea route round Africa, linking the Atlantic with the Indian Ocean: 'One has certain proofs of this communication, although one has not been able to confirm it by sight.'

Almost five centuries later, he would be proved right.

FIVE

On the Silk Route to Cathay

Let me tell you next of the personal appearance of the Great Lord of Lords whose name is Kubilai Khan. He is a man of good stature, neither short nor tall but of moderate height. His limbs are well fleshed out and modelled in due proportion. His complexion is fair and ruddy like a rose, the eyes black and handsome, the nose shapely and set squarely in place.

—Marco Polo, *Description of the World* (1298)

WHILE ARABS and all other Muslims retained a freedom to travel from the western Mediterranean to the Sea of China, the western Christians found their horizons more restricted than ever as the second millennium of their faith advanced. Behind the barriers of hostility raised by the crusades, European ignorance of the geography of the wider world remained almost absolute.

Moreover, notions about the shape or size of countries, even ones close at hand, were vague and confused. Map-making had scant regard for scale, journeys were measured by the time they took rather than the distance covered, and the whole subject was bedevilled by those theological theories about the world having a flat, plate-like shape, with Jerusalem at its centre.

As for the inhabitants of distant lands, any fantasy was believable. Europe's appetite for the grotesque was sustained by the inclusion in many medieval writings of excerpts from the work of Caius Julius Solinus, who in late Roman times had plagiarized Pliny's *Natural History*, assembled many ancient myths about human and animal monsters, then spiced them all up with his own imaginings. Another proponent of the fantastic was Osorius, a fifth-century priest in Spain whose main purpose in his 'world encyclopaedia' was to vilify all non-Christians. Through such works, much of Asia, and all of Africa, became peopled with 'troglodytes', who lived underground and 'jibbered like bats' in an unknown tongue. There were also half-human creatures looking like

39

hyenas, men with four eyes, and others with only half a head, one arm, and one leg upon which they could jump to astounding heights.

All these improbabilities went unchallenged in Europe because there were virtually no eye-witness accounts of the world beyond Egypt and Palestine. Although many Arabic works, such as medical textbooks, had already been translated into Hebrew or Latin, the Arab geographers seem to have been largely ignored. The only non-Muslims able to travel with little hindrance across the boundaries of the two dominant religions were certain Jewish merchants, whose trading networks stretched out to the East from Alexandria and the cities of the Levant. Yet they were intensely secretive about where they went and what they had seen.

One rare exception was a rabbi named Benjamin of Tudela.[1] In the twelfth century he spent twelve years travelling from northern Spain to Baghdad, Basra, the cities of Persia and parts of India. Benjamin writes about Christians with bitterness, but is conspicuously warm towards Muslims: the caliph of Baghdad is called 'an excellent man, trustworthy and kind-hearted towards everyone', as well as 'extremely friendly towards the Jews'. The rabbi's principal aim was to compile a register of the Jewish communities in as many cities of Asia as he could reach (the results were gratifying to him, because he found them to be numerous and prospering everywhere).

He gives a vivid impression of life in Persia, then goes on to explain in detail how merchants arriving in the great South Indian port of Quilon were assured of security by the ruler. His narrative also describes the growing and processing of pepper and other spices in the countryside round Quilon. Although the rabbi did not go as far as Ceylon, which he called Kandy (after one of the kingdoms on the island), he established that even it had 23,000 Jewish settlers. He added: 'From thence the passage to China takes 40 days.' It is the earliest known use of this name by a medieval European writer to identify the greatest power of the Orient. Benjamin wrote a level-headed narrative, and monsters have no place in it, apart from the ubiquitous *rukh*, which he claims swoops down on sailors shipwrecked on the way to China, then flies away with them in its claws to eat them at leisure; some sailors had been clever enough, after being deposited on dry land by the bird, to stab it to death.

On his way home Benjamin took ship across the Indian Ocean to Yemen. There he collected some hearsay information about the source of the Nile, 'which comes down here from the country of the blacks'.

The yearly rise in the level of the river was caused by floods from Abyssinia, also known as Ethiopia:

> This country is governed by a king, whom they call Sultan al-Habash, and some of the inhabitants resemble beasts in every way. They eat the herbs which grow on the banks of the Nile, go naked in the fields, and have no notions like other men; for instance, they cohabit with their own sisters and with anybody they may find. The country is excessively hot; and when the people of Aswan invade their country they carry wheat, raisins and figs, which they throw out like bait, thereby alluring the natives. They are made captive, and sold in Egypt and the adjoining countries, where they are known as black slaves, being the descendants of Ham.[2]

In the terminology of his time, Rabbi Benjamin spoke of Ethiopia as belonging to 'Middle India', which extended up to the east bank of the Nile, with Africa starting only on the west bank. The shape and size of India, suspended from the great bulk of Asia, was still a mystery, but the term itself was liberally applied to lands bounding the ocean which took its name. 'Greater India' was the south of the sub-continent and lands further east. 'Lesser India' lay to the north. 'Middle India' included the southern parts of Arabia as well as Ethiopia − a name with Greek origins. 'India Tertia' covered East Africa, as far as its existence was known, and sometimes Ethiopia as well, which was imagined to be in the southern hemisphere.

In the century following the travels of Rabbi Benjamin, merchants in Europe had begun to ponder ways of finding some unimpeded route to the wealth of the East. After the defeats inflicted on the crusaders by the armies of Saladin, the great Kurdish leader, all access to the Red Sea was strictly denied to Christian traders. Goods from India and China could be bought from Arab merchants in Alexandria and other ports of the eastern Mediterranean, but prices were high and payment must always be in gold. Moreover, this business was dominated by Venetians, whose Adriatic republic felt strong enough to flout the papal prohibitions about trading with Islam.

So in the spring of 1291, a small flotilla of ships left Genoa, the leading rival of Venice, and headed westwards through the Mediterranean. They were captained by two brothers, Ugolini and Vadino Vivaldi, men with a bold scheme in mind. They intended to sail through the Strait of Gibraltar, follow a southerly course down the coast of Africa, and keep on until they made a landfall at last upon the shores of India or Persia. Considering the meagre geographical knowledge in the Europe of their time, this plan could only have been based upon intuition and reckless courage. Nevertheless, the purpose was practical enough: if they could open such a route, they might break the Venetian stranglehold.

A few Genoese were already living in Persia, which had been conquered seventy years before by the Mongols under Chinghiz Khan. Although these compatriots were on friendly terms with a king named Arghon, who ruled the vast western empire of the Mongols, there was as yet no unimpeded way of sending home merchandise.

The Vivaldis sailed past Gibraltar, and were seen heading south along the Moroccan coast. After that, they were never heard of again. Their frail vessels, propelled by oarsmen and sails rigged for Mediterranean weather, were no match for the Atlantic currents and storms. The doomed Genoese could never have guessed at the African continent's immense length and the perils to be faced in trying to circumnavigate it.

The Vivaldi brothers were two centuries ahead of their time. For many years after their disappearance, members of their family sought in vain for news of them. There were even rumours, but never any proof, that they had managed to sail round Africa, only to be wrecked at the mouth of the Red Sea.

The much-discussed disappearance of the Vivaldis would have been of more than passing interest to a prosperous Venetian merchant brought to Genoa a few years later, in 1296, and put under guard in a castle overlooking the harbour. His name was Marco Polo, and he had been taken prisoner during a sea battle in the Adriatic, just after returning to Europe from twenty years in the East.

The Venetians made a habit of being condescending about their Genoese enemies, so Marco would almost certainly have dismissed the Vivaldis' idea of reaching Persia or India by sea as absurd. He knew the straightest route from Europe to those places as well as any man, and it went overland from the Black Sea port of Trebizond. He had twice sailed across the eastern half of the Indian Ocean (and apart from the nameless flotsam of history was perhaps the first European to have done so for many centuries); but he would never have dared to venture into the 'Torrid Zone' of Africa.

As he was to assert – with some exaggeration – in his memoirs, ships could not sail to the far south, 'beyond Madagascar and Zanzibar', because 'the currents set so strongly towards the south that they would have little chance of returning'. Marco had heard discouraging tales about the perils of the southern seas of the Indian Ocean, and even less was known about the waters encompassing Africa on its Atlantic side. The Vivaldis had paid with their lives for confronting these mysteries.

Marco's anecdotes on faraway lands were countless, and fortunately he was to share his two years of imprisonment in Genoa with a companion only too ready to hear them. The man cast by fortune to be Marco's scribe and literary helpmate was a certain 'Rustichello of Pisa', whose slender reputation as a writer rested upon translations of Arthurian romances into Old French. Little is known about Rustichello, why he was in prison, or if he ever came out alive; but he may have travelled earlier in life to Palestine, and even to England, where his patron was reputedly the prince who later became Edward I.

It is thanks to this dauntless scribbler that the fame of his Venetian fellow-prisoner has lived on. The two men were to occupy many idle months in working together on a manuscript, written in Italianate French, which Rustichello boldly entitled *A Description of the World*.[3] Left to himself, Marco might never have written a thing. He came from a family of merchants, joined his father in business at the age of seventeen, and his interests were anything but literary. After parting from Rustichello when he was released by the Genoese, probably in return for ransom money, he lived on for a quarter of a century, without composing another sentence on his travels. (There was, admittedly, scant incentive; before the era of printing an author could hope for few direct rewards.)

Much of what Marco dictated to his scribe about Cathay was well calculated to arouse the envy of other European merchants, as when he describes the port of Zayton:

> And I assure you that for one shipload of pepper that goes to Alexandria or elsewhere to be taken to Christian lands, there come a hundred to this port of Zayton. For you must know that it is one of the two great harbours in the world for the amount of its trade. And I assure you that the Great Khan receives enormous revenues from this city and port, for you must know that all the ships that come from India

pay ten per cent, namely a tenth part of the value of all the goods, precious stones and pearls they carry. Further, for freight the ships take 30 per cent for light goods, 44 per cent for pepper, and 40 per cent on aloes-wood, sandalwood, and other bulky goods.

And I assure you that if a stranger comes to one of their houses to lodge, the master is exceedingly glad. He orders his wife to do everything the stranger may desire . . . And the women are beautiful, merry and wanton.'

Such practical information abounds, but is artfully juxtaposed with jocular anecdotes, as when describing his youthful memories of a place in central Asia where husbands offered their wives to guests. The relish with which Rustichello inserted such vignettes into the *Description of the World* is perceptible, but the raconteur himself remains unmistakably a figure to be viewed with respect.

There was good reason, for although there were many prosperous and well-born Venetian merchants, Marco Polo had always been notably privileged. As a youth of seventeen, in 1270, he had welcomed home his father Nicolo and his uncle Maffeo from their first journey to Cathay. They were bearing a golden tablet of authority from Kubilai Khan, the Mongol ruler. From that moment it counted for a great deal to belong to the Polo family.

Earlier in the thirteenth century, Europe had been terrified of the all-conquering Mongols (generally known as Tartars).[4] Opinions of them had changed entirely by the time Marco's father and uncle arrived in Italy from Cathay with Kubilai Khan's golden tablet. The Mongols were now seen as potential allies, with whom the lost fervour of the Crusades might be rekindled; since the time of Pope Innocent IV (1243–53) hopes had been nurtured of converting the Mongols to the Catholic teaching, for some already had Christian leanings, albeit of an heretical kind. The Great Khan was a figure of almost mystical significance for Europe's rulers, and the Polo brothers were honoured to be his chosen emissaries in the latest attempt to forge permanent links between East and West against the common enemy: Islam.

Fifteen years before the Polos arrived back from Cathay, a Flemish friar named William of Rubrouck had been sent to Cathay by Louis IX of France. The friar's mission had been to offer the Mongol emperor a pact with Christendom, and he returned with remarkable stories about people from Europe who had been swept like dust across the world when the Mongols drew back into Asia.

In remote Karakorum, traditional gathering place of the Mongols, the friar encountered a woman called Paquette, from Metz in Lorraine, who had been taken prisoner in Hungary, but was now happily married to a Ukrainian carpenter, and had three children: 'She found us out and prepared for us a feast of the best she had.' Also in Karakorum were the Hungarian-born son of an Englishman, a Greek doctor, and a goldsmith from Paris named Buchier, who had made for the Great Khan a silver tree, with an angel on the top blowing a trumpet and at the base four guardian lions whose mouths spouted mare's milk, a staple item of the Mongolian diet.

Although Friar William had failed in the main aim of his mission, the auguries for an East-West alliance were more promising when the Polo brothers reached Europe. The Great Khan was asking, among other things, for a hundred learned men of the Christian faith to be escorted back to him by the Polo brothers. It might have seemed too good a chance to miss, but at that crucial moment one Pope died and there was a dispute over who should succeed him. When Gregory X was eventually installed he chose only two scholarly friars to go to Cathay. Even these were not up to the task. After setting off with the Venetian merchants, accompanied now by young Marco Polo, the friars turned back after travelling only as far as Armenia, where a war threatened.

The Polos rode on. They still had to deliver Pope Gregory's message of good-will to Kubilai Khan, and this gave them, by thirteenth-century standards, a sense of urgency. They decided that the sea route through the Indian Ocean would be quicker than a long, exhausting journey across central Asia's deserts, whose hazards Nicolo and Maffeo knew only too well. So they travelled first to Baghdad (which the Mongols had sacked a few years earlier, massacring all the Muslims but sparing the Christians). From there they crossed into Persia, then rode south to the great port of Hormuz at the mouth of the Gulf. This was Marco Polo's first sight of the Indian Ocean, but he was not impressed.

Hormuz had an excellent harbour, and it had taken over much of the trade controlled three centuries earlier by Siraf, birthplace of the story-teller Buzurg ibn Shahriyar. Merchants came to Hormuz from 'the length and breadth of the world' to deal in pearls, cloth and dried fruits, spices from Malabar and Ceylon, Chinese ceramics and African ivory. Arabian horses were shipped from here to India: steeds chosen for their strength, powerful enough to bear men in full armour. However, as Marco would remember it many years later, the climate of Hormuz was torrid and unhealthy. Sometimes in summer, winds blew from the deserts lying on every side with such unbearable heat that there was only one way to survive: the local people lived outside the city in summer, beside lakes and waterways, so that when the hot winds approached they could 'plunge neck-deep into the water to escape'.

With his medieval fondness for the gruesome he goes on to tell a story to illustrate the infernal heat of the place:

> As the king of Hormuz had not paid his tribute to the king of Kerman, the latter got ready 1,600 horse and 5,000 foot, sending them across the region of Reobar, to attack the others by surprise. This he did at the time when the people of Hormuz were living outside the city in the country. One day, the assailants, being wrongly guided, were unable to reach the place appointed for passing the night, and rested in a wood not very far from Hormuz. When, on the next morning, they were about to set out again, that wind caught them, and suffocated them all . . . When the people of Hormuz heard this, they went to bury them in order that all those corpses should not infect the air. But the corpses were so baked by the immense heat, that when they took them by the arms to put them in the pits, the arms part from the bodies. It was hence necessary to make the pits next to the bodies and to throw them in.

The Polos stayed some while in Hormuz. According to Marco the people were 'black' – darker, he meant, than the northern Persians – and 'worshipped Muhammad' (he always used this term, calculated to enrage any Muslim). He described the Hormuzians as living mainly on dates, tunny-fish and onions. They brewed an excellent date wine which purged the bowels.

The Polos' clear purpose in coming to Hormuz was to take a ship across to Cambay in India, then down the Malabar coast to one of the ports from where convoys sailed straight to China. Instead, they turned back and chose the overland route after all. Marco does not explain why outright, but the reason for this retreat is plain enough. The 'sewn boats', the traditional craft of the Indian Ocean, looked too dangerous: 'Their ships are very bad and many of them are wrecked, because they are not fastened with iron nails but stitched together with thread made of coconut husks . . . This makes it a risky undertaking to sail in these ships. And you can take my word that many of them sink, because the Indian Ocean is often very stormy.'[5]

Even if a vessel stayed afloat, the voyage would be anything but agreeable: 'The ships have one mast, one sail and one rudder, but no deck. After they are loaded, however, the cargo is covered with a piece of hide, and on top of the cargo thus covered are placed the horses that are taken to India to be sold.' Marco notes as a gloomy afterthought that the boats were not caulked with pitch, but 'greased with a fish oil'.

The sea voyage had seemed impossibly hazardous, yet the Polos barely survived their two-year journey overland to Cathay. After many mishaps they finally bowed before the Great Khan, to be welcomed with all the honour due to emissaries from Christendom. There was little incentive to hasten back to Venice, and Marco began collecting the material which for three centuries was to have an unequalled influence upon Europe's thinking about other races and continents.

SIX

A Princess for King Arghon

Gold and silver to fill my storehouse year by year;
Corn and rice to crowd my sheds at every harvest.
Chinese slaves to take charge of treasury and barn,
Foreign slaves to take care of my cattle and sheep.
Strong-legged slaves to run by saddle and stirrup when I ride,
Powerful slaves to till the fields with might and main,
Handsome slaves to play the harp and hand the wine;
Slim-waisted slaves to sing me songs, and dance . . .

—a bridegroom's dream, in *Ballads and Stories
from Tun-Huang* (c. A.D. 750 trans. Arthur Waley)

THERE ARE too few guidelines in his book to tell precisely where Marco Polo travelled during his twenty years in the East, yet he certainly saw much of China, and journeyed beyond its borders, apparently to carry out diplomatic tasks for the Great Khan.[1] One mission took him to India by sea, but the ship in which he was a passenger seems to have reached Sumatra too late to catch the summer monsoon. He had to wait on the island for five months, until the wind began blowing again towards the north.

Marco filled his time by learning all he could about this unfamiliar part of the world. He describes the woods and spices produced in the region of Sumatra and 'Malayur', for he is always thinking of the trading possibilities. (At one point he steps outside his narrative to mention having brought a particular variety of seed back to Venice in the hope of cultivating it there; but the climate had defeated him.)

On the other hand, Marco – doubtless encouraged by his scribe Rustichello – never misses a chance to dwell upon the macabre. He denounces as fraudulent several embalmed specimens of tiny 'pygmies' which had reached Europe from the East and caused much amazement. Having been where they were made, he knows they are nothing but small monkeys with faces like humans. The Sumatrans were experts at 'doctoring' the monkey corpses to make them look more convincing.

He goes on to tell of a kingdom called Dagroian, where the people had one 'particularly bad' custom. When a sick patient was considered unlikely to recover he was suffocated and cooked: 'Then all his kinsfolk assemble and eat him whole. I assure you that they even devour all the marrow in his bones.' He discerned a religious purpose here, for if any flesh were left it would breed worms, the worms would die of hunger and the dead man's soul would suffer torment because so many souls 'generated by his substance' had met their deaths.

When Marco was finally able to sail on from Sumatra he showed none of his earlier fear of the Indian Ocean, doubtless because he was now on board a large Chinese junk, markedly different from the filthy horse-boats of Hormuz. It was from his narrative that Europe was to gain the first detailed description of these oriental ships, by far the world's most advanced sea-going vessels at that time. They carried crews of up to four hundred, were propelled by sails made of split bamboo cane on as many as four masts, and the hulls had strong watertight bulkheads to limit the flooding if the sides were pierced by reefs. Unlike the Arab and Persian ships, in which passengers had a wretched time, the junks were described by Marco as planned for comfort, 'with at least sixty cabins, each of which can comfortably accommodate one merchant'.

The young Venetian travelled up both sides of India, going from port to port and giving a precise account of the trading prospects there. Since the old fantasies about monstrous beasts and bizarre humans still fascinated Europe, the lack of them in Marco's memoirs may have been a disappointment to some of his readers; on the other hand, this first coherent account of India's exotic richness was destined to arouse much excitement among both monarchs and merchants.

His first stopping-place had been Ceylon, and what impressed him there was the abundance of rubies, sapphires, topazes and other gems. One ruby, the length of a palm and as thick as a man's arm, was so famous that the Great Khan sent emissaries to buy it; but the king of Ceylon turned them away. Marco's detailed account implies that he may have been among these emissaries.

As he voyaged up the west side of India, along the Malabar coast, Marco marvelled at the immense production of pepper, cinnamon, ginger and other spices. Some regions produced cotton, and everywhere it was possible to buy beautiful buckram, as delicate as linen, and fine leather, stitched with gold and embossed with birds and beasts. The merchants of India, known as *banians*, from an old Sanskrit word, were scrupulous in their trading, and goods could be left with them in complete safety; so it was not surprising that ships came to Malabar from many lands. Towards the end of his journey Marco visited the great Gujarati port of Cambay, the terminus for much of the trade across the western half of the Indian Ocean. The merchants of Cambay regularly travelled as far as Egypt, and many of their goods were sold on to the Mediterranean countries.[2]

About the time when Marco was in India, the ruler of Ceylon, named Buvanekabahu, had sent an envoy to Cairo in a bid to win a share of this trade. His message to the Mamluke rulers said: 'I have a prodigious quantity of pearls and precious stones of every kind. I have vessels, elephants, muslins and other cloths, wood, cinnamon, and all the objects of commerce which are brought to you by the *banian* merchants.'[3] However, the Indian monopoly was to prove far too strong for him to break, although the discovery of Ceylonese coins near Mogadishu, in the Horn of Africa, suggests that Buvanekabahu may have had some success in expanding his island's trade.

Marco was impressed by India's exports of cotton and imports of gold; one of the shipping routes took merchants directly across the ocean, to exchange brightly-coloured cloth for the gold of southern Africa. A trade which continued to fascinate him was the traffic in horses from Arabia and Persia. 'You may take it for a fact that the merchants of Hormuz and Kais, of Dhofar and Shihr and Aden, all of which provinces produce large numbers of battle chargers and other horses, buy up the best horses and load them on ships and export them.' Some were sold for as much as 500 *saggi* (about 2,500 grams) of gold, and one kingdom alone on the Coromandel coast imported about 6,000 horses a year. By the end of the year no more than 100 would still be alive, because the Indians had no idea of how to care for them. According to Marco, the merchants who sold the horses did not allow any veterinarian to go with the animals, because they were 'only too glad for many of the horses to die'.

The social customs of India are also recounted in the *Description of the World*, including the practice of suttee, by which widows flung themselves on the funeral pyres of their husbands. Marco notes how Hindu superstitions governed business deals; the appearance of poisonous spiders or the length of shadows were taken as omens. He tells of the behaviour of yogis in great detail, and while their beliefs seemed bewildering at times – even green leaves had souls, so it was a sin to eat off them – he had come across many strange things on his travels and was usually too broad-minded to scoff.

The Indian people were 'idolators', and the inquisitive Venetian soon discovered what went on at Hindu festivals. True to form, he took a particular interest in the temple maidens, who did a great deal of dancing to conciliate the gods and goddesses: 'Moreover, these maidens, as long as they are maidens, have such firm flesh, that no one can in any way grasp or pinch them in any part of their bodies. And, for the price of a small coin, they will let a man try and pinch them as hard as he likes. When they are married, their flesh remains firm, but not quite so much. On account of this firmness, their breasts do not hang down, but always remain stiff and erect.

Amid such diverting ribaldry there was ample proof that the riches of the East were indeed beyond compare. What had Marco said about Beijing? 'It is a fact that every day more than 1,000 cartloads of silk enter the city; for much cloth of gold and silk is woven here.' Almost anywhere in the East, it seemed, a few groats would purchase treasures worth a fortune, if they could be brought back to Europe.

Marco never set foot in Africa, but he had collected a hotchpotch of facts and falsehoods about it during his travels. He begins his description of the continent by giving an accurate account of Socotra island, with its population of Nestorian Christians. However, he is far from clear about Socotra's position, putting it 'about 500 miles' to the south of two completely mythical places, about which absurdities had been written for centuries: the Male and Female islands, whose inhabitants met once a year for sexual congress.

He next tells how whales are hunted in the Indian Ocean, with so much detail that the account reads more like recollected experience than hearsay. One part tells what the hunters do after drugging a whale with a concoction of tunny fish:

> Then some of the men climb on to it. They have an iron
> rod, barbed at one end in such wise that, once it has been
> driven in, it cannot be pulled out again ... One of the
> hunters holds the rod over the whale's head, while another,
> armed with a wooden mallet, strikes the rod, straightway
> driving it into the whale's head. For, on account of its being

drunk, the whale hardly notices the men on its back, so that
they can do what they will. To the upper end of the rod is
tied a thick rope, quite 300 paces long, and every fifty paces
along the rope, a little cask and a plant are lashed. This plank
is fixed to the cask in the manner of a mast . . .

Marco goes on to remark upon the amount of ambergris found in
that part of the Indian Ocean, rightly saying that it comes from the
whale's belly.

He calls Madagascar 'one of the biggest and best islands in the whole
world', about 4,000 miles in circumference. This almost doubles Madagascar's true size, but is a geographical revelation, considering the time
when he was writing. He could have collected such details only from
Indian or Arab captains who had sailed to the island. Marco then goes
on to air that persistent myth of the *rukh*, living in Madagascar. Calling
it a gryphon, Marco rejects reports that it is a cross between a lion and
an eagle, asserting that 'actual eye-witnesses' describe it as like an 'eagle
of colossal size'. He then adds a brief, intriguing aside, saying that the
Mongol emperor had despatched emissaries to Madagascar and Zanzibar
to 'learn about the marvels of these strange islands'. The first was
imprisoned, so a second was sent to have him freed.

One of Marco's worst errors was to mix up Madagascar and Mogadishu in the Horn of Africa: 'The meat eaten here is only camel-flesh.
The number of camels slaughtered here every day is so great that no
one who has not seen it for himself could credit the report of it.' This
is exactly true to Mogadishu, but certainly not of the great island 2,000
miles to its south. (It is testimony to the influence of Marco Polo that
the name Madagascar, taken directly from his writings, has survived
despite being based upon a total confusion.)

When he goes on to talk of Zanzibar island, he seems to confuse it
with the entire Zanj region, claiming that it is 2,000 miles in circumference. Of the Africans he says: 'They are a big-built race, and though
their height is not proportionate to their girth they are so stout and so
large-limbed that they have the appearance of giants. I can assure you
that they are also abnormally strong, for one of them can carry a load
big enough for four normal men. And no wonder, when I tell you that
they eat enough food for five.' Their hair was 'as black as pepper' and
they 'went entirely naked except for covering their private parts'.

His description of their physical features leaves no doubt that Marco had met and studied Africans, for many were held in slavery in India, and others employed as mercenaries. He may also have encountered them in China, where by the thirteenth century it was not uncommon for the rich to have black 'devil-slaves'. They were, he says, good fighters who 'acquit themselves very manfully in battle'.

His narrative turns next to Abyssinia, 'Middle India', whose king is correctly identified as a Christian, with six vassal monarchs within his empire. The Muslims lived 'over in the direction of Aden', and Marco relates how the sultan of Aden ('one of the richest rulers in the world') enraged the king of Abyssinia in 1288 by seizing one of his bishops and having him forcibly circumcized 'in the fashion of the Saracens'. As a result, the Abyssinian Christians declared war and won a momentous victory, 'for Christians are far more valiant than Saracens'. The story ends with a description of the lands laid waste to avenge the mutilated bishop, then is rounded off with a flourish which has a ring of the scribe Rustichello: 'And no wonder; for it is not fitting that Saracen dogs should lord it over Christians.'

In the closing decade of the thirteenth century, when his long stay in the East neared its end, Marco sailed once more across the Indian Ocean, with his now elderly father and uncle. They were travelling in great style and comfort, in a fleet of fourteen junks fitted out to the orders of Kubilai Khan, and were on their way to Persia, to the court of King Arghon.

The task given to the Venetians was to present Arghon, whose Christian wife had died, with a new bride selected by Kubilai Khan; she was a seventeen-year-old princess 'of great beauty and charm' named Kokachin. However, for some unexplained reason the fleet took almost two years to deliver the princess to Persia, by which time Arghon had died in battle. His brother Gaykhatu, now ruling in his place, told her escorts that Kokachin should instead become the bride of Arghon's young son Ghazan, who happened to be away at the time fighting a war at the head of 60,000 troops. This instant solution seems to have satisfied everyone, including the princess. The Polos set off again towards the west, to Europe and home, their duty done.

It was a misfortune for them that they had reached Persia just too late to meet Arghon, for no Mongol ruler had ever been keener to unite with European Christianity in a great war to vanquish Islam (which was, at that moment, temptingly weak and disunited). In the course of

his seven-year reign Arghon sent four missions to Europe, vainly appealing for a commitment to a simultaneous assault on both flanks. One
mission was led by a Genoese named Buscarel, who arrived in his home
city a year before the Vivaldi brothers set out to circumnavigate Africa.
His stories of the riches of the East may well have encouraged the
Vivaldis to embark upon their ill-fated voyage.

The most eminent of Arghon's envoys was Rabban ('Master') Sauma,
a Chinese Christian of the Nestorian faith.[4] His formidable journey
illustrates how contacts between Asia and Europe flourished during the
brief outward-looking interlude of Mongol power towards the end of
the thirteenth century. Sauma had been born in Canbaluc (later called
Beijing), and after long years of religious study travelled to Persia. His
companion was a prominent fellow-Christian named Yaballaha, who
was a Mongol. They had reached Baghdad, religious capital of the
Nestorian sect to which they belonged, just as their patriarch was dying;
Yaballaha was chosen to replace him.

The new patriarch fervently supported Arghon's plans for a combined
onslaught on Islam, so he put forward his friend Sauma as the best
person to go to Europe to advance this cause. Helped on his way by
King Arghon's gifts of gold and thirty horses, Sauma rode the well-used
route to the Black Sea port of Trebizond, then to Constantinople and
on to Italy and Rome. Wherever he went he noted down everything
of interest: the eruption of Etna as his ship sailed up the coast of Sicily,
a sea battle off Naples, the beauties of the country round Genoa ('a
garden like Paradise, where the winter is not cold, nor the summer
hot'). The northernmost point of his itinerary was Paris, where he met
Philippe IV and was impressed to learn that the University of Paris had
30,000 students.

From there he rode to Bordeaux to present gifts to Edward I of
England. He had some trouble with the names, recording him as 'King
Ilnagtor in Kersonia'; that is, King of Angleterre in Gascony. But Edward
was so gratified by the message borne by his Chinese visitor that he
wrote a letter promising to fight in the proposed conflict to extirpate
the 'Mohometan heresy' for good. Back in Rome in February 1288,
Sauma met the newly-elected Pope, Nicholas IV, and 'wept with joy'
when Nicholas gave him the Eucharist.

In the end, Sauma's diplomatic efforts were as fruitless as all the rest.
Although the Mongols had once believed that the sky-god Tenggeri
had chosen them to conquer the entire world, when their enthusiasm

for the task waned they turned in upon themselves and retreated to the steppes. The Silk Route was closed to Europeans and the Indian Ocean, with all its bustling commerce, remained even less accessible. The wondrous world the Polos had known once again became little more than a tantalizing legend for the Christians of the West.

SEVEN

The Wandering Sheikh
Goes South

> The people of Greater India are a little darker in colour than we
> are, but in Ethiopia they are much darker, and so on until you
> come to the black negroes, who are at the Equator, which they
> call the Torrid Zone.
>
> —Nicola de' Conti, quoted in *Travels and Adventures of
> Pero Tafur*, 1435–39

THE YEAR AFTER Marco Polo died, a young Berber lawyer bade
farewell to his family and friends in Tangier before setting off on a
lifetime of travel. Just as it was claimed for the Venetian merchant in
his lifetime that no other man had 'known or explored so many parts
of the world', so it would be said on Ibn Battuta's behalf that 'it must
be plain to any man of intelligence that this sheikh is the traveller of
the age'. Both men went to China and India, both sailed across the
Indian Ocean, but Ibn Battuta went further, by making two visits to
Africa. He probably travelled 75,000 miles to Marco Polo's 60,000; but
the cultural dominance by Christian Europe has bestowed fame upon
the Venetian merchant, whereas the rumbustious Moroccan judge has
fallen into relative obscurity.

As their lives overlapped, so did their routes in many distant corners
of the world. Moreover, they have much in common as narrators.
Both enjoy telling outlandish anecdotes, although Marco's tales often
have that typically medieval mixture of farce and earthiness found in
Chaucer and Boccaccio, whereas Ibn Battuta, as befits his profession
and Muslim piety, is more reserved as a story-teller, while never hiding
his enthusiasm for life. The most marked difference is that Ibn Battuta
uses the first person singular liberally and keeps himself constantly at
the centre of the stage. His narrative is a mixture of travelogue and
autobiography.

Although both men exaggerated now and then about the populations of faraway cities, the numbers killed in wars or the riches of foreign potentates (which may be the origin of Marco's nickname 'Il Milione'), whenever their memoirs can be checked against independent evidence both turn out to be substantially accurate. On occasion their descriptions of places and customs are so similar that it seems almost beyond coincidence.

Ibn Battuta never reveals whether he had heard of Marco Polo, or if he was conscious of so often following closely in his footsteps. Possibly he did know of him, for Ibn Battuta's own links with Europe were especially strong, and by the time he was planning his first journey the Polo manuscript had already been translated into several European languages. The Moroccan lawyer had been born into a family of the Berber élite, and Berbers had been settled in Spain for six centuries – ever since 711, when they crossed the narrow straits from Africa in the forefront of the all-conquering Arab armies. The intellectual heart of his world lay in Cordoba, an Islamic but cosmopolitan city with seventeen libraries containing 400,000 books; no other place in western Europe rivalled it as a centre of learning. (Academies in the Christian parts of Spain were dedicated to acquiring from Cordoba and other Andalusian cities the Arab manuscripts containing the great works of Greece and Rome, then translating them into Latin.)

Although a renewed struggle to drive the 'Moors' from Spain had deepened the cleavage between opposing religions in the Mediterranean region, differences were often still only of degree, even on such a basic human issue as slavery. While Marco Polo never speaks of owning slaves, apart from granting freedom in his will in 1224 to a man identified as Peter the Tartar, his 'Serene Republic' had for centuries thrived on the trade. Venice shipped the captives of European wars to Alexandria, where they were exchanged for the silks and spices of the East. There was also an active slave market in Crete, a Venetian colony, and another in Cyprus selling negroes shipped to Spain from North Africa, then brought along the Mediterranean in galleys.[1]

For his part, Ibn Battuta talks freely about the slaves who were always in his entourage, including one or more concubines. While travelling in Turkey, he remarks as an afterthought about a city he had passed through: 'In this town I bought a Greek slave girl called Marguerite.' Since she was merely a slave, the reader hears no more of Marguerite; however, Ibn Battuta took care of his slaves, for when a ship he is in starts to sink, his first thoughts are for his two concubines.

Ibn Battuta had left Tangier when he was twenty-one simply to make the pilgrimage to Mecca. He wandered at a leisurely pace through Egypt, the Levant, Syria, Iraq, Iran and Arabia. While crossing the Mediterranean he travelled in a Genoese ship, and praises the captain for his kindness. His trip to Mecca was extended into a stay of more than two years, which served to enhance his prestige as a *qadi*, or judge of Islamic shar'ia law; this status, proclaimed by his ceremonial cloak and tall hat, was to make travelling much easier for Ibn Battuta, entitling him to respect and hospitality from Muslim rulers or merchants wherever he chose to stop. It also allowed him to offer himself for the post of *qadi* whenever he reached a town where a judge had died or the incumbent had fallen into disfavour.[2]

Until the moment when he decided to visit the Land of Zanj he had travelled mainly on land, and only to places that might not have seemed unduly perilous to a young, educated Muslim with some spirit. By his own testimony, Ibn Battuta found it easy to make friends, but had a weakness for political intrigue; he was generous, yet ambitious, and his public piety was balanced by private indulgence. Most of all he was impetuous, always capable of being swept along by sudden enthusiasms, and his decision to go on a long sea voyage to a remote area of the Indian Ocean revealed the true adventurer in him. Despite being African in a strictly geographical sense, he would have regarded his bustling Tangier birthplace as a world away from Zanj, about which there were many dire rumours. Sometimes it was called Sawahil al-Sudan or just Barr al-'Ajam (Land of the Foreigners).[3]

His first experience of Africa was certainly discouraging. He crossed from the prosperous port of Aden to a town called Zeila, on the Red Sea side of the Horn. 'It is a big city and has a great market, but it is the dirtiest, most desolate and smelliest town in the world. The reason for its stink is the quantity of fish, and the blood of the camels they butcher in its alleyways. When we arrived there we preferred to pass the night on the sea, although it was rough.' An additional reason for Ibn Battuta's distaste was that the people of Zeila were what he called 'Rejecters', since they belonged to a heterodox branch of the Shi'a belief. He was a devout Sunni, his loyalty having been strengthened during his long stay in Mecca. The people of Zeila he dismissively described as 'negroes' of the 'Berberah'. (They were certainly not to be confused with his own Berber people, who were fair-skinned and sometimes had blue eyes.) What he did not say about Zeila was that it served as an assembly-point for prisoners taken in the constant wars against the Christian kingdom of Ethiopia, lying to the west; they were shipped from Zeila to Aden as slaves.

The dhow in which Ibn Battuta was a passenger quickly set sail again from Zeila, eastwards into the Indian Ocean, then south along the desert coastline to Mogadishu; it was a fifteen-day voyage. For someone of his background, Mogadishu also seemed a fairly brutish place, where killing camels to supply meat for Arabia was one of the main occupations. (As Marco Polo had said, the camel-slaughtering was so great in Mogadishu that it had to be seen to be believed.)

However, this time the young Moroccan was happier to go ashore. One of his companions on board had shouted to the touts who came out to the boat: 'This man is not a merchant, but a scholar.' The news was passed to the local judge, who hurried down to the beach to offer a welcome. As Ibn Battuta stepped on to the beach he was warmly embraced by his fellow-*qadi*, an Egyptian. The salaams acknowledged his status: 'In the name of God, let us go to greet the sultan.'

The visitor was at once caught up in an elaborate series of rituals, one of which involved being sprinkled with Damascus rosewater by a eunuch. He was then given hospitality in the 'scholar's house' (merchants staying in Arab ports had quarters known as *funduqs*). It was not until after Friday prayers in the main mosque that Ibn Battuta came face to face with the sultan, who said with traditional courtliness: 'You are most welcome. You have honoured our country and given us pleasure.' Ibn Battuta joined in the formal procession from the mosque, and as a mark of respect was allowed, along with the sultan and the *qadi*, to keep on his sandals. Drums, trumpets and pipes led the way to the audience chamber. There the formal manner of greeting the sultan was like that in the Yemen, by putting an index finger on the ground, then raising it to the head and declaiming, 'May Allah preserve your power.'

Other ceremonies in Mogadishu were unlike anything Ibn Battuta had yet seen in his travels. As the sultan walked along in fine silken robes topped by an embroidered turban, a coloured canopy was held above him, with a golden statuette of a bird at each corner. It was also surprising to a visitor that men in Mogadishu wore no trousers, but wrapped sarong-like cloths around themselves. (Several social customs mentioned by Ibn Battuta suggest there was a strong Indian or Indonesian influence at work.) But most firmly fixed in Ibn Battuta's mind, when he came to commit his memories to writing more than twenty years later, was the stupendous amount of food consumed in Mogadishu. He was able to recall the typical meals served up to him three times a day in the scholar's house: 'Their food is rice cooked in fat and placed on a large wooden dish', with dishes of chicken, meat, fish and vegetables placed on top. Then there were further courses of green bananas cooked in milk and pickled chillies, lemons, green ginger and mangoes, all eaten with rice. Ibn Battuta estimated that a whole group of people in Morocco would eat no more at a sitting than any man in Mogadishu: 'They are extremely corpulent and large-stomached.'

Shortly after leaving the desert country of the Horn the ship crossed the equator: in those times an awesome moment for the superstitious, because unfamiliar constellations began appearing in the night sky. Ibn Battuta did not think it worth mentioning: 'Then I sailed from the city of Mogadishu, going towards the land of the Sawahil, intending to go to Kilwa, which is one of the cities of the Zanj.' His ship, its lateen sail billowing before the north-east monsoon, passed a succession of ports founded by the immigrants from Arabia. The names of only a few of these places, such as Mombasa and Malindi, had been heard of in the outside world. About this time there were even rumours in Egypt that Mombasa had been taken over by monkeys, who marched up and down like soldiers. The Swahili coast was not on a route to anywhere else, so scholarly visitors were distinctly rare.

Ibn Battuta's interest in Kilwa, apart from its pre-eminence on the coast at that time, may have been stirred by his more general curiosity about the African gold trade. In 1324, the year before he passed through Cairo, an African emperor, making the pilgrimage to Mecca, had come there with so much gold that amazement had gripped the Arab world. The ruler was Sulaiman, the Mansa Musa, and he arrived in Egypt with 8,000 warriors, 500 slaves bearing golden staffs, and 100 camels carrying a total of 500,000 ounces of gold. Sulaiman's profligacy with his wealth depressed the price of gold in Egypt for a decade. It was known that he controlled mines somewhere on the southern side of the Sahara desert, but the extent of Africa was such a mystery, and the dimensions of the world so misconceived, that it was easy to think that gold exported from Zanj came from the same source. (The West African mines were, in fact, an immense distance from Zimbabwe, but that would not become clear for almost two centuries.)

Ibn Battuta's visit to East Africa may also have been in response to an invitation from one of its leading citizens. The sultan of Kilwa, al-Hasan ibn Sulayman, had been to Mecca and spent two years in Arabia studying 'spiritual science'. There was great prestige attached to having made the pilgrimage from somewhere as remote as Zanj; being able to welcome to one's own town a learned stranger met while travelling would have been an additional cause for pride for the sultan.

Certainly, by his own account, Ibn Battuta seemed eager to reach Kilwa, for his description of a port where he stopped overnight on the way is perfunctory. He says it was Mombasa, but at once makes this unlikely by describing it as 'an island two days' journey from the coast'. This is clearly a confusion with some other place, perhaps Pemba, Zanzibar or Mafia. He remembered that the people of the island lived mainly on bananas and fish, augmented by grain brought from the coast, and that the wooden mosque was expertly built, with wells at each of its doorways, so that everyone who wished to go in could wash his feet, then rub them dry on a strip of matting supplied for the purpose.

His journey further southwards, past a coastline shrouded in mangrove swamps, brought Ibn Battuta at last to Kilwa. He described it as 'amongst the most beautiful of cities, and elegantly built'.[4] His first view of it, in early 1331, would have been as the ship entered the channel between the island and the mainland. Here was a superb natural harbour in which vessels of every kind could anchor or be run up on the beaches. Within sight further away were several smaller islands; a large settlement on one of these, called Songo Mnara, was also part of the sultan's domain.

The main town of Kilwa, with its defensive bastions, stood well above the sea, directly facing the mainland. Many of its houses were closely packed together, but others were surrounded by gardens and orchards. In the gardens were grown all kinds of vegetables, as well as bananas, pomegranates and figs. The surrounding orchards provided oranges, mangoes and breadfruit. Almost the only foodstuff brought over from the mainland was honey.

When Ibn Battuta arrived, in February, there would have been no lack of lush vegetation, for it was the middle of the wet season, whose ferocious downpours are not easily forgotten. 'The rains are great,' he recalled. Yet at moments his memory utterly fails him, for he says that the city was entirely built of wood. That certainly was not the case by the time of his arrival, since the first stone mosque had been built on the island two centuries earlier. That mosque was later replaced by a much grander building with five aisles and a domed roof supported on stone pillars; it would have been the envy of all neighbouring ports, which had nothing to compare with it.

There was also a huge palace, to the north of the town, with many rooms and open courtyards.[5] One of its features was a circular swimming pool. This building, superbly designed, followed the gentle fall of the ground to the edge of a cliff, below which boats could anchor. It was the home of the sultan and Ibn Battuta must have been received there. He would have dined off Chinese tableware, green celadon and blue-and-white porcelain adorned with chrysanthemums, peonies and lotus flowers: oriental ware was being imported in such quantities that many wealthier residents of Kilwa had taken to cementing them into the walls of their buildings as ornaments.

Kilwa would have needed vast amounts of African labour to build and maintain it. Many of the inhabitants were Zanj, 'jet black in colour' and with tribal incisions on their faces; most were slaves. There were also people of other nationalities to be seen in the busy streets, including visiting merchants and their servants. Lodgings with rooms for trading were provided close to the mosque for the merchants. But not all the merchants were Muslims: some were Hindus, who had sailed directly across the ocean from India with the north-east winter monsoon. They came from the great Gujarat port of Cambay and other trading centres further south along the Malabar coast. Apart from cloth and other manufactures, their ships carried rice, on which the profits were high.

According to Ibn Battuta, the sultan of Kilwa was constantly engaged in a 'holy war' with the Muli, the people of the mainland: 'He was much given to armed sweeps through the lands of the Zanj. He raided them and captured booty.' Put more bluntly, Sultan al-Hasan ibn Sulayman was busy with slave-raiding, but this did not seem in the least shocking in an age when slavery was an integral part of life. In Ibn Battuta's eyes, the sultan, also known as Abu-al-Mawahib (Father of Gifts), was a man true to his beliefs, for he always set aside a fifth of the booty from his raids on the Zanj, and gave this to visiting *sharifs*, descendants of the Prophet. Confident of the sultan's generosity, the *sharifs* came to visit him from as far away as Iraq. 'This sultan is a very humble man,' concluded Ibn Battuta. 'He sits with poor people and eats with them, and gives respect to people of religion and Prophetic descent.'

The young Moroccan lawyer chose not to venture as far as Sofala, which a merchant told him was several weeks' sailing further south. The uncertainties of the weather between Sofala and Madagascar, the land of the heathen Waqwaqs, meant that he risked being unable to sail back across the equator with the arrival of the south-west monsoon. There was also the danger of cyclones in the southern part of the ocean. So when the monsoon changed, Ibn Battuta did not linger, because in the middle months of the year there was a likelihood of violent storms. He boarded another ship, which headed across the open sea to Arabia; from there he went on by a roundabout route to India.

Ibn Battuta's journey to East Africa in 1331, his first venture into the arena of Indian Ocean civilization, provides an eye-witness account of the coast after a gap of several centuries. For him it was the turning point of his career. From now on his lifelong urge to find out what lay beyond the next mountain, past the next town, across the next sea, was to make him, in Islamic eyes, the doyen of adventurers in pre-modern times.

EIGHT

Adventures in India
and China

> He who stays at home beside his hearth and is content with the
> information which he may acquire concerning his own region,
> cannot be on the same level as one who divides his lifespan
> between different lands, and spends his days journeying in search
> of precious and original knowledge.
>
> —Al-Mas'udi, *The Meadows of Gold*

WHAT DISTINGUISHES the memoirs of Ibn Battuta from many other
humdrum travel diaries is not merely his flair for recording what is
bizarre, exotic or absurd, but also the way he lays bare his personality:
at times he is swashbuckling and boastful, at others vulnerable and
indecisive, then ready to laugh at his own folly in inviting misfortune.
After six centuries, in translation from the Arabic, his individuality asserts
itself. His capacity for self-revelation is closely related to a gift for capturing in one or two sentences the manners and customs of other people.

His description of life aboard the big Chinese trading junks, which
were more and more to be seen sailing to Indian Ocean ports, epitomizes
his skill. Ibn Battuta writes approvingly, echoing Marco Polo, about the
amenities for merchants: 'Often a man will live in his cabin unknown
to any of the others on board until they meet upon reaching some
town.' These cabins, consisting of several rooms and a bathroom, could
be locked by the occupants, 'who would take along with them slave
girls and wives'. He adds a glimpse of lower-deck life: 'The sailors have
their children living on board ship, and they grow lettuces, vegetables
and ginger in wooden tubs.'

In the Chinese custom, the most important figure in running these
behemoths, with their twelve masts and four decks, was not the captain
but a superintendent acting for the owner. In Ibn Battuta's words, the
superintendent was 'like a great emir', and when he went ashore he

was preceded by archers and armed Abyssinians beating drums and blowing trumpets and bugles.

This mention of Abyssinians aboard Chinese ships in the fourteenth century is revealing, for the term always identified a person as coming from somewhere on the eastern side of Africa. Elsewhere, Ibn Battuta says Abyssinians were used throughout the Indian Ocean as armed guards on merchant ships; the presence of merely one was enough to frighten away pirates. He also tells of an Abyssinian slave named Badr, whose prowess in war was so phenomenal that he was made the governor of an Indian town: 'He was tall and corpulent, and used to eat a whole sheep at a meal, and I was told that after eating he would drink about a pound and a half of ghee [clarified butter], following the custom of the Abyssinians in their own country.'

Many Africans were taken to India in the retinues of the Arab merchants who were settling in its ports during the fourteenth century. Others were transported to serve as palace guards. There was also a human flow in the opposite direction: Hindu merchants from the great port of Cambay, in north-west India, crossed the ocean to live in Kilwa, Zanzibar, Aden and ports on the Red Sea.

When Ibn Battuta reached India the fabric of its ancient culture was being torn to shreds. The entire sub-continent was under threat from the war-loving Turks of central Asia, who had invaded India through the mountain passes and the Afghan valleys of the north. One after another they were destroying the ancient Hindu kingdoms lying in their path. However, since the conquerors were Muslims, many doors were open to Ibn Battuta, and this enabled him to give a unique account of the tyranny with which his co-religionists were ruling amid the splendours of northern India. Since his hosts were not Arabs, he was able to view them fairly dispassionately.

By 1333, when Ibn Battuta arrived in Delhi, the throne was occupied by Sultan Muhammad ibn Tughlaq, who called himself by the grandiose title 'Master of the World'.[1] The sultan had murdered his father to gain power, and had his half-brother beheaded when he suspected him of disloyalty. Ibn Battuta's experiences with the sultan during several years in Delhi were to contain all the menace of being trapped in a cage with a man-eating tiger.

Shortly before Ibn Battuta's arrival, the sultan had depopulated his capital as a punishment for its citizens' enmity towards him, made plain in written messages tossed every night into his audience hall. In his rage Muhammad ordered all the people of Delhi to leave at once for a distant region: then he decreed a search for anyone who had not obeyed. As Ibn Battuta tells its, the sultan's slaves 'found two men in the streets, one a cripple and the other blind'. The two were brought before the sultan, who ordered that the cripple should be fired to his death from a military catapult and the blind man should be dragged from Delhi to Dawlat Abad, forty days' journey away. 'He fell to pieces on the road and all of him that reached Dawlat Abad was his leg.'

Ibn Battuta makes a half-hearted attempt in his narrative to excuse the sultan for his savagery, by giving examples of his lavish treatment of strangers. For a time he enjoyed this generosity himself, but then it seems to have gone to his head, because by his own admission he began behaving in a reckless fashion. When the sultan decided to go hunting, he went too, hiring a vast retinue of grooms, bearers, valets and runners. Soon the constant extravagance of the young Moroccan judge became the talk of the court. As Ibn Battuta unashamedly relates, the 'Master of the World' eventually sent him three sacks, containing 55,000 gold dinars, to pay off his creditors. This may also have been the sultan's way of making up for having executed a rebellious court official, the brother of a noblewoman named Hurnasab, whom Ibn Battuta married soon after reaching Delhi.

His volatile friendship with the sultan took a turn for the worse when Ibn Battuta went to stay as a penitent with Kamal al-Din, an ascetic Sufi imam known as the 'Cave Man', living underground on the outskirts of Delhi. The sultan distrusted the 'Cave Man' and eventually had him tortured and put to the sword. Before doing so he summoned Ibn Battuta and announced: 'I have sent for you to go as my ambassador to the king of China, because I know your love of travel.' His difficult guest was quick to accept the proposition; each of them was glad that they would soon be seeing the last of the other.

As a prelude to departure, Ibn Battuta divorced Hurnasab, who had just borne him a daughter. Clearly, domesticity counted for little beside the task of leading an imposing expedition across land and sea. Fifteen envoys had lately arrived from the Great Khan of China, bringing gifts which included 100 slaves, many loads of silk and velvet cloth, jewelled garments and sundry weapons. The sultan was not to be outdone, sending in return 100 white slaves, 100 Hindu dancing girls, 100 horses, fifteen eunuchs, gold and silver candelabra, brocade robes, and numerous other treasures. Ibn Battuta's fellow-ambassadors were a learned man named Zahir ad-Din and the sultan's favourite eunuch, Kafur the cup-bearer. Until they reached their place of embarkation on the west coast of India they were to have an escort of 1,000 horsemen.

This cavalcade, incorporating the fifteen Chinese emissaries and their servants, travelled for only a few days before reaching a town under attack from 'infidels'; that is, Hindu enemies of the sultan. Ibn Battuta and his colleagues decided to use their escorting force to mount a surprise counter-attack. Even allowing for some boasting on his part, this was a considerable success. The infidels were cut to pieces. But one important casualty was the eunuch Kafur, whose special responsibility had been to look after the presents for the Chinese ruler. A messenger was sent back to Delhi, telling the sultan what had happened.

Meanwhile, Ibn Battuta became caught up in a series of skirmishes with the enemy, and it was not long before calamity befell him. He became separated from his cavalry troop, was chased by the Hindus, hid in a ravine, lost his horse, and was soon taken prisoner. All his costly clothes and weapons were removed, including a gold-encrusted sword, and he expected at any second to be killed.

At the crucial moment a young man helped him to escape, and from then on Ibn Battuta's account of his tribulations takes on a dreamlike quality. He wanders through ruined villages, eating berries and looking for water. He hides in cotton fields and abandoned houses. In one house he finds a large jar, used for storing grain, and climbs into it through a hole in the base. There is some straw in the jar, and a stone he uses as a pillow. 'On the top of the jar there was a bird which kept fluttering its wings most of the night. I suppose it was frightened, so we were a pair of frightened creatures.'

After eight days of wandering, Ibn Battuta found a well with a rope hanging over it. Desperate to relieve his thirst he tied to the rope a piece of cloth used to shield his head from the sun, then lowered this down the well. After pulling up the cloth he sucked the water from it, but thirst still afflicted him. He then tied one of his shoes to the rope, and pulled this up full of water. At the second attempt he lost the shoe, then started to use the other one for the same purpose.

In this dire moment a 'black-skinned man' appeared beside him and gave the Muslim greeting, 'Peace be upon you.' Salvation was at hand, for the stranger not only produced food from a bag he was carrying and drew up water from the well in a jug, but even carried Ibn Battuta when he collapsed. Then this mysterious figure vanished, having deposited his human burden near a Muslim village.

After rejoining his companions and resuming his ambassadorial role, Ibn Battuta learned that the sultan had sent another trusted eunuch to replace the ill-fated Kafur. Then the expedition resumed its journey towards the coast. Progress now being relatively uneventful, there was time for him to study the behaviour of Indian yogis. They are as astounding to Ibn Battuta as they had been to Marco Polo: 'The men of this class do some marvellous things. One of them will spend months without eating or drinking, and many have holes dug for them in the earth which are then built in on top of them, leaving only a space for air to enter. They stay in there for months, and I heard tell of one of them who stayed thus for a year.'

Progressing from city to city, the expedition reached the coast near the great harbour of Cambay and boarded a fleet of ships.[2] In these it travelled south, calling at many of the ports Marco Polo had visited half a century before. One was Hili, which Ibn Battuta names as 'the farthest town reached by ships from China'. He adds that it was on an inlet which could be navigated by large vessels; his Venetian predecessor had described the port as being on 'a big river with a very fine estuary'.

At the end of this voyage, the sultan's mission to China, with all its slaves, eunuchs and horses, was to be transferred to junks. These were to sail south-east to Sumatra, then north towards Zayton (Quanzhou), the port in south-east China where most foreign ships unloaded their cargoes. The natural place to switch to the junks was Calicut, a port founded some forty years earlier and already dominant in the export of pepper from the entire Malabar coast. Much of the pepper and other spices traded here were destined for Europe.

Calicut (more accurately, *Koli Koddai*, the 'fortress of the cock') would eventually be destined to play a central role in the history of the Indian Ocean. Its very name was to become a tantalizing challenge, almost a synonym for the wealth of the Indies. As Ibn Battuta's expedition entered Calicut harbour, he counted thirteen large junks lying at anchor. There were also many smaller Chinese ships, for each junk was accompanied at sea by supply and support vessels. He now had three months to wait before the monsoon winds would blow in the right direction for the voyage, so he passed the time by learning all he could about the place.

The ruler of Calicut was an old man, with a square-cut beard 'after the manner of the Greeks', bearing the hereditary title of Zamorin, meaning Sea-King. One explanation for Calicut's growing popularity with merchants and captains was that when a ship was wrecked on any part of the coast under the Zamorin's control, its cargo was carefully protected and restored to the owners; almost everywhere else along the coast any goods washed up were simply expropriated by local rulers. The Sea-King was a Hindu, not a Muslim, but he provided houses for all Sultan Muhammad's emissaries.[3] When the monsoon was due to start blowing southwards, and the time for the voyage to China was at hand, he saw to it that they were fittingly accommodated in one of the largest junks.

However, a disaster exemplifying the hazards of Indian Ocean travel was about to occur. Ibn Battuta survived it only by chance, through his insistence on his personal comforts. He had told the commander of the junk: 'I want a cabin to myself because of the slave-girls, for it is my habit never to travel without them.' The Chinese merchants had taken all the best cabins, however, so he decided to switch with his retinue to one of the support vessels.

The junk, anchored offshore, was about to sail when a violent storm blew up. The great vessel was hurled on to the coast in darkness. Everyone on board was drowned, including the learned Zahir ad-Din and the second eunuch appointed to guard the presents intended for the Chinese ruler.

Ibn Battuta had delayed boarding the support vessel because he had wanted to go to the local mosque for the last time before the journey, so he was one of those who went out after the storm and found the beach strewn with bodies. The support vessel had escaped disaster by reefing its sail and heading off down the coast – leaving Ibn Battuta on land, but carrying away all his slaves and goods (he mentions the goods first in his narrative). He was left with only a former slave whom he had just freed, a carpet to sleep on, and ten dinars. As for the former slave, 'when he saw what had befallen me he deserted me'.

The expedition to China, which had set off with such pomp, was now in ruins. Ibn Battuta thought first of turning back to Delhi, then decided that the half-crazed sultan might well vent his rage upon him for the disaster. Anxious about his goods and his slaves he set out southwards towards the port of Quilon, having been assured that the support vessel would have called in there. Part of the journey was by river, and he hired a local Muslim to help him on his way. But every night his new servant went ashore 'to drink wine with the infidels' and infuriated Ibn Battuta with his brawling.

Despite the plunge in his fortunes, Ibn Battuta managed to pay heed to the passing scene, noting for example that one hilltop town was entirely occupied by Jews.[4] But when he reached Quilon after ten days there was no trace of the ship he had hoped to find there, so he was driven to live on charity. Some of the Chinese ambassadors who had accompanied him from Delhi turned up in equal straits: they had also been shipwrecked, and were wearing clothes given them by Chinese merchants in the town.

Having no compatriots to turn to for succour, Ibn Battuta was at a loss about how to escape from his state of beggary. His credentials as the sultan's ambassador were gone, and all the presents for the Great Khan of China were either at the bottom of the sea or dispersed. As a *qadi*, a law-giver, he had the status which put an obligation on Islamic rulers to offer him hospitality, but without the conventional entourage of slaves, or the clothes and other regalia of his profession, it was hard to win much respect. Eventually he decided to try his fortunes with a ruler further up the coast in the port of Hinawr: 'On reaching Hinawr I went to see the sultan and saluted him; he assigned me a lodging, but without a servant.'

This was a cruel humiliation, but the ruler did ask Ibn Battuta to recite the prayers with him whenever he came to the mosque. 'I spent most of my time in the mosque, and used to read the Qur'ān through every day, and later twice a day.' The help of Allah was badly needed.

Matters only began to improve when the sultan decided to start a *jihad* against the Hindu ruler of Sandabur (later known as Goa). Ibn Battuta opened the Qur'ān at random to find an augury and saw at the head of the page a sentence ending with the words 'and verily God will aid those who aid him'. Although not by nature a fighting man, he was convinced by this that he should offer his services for the *jihad*. There was a brisk but brief seaborne assault, then the palace was captured after being attacked with flaming projectiles: 'God gave victory to the Muslims'.

Ibn Battuta had shown his mettle. His fortunes started to rise again, and on returning to Calicut he was even able to respond with a measure of calm to the news he received from two of his slaves who were aboard the Chinese support ship when it sailed away during the calamitous storm: the ship reached Sumatra safely, but a local ruler had taken his slaves; his goods were likewise stolen. All Ibn Battuta's surviving companions from the expedition were scattered, some in Sumatra, others in Bengal, and the rest were on their way to China. The worst news was that a slave-girl who was about to have his baby was dead; his child by another slave-girl had died in Delhi.

Following this series of disasters, Ibn Battuta abandoned all thought of going to China for some years. Instead, he travelled aimlessly about southern India and Ceylon, attaching himself as the opportunity arose to various Muslim, Hindu and Buddhist rulers. He was repelled by the lawlessness he encountered on both land and sea, and by the cruelties inflicted upon men, women and children alike. But this way of life offered many possibilities for someone of his experience and with his gift for seizing the opportune moment.

At times the situations he encountered could be almost too demanding, as happened when he visited the Maldive islands, lying several days by sea to the south-west of the Indian mainland. These hundreds of coral outcrops, with their palm-trees and sandy beaches, would have reminded him of the islands off the African coast. The Maldives were prosperous, partly because of a seemingly endless supply of cowrie shells lying in shallow water off the beaches: for many centuries the shells had been exported to northern China to be used as currency, and shiploads were sent in the opposite direction every year to Africa for the same purpose.[5]

Islam's roots were not deep here, the faith having been introduced by a visitor from Persia in 1153; before that the population had followed a mixture of Hinduism and Buddhism. Ibn Battuta claims that he tried to disguise his identity on arrival, through a fear that the Maldivian rulers might prove loath to let him leave again, because they lacked a qualified Muslim law-giver. He was quickly recognized none the less: 'Some busybody had written telling them about me and that I had been *qadi* in Delhi.' The suspicion that, in truth, he was only too ready to be asked to offer his services is hard to avoid.

Presents were soon being showered upon him by the Maldivian chief minister and other notables: two new slave-girls, silk robes, a casket of jewels, five sheep and 100,000 cowries. Soon the highly-prized Moroccan finds himself being offered wives from among the rival ruling families, and accepts four, the most a good Muslim can have at any one time. In all, during his eight months in the Maldives he had six different wives. This was entirely in accord with the custom of the islanders: 'When ships arrive, the crews marry wives, and when they are about to sail they divorce them. It is really a sort of temporary marriage.'

Given little option, Ibn Battuta soon donned his robes as the islands' chief justice and set about his duties with a will. His interpretation of the shari'a law was much stricter than anything the easy-going islanders had been used to. When he sentenced a thief to have his hand cut off, several people fainted in the courtroom. Anyone who was found to have been absent from Friday prayers was beaten and paraded through the streets. Husbands who kept divorced wives with them until they found new husbands were also beaten. Only one edict by the strict new judge came to nothing: he tried to stop the women walking around bare-breasted, 'but I could not manage that.'

If Ibn Battuta had set out deliberately to make himself unpopular and stir up rival factions, so easing his departure, then he was successful. The breaking point came when he ordered that an African slave belonging to the sultan should be beaten for adultery; he then publicly rejected the chief minister's appeal for the order to be rescinded. Even this did not remove all obstacles to his departure, for there was now a suspicion that when he returned to the Indian mainland he might incite potential enemies there to amount an invasion of the islands. (Such fears were justified, for as Ibn Battuta admits – or rather, boasts – he became immersed in intrigue and later came close to mounting just such an attack.) Eventually, he agreed to make a tour of the islands while emotions cooled. Then he went to say farewell to the chief minister: 'He embraced me, and wept so copiously that his tears dropped on my feet.'

A leisurely voyage through the Maldives gave the embattled *qadi* time to collect material for the earliest surviving description of the islands. At last he reached an islet where there was only one house, occupied by a weaver:

> He had a wife and family, a few coco-palms and a small boat, with which he used to fish and to cross over to any of the islands he wished to visit. His island contained also a few banana trees, but we saw no land birds on it except two ravens, which came out to us on our arrival, and circled above our vessel. And I swear I envied that man, and wished that the island had been mine, that I might have made it my retreat until the inevitable hour should befall me.

Ibn Battuta eventually slipped away from the Maldives after divorcing all his four current wives (one was pregnant). However, he kept his slaves. His ship sailed off-course and put into harbour in Ceylon, instead of reaching the coast of India. So he took the opportunity to collect facts about the island, noting among other things that the most powerful man in the large town of Kalanbu (Colombo) was a pirate named Jalasti, with a force of 500 Abyssinian mercenaries.

The wandering judge was tempted to Adam's Peak, a place of pilgrimage for Muslims, Buddhists and Christians alike. At the top was a depression claimed to be the footprint of the first man, and to reach it the pilgrims had to go up a steep stairway with the aid of chains fixed to the rock. Marco Polo had also described Adam's Peak, but Ibn Battuta's account of struggling to the mountain-top has infinitely more drama. As he stared down from the peak through the clouds to the vivid greenery of Ceylon he remembered that he had been away from his Moroccan homeland for almost twenty years, but he was still little more than halfway to China, the ultimate goal. There was also a lingering sense of duty towards that self-styled 'Master of the World', the mad sultan in distant Delhi.

The route Ibn Battuta took to get to China was typically circuitous. First he made his way up the eastern coastline of India, almost being shipwrecked at one point and risking his life to rescue his slave-girls. He even dared to return to the Maldive islands, contemplating taking away his two-year-old son by the senior wife he divorced there, but soon thought better of it and sailed to Bengal – a 'gloomy' country where food was cheap. Next he went to Assam to meet a holy man, then arrived in Sumatra, where he stayed with a Muslim ruler and clearly felt far more at ease than Marco Polo had done during his time in the same land. Finally he landed in the port of Zayton and immediately had the luck to meet one of the Chinese ambassadors who had come to Delhi with presents from the Great Khan.

Although Ibn Battuta strives to convey the idea that he was at once elevated to the status of a visiting ambassador, and was taken in magnificent style to see the Great Khan at Peking, this part of Ibn Battuta's memoirs lacks the vivacity of the rest. He does admit that he never saw the Mongol ruler, saying that this was because of a rebellion spreading disorder throughout north China. For all that, he is able to give a convincing account of the burial of the deposed monarch with a hundred relatives and confidants, ending with a grisly description of horses being slaughtered and suspended on stakes above the graves.[6]

Ibn Battuta was constantly impressed by the wonders of China, but unlike Marco Polo he did not enjoy life there: 'Whenever I went out of my house I used to see any number of disagreeable things, and that disturbed me so much that I used to keep indoors and go out only in case of necessity. When I met Muslims in China I always felt as though I was meeting my own faith and kin.' The nub of his unease lay in being totally outside the *Bilad al-Islam*, and discovering that 'heathendom had so strong a hold' in what was plainly the most powerful country in the world.

An emotional moment came when he met in Fuchow (Fuzhou) a Muslim doctor from Ceuta, the Mediterranean port only a few miles from his Tangier birthplace. At this encounter on the far side of the world they both wept. The doctor had prospered greatly in China: 'He told me that he had about fifty white slaves and as many slave girls, and presented me with two of each, along with many other gifts.' Some years later Ibn Battuta was to meet the doctor's brother in West Africa.

Ibn Battuta returned safely by sea from China to Calicut, and there faced a delicate decision. At one moment he felt duty-bound to return to Delhi to report to the sultan all that had happened, then the idea grew too alarming: 'on second thoughts I had some fears about doing so, so I re-embarked and twenty-eight days later reached Dhofar.' This was in the familiar territory of Arabia. From there he began making his way home to Tangier by way of Hormuz, Baghdad and Damascus (with a detour for one more pilgrimage to Mecca).

Shortly before he reached Tangier his mother, long a widow, died from the Black Death.[7] Much had changed in Morocco during the quarter of a century he had been away and little attention was spared for a weatherbeaten *qadi* whom most people had forgotten. Anxieties were running deep about events across the Strait of Gibraltar, because after almost 700 years Islam was yielding its control, step by step, of southern Spain.

Seemingly at a loss as to what he should do next, Ibn Battuta crossed to the European side of the Mediterranean and joined briefly in the *jihad* against the advancing Spaniards. His experiences there were far from happy: in one incident, Christian bandits almost took him prisoner near 'a pretty little town' called Marbella. He soon returned to the safety of Morocco and decided on one last adventure. He headed southwards across the Sahara desert, along trade routes pioneered by his Berber ancestors in Roman times.

He travelled for another two years (1352–53), covering thousands of miles by camel, donkey and on foot, visiting Mali and other powerful West African kingdoms. It was the region from which the fabulous Mansa Musa had emerged twenty-five years earlier to astound Egypt with his wealth. This part of Africa had been won for Islam, but it was strikingly different from the cities Ibn Battuta had visited two decades before on the Indian Ocean side of the continent. There the rulers were Arabs, controlling an African population but holding firm to a non-African culture. In West Africa the culture was indigenous, and the rulers had adapted Islam to fit their own traditions.

He was astonished by the riches of West Africa, at that time the world's greatest gold producer, and by the scholarship he found in Timbuktu, on the bend of the Niger river.[8] He commented: 'The Negroes possess some admirable qualities. They are seldom unjust and possess a greater abhorrence of injustice than any other people . . . There is complete security in their country. Neither traveller nor inhabitant in it has anything to fear from robbers or violent men.'

Sadly, his conclusions about the geography of Africa were wildly astray, because he believed that the Niger, flowing eastwards at Timbuktu, later became the Nile, which he had seen flowing northwards in Egypt. (In this error he was following the theory of the twelfth-century writer al-Idrisi, and many other Arab geographers, that there was a 'western Nile' flowing from the direction of the Atlantic.) Ibn Battuta may even have thought that the Nile was also joined to the Zambezi. Recalling his experiences in East Africa he said that Sofala was a month's journey from the gold-producing land of Yufi. When he came to describe what he believed to be the course of the Nile he declared: 'It continues from Muli to Yufi, one of the greatest countries of the black people, whose ruler is the most considerable of kings of the whole region.'

He went on: 'Yufi cannot be visited by any white man, because they would kill him before he got there.' Since Ibn Battuta regarded himself as 'white' in both colour and culture this was simply a way of explaining why he had failed to make a trip to see the gold-mines, the subject of so much speculation.

When Ibn Battuta finally returned from West Africa to Fez, the Moroccan capital, he was able to claim that he had visited every region of the world where Muslims either ruled or had settled. Many people in the court insisted that it was impossible for one man to have travelled so far and survived so many dangers. These arguments were silenced by the sultan's chief minister, who gave Ibn Battuta several scribes to whom he could dictate as he pleased, as well as a young court secretary, Muhammad ibn Juzayy. It was Ibn Juzayy, proud of his own modest journeys abroad, who wrote in admiration of his elderly charge: 'It must be plain to any man of intelligence that this sheikh is the traveller of the age.'

The old adventurer took his time, living near the palace, sifting through his memories and dictating to the scribes. These labours seem to have been stretched out over almost three years. At times he faltered in remembering the names of people and places, but could still recall vividly those parts of India where the women were especially beautiful and 'famous for their charms in intercourse'. Ibn Battuta was eventually despatched to be the law-giver in an unidentified Moroccan town. No more is on record about him, except that he is thought to have died in 1377 in the ancient city of Marrakesh, aged seventy-three.

By that time a momentous change had overtaken those distant lands through which he and Marco Polo had travelled. The Great Khan was no more, for Mongol rule in China had ended as swiftly as it began. The people whose mounted armies had swept irresistibly across Asia and much of Europe in the middle of the thirteenth century now vanished from the world stage. The Ming dynasty had taken power in the 'Central Country' and would hold it for the next 300 years.

NINE

Armadas of
the Three-Jewel Eunuch

Your Master the Lord of China greets you and counsels you to
act justly to your subjects.
—Chinese envoy, addressing the Sultan of Aden, 1420

THE DRIVING FORCE behind China's most dramatic display of sea-power in its history was a singular figure, the Grand Admiral Zheng He. Described by contemporaries as handsome, tall and burly, with fierce eyes, long earlobes, and a voice 'as loud as a bell', Zheng was also a eunuch. They called him the Three-Jewel Eunuch (or, more formally, the Eunuch of the Three Treasures, a title derived from Buddhism which is literally translated as 'the Three Jewels of Pious Ejaculation'). Yet he was not a Buddhist, his original surname was not Zheng, and ethnically he was not of Chinese descent.

He was born in 1371 in the south-western Kunyang county, in the province of Yunnan. Kunyang is remote from the sea, but his family is thought to have originated even further away, beyond the Great Wall in a distant part of central Asia, and to have come to Yunnan with the Mongols. At all events, they were Muslims, both his father and grand-father having made pilgrimages to Mecca – a great achievement at that time. The family name was Ma, a common one among Muslims in China, and the boy had an elder brother and four sisters. When he was born the Mongols were still holding Yunnan, but were finally driven out by the armies of the Ming emperor Hongwu in 1382.

This was to be the turning-point in the life of the Ma family's eleven-year-old son. A visiting general chose him, for his looks and his intelligence, to be taken to Nanjing, then the Chinese capital. Once in Nanjing, he was made a page to the prince of Yan, the future emperor Yongle. He was given the new surname of Zheng, and castrated.

The creation of eunuchs to be the personal attendants of China's rulers was a tradition, dating back to the earliest empires. At first only criminals were castrated, and were then sent to serve in the palace; this was called *gongxing*, palace punishment. Gradually the stigma was removed. Eunuchs were found to be unwaveringly loyal, never liable to suspicion of plotting to found dynasties of their own; all their energies were dedicated to whatever tasks were set for them. The most obvious role for a eunuch of a menial type was as 'guardians of the harem'. Sometimes courtiers and confidants of much higher status chose to be castrated, to rule out any danger of being accused of sexual misconduct.

The Yongle period was the heyday of the eunuchs, who had played a decisive role in the intrigues which helped the emperor to seize the throne in 1403. They came to have far more say in palace circles than the traditional wielders of power, the Confucian bureaucrats, and none was more influential than Zheng He. While still in his mid-thirties he became a senior officer in the army garrison at Nanjing, on the Yangtze river, after putting down a rebellion in his home province.

When the new emperor decided to implement the long-discussed plans for a naval venture into the Indian Ocean, he turned to Zheng whose religion made him a natural choice since so many of the 'barbarian' lands round the ocean were reputed to follow the rites of the 'Heavenly Square' (the Ka'ba in Mecca). There had been a pretence at first that Zheng He was merely being sent to look for Huidi, the deposed emperor, but this was soon abandoned. The Chinese were primarily looking for markets for the surpluses of their great factories.[1]

There is no knowing whether Zheng was ever a naval commander before being appointed to lead the first expedition. Perhaps he had seen action in sea fights with Japanese pirates (*wokou*), who wreaked havoc among Chinese merchant shipping; the junks of the coastal defence fleet carried warriors trained to board the pirate ships and slaughter their crews. Even if Zheng was no seafarer he must have been well acquainted with naval activity, since Nanjing was near the ocean. Stupendous efforts had been made there for several decades to build up China's fleets.

A previous emperor, Taizu, had ordered the planting on mountainsides inland from Nanjing of millions of trees, to provide wood suitable for ships. By the time of Yongle, the imperial navy consisted of 400 vessels stationed at Nanjing, 2,800 coastal-defence ships, a 3,000-strong transport fleet, and 250 'treasure ships', showpieces of Chinese technology. Although the Mongol rulers had been able to assemble 4,400 ships for a failed attack on Japan a century earlier, and 1,000 for a punitive expedition to Java, most of these would have looked puny alongside the vessels now put at the disposal of the 'Three-Jewel Eunuch'.

Armed with the emperor's edict, Zheng prepared the first of his seven expeditions with a bravura that was to be characteristic of his entire career. The fleet assembled at Dragon River Pass (Liujiajiang) near the mouth of the Yangtze in 1405; this was to be the pattern for the next quarter of a century. The stately 'treasure ships', each weighing more than 500 tons, borne along by the wind in their twelve sails, and carrying hundreds of men, had names such as *Pure Harmony*, *Lasting Tranquillity* and *Peaceful Crossing*.[2] Under full sail they were likened to 'swimming dragons'. These were the floating fortresses of the fleet, their crews armed with 'fire arrows' charged with gunpowder, as well as rockets and blunderbusses firing stones. By 1350 the Chinese had also invented bombards, known as 'wonder-working long-range awe-inspiring cannon', although these were not highly valued for naval use.

The number of big junks sailing in each of the expeditions varied from about forty to more than a hundred, and each had several support vessels. These armadas of the Xia Xiyang ('Going Down to the Western Ocean') were the wonders of the age. The ships carried doctors, accountants, interpreters, scholars, holy men, astrologers, traders and artisans of every sort: on most of his seven expeditions Zheng had as many as 30,000 men under his command, in up to 300 ships of varying types. Flags, drums and lanterns were used to send messages within the fleet. To work out positions and routes the heavens were studied with the use of calibrated 'star plates', carved in ebony.

As with all convoys, the slowest vessels dictated the speed, and this was often no more than fifty miles a day, despite the use of huge oars when winds were slack.[3] Enough rice and other foodstuffs to last for a year were in the holds, lest provisions were lacking in the barbarian lands. Fresh water was stored in large tanks deep in the hulls. As a matter of pride, the Chinese never cared to feel at a disadvantage in foreign parts.

At first the Three-Jewel Eunuch ventured no further than Ceylon and the Malabar and Coromandel coasts of southern India, sending his huge fleets into such ports as Calicut and Quilon, with which Chinese merchants had been familiar for a century. By this time the South Indian pepper port of Calicut (called Kuli by the Chinese) was recognized as the most important emporium in the 'Western Ocean'; when Calicut's emissaries went to Nanjing in 1405 its ruler, the Zamorin, was rewarded with an elevated Chinese title. The attention Zheng's fleets paid to this thriving city proves the commercial purpose behind his expeditions.

There were also less mundane reasons for visiting local rulers. In 1409 the Chinese invaded Ceylon, penetrated the country as far as the mountain capital of Kandy, and captured the Sinhalese king, Vira Alakesvara, together with his queen and members of the court. This was a direct punishment for the king's refusal, several years before, to hand over to the Chinese emperor a precious relic, the tooth of the Buddha. In his time the Mongol ruler Kubilai Khan had also tried to acquire the tooth, but in vain. The king and the other captives were taken back to China as hostages and kept there for five years (although Zheng never did manage to lay hands on the holy tooth). As a reminder of this violent interlude the expedition left behind at the port of Galle a tablet inscribed in three languages, Chinese, Tamil and Persian, respectively praising Buddhism, Hinduism and Islam.

News of this hostage-taking must soon have spread along the trade routes of the Indian Ocean, ensuring that other rulers would be suitably submissive and hand over tribute, thus in effect conceding that they recognized the Chinese emperor as supreme ruler of the universe. When dealing with foreigners, the envoys from Beijing sometimes failed to hide the superiority they felt. One who went ashore in Aden could not bring himself to kiss the ground, as was customary, at the start of his audience with the sultan. This was taken by the Arabs as an insult; for their part, the Chinese thought the people of Aden 'overbearing'.

However, the rewards were great for foreign monarchs willing to pay tribute to the emperor and acknowledge him as their ultimate overlord and mentor. They would be invited to send emissaries to China aboard one of the great treasure ships; in due course the emissaries would return with gifts more valuable than any they had taken with them, to press home the fact of Chinese superiority. An imperial edict explained: 'They come here out of respect for our civilizing ways.' The gifts they brought with them were seen as tribute, a proof of submission.

Yet if this was imperialism, it was of a curiously impermanent nature. Although Zheng sometimes sent punitive parties ashore – one was landed at Mogadishu in Somalia to teach its truculent sultan a lesson – he never installed a permanent garrison anywhere.[4] When each expedition was finished, the entire fleet would turn away eastwards, sail back through the straits of Malacca, head north through the more familiar waters of East Asia, and finally drop anchor in the home port of Nanjing.

The treasure ships carrying the envoys from the Indian Ocean lands were known as 'Star Rafts', a term used by a certain Fei Xin in the title of his account of one expedition: *Triumphant Sights from the Star Raft*. This in turn came from an ancient belief, dating back at least twelve centuries, that if a ship sailed far enough it would eventually leave the earth, reach the Milky Way and come to a galactic city wherein sat a maiden spinning (the traditional representation of Vega in the Lyra constellation). Such heavenly images are mirrored in the wording on a column at Dragon River Pass commemorating Zheng's expeditions: 'Our sails, loftily unfurled like clouds, day and night continued their course, rapid like that of a star, traversing the savage waves.'

Although Zheng was a devout Muslim, he saw no inconsistency in erecting a column in a temple dedicated to the Taoist goddess Tianfei (the Celestial Spouse). The inscription boasts that countries 'beyond the horizon and at the ends of the earth have all become subjects', and goes on to thank the Celestial Spouse for her protection. The miraculous and majestic powers of the goddess 'whose virtuous achievements have been recorded in a most honourable manner in the Bureau of Sacrificial Worship' quelled hurricanes and saved the fleets from disaster. Her presence was revealed in times of extreme peril by a light shining at the masthead.

This inscription at Dragon Pass River also reveals how total were the powers vested in the eunuch 'aristocracy'. The tribute to the Celestial Spouse was in the names of Grand Eunuchs Zheng He and Wang Jinghong, the assistant envoys, the Grand Eunuchs Zhu Liang, Zhou Fu, Hong Bao and Yang Zhen, and the Senior Lesser Eunuch Zhang Da. Probably all of Zheng's senior captains were eunuchs.

The fourth expedition, launched by an imperial edict in December 1412, extended Zheng's sphere of influence westwards beyond India, to Arabia and Africa. The commander himself only went as far as Hormuz and the Persian Gulf, but another part of his fleet was detached near Sumatra and sailed straight across the Indian Ocean to East Africa (the route taken centuries before by the Waqwaqs).

Despite some misconceptions and prejudices, the Chinese clearly knew, even before Zheng's expeditions, far more about Africa than did their European contemporaries. Most remarkable are two maps surviving in Chinese archives. These accurately portray the triangular shape of the African continent, sharply pointed at the southern tip. One is dated 1320 and the other 1402, a time when China still regarded itself as the 'Central Country' in a single landmass, of which Africa was one extension. Both maps show rivers flowing northwards through Africa, and one has a great lake in the heart of the continent. At the time when they were drawn, Europe was still totally ignorant about the overall shape of Africa.[5]

Zheng's purpose in reaching out for the first time as far as the Red Sea and the Zanj coast was largely so that Chinese merchants could make their first direct contact with these remote markets. Through intermediaries they had been buying the products of Africa for many centuries, and as early as the eleventh century the first envoys from East Africa had appeared in China. They were described as coming from Cengtan (Zangdan; that is, the Land of Zanj) and because it was such a great distance they were rewarded by the Song emperor with especially opulent gifts in return for their tribute. It had been thought worthy of note that these 'barbarians' were casting their own coins, which indeed was just starting to happen, and the language of Zanj (early Swahili) was described as 'sounding like that of the Arabs'. The despatch of envoys from East Africa at that early date is less surprising than might at first appear: its ivory, ambergris and rhinoceros horn had reached China through Oman, which had itself sent a series of trade missions to the *Sahib al-Sín*.

In the late twelfth century the author Zhou Qufei had written about the slave trade centred in the offshore islands of East Africa, which he called Cenggi Kunlun (Land of the Blacks). By the early thirteenth century a senior trade official, Zhao Rugua, had been able to put together a fairly detailed account of East Africa's imports, saying that many ships went there from India and Arabia, carrying white and red cotton cloth, porcelain and copper, probably in the form of cooking-pots, lamps and ornaments.

The East African town with which the Chinese were to have most contact was Malindi, which Arab chroniclers had called the 'capital of the Land of Zanj', renowned for its wizards. (Ibn Battuta never mentioned Malindi, perhaps because it inclined towards religious practices, derived from strong links with Persia, of which he could not approve.)

This port on the Zanj mainland was well placed to take advantage of trading opportunities in the Indian Ocean, being only a few days' sailing below the equator and less than a month's voyage across the sea from Calicut. In an age when open-sea navigation relied mainly on latitudes estimated by the stars, a ship going to Africa from Calicut could stay on the latitude of 10°N, make its landfall near the tip of Somalia, then follow the coastline south-west to Malindi, the first major Zanj entrepôt. Otherwise it could sail south to the equator, then turn due west and head for the African shore, to reach Malindi at 3°S.

The rise of Malindi had mirrored the growth of Calicut. Now it was to become renowned as the source of wondrous auguries, brought to the emperor of China in the treasure ships of the Three-Jewel Eunuch.

TEN

Ma Huan and
the House of God

> You must know that the giraffe is short in the body and slopes
> down towards the rear, because its hind legs are short . . . It has
> a small head and does no harm to anyone. Its colour is dappled
> red and white. And a very pretty sight it is.
> —Marco Polo, *Description of the World* (1298)

ON 20 SEPTEMBER 1414, the first giraffe ever seen in China trod
delicately along the road leading to the palace in Beijing. It was a gift
from the sultan of Bengal, Saif-ud-Din, who in turn had been given it
by the sultan of Malindi. At the outset the response of the emperor
Yongle was cool. 'Let congratulations be omitted,' he replied, as courtiers vied to assure him that this long-awaited vision was proof of imperial
virtue and wisdom. Good government depended upon peace, said the
emperor, not upon the appearance of an animal which was being hailed
as the magical *qilin*. His ministers should simply work harder 'for the
welfare of the world'. In any case, the emperor knew, and even his
most sycophantic courtiers knew, that this was nothing like a *qilin*, that
legendary, single-horned animal with the 'body of a deer and the tail
of an ox', the Chinese equivalent of the unicorn.

The giraffe was just the most extraordinary of all the creatures being
sent at this time to Beijing from distant barbarian countries. Chinese
official records soberly called it a *zulafu*, which was as close as they
could come to the Arabic word *zarafa*, but exotic animals like these had
fascinated China from the earliest times. During the Western Han dynasty (206 B.C. to A.D. 24) there had been a vast imperial park, with a
perimeter of 130 miles, full of zoological and botanical rarities. The
animal-loving mother of one of the Han emperors had been buried
with a rhinoceros, a giant panda and other creatures. Envoys going to
distant lands were always enjoined to bring back unfamiliar species, and

many old geographical works by Chinese scholars contain sections in which real and mythical beasts are jumbled together.[1]

Although the mythical *qilin* had been written about for 4,000 years – some accounts saying it had blue eyes and red-tipped horns with magic qualities – a realistic description of the giraffe had been lacking until the foreign trade official Zhao Rugua gave a hearsay account. This was undoubtedly garnered from Arab merchants: 'There is also in this country [the Horn of Africa] a wild animal called *zula*; it resembles a camel in shape, an ox in size, and is of a yellow colour. Its forelegs are five feet long, its hind legs only three feet. Its head is high up and turned upwards.' Zhao Rugua also noted that the giraffe's skin was very thick, which is true; it is often used for making whips.

Public delight with the first African giraffe ever seen in China was to prove stronger than the imperial desire to belittle it as a portent. Although, in these early years of the Ming dynasty, there was a widespread interest in natural science – the emperor's own brother had written a serious work on botany – the people had long awaited a *qilin*, and the giraffe seemed as near to one as the animal kingdom was likely to provide. A member of the Imperial Academy called Shen Du caught the mood with his poem, which was prefaced by a flowery dedication to the emperor: 'I, Your Servant, joining the throng, behold respectfully this omen of good fortune and kneeling down a hundred times and knocking my head on the ground I present a hymn of praise as follows.' Amid a welter of rhetoric comes Shen Du's highly fanciful description of the giraffe:

> In a corner of the western seas, in the stagnant waters of a
> great morass,
> Truly was produced a qilin whose shape was fifteen feet
> high,
> With the body of a deer and the tail of an ox, and a fleshy
> boneless horn,
> With luminous spots like a red cloud or a purple mist,
> Its hoofs do not tread on living creatures.

This apparent harmlessness (although its hind legs do possess a lethal kick) was the characteristic the giraffe most visibly shared with that mythical unicorn.[2] The admiring crowds had no fear as this latest gift from foreign lands walked through Beijing with its curious, camel-like stride. Its head, far above the admiring crowd, turned constantly from side to side as it sniffed the autumn air. In the words of Shen Du: 'Ministers and people gathering to behold it vie in being the first to see the joyful spectacle.' Another courtier wrote in a similar vein: 'Its two eyes rove incessantly. All are delighted with it.' The creature was strange in so many ways: despite having a tongue nearly as long as a man's arm, it could not utter the faintest sound. A Chinese painting survives in which the animal is being led on a rein by the Bengali keeper who has accompanied it across the seas; he looks up devotedly at his charge.[3]

So when yet another tame giraffe appeared, directly from Malindi, in the following year – the precise date, 10 October 1415, can be calculated from Chinese records – the emperor had to yield to the enthusiasm of the populace. He went himself to welcome it. Two other most auspicious creatures were being led towards him behind the chestnut-coloured giraffe: a 'celestial horse', a zebra, and a 'celestial stag', an oryx. This time the emperor's pronouncement was less dismissive, but suitably modest. He attributed this symbol of harmony and peace to 'the abundant virtue of the late emperor, my father', enhanced by the support of his own ministers. From now on, it would be his duty to hold ever more resolutely to virtue, and the duty of his ministers to remind him of any shortcomings.

A certain testiness can be discerned in the emperor's comments on the excitement aroused by Malindi's giraffes. After all, the transporting of gifts was only incidental to the intensely serious business of the great expeditions. The giraffes are not even mentioned by Ma Huan, a chronicler who went with Zheng He on several voyages. Ma Huan was intent on describing the countries he visited, and without his book, *Yingyai Shenglan* (*Triumphant Visions of the Ocean's Shores*), the reputation of his master would rest only upon fragmentary writings.

Ma Huan was also a Muslim, his surname being the same as the one Zheng had originally possessed, although he is not known to have been a eunuch. He was recruited at a time when Zheng was coming to realize that the further he sailed the harder it would be to understand the languages of the barbarian envoys brought back to the imperial court. (Sometimes it was proving necessary to resort to 'double translation', in which the envoys' messages were relayed through two interpreters before a Chinese version could be conveyed to the emperor.) Zheng had already set up a foreign languages school in Nanjing, and Ma Huan was one of a corps of seagoing interpreters whose first duty was to be in attendance when audiences were held with foreign monarchs. The interpreters would also help the Chinese merchants accompanying Zheng's fleets.

In personal references in his book, Ma is self-deprecatory in the typical Chinese style of the time. He calls himself a 'simpleton' and a 'mountain-woodcutter', for whom the expeditions were 'a wonderful opportunity, happening once in a thousand years'. Nevertheless, Ma was well educated, with a mastery of written and spoken Arabic. His book begins with a laudatory poem, with these opening lines:

> The Emperor's glorious envoy received the divine
> commands,
> 'Proclaim abroad the silken sounds, and go to the barbarous
> lands'.
> His giant ship on the roaring waves of the boundless ocean
> rode,
> Afar, o'er the rolling billows vast and limitless, it strode.

The poem goes on to list some of the twenty countries he saw on the expeditions, and declares that the foreign peoples were 'grateful, admiring our virtue, showing themselves loyal and sincere'. He says proudly that merchants from the 'Central Glorious Country' were now travelling as far as Misr (Egypt).

Measured by the information his book gives on social customs, trade and current affairs, Ma is on a par with Marco Polo and Ibn Battuta. Since less than a century separates them, it is especially rewarding to set Ma's accounts of the Indian Ocean alongside those of Ibn Battuta. For example, both exerted their descriptive talents in praising Calicut and its people.

By the time Ma came to Calicut in 1414, the port had grown to become a city-state, and with some hyperbole he called it 'the great country of the Western Ocean'. Almost a tenth of his entire book is devoted to Calicut, which the grand eunuchs leading the expeditionary fleets used as the pivot of their operations. One reason for Ma's praise for Calicut (apart from an eagerness to mirror the judgement of his superiors) was the strong Islamic leanings of a town which had more than twenty mosques and a settled Muslim population of 30,000. Everywhere in its streets Arabic could be heard. To a young Chinese Muslim, one of whose main goals in life was to make a pilgrimage to Mecca, Calicut's atmosphere must have been exhilarating. Arabia was just across the ocean, no more than a fortnight's voyage away with a fair wind.

It may have been a desire to please Chinese readers that led Ma to assert that the Zamorin, the Sea-King of Calicut, was a Buddhist. In fact he was a Hindu. But the 'great chiefs' who advised the ruler were all Muslims, and the two most senior had been given high awards by Zheng He on the emperor's orders. The envoys of Calicut were granted precedence over all others when they went to China to present tribute. Ma applies a string of laudatory epithets to the people of the city: honest, trustworthy, smart, fine and distinguished. He gives a detailed picture of the way trade was conducted between the representatives from a Chinese 'treasure ship', bringing ashore their silks, porcelains and other goods, and the local merchants and brokers. It was a slow process, taking up to three months, for prices had to be agreed separately, but eventually all parties would clasp hands and swear that the settlement would never be repudiated. The presence of 'His Excellency the Eunuch' at the hand-clasping ceremony confirms the importance attached to trade on the expeditions, notwithstanding all the grandiose rhetoric about their civilizing role.

It intrigued Ma – he calls it 'very extraordinary' – that the merchants of Calicut did not use an abacus in the Chinese fashion when making calculations: 'They use only their hands and feet and the twenty digits on them, and they do not make the slightest mistake.'

He goes into detail about the vegetables grown in Calicut, about which animals are bred for food, the varieties of rice planted and the imports of wheat. He notes that the wealthy people invest in coconut plantations, some growing as many as 3,000 trees; the numerous uses of the coconuts and the trees themselves are carefully listed. The cultivation of pepper on hillside farms, the time of year when it is picked and dried, the prices paid and duties levied by the king; all these are recorded. Ma even gives an account of Indian music, conceding that 'the melodies are worth hearing'.

He ends his portrayal of Calicut with a graphic account of a gruesome 'boiling oil' method used to test the innocence or guilt of miscreants. A cooking pot of oil is heated until leaves thrown into it shrivel up with a crackling noise.

> Then they make the man take two fingers of his right hand
> and scald them in the oil for a short time; he waits until they
> are burnt then takes them out; they are wrapped in a cloth
> on which a seal is affixed; he is kept in prison at the office.

Two or three days later, before the assembled crowd, they break open the seal and examine him; if the hand has a burst abscess, then there is nothing unjust about the matter and the punishment is imposed; if the hand is undamaged, just as it had been before, then he is released.

Although Ma's chapter on Calicut stands out from the rest of his book, wherever he goes the oddities of life capture his attention. At times he can be as earthy as Marco Polo in describing social customs, notably in his account of the popular Thai manner of enhancing masculine charms:

When a man has attained his twentieth year they take the skin which surrounds the penis and with a fine knife shaped like the skin of an onion they open it up and insert a dozen tin beads inside the skin; then they close it up and protect it with medicinal herbs. The man waits until the opening of the wound is healed, then he goes out and walks about. The beads look like a cluster of grapes. There is indeed a class of men who arrange this operation; they specialize in inserting and soldering these beads for people; they do it as a profession. If it is the king of the country or a great chief or a wealthy man who has the operation, then they use gold to make hollow beads, inside which a grain of sand is placed, and they are inserted in the penis; when the man walks about they make a tinkling sound, and this is regarded as beautiful. The men who have no beads inserted are people of the lower classes.

He ends blandly: 'This is a most curious thing.'

Sometimes his anecdotes closely echo those of Marco Polo: 'If a married woman is very intimate with one of our men from the Central Country [China], wine and food are provided, and they drink and sit and sleep together. The husband is quite calm and takes no exception to it; indeed, he says, "My wife is beautiful and the man from the Central Country is delighted with her."'

When Ma comes finally to conduct his readers through Arabia and Mecca, all such hints of raciness are absent. It was not merely that as a Muslim he was filled with a sense of reverence for the holy places of his religion, but also that two decades had passed since he first went to sea with one of the great Indian Ocean fleets; he was now in his fifties, accompanying the last of Zheng's expeditions. Ma must have been surprised that the Three-Jewel Eunuch had won consent, after a gap of ten years, to mount another huge and costly venture to distant lands, because the death of the Yongle emperor in 1424 had seemed to mark the end of an era.

The coterie of predominantly Muslim eunuchs round the emperor had now been challenged by a rival élite, the Confucian civil servants. For six of the intervening years Zheng had been posted as garrison commander at Nanjing, watching his great treasure ships swing idly at their moorings in the Yangtze river. There were signs that the court of the Xuande emperor had turned its back on the idea of asserting a permanent mastery over a vast and dangerous ocean which nowhere touched China's own borders.

Somehow, however, Zheng managed to override this indifference, and in January 1431 his final voyage began. Many of the veterans of former expeditions were among the 27,550 men under his command; others were performing compulsory service, in obedience to the laws of the Ming era, to expiate crimes committed by their fathers or grandfathers. Calicut was once again the base for the main fleet, and detachments were sent off to various countries. Ma Huan probably went to Arabia as the interpreter for a group of Chinese who took musk and porcelain as their trade goods and returned with sundry 'unusual commodities', as well as ostriches, lions and yet another giraffe; such animals were easily transported across the Red Sea from Ethiopia.

As might be expected, Ma offers no criticism of life in Arabia: 'The customs of the people are pacific and admirable. There are no poverty-stricken families. They all observe the precepts of their religion and law-breakers are few. It is in truth a most happy country.' When he describes the Ka'ba (House of God), there are many similarities to an account Ibn Battuta had given a century earlier. Ma even goes to the trouble of listing the number of openings (466) in the wall around the Ka'ba, and the exact number of jade pillars on each section of the wall. Although generally accurate, he makes some curious mistakes, saying that Medina, the site of Muhammad's tomb, was a day's journey west of Mecca, whereas it was ten days' distance to the north. He goes on to describe the holy Well of Zamzam as being beside Muhammad's grave, whereas it is in the centre of Mecca. This must arouse the suspicion that although he certainly went to Arabia he never reached Mecca itself, perhaps because of fighting near the southern end of the Red Sea.

It was a time when Aden was challenging the Mamluke monarchs of Egypt for control of western Arabia, including Mecca and Medina. The instability this caused is shown by the predicament of two large junks, loaded with trade goods, when they reached Aden in June 1432. Their captains wrote letters to the sharif in Mecca and the port controller in Jeddah, seeking permission to sail up the Red Sea. These officials in turn sought the approval of the ruler in Cairo, al-Malik al-Ashraf Barsbay, who said that the junks should be 'welcomed with honour'. It is not recorded that the ships ever did reach Jeddah; it may have been this disorder which forced Ma in the end to rely upon hearsay about Mecca and Medina.

In March 1433, as the great fleet was reassembling to return to China, the Three-Jewel Eunuch died in Calicut. His body was carried home in one of the treasure ships, to be buried in Nanjing; as was the custom with Chinese eunuchs, his genitals – kept in a sealed jar since his castration – were buried with him, so that he could go complete into the afterlife.

Never again would the great fleets make their majestic progress across the Indian Ocean. Only memories lingered: according to an Arab ambassador who visited India in 1441, the 'adventurous sailors of Calicut' liked to call themselves *Tchinibetchegan* (Sons of the Chinese); by the end of the fifteenth century there were only confused legends of men with strange beards who had arrived in huge ships and came ashore carrying their weapons.

Despite all the imperial honours bestowed upon Zheng He, his life-long efforts to forge permanent bonds with the lands of the Indian Ocean had come to nothing. China retreated into itself, once more indifferent to the world beyond the straits of Malacca.[4] After his death the silken screens of Confucian authority closed around his reputation, and the 'Star Raft' records were destroyed. When another influential eunuch, hoping to organize a seaborne attack on Annam, asked to see them, he was told they could not be found. Only at the end of the sixteenth century, 160 years after Zheng's death, did the author Luo Maodeng try to restore his fame with a 1,000-page novel called *The Western Sea Cruises of the Eunuch San Bao* (San Bao means Three Jewels). It contained a portrait of the grand admiral, seated aboard his flagship, his features awesome. But the book made little impact, for the civil servants had done their work well, and China's greatest naval commander was consigned to oblivion. As for Ma Huan, he finally managed to have his book printed in 1451, when he was in his eighties; although he had spent his later life lecturing about his travels, his name was soon forgotten.

Viewed in historical perspective, Zheng's seven expeditions seem a perplexing, almost irrational, phenomenon. The Indian Ocean in the fifteenth century was a trading arena of great wealth (no other region of the world had a comparable output of manufactured goods and raw materials); into this arena the Chinese intrusion had been sudden, massive and forceful. Yet just as suddenly it ended, leaving scarcely a trace behind. Indeed, there is only one known piece of tangible evidence throughout the whole of the Indian Ocean to prove that Zheng was ever there with his vast armadas and tens of thousands of men: that is the trilingual tablet set up in Ceylon in 1410.[5]

The rest of the tantalizing evidence survives in China, and apart from narratives such as Ma Huan's book and the temple pillars there is a nautical chart more than five metres long. This was compiled during the expeditions and names more than 250 places in the Indian Ocean, from Malacca to Mozambique. Although known as the Mao Kun map, it is not a map in the normal sense, but lists ports, landmarks, bays, havens and dangerous rocks along a course drawn from right to left. There is no scale, and the space devoted to various regions varies according to the data available; thus China has three times as much as Arabia and East Africa combined. The correct routes are carefully defined, giving currents, prevailing winds and depth soundings. By means of compass bearings and the positions at precise times of sun and guiding stars (*jian xing fa*) the compilers were able to show with astonishing accuracy the sea lanes of the fifteenth century.

The map was probably assembled from the records of Zheng's commanders.[6] However, there is no way of knowing from it exactly where all the flotillas sailed, or how many of them never returned. There are hints that some may have swept in a great arc through the southern seas, looking in vain for land, and that others could have followed the African coastline past Sofala. The Mao Kun map says that storms stopped fleets going beyond 'Habuer', which appears to be a small island south of Africa.

Momentarily, the cloak of Chinese power was spread across the world, almost touching the borders of Europe. The merchants who went as far as Cairo stimulated the demand in Europe for oriental silks and porcelains. In China itself a cosmopolitan atmosphere was created as crowds of envoys from remote countries were brought back in the treasure ships. Processions of men speaking unknown languages and wearing strange costumes were seen in the streets of Nanjing and Beijing. They brought jewels, pearls, gold and ivory, and scores of animals. The keepers of the imperial zoological gardens were much occupied with the unfamiliar tribute being offered to the Sacred Emperor.

The place to ponder on the forgotten achievements of Zheng He is Dondra in Ceylon; it is the southernmost point of the Indian sub-continent. Close by the headland is a rocky beach, where the crumbling graves of shipwrecked mariners are shaded by coconut palms. Once Dondra had a great temple for a recumbent Buddha made entirely of gold, with two great rubies as eyes, and every night 500 maidens sang and danced before it. A short distance to the west is where Zheng's tablet in three languages was set up. When the Chinese fleets, sailing west, sighted the gilded temple roof at Dondra Head they knew it soon would be time to turn north, towards Calicut and the Arabian Sea.

From here the Indian Ocean stretches away southwards, beyond countless horizons, to the bottom of the world. South-east lies the route back to Sumatra and China; far to the south-west is Madagascar. Beyond that is the cape where Africa makes its sudden turn into a more hostile ocean, so long unconquered by ships from either East or West.

ELEVEN

The King of
the African Castle

Mombaza, Quiloa and Melind,
And Sofala (thought Ophir) to the realm
Of Congo and Angola farthest south.
—John Milton, *Paradise Lost*, Book II

IF THE REST OF AFRICA can put forward any rivals to the pyramids
of Egypt in monumental building, Great Zimbabwe must rank high
among them. The grey granite outlines of this African capital, 1,200
miles south of the equator, are strewn on the edge of the high plateau
between the Zambezi and Limpopo rivers; the names of the men who
ruled here, 700 years ago, are long forgotten. (So is the original name
of the place itself. Zimbabwe comes from the title given it by later
inhabitants of the region: *dzimbahwe*, house of stone.) Yet even in a
state of ruin, when first sighted by European colonizers in the nineteenth
century, the place was so impressive that credit for its construction was
given to Phoenicians, Egyptians, Indians, anyone but Africans.[1] This
revived the ancient legend that the gold-producing regions of southern
Africa were Ophir, the destination of King Solomon's ships.

Gold had certainly been a stimulus in the surge of activity which
created Zimbabwe.[2] The Indian Ocean port of Sofala was reached by
a twenty-day journey, down from the plateau and due east across the
coastal lowlands. At the coast the merchants waited with Syrian glass-
ware, Persian and Chinese bowls, beads, cowrie shells, spoons and bells.[3]
The dhows, arriving on the monsoon, also brought cargoes of bright-
coloured cloth, known as *kambaya*, from the great Indian port of Cambay. For centuries such goods had been an irresistible lure for the people
of the interior.

Great Zimbabwe was occupied continuously for 400 years, and during
much of this time it controlled the gold trade with Sofala. The rulers

grew rich. They wore garments of imported silk (traditionally, coloured blue and yellow), but also had long capes of stiff cloth, woven locally from cotton grown in the Zambezi valley. When they gave judgement in disputes they sat on carved, three-legged stools, and were often hidden, speaking from behind a curtain. Gongs were sounded to announce their arrival, and petitioners had to crawl forwards on the ground, clapping their hands as they spoke, and never looking at the king. It was expected of a ruler, because of his divine powers, to keep a vast number of wives – perhaps as many as 300. He was also the custodian of all the nation's herds, and ordinary people had use of the cattle as an act of royal patronage. Animals were slaughtered on the orders of the king to meet the needs of his subjects.

Between the twelfth and fifteenth centuries, Great Zimbabwe was the most powerful capital in southern Africa, but there were dozens more stone-built settlements on the eastern side of the plateau, from which cattle were taken down to the lowlands to graze. Near the Limpopo river the earlier *dzimbahwe* of Mapungubwe was surrounded by terraced farmland, its rulers ate off celadon dishes from China, and relics found in graves include a sculpture of a rhinoceros, six inches long, completely sheathed in gold leaf. Only in Great Zimbabwe's maturity did its rulers develop a similar interest in making ornaments out of the metal, rather than simply selling it as dust or nuggets.

What distinguished Great Zimbabwe, from about A.D. 1200, was an ability to plan and carry through construction work on a massive scale, with a steady advance in techniques. Blocks used for building were fitted together without the use of mortar, and as skills progressed, walls became adorned with various patterns; most pervasive was the chevron, a symbol of fertility.[4]

The origin of Great Zimbabwe lay in the building of a stone acropolis amid granite boulders on a hilltop surveying the countryside in all directions. This acropolis with its towers and turrets was, in effect, the palace, and meant that the king's subjects knew that he was literally looking down on them. At night they could see the glow of his fires. The climb to the royal presence was steep and exhausting. Entry was controlled by spear-carrying warriors; the doors in walls mounted on the natural rock were so small that a man could go in only by crouching low.

In the valley below were many enclosures, probably occupied by the king's wives and powerful retainers. The walls of the biggest were six times the height of a man and had drainage channels from the interior floor levels. To make them, a million pieces of dressed granite had been shaped and carried to the site. Inside were circular thatched houses built in the typical African style, with walls of *daga*, a cement-like earth often taken from anthills. It was customary to paint these walls with bright geometric patterns. Clustered round the enclosures were the huts of the lowly subjects and the slaves, captive survivors from raids on neighbours. The population of the capital grew to as much as 20,000.

The Zimbabwe gold trade was to set off a chain reaction far across the continent. Elephant tusks, dried salt, and iron weapons and implements were carried along forest paths from one market to the next, until they gained a maximum barter value in the more densely-populated districts. Even 1,000 miles away, north of the Zambezi watershed, copper deposits which had been neglected for 300 years were again worked intensively.

The king of Great Zimbabwe ruled a warlike people known as the Karanga. He and the subject chieftains, who lived round the plateau in less imposing settlements, held sway over an area almost the size of France. Their territories spread into what today is Botswana on one side, into Mozambique on the other, and across the Limpopo into what is now South Africa; the granite ruins are their monuments.

The growth of Great Zimbabwe had happened in total isolation from the formation of city-states at much the same time far away on the western side of Africa. The empires of Ghana, Mali and Songhay which rose and fell beside the Niger river might as well have been on another continent. They were almost as far to the north of the equator as Great Zimbabwe was to the south, and much of the 3,000 miles separating them was almost impenetrable tropical forest. Beside central Africa's inland seas, from which the Nile takes its source east of the Ruwenzori ('Mountains of the Moon'), lay cultures far more closely allied to Great Zimbabwe. Settlements almost on the same scale seem to have developed there concurrently, to gauge from massive earthworks and irrigation systems; but since their buildings were of wood and thatch, almost all the evidence has vanished in the intervening centuries. The people who lived in them seem, moreover, to have had no connection at all with the trade of the Indian Ocean.

However, one link is clear. In the great lakes region, as was the case 1,500 miles further south, iron-mining and smelting were central to the economy. Great Zimbabwe had grown rich from gold – there were

more than 4,000 small gold-mines on the high plateau – but iron ruled
the lives of ordinary people. Whereas most of the world first smelted
copper, then progressed over many centuries to the making and harden-
ing of iron, Africa took a single leap straight out of the stone age. This
new ability spelled power, for wrought-iron weapons transformed the
ways in which wars were fought and wild animals hunted; with iron
axes men could chop down forests and with hoes dig more land to
grow crops.

How iron-age technology developed in the interior of Africa, whether
invented independently or acquired from outside, is much debated. It
seems to have been used there at least as early as in Egypt or much of
Europe. The first known iron-makers in sub-Saharan Africa lived to
the west of what is now called Lake Victoria, just below the equator.
Others were settled amid the hills of Rwanda and Burundi, in a fastness
of extinct volcanoes capped with snow, of deep lakes and heavily-
forested hills rich in red, haematite ore. The first traces of smelting in
that remote region may date back to 1000 B.C.[5]

The identity of the smelters remains a mystery. They certainly did
not come from among the bushman or pygmy communities, the 'hunting and gathering' aborigines, since they kept humpbacked *zebu* cattle
(an Asiatic breed) and knew how to grow simple crops. Each clay iron
furnace was small but elaborate, with access points all round the base
for hand-worked bellows to drive up the heat of the charcoal fire.
Swathes of primeval forest were brought down to keep the furnaces fed
with hardwood, because the demand for iron tools was unending. It
was a pattern which would be repeated in many parts of Africa.

The mastery of smelting may have spread southwards from the Nile
valley, from the Nubian city of Meroë, mentioned by the Greek historian Herodotus in 450 B.C. On the outskirts of Meroë are huge mounds
of iron-slag – the city has been called the 'Birmingham of ancient Africa'.
However, the earliest evidence of iron at Meroë is dated at about
500 B.C. Another possibility is that the pioneer iron-workers may have
migrated to Rwanda and Burundi from the Red Sea, herding their cattle
for as much as 2,000 miles until they halted in the fertile heart of the
continent. Iron-hardening methods had been 'discovered' in Assyria in
about 2000 B.C., and the secret spread southwards from there to Arabia.

Once the skill was established at the equator, it advanced steadily
southwards along the rocky backbone of Africa. By A.D. 300 iron was

being smelted almost at the Cape. In some areas, the remains of hundreds of furnaces are discernible, proving the existence of highly-organized village industries. Iron hoes, like cattle, could be used to buy a bride. The metal-workers formed themselves into guilds, being regarded as men apart. It was the rule that they must practise sexual abstinence before the ores were smelted, and goats were sacrificed when a deposit was discovered. The spirit of the clay furnaces was always female; some were built with protuberances on the outside representing breasts.

At Great Zimbabwe, teams of metal-workers were constantly at their tasks. Those not making iron tools or spears were busy casting the capital's distinctive H-shaped copper ingots, which served as a form of currency. Smoke from many furnaces hung in the air. Like most other daily activities, smelting was closely concerned with magic. It could well be imagined that restless spirits had been active inside the furnace if the metal proved impure. Rituals must be performed to set them at peace.

The king and his close advisers took divine guidance on such matters at their religious shrines in the acropolis, where the spirits of royal ancestors were worshipped.[6] The time of the new moon was most auspicious. The senior sister of the king played a main role, for like the king she was regarded as being in direct contact with the ancestors. At Great Zimbabwe the shrines were adorned with green soapstone carvings of mysterious creatures, part bird, part beast, adorned with beads and tautly stylized. Since each is different they may represent the spirits of former kings. These carvings were set on tall monoliths round the shrines and below one of the birds a lifelike crocodile crawls up the pillar. The beaks of the birds are like those of eagles: in Karanga belief, the eagle carries messages between the earth and Murenga, the deity.

Other artistic remnants of the religious rituals are contorted sculptures of men and women, made in soapstone brought from a hundred miles away. The stone was also carved to form circular bowls, twenty inches across, with hieroglyphic-like designs of animals, such as zebra, baboons and dogs, on their vertical sides.

The stone-working skills of the Great Zimbabwean craftsmen, and their ability to make ornaments in gold and copper, had grown out of the traditions of wood-carving and moulding in terracotta. Wooden artefacts have been lost to time and the African climate, but proof of the depth of artistic tradition in southern Africa is to be found in the fired earthenware sculptures discovered on the edge of South Africa's Drakensberg mountains. Made in or before A.D. 600, what are called the 'Lydenberg Heads' were elaborately moulded masks, big enough to be worn completely over the head. The biggest is fifteen inches tall and still bears traces of painted decoration on the terracotta. These heads, dating to at least seven centuries before Great Zimbabwe's maturity, show an aesthetic sophistication which must have even earlier roots.

Most puzzling of the stone structures at Great Zimbabwe is a conical tower, dominating the largest enclosure. Built of granite blocks, with a core of rubble, it hides no treasure, nor does it guard a royal grave. Meaningless today, the tower was so carefully constructed that it must have carried a precise message to all who saw it in the capital's time of greatness. Perhaps this represented an African grain store, to assure the people that the king cared about their welfare and would never let them starve. Legend says that this enclosure, more than 800 feet in circumference, within which the tower stands, was built for the ruler's senior wife. So this might have been yet another symbol proclaiming the virility of the royal line. Two entrances to the enclosure were marked with male and female symbols: a horn and a groove.

For the king's humbler subjects, in their clusters of huts below the acropolis, life was little different from that in any village on the plateau. Water still had to be carried by the women from the nearest stream, firewood collected, grain pounded and cooked, the dark red earth of the gardens hoed; children looked after the goats and chickens; menfolk herded cattle, hunted game, moulded clay cooking pots, and prepared for war with their spears and clubs when orders came down from the acropolis. Much beer was drunk, especially on feast days such as the new year, when the king's fire was rekindled and all other fires lit from it.

Existence was governed by fantasy and superstition. When the rainy season did not start on time the people took part in sacrifices at shrines where unseen 'owners of the land' had to be appeased. If such sacrifices failed to induce enough rain, women spirit mediums were consulted.

It was a mark of their spirit power – and, without doubt, their ruthlessness – that Great Zimbabwe's monarchs held their subjects together for centuries around the nucleus of a city-state. But there was a fatal limitation: the ability to keep records was never mastered, nor was any form of writing borrowed from the Indian Ocean cultures with whom the gold trade had put its rulers in touch. In the course of more than three hundred years, countless trade caravans were sent to the coast, where the leaders would have seen accounts being recorded in Arabic. Emissaries must likewise have travelled inland, bearing written messages to be read out to the king of what the Arabs called 'Zabnawi, the land of gold'. More than any other sub-Saharan society, Great Zimbabwe had the opportunity and the need to start keeping written records, yet failed to take the decisive step to literacy.[7]

Instead, it was stultified by clinging to the oral culture of African rural life. When a ruler felt the need to send tidings or commands to an outlying village he would choose a courier who could be relied upon to memorize his words. During a long journey the courier would tie knots in a string to record how many days it had taken, and on his return the string was saved for future reference. Various methods of arithmetic were used and bundles of sticks tied with cords or marked with notches were used as tallies in trade.

Religious practices remained simple: there was no scholarly priesthood dedicated to setting down the precise form of rituals and the days in the calendar when they must be performed. The lunar months were divided into three weeks, made up of nine or ten days. Law-giving was not based upon written statutes, but on social customs, and the interpretation of signs. Above all, the spirits of the ancestors permeated everything in life: the spirit world was indivisible from reality and existence was as repetitive as the seasons. The keeping of records would have meant a linear progression in time, a rejection of the past, but the presence of the spirits weighed heavily against that.

A civilization could not be built on the shifting sands of memory alone, and black Africa's only literate people, apart from the Muslim converts of West Africa and the Zanj coast, remained the Ethiopians, far away in the north-east, using their ancient Ge'ez language. All the wealth of the gold trade had failed in the end to transmute the fundamental nature of Great Zimbabwe's society.[8]

As Al-Mas'udi had discovered in the tenth century, wealth in cattle was what always mattered most in southern Africa: from early times, figurines of oxen had been revered and cattle were ceremonially buried. The king ruled the herd as he ruled the people; he was, in reality, just the most powerful pastoralist. So when some insoluble problems confronted the state, shortly after 1400, Great Zimbabwe was simply abandoned. With his cattle and his people, the king moved on.

What tolled the knell of Great Zimbabwe can only be guessed at. It may have been a conflict among the rulers over the succession, or a long drought and the exhaustion of the soil. Equally possible, there was a sudden advance of the lethal tsetse fly from the lowlands, attacking both the cattle and the people.

The king who ordered the abandonment of Great Zimbabwe after almost four centuries is said to have been called Nyatsimba Mutota. He went north, nearer to the Zambezi river and the gold-mines of the high plateau, and founded the empire of the Mwene Mutapa. This became translated as Monomotapa, and was to appear on maps for many centuries as a mighty state of the African interior. Yet Monomotapa was never as powerful as Great Zimbabwe, whose flecked grey stones leave so many questions unanswered.

The acropolis and the enclosures may have been an almost chance response to economic prosperity: there merely happened to be more stone available than wood, since so many trees had been cut down to make charcoal for smelting. Alternatively, Great Zimbabwe could be seen as the unfulfilled prelude to the development of a distinctly African civilization; in their new home the Karanga people might have gone on to adapt to literacy and organize a fully-fledged state based upon it. History did not grant time for such possibilities to be resolved, because Africa south of the equator was about to enter a new era.

PART TWO

The Cannons
of Christendom

TWELVE

Prince Henry's
Far Horizons

Bell, book and candle shall not drive me back,
When gold and silver becks me to come on.
—Shakespeare, *King John*, III, iii

THE YEAR 1415 was memorable for the kings of Portugal and England, for each had a feat of arms to celebrate. In August an armada of small ships from Lisbon had captured the Moorish town of Ceuta, on the North African coast, and in October the bowmen of England routed the French at Agincourt. For Henry V, victory had been hard won, whereas John of Portugal's losses – only eight men killed – were almost absurdly light. This was because the governor of Ceuta, having summoned a Berber force to help defend the town, sent it home too soon; he had decided that the attack was never going to materialize because of reports that the 240 Portuguese craft sailing towards him were too tiny and ill-manned to contend with the winds and currents in the Strait of Gibraltar. (The ships were a motley assortment, some being hired from England for the occasion against a promise of payment in consignments of salt.)

In the event, a good number of Muslims were slaughtered, their houses and stores were thoroughly looted, and the Pope declared the undertaking to be a holy crusade. The main mosque was turned into a church. King John proudly declared that he had 'washed his hands in infidel blood', to make amends for any offences he might have committed against God in his daily life, and set about celebrating the thirtieth anniversary of his reign.[1]

It was certainly spectacular to capture and keep a town in North Africa, especially one so strategically placed only fifteen miles across the water from Gibraltar. Ceuta, just east of Tangier, boasted a history going

back to Roman times, and the Arabs had used it in the past to control
shipping in the western Mediterranean. The Portuguese were also happy
to outshine their rivals the Castilians, who sixteen years earlier had
raided Tetuan, a town not far from Ceuta; half of Tetuan's citizens were
massacred and the rest enslaved, but then the Castilians withdrew. The
aims of the new masters of Ceuta were less fleeting.

Portugal was small, poor and ignorant, but its pride was formidable.
The ruling dynasty had won the loyalty of the people, shortly after
coming to power, for having fought off Castile's attempt to conquer
them in the final decades of the previous century. Confidence had also
been raised by the king's marriage ties with England: his queen was
Philippa of Lancaster, and among courtiers in Lisbon the legends of
Camelot and its knights were favourite reading. The eldest of the Portuguese princes, Duarte, Pedro and Henry, took part in the fighting at
Ceuta and immediately after its capture they were dubbed knights by
their father. Queen Philippa had encouraged them in feats of arms (not
for nothing was she the daughter of John of Gaunt) but was denied the
pleasure of welcoming them home from their triumph at Ceuta; as they
were returning she died of the plague.

In their plundering of Ceuta's well-built houses the Portuguese were
astounded by the silks from China, the silver-embroidered muslins from
India and many other luxuries. 'Our poor homes look like pigsties in
comparison,' admitted one Portuguese chronicler. The curiosity of the
royal princes was aroused by the stories they heard from their captives
about the interior of Africa, beyond the peaks of the Rif mountains
overlooking Ceuta. They learnt about the Sahara desert to the south,
across which the camel caravans journeyed to a 'River of Gold'.[2] One
account said that on the river bank there were ants the size of cats,
digging up gold and leaving it in heaps for humans to collect. This
ancient myth of gold-digging ants was readily believed. Like everyone
else in Europe, the Portuguese knew virtually nothing about Africa and
assumed it to be populated by monsters and cannibals.

Depictions of Mali's long-dead king, the Mansa Musa, seated on a
golden throne, had been inserted on medieval maps of Africa merely
to fill up space and hide the ignorance of cartographers. As recently as
1410, Ptolemy's *Geography* had been 'rediscovered' from Arab sources,
but it was more misleading than helpful. A few secretive Genoese,
Catalans and Jews controlled the northern end of the desert trade in
gold, in towns where caravans reached the Mediterranean, but even

they knew little about the source of the metal. Isolated in their tiny enclave at Ceuta, the Portuguese had no way of taking part in the Saharan trade.

Every rumour picked up in Ceuta about African gold was of compelling interest to King John, because his country was so painfully short of the metal. The price of gold had risen several hundred times in Lisbon within a few decades.[3] It was a matter of pride for any country to mint its own gold coinage, acceptable as payment for imports, but John's treasury was too empty for that; so Portugal used the currency of richer neighbours, including that of 'infidel' Morocco.

The prestige earned by Ceuta's capture was soon overlaid with greater issues in Europe. The Catholic Church was convulsed by the 'Great Schism', with rival popes contending for power, and by a surge of revolt against the dictates of Rome; a famous Bohemian heretic, Jan Hus, had been burned at the stake a few weeks before the occupation of Ceuta. Any attention that could be spared from religious disputation tended to be directed towards the east, and the advance into Europe of the Otto-man Turks, former nomads from the Asian steppes. Constantinople was in peril. The Turks had by-passed Byzantium's great citadel, choosing instead to cross the Bosphorus into Europe and overrun most of the Balkans; but everyone knew that they would, in their own time, turn back to lay siege to Constantinople itself. Despite the Castilian reconquest of almost all of Andalusia, rarely had the threat to Christendom seemed greater. The thirteenth-century dreams of an all-conquering alliance with the Mongols were dead. Islam was resurgent and the Ottoman Turks were its spearhead.

This was, in consequence, a moment when the known world, stretching from China to the Atlantic, was more physically divided than ever. Asia's overland route, along which Marco Polo and countless other merchants once travelled and which the Mongols had kept open, had been effectively shut to Christian travellers for a century. A few missionaries struggled as far as Samarkand, but could go no further. Only the most daring European travellers tried to reach the lands around the Indian Ocean by way of the Black Sea or Syria or Egypt, and few returned. For centuries hopes had flickered of somehow reaching the East by sea, yet medieval geography was so irrational that there was no clear idea of which direction to take.

Until some route could be found it was likely that a virtual monopoly of Europe's trade with the East would remain in the hands of glittering

Venice, 'La Serenissima'. Its merchants were stationed in the ports of the eastern Mediterranean, and in Constantinople itself, bargaining with their Muslim counterparts for the pepper, cinnamon, ginger, nutmegs, rubies, pearls and silks brought from beyond the barriers of Islam. As recently as 1413 the ruler of the Turks, Mehmet I, had signed a fresh treaty with Venice, guaranteeing the security of its trading colonies. The unique power of the Venetians was resented by their rivals, but there seemed little to be done.

Europe's passion for culinary spices – which were believed to have medicinal value and to purify mouldering foods – had continued to grow since the Crusades, so the prices were high. Most valued of all was pepper, used both in cooking and as a preservative. Pepper was rubbed into meat, together with salt, when the farmers slaughtered large parts of their herds and flocks at the start of winter. Cloves were similarly valued, their pungent 'nails' being pressed into meat when it was roasted. By the fifteenth century the words 'spices' had come to embrace a wide range of exotic goods from Asia, including scents, cosmetics, dyes, glues, pomanders to ward off the plague, even sugar and fine muslins. The volume of Chinese silks and porcelains reaching Europe had also risen sharply, although Europe did not know why (that these luxuries were brought in bulk to the Indian Ocean ports by the fleets of Zheng He).

So galling was the supremacy of Venice, so tantalizing the wealth it had acquired, that various rivals sought to break its grip. The Genoese tried hardest of all, but their long wars with Venice had ended in costly failure by the start of the fifteenth century. For the moment Portugal counted for nothing in these great rivalries. It did not even have a Mediterranean coastline, but lay on the outer rim of mainland Europe, its ports facing the restless Atlantic. In the scales of political influence, Portugal lacked both wealth and manpower. Moreover, its clergy were despised in the higher reaches of the Church, generally held to be ill-educated and too fond of keeping concubines.

Yet the knightly ardour of King John and two of his sons, Pedro and Henry, had been fired by their venture across the narrow straits between Europe and Africa. Prince Henry, in particular, saw Morocco as an outlet for his ambitions. Being a third son he was never likely to be king, but he had implicit faith in his horoscope, and court astrologers had declared that because of the positions of Mars and Saturn at his birth he was destined to 'discover great secrets and make noble conquests'. This prophecy would be remembered when Portuguese historians told how he had sown the seeds of his country's achievements on the high seas and in distant lands.

At the age of twenty-five, the thin and temperamental Henry took himself off to Cape St Vincent in the Algarve. It was the south-westerly tip of Europe, a headland thrusting into the Atlantic like the prow of a ship. Legends which later grew up around Henry were closely linked to Cape St Vincent and Sagres, a village sheltered from the ocean gales by its cliffs. It was said that he built a castle at Sagres, and gathered round himself a cabal of wise men such as map-makers, astronomers and mariners. That picture owes a lot to imagination. Henry did build a fortified camp at Sagres, as accommodation for sailors waiting behind the cape for calm weather, but most of his time in the south was spent at Lagos, a port fifteen miles further east. (As for the prince's romantic title, 'Henry the Navigator', that was bestowed upon him by a German historian in the nineteenth century; he was not a practical navigator and never captained a ship in his life.)

However, Cape St Vincent was certainly a place to dream of deeds of chivalry, of felling the hordes of the 'abominable sect of Mohamed'. So obsessed did the prince become with ideas of valour and piety that it was even said he had taken a vow of chastity. All around were reminders of the time, little more than a century earlier, when the Algarve was governed by Muslims. The queen heightened Henry's visions by giving him what was said to be a piece of wood from the cross on which Jesus had died, and the king put him at the head of the Order of Christ, a religious and military society created in Portugal with the papal blessing in 1319. The Order of Christ replaced the discredited Knights Templars, and its purpose was to 'defend Christians from Muslims and to carry the war to them in their own territory'. The Portuguese had already put their hands to this holy task, and it was to become the justification for all their bloodiest deeds.

Henry looked back fondly, as did his contemporaries in Lisbon, to the world of Charlemagne and the Arthurian romances, but was realistic enough to see that gunpowder, one of the inventions that had filtered across the world from China, was about to transform the arts of war. The formula for gunpowder had been widely known for at least a century (the English philosopher and scientist Roger Bacon possessed a 'secret recipe' as early as 1260), but the skills for exploiting it grew only slowly. At Ceuta and Agincourt in 1415, guns played no part, although earlier in the year the English had used primitive bombards, firing stone balls, when they successfully besieged the port of Harfleur. Guns were hard work to move in an age when roads scarcely existed, and their range was short, so on land they were as yet only effective in sieges, when the attackers had ample time to set them up.

The value of guns at sea was more quickly apparent. Once these cumbersome weapons were fixed to the deck, ready for action, the ship itself gave them mobility. The English, as a seafaring nation, pioneered the use of guns at sea – although they were too small to have much effect – during the battle of Sluys in 1340. A generation later, naval gunfire had grown more lethal: a Danish prince was killed by a stone ball shot from a German ship. Soon afterwards the Venetians began installing bombards in their war galleys, firing forwards over the bows.

Early in the fifteenth century the English were designing large ships armed with cannons. Some were built in Bayonne, the port in south-west France still held by Henry VI. His Portuguese namesake and kins-man would undoubtedly have been made aware of their potential, and by 1419 the Portuguese were able to deploy vessels armed with guns to deter a Spanish Muslim fleet sent to try and recapture Ceuta.

It is not known what first steered Henry's thoughts towards the challenge of the Atlantic and the mysteries of Africa, for he was the most secretive member of a tight-lipped family. However, the improve-ments in ship design, combined with the advances in gunnery, were to bring consequences for Portugal which even he could never have dreamed of. History had portrayed Henry as a visionary; rather, he was ruthlessly ambitious. The exhortations of the Order of Christ for the launching of a holy war against the Muslims in their own lands merely bestowed on his ambitions the aura of sanctity.

At first, his interests lay close at hand. Only two days' journey across the water from Cape St Vincent was Tangier. Although he might never be the king of Portugal, at least he thought he could make himself the viceroy of wealthy Morocco. To drive the infidels from it would be a sweet revenge for their eight centuries of rule in the Iberian peninsula. When his father, the king, rejected these schemes as too risky and vainglorious, the rebuff encouraged Henry to direct his thoughts beyond Morocco, across the desert to the 'River of Gold'.

An Arab prisoner taken by the Portuguese gave some details of the trade routes across the deserts, and even told of lakes in the heart of Africa. Henry knew that Muslims would never let Christians go to the fabled Rio del Oro by land; but since the river presumably flowed into the Atlantic, it might instead be reached by following the coast of Africa southwards.

He kept courtiers around him who could be despatched on such missions in spring and summer, when the winds blew from the north-east. The prince had control of several ships, which regularly went on trading and fishing voyages from Sagres and Lagos. Most important were the documents he had collected about the vessels of those other nations which had tried to explore southwards, down the African coast.[4]

The fate of the Vivaldi brothers of Genoa was well remembered. Men still wondered where their expedition had come to grief after it sailed through the Strait of Gibraltar in 1291 to search for a way around Africa to India. A Catalan map made half a century later bore an inscription saying that a certain Jaime Ferrer from Majorca had sailed past a Moroccan landmark known as Cape Bojador (at 26°N) where the shoreline was desert and the 'Land of the Blacks' began. Ferrer had also vanished without trace, and sailors claimed that any ship going beyond Cape Bojador – in Arabic Bon Khatar ('Father of Danger') – could never return.[5] Several French fishing-boats from the port of Dieppe had also disappeared in those waters in more recent years. Superstitious people asserted that these adventurers had paid with their lives for sailing into the 'Torrid Zone', one of five climatic regions into which medieval geographers divided the world.

Henry's pride was challenged by the activities of other nations on the African coast. The French, looking for new fishing grounds, seemed a particular threat, because as early as 1401 a party of French seamen had gone ashore near Cape Bojador in a small boat, captured some African villagers, then carried them back to the Canary islands. A year later a Norman knight, Jean de Béthencourt, occupied the Canaries and proclaimed himself king.[6] The Castilians, who saw the islands ultimately as a prize for themselves, had encouraged him. The Portuguese tried to seize the islands, since they were strategically placed near the coast, but failed. Henry decided to push on southwards.

Year after year he sent his ships towards Cape Bojador. They were only small cargo vessels, little more than rowing boats with sails, and when they found themselves caught in strong currents they fled back towards Portugal. The main reward lay in plundering any Moroccan craft encountered along the coast. For fifteen years the prince sent his courtiers on these expeditions, and at last Cape Bojador was rounded. A squire named Gil Eanes sailed out into the Atlantic, to avoid the coastal currents, then made a landfall to the south of the fearsome cape. The Portuguese had at last touched the fringe of the 'Land of the Blacks'. The year was 1434, almost twenty years after the first step into Africa, the capture of Ceuta.

THIRTEEN

Commanding the Guinea Coast

The city belongs to God.
—Prince Henry, when asked why Ceuta would not be exchanged for
his brother Fernando, captured by the Moroccans (c. 1440)

FOR A WHILE, Prince Henry was diverted from exploring Africa's
coastline. King John was dead and his eldest son Duarte sat on the
throne. A mild man, known as the 'philosopher king', Duarte gave way
at last to Henry's demands that Portugal should try to extend its power
in Morocco by capturing Tangier.

The attack took place in 1437 and was a calamity. The army under
Henry's command was cut to shreds and his youngest brother, Fernando,
was captured and taken as a hostage to Fez. These events so shocked
Duarte that his health gave way and he succumbed to the plague the
following year. The Moroccans offered to free Fernando if the Portuguese would evacuate Ceuta, but Henry scorned the suggestion.[1]
Although the captive prince sent pleading letters home, he was abandoned to God's mercy and died after five years in a dungeon. The
Portuguese proclaimed him a Christian martyr.

The second of Portugal's royal brothers, Pedro, had been far keener
than Henry to strike a bargain for the release of Fernando, but otherwise
held himself aloof from the Tangier disaster. During a tour of Europe
he had done his share of fighting some years earlier, against the Ottoman
Turks invading Hungary.

The Turks had shown themselves far fiercer than the Muslims of
Andalusia and Morocco, so it had been something of a relief for Pedro
when he left Hungary and travelled south to Venice. The newly-elected
Doge, Francesco Foscari, chose to welcome the Portuguese prince in
extravagant style, since there was an awareness that this visitor might
easily become a king, given the uncertainties of the time. In any case,
the Doge had a fondness for pageantry.[2]

113

At one banquet, Pedro was dazzled by the sight of 250 women from the city's most patrician families dressed in the finest silks from the Orient. He had arrived at the banquet in the great state barge, with swarms of lesser craft escorting it. During his stay the prince attended many balls and feasts; he also inspected the ships under construction around the Lagoon, being like his brother Henry a keen follower of maritime innovations. Pedro envied the voluptuous wealth of Venice, built upon its long trade with the East.

As a parting gift the Doge handed him a rare manuscript of the memoirs of Marco Polo, doyen of Venetian travellers. This was a gesture of greater significance than either could have foreseen, for in years to come the Portuguese would be urged on by Marco Polo's descriptions of the East to feats which would spell the economic ruin of Venice.

His disaster at Tangier had driven Prince Henry back to the Algarve, back to scheming about how to reach the 'River of Gold'. Until 1440 this was the limit of his ambitions, but shortly afterwards his mind began racing ahead to more grandiose goals. He was emboldened by the development of a new kind of ship, the caravel. Usually no more than 60 feet long, yet strong and fast, the smooth-hulled caravels were a leap forward in design from the cumbersome clinker-built 'cogs' or the primitive *barchas* using oars and sails.

The early caravels were never designed to be cargo carriers and their capacity was little more than 50 tons, but they were ideal as ocean trail-blazers. Since they drew only six feet they could be used close inshore, but with their high prows they were equally able to face Atlantic storms. They needed a complement of only twenty-five men, and although the sailors had to sleep as best they could on the open deck or in the hold, there were rudimentary cabins for the officers in the stern 'castle'. Mariners grew more daring in these craft.

The caravel was designed to exploit the advantages of its triangular lateen sail by steering closer to the wind (the sail had been adapted from the typical Arab rig by Italian mariners and from them came the name 'latin' or 'lateen'). Advances in navigation and the caravel's sail made it easier to return to Portugal from south of Cape Bojador by sailing westwards and north-west into the Atlantic wind-system, far from the sight of land, towards Madeira and the Azores (which so came to be discovered and occupied). The Portuguese coast was then approached across the prevailing wind from the west.[3]

The country whose ships had barely managed to reach Ceuta in 1415 was emerging as a conqueror of the ocean: the waves pounding on the Portuguese coasts were a ceaseless reminder of the challenge beyond the horizons. There was nothing to be discovered in the Mediterranean, for its every island, every harbour, had been known since Roman times. Instead, the Atlantic became Portugal's hunting-ground, an ocean of boundless possibility. Somewhere beyond it, either to the west or the south, nobody quite knew, lay the tantalizing Indies and the land of the Great Khan which Marco Polo had visited a century and a half before.

By the 1440s there was already a scent of the profits in these Atlantic voyages, for Portuguese ships were sailing well beyond Africa's desert shoreline and nearing the mouths of the Senegal and Gambia rivers. Not only were they reaching waters where the fishing-grounds were rich, but in the coastal villages their trade goods could be exchanged for Malian gold, ivory and exotic spices. Foreign captains – mostly Venetians and Genoese – were told by Henry when he hired them that their first duty was to bring back gold. Part of the gold was used to buy English and French goods such as cloth and tin bowls, which the Portuguese then used for trade with the Africans.

Most rewarding was slave-raiding. Portugal had only a million people (in contrast, Spain had eight million and France sixteen million) and labour was needed for plantations in the Algarve and the Azores, where sugar had been found to flourish. As freebooters of various nations had already done in the Canary islands, armed gangs of Portuguese began storming ashore in Africa, to attack unsuspecting villages, seize the young men and women, and haul them back to the ships. The communities in these coastal villages were simple, far removed from the highly-organized Islamic kingdoms of the interior. The inhabitants had originally greeted the white visitors with friendly awe, but this soon changed to terror.

The very first blacks brought back were simply 'for the amusement of Prince Henry'. The date was 1441. However, the idea soon took hold; after being baptized some black prisoners were sent home as hostages for more of their own people. A Portuguese chronicler, Gomes Eannes de Zurara, relates how 200 or more black slaves were auctioned in 1445 in the Algarve port of Lagos. The prince himself made an appearance, riding down to collect forty-six Africans, his one-fifth entitlement. The Franciscans, who had a monastery near Cape St Vincent, were also given some. Since horses were much in demand in West Africa, and these were plentiful in Morocco, it was found possible to use them for barter. At first it was possible to exchange one horse for fourteen slaves, but later one for six became the norm.[4]

There were no moral doubts in Portugal about the slave-trading conducted by the caravel captains, for slavery was already well established all across southern Europe. The Venetians used slaves in large numbers to grow sugar in Crete, their largest colony. Greeks, Tartars and Russians were regularly offered for sale in Spain by Italian merchants. Moreover, after eight centuries of Islam in the Iberian peninsula, the custom was entirely familiar, and prisoners taken in battle thought themselves fortunate to be sold rather than slaughtered.

However, the Portuguese were notably scrupulous about having their heathen captives baptized into Christianity, to save their souls from damnation. (In later years the slaves were baptized before they left Africa's shores, lest they died in transit.) There was a duty to bring all mankind to the true faith, so the enforced conversion of slaves served God's will. Henry decided to take his religious obligations further, by ruling that a twenty-first part of all merchandise brought from Africa should go to the Order of Christ. He listed slaves first, ahead of gold and fish.

Among the many Italians sailing in the Portuguese caravels was a young Venetian, Alvise da Cadamosta. He made two voyages to Senegal and Cape Verde in the 1450s, then wrote the first known eye-witness account by a European of daily life in black Africa. Educated, inquisitive and humane, Cadamosta visited coastal villages, questioned the chiefs about their domestic arrangements, sampled an elephant steak, and studied how birds built their nests in palm-trees. One day he went to a market: 'I perceived quite clearly that these people are exceedingly poor, judging from the wares they brought for sale — that is, cotton, but not in large quantities, cotton thread and cloth, vegetables, oil and millet, wooden bowls, palm leaf mats, and all the other articles they use in their daily life.'

Cadamosta's presence in the villages caused something of a sensation:

> These negroes, men and women, crowded to see me as though I were a marvel . . . My clothes were after the Spanish fashion, a doublet of black damask, with a short cloak of grey wool over it. They examined the woollen cloth, which was

new to them, and the doublet with much amazement: some touched my hands and limbs, and rubbed me with their spittle to discover whether my whiteness was dye or flesh. Finding that it was flesh they were astounded.

In many ways the Africans delighted him: 'The women of this country are very pleasant and light-hearted, ready to sing and to dance, especially the young girls. They dance, however, only at night by the light of the moon. Their dances are very different from ours.'

Yet Cadamosta did his share of fighting, and had no compunction about bartering horses for slaves. When a baptized slave brought out from Portugal to act as an interpreter was put ashore at a spot where the caravels hoped to trade, he was instantly killed by the local people. Without realizing it, Cadamosta had been taking part in the first stages of an historic confrontation, the Atlantic slave trade.

When he returned to Portugal the Venetian was personally welcomed by Henry, to whom he presented an elephant's foot and a tusk 'twelve spans long'. These the prince passed on to his sister, the duchess of Burgundy. Dutifully, Cadamosta praised Henry's virtues, his readiness to 'devote all to the service of our lord Jesus Christ in warring with the barbarians and fighting for the faith'.

The Portuguese badly needed to recruit foreigners of Cadamosta's calibre, but as their caravels explored further into unknown waters the desire for secrecy became an obsession. This was demonstrated when a ship's pilot and two sailors fled to Castile after a voyage to West Africa. They were accused of theft, but the real fear was that they would 'disserve the king' by revealing navigational secrets. They were followed; the two sailors were beheaded and the pilot was brought back 'with hooks in his mouth' to be executed. His body was quartered and put on display to discourage any more intending turncoats. Death was the accepted penalty for giving away the details of charts; it was equally forbidden to sell a caravel to any foreigner.

The Castilians were warned to leave Africa to the Portuguese by a papal bull issued in 1455 by Nicholas V. This gave Portugal exclusive rights of conquest and possession in all 'Saracen or pagan lands' beyond Cape Bojador. The bull was issued in response to appeals from Prince Henry, after Castile had laid tentative claims to the 'Guinea coast' (a term newly coined by European mariners). The Pope declared that

Henry believed he would best perform his duty to God by making the sea navigable 'as far as the Indians, who are said to worship the name of Christ, and that he thus might be able to enter into relations with them, and to incite them to aid the Christians against the Saracens and other such enemies of the faith'. Thus the Vatican openly proclaimed Henry's ultimate goal: to sail to India by circumnavigating Africa.

The papal bull had been issued two years after the fall of Constantinople to the Ottoman Turks, a moment when Europe was quaking at the thought of where the 'Mohamedans' might strike next. Western Christendom had quarrelled down the centuries with Byzantium, over religious doctrine and more material matters, but all too late regretted its demise, its martyrdom. The Portuguese had responded with a unique militancy to the Pope's call to Christian nations to unite to recover Constantinople. Despite claims of a revelation from God that the victorious Sultan Mehmet II would be defeated and brought as a prisoner to Rome, to be 'stamped under the foot of the Pope' and forcibly baptized, only in Lisbon was there any eagerness for a new 'crusade against the Infidel'. The fervent Portuguese proclaimed that they would raise an army 12,000 strong. They also minted a coin, made with West African gold, and called it the *cruzado* (crusade).

For the merchant states of Italy, the fall of Constantinople was of far more immediate moment, because it struck at the heart of their trade. All over the Mediterranean, Christian ships went in fear of being captured or sunk by Turkish raiders. Since the Turks never ventured beyond the Strait of Gibraltar the geographical good fortune of the Portuguese grew ever more apparent. Their caravels feared only the challenge of marauding Castilians as they advanced doggedly southwards in the Atlantic and down the West African coast.

In 1456, another bull had granted the Order of Christ jurisdiction 'all the way to the Indians'. This steady flow of papal encouragement entrenched in the minds of the royal family in Lisbon that it was their destiny and religious duty to find the route to the East. The young King Afonso proclaimed extravagantly that his uncle, Prince Henry, had 'conquered the coasts of Guinea, Nubia and Ethiopia, desirous of winning for God's holy church, and reducing to obedience to us, those barbarous peoples whose lands Christians had never before dared to visit'.

However, the last events in Henry's life had nothing to do with this vision. In 1458 he returned to the scenes of the first Portuguese venture into Africa, when he helped Afonso capture Alcacer Ceguer, a town next to Ceuta. The army used for the purpose was the one originally raised to help liberate Constantinople from the Turks, but never despatched because all other European countries drew back from action. For Henry the assault on Alcacer Ceguer was heart-stirring, since all his brothers were dead and he was one of a diminishing few who could recall the victory at Ceuta, more than forty years earlier.[5]

Two years later Henry died, at the age of sixty-six. His dream of reaching the 'land of the Indies' was unfulfilled, although black slaves were now being brought back to Portugal at a rate of 30,000 a year, many for re-export to Spain and Italy. By the time of Henry's death the caravels were exploring 1,500 miles beyond Cape St Vincent. They had rounded the great bulge of West Africa and were following the coastline almost due east. It seemed, deceptively, that the route to the Indies lay straight ahead.

After Henry's death the task of carrying forward the voyages of discovery was contracted out to a Portuguese businessman, Fernando Gomez, on terms that would financially benefit the crown. The arrangement left King Afonso free to concentrate on ways to strike another blow in Morocco. By 1471, he was ready to attack an enemy temptingly weakened through the incompetence of its sultans. A 30,000-strong army boarded 300 ships: caravels and the larger armed merchant vessels known as carracks. The destination was Arzila, a seaport on the Atlantic coast some forty miles south of Tangier. It was in no way a military bastion, and had little chance of defying the heavily-armed Portuguese attackers. After a brief resistance, the population surrendered and awaited its fate. Afonso quickly settled that: 2,000 inhabitants, men, women and children, were put to the sword, and 5,000 were carried off as slaves.[6]

News of the massacre spread north to the city of Tangier, whose people knew that their turn must be next. Panic took hold and the population fled either by land or sea, carrying with them what they could. Other nearby towns capitulated without a fight. The Portuguese marched in unchallenged. Prince John, the sixteen-year-old heir to the throne, was taken by his father on this exhilarating crusade, a revenge for the humiliation inflicted upon Prince Henry at Tangier more than thirty years earlier.

Viewed from the Moroccan side, the loss of Tangier, in particular, was a catastrophe. The city's 700-year-old role as the gateway to Europe, to Andalusia, had been reversed. The birthplace of Ibn Battuta now became a point of departure for Afonso's onslaughts. Since it was customary to honour monarchs with a soubriquet, the conquering hero of Arzila and Tangier became entitled 'Afonso the African'.

The Moroccan crusade in the final decades of the fifteenth century was to set the pattern for Portugal's behaviour in later conquests much further afield. Many of the young knights – the noble *fidalgos* – received unforgettable lessons in plundering, raping and killing without mercy. They came to accept that the lives of Muslims, men, women and children alike, counted for nothing because they were the foes of Christendom.

So 1471 had been memorable for the victories in Morocco, and it was momentous in another way. Far to the south, in waters where no European had ever sailed before, a captain called Alvaro Esteves crossed the equator, close to an island he named São Tomé. What was more, he found that the African coastline had changed direction again; his caravels' bows were once more pointing due south. On his seaward side the ocean seemed endless. To landward, the snake-green forest was impenetrable, hiding everything beyond the shoreline.

Although the entrepreneur Gomez had met his side of the bargain, extending the range of the caravels for another 1,500 miles, his contract was ended in 1475. By that time Portugal was facing a critical challenge along the Guinea coast from the Spaniards. Prince John took charge of driving them out. Fighting between the rival caravels for the right to exploit the African trade was savage. Prisoners were never taken; captives were hanged or thrown overboard.

The Spaniards had more ships, the Portuguese were more ferocious. In 1478 a thirty-five-strong Spanish fleet arrived off West Africa to do battle, and it was defeated. The Portuguese monopoly of the route to the Indian Ocean was secure.

FOURTEEN

The Shape of the Indies

> They report therefore that there were in Inde three thousand
> Townes of very large receit, and nyne thousand sundry sorts of
> people. Moreover it was believed a long time to be the third part
> of the world.
>
> —Caius Julius Solinus, *c.* A.D. 300. trans Arthur Golding (1587)

DURING THE LAST TWO DECADES of the fifteenth century the Portuguese sailed ever onwards through the South Atlantic; yet the further they explored beyond the Guinea Coast the more meagre were the material rewards: good harbours were scarce and the inhabitants of coastal villages vanished into the forests before landing parties could capture them.[1] Africa seemed both hostile and never-ending. King Afonso, notorious for the waxing and waning of his enthusiasms, began losing faith in this costly venture into the unknown. His doubts infected the court.

The Portuguese also had deeper anxieties. When they looked beyond the Atlantic, to the time when Africa's geography might finally be conquered, they saw vast gaps in their knowledge of what they must then confront. What should be their strategy upon reaching the East, that wondrous goal? Facts were so scanty that 'Indies' was a term often used to embrace all the world from the Nile to China.

India itself was sometimes reputed to be an immense country, at others a patchwork of many fertile isles. Regarding the seas round the Indies – their extent, their winds, their currents – even less was known. The names of a few Indian Ocean ports were common currency, but there was little idea of where they were in relation to one another.

The Portuguese could have learned a great deal from accounts by Arab travellers such as Ibn Battuta, but these seem to have been out of reach. By far the best source on the Indies was still the thirteenth-century narrative by Marco Polo. A few missionaries had found their way to the East since his time, but their accounts were fragmentary. Most of what the Greek and Roman historians once knew was now lost or surviving only in garbled forms, such as the much-translated work of Solinus.

For decades the Portuguese brooded over every scrap of information. After the fall of Constantinople it had even become perilous to set foot in the Muslim lands flanking the eastern Mediterranean – Turkey, Syria and Egypt – which before 1453 could still be visited by adventurous Christians whose purpose, or excuse, was to see the holy places of Jerusalem. The triumph of the Ottoman Turks over Byzantium had closed many windows on the East.

Yet there were clues to be garnered from the memoirs of Europeans who had visited those lands shortly before Constantinople fell. Most detailed of all was the narrative of a French knight, Bertrandon de la Brocquière, an intimate of the Duke of Burgundy. With several friends he went to Venice by way of Rome in the spring of 1432, and from there to Palestine. When his aristocratic companions turned for home, la Brocquière set off to Damascus, where he found that European merchants were locked into their homes at night and closely watched. 'The Christians are hated at Damascus,' he wrote.

Dressed as an Arab, la Brocquière spent months wandering through Turkey. By his own account he was many times lucky to escape assassination, and although he once came to a valley where the road led to Persia, he did not dare take it. The military strength and confidence of the Turks was far greater than he had expected, although when safely back in Burgundy he felt it his duty to put forward a scheme for defeating them. (It involved bringing together the best bowmen of France, England and Germany, supported by light cavalry and infantry armed with battleaxes. After driving the Turks from eastern Europe this army might, 'if sufficiently numerous', even march on to take Jerusalem.)

While in Damascus the Burgundian had watched a caravan of 3,000 camels arrive in the city, with pilgrims from Mecca. He learned that spices from India were brought up the Red Sea 'in large ships' to the coast near Mecca. 'Thither the Mohammedans go to purchase them. They load them on camels, and other beasts of burden, for the markets of Cairo, Damascus and other places, as is well known.'

This was the trade which Portugal yearned to usurp. In those Arab markets the main buyers of pepper and silks and other oriental products had always been merchants from Italy, and the Venetians above all. If truth about the Indies was to be sifted from fantasy, then Venice was surely the place for the Portuguese to begin their investigations.[2] More-over, relations between Lisbon and the mighty republic had been cordial ever since the visit of Prince Pedro in 1428.

Italy did not fail the Portuguese. Shortly before the middle of the fifteenth century a Venetian named Nicolo de' Conti had appeared in Rome after twenty-five years abroad. His first action was to ask for an audience with the Pope, to seek absolution for having (as he claimed, to save his life) renounced Christianity in favour of Islam during his travels. The Pope, Eugene IV, was sympathetic to Nicolo, and the penance he imposed was mild: the Venetian must recount his experiences to the papal secretary, Poggio Bracciolini.

With his inquisitive and rational mind, Poggio typified the new spirit of the Renaissance. He was preparing a world encyclopaedia entitled *On the Vicissitudes of Fortune*, and his interest in geography was keen. In the past he had written to Prince Henry of Portugal, congratulating him extravagantly for his maritime explorations: by penetrating regions unknown, Henry was even 'exceeding the deeds of Alexander the Great'.

Nicolo de' Conti had much to relate about a career which had taken him to the borders of China. In 1419, when he was a young man, Nicolo had gone to Damascus, set up as a merchant, then decided to travel eastwards with a trading caravan. But unlike Bertrandon de la Brocquière, he did not turn back at the decisive moment. Adopting Persian dress, and speaking Arabic and Persian, Nicolo found his way to India. From there he spent many years sailing from port to port round the Indian Ocean. He made his home in India, where he married and raised a family.

Nicolo's travels in India itself had been wide-ranging. He knew the ports of the sub-continent, and had also travelled far inland. The great 'maritime city' of Calicut was 'eight miles in circumference, a noble emporium for all India, abounding in pepper, lac [crimson lake], ginger, a larger kind of cinnamon'. Although he was not slow to criticize Indians, describing the practice of suttee in gruesome detail and maintaining that they were 'much addicted to licentiousness', he was equally ready to report that they regarded the Franks (Europeans) as arrogant for thinking they excelled all other races in wisdom.

He recounted the scenes of daily life in India, even describing how women arranged their hair, sometimes using false locks, 'but none paint their faces, with the exception of those who dwell near Cathay'. In

Calicut there was fondness for polyandry, with one woman having as many as ten husbands; the men contributed among themselves to the upkeep of the shared wife, and she would allocate her children to the husbands as she thought fit.[3]

Nicolo's years of living and travelling in the Indian Ocean lands corresponded precisely with the visits by Zheng He's fleets, and several of his accounts of local customs closely match those of Ma Huan, the Chinese interpreter. The two describe, almost word for word, the Indian test for guilt or innocence, by which an accused person's finger was dipped in boiling oil. Like Ma, the Venetian could not refrain from telling how men in Thailand had pellets inserted in their penises; unlike Ma he even dared to explain how this was intended to gratify their womenfolk. The Pope's secretary dutifully wrote it all down.

Nicolo never referred directly to the Chinese, but his knowledge of them appears in the memoirs of a Spaniard named Pero Tafur, who had encountered him in Egypt. There is a familiar ring of truth when Tafur quotes what Nicolo had told him about vessels in the Red Sea: 'He described their ships as like great houses, and not fashioned at all like ours. They have ten or twelve sails, and great cisterns of water within, for there the winds are not very strong; and when at sea they have no dread of islands or rocks.' This is, unmistakably, a description of an ocean-going Chinese junk. When questioned by Poggio the Venetian explained how these giants of the Indian Ocean were made: 'The lower part is constructed with triple planks. But some ships are built in compartments, so that should one part be shattered, the other part remaining entire they may accomplish the voyage.'

While Nicolo was making his way back to Europe he had dared to join a pilgrimage to Mecca. He seems also to have visited Ethiopia, since he tells of seeing 'Christians eating the raw flesh of animals' – a distinctively Ethiopian habit. The last stage of Nicolo's long journey home was marred by tragedy: in Egypt his Indian wife and their children died, probably from the plague, and he lingered in Cairo for two years, working for the sultan as an interpreter.

As an informant, Nicolo was both practical and entertaining. Being a merchant he could tell Poggio a lot about the cities and trading practices of the Indian Ocean; he also had an eye for local customs. He might even have matched his compatriot Marco Polo as a story-teller, if only fate had given him an amanuensis on a par with Rustichello of Pisa and all the leisure granted by a spell in prison. However, within the constraints imposed by his other duties, Poggio drew out of the Venetian a lively, coherent account of life in the East.

It was two or three years before the papal secretary found time to complete his encyclopaedia, which was written in Latin: what Nicolo had told him was included in Book IV. Copies in both Latin and Italian soon reached Lisbon, where they were closely scrutinized. Soon the Venetian's memoirs were extracted and distributed separately, under the title *India Rediscovered*. Some years later, after the invention of printing, they would be published in Portuguese.

The Portuguese went on hunting for every source of information about the Indian Ocean.[4] One highly-placed friend, and a keen collector of geographical news, was a Florentine banker, Paolo del Pozzo Toscanelli, whose ideas would later influence Christopher Columbus. Since Italy led the way in cartography, it was to there that Lisbon turned for a visual compilation of all that was now known about the East. They wanted to see their own discoveries embodied in this work (without revealing too much to potential rivals), and because their ambitions were boundless they wanted a map not merely of the Indian Ocean and its environs, but of the entire known world: a *mappa mundi*.

The result of Portuguese curiosity was the making of one of the most intricately ornate maps in existence. The artist was a monk, Brother Mauro, at S. Michele di Murano, a monastery outside Venice. He had been renowned for many years as a physician, mathematician and 'cosmographer', but only towards the end of his life did he concentrate upon his masterpiece, the detailed *mappa mundi*, almost two metres across. Adorned in colour with fanciful paintings of towns and sprinkled with finely-scripted explanatory legends, it is as much a work of art as a piece of cartography, a *mélange* of true research and medieval imaginings. In some ways, Mauro's ideas were decidedly old-fashioned: his world, which he portrayed 'upside down', with north at the bottom, is depicted as flat and nearly circular, with the sides of the continents following its circumference, yet always enclosed by an outer seas.

The Portuguese paid Brother Mauro's monastery to hasten the *mappa mundi*. When the map was finished the original was sent to Lisbon and the monastery kept a copy. (Their intermediary with the papal secretary Poggio had probably been a certain Dom Gomez, head of the Camaldolite Order in Portugal, the very order to which Brother Mauro belonged.)

Naturally, the Portuguese were anxious for any clues as to whether

ships might be able round the furthest extremity of Africa, wherever
that was. Brother Mauro did not fail them. In the Indian Ocean a junk
is depicted, and the legend says: 'About the year 1420 an Indian vessel,
or junk, which was on her way across the Indian Ocean to the Islands
of Men and Women, was caught by a storm and carried for 40 days,
2,000 miles, beyond Cavo de Diab to the west and southwest, and when
the stress of the weather had subsided, was seventy days in returning to
the Cape.' The source of this vignette, written in a monastery close to
Venice in 1459, must surely have been that lately-returned Venetian
traveller, Nicolo de' Conti. In his conversations with Poggio Bracciolini,
the Venetian had even talked of the mythical 'Islands of Men and
Women'; following the lead of Marco Polo he said they were near the
island of Socotra, off the Horn of Africa.

Mauro's masterpiece inevitably owes much to Marco Polo. 'Cathay'
is crowded with exquisitely executed miniature paintings of walled cities,
each different from the next, and all conceived as being like cities in
Italy. But the map also paid particular attention to Africa. One legend
says that he had access to the 'charts of Portuguese navigators' (which
could only have defined, at the time when he was working, the African
coast as far as the Gulf of Guinea). The shape of Africa was almost total
guesswork, with the whole continent being inscribed as Ethiopia, except
for some western and central parts. Along the east of Africa is a large
island called Diab; although this might be taken for Madagascar, the
name is never found anywhere else and is possibly a confusion with
Dib, the Arab word for the Maldives.

One region was even given over to the Bnichilebs, the 'dog-faced
people' of classical mythology. On the Nile were the so-called 'Gates
of Iron', which the Ethiopians were said to open once a year out of
the goodness of their hearts, allowing the waters to flood down to
Egypt.

Apart from such confusions and remnants of ancient legends, the map
was a great advance in thinking about Africa. Foremost was the faith it
showed in the possibility of sailing round the end of the continent into
the Indian Ocean. Most significant of all, several towns are marked
along the eastern seaboard of Africa, including Kilwa and Sofala; never
before had a European map borne these names, and as far as is known
no European had ever set eyes on them. Who had been Mauro's source?
Most probably Nicolo de' Conti once again, for those great Indian ports
he had lived in, such as Calicut, faced the coast of East Africa.

The Portuguese had every reason to be pleased with their purchase from the monastery of San Michele di Murano. They struck a medal in honour of 'Frater Mauro, Cosmographus incomparabilis'.[5] In years to come, simplified copies of his map would be handed to the caravel captains, to check against their discoveries.

FIFTEEN

The Lust for Pepper,
the Hunt for Prester John

> I gave to this subject six or seven years of great anxiety, explaining,
> to the best of my ability, how great service might be done to our
> Lord, by this undertaking, in promulgating his sacred name and
> our holy faith among so many nations . . . It was also requisite to
> refer to the temporal prosperity which was foretold in the writings
> of so many trustworthy and wise historians, who related that great
> riches were to be found in these parts.
>
> —Christopher Columbus, in a letter to King Ferdinand
> and Queen Isabella of Spain (1499)

AFTER 1481 the pace of Portuguese exploration was transformed, for
John II came to the throne in that year. As a sixteen-year-old prince
he had exulted in the massacre at Arzila, and ten years later proved
implacable in his use of power. At home, John openly challenged the
nobles who had bent his weak father to their will. Abroad, he showed
himself adroit, especially in improving the old ties with England. Most
of all, he ordered that the caravels should once more push boldly into
the southern hemisphere. Their captains began charting league upon
league of the African coast. Any doubts his courtiers showed were
brushed aside.

This confidence was sustained in 1483 when a caravel captained by
Diogo Cam reached six degrees south and came to the mouth of a vast
river, the Congo. Its waters, pouring down from the African interior,
etched a brown pathway far out from the shore, until they grudgingly
merged into the Atlantic. It seemed to the Portuguese mariners that the
river might offer a route to 'Ethiopia' and the Indies, so they set up a
stone pillar on a headland, bearing the arms of their homeland. These
hopes were foiled by sandbanks and rapids, but Cam did discover a
well-organized African kingdom just south of the river. On his second
journey to the Congo, in 1485, he bore lavish gifts from King John for

King Nzinga Nkuwu, called the Manicongo, with a message of good-will urging him to embrace Christianity. This pioneering bid for friend-ship with a non-European monarch might have seemed a portent of what would happen in the Indies: the Manicongo's son was baptized with the name Afonso, black clerics were trained, and teams of artisans sent out from Lisbon to help Portugal's new friends. (Significantly, the early promise was not to be fulfilled, for the Congo kingdom was soon ravaged by slave-trading.)

John II's resolve was equally sustained by a dramatic advance in navigation, which allowed the caravels to work out their latitudes accu-rately, even when far south of the equator and unable to see the stars of the northern hemisphere.[1] The king had turned for help to Jewish astronomers and mathematicians, especially the famed Professor Abra-ham Zacuto of Salamanca in Spain. The professor devised tables giving the sun's maximum altitude on every day of the year at every latitude. These calculations were first written in Hebrew, then translated into Latin and finally into Portuguese as *O Regimento do Astrolabio*. The king sent his personal physician, Master Joseph, on a voyage to Guinea to test them there; he reported that Zacuto's figures were faultless.

John II sensed the culminating moment must be at hand, almost seventy years after his great-grandfather, his namesake, had led Portugal into Africa by capturing Ceuta. His methodical mind was already pon-dering how to treat with a ruler he only knew as the 'Rajah of Calicut'. A Genoese named Columbus, who was living in Portugal, had come to the Lisbon court in 1484, offering to command a voyage westwards across the Atlantic in search of the Indies. The manner in which he was rejected, making him turn instead to Spain, reflected John II's confidence that his caravels were nearing success.

The one constant impediment, slowing down progress, was a lack of numbers. Even to man their ships going to the Guinea the Portuguese had been driven to recruit desperadoes from other parts of Europe. Such crews had been equal to their task, for the caravels then only faced black pagans armed with spears and arrows, and gunfire had easily wrought havoc among them. In the Indian Ocean, however, there might well be far more formidable enemies, and the Portuguese would be alone, at the extremity of sea routes stretching back for thousands of stormy leagues.[2] The Pope was telling John II to 'take the Ottoman Turks in the rear'. But their conquests in Egypt and Arabia had already brought the Turks close to India; by the 1480s they were advancing along the

Black Sea towards Persia, and their performance in the Mediterranean proved that they could use guns at sea as formidably as on land. 'Taking the Turks in the rear' was unlikely to be an easy matter.

Having all the odds against them might have driven the Portuguese, so lacking in numbers, to put aside all heroic visions of striking a blow in the East for Christendom. The alternative was to go to the Indies as humble merchants, buying up cargoes of spices wherever the chance arose. Yet such a mundane role was never contemplated by King John, for he was implacably sure that Portugal would not be alone in facing the followers of the 'false prophet Mohammed'.

Worldly-wise and ruthless, a Renaissance figure whom Machiavelli might well have admired, John II was known to his Portuguese subjects as 'the Perfect King'. Nevertheless, he was still able to believe implicitly that 'Prester John', the fabled priest-king of the East, was waiting eagerly in the Indies to join hands with European Christendom. The Portuguese could put their trust in this legendary figure because the readiness to elevate make-believe above verifiable truth still flourished. Scientific thought counted for less than alchemy, witchcraft or miracles.[3]

The Prester John story was one of the most persistent fantasies of the Middle Ages, invented to shore up religious morale in a time of frailty, then given new impetus by a literary hoax. The readiness of the 'Perfect King' to put his faith in it can only be understood as the culmination of a dream, affecting the course of history. This directly influenced the European seaborne assault on Asia, and to a lesser extent the westwards search leading to the discovery of the New World. There would even be, in the end, a curious vindication.

The origins of the legend can be traced back to a tale about an apocryphal visit to Rome by a 'Patriarch of the Indians' spread in 1144 by Hugh of Jabala, a French-born Catholic bishop stationed in the Levant. He told of a 'priest and king' named John who dwelt 'beyond Persia and Armenia in the uttermost East and [who], with all his people, is a Christian but a Nestorian'; this brave ruler had fought and defeated the Persians.

The decisive myth-making came soon after, with the appearance of a 'Letter from Prester John' addressed to the Pope, as well as to Emperor Manuel of Constantinople and Emperor Frederick of the Romans. All the evidence suggests it was concocted by an Archbishop Christian of Mainz, who claimed to have translated it from Greek into Latin. A Greek original was never found, and the archbishop may well have hit upon the idea of this pretence during a visit to Constantinople.

A masterpiece of invention, the letter tells of Prester John's domain, with its crystal waters, great caches of precious stones and forests of pepper trees.[4] On a mountain of fire, salamanders spin threads for the precious royal garments. Prester John speaks of his beautiful wives, and of how he limits his congress with them to only four times a year; for the rest of the time he sleeps on a 'cold bed of sapphire', to subdue his lust.

In a magic mirror outside his palace, says Prester John, he can discern all the intrigues of his enemies. The letter ends in a grandiose biblical vein: 'If thou canst count the stars of the sky and the sands of the sea, judge the vastness of our realm and our powers.' Such imagery played upon Europe's vague notions of the lurking might of Asia.

One defence of Archbishop Christian, if he were indeed the author, is that fictitious letters were an accepted literary device in the Middle Ages. What made the Prester John forgery so much more potent was the desire in Europe, among kings, priests and peasants alike, to hold it as the truth. At a time when the Crusades had begun to falter and all the prayers asking God to intervene on the side of Christianity seemed in vain, it restored faith in the bond between religion and valour. The mysterious presbyter was an oriental counterpart of those bishops who rode into battle with studded maces in their mailed fists. He was also immensely rich, making popes and archbishops see him as a person after their own hearts, spreading a message which could be set against the urgings of Jesus to be poor and humble.

A few brave spirits, such as the philosopher Roger Bacon, were openly sceptical, hinting that the priest-king might not exist. They went unheeded. Soon the letter was being translated from Latin into almost every European language and dialect; there was even a Hebrew version. Then scribes began weaving their own fancies into it. The next stage was the invention of tales by imaginary travellers of visits to the domain of the divine monarch, and even of interviews with him. Naturally enough, all travellers to the East – especially the friars sent to Cathay by the Church – were told to look out for the Prester. They were questioned on their return: did they see him or, at the very least, did they hear about him? Few dared say no.

Marco Polo had embellished the legend in a rather discouraging way, by declaring that Prester John was long since dead, killed by the Mongol leader Chinghiz Khan in 'one of the greatest battles ever seen'. The

Prester himself had been a Mongol, albeit a Christian, and Marco turned him into a somewhat unpleasant figure whose arrogance led to his own downfall; when Chinghiz had politely asked for his daughter as a bride, Prester John replied fiercely that he would rather 'commit his daughter to the flames'. That had led to the disastrous war. The descendant of Prester John was a king named George, a mere vassal of the Great Khan.

Even if Marco's account was highly confused, there was a certain historical basis for it, because back in 1141 an immense battle had indeed been fought in the Katwan valley near Samarkand between the followers of a nomad from north China named Yelu Dashi and the army of Sanjur, a Muslim sultan; the opposing sides were reputed to have thrown a total of 400,000 horsemen into the field, and when Yelu Dashi emerged triumphant he went on to capture Samarkand. Although not a Christian, he was supported by the heretical Nestorians and was sympathetic towards them (even calling one of his sons by the suitably warlike name of Elijah). It is likely that Nestorian merchants had brought news of Yelu Dashi's victory westwards to the Levant, since it was only three years later that Bishop Hugh of Jabala had travelled to Rome and told there how a great victory had been won 'in the uttermost East' by a Christian king named John.

If by the start of the fourteenth century Marco Polo had declared Prester John to be dead – and by any rational judgement, he had to be – the time might seem to have arrived for Europe to stop believing in him. On the contrary, his fame was fanned into new life by 'Sir John Mandeville', an imaginary English knight whose fictitious memoirs claimed to be an account of thirty-four years spent travelling in the East.

Who wrote the Mandeville text remains an enigma, but it was someone with a talent close to genius. He was possibly an Englishman born in St Albans, north of London, who in about 1350 had fled across the Channel to Liège – another cathedral city – after committing some grave crime. Perhaps he was a dealer in precious stones, for his narrative reveals a compulsive interest in diamonds. His 70,000-word *tour de force* was written in French a few years before he died in 1372. At his deathbed was a Liège lawyer and fellow-writer, Jean d'Outremeuse, who has sometimes been wrongly named as Mandeville's creator.

The surname of the fictitious Sir John could have been derived from William de Mandeville, Earl of Essex, a twelfth-century crusader who sailed from England to the Holy Land with a fleet of thirty-seven ships.

(While on this expedition he had helped the Portuguese to fight against the Muslims in a battle during which 40,000 men were killed.) But the stratagems by which the Mandeville author hid his own identity scarcely matter beside the impact of his work on all levels of European society for several centuries. He was not recognized for what he was – a brilliant confidence-trickster who had pillaged the memoirs of many real travellers, Marco Polo among them – but was revered as a trustworthy witness to the world's wonders.

Mandeville's Travels was destined to be the first book ever printed in Europe in a language other than Latin, when a Dutch version came out in 1470; by 1500 at least twenty-five editions had appeared. Part of the narrative's success derived from its grotesque stories, sometimes with a sexual element; even the familiar Roman and medieval tales of lands where husbands invite other men to lie with their wives are worked over once more. This was the kind of earthy secular writing which the Church condemned yet never quite managed to outlaw. The author knew how to forestall religious criticism: as the climax of his story, readers are introduced to the country of Prester John, most virtuous of Christian monarchs.

The writer of the original Prester John letter had motives easy to understand. He wanted to tell the beleaguered Christians of Europe that they were not alone, that succour might be at hand. The motives of whoever called himself Sir John Mandeville are more intriguing, for there was small prospect of financial reward. Perhaps he was merely an 'armchair traveller', amusing himself in his last days by drawing together the favourite tales of a lifetime's reading. Indeed, his closing sentences are distinctly plaintive, talking of 'rheumatic gouts' and of 'taking comfort in wretched rest'. He ends by asking his readers to pray for him; then he will pray for them. If within the work there lies some religious or political motive, it is hard to discern across a gulf of six centuries.

Had he lived to see it, the Mandeville author would have marvelled at the huge and lasting success of his travelogue. One sure result was to sustain the Prester John myth in the minds of those European powers, and in particular, the Portuguese, who were looking for new routes to the Indian Ocean lands of pepper, spices and jewels. To find the priest-king would be a service to God, while acquiring earthly wealth. Thus a medieval legend was destined to buttress the needs of the Age of Discovery: even Columbus, crossing the Atlantic in search of Cipango (Japan) and the land of the Great Khan, had carefully studied Mandeville.

It is unlikely, however, that Columbus really expected to meet Prester John, if only because Mandeville had moved the priest-king westwards from where Marco Polo had placed him to become the 'great emperor of India'. Moreover, the name of the elusive monarch was no longer seen as belonging to an individual; that would strain gullibility too far.

So 'Prester John' became a title, for bestowal upon the ruler of any suitable Christian kingdom discovered in the East. The name was used in precisely such a way in the Mandeville story: 'This emperor, Prester John, takes always to wife the daughter of the Great Khan; and the Great Khan also in the same wise the daughter of Prester John. For they two are the greatest lords under the firmament.' (It demonstrates Europe's ignorance of events in Asia that the writer seemed unaware that the Mongols, whose ruler was the 'Great Khan', had fallen from power almost a century before he was writing.)

As early as 1306, when the Mandeville author had yet to put pen to paper, one scholar had already pointed to Ethiopia as the kingdom of Prester John. It happened because of a remarkable visit to Europe by a thirty-strong Ethiopian delegation sent to the Pope and 'the King of the Spains' to seek help against the Muslims. Spain may have been chosen from all the European countries because there was an active Catalan trading station in Alexandria, as well as an Orthodox patriarch who traditionally appointed the head of the Ethiopian Church. If Spanish aid were forthcoming, said the Ethiopians, they were ready to join in a war against the infidels.

The mission apparently gained little, apart from expressions of friendship; but on their way home from Rome and Avignon, where they had been received by Pope Clement V, the Ethiopians were delayed in Genoa by bad weather. A learned priest, Giovanni da Carignano, took the chance to interrogate these strangers, whose looks were so unfamiliar. Being a cartographer, he was keen to learn all he could about the geography of Ethiopia, as well as its customs and religious rites. The Ethiopian king, according to Father Giovanni, was Prester John. Since the visitors would never have called their own king Prester John (his name was Wedem Ar'ad), the title must have been bestowed by Giovanni; since the Prester was by then regarded as being in India, and Ethiopia was commonly called Middle India, this was a reasonable assumption.

Another priest who decided to place the legendary Christian king in India was a Dominican named Jordanus, from the town of Séverac in southern France. His life-story is obscure, but by his own account he made two hazardous journeys to the East in the early part of the four-teenth century and was granted the title by his religious order of 'Bishop of Columbum in India the Greater'. ('Greater India' was probably seen by Jordanus as embracing South India, Sri Lanka and Thailand; Colum-bum was the port of Quilon, near Calicut.)

There were Christian communities in southern India, reputedly dating back to the time of St Thomas; the saint is said to have gone to India in A.D. 52 to spread the Gospel and eventually died there. Jordanus was being sent to cajole these wayward believers towards Roman orthodoxy, as well as to win new converts. All the evidence suggests that he made little headway; moreover, although the stories of Prester John and St Thomas had often become tangled together, the adventurous Domini-can had been disappointed to find no trace at all of the Christian emperor in India the Greater.

The answer lay elsewhere, and on his return home Jordanus pointed confidently to Ethiopia. While not claiming to have visited their country, the friar had been in 'Greater Arabia', where he had learned that the Ethiopians were 'all Christians, but heretics'. He had a fondness for monsters: 'Of Aethiopia, I say that it is a very great land, and very hot. There are many monsters there, such as gryphons that guard the golden mountains . . . The lord of that country I believe to be more potent than any man in the world, and richer in gold and silver and in precious stones. He is said to have under him 52 kings.' Jordanus also offered a description of East Africa, which he called 'India Tertia': it was inhabited by dragons breathing fire, unicorns so fierce that they could kill an elephant, and 'black, short, fat men'.[6]

What Jordanus said about Ethiopia in 1330 marked a decisive stage in relating the legend to a semblance of truth. The friar had almost certainly been helped in his travels by Genoese merchants, and a 1339 map drawn by Angellino da Dalorto, a Genoese, said that the Muslims of Nubia were 'warring continuously with the Christians of Nubia and Ethiopia, who are ruled by Prester John, a black Christian'.

At last, the kingdom of Prester John, having been sought all across Asia, had come to rest in Africa. While the reality might be far more humble than three centuries of grandiose exaggeration, it was enough to bear Portuguese piety and commercial enterprise along upon the same optimistic wind.

*   *   *

By the fifteenth century there was a small colony of Europeans living
in Ethiopia. Almost all were Italians, mainly from Venice, Florence and
Genoa. Some had gone to the 'land of Prester John' in the hope of
acquiring precious stones; others may have become stranded while trying
to reach the Indian Ocean by way of the Nile and the Red Sea. One
of the earliest visitors whose name has survived is Pietro Rambulo,
sometimes referred to as 'Pietro di Napoli' (he actually came from
Messina, in Sicily, then part of the state of Naples). Rambulo reached
Ethiopia in 1407 as a young man, took a local wife soon afterwards,
and lived there for forty years.

His influence upon relations between Europe and his adopted home
were to be considerable, as first appeared in 1428 when an Ethiopian
mission reached Alfonso V of Aragon. The decision by the Ethiopians
once again to approach a Spanish ruler, as they had in 1306, was most
probably due to lobbying by Rambulo, because Alfonso held Sicily and
was on the point of acquiring Naples as well. The emissaries proposed
on behalf of Yishaq, the king who had sent them, that the two royal
families should be united by marriage: Alfonso should send one of his
sons to marry an Ethiopian princess, and an Ethiopian prince would be
married to a daughter of Alfonso. The king side-stepped this proposition,
but did agree to supply a team of artisans (who all died on the way).

Two years later Rambulo is recorded as accompanying a delegation
sent to Ethiopia by the Duc de Berry, who had Spanish connections.
In 1432 Rambulo halted near Constantinople, and there met the Burgundian traveller Bertrandon de la Brocquière. Since his companions
on the delegations had died, Rambulo was doubtless hoping to recruit
at least one extra European to present to the Ethiopian monarch. So
he 'made many efforts' to induce la Brocquière to come with him to
Axum, the Ethiopian capital. Although the Burgundian remarks in his
memoirs that he had met Rambulo before (without saying where), he
also speaks deprecatingly of the fondness of 'Pietro di Napoli' for con-
cocting outrageous stories, such as the Ethiopian scheme to divert the
Nile and starve out Egypt. Pietro's offer was turned down.

The failure of the mission to Spain did not seem to lower Rambulo's
standing with Zara-Yacob, the new emperor of Ethiopia, for his next
diplomatic mission was to India and China. In 1450 he was again
despatched to Europe, with an Ethiopian envoy named Brother Michele,
and after a gap of twenty years was once more received in audience by
Alfonso of Aragon.

Rambulo now took the opportunity to visit his birthplace. In Naples he was interviewed by a Dominican monk, who wrote down a brief account of the career of this intriguing character. The monk describes Rambulo as being tall, tanned by the sun, handsomely attired and white-haired. This is the last glimpse of him that history affords.

The good fortune of Rambulo had been that he was often allowed out of Ethiopia, whereas other foreigners who came there were not: Zara-Yacob treated them well, giving them wives and land, but refused to let them leave. He may have feared that while on the road they would be captured and tortured by the Muslims to extract information useful in war. Escape for his 'prisoners' was impossible, since there was only one route out, northwards to the Red Sea port of Massawa, and that was both hazardous and well guarded.

Such facts as the Portuguese had collected about the country were fragmentary enough to let them cling to the Mandeville fantasies of Prester John's invincibility: 'This emperor, when he goes into battle against any other lord, has no banners borne before him; but he has three large crosses of gold full of precious stones; and each cross is set in a chariot richly arrayed. And to keep each cross are appointed ten thousand men of arms and more than one hundred thousand footmen.'

Undeterred by the dangers, several Franciscan missionaries now managed to reach Ethiopia and make their way to the king's court. Although one Venetian friar who wrote an account of the trip felt obliged to talk of 'the great king Prester John', his opinion of Ethiopia was decidedly low:

> This country has much gold, little grain, and lacks wine; it has a very large population, a brutish people, rough and uncultured. They have no steel weapons for combat. Their arrows and spears are of cane. The king would not take the field with a force of less than 200,000 or 300,000 people. Each year he fights for the faith. He does not pay any of those who take the field, but he provides their living and exempts these warriors from every royal taxation. And all these warriors are chosen, inscribed and branded on the arm with the royal seal. No one wears woollen clothes because they have none, but instead they wear linen. All, both men and women, go naked from the waist upwards and barefoot; they are always full of lice. They are a weak people with little energy or application, but proud.

Had he read them, these contemptuous judgements would have enraged Zara-Yacob, the most powerful Ethiopian ruler in the fifteenth century, since he was expanding his domains by driving the Muslims back towards the Red Sea. Zara-Yacob was also brandishing at Egypt the wildly improbable but oft-repeated threat that he would divert the course of the Blue Nile. In a letter to Cairo in 1443, he warned Sultan Jamaq that he could do so at that very instant; only his fear of God and reluctance to cause human suffering held him back.

Zara-Yacob was annoyed on hearing that Europeans were calling him Prester John, remarking that he had a perfectly good name already, meaning 'Seed of Jacob'. The emperor also conceded nothing in terms of piety: his subjects were ordered to have the renunciation of the devil tattooed on their forehead, and any who demurred were beheaded.

How much the Portuguese knew of such matters is uncertain. There was quite enough to convince them, however, that Prester John really did exist. The exact position of his Ethiopian kingdom remained obscure, but it would surely be a place of succour on the way to India. All caravel captains had orders to seek news of this Christian king wherever they stepped ashore in Africa. Since on Brother Mauro's map almost all of the continent had been delineated as Ethiopia, dotted with imaginary cities and fanciful drawings, the court in Lisbon started thinking of ways to collect more precise information.

SIXTEEN

The Spy Who
Never Came Home

> So geographers, in Afric maps,
> With savage pictures fill their gaps,
> And o'er unhabitable downs,
> Place elephants for want of towns.
> —Jonathan Swift, 'On Poetry, a Rhapsody' (1733)

DURING THE AUTUMN OF 1487, two Moroccan merchants lay ill with fever in the Egyptian port of Alexandria. Their deaths seemed so certain that the city governor did not bother to wait on the event, but exercised his right to confiscate their possessions. To his dismay the Moroccans recovered. They reclaimed their goods, including numerous jars of Neapolitan honey, then hurried off to Cairo.

This had been an unpromising start to what was to become one of the most spectacular feats in the history of espionage. The two men were neither Moroccans nor merchants, but agents of the Portuguese government. Their orders were to spy out the ports of the Indian Ocean, investigate the routes by which pepper and other spices reached the Mediterranean, and make contact with 'Prester John', ruler of Ethiopia. The senior of the two agents, named Pêro de Covilham (sometimes written Covilhã or Covilhão), had been given a chart on which he was ordered to note down everything the two managed to learn about navigation in the Indian Ocean.[1] In particular, he had been told to find out whatever the Arab and Indian sea-captains might know about a route round the southern tip of Africa.

On the day of their departure, Covilham and his companion, Afonso de Paiva, had been assured by the Portuguese king, John II, that he knew they were embarking on a 'difficult mission'. This was an understatement. Although both spoke Arabic, were using Muslim names, and had assumed the appearance of itinerant merchants, the price of having their identities discovered would almost certainly be death; the best they could hope for, if they were found out, would be enslavement. To ensure they had perfected their new roles they took time over the journey from Portugal to Egypt, by way of Valencia, Barcelona, Naples and Rhodes, where they boarded a ship for Alexandria with their jars of honey.

From that moment on there was no way of sending messages back to Lisbon, other than risking the use of a slow and uncertain courier system maintained between Jewish merchants in Europe and their compatriots in the lands of the East. There was a large Jewish community in Cairo, which had been the foremost city in the Muslim world until Constantinople was captured by the Turks some thirty-five years earlier; it was to Cairo that Covilham and Paiva planned to return when their work was complete. Now their aim was to travel up the Nile, cross to the Red Sea with a trading caravan, then take a boat down to Aden at the entrance to the Indian Ocean.

Selling honey as they went, they reached Aden safely in August 1488, and there agreed to part. They would never see one another again, and neither would return to Portugal. Paiva crossed over to the port of Zeila on the African mainland, to make his way into Ethiopia. This was a hazardous route for a Christian disguised as a Muslim, since it went through territory occupied by the Arab armies who were confronting the Ethiopians in their mountain fastnesses.

Now on his own, Covilham booked his place in one of the hundreds of small Arab dhows leaving at that season from Aden to India, with the south-west monsoon in their sails. This was to be the first of a series of journeys that would last more than two years, as Covilham repeatedly criss-crossed the Indian Ocean, furtively making notes on the chart he kept in his baggage.

Behind him lay a career in espionage and diplomacy which made him a natural choice for such a venture. By now in his late thirties, he had risen from poverty to be a knight in the royal household. His birthplace, from which he took his name, was the mountain town of Covilham, close to the border with Spain. In his youth he had served in the court of the Castilian duke of Medina Sidonia, but returned to Portugal in 1474. A natural linguist, he accompanied King Afonso V on a visit to France, and so impressed his superiors that he was sent back to France on his first espionage mission. One of his contemporaries described him as 'a man of great wit and intelligence', and a vivid raconteur. Covilham was taken up by John II, who sent him to Morocco as an ambassador. There his task was to negotiate with the sultan of Fez for the return to Portugal of the bones of the 'martyr' Prince Fernando, who had died in a Moroccan dungeon after being captured at Tangier in 1437. This spell in Morocco allowed Covilham to master Arabic and study the Islamic way of life.

What had especially endeared Covilham to the new king was the work he next carried out; he was sent to Castile to keep an eye on the activities of the fugitive Braganza family.[2] As a chronicler put it, John II wanted Covilham to 'spie out who were those gentlemen of his subjects which practised there against him'. The hatreds around the throne at the time were intense, for the king had ordered the execution of his cousin the Duke of Braganza for plotting, and had personally stabbed to death another disloyal duke, notwithstanding that he was the queen's brother. Amid this royal blood-letting, Covilham always stayed true to the king.

The decision to send spies to the East had been taken early in 1487, and simultaneously three caravels were being prepared for a decisive effort to reach the southern end of Africa and find a way into the Indian Ocean. This was the culmination of seventy years of Portuguese effort, during which geography had proved a far more frustrating obstacle than could ever have been imagined by the long-dead Prince Henry. Already the voyages of exploration went as far beyond the equator as Portugal was to the north of it, yet still the African coastline ran due south.

The Portuguese captains continued to put up stone pillars, surmounted by crosses, on prominent headlands. These landmarks in the unknown were reassurances to the men who came by on subsequent voyages, and challenged them to go further. The captains were always anxious about the moods of their crews, in cramped and comfortless ships amid stormy seas. The greater the distance from Europe, the greater the risk of mutiny. Superstitious sailors feared they might sail off the end of the world into oblivion.

The tested and resourceful captain chosen to lead the three caravels to the end of Africa was Bartolomeu Dias. Although Covilham must have known him, or at least have heard of his plans, there is little likelihood that they would have discussed the chance of meeting somewhere in the Indian Ocean during their respective journeys. With success seemingly so close, and fears of Spain's jealous rivalry so strong, few confidences were exchanged in Lisbon during the fifteenth century's closing decades.

The small group who gave Covilham and Paiva their final instructions met in 'great secrecy' in the house of an aristocrat, Pêro de Alcacova. Present were the future king, Manuel, then Duke of Beja, and two Jewish 'master doctors', Moses and Roderigo. One of these was a royal physician, and both were renowned cosmographers. The importance plainly being attached to the covert expedition shows how the Portuguese still feared there were unknown hazards which might yet snatch away success. The orders to make contact with 'Prester John' equally reflected the hope of forging an alliance with a friendly monarch whose ports could offer safe havens to the Portuguese caravels.

Seemingly never in doubt was the prospect of 'breaking through' to the Indian Ocean. The two cosmographers told Covilham that they had found a document (nothing more is said about it) regarding the passage between the Indian Ocean and the Atlantic. The existence of Sofala, the southernmost port on the eastern coast of Africa, was by now well known – although it had never been seen or described by any European – and that was one of the places Covilham knew he must visit in due course.

However, when he sailed eastwards from Aden in an Arab dhow, after saying farewell to Paiva, he was following the priorities laid down by Prince Manuel. First he must collect information on the prosperous ports of western India, since they held the keys to the 'spiceries' which Portugal hoped to monopolize. The destination of the boat in which he travelled was Cannanore,[3] in the pepper country of India's Malabar coast; from there he had to make only a short journey to reach Calicut, the famous city that was one immense marketplace, renowned throughout the Indian Ocean. Half a century before Covilham's visit, this was the port from which Admiral Zheng He had sent his junks to Persia, Aden and Africa.

Nicolo de' Conti, the Venetian wanderer, had told his interrogator in Rome about the grandeur of Calicut, and his description was known to the Portuguese. More recently, a Genoese emissary who had managed to reach Persia reported that merchants of all nations came to the city.[4] Behind its foreshore lined with warehouses and shops, Calicut's stone-built houses were set in large gardens; pepper was cultivated everywhere. Inland the country was mountainous. Calicut lacked a good harbour, but there were, as Ibn Battuta had recorded more than a century earlier, well-protected bays along the coast where merchant ships could seek refuge from the monsoon storms.

Every kind of spice could be bought in Calicut. In exchange for pepper the dealers demanded gold coins: ducats or sequins from Venice, ashrafis from Egypt, or dinars from Arabia. Copper was the currency for buying ginger. There were many other treasures to be found in this emporium, especially diamonds, pearls and the precious stones of Ceylon, including sapphires, emeralds, tiger's eyes and zircons. From Africa came ivory, slaves and gold. Covilham would also have seen trade goods from the Mediterranean on sale in the Calicut markets. These reached the Indian Ocean by a variety of tortuous routes and were mainly weapons, ornaments and mirrors.

For those zealous Europeans who saw it as their right and duty to convert all mankind to Christianity, as well as to trade, there were special attractions in the Malabar region: the Christian communities whom Jordanus of Sévérac had vainly sought to convert to Catholic orthodoxy were still living harmoniously alongside other religions. The Zamorin of Calicut was a Hindu, and his city was dominated by a temple of his faith clad in copper, but he had set aside a special audience room for Christians.

Continuing his reconnaissance, Covilham made his way northwards from Calicut to the port of Goa, a centre for the trade in horses from Persia and Arabia; the belligerent princes of India were insatiable in their demand for imported war-chargers, just as they were for trained elephants from Ceylon. Further north, well beyond Goa, were the cities of Gujarat, the greatest manufacturing centre anywhere in the Indian Ocean. Gujarat's many-coloured cotton textiles, especially those from Cambay, were exported westwards to the Red Sea ports and Africa, and eastwards to Indonesia, as well as serving the vast internal market of India itself.

A few adventurous Europeans, mostly Genoese and Venetians, had travelled in India before Covilham, but none had made a systematic assessment, designed to serve the goals towards which Portuguese energies were now being directed. Secrecy was the watchword, so while Covilham was carrying out his mission his masters in Lisbon were throwing dust in the eyes of Christopher Columbus, who was once again loitering about the Portuguese court. John II told Columbus of a great discovery by Bartolomeu Dias, who had sailed home in December 1488 after rounding what was already being called the Cabo de Boa Esperanca. (Admittedly, Dias had gone only a small way beyond the Cape, because his men were afraid, exhausted and mutinous, but the strong Agulhas current was so warm that it must have come from tropical regions.) The deliberate lie told to Columbus, in the confidence that it would quickly get back to Spain, was that the Cape was 45 degrees south of the equator. This was an exaggeration by more than ten degrees, and served to make the Cape route to the Indies seem even longer and less inviting than it really was. Columbus had calculated, quite wrongly, that Japan was a little over 4,000 miles from Europe, for a ship sailing westwards round the globe; the Indies by way of Africa could be four times as far.

The Portuguese engaged so shamelessly in subterfuge because by this time they were ready to believe that somewhere beyond the Azores a landmass did exist which was neither China nor India. They were happy for Columbus or some other captain in the service of Spain to go off and find it, because this would improve Portugal's chance of not having to fight to enjoy the rewards of its own discoveries. Portugal was too small for such a contest, and could not afford it, having already dissipated much of the wealth earned from West Africa on intermittent wars with Spain and Morocco.

Fear of war with her bigger Iberian rival was only one of the reasons for nervousness in Lisbon about the costly next step of sending a fleet right into the heart of the Indian Ocean. What if the caravels could not get back round the Cape of Good Hope because of contrary winds? What if Muslims, the infidel foes, controlled all the ports, so that the Portuguese could find nowhere to take on food and water and repair their vessels? How strong would the opposition to the newcomers be? These were daunting questions. On the positive side, John II and his small group of confidants knew they could muster captains and crews ready to risk everything, if the rewards were good enough.

These men would sail for many weeks out of sight of land, crowded together in squalor, living on a diet of biscuits, rough wine, salt beef and pork, and such fish as they could catch. They were ferocious fighters when the opportunity arose. The Portuguese were developing the use of guns at sea with an effectiveness undreamed of half a century earlier: by mounting their cannons on runners to absorb some of the recoil, the caravels could now fire broadsides without risk of capsizing, their shots skimming low over the water.

Even so, the king was uneasy, impatient to know from Covilham and Paiva whether Prester John had a coastline on the Indian Ocean. The Dias expedition took with it four negresses captured in West Africa and trained up to promote the Portuguese cause. One woman was put ashore in what is now Namibia and ordered to look for Prester John; she was impressively dressed and carried samples of spices, gold and silver, so that she could ask the inhabitants whether such items were to be found locally. There is no record that she was given any useful answers. By the time the expedition had rounded the Cape, one of the three remaining women had died, but the last two were put ashore near some Khoi ('Hottentot') women collecting shellfish. What happened to them is also unknown, but they certainly never had a chance of finding 'Prester John', 3,000 miles to the north.

As for Covilham, learning about the extent of Ethiopia was not among his duties, since Paiva had been given that task. So from India he made his way to Persia. The ship in which he took passage sailed from Cambay across the Arabian Sea, past the delta of the Indus river, until it dropped anchor at Hormuz. This was the venerable city whose arid heat had so appalled Marco Polo two centuries earlier. While travelling on this route Covilham was able to appreciate the strategic value of Hormuz, standing at the mouth of the Persian Gulf.

Many parts of Covilham's spying itinerary are obscure. His story can be pieced together only from Portuguese chronicles written several decades later, but it seems he sailed back across the Indian Ocean from Hormuz and stayed some while in Cairo, 'where he learnt about some other things'. Presumably he had been hoping to meet Paiva there, or at least have news of him; it seems he did not find out that Paiva was already dead. Although the evidence is lacking, it would have been logical for Covilham to have tried to send a report back to Lisbon about his travels so far.

By the end of 1489 he was once more travelling down the Red Sea, to the port of Zeila. This time the Zanj coast and the distant port of Sofala were to be his objectives. He had now been living and travelling as a 'Moor' for well over two years, so he had no difficulty in joining up with a group of Arab merchants intent on doing business along the African coast.

From Zeila to Sofala and back was more than 5,000 miles. This voyage may have taken more than six months, past Mogadishu, Pate, Malindi, Mombasa, Zanzibar, Kilwa, and the mouth of the Zambezi

river, until at last Covilham reached the remote and ancient port spoken
of by Buzurg ibn Shahriyar, more than 500 years earlier. Although Great
Zimbabwe was by now abandoned, Sofala was still thriving, because it
had broken away from the domination of the Kilwa sultans and was
trading directly with ships from India and Arabia. This was one place
from where Arab merchants were beginning to venture into the interior
of eastern Africa, to attend the fairs held in tribal areas along the edge
of the Zimbabwe plateau. Small boats also travelled up the main rivers
to barter for gold, ivory and copper wire.

Knowing how avid his country was for gold, Covilham must have
closely studied the prospects for taking control of Sofala. Despite its
antiquity, it was not an impressive town, with only a few stone houses,
and there were no defences because attacks by enemies were never
expected. Significantly, it was not on an island, and Arab influence
was smaller than in such places as Kilwa and Zanzibar. Sofala and the
neighbouring ports served as intermediaries between the Indian Ocean
world and mainland African society; they operated at the pleasure of
the rulers controlling the routes between the coast and the Zimbabwe
gold-mines.

The ocean routes to Sofala were hazardous: coral reefs and shoals
lurked off the coast, and cyclones swept across the sea. Several days'
sailing to the east was the great island of Madagascar (al-Qumr to the
Arabs, but named as Diab on the map of Brother Mauro). Further south
were latitudes the Arabs rarely visited. Although Covilham could not
have known it, the point on the South African coast where Dias had
been forced to turn back two years earlier was more than a thousand
miles south of Sofala. This was the gap still unbridged.

Covilham would have noted that the monsoon still blew at Sofala,
though more erratically than it did further north. So in the right month
of the year, ships arriving from the south, from the Cape, would find
it easy sailing to Calicut. His contemporary Fernando de Castanheda
summed up Covilham's discoveries: he was now able to

> inform the King about all he had seen along the coast of
> Calicut, and about the spices, and Hormuz, and the coast of
> Ethiopia and Sofala, and the big island, saying finally that if
> his caravels, which were accustomed to sail to Guinea, went
> on navigating along the coast and asked for the coast of that
> island [sic] and of Sofala, [they] could easily penetrate to

those eastern seas and reach the coast of Calicut, for it was
sea all the way, as he had learned.

To send home his report, Covilham had to return to Cairo once
again. He set off from Sofala around the middle of 1490, travelling
northwards to Aden along the African coastal route. On arrival in Egypt
he received the news he surely was expecting: Paiva was dead. His
instinct must have been to go back to Portugal with all speed, to recount
to John II everything he had found out. There was no messenger in
Cairo that he could trust, so if he should also die the whole purpose of
the expedition would be thrown away.

At this moment, as Covilham prepared to join a party of traders on
the way to Alexandria, he 'had news that there were two Portuguese
Jews who were going about looking for him'. They had been secretly
searching all through Cairo. 'By great cunning they knew each other'
– Covilham in his Muslim disguise, and the two Jewish agents, a certain
Rabbi Abraham, and a shoemaker known as Joseph of Lamego. Proofs
of identity were doubtless given from both sides in the usual way, by
uttering prearranged and memorized sentences. The master-spy was
then handed letters from the king.

Although Jews were able to travel freely in Arab countries, Joseph
of Lamego was no ordinary cobbler, for he had already been to Baghdad
and had told the Portuguese king about it, face to face. The king declared
himself pleased with information Joseph had also gathered about the
Persian port of Hormuz.

Covilham's plans now changed. The letters, addressed to him and
Paiva, said that if the two had carried through all the tasks set for them
they should come home, where they would 'receive many favours'. If
not, they must strive to complete their tasks; in particular, they must
visit Prester John in Ethiopia. The king's letters also mentioned that the
Rabbi Abraham wanted to visit Hormuz. So instead of returning to
Portugal (where he had a wife and family), Covilham wrote a report
about the Indian Ocean, then handed it to Joseph, together with the
much-travelled chart. The shoemaker began his return journey to
Lisbon, while Covilham and the rabbi set off in the opposite direction,
for Hormuz.[5]

After escorting Rabbi Abraham to Hormuz, the tireless spy sailed
back with him to Aden. There they parted, the rabbi going on to
Portugal to report to the king. Covilham's next action strongly suggests

that by now he was addicted to the east, and the excitements of a wandering life, because he decided that before going to Ethiopia he must see Mecca. It was never part of his brief from the king; but dressed in white and with his head shaved, Covilham successfully attached himself to a band of Muslim pilgrims on the way to their holy city. From Mecca he visited Medina and Mount Sinai, before reaching Ethiopia at last through the Red Sea port of Massawa.

Having entered this mountainous land, a lonely bastion of Christianity surrounded by Muslim foes, he was told he could never leave. It was a rule the Ethiopians imposed on all who entered their country, to guard the secrets of their defences. Even Covilham's resourcefulness was now defeated. Seemingly reconciled, he became a close friend of Helena, dowager empress of Ethiopia, who saw to it that he was given a wife and large tracts of land. He settled down to live like an Ethiopian nobleman, far removed from the intrigues of the Portuguese court.

Thirty years later a Portuguese priest, Francisco Alvares, would find Covilham still living in Ethiopia: 'He is one who knows all the languages that can be spoken, both of Christians, Moors, Abyssinians and heathens, and got to know all the things for which he was sent [by the king]; he gives an account of them as though he had been present before him.' Alvares' admiration for the elderly Covilham was unbounded, because 'there was no one else like him' in Prester John's court.

SEVENTEEN

Kings and Gods
in the City of Victory

Thrice in the year they keep festivals of especial solemnity. On
one of these occasions the males and females of all ages, having
bathed in the rivers or the sea, clothe themselves in new garments
and spend three entire days in singing, dancing, and feasting . . .
There are also three other festival days, during which they sprinkle
all passers-by, even the king and queen themselves, with saffron
water, placed for that purpose by the wayside. This is received by
all with much laughter.

—Nicolo de' Conti, describing life in Vijayanagara (c. 1420)

ALTHOUGH PÊRO DA COVILHAM sailed several times across the
Indian Ocean, he is likely to have had only vague ideas about its shape
and size. Distance at sea was measured by the days or weeks taken to
sail from one port to another, just as the extent of a kingdom on land
was best judged by how long armies could march before coming face
to face with their enemies. Cartography remained an imprecise skill.
Until he was trapped inside it, Covilham could have understood little
about Ethiopia, how large it really was or where the borders lay. The
later actions of his compatriots suggest that he was never able to tell
them that the 'empire of Prester John' was virtually landlocked, and
that it lacked any coastline on the Indian Ocean, as they had long
imagined.

The Portuguese would need time to grasp the geography of the East,
yet there was one fact about it on which they could never have had
doubts: this was the strength of Islam, the religion they were sworn to
extirpate. It held power almost everywhere Covilham had travelled, and
embraced many races (which had made it easier for him to escape
detection in his disguise as a Muslim merchant). Islam dominated
the Indian Ocean from Bengal to Kilwa, from Aden to Sumatra and
beyond. Earlier visitors from the west, such as Marco Polo and Ibn

Battuta, had seen it advancing; now the process was almost complete.

Christianity held out in Ethiopia's mountains, and in a few enclaves elsewhere, but the greatest loser was Hinduism, for many parts of northern India had been under Muslim rule for more than two hundred years. The most ancient civilization of the Indian Ocean world was in retreat before the youngest of the prophetic religions. As far away as Indonesia, where Hinduism had held sway for a millennium, it was being extinguished in all but a handful of the 6,000 inhabited islands.

By its nature, Islam had many advantages in this context, since it looked to a single god of all-embracing authority. In contrast, Hinduism worshipped many deities, and its complex polytheism was replicated within societies and even individuals. Down the centuries, India's kings had fought one another, using phalanxes of cavalry and elephants, but their armies were ill-equipped to meet the invaders. Muslims proclaimed all men were equal in the sight of Allah, whereas Hinduism was riven by the caste system. In times of peace, Islam won converts who were escaping the tyranny of caste. In battle, Muslims were united by their confidence in the glories of martyrdom.

Although Buddhism had long ceased to be the religion of India, surviving only on the margins in Ceylon and the Himalayan kingdoms, one of its crucial tenets was shared by Hinduism: *ahimsa*, non-violence. Many Indians showed little heart for fighting and believed that war was best left to professional soldiers, the *Kshatriya* class, whose origins lay far in the past. Hinduism was suffused with memories, and epic poems celebrated the long-dead empires of the northern plains, where the Persian hordes of Cyrus and the Greeks led by Alexander had come and gone. For all that, Hindus could not close their eyes to the reality of the previous two centuries: the plundering of their cities, the tearing down of temples, the smashing of ancient statues, the methodical killing of Brahmin priests, the calculated slaughter of sacred cows. As each victorious Muslim army retired northwards, it took away the treasure, war-elephants, horses and slaves of ruined kingdoms.[1]

At the end of the fifteenth century Hinduism was holding a defensive line on the 'waist' of the sub-continent, along the Krishna river, which flowed eastwards into the Bay of Bengal. To the west lay the *ghats* (mountains), running parallel to the Indian Ocean and forming a barrier against any attempts to outflank this river line. Even the Deccan, the sub-continent's central plateau, had been abandoned to Islam. Only the diminishing triangle of the south was left.

However dire the prospect, Hinduism's independence was being granted a reprieve, time to recruit its strength, because of the disarray in the ranks of its enemies. Rival sultans were more concerned to wage war among themselves than to campaign and pillage in the south. When they did campaign, their cruelties served to unite all Hindus against them. Most notorious of these sultans was Ahmad Shah, ruler of the Deccan in the early fifteenth century; his brutalities were not reserved for Hindus alone, as shown when he ordered the poisoning and strangling of his younger brother.

Revolted by endless cycles of violence, of entire cities being put to the sword, mystics and philosophers from both Islam and Hinduism had begun searching for a synthesis between two religions so profoundly different. Foremost among the advocates of reconciliation was Kabir, a Muslim poet born in about 1440. He dared to condemn many elements of both faiths, including his own religion's exclusive trust in the Qur'ān and insistence upon the pilgrimage to Mecca. Turning to Hinduism, he denounced the adoration of idols and the caste system. Kabir was at one and the same time a Sufi Muslim and a disciple of the Hindu saint Ramananda, so for him Allah and Rama were only different names for the same god. He urged his followers to search for a world religion, acceptable to people of all races. Contemporary with Kabir was the guru Nanak, who equally insisted that there was only one god. His teachings led to the creation of an entirely new religion, Sikhism.

However, such ideas were able to evolve only in a dimension outside the spectrum of Hindu faith, which permeated every part of life and could never change. Even during the final phase of the contest with Islam, the trust in this faith was expressed by the building of a city to which all of beleaguered southern India could pay homage. This was no ordinary capital, but the symbol and citadel of Hinduism's last religious empire. Vijayanagara, the bravely-named City of Victory, founded in 1336, was designed on an awe-inspiring scale, for its occupants were to include gods and kings, as well as half a million lesser beings.[2]

Vijayanagara stood on the south bank of the Tungabhadra river in a terrain broken with granite rocks and hillocks. This was the western end of the Hindu defensive line, and the rajahs who ruled there relied for much of their military strength on support from Hindu kingdoms of the interior, stretching southwards towards Ceylon; in times of war they could put a million men into battle. It was not an empire shaped by a central power, but one summoned into being by religion.

The nearest point to Vijayanagara on the Indian Ocean was Goa, 150 miles to the west, but this had fallen into Muslim hands by the fifteenth century. So the main links with the outside world were through Calicut and other Malabar ports, lying further south. The City of Victory also relied upon the countryside behind the Malabar coast for rice and other food. Malabar was the most fertile land in India, because of the heavy rainfall brought to it each year by the south-west monsoon.

The first description by a foreigner of the City of Victory is by the Venetian wanderer, Nicolo de' Conti. According to him, Vijayanagara (which he called Bizenegalia) was sixty miles in circumference and garrisoned by 90,000 soldiers, but he gives few details about its design. Much of his recollections, as taken down twenty years later in Rome, concern the rajah's 12,000 wives, the practice of suttee following a monarch's death, and the enthusiasm with which citizens sacrificed themselves under the wheels of chariots carrying the effigy of a god.[3]

More substantial is the eye-witness account by Abd-ur-Razzaq, an ambassador sent to southern India from the Persian court in 1442. He went first to Calicut and there a letter arrived saying that the rajah of Vijayanagara wanted to meet him. Abd-ur-Razzaq explains that Calicut was not subject to the laws of Vijayanagara, but its ruler respected and feared its power. After a month's journey by sea and land the ambassador reached the great city. It was such 'that the pupil of the eye has never seen a place like it, and the ear of intelligence has never been informed that there existed anything to equal it in the world'. There were seven citadels, surrounded by seven walls, and the ambassador estimated that the city was seven miles across. Between the outer boundary walls were gardens and houses, while further in towards the royal palace were more densely populated districts.

> In the space from the third to the seventh [wall] one meets
> a numberless crowd of people, many shops, and a bazaar. By
> the king's palace are four bazaars, placed opposite each other
> ... Above each bazaar is a lofty arcade with a magnificent
> gallery ... Roses are sold everywhere. These people could
> not live without roses, and they look upon them as quite as
> necessary as food ... Each class of men belonging to each
> profession has shops contiguous the one to the other; the
> jewellers sell publicly in the bazaars pearls, rubies, emeralds,
> and diamonds. In this agreeable locality, as well as in the

king's palace, one sees numerous running streams and canals formed of chiselled stone, polished and smooth.

Abd-ur-Razzaq was in a city laid out in obedience to the circular concept of the mandala, the structure of the universe. The Shastras, ancient Sanskrit writings, ordained its overarching design, with two centres, one sacred and one royal. Vijayanagara was adorned with temples, statues and palaces. The greatest temple, where the rajahs worshipped, was covered in with bas-reliefs and dedicated to Rama, the god of heroic legend. Rama's temple was like the hub of a wheel, where many roads came together. Pathways beside the river on the edge of the town recreated elements of the Ramayana story.[4] It was from this place, according to Hindu belief, that Rama had set out to save his wife Sita from the grip of the demon Ravana. In his odyssey he is helped by a loyal aide, the monkey Hanuman, honoured in bas-reliefs in the City of Victory. (The whole area is still one of the main centres of Hanuman worship in India.)

Vijayanagara's inhabitants, numbering half a million, were entertained in their religious festivals by musicians, story-tellers, jugglers, dancers and jousting soldiers. While the ambassador was in the city, the rajah invited kings and generals from all parts of the empire to present themselves at his palace. They came with 1,000 war-elephants wearing brilliant armour and castles on their backs. It was a scene to excite the empire's female warrior-poets, women who combined literary skills with courage in war.

The city was also a great trading centre, so that columns of loaded oxen were constantly coming and going on its wide avenues.[5] Along one avenue were stone carvings of lions, tigers, panthers and other animals, surmounted by stone platforms: 'Thrones and chairs are placed on the platforms, and the courtesans seat themselves thereon, bedecked in gems and fine raiment.' In the heat of the day, Vijayanagara's nobles and their women spent hours disporting themselves in sunken baths.

Before he left the city Abd-ur-Razzaq was received by the king, Deva Rajah II, (Deva means 'divine'). After passing through rooms whose walls and roofs were panelled with gold 'as thick as the blade of a sword', embellished with jewels and fastened with golden nails, he came in sight of the rajah's huge throne. This was also of gold, and 'enriched with precious stones of extreme value'.

The Portuguese may have had some inkling, at least from the memoirs of Nicolo de' Conti, that in India existed a city whose ruler possessed great riches, commanded an immense army and was an implacable foe of Islam. Moreover, the bejewelled rajahs of Vijayanagara were strikingly similar to the Prester John of the Mandeville legend, for each possessed huge armies and seemingly limitless wealth. The Vijayanagara empire had much to commend it as a natural ally.

Yet fragmentary tales of the City of Victory could not rival all the evidence Lisbon was amassing about the 'Pepper Coast' and the great port of Calicut. According to Nicolo de' Conti, this was a 'noble emporium' for the whole of India, and all the thoughts of the Portuguese were directed towards it. They were not yet aware how much the ruler of Calicut was in the hands of the Muslim merchants settled in his city.

EIGHTEEN

Da Gama Enters
the Tropical Ocean

~~❧~~

> What distinguished the captains, crews, and explorers of Europe
> was that they possessed the ships and the firepower with which
> to achieve their ambitions, and that they came from a political
> environment in which competition, risk, and entrepreneurship
> were prevalent.
>
> —Paul Kennedy, *The Rise and Fall of the Great Powers* (1988)

WHEN THE CAPE OF GOOD HOPE was rounded by Bartolomeu Dias
the stage was set for his country's emergence as a world power. Strangely,
Portugal seemed to hesitate for the best part of a decade before taking
the final step. Dias had proved what Covilham reported: that it was 'sea
all the way' from southern Africa to India. The route to the East was
open; but in the momentous first half of the 1490s, during which Columbus twice sailed across the Atlantic, the Portuguese appeared to do
nothing. The truth is that secretly they were doing a great deal.

Just as it is likely that other Europeans reached America before
Columbus, there can be little doubt that unrecorded Portuguese voyages
were made into the Indian Ocean between the return of Dias to Lisbon
in 1488 and the start of Vasco da Gama's historic voyage in 1497. The
clues lie in the Portuguese archives, where still surviving are royal orders
for ships' biscuits – the 'hard tack' handed out to the caravel crews.
From 1488 onwards these consignments cover eighty separate voyages,
but often the destinations are not disclosed. Thus in August 1489, nine
months after the return of Dias, there were successive orders from the
royal treasury for forty tons and sixty tons of these biscuits, each enough
to supply two caravels for voyages of eighteen months or more (the
voyage by Dias took exactly that long). Instructions with an order for
sixty tons of biscuits noted enigmatically that they should be delivered
to 'whom our lord the King will say'.[1]

Only the experience gained in such secret voyages explains the assurance with which Vasco da Gama's ships were to sail south-west across the Atlantic, out of sight of land for three months, then turn south-east with the trade wind in their sails, and make (with the help of Professor Zacuto's tables in his *O Regimento do Astrolabio*) an accurate landfall about a hundred miles north of the Cape of Good Hope. It was an unbroken run of 4,500 miles, without equal in the annals of European seamanship. The route was completely different from the one taken ten years before by Bartolomeu Dias, whose caravels had stayed closed to the African coast, painfully beating their way southward against headwinds.

It was said that Vasco da Gama had been chosen to command the historic expedition because he was 'experienced in the things of the sea'; but no surviving account tells of any such experience, apart from a brief trip to seize some French ships off the Portuguese coast in 1492. It also happens that all records belonging to the Portuguese royal chancery are missing for the years 1493–95. The assumption must be that Vasco da Gama learnt about the 'things of the sea' by commanding one of those long, unrecorded voyages during the decade of seeming inactivity after Dias had reached the Cape.

A document telling the story from the Indian Ocean side is a prose-poem written in 1500 by an Arab sea-captain, Ibn Majid. Entitled the *Sofaliya* ('The Sofala Route'), it is partly a guide to the East African coast, but also describes the arrival of the Portuguese. At one point Ibn Majid has this to say:

> It was here [near Sofala] that the Franks [Portuguese] stumbled, because they trusted the monsoon, on the day of the feast of Michael, it seems . . . The waves fell on them, throwing them to the opposite side of the rocks of Sofala. And the masts submerged, and the ships overflowed with water. Some were seen to drown . . . [much further north] sailed the ships of the Franks in the year 900. They navigated during two whole years and they always intended to reach India.

When the Islamic year 900 is converted to the Christian calendar it becomes 1495–96, two years earlier than Vasco da Gama's acclaimed voyage; and the feast of the Archangel Michael (a purely Christian festival, although Ibn Majid knew of it) is on 29 September, just when the monsoon reverses its direction.

So Ibn Majid's *Sofaliya* suggests that the Portuguese, unacquainted with the Indian Ocean wind patterns, did not pioneer the route to the East without suffering losses. The truth was never revealed in Portugal, yet Ibn Majid must have known, because of the close dealings he later had with the 'Franks'.

There are other reasons why the decisive expedition, by which Portugal stood to gain or lose so much, was long delayed. One was the need to 'divide up the world' with Spain after Columbus had returned from the Caribbean in 1493. Only when this had been done could the Portuguese feel protected against a stab in the back from their larger neighbours. To push forward such an agreement, John II had threatened in April 1493, a month after Columbus returned, to despatch an armada to claim all lands west of the Azores, because Spain had 'infringed Portuguese rights'. This bluff worked: Ferdinand and Isabella of Spain condescended to come to terms. They could afford to be generous after the capture of Granada from the Spanish Muslims and the triumphant return of Columbus.[2]

The result was a ruling by the Pope embodied in the Treaty of Tordesillas (signed in June 1494).[3] The dividing line agreed was the meridian of longitude passing 370 leagues west of the Cape Verde islands. Everything beyond that – the lands newly discovered by Columbus – was to be exploited by Spain. All the world to the east of the 'Pope's line' went to Portugal; this embraced Africa and the entire Indian Ocean.

The building of several fine ships was now ordered. They must be designed to undertake a voyage longer than any ever recorded in European history. Carefully-chosen oak for the hulls was cut and taken to Lisbon, where Bartolomeu Dias, the captain who had rounded the Cape, was put in charge of all preparations. He took this task seriously, designing two strong, square-rigged ships larger than caravels.

These ships (called *naus*) would be more comfortable for the crews and, if India were reached, their holds would have greater capacity for bringing back spices and other oriental luxuries. The ships were to be equipped regardless of cost. Dias insisted that all the parts of the two ships should be interchangeable and each had two complete sets of rigging. The flagship was to be a floating fortress, with twenty cannons, strongly built to take the strain of firing broadsides. Each vessel was also well supplied with matchlock guns and small hand-held cannons, effective at close range.

King John, so ambitious for his nation, never saw the ships set out to sea. By the end of 1494 he was ill with dropsy, and died nine months later.[4] His son and heir, Afonso, had died after falling from a horse, so John was followed on the throne by his brother-in-law, the vain and jealous Manuel, one of the group who had secretly briefed Covilham and Paiva seven years earlier.

Manuel had a fervent desire to conquer the Indian Ocean; but there was more urgent business to settle first. It concerned Portugals Jews and Muslims. Three years earlier an example had been set by Ferdinand and Isabella: all non-Christians were expelled from Spanish soil, even those whose forebears had lived in the country for centuries. Hundreds of thousands of them, Jews and Muslims alike, fled to the safety of Ottoman domains. At least 100,000 Jews – equal to about a tenth of the country's existing population – fled into Portugal. The new king, Manuel, had taken as his bride the young widow of the unlucky Prince Afonso. She was the daughter of the formidable rulers of Spain and their main condition for consenting to the marriage was that Portugal must now apply the same religious rules.

So it was decreed in 1496 that every Jew and Muslim who not been 'baptized into the Christian faith' must leave Portugal within ten months. This edict applied both to the refugees from Spain and to the permanently-settled non-Christians – doctors, merchants and artisans. All Jewish and Muslim children under the age of fourteen were to be forcibly baptized; many were dragged screaming into churches for the ceremony. Faced with the prospect of never seeing their children again if they escaped to some other country, tens of thousands of adult Jews chose to be baptized themselves. They became known as the 'New Christians' and took Portuguese names. However, this did not win them acceptance: they were derisively called 'Christians from the teeth out'.

Apart from the human misery, these events caused convulsions in Lisbon's commerce. However, there were immediate benefits for Manuel (known as 'the Fortunate'), because the businesses of ousted Jews and Muslims were then expropriated by the Order of Christ, which had been an instrument of the royal family since the days of Prince Henry. There was an irony in these measures, since non-Christian scholars had done much to help Portuguese sailors find their way across the open seas. However, most of the seized businesses were leased to Italians from Florence, so providing timely funds for the royal purse.

Manuel needed the money, particularly to finance the expedition that Vasco da Gama would lead.

By the time the Jewish question had been settled to Manuel's satisfaction, Vasco da Gama was ready. All his 148 crew members, so carefully selected, were paid far more than men aboard ordinary Portuguese ships. A respected caravel captain, Duarte Pacheco Pereira, writing a few years later, could scarcely hide his jealousy: 'The money spent on the few ships of this expedition was so great that I shall not go into detail for fear of not being believed.' One account says that Vasco da Gama, as captain-major (admiral), was given 2,000 gold *cruzados* before sailing – a fortune for the time. The same amount went to his elder brother, Paulo, who was second-in-command. All members of the crews were given large advance payments for the maintenance of their families while they were away. Everything was planned to the last detail. The ships carried food to last for three years, and daily rations allocated for each man were generous: one and a half pounds of biscuit, a pound of beef or half a pound of pork, two and a half pints of water, one and a half pints of wine, and oil and vinegar. Other stores included flour, sardines, dried plums, almonds, garlic, salt, mustard, sugar and honey.[5]

By early 1497 all was prepared. It was now a matter of waiting until the middle of the year, the best time to catch favourable winds. Their flagship, the *San Gabriel*, had a capacity of less than 300 tons, and her companion, the *San Rafael*, was even smaller. But they made a proud sight as the wind filled their white sails, embellished with the blood-red crucifix of the Order of Christ. The name of the flagship proclaimed Vasco da Gama's faith in his mission, for the archangel Gabriel was Heaven's messenger, bearer of divine truths. The two other ships of the squadron were a traditional caravel, the *Berrio*, and a large unarmed storeship, designed to be unloaded and broken up as soon as the two main vessels had used up enough provisions to take her cargo into their holds.

Most of the total 180-strong complement were mariners chosen for their ocean-going experience, or soldiers capable of doing duty on land or sea. There were artisans, especially carpenters and gunsmiths, but also West African negro slaves who might be able to win the friendship of native peoples on the far side of the continent. Most vital of all were the pilots and navigators, men who had previously travelled far down Africa, including a certain Pêro de Alenquer; he had sailed to the Cape with Dias. Highly expendable, and useful for putting ashore in unknown places to discover what kind of welcome might be expected from the inhabitants, were a dozen criminals, known as *degredados*; most of them had escaped execution by volunteering for the expedition. Several were selected for their grasp of Arabic, which by now was known to be the language most commonly spoken around the Indian Ocean.

Vasco da Gama spent the night before the ships set sail in prayer with his officers at a chapel built by Prince Henry. An aura of messianic fervour infused this moment, for oaths had been sworn that death was the only alternative to success: the ships would never return to Portugal without having borne the standard of King Manuel and the sacred symbol of the Order of Christ through the oceans of the East. In the early morning the captain-major led a solemn procession through the Lisbon streets to the water's edge. He and his men were barefoot and wore nothing but plain tunics to their knees. They carried candles in their hands. Then they knelt to receive absolution for all their sins, and this was followed by the reading of a papal bull for men voyaging to unknown destinations. Drums were sounded, priests chanted, and the onlookers wept. Vasco da Gama was gripped by religious emotion: his eyes blazed from a sallow, heavily-bearded face. On his breast was a gilded cross, suspended from a scarlet neckerchief, for he was embarking upon a voyage of discovery which was also a holy crusade.

Accompanied for a while by smaller boats carrying relations waving and shouting their last farewells, the expedition sailed down to the mouth of the Tagus; but the wind was not in the right quarter, so Vasco da Gama had to keep his ships at anchor for three days. When the wind changed on 8 July 1497, and the expedition set off on the first stage of the voyage, to the Cape Verde islands, the crews had total faith that the Lord was keeping for them a prize more valuable than that bestowed upon Columbus the Genoese, four years earlier.

'In the name of God. Amen!' These are the opening words in the diary kept by Alvaro Velho, one of Da Gama's soldiers. His eye-witness account of the expedition (no other survives) is lucid and literate, although sometimes prosaic. He is astonishingly casual about the ninety-day journey, without a sight of land, from the Cape Verde islands into the southern Atlantic (by comparison, Columbus had been out of sight of land for only thirty-three days on his voyage of discovery in 1492); this strongly suggests that some of Velho's companions had sailed on that daunting route before.

Africa's shoreline was sighted near the Cape of Good Hope on 4 November, after the run of more than 4,000 miles. This feat of navigation was celebrated by decking out the ships with flags, and the men put on their 'gala clothes'. Then a week was spent on cleaning the cramped and stinking ships.[6] There were encounters with the local inhabitants: a child was captured and handed over to the negro slaves, known as 'ship's boys'; they were ordered to treat him well. The locals were not submissive to the strangers, and in one clash da Gama himself was slightly wounded by an assegai.

The journey resumed, and on 27 November the much-feared Cape was rounded. Then for several weeks the ships had to struggle with stormy weather and the strong current. They began to take in water, and off the coast of Natal (given this name because it was reached on Christmas Day), there was a conspiracy of the kind that had defeated Dias nine years earlier. Some of the crews wanted to return to Portugal, rather than go on battling against the unknown. Da Gama responded by putting the ringleaders in chains.

The expedition made one halt to break up the storeship and reload its supplies, and several more to barter with friendly African communities living on the coast; two of the *degredados* were put ashore to explore for Prester John and survive as best they might. Finally, the three remaining vessels dropped anchor somewhere near the delta of the Zambezi river. By accident or design they had sailed straight past Sofala, the ancient gold port reported upon by Covilham. Now, at last, the Portuguese encountered men who spoke some Arabic, wore flowing clothes of cotton and silk, and explained by sign language that other ships sometimes visited them from the north. This was the moment Vasco da Gama had been waiting for; he now knew, at the end of the January 1498, that the last gap was closed and the sea route round Africa had been forced open. The inlet where the ships had anchored was given a name, Rio dos Bons Signaes, River of Good Omens. They halted for a month for repairs and to give the crews a chance to recover from scurvy and other illnesses.

A week's sailing further north brought the expedition to Mozambique, a small port from which an entire country would ultimately take its name. The town, on an island just off the coast, was mainly of mud huts thatched with the leaves of coconuts palms. But several stone-built houses were visible. In the harbour were four Arab dhows. Da Gama and his men were overcome by this scene. They wept at the thought of the riches within their grasp. The European conquest of the Indian Ocean was about to begin.

'We shouted with joy,' writes Alvaro Velho. 'We begged God to grant us health, so that we might see what we all so desired.' He meant not only the land of spices, India itself, but also the Christian kingdom of Prester John, about which the Portuguese explorers asked repeatedly, but in vain, wherever they stepped ashore in Africa.

It was plain that there were no Christians in Mozambique town; moreover, the Portuguese soon realized that the local sheikh was assuming that they must be Turks, and fellow-Muslims. Without qualms, Vasco da Gama decided that the fullest advantage be taken of this misunderstanding. The elderly sheikh, smiling and courteous, seemed eager to make friends with his light-skinned visitors in their unusual ships. He first visited the caravel, the *Berrio*, and as a fulsome display of good-will and trust handed the captain his personal religious beads (called *masbaha* in Arabic). Gifts were exchanged, the Portuguese sending ashore yellow jackets, brass tankards and hats. In return they received jars of Arab sweetmeats. When the sheikh came aboard the flagship, the *San Gabriel*, he was treated with ceremony: flags were flown and trumpets sounded. The crew were paraded in their breastplates and best attire, and those men who were ill were kept well out of sight.

The sheikh was an impressive sight in his long white gown, his embroidered waistcoat and silk turban adorned with gold thread; in his hand he carried a ceremonial silver sword. He explained through an interpreter that his overlord ruled in Kilwa, the powerful city lying some days' sailing further north. Politely, he asked if he might look at Vasco da Gama's copy of the Qur'ān. Unfortunately, responded the captain-major through the interpreter, he had left his copy of the holy book in his homeland, which was near Turkey, because he did not carry it with him on a voyage. Seeking to explain away his sudden arrival on the East African coast, da Gama lied boldly: his few ships were part of a much greater fleet, from which they had been parted in a storm. His homeland, he declared, was the most powerful country in the world, and its monarch had despatched the fleet to look for the Spice Lands.

The sheikh was completely taken in by these inventions. He told the visitors that they would have no difficulty in buying pepper and all other spices when they reached India, as long as they had gold and silver. Da Gama replied that he possessed ample supplies of both, but needed pilots to help him cross the ocean. The sheikh promised to provide these, as long as they were paid in advance and treated well.[7] He then returned to the town in his own boat, with an entourage playing tunes on ivory horns.

The diarist Velho noted:

> The men of this land are russet in colour and of good phys-
> ique. They are of the Islamic faith and speak like Moors.
> Their clothes are of very thin linen and cotton, of many-
> coloured stripes, and richly embroidered. All wear caps on
> their heads hemmed with silk and embroidered with gold
> thread. They are merchants and they trade with the white
> Moors, four of whose vessels were here at this place, carrying
> gold, silver and cloth, cloves, pepper and ginger, rings of
> silver with many pearls, seed pearls and rubies and the like.

The references to 'russet-coloured men' and 'white Moors' well describe the Swahili culture, part-African and part-Arab, which had been evolving for several centuries along the East African coast, the erstwhile Land of Zanj.

The local boats, held together in traditional Indian Ocean style with coconut cording, were objects of curiosity; in contrast to the Portuguese ships they were virtually unarmed, and in any case their hulls could never have withstood the strain of firing heavy guns. The newcomers were quietly exultant as they looked them over. They now knew that the firepower at their own command meant they had nothing at all to fear in these waters.

Still pretending to be Turks, they bartered for chickens, goats and fruit. The sheikh was sent more gifts: a mirror, yards of scarlet cloth, Flemish brass bells and other oddments. But the deception could not last. One of the local pilots saw the crews preparing to hold a religious service, and recognized them as Christians. When this news reached the sheikh, and he realized how he had been deceived, he was incensed, so the Portuguese swiftly decided to stand off from the town. They dropped anchor near another island and named it after St George.

The new mood of bitterness and suspicion was tested by da Gama in person when he set off for the town in a flotilla of several small boats, after one of the two local pilots fled ashore. The Portuguese had paid in advance for the pilots, and were resolved that the bargain should be kept. But the sheikh's men were waiting, and several dhows tried to mount an attack with bows and arrows and spears. The Portuguese responded with their matchlocks. Then the caravel *Berrio* joined the fray: with its shallow draught it could move in close, and when its heavier guns opened fire the startled Swahilis fled.[8]

The expedition weighed anchor and set off north, with the aim of reaching Kilwa. This island city-state, whose name was inscribed on the charts given to da Gama in Lisbon, was known to be among the most important East African trading centres. Kilwa acquired even more significance when the Portuguese were told by the remaining pilot from Mozambique that its populace included Christians as well as Muslims. A desire to make contact with true believers burned strongly in da Gama, for if such people could be found they would surely guide him to the kingdom of Prester John. The tantalizing rumour that Christians lived in these parts kept recurring, and they were strengthened when a reputedly 'Christian Indian' was led into the captain-major's cabin, saw a picture of St Gabriel hanging on the bulkhead, and flung himself to the ground.

In reality, these 'Christians' were Hindus, many of whom came to East Africa during the fifteenth century as traders, money-lenders and craftsmen. To local Muslims and Africans, the practices of Christians and Hindus might easily be confused, because both religions worshipped before gilded statues and pictures of gods and saints; this clearly marked them off from Islam, to whom such images were abhorrent. The mistaking of Christ for Krishna, second in the Hindu trinity, was also an easy matter.

As it turned out, the expedition was saved a religious disappointment in Kilwa, because the monsoon was still blowing from the north-east. After several days the Portuguese found themselves driven backwards and once more were lying off Mozambique. Although the sheikh asked for an end to hostilities, there was soon more trouble when da Gama sent men to fetch drinking water, and to protect them stationed armed boats close to the shore. The townspeople had erected a high wooden palisade on the water's edge, but when they saw that this was no defence against gunfire they all fled to the mainland. A party of soldiers were landed to take hostages and search for a runaway West African slave from one of the ships. Four Africans were captured, but there is no record of whether the slave was caught. The landing party then returned with some modest loot, including sacks of grain, a large bowl of butter, glass beakers, bottles of rosewater, and several books in Arabic. There was nothing more to stay for, but as a farewell gesture the three ships sailed up and down in front of the deserted town and thoroughly bombarded it. It was the first calculated display of European power in the Indian Ocean.

The one local pilot still held aboard the *San Gabriel* was proving far from satisfactory. Kilwa was overshot and efforts to tack back to it were in vain because the monsoon had turned and was blowing from the south. Vasco da Gama suspected the pilot had deliberately passed Kilwa to keep the Portuguese away from its reputed Christians. Perhaps it was true, and the pilot was simply enjoying some revenge, because earlier he had been given a lashing for mistakenly saying that three small islands were part of the mainland. With heavy humour, one of the islands was named Ilha do Acoutado (Island of the Flogged).

The wind filling their sails, the Portuguese pioneers made fast progress towards Mombasa, a place destined to play so large a part in their nation's history. They arrived there towards dusk on 7 April 1498, in time to see the sun going down behind the hills on the mainland. To bid them welcome a boat was sent out, bearing fruit, chicken and goats. A message from the sultan invited Vasco da Gama to sail straight into the inner harbour. Ever suspicious, the admiral declined the offer, for he knew that at close quarters his men might be overpowered by sheer numbers. Yet he still clutched at the hope of finding Christians in Mombasa, because the next day was Palm Sunday and his men's spirits would be much uplifted by celebrating mass in a chapel on dry land.

It was not to be. Although two men making dubious claims to be Christians appeared, any idea of finding a community here owning allegiance to Prester John was soon abandoned. Nevertheless, Mombasa was impressive, its strength as a trading centre having finally outstripped Kilwa, Zanzibar and all other ports along the Swahili coast. The town possessed many stone houses, interspersed with traditional buildings of mud and thatch. There were elementary defences, but Mombasa's rulers obviously did not imagine they had foes who might want to launch an attack from the sea.

As described by the chronicler Duarte Barbosa, writing less than twenty years later, this was

> a very fair place with lofty stone and mortar houses, well aligned in streets. The wood is well-fitted with excellent joiner's work. It has its own king, himself a Moor. The men

are in colour either tawny, black or white, and also their women go very bravely attired with many fine garments of silk and gold in abundance. This is a place of great traffic, and has a good harbour, in which are always moored craft of many kinds and also great ships . . . The men thereof are oft-times at war and but seldom at peace with those of the mainland, and they carry on trade with them, bringing thence great store of honey, wax and ivory.

There was little chance for da Gama's men to enjoy their first visit to a thriving Indian Ocean city. News of events in Mozambique had already been brought to Mombasa by local craft, and boatloads of armed men circled the Portuguese ships in the darkness. Two *degredados* were landed as emissaries, but although they were taken to the sultan's palace, and given a tour of the main streets, they came back little the wiser about what might happen next.

During an attempt to move closer into the harbour, the *San Gabriel* nearly ran aground and the pilot from Mozambique took advantage of the confusion. He escaped by jumping into the water. Other local people who were on board did the same, but not all got away.

By now da Gama's suspicions were fully aroused. The soldier-diarist takes up the story:

At night the captain-major questioned two Moors we had on board, by dropping boiling oil upon their skin, so that they might confess any treachery intended against us. They said that orders had been given to capture us as soon as we entered the port, and thus to avenge what we had done at Mozambique. And when this torture was being applied a second time, one of the Moors, although his hands were tired, threw himself into the sea, whilst others did so during the morning watch.

Beyond physical pain, the torture had an additional anguish for da Gama's Muslim victims: he used boiling pork fat.

Boatloads of men came alongside to attack the ships. Others swam out at night to try and cut the anchor cables. 'Wicked tricks' were used by 'these dogs', records Velho. 'But our Lord did not allow them to succeed, because they were unbelievers.'

NINETEEN

A First Sight of India

The stern-brow'd Turk shall bend the suppliant knee
And Indian Monarchs, now secure and free,
Beneath thy potent Monarch's yoke shall bend,
Till thy just Laws wide o'er the East extend.
—Luis de Camöens, *The Lusiads*, Book II (trans Mickle, 1778)

IN APRIL 1498, Vasco da Gama's tiny fleet continued to push its way northwards along the East African coast towards the equator, which it had crossed nine long months before while sailing southwards in the Atlantic. Every league added to a feeling of loneliness, of remoteness from familiar waters and the Portuguese homeland. Although the pause at Mombasa had restored the health of some sick men, the 180-strong complement with which the voyage had started was being steadily reduced by scurvy, desertions and skirmishes with hostile Muslims. The religious isolation was hardest of all to bear for men who relied heavily, whatever the physical hardships, on a messianic faith in their Christian purpose.

The prospect of joining hands with Prester John, an inspiration since the time of Henry the Navigator, had seemed so close to fulfilment after the Cape was rounded: every chance had been taken to send emissaries ashore in search of news of that holy and warlike ruler, yet always in vain. The inquiries after Prester John may have helped Vasco da Gama for a while to sustain morale, by encouraging his companions to believe that round every headland a friendly Christian port might be waiting to greet them; but when they had travelled almost 3,000 miles northwards from the Cape such hopes were ebbing, for Arab influence on the Swahili coast could be seen to be growing steadily stronger. The men knew they were sailing towards the heartlands of Islam.

The dependence of da Gama and his men upon their faith, and their obsessive hatred of all Muslims have to be seen against a background of centuries of religious conflict in the Iberian peninsula and Morocco.

Holy war was the relentless theme of sermons upon which they had been spiritually reared, and the absolute superiority of the Christian message was never to be doubted. Moreover, the entry into the Indian Ocean was taking place just as the rivalry between the two great religious forces of Europe and the Near East was at a climax. Da Gama believed, as did Columbus, that the world's conversion to Christianity was ordained by the Scriptures; their voyages served God's purpose to that end. Equally, the Ottoman Turks believed that Allah had chosen them to spread Islam throughout the world; the capture of Constantinople was merely a step on the way to that goal.

The Portuguese Catholics and the Ottoman Turks viewed dissenters within their ranks as heretics to be dealt with ruthlessly; but whereas the Turks were commended by the Qur'ān to regard their Christian foes as believers, 'people of the Book', the Portuguese Catholics made a precise distinction between Muslims, whom they held to be damned souls in the devil's grip, and other unbelievers; the former must be destroyed to please God, the latter were merely awaiting conversion to the true faith. This premise had governed the fulsome Portuguese attitude to the Manicongo and his heathen subjects, just as it would dictate the treatment to be handed out to the peoples of the Indies.

There were times, however, when prejudice must yield to immediate needs, as Vasco da Gama showed when he halted off the port of Malindi a few days after fleeing from Mombasa. The Portuguese had discovered that there was rivalry between these two Swahili cities and now decided to exploit this to their own advantage. Beyond doubt, Malindi was a Muslim place, but the desire to make friends somewhere along the East African coast forced the far-travelled Christians to close their eyes to that. On board the *San Gabriel* was a hostage, a 'man of some standing' from Malindi, who had jumped into the sea and been pulled out with a boat-hook when the Portuguese caught and plundered a passing dhow. This hostage had urged da Gama to steer for his home port, saying that pilots well acquainted with the route to India were easy to find there.

After some hesitation, the sultan and leading citizens of Malindi showed themselves astute enough to welcome the overtures of these curious strangers. Self-preservation was one motive, for accounts of Portuguese belligerence and prowess had quickly travelled up the coast. Beyond that, the sultan was always looking for new allies against Mombasa. Although Malindi was dotted with more than a dozen mosques, it had long been a cosmopolitan city, enjoying strong links with India,

Bengal and Persia (like the Persians, the Malindians followed the Shi'a rites). The giraffes which had so amazed China eighty years before had come from Malindi.

Da Gama realized at once that the Malindi harbour did not compare with that of Mombasa; but it was safe enough in calm weather. The view of the shore was impressive: 'This city stands in a broad field along the seaside, and round about it are many palm-trees, with many other sorts of trees, which all the year grow green; also many gardens and orchards.' Looking for a way to persuade the Malindians of their good intentions, the Portuguese set free their captive, placing him on a sand-bank near the beach. He was told to assure his fellow-citizens that the strangers were peaceable and had sailed for two years to reach East Africa (both considerable exaggerations). Da Gama then sent messages ashore, asserting that his king was the 'greatest Christian sovereign in the world', and that the three ships lying off Malindi belonged to a fleet of a hundred vessels taking part in a great voyage of exploration.

The sultan, impressed, made the first gesture by despatching a boat loaded with goats, oranges and sugar cane. Da Gama responded by ordering one of the *degredados* ashore with a yellow coat, a hat, some necklaces, brass beakers and various trinkets. This wary process went on for several days, until the sultan came out in a ceremonial craft, bedecked with tapestries, and tied up alongside the *San Gabriel*. He was welcomed by da Gama, resplendent in his crimson cloak, and shown around the ship, whose cannons were fired in his honour. The Portuguese admired the brightly-coloured silken clothes worn by the sultan, his sword in a silver scabbard borne by an ancient retainer, the vast red sunshade held over his head, the brasswork on his throne, the corps of musicians blowing on trumpets and elephant tusks. But fearing a trick, da Gama refused an invitation to step ashore, only allowing some of his men to visit the sultan's palace; hostages were given as a guarantee of their safe return. The diarist Velho wrote nostalgically that Malindi reminded him of Alcochete, a town on the banks of the Tagus.

There was a saying on the Swahili coast: 'The men on horseback in Mombasa, and the women of Malindi.' This meant that one city boasted better warriors, while the other had the more beautiful women. The Portuguese were given scant opportunity in their nine-day stay to become familiar with Malindi's women, but they could at least admire the civilized quality of life in the city. According to one chronicler, the gardens had 'all kinds of herbs and fruit', especially large oranges 'very sweet and pleasant to taste'. The houses were built of lime and stone, along tidy streets.

Most of the inhabitants were black, but among them were merchants from Arabia and India. Since India was the goal of the Portuguese, and they had persuaded themselves that most of its people were Christians, they studied the sailors in nearby ships: 'These Indians are tawny men. They wear but little clothing and have long beards and long hair which they braid. They told us that they ate no beef. Their language differs from that of the Arabs, but some of them know a little of it.'[1]

During festivities in which both the locals and their guests took part, the aged and half-blind former sultan was carried down to the shore in a sedan chair. Local gallants galloped along the beach on horseback.[2] After nightfall, rockets were fired into the sky from the Portuguese and Indian ships.

Despite these contests of goodwill, da Gama was eager to seize his advantage and be gone. Although he had sworn to his king that he would reach Calicut, his crews were homesick and knew that India was several weeks more sailing away. So it had been a great relief to da Gama when he recruited a willing pilot, experienced in making the crossing, for all the Swahili mariners he had earlier tried to persuade to pilot his tiny fleet to India had refused outright, either through fear or defiance – 'even though they were put to torture'.

In Malindi, fortunes had changed. An Arab sea-captain, whose name was written down by Velho as Malema Cana or Canaqua, was produced by the sultan. This elderly 'Moor of Gujarat' was well acquainted with the route of Calicut, and declared himself willing to guide the Christian newcomers. He displayed his navigational aids for finding positions at sea, had a chart of the western side of India, and was in no way over-awed when shown an astrolabe.

Before da Gama left Malindi he again put ashore one of the *degredados*, giving him some money and a warrant to say that he represented Portugal. This unnamed man, probably a well-educated miscreant, qualifies as the earliest European resident of East Africa. Told to discover all he could about the mainland (and, doubtless, to ask after Prester John), he was promised that if he survived and returned to Lisbon, he would be rehabilitated as 'a gentleman of the king's household'; there is no record of his fate.

The sultan bade the Portuguese farewell, and their pilot set course for the north-east, keeping within sight of the coast. Soon the land began to change, from the lush greenery of palms and mangrove trees to dry, arid beaches. But da Gama's crews were cheered to discern from the heavens that they were again in the northern hemisphere: 'The next Sunday our men saw the North, and they also saw the south, of which good fortune they thanked God.' After five days the ships reached a long beach, known to the pilot as the Saif al-Tawil, and there he turned away from Africa and steered almost due east.[3] The Portuguese sailors were impressed by the navigational instruments he used, and his cheerful self-confidence. They also knew that their fate lay in his hands.

After twenty-three days of good weather, the lookouts shouted that the coast of India was in sight. Da Gama had fulfilled his destiny, after the longest sea voyage in history. The date was 18 May 1498. Now he must make ready for meeting the man he knew to be the most powerful ruler on the Indian coast, addressed as the 'Rajah of Calicut' in the letter he bore from King Manuel. It was not going to be easy for da Gama to present himself with dignity in his three small weatherbeaten ships. He must also have realized by now that the gifts reserved for the rajah would seem meagre and tawdry when unpacked from their watertight boxes. But he was sustained by a dual faith, in his God and his guns.

The pilot had made his landfall a short distance north of Calicut. The depth was sounded at forty-five fathoms, then the ships turned south amid thunderstorms. When they anchored off Calicut it was exactly as they would have been led to expect from the accounts by Pêro da Covilham and Nicolo de' Conti: an open harbour filled with many kinds of vessels, a beach dotted with shops and warehouses, and behind that a vast city. Flanking the harbour were inlets where ships could shelter from rough seas.

The arrival of the Portuguese, their vessels unlike anything seen before in India, caused excitement. Small craft came out filled with sightseers, bringing their children 'merrily to see the ships'. Other boats were 'selling fish, coconuts and poultry for biscuits and money'. Although da Gama's men were at their furthest point from home, their spirits rose: 'They little think in Portugal how honourably we are received here.'

The first man sent ashore was, in the usual fashion, one of the *degredados*. He was Joao Nunez, a 'New Christian' who spoke Hebrew, Arabic, Portuguese and Spanish; 'a man of subtle understanding.' While he was preparing to hand over the letter from King Manuel he was astonished to be addressed in Castilian by an onlooker: 'May the Devil take you! What has brought you hither?'

The identity of the speaker differs in various accounts of the incident. According to one he was a Sevillian named Alonso Perez who had been captured by the Arabs during the wars in Spain, was held captive in various places, and was freed after converting to Islam. Another version says that the man who uttered this robust greeting was a Tunisian trader named Bontaybo, who later took Nunez to his house, and gave him a meal of bread and honey. Whichever is true, it illustrates how freedom of travel existed within the Muslim world. According to Nunez, reporting back to da Gama, he had answered the question about why the Portuguese had come to India by saying: 'We seek Christians and spices.' As an enforced convert from Judaism, convicted of some offence for which he could still be hanged if he displeased the intensely religious admiral, Nunez did well to put the Christians first.

The Portuguese were taken aback by the opulence of Calicut. A crowded street, called the Nadakkava (Avenue of Trees), led to the palace. The ground was strewn with white blossom from the trees. The palace itself covered an area of a mile square and was surrounded by brightly lacquered walls. People of importance were borne around the city on litters, preceded by men blowing on trumpets to clear a path. Depending on the status of the person in the litter, the trumpets were either of gold or of brass.

It was plain to the Portuguese that Arab traders and ship-owners played a dominant role in this rich Indian Ocean emporium. Their houses were vast and some owned as many as fifty ships capable of crossing to the Red Sea, carrying cargoes and pilgrims for Mecca; it was said that the Muslims had taken control of the ocean routes from India, to both east and west, because the tenets of Hinduism inhibited its followers from making long sea journeys. Many powerful Arabs from as far away as Egypt were settled in Calicut, but they took care to honour the religious beliefs of their hosts, showing respect to cows and never eating beef. On the other hand, there were many Hindu converts to Islam who were escaping from the caste system.

Although da Gama had always refused, since leaving Lisbon, to go ashore to meet local rulers, he knew that he could not maintain such a stance in Calicut. A display of respect to its ruler was vital. He had time to prepare himself, because Nunez returned to tell him that the 'rajah' – the Zamorin, the Sea-King – was away on a journey.[4] On receiving a message that the Zamorin was back and awaiting him, da Gama put on a scarlet cloak reaching to the ground, a blue satin tunic, white buskins and a blue velvet cap adorned with a feather. As a guarantee of his safety a group of Nairs, the Zamorin's high-caste warriors,[5] was sent out to the Portuguese ships and would be held hostage for his safe return.

As da Gama took his first steps on to Indian soil, with his escort around him, a palanquin was waiting, and crowds lined the roads to see the procession pass. On the way a Hindu temple was sighted, and the Portuguese were delighted, because they mistook it for the church of 'Christian heretics'. Da Gama stepped down from his palanquin, entered the temple, and knelt in prayer before a statue of a mother holding a child – Devaki nursing Krishna. One of his aides warned him that he might be bowing down before a 'false god'.

When the palace gates were reached, the Zamorin watched from a balcony as da Gama was helped down from his palanquin by a page in red satin. The Portuguese admiral walked slowly forward, his escort leading the way. A turning-point in the history of the Indian Ocean is crystallized in this scene. Patterns of life and commerce which had held good for many centuries were about to be shattered.

Da Gama was led with elaborate ritual through a series of ante-rooms with massive golden doors, until he came to the royal chamber. The Zamorin, Mana Vikrama, lay on a green couch below a silken canopy. He was naked above the waist, and was chewing betel-nut. On his left arm, above the elbow, glittered a bracelet from which hung an immense diamond, and round his neck were strings of pearls. He also wore a heart-shaped emerald surrounded by rubies, the *pathakkam*, insignia of royalty in Malabar.

From time to time the Zamorin spat into a gold cup held by a page. Behind him stood another page holding a drawn sword and carrying a red shield bordered with gold and jewels. Before discussions began through interpreters, bowls of fruit were handed round. During the meeting, which was to be the prelude to so many cataclysmic events, da Gama knelt and presented a letter from King Manuel. He swore that if he had returned to Portugal without reaching Calicut, his king would have him beheaded. His only wish was to buy spices, to load his ships and depart peaceably. The Zamorin replied that he was ready to exchange 'cinnamon, cloves, pepper and precious stones' for gold, silver and cloth of the kind da Gama was wearing. The mood changed when the Portuguese produced their gifts: wash-basins, strings of coral, hats, scarlet hoods and jars of honey. The Zamorin did not express any pleasure, and an Arab with whom da Gama's escort was lodged that night said derisively that the 'poorest merchant from Mecca would have given more'. After all, the Zamorin was also known as Kunnalkkonathiri (Lord of Hills and Waves), and many of the surrounding Malabar ports were subject to his authority. The most exquisite products of all the lands of Asia were his for the asking; such items as wash-basins and jars of honey were altogether too paltry. Contempt was implicit in them.

One member of the escort was the soldier–diarist Alvaro Velho, and he gives a vivid glimpse of how he and his comrades behaved next morning while waiting to go back to the palace. Despite the heat, 'we diverted ourselves by singing and dancing to the sound of trumpets'; but such gaiety was not to last. When da Gama climbed into the palanquin to be borne back to his ship, he and his men were instead led away into captivity. There was no way of resisting, because the escort had come ashore carrying sticks in place of weapons – the accepted way of showing they were without hostile intent.

The Portuguese were held for several days in a house surrounded by men with battleaxes, swords, and bows and arrows. The conditions were hot and uncomfortable. A West African, one of the slaves included in the expedition, was sent in secrecy to raise the alarm. He slipped away, managed to hire a small fishing boat and under cover of darkness reached the fleet. Intricate negotiations then began between Paulo da Gama, who had taken charge of the ships during his brother's absence, and the Zamorin. For someone of da Gama's violent temper, his impotence was an intolerable humiliation.

The leading Arab traders in Calicut were soon to be revealed as being behind this turn of events, for news had already reached them from East Africa about the behaviour of the Portuguese. The Muslims must also have heard of the wars waged by the Portuguese in Morocco for almost a century. They knew that these Christian newcomers were too few in number to start a fight at the moment, but now that they had finally found the sea route to India they would surely come back in greater force. Some of the captors may have wanted to kill the leader of the 'Christian Franks', while he was in their grasp; but that was no solution. The three ships lying off Calicut would sail home to tell the tale and revenge would be certain.

If the entire Portuguese expedition could have been wiped out at this moment, leaving its fate a mystery, the Indian Ocean peoples might have been granted a short reprieve. However, the Zamorin would have vetoed any attempt to annihilate his uninvited guests, because such a deed would have flouted those principles which had brought Calicut to prosperity: free trade and respect for foreign shipping. There was also a practical restraint: the Portuguese ships' cannons, pointing shorewards. The three ships would have to be boarded and their crews overcome in hand-to-hand fighting, for Calicut had no cannons of its own: the recipe for gunpowder was well known, but used mainly for fireworks.

The Zamorin was encouraged to free da Gama by the four Nair warriors who had been accepted as hostages but shrewdly released by Paulo da Gama. Standing before their ruler, they demanded to be beheaded, failing which they would kill themselves, because they had been given to the Portuguese as pledges of the Zamorin's good faith, and had 'staked their heads on it'. So before the Portuguese admiral went back aboard his flagship, lavish presents were sent to him from the palace, together with messages of apology. He was invited to fill his ships with spices.

All the Zamorin's attempts at reconciliation were futile: da Gama was never one to forgive. His heart burned for revenge at this insult to his honour. On the deck of the *San Gabriel* he embraced his brother, as the crew looked on and wept in relief. After spices had been bought the ships prepared to leave Calicut for the long voyage home, 'everyone greatly rejoicing', wrote Velho, 'at their good fortune in having made a great discovery'. Just before the anchors were raised, the Castilian who had greeted Nunez, asking 'what had brought them hither', made his way to the palace. The Portuguese would certainly be back, he said, to punish Calicut. The Zamorin was seized by foreboding.

He sent a message to da Gama, pleading with him to stay longer and load more spices; those who had taken him hostage would be punished. In an ominous response, the admiral ordered his gunners to fire broadsides above the city; then the white sails, with their blood-red crosses, were unfurled. The time would come, said da Gama as he left, when the Zamorin would 'repent still more'.

Only one matter-of-fact account of this momentous visit survives from the Indian side: 'Three Firingis [Frankish] ships came to Pandaram Kollam [near Calicut] . . . at this time they did not trade, but returned to their own country, Portugal.'

The journey homewards was plagued by contrary winds, because the Portuguese did not yet understand the monsoons and were now without the pilot who had brought them from Malindi. During their meanderings off the Indian coast they took shelter in the Laccadive islands. There they had an unexpected visitor, an Italian-speaking emissary from the mainland state of Goa. This tall, white-bearded figure was quickly suspected of being a spy, and was taken prisoner. Under torture he told the Portuguese that forty small warships were hard on their trail, and were only waiting for him to give the order to attack. As for himself, he was a Polish Jew who had travelled to the East by way of Alexandria and Mecca. Readily betraying his Indian masters, on the grounds that he had 'always been a Christian at heart', this new friend revealed to da Gama exactly where the Goanese vessels lay in hiding.

Sailing in silently by night, the Portuguese threw grenades packed with gunpowder among the serried lines of the enemy fleet, whose crews were sleeping. There were scenes of panic as the Portuguese overran their enemies: the Indians jumped into the sea, and many began swimming to nearby islands. In the grey light of dawn, da Gama led his men on a mission of slaughter. Using the ships' boats, they 'went about the sea killing them all, and they went to kill as many as were in the islets, for they spared nobody'. Having loaded up with rice, dried fish and coconuts from the abandoned craft, the Portuguese assembled the slaves who had been at the oars. They selected the strongest to man the pumps in their own ships. The rest they executed.

Da Gama took care that local fishermen were looking on, so they might spread the news of how the Franks took vengeance. He then showed his gratitude to the turncoat who had handed him this success. Assuming the role of godfather, he instructed his chaplain to baptize the Pole with the name Gaspar. The so-called 'Gaspar da Gama' or 'Gaspar of the Indies' was to become a renowned figure in Portuguese legend.

The voyage back across the Indian Ocean was calamitous. In the words of the diarist Velho, 'we were face to face with death'. Perplexed by the lack of constant winds and seemingly unable to work out their latitudes, the Portuguese took three months to cover what had taken scarcely more than three weeks going eastwards. The elation da Gama's men had earlier felt darkened into despair. Christmas Day 1498 was half-heartedly celebrated and the year ended without sight of land. At last, on 2 January 1499, the African coastline was reached. A third of the ninety survivors who had set out homeward from Calicut were dead and many more were sick; there were barely enough able-bodied men to work the ships.

Since his own navigators had died, da Gama had only the vaguest idea of his position, thinking he was off Mozambique. On sighting a large port and realizing it was Mogadishu (more than 1,500 miles north of Mozambique) the Portuguese bombarded it. Their aggression was probably due to weakness, the aim being to deter any local ships from coming out to attack them. Further south, near Lamu, they were approached by a small fleet of Arab vessels. Once more, their cannons roared.

When Malindi came in sight there was at last some hope of respite, and the sultan was still friendly, but da Gama was now desperate to hurry round the Cape of Good Hope into the more familiar Atlantic waters. His shrinking band ate their fill of eggs, chicken and oranges, but they kept on dying; seven more in a week. The sultan presented a large elephant tusk, carved into one of the musical horns played by his trumpeters, as a gift for King Manuel. He also supplied pilots, who would show the Portuguese the best routes south along the African coast, then accompany them back to Lisbon.

Da Gama did not want to stop anywhere, but a few days south of Malindi the *San Rafael*, his brother's command, began to leak so badly that it had to be abandoned. The crew and their possessions were distributed between the flagship, the *San Gabriel*, and Nicolo Coelho's small but sturdy caravel, the *Berrio*. The empty ship was set ablaze and the journey southwards was resumed.

The two vessels, navigated by the local pilots, kept within sight of land. It was the time of year when that part of East Africa is always lashed by rainstorms, but da Gama insisted on halting at Mozambique island to erect one of the landmark pillars. Velho notes sadly in his diary that 'the rain fell so heavily that we could not light a fire for melting the lead to fix the cross, and it therefore remained without one'.

When they had gone well beyond Mozambique another halt was made in a quiet bay, to slaughter seals and shoot birds. These were salted and stored below decks for the long final lap, from the South Atlantic to Lisbon.

The Cape was rounded by the end of March and sails were set for the equator and the Guinea coast. In little more than a month the Cape Verde islands were reached and da Gama knew he had triumphed, for the islands were almost home waters to the Portuguese. Yet the human cost had been severe: only a third of those men, hand-picked for resilience and courage, who had set out with him were still alive. The final victim was to be his own brother, Paulo. When he saw that Paulo's strength was ebbing away, da Gama ordered the caravel *Berrio* to hurry homewards with the news of their success. Then the two brothers disembarked from the leaking, weather-worn *San Gabriel* and hired a small, fast vessel to take them to Lisbon by way of the Azores. It was there that Paulo died.

The proud but grieving da Gama was welcomed by King Manuel as 'Almirante Amigo'. He threw himself to the ground, wrapped his arms around the king's legs and cried, 'Sire, all my hardships have come to an end at this moment and I am altogether satisfied, since the Lord has brought me to the presence of Your Highness at the end of all, very well as I desired.' Showered with honours and rewarded with 20,000 gold *cruzados*,[6] da Gama then cut his beard to symbolize the fulfilment of a great task, for he had not trimmed it since leaving Portugal more than two years before. His voyage of 24,000 miles had in all been four times longer than that made by Columbus to discover the New World, and more than twice as far in seas previously unknown to European mariners.

As for King Manuel, he took the triumph personally, at once proclaiming himself to be 'Lord of Guinea, and of the Conquest, the Navigation and Commerce of Ethiopia, Arabia, Persia and India'.

TWENTY

The Fateful Pride
of Ibn Majid

My attention has been so devoted to the shining of the stars,
That when I am away from them, they ask after me.
When rising, one is given a greeting by them:
My day ends with bidding them farewell.
—Ibn Majid, in 4th Fa'ida of the *Kitab al-Fawa'id* (c. 1490)

WONDERFUL THOUGH da Gama's feat had been, there is no doubt that a main contributor to its success had been a religious enemy, the elderly Muslim pilot who had shown the way across the Indian Ocean to Calicut. On their own during the return journey, baffled by the winds and currents, the Portuguese ships had come close to destruction.

Later, the Arabs displayed an understandable bitterness towards the pilot, a man of their own race, who had so willingly shown the 'cursed Franks' the route to India. To them this was the basest treachery, for without him these belligerent newcomers might have wandered aimlessly round the sea, without knowing the monsoon or the currents, or the latitude of the city which was their goal. To the Portuguese the pilot was merely an amiable employee whom they nicknamed Malema Canaqua, 'Captain Astrologer', a tribute to his skill in reading the stars.

The so-called Malema Canaqua is twice mentioned in *The Lusiads*, the epic poem by Luis de Camöens celebrating the Portuguese discovery of India. The first reference is as the three ships leave the African coast:

> Full to the rising sun the pilot steers,
> And far from the shore through middle ocean bears.

Then when the men in the crow's nest spy land ahead:

> Aloud the Pilot of Melinda cries,
> Behold, O Chief, the shores of India rise!

The real name of the venerable pilot was Ahmad Ibn Majid. His identity was first revealed by a fellow-Arab, Qutb al-Din al-Nahrawali, in his history of the Ottoman conquest of the Yemen. The relevant passage says:

> At the beginning of the tenth century of the Hegira [1495–1591], among the astounding and extraordinary occurrences of the age was the arrival in India of the curst Portugals, one of the nations of the curst Franks. While in East Africa the Portuguese continually asked for advice regarding the sea of West India [the western Indian Ocean] until the moment when they used for a pilot a skilful mariner named Ahmad ibn Majid, with whom the chief of the Franks named Almilandi [Almirante] made acquaintance, and he became bewitched with the Portuguese admiral. This mariner, being drunk, showed the route to the admiral, saying: 'Do not approach the shore on this part of the coast, steer straight for the open sea and be sheltered from the waves.' When they followed these directions, a large number of Portuguese ships avoided shipwreck and many reached the sea of Western India . . . They took every ship by force, thereby causing great losses to the Muslims, taking prisoners and looting.

Yet there are other, less controversial, reasons why Ibn Majid's name should be remembered, for he is among the most prolific writers of any race or period on nautical matters. This son and grandson of Arab sea-captains is credited with at least forty works, almost all in various verse forms and mixtures of prose and verse.[1] More than half of these have survived in various manuscript collections. It was with good reason that the Portuguese called him Captain Astrologer, for Ibn Majid's long poems go into greatest detail about the science of stellar measurement to fix a ship's latitude.[2] Navigational skills on the busy Indian Ocean routes were already highly developed when the Portuguese arrived, but Ibn Majid makes it plain that he regards himself as a supreme authority.

In his best-known work of instruction for mariners, the twelve-part *Fawa'id* (its full title means *The Book of Useful Facts Concerning the First Principles and Rules of Navigation*), he tells the reader again and again that he has spent his whole life at sea, has constantly measured the stars, and that his guidance should be followed by all who seek to avoid disasters. He is far from modest, but with fair reason. His ability was such that even when the Pole Star was hidden behind the clouds he could work out its exact position by measuring the altitude of ten or more other stars which could still be seen. At one place he pens a poem about himself:

> I have exhausted my life for science and have been famous for it.
> My honour has been increased by knowledge in my old age.
> Had I not been worthy of this, kings would not have
> Paid any attention to me. This is the greatest aim achieved.

However, not all of Ibn Majid's verse is in so solemn a vein. He intersperses his nautical teachings with short poems which show him to be of a distinctly pleasure-loving disposition. A typical example reads:

> Behold, the maiden of beauty, perfect,
> A maiden of fourteen, completely matured.
> The wine and the stringed instruments are ready,
> My good fortune is clear; hence my boasting.
> The turtledove sings on its branch, its voice
> Sways with rapture, living yet tender.
> The surface of the plain blossoms as a rose;
> The flowers of the meadow as the flowers of Paradise.
> The vine makes a bower with its leaves,
> And the drinking companions say, 'Surely this is the place.'
> I arose then to enjoy the pleasure of youth,
> Mixing the water of the vine with the water of the tongue.
> I plucked the pomegranate of her breast
> A fruit from a sapling, pleasing and tender.
> I attained what no one else can name
> What no one else had ever yet attained.

Some admirers of Ibn Majid's writing have suggested that he might not, after all, have been the pilot who guided the 'curst Franks' to India. They could draw some support from the Portuguese references to him. In these he is always called Malema Canaqua, or some variant of the nickname, but never Ibn Majid. He is also described as the 'Moor of Gujarat', implying that he came from an Arab community in one of the cluster of thriving ports north of Goa, whereas his most likely birthplace was Arabia. A reliable source about the identity of the pilot might well have been the soldier-diarist Alvaro Velho, but his confused remarks only compound the mystery. Describing the departure from

Malindi he says: 'We were much pleased with the Christian pilot whom the king has sent us.' He claims that Canaqua or Kanaka was the name of the pilot's caste, although a 'Moor of Gujarat' could scarcely have been a Christian, nor could he have belonged to any caste. Ibn Majid may simply have hinted at belonging to some heretical Christian sect to please his hosts.

However, his writings do confirm that he had sailed to Gujarat count-less times, and the most likely explanation is that when the Portuguese found him in Malindi he had just captained a ship across the Indian Ocean to Africa for one of the many rich Gujarati merchants. His vanity would have been stirred by the idea of displaying his prowess to these formidable strangers, for although he was well into his sixties, he was still full of vigour and pride. A professional curiosity about their ships may also have drawn him towards the Franks, not to mention the discovery that they had good stocks of wine aboard:

> The yellow wine is shining bright like fire. I can never see it
> In the cup but that I banish sorrow and my cares.

One last proposition exists for acquitting Ibn Majid of having betrayed the secrets of the Indian Ocean: that he was named merely as an act of revenge in some forgotten feud. A religious antagonism is certainly possible, since Ibn Majid belonged to the Shi'a branch of Islam, and was not notably devout, whereas his principal accuser, Qutb al-Din al-Nahrawali, lived in Mecca and was almost certainly a Sunni.

It is in Ibn Majid's own writing, however, that the real evidence has long lain hidden, and specifically in his last poem, the *Sofaliya*. The existence of the *Sofaliya* was unknown until the middle of the twentieth century, when it was discovered by a Soviet scholar in the archives in Leningrad (St Petersburg). Probably written in the year 1500, this is the same work which relates how Portuguese ships had, several years before da Gama's expedition, come to grief after rounding the Cape and sailing almost to the Mozambique port of Sofala.

The *Sofaliya* tells much more about the Portuguese, and about Ibn Majid's connections with them. It is a rather rambling poem, repeating many details from his earlier compositions. Again and again he returns to the doings of the Portuguese in the Indian Ocean, describing how they came to attack and capture one place after another. Their first appearance, according to his dating, converted from the Islamic calendar, was in 1495–96, when one of their ships had come to grief off Sofala:

'They had been sailing this way for two years and were of course heading for India.' Then they reappeared, reached their goal, and 'returned from India to Zanj'.

Ibn Majid describes the arrival of the Portuguese at Calicut:

> There they sold and bought, showed their power, bribed the
>   Zamorin and oppressed people.
> With them came hatred of Islam! And people were afraid and
>   anguished.
> And the land of the Zamorin was torn from that of Mecca and
>   Guardafui [the cape at the entrance to the Red Sea] . . .
> People doubted them, wondering whether they were wise men
>   or demented thieves.

He leaves the reader in little doubt of his close contacts with the Portuguese, using such phrases as 'this also was told us by the Franko-Portuguese'. Then comes his account of the early part of the Portuguese voyage, through the Atlantic:

> In the first place, leaving their land, the Franks, as they told me,
> Navigated out to the south-west, a ten-day route . . .
> They told me: after a day they saw islands behind them.
> Afterwards they navigated to the south for ninety days . . .

That is precisely the time recorded by Alvaro Velho in his diary as having been taken for the non-stop voyage from the Cape Verde islands, through the southern Atlantic, to the Cape. The only possible way in which Ibn Majid could have become privy to such a piece of information from the secretive Portuguese was by living among them, as he did on the three-week crossing from Malindi to Calicut.

Ibn Majid says he admires the Portuguese for their 'science', their skills in navigation, and he urges his Arab readers to learn from them 'after my death'. But near the end of the poem comes one poignant cry of regret:

> Oh! Had I known the consequences that would come from
>   them!
> People were surprised by what they did!

Ibn Majid is believed to have died only a year or two after he wrote the *Sofaliya*.

TWENTY-ONE

Sounds of Europe's Rage

> The carracks, piled high with loot – pepper, cinnamon, mace, silks, pearls, rubies – aroused the lust of Europe. The Portuguese made the breach through which the jackals raced to get their fill. Few European historians will face up to the consequences of the murderous Western onslaught on India and the East, which broke not only the webs of commerce but of culture, that divided kingdoms, disrupted politics and drove China and Japan into hostile isolation.
>
> — Professor J. H. Plumb, Introduction to *The Portuguese Seaborne Empire* by C. R. Boxer (1969)

WHEN THE FIRST SURVIVORS from da Gama's expedition arrived in Lisbon in the caravel *Berrio*, the Portuguese king could hardly contain his pride and excitement. Manuel hurriedly wrote a letter to Ferdinand and Isabella of Spain telling them about the achievements of his sailors in the Indian Ocean. The Spanish monarchs had, for the moment, grown disillusioned with the discoveries made a few years earlier on their behalf by Columbus, so Manuel did not need to hint that his half of the world seemed the more promising. It was all too obvious. His men had been to India and returned with its spices as the proof, whereas the islands Columbus found certainly were not India and his ships had brought home scarcely anything of value. The Portuguese had met the bejewelled 'Rajah of Calicut' in his glittering palace, but the islanders on the western side of the Atlantic were only poor, backward and heathenish.

Manuel ordered religious processions throughout his little kingdom to celebrate this triumph, this victory for Christendom. He assured Ferdinand and Isabella that there were many Christians in India, 'although not yet strong in the faith or possessed of a thorough knowledge of it'. But as soon as the Portuguese brought them to the true Catholic beliefs 'there will be an opportunity for destroying the Moors of these parts'. Manuel knew that this would strike a chord, for it was only seven years since the recipients of his letter had driven the last Muslims from Castile. Ferdinand and Isabella were game to go on fighting 'Moors' anywhere they might be found, thus it was something of an anti-climax for them that none seemed to exist across the Atlantic. So it was Manuel's joyful prerogative to extend the holy struggle in distant regions: the war would be 'pushed with more ardour', he promised, 'in the lands conquered by us'.

The sense of divine mission which possessed Manuel was heightened because the end of the century, the mid-point of the second millennium, was so near. In an age of superstition there was talk of Christ returning, of earthquakes, floods and plagues to punish the wicked. Many Portuguese held to a mystical belief in a 'Hidden One', who would appear and bestow on them the right to rule the entire world. It was a time of religious ferment, with mounting demands for reform of the Catholic Church. The dying century had also seen both victory and defeat in the holy war against Islam: the Muslims had been expelled from the soil of western Europe, but to the east the Turkish crescent was ever more in the ascendant. By sailing into the Indian Ocean the Portuguese were not only poised to take the spice trade from Venice, but also to outflank Islam and shatter the Ottoman dream of world conquest. This fired their visions of linking up with Prester John to make a combined assault to destroy Mecca, the 'citadel of the infidels'.

Manuel was proud that the arrival of da Gama's little fleet had caught the Indian Ocean region by surprise. This was partly a tribute to the artfulness of successive monarchs in Lisbon, but there was another factor. The sharper division between Christendom and Islam created by the Turkish capture of Constantinople in 1453 meant that the flow of information between the Mediterranean to the East was far more scanty; and with the fall of Granada in 1492 the Muslims had lost their last listening post on the mainland of western Europe. Even the Venetians, who had their spies in Lisbon, seem not to have spread any rumours about the momentous event which was to be so fatal to their own monopoly of the European spice trade.

Now the time for secrecy was past. Italian merchants and bankers began sending news home from Portugal about the expedition, with eye-witness descriptions of Indian life. According to one such report, Calicut was 'bigger than Lisbon'.

Keen to deter any rivals hoping to usurp his rights, Manuel ordered that a second fleet should sail to India at the beginning of the next spring, and whereas da Gama had been given only three ships with a complement of fewer than 200, the new commander would have thirteen ships and 1,200 men.[1] Twelve of the ships would be *naus*, able to carry large cargoes, since it was plain from what da Gama had paid for spices in India, compared to their cost in Europe, that immense profits were in prospect. It confirmed Manuel's hopes that the divine task of destroying Islam would agreeably partner the earthly benefits of cornering the spice trade; not for nothing was Manuel soon to be derided by his royal counterpart in France as the 'grocer king'.

The fleet commanded by Pedro Alvares Cabral, an aristocrat in his early thirties, sailed from the Tagus on 8 March 1500. This was early in the year for setting out, but the king was insistent. During a storm one ship lost contact with the rest and returned home, but Cabral pushed on, taking an even wider arc through the Atlantic than da Gama's route in 1497. To make up for his own lack of experience he had captains in some of his ships who knew these regions well. One was Bartolomeu Dias, who had rounded the Cape almost fifteen years before; another was Nicolo Coelho, who had taken the caravel *Berrio* to India and back with da Gama.

So far westward did Cabral go that he touched the coast of Brazil, and his fleet halted there briefly before tackling the Cape of Good Hope.[2] (Almost certainly, Brazil had been discovered two years earlier by Duarte Pacheco, but for the moment Portuguese interest in it was slight.) The fleet sailed on, making a fast passage, but near the Cape it was struck by a violent storm. Four ships went down with the loss of all on board, including the one captained by Dias.

After this setback Cabral made his way up the Natal coast, looking for Sofala, renowned as the port from which African gold went to India. The Portuguese realized that by monopolizing Sofala's trade they might acquire gold more cheaply than it could be bought in Europe, then they could use it to pay for India's spices, so multiplying their ultimate profits; if Dias had lived, he was to have become Portugal's governor in Sofala. It was decided to abandon for the moment any idea of founding a settlement there: the harbour was hard to enter, so Cabral may have been frightened of the shoals close by it, because the ships directly under his command now numbered only six, the others having been blown out of contact. One vessel did call at Sofala, then made a brief, inaccurate report: 'This is an island near the bar of a river wherein dwell many merchants; infinite gold is brought thither from the interior of Africa by men of low stature, but strong, very ugly, with small voices, who eat human flesh, mainly that of their enemies.' Sofala 'belonged to the King of Kilwa'.

Cabral set a determined course for Kilwa. He was now sure that this was one of the three main towns along the East African coast, the others being Mombasa and Malindi. His instructions were to set up a trading station there and demand that the population accept Christianity forthwith. However, reports of the reappearance of the Portuguese in the Indian Ocean had already evoked fear in Kilwa: its ruler, Sultan Ibrahim, was all too clear about the tactics the Franks were likely to use. He had built up his defences and recruited hundreds of African bowmen, bringing them across the narrow stretch of water dividing the island from the mainland. For all that, his first actions were conciliatory when the uninvited guests appeared. He sent out boatloads of food, including live goats, and invited the admiral to come ashore for talks.

Cabral declined, saying that he never stepped ashore, other than for fighting. Instead, the sultan should come to him. Fearful that the Christians were going to take him hostage, the ruler of Kilwa refused. For two days there was stalemate, during which time Cabral moved closer inshore and kept his cannons trained on the town. The Portuguese had ample time to study Kilwa, albeit from a distance, and were impressed, just as Ibn Battuta had been 150 years earlier. The houses were 'built in our ways' with beautifully carved doors, noted a later chronicler. The wealthier citizens wore 'gold and silk and fine cotton clothes'. Around the town were orchards and gardens with 'many channels of sweet water'. The palace, a complex of audience chambers and private rooms, surrounding a central pool with fountains, overlooked the ocean and had its own landing-place.

After two days the sultan announced that he was willing to meet the admiral on the water. With a big entourage, all lavishly dressed and wearing ceremonial daggers at their waists, he sailed across the harbour on a raft made from two boats. His musicians blew blasts on elephant horns and the Portuguese replied with their trumpets. As a show of strength Cabral fired off his cannons; their thundering roar, unlike anything ever heard before in Kilwa, aroused panic. Then he handed the sultan a letter in Arabic from King Manuel, saying that Portugal desired Sofala's gold and planned to set up a trading post in Kilwa. Finally there was the matter of abandoning Islam, no small demand to make on a town with the biggest mosque on the whole of the Swahili coast.

The sultan said he must think about signing a treaty on these matters, and consult his advisers; but some of them were away on the mainland, waging war against the 'kafirs of al-Muli'. Then he retired to his palace on the island. As the Portuguese later discovered to their chagrin, the 'sultan' was only a pretence. A sheikh named Lukman Ali Malik had gallantly volunteered to act the part, in case the visitors tried to kidnap Sultan Ibrahim.

The admiral waited impatiently for a reply to his proposals. None came. The Portuguese were told that their trade goods were uninteresting. When they asked for water it was brought to the beach in pottery jars, then the jars were all smashed. The work of a lunatic, explained the sultan, but offered no more. Cabral conferred with his captains. It was agreed to weigh anchor and sail on. Truculent Kilwa would be dealt with later.

A few dhows were seized on the way north, but the fleet stayed clear of Mombasa and was guided to Malindi by the veterans who had voyaged with da Gama. As before, the sultan was hospitable, but complained that Mombasa was making war on him, as retribution for his friendship with the Franks. Cabral was sympathetic; Mombasa would have to be dealt with later.

The Portuguese paused for only five days before tackling the Indian Ocean crossing, but their stay, according to the chronicles, was taken up with inordinately lavish festivities. Such accounts must be treated with reserve, since exaggerating the splendour of friendly monarchs made them seem more worthy of Manuel's benevolent attentions; furthermore, they compensated for the failure to have yet made contact with Prester John.

One of Cabral's final acts in Malindi was to send ashore two more *degredados*, with orders to travel inland until they reached the land of Prester John.[3] Had they managed to do so, it would have been an astounding feat. The Portuguese knew nothing about the interior of Africa and even their ideas about its coastline were still hazy. One contemporary account asserted: 'These two kingdoms, Kilwa and Malindi, are on the west side of the Red Sea, adjacent to the territories of the gentiles and Prester John.' The entrance to the Red Sea was more than a thousand miles north of Malindi.

As Cabral sailed on towards India he could have been in little doubt that the Muslim merchants of Calicut would view the Portuguese as enemies in both religion and trade. On the other hand, Vasco da Gama had suggested to King Manuel that the Zamorin, the ruler of the great port, might prove to be an heretical Christian, able to be won over to the true Catholic faith. This proposition flew in the face of everything the Portuguese had seen in Calicut, but is understandable in the context of the obsession with finding a Christian ally in the Indian Ocean.

The idea of an alliance with the Zamorin, on Portuguese terms, much appealed to the king. He saw it as the easiest way to assure himself of a constant flow of marvellously profitable shiploads of pepper, nutmeg and cinnamon. So he supplied Cabral with an array of gifts so lavish that they could quite wipe out the memory of da Gama's poor offerings. As a further incentive to the Zamorin, several captive Indians, survivors of da Gama's massacre of the fleet from Goa, were being brought back so they they could expound upon the wonders of Europe. There was, however, a *sine qua non* for friendship: the Zamorin and his countrymen must agree to expel all Muslims living in Calicut, and sell spices only to the Portuguese.

A pretence was briefly maintained that this capitulation might be achieved without fighting, that the Arabs who stood in the way of Cabral's designs would quietly give up their established rights. If not, the admiral was ready to fight and be sure of the outcome, given da Gama's satisfying discovery that beyond the Cape of Good Hope there was no power on land or sea able to contend with European gunfire. Their military superiority would enable Cabral and his successors to impose an idea never dreamed of before their coming: ownership of the sea. By merging their cannon's roar with Christian dogma they were asserting a right to decide who should be granted the use of nature's gifts, the monsoons and the currents, that is, who might earn a living by trading from port to port. As a first step, Cabral was ordered to capture the ships of the 'Moors of Mecca' whenever possible, then sink them. Until now, the freedom of traders to go about their business unhindered had been the very pivot of Indian Ocean life.

The aim of creating a hegemony over the Indian Ocean went far beyond the casual pillaging of small craft unlucky enough to be caught on the open sea. Later, the historian Joao de Barros would carefully set out a justification:

> It is true that there does exist a common right to all to navigate the seas, and in Europe we acknowledge the right which others hold against us, but that right does not extend

beyond Europe, and therefore the Portuguese by the
strengths of their fleets are justified in compelling all Moors
to take out safe-conducts under pain of confiscation and
death. The Moors and the Gentiles are outside the law of
Jesus Christ, which is the true law which everyone has to
keep under pain of damnation to eternal fire. If then the soul
be so condemned, what right was the body to the privileges
of our laws?

Although Cabral had lost several ships, the surviving vessels made
good time on the long voyage, reaching Calicut only six months after
leaving Lisbon. If the Zamorin proved co-operative, they could be
home again with their loads of spices by the middle of the year 1501.
At first, the Portuguese were encouraged: 'One league from the harbour
of Calicut, the citizens and gentlemen of the King came to greet them
with great festivities.' Cabral decided to lower his anchor directly in
front of the city, then advertised his presence by firing a salute with his
cannons – 'which caused great admiration among the inhabitants'. The
Portuguese doubtless wished to cause other feelings as well.

The best account of Cabral's subsequent progress is a long letter
allegedly written to Ferdinand and Isabella of Spain by King Manuel (it
was circulated in Rome and, if not genuine, was certainly derived from
eye-witness accounts). After hostages had been exchanged, Cabral went
ashore and was carried up the beach and borne to the palace on a litter
covered with purple silk. Unlike his demeanour during da Gama's visit,
the Zamorin, Mana Vikrama, was not lying on a couch, but sitting on
a silver throne which had arms of gold and was studded with precious
stones. The monarch was wearing only a sarong, but his fingers were
covered with rings and the pearls in his earrings were 'as big as hazelnuts'.
The throne room was lit with 'six Moorish lamps of silver, which burned
day and night'.

The Zamorin declared his pleasure at this second appearance of the
Franks at Calicut, and Cabral responded by offering gifts far more fitting
than those brought by da Gama: costly bowls, carpets, brocade, fine
cloths and royal sceptres. Without more ado a simple treaty of friendship
was agreed upon and written upon a beaten silver sheet bearing the
Zamorin's seal in gold; but the messages Cabral bore from his monarch
made the treaty meaningless. The Zamorin was told that 'to comply
with his duty as a Christian king' (an echo of da Gama's notion that

Hindus were believers, but heretics) he must expel all Muslims from his kingdom, for it was the intention of the Portuguese to make war on them, being 'a people with whom we have so great and so ancient an enmity'.

In a long exhortation speaking of 'God's will' in every sentence, Manuel had threatened:

> And if it should happen that owing to ill-will and minds obstructive of good, which are never lacking, we find in you the contrary of this . . . our fixed purpose is to follow the will of God rather than that of men, and not fail through any contrarities to prosecute this affair and continue our navigation, trade and intercourse in those lands which the Lord God wishes to be newly served by our hands.

Hindu accounts of the Zamorin's response have not survived, due to the custom on the Malabar coast of writing on fragile palm-leaf sheets, but the Portuguese historians recognize this as a crucial moment. An ominous mood enveloped Calicut as the truth of what the visitors were truly demanding sank in. Five hostages being held in the Portuguese flagship took fright and tried to escape by jumping overboard. They were speedily caught and put back on board.

The *casus belli* came after the landing of seventy Portuguese, including three Franciscan friars, to establish a trading station under the command of Cabral's agent, Ayres Correa. For fully two months Cabral fretted at anchor, then permission was at last given for the agent to start buying spices; the north-east (*azyab*) monsoon was now blowing, ideal for the westwards crossing of the Indian Ocean to Africa's coastline. The fearful Zamorin had promised that when the time came to bid for spices the Portuguese would be given precedence, even over the powerful and long-established Arab merchants living in the city. However, the wind was also perfect for sailing to the Red Sea, and a large 'Mecca ship', already loaded with cargo, was seen preparing to leave for Aden.

It was a fatal moment. Cabral seized the ship, and a riot broke out in Calicut. The Portuguese 'compound' was attacked and fifty-three of the seventy Portuguese were killed, including the three friars. Their compatriots in their ships offshore could not help them, but as dawn rose over Calicut the Portuguese cannons roared in earnest. Cabral's six ships hurled broadside after broadside into the heart of the city. There were ten merchant ships lying nearby, and these were taken captive.

Most of the crews were slaughtered at once, but some were saved for a worse fate: they were tied up, then burnt alive in the sight of the people ashore. The effects of a ceaseless two-day bombardment were so severe that Mana Vikrama had to flee from his palace – a humiliation he would never forget. As for the Portuguese, they swore never to forgive the massacre of their compatriots, landed in good faith after the Zamorin had signed a treaty of friendship.

In one of the captured ships the Portuguese had found three tame elephants, and might have carried at least one back to Lisbon as unusual booty to delight the king. But provisions ran short, so all the elephants were killed and eaten.

After causing enough damage to Calicut and a neighbouring town to meet the immediate duty of revenging the deaths of his fifty-three men, Cabral sailed southwards to the port of Cochin. The Portuguese understood by now that its rajah, Unni Rama Varmah, chafed under the dominance of Calicut, so the tactics da Gama had used in East Africa, of making an alliance with Malindi after crossing swords with the more powerful Mombasa, was copied by Cabral.[4] Although Cochin was far less important than Calicut, it had the virtue of a deepwater harbour, within which lay an easily defensible island. It was also a place where spices could be bought.

The rajah welcomed Cabral obsequiously. Faced with a choice – bombardment if these visitors were rebuffed, or possible retribution from Calicut for siding with its foes – he saw this as the moment for asserting his independence. The Portuguese ships were loaded with Cochin's spices, payment being made with gold coins. The prices he paid told Cabral that the royal coffers in Lisbon would soon be filled by this trade, so his foremost desire was to find his way safely to the Cape and hurry northwards. As he left Cochin there was news that a fleet of eighty vessels sent by the Zamorin was sailing south to do battle. It was unlike the Portuguese to shirk a challenge to arms, but Cabral knew that his priority was to bear the spices home.

The fleet reached Lisbon on 21 July 1501. Their cargoes delighted Manuel, as did Cabral's report that Indians holding indisputable Christian beliefs lived in the countryside near Cochin. Here were souls to be brought into the Catholic Church, as he assured Ferdinand and Isabella.

Elsewhere in Europe, prospects of the souls Manuel might win were less important than his spices. The size of the cargoes brought home by Cabral was proof that the new trade route to India was practicable.[5]

The news quickly reached Venice, where the banker Girolami Priuli wrote in his diary: 'And if this voyage should continue, since it now seems to me easy to accomplish, the King of Portugal could call himself the King of Money.'

Priuli estimated that what might be bought for a ducat in Calicut cost sixty or a hundred ducats when it reached Venice by the Red Sea route, because of all the customs duties and bribes to be paid on the way. The Cape route was far longer, but the savings were immense. His fellow merchants had been 'stupified' by the news from Lisbon, and he rightly forecast that Venice was about to be ruined.

TWENTY-TWO

The Vengeance of da Gama

To Vasco da Gama ... we can trace the beginning of a new
civilization which began to spread among the natives ... the
darkness of ignorance, which prevailed among many, began to be
dissipated by the science of the west: and who can enumerate all
the social changes for the better which are to be traced to this
event?

> —The Reverend Father Maffei, SJ, speaking in Calicut (1897), at the
> fourth centenary of the first Portuguese landing

THE FRENZY of ship-building in Portugal during the early years of the
sixteenth century was the wonder and envy of other nations. King
Manuel had quickly realized that he must send fleets to the Indian
Ocean every year, to assert his total monopoly of the European spice
trade. But although his ambitions were limitless his treasury was meagre,
so he invited the wealthier merchants of Lisbon to join in the venture.[1]
They needed little encouragement when they realized that the landed
price of a *quintal* (128lb) of pepper in Lisbon was a fraction of that paid
in Alexandria for a like amount brought from the Indian Ocean by the
traditional route, in Red Sea dhows and on the backs of camels.

Even before the survivors of Cabral's fleet arrived home, a squadron
of four ships had left the Tagus under the command of an experienced
captain, Joao da Nova. His principal role was to help collect the African
gold brought to the coast at Sofala. Cloth, mirrors and trinkets from
Portugal were to be bartered for the gold, which in turn would be used
to buy spices in India. Da Nova assumed that this trade was already
being supervised by Bartolomeu Dias, because it was not yet known in
Lisbon that the conqueror of the Cape had gone down with his ship.

On the way to Sofala the four ships stopped in a bay just beyond the
Cape, and there they had the remarkable fortune to find, on this alien
strand, a letter in a shoe. The letter had been left by one of Cabral's
officers, and told of the disaster which had befallen Dias. So the
expedition sailed directly to Kilwa, where it was greeted by one of the

degredados left behind in Malindi two years earlier by Cabral. This man, Antonio Fernandes, had made his way south in Arab coastal vessels, and was now living contentedly in the house of a local sheikh. Cabral's instructions to Fernandes and another convict, to travel into the African interior until they found Prester John, had clearly not appealed to them. Since Fernandes was a useful informant he was left in Kilwa, then da Nova sailed on to India.

Cabral's method were diligently copied. Calicut was bombarded and every Muslim ship sighted was fair game to be boarded and looted. On one, off Calicut, the captains discovered 1,500 pearls, many jewels and fine navigational instruments. Only the pilot was spared, in case his skills might prove useful on the return voyage, and the rest of the crew were burned to death in their ship.

In another ship captured off the Indian coast was found 'a Jewess from Seville'. She had fled from Spain to escape persecution and reached India by way of Egypt. She recounted what she had been told about the reasons for Cabral's troubles in Calicut: Arab merchants had persuaded the Zamorin that the newcomers 'were thieves and were going to destroy his country'. After hearing her out the Portuguese decided to spare the woman and take her with them, but after a few days she threw herself into the sea.

The incident may almost seem to symbolize a mood of helplessness which had started to seep through the Indian Ocean world. A way of life which had seemed as immutable as the coming and going of the monsoons was about to vanish. With his sense of history the Portuguese soldier and scholar Duarte Pacheco expressed this succinctly, in the course of praising his monarch for sending powerful fleets to the East: 'With these he has conquered, and daily conquers, the Indian seas and the shores of Asia, killing, destroying and burning the Moors of Cairo, of Arabia and of Mecca, and other inhabitants of the same India, together with their fleet, by which for over 800 years they have controlled their trade in precious stones, pearls and spices.'

The pattern of killing, destroying and burning was soon to be given the imprimatur of Vasco da Gama himself, when in the middle of 1502 he sailed once more into the Indian Ocean. The king's 'almirante amigo' now commanded twenty-five ships, the ten largest containing 'much beautiful artillery, with plenty of munitions and weapons, all in great abundance'. Thirteen of the ships under da Gama's command belonged to wealthy Portuguese merchants. Since his first appearance less than five years before, in command of three small vessels groping their way towards an uncertain goal, everything had changed. Da Gama was now clear about where he was going and what he meant to do. The Zamorin had 'treated him with contumely', so he 'felt in his heart a great desire to go and make havoc of him'.

Originally it had been planned to put the armada in the charge of Cabral, who was also keen to punish Calicut further. But he had fallen out with the Portuguese king, who superstitiously branded him as being 'unlucky at sea'. So da Gama, always the courtier, won for himself this coveted commission.

His first moment of satisfaction came just after crossing the Indian Ocean with nineteen ships of his fleet (six having been diverted northwards with orders to 'stop up' the Red Sea). A large merchant vessel named the *Merim* was intercepted and its owner was discovered to be the richest Arab in Calicut, a man related to the sultan of Egypt. The ship, laden with cargo, was bringing back pilgrims from Mecca; 'many honourable Moors' were among the passengers. Da Gama ordered his men to unload all the cargo and transfer it to the holds of his own vessels. His purpose was never in doubt.

The sixteenth-century historian Gaspar Correa[2] tells what happened next. The captain of the *Merim*, whose name is given as Joa Fiquim, was led before da Gama when the unloading of his ship was nearly complete. The captain, a man of high repute, pleads as best he can:

> Sir, you gain nothing by ordering us to be killed. Command
> that we be put in irons, and carry us to Calicut, and if there
> they do not load your ships with pepper and drugs, without
> your giving anything for them, then you may order us to be
> burned . . . And consider that in war they pardon those who
> surrender, and since we did not fight, do you put in practice
> the virtue of knighthood.

The appeal to chivalry counted for nothing. 'Alive you shall be burned,' replied da Gama, 'because you counselled the King of Calicut to kill and plunder the Portuguese. I say that for nothing in this world would I desist from giving you a hundred deaths, if I could.' In desperation, the Arab captain tries another argument. If only da Gama reprieves the passengers he will be able to extract much more wealth from them in ransom money.

The response is the same: the great ship will be primed with gunpowder, fired and sunk, with its 700 passengers and crew. At this, the doomed Arab sailors begin to fight, 'preferring to give up their lives to the sword, sooner than to the tortures of fire'. As the order comes to set the ship ablaze, survivors jump into the sea. Many are women and children. Da Gama tells his men to lower boats and complete their work. They use their lances until the sea is red. However, the holy duty of the armada's Franciscan fathers receives its due: 'Twenty children were spared to be turned into Christians.'

Even before da Gama reached Calicut, the frightened Zamorin was sending emissaries to plead for peace. All such efforts were futile, because the admiral's mind had been fixed, before he left Lisbon, as to the punishment his 'beautiful artillery' was going to inflict. On his first voyage he had been the suppliant, seeking the Zamorin's favour, and even imagining him to be a Christian, a potential ally against the Muslims. This time the Zamorin was the suppliant, and da Gama now knew him to be a heathen. God's work would be done.

When the fleet anchored off Calicut the Zamorin sent out his most persuasive emissary, a Brahmin (the Portuguese accounts call him 'the friar'; it took time to shake off the impression that Hinduism was an heretical form of Christianity). The Brahmin argued that the Portuguese had already inflicted more damage on the city than they had suffered, so it would be honourable for both sides to draw a veil over the past and make a pact for peaceful trade. Da Gama was merely enraged at what seemed to him a calculated insult. At that, the Brahmin went further: the Zamorin would hand over twelve leading Arab merchants of Calicut to be sacrificed for the killing of the Portuguese during Cabral's visit, and he would also pay a vast sum of money as compensation. Da Gama spurned these offers. The unhappy envoy was made captive, and orders given for a bombardment to begin.

Able to call upon several times more firepower than Cabral, and having a more ruthless nature, da Gama proceeded to devastate Calicut. As Manuel later wrote with pride to the Spanish monarchs, the admiral did 'inestimable damage'. As cannon-balls hurtled out of the sky, bringing down houses, shattering temples, crushing all in their path, there was nothing the people of the city could do but flee or cower among the ruins. The Zamorin, anticipating what might happen, had earlier ordered that barricades of palm-trees should be built up facing the sea, but these were a futile defence against a cannonade lasting for three days. The Portuguese were displaying a fierceness unimaginable until now on the Malabar coast, where wars had traditionally been almost ceremonial affairs. The Zamorin proclaimed that he would 'expend his whole kingdom' to resist the Franks.

After slaking his appetite for bombardment, da Gama turned to the twenty trading vessels he had found anchored off Calicut when he arrived. These had all been rounded up by his caravels. A few were allowed to depart unharmed, because they came from Cannanore, a port which had shown friendship to the Portuguese. The rest were plundered of their cargoes – rice, jars of butter and cloth – and the crews, about 800 men, were taken prisoner.

With Calicut at his mercy, da Gama might have sent his soldiers ashore to put to the sword as many of its citizens as they could seize. Instead, he told his men to parade the prisoners, then to hack off their hands, ears and noses. As the work progressed, all the amputated pieces were piled up in a small boat. The Brahmin who had been sent out by the Zamorin as an emissary was put into the boat amid its new, gruesome cargo. He had also been mutilated in the ordained manner.

The historian Gaspar Correa describes what da Gama did next:

> When all the Indians had been thus executed [*sic*], he ordered their feet to be tied together, as they had no hands with which to untie them: and in order that they should not untie them with their teeth, he ordered them to strike upon their teeth with staves, and they knocked them down their throats; and they were put on board, heaped on top of each other, mixed up with the blood which streamed from them; and he ordered mats and dry leaves to be spread over them, and the sails to be set for the shore, and the vessel set on fire . . . and the small vessel with the friar [Brahmin], with all the hands and ears, was also sent ashore, without being fired.

A message from da Gama was sent to the Zamorin. Written on a palm leaf, it told him that he could make a curry with the human pieces in the boat.

The bigger ship, engulfed in flames, drifted towards the shore. The families of the men aboard came crying to the beach, trying to put out the fire and rescue any of those still alive, but da Gama had not quite done. He drove off the families, and had the survivors dragged from the boat. Then they were hung up from the masts, and the Portuguese crossbowmen were ordered to shoot their arrows into them 'that the people on shore might see it'.

The transfixing of men hung in mid-air was one of the admiral's favourite forms of execution, since it gave his soldiers good practice. However, there was a strange incident when three among a group of captured sailors from the Coromandel coast threw their hands up to heaven and told him that they wanted to become Christians. Da Gama, unmoved, ordered the interpreter to tell them 'that even though they became Christians, yet still he would kill them'. The ship's priest was allowed to baptize them none the less, and as he declaimed the Pater Noster and the Ave Maria they recited his words. 'When this was done, then they hanged them up strangled, that they might not feel the arrows.' The crossbowmen transfixed the rest of da Gama's victims strung from the yardarm; but the arrows which struck the newly-baptized trio 'did not go in, nor make any mark'. At this, the admiral seemed troubled. The three bodies were shrouded and thrown into the sea, which the chronicler of this event called the Lord's 'great mercy' to gentiles. The priest said prayers and read psalms.

However, da Gama was troubled only briefly. When yet another Brahmin was sent from Calicut to plead for peace, he had his lips cut off, and his ears cut off; the ears of a dog were sewn on instead, and the Brahmin was sent back to the Zamorin in that state. He had brought with him three young boys, two of them his sons and a nephew. They were hanged from the yardarm and their bodies sent ashore.

Keen to win approval, da Gama's captains did their best to match his deeds. One of them, Vincent Sodré, decided to make a special example of an Arab merchant whom he had been lucky enough to capture. This important prisoner, Coja Mehmed Markar, traded throughout the Red Sea and down the East African coast. His home was in Cairo.

The account tells how Sodré had him lashed to the mast by two black sailors, then beaten with tarred ropes 'that he remained like dead, for he swooned from the blood that flowed from him'. When the prisoner was revived his mouth was held open and stuffed with 'dirt' (of an unspecified kind), despite the pleas from other Arab prisoners forced to look on. Then bacon was fastened over his mouth, which was gagged with a short stick; he was paraded with arms pinioned, then finally set free.

Unsurprisingly, Coja Mehmed became a relentless enemy of the

Portuguese, devoting himself to persuading the Ottoman Turks to take up arms against them.

Amid the atrocities, da Gama went out of his way to acquire some friends in the Indian Ocean, most notably in Cochin, whose ruler had already shown a readiness to ally himself with the Christians against his great rival, the Zamorin. Elaborate gifts were exchanged in Cochin, the finest present of all from King Manuel being a circular tent, 'a very pretty thing', lined with coloured satins. It was set up behind the palace.

The Portuguese were now so confident of their prowess that da Gama decided, before sailing for home with holds filled with spices, to leave five ships behind in Cochin. A resolute body of soldiers and craftsmen, commanded by the scholarly veteran Duarte Pacheco, was stationed ashore. The ships were anchored nearby to protect them.[3]

The year was 1503. For the first time since the days of the Roman empire, there was a permanent European presence in the Indian Ocean. The Cochin settlement was the precursor of four centuries of white colonialism.[4]

TWENTY-THREE

The Viceroy in East Africa

There are many storeyed houses stoutly built of masonry and
covered with a plaster that has a thousand paintings.
—Kilwa, described by an anonymous Portuguese diarist (1505)

KING MANUEL had the spices of the East within his grasp, but he
wanted more. He wanted an empire. Portugal must keep on equal terms
with Spain, simultaneously taking possession of the New World. Equally
important was to send a message to the rest of Europe, and in particular
to Venice, that the Portuguese were no longer just merchants, but lordly
conquerors. Manuel knew that the Venetian senate had set up a special
committee to make proposals for action 'lest the King of Portugal take
the silver and gold from our hands, to the destruction of our commerce
and prosperity'. He was confident, however, that Venice could do little,
despite having signed a new treaty with the Turks and having sent a
spy to Lisbon expressly to study how Portugal was selling its pepper.

Manuel showed his imperious spirit when Sultan Qansuh al-Gawri
of Egypt threatened to expel all Christians and destroy the holy places
in Jerusalem if Portuguese ships went on interrupting trade between
India and the Red Sea. The sultan's emissary was the prior of
St Catherine's monastery on Mount Sinai. After reciting this message
to the Pope, the prior went on to repeat it in Lisbon. The king responded
with a familiar threat: let the sultan be warned that Portugal intended
to do its Christian duty by entering the Red Sea, laying waste to Mecca,
destroying the tomb of the 'false prophet Muhammad' and carrying
away his remains.

Manuel decided what he would call his empire: Estado da India, the
State of India. For a king ruling one of Europe's smallest countries this
might have seemed an unattainable dream, embracing not simply the
Indian sub-continent, as far as that was understood, but also the lands
all round the Indian Ocean: Arabia, Persia, Africa, and places further

east which were still to hear the sound of Portuguese guns. Yet Manuel, at the age of thirty-six, was suffused with vigour and ambition. After all, had not the Treaty of Tordesillas awarded half the world to Portugal?

However vague the extent of the Estado da India might be on land, Manuel was quite clear that it meant ruling the ocean. As he had arranged with the king in advance, Vasco da Gama took the decisive step of leaving five ships behind at Cochin when his second expedition turned for home. They were the index of Portugal's purpose. Now a new armada of twenty-two fighting ships was being assembled in Lisbon: 1,500 hand-picked sailors and soldiers would sail in them to Africa and India. Some of the ships were armed with German-made bronze cannon, more costly but safer than the iron guns produced by Portuguese foundries. The aim was to stamp Portuguese authority permanently on the region and shatter opposition wherever it might show its head. Naturally, commerce kept in step with this task: just as Germany had supplied cannons, so the cost of building three large ships was borne by German trading companies in return for privileges in the spice trade.

Chosen to lead the armada was Dom Francisco de Almeida, a nobleman of even more violent a disposition than da Gama. He was given the title of viceroy and handed lengthy orders as to the conduct of the fleet, discipline, plunder, strategic points where forts should be established and how the system of passports (*cartazes*) should be imposed on all shipping. Any ship – especially any Muslim ship – caught on the high seas without a Portuguese pass, should be seized, plundered and sunk. The mouth of the Red Sea should be closed with a fort to stop any spices being sent to Europe by that route, and to 'persuade all the people of India to put aside the fantasy that they can ever again trade with any but ourselves'.

Almeida, who had shown himself fearless during the wars in Morocco, was given complete charge of the embryonic empire for three years. He knew that the forces opposed to Portugal were gathering their strength, but promised to carry through all the appointed tasks. His son Lourenco, already famed for courage, was joining the expedition to share in the glory. The king, some ten years younger than Almeida, wrote to him: 'I give you power as though it were to my own person.' He promised that while he reigned no other man but Almeida would hold the title of viceroy.

Fine weather, and the experience gained by earlier fleets, large and small, allowed the armada to make good speed to the Cape. On the way Almeida stopped briefly at Brazil, which Cabral had visited before him (and which, because of the line of longitude agreed at Tordesillas, fell within Portugal's half of the world). Leading the way into the Indian Ocean with several heavily-armed *naus*, the viceroy headed straight from the Cape to Kilwa. If the island's ruler, Sultan Ibrahim bin Sulaiman, was not flying a Portuguese flag forcibly bestowed on him by da Gama three years earlier, he was to be punished. Almeida also intended to build a fort on the island and leave behind a contingent of troops.

With a threat to bombard Kilwa town into ruins, da Gama had already terrorized the sultan into signing a treaty by which he declared himself a vassal of Portugal and promised to pay tribute every year in gold. He was warned then that if he proved defiant the Portuguese would take him to India and parade him there with an iron collar round his neck; but when a caravel tried to collect the tribute due in the following year, Ibrahim had shown himself evasive. Clearly, firm treatment was now needed.

Almeida announced his arrival with a salvo of cannon-fire over the town. The sultan quickly sent out fruit for the crews, but the viceroy was not appeased, for the Portuguese flag was nowhere to be seen. There were also signs that Kilwa was ready to fight. Da Gama had made contact with one of the sultan's enemies, an elderly sheikh named Mohamed Ankoni, and this man secretly despatched a message that hundreds of African bowmen were being brought over from the mainland.

When Almeida demanded to know what the sultan had done with King Manuel's flag, the sultan replied that it had been given to a ship sailing to Sofala, to fly for self-protection, but the ship had been stopped on the way by a Portuguese vessel and the flag taken away. Despite his displeasure, Almeida decided to give the sultan a last chance. He went ashore, and with his senior officers grouped around him under a canopy of scarlet silk, waited for Ibrahim to come and talk.

Doubtless remembering the threat that he might be taken to India with an iron collar round his neck, the sultan did not appear. He sent a messenger to say that he had guests; moreover, a black tomcat had walked in his path and it meant that any agreements reached would not be long-lasting. That was enough. In the evening Almeida circled the island in his flagship and prepared for his first battle in the Indian Ocean. After four months crowded together at sea, the men under his command relished the prospect of going ashore to plunder this rich and handsome town, whose whitewashed houses they could see amid the palm-trees.

The Portuguese attacked at daybreak. Almeida's son, Lourenco, landed with 200 men near the great palace, Husuni Kubwa, outside the town. A larger force swarmed into the narrow streets. But they met no opposition. One of the few signs of life was a man leaning out of his window waving the elusive Portuguese flag.

According to an anonymous diarist,[1] the looting was thorough, the attackers smashing down the heavy wooden doors and taking 'a great quantity of merchandise and provisions'. A German eye-witness named Balthasar Sprenger, a gunner with the fleet, relates how the soldiers 'shot several heathen dead and plundered the town at the same time and found many treasures including gold, silver, pearls, precious stones and costly clothes'. However, there was a disappointment at the palace, for Sultan Ibrahim had slipped away to the mainland with his wives and jewels. All valuables he left behind were expropriated for King Manuel.

Two Franciscan friars went ashore carrying crosses and crying, 'Let us praise the Lord!' A large house was chosen for Almeida to occupy and a cross erected on its roof. Men who had started setting fire to houses after looting them were called to order and the plunder was assembled to be divided up according to custom. The viceroy claimed for himself only a single arrow, as a memento of his first triumph.

The Portuguese were impressed by all they saw about them. Kilwa was less powerful politically on the East African coast than it had been 170 years earlier when Ibn Battuta paid his visit; this was mainly the result of bitter rivalries among its ruling élite and a decline in the Sofala gold trade. Even so, it was a mature, prosperous town.

The viceroy wrote to his king: 'Sire, Kilwa, of all the places I know in the world, has the best port and the fairest land that can be ... In it are lions, deer, antelopes, partridges, quail and nightingales and many kinds of birds and sweet oranges and pomegranates, lemons, green vegetables, figs of the land, coconuts, and yams and marvellous meats and fishes and very good water from the wells.' Although Almeida was exaggerating about the lions, he had arrived at a time of year when skies were clear and the gardens were filled with flowers and fruit.

After the many weeks at sea on salt meat and hard biscuits, the anonymous diarist was also delighted by the gardens, describing the 'radishes, tiny onions, sweet marjoram and sweet basil'. There was also honey, butter and wax. 'All the gardens are surrounded by wooden fences ... the hay is the height of a man. The soil is red on top and there is always some green thing to be seen.' Cotton was grown and cloth was made; perfumed water was produced for selling abroad. Most of the work was done by black slaves, owned by 'white Moors'.

This account gives a vivid picture of life in Kilwa, even telling how the 'Moors of quality' chewed betel: 'These leaves turn the mouth and teeth a deep red and it is said to be very refreshing.' All the people 'slept off the ground' on hammocks made of palm nets 'that held one person'. In Kilwa's humid climate the Arabs wore two cotton garments, one from the waist reaching to the ground, and another thrown loosely over their shoulders. All carried praying beads.

There was more to do in Kilwa than study the daily lives of its inhabitants. Almeida decided without delay that the sultan who had fled was to be deposed and replaced by his enemy, Sheikh Ankoni. A platform decked with flags was set up and the sheikh was dressed up in a Portuguese robe, coloured purple and stitched with gold thread. During the ceremony the viceroy briefly placed on the new sultan's head a golden crown, destined to be given in due course to the Rajah of Cochin. Then there was a procession through the town, the sultan riding a Portuguese horse and preceded by the Portuguese flag. A treaty drawn up in Arabic and Portuguese proclaimed that Kilwa would be subject for ever to the King of Portugal.

The fleet stayed at anchor off the island for more than a fortnight while work was begun to make a square fort with four bastions. After the building had begun to take shape it was blessed in a solemn mass. The viceroy chose a commandant, gave him a garrison of 150 men and a caravel, then set sail again northwards.[2]

Mombasa, the biggest city on the coast, was now Almeida's goal. Ever since Vasco da Gama was met there with hostility on his first voyage, the Portuguese had given it a clear berth and made instead for Malindi. They knew, however, that Mombasa had two fine harbours, whereas ships were exposed to monsoon storms when lying offshore at Malindi. Moreover, it was vexing that Arab vessels which might have eluded the patrolling caravels on the open sea could hide in the recesses of the Mombasa harbours, which the Portuguese dare not enter without risking a full-scale conflict. Many Arab vessels heading towards Mombasa had already been caught and their cargoes were confiscated; often the crews did not escape with their lives. Others used their knowledge of the East African shoreline to hide in the mangrove swamps, then slip into Mombasa at night.

The Mombasa sultan realized that his time of tribulation was coming. So where Mombasa island faced eastwards to the open sea, a fort with two bastions was built on top of a steep bank of coral rock. Hurriedly adjusting to the warfare of a new era, the city's inhabitants then salvaged six or seven cannons and a good supply of cannonballs from a Portuguese ship which had been wrecked close by on the coast in 1501. With the guidance of a fugitive Portuguese sailor who had converted to Islam, the cannon were set up in the new fort to await the onslaught of the Franks.

A party of soldiers went ashore to reconnoitre Mombasa's defences. They were landed from small boats and came back to report that their renegade compatriot had shouted to them from the fort: 'Tell the admiral that he will not find Mombasa like Kilwa, with chickens waiting to have their necks wrung.' Thousands of warriors, including 500 African archers, were ready to defend the city, and the sultan was determined to resist to the end. As Vasco da Gama had realized, Mombasa was a place worth fighting for, and Almeida's fighting men looked hungrily towards it. The viceroy himself went pale with fury when the renegade's taunt was repeated to him.

The chronicler in Almeida's fleet describes the fine stone-built houses where the rich merchants lived, interspersed with smaller buildings thatched with palm-leaves, for slaves, cattle and other animals. The island and the adjoining mainland produced fruit, honey, rice and sugar cane: 'According to the Moors, this city was the finest of the whole coast.'

Before the real battle began, two of Almeida's smaller ships, sent to take soundings in the harbour, were damaged by cannonballs from the fort. To the consternation of the defenders a lucky answering shot from one of the ships hit the powder magazine, which caught fire and blew up. This was the disastrous end of Mombasa's first fort, although not of resistance from the city itself. In a four-pronged attack the Portuguese fought their way against stiff resistance towards the sultan's palace, looting and killing as they went. Almeida's son Lourenco took a leading part in the assault. Defenders on the rooftops slowed their advance by hurling stones down into the narrow streets. The two Franciscan friars, so fervent in Kilwa, were once more in the van of the battle. When the palace was reached they climbed to the top of the roof and erected a cross.

As a last resort the Swahili defenders drove two wild elephants into the battle, but the Portuguese were not to be denied. They looted until they were exhausted, finding 'a great number of very rich cloths, of silks and gold, carpets and saddle-cloths, especially one carpet that cannot be bettered anywhere and was sent to the king of Portugal with many other articles of great value'. Almeida gave each of his captains an area of the city to plunder and everything was piled up in front of the palace to be shared out according to rank. There was more than could be carried off.[3]

Finally, Mombasa was put to the torch, the buildings thatched with palm-leaves making it a simple matter. As recorded, 'the whole city burned like one huge fire that lasted nearly all night'. The sultan and some of the leading citizens looked on from a palm-tree plantation at the far end of the island. Many larger houses collapsed in the flames 'and great wealth was burned, for it was from here that the trade with Sofala and Cambay was carried on by sea'.

Putting aside old rivalries, the defeated sultan gave his version of events in a letter to the ruler of Malindi:

> Allah keep you, Said Ali. I would have you know that a great lord passed here, burning with fire. He entered this city so forcefully and cruelly that he spared the life of none, man or woman, young or old or children no matter how small ... Not only men were killed and burned, but the birds of heaven beat down upon the earth. In this city the stench of death is such that I dare not enter it, and none could give account of or assess the infinite wealth they took.[4]

TWENTY-FOUR

Defeating the Ottoman
Turks at Diu

%

The Portuguese of the 16th and the 17th centuries had nothing
to teach the people of India except improved methods of killing
people in war and the narrow feeling of bigotry in religion. Surely,
these were not matters of such importance as to make it necessary
for Indians to feel grateful towards Vasco da Gama or his successors.

—K. M. Panikkar, *Malabar and the Portuguese* (1929)

WELL BEFORE Francisco de Almeida began making his presence felt
in the Indian Ocean, the Egyptian sultan in Cairo and his Turkish
overlords had decided upon an all-out challenge to the Christian
intrusion. But since this response had to be on the sea, there were
pressing dilemmas. The first of these was to learn what kind of vessels
a Muslim fleet would be facing. Portugal was a country remote from
the eastern Mediterranean and the Turks had never been given the
chance to examine its ships at close quarters; they knew only from the
reports reaching Egypt that the Franks possessed terrifying firepower
and used it mercilessly.

The Turks would have realized at once that merchant ships plying
the routes between India and Arabia were useless for any warlike task,
since their hulls were too frail to carry guns big enough to stand a
chance against the Portuguese. There was no source of suitable ships
anywhere round the Indian Ocean. The only answer was to build a
fleet on the shores of the Red Sea (the Turks had not yet fought their
way to the Persian Gulf) and sail out into the ocean from there to do
battle.[1]

This solution presented, in its turn, a difficulty. No wood suitable
for making the hulls of ocean-going ships grew either in Egypt or
Arabia. It would have to be transported in cargo boats across the Medi-

terranean to Egypt from Anatolia or the Balkans, then carried on camels to a Red Sea port. Cannons and cannonballs would also have to be brought from Turkey, because the Mamluke military caste which ruled Egypt made guns designed only for defensive use on land. The Mamelukes were contemptuous of warfare at sea and clung to an ethos of honour and chivalry which shortly would prove their undoing.

Although 260 Turkish galleys had fought and beaten 170 Venetian craft as recently as 1499 in a sea battle off the Greek town of Sapienza, it was to Venice that the Turks now turned for help. There was a mutual interest in driving the Portuguese out of the Indian Ocean, and both also realized that the typical Mediterranean galleys in which they had fought one another would be useless against the 'floating fortresses'. The galleys would be blown to pieces long before they could get close enough for their soldiers to have the chance to climb aboard the enemy ships and hurl themselves into close combat.

The Venetians had at one stage thought of urging the Egyptians to dig a canal through the Suez peninsula as the easiest way to put ships into the Indian Ocean. They withdrew the idea, fearing that the sultan would suspect them of wanting to open a route for their own trade. Instead, Venice gave him advice about the Portuguese, based on what had been learned in Lisbon by its agent Leonardo di Ca' Massa. It also allowed timbers cut in the Dalmatian forests to be shipped to Suez. Finally, a team of Venetian gunners was put at the sultan's disposal.

While the Egyptian fleet of twelve large warships was being built at Tor on the Sinai peninsula, Almeida was sailing unhindered up and down the Indian coast, which he had reached in October 1505. One of his first calls was at Cochin. Its rajah still gave loyalty to Portugal, despite having at one time been driven to take refuge in a Hindu temple to escape the Zamorin's troops. A wooden fort dominating the harbour had been held against great odds by the Portuguese garrison commanded by Duarte Pacheco. When efforts were made to starve out the garrison, Pacheco had kidnapped the leading Muslim merchant in Cochin and held him hostage until rice supplies were handed over. Outside the town a small force of Portuguese had defended a river crossing for more than three months, until the Calicut army withdrew with heavy losses. As a show of triumph a mosque beside the ocean was demolished and a church built on the site.

The gold crown which had briefly adorned the brow of the sultan imposed upon Kilwa was now placed upon the rajah's head. However,

Almeida soon found himself, after that gratifying interlude, deep in the throes of the politics of the Indian mainland. Nominally, Calicut was part of the great Hindu empire of South India, named after its capital, Vijayanagara, the holy City of Victory. But Calicut behaved as though it were almost totally independent. For their part, devout Hindus regarded the Zamorin as a creature of the Muslim merchants surrounding him. Moreover, Vijayanagara was an empire under intermittent attack from Muslim kingdoms to its north, and its king cared little about what might be happening to the pepper ports hundreds of miles further south. At first the Portuguese had hopes of inciting him to attack Calicut, but such hopes were always unrealistic.

Had his own forces been greater, Almeida might have offered to fight alongside the armies of Vijayanagara against their Muslim enemies. This he dared not do, for he was the strongest proponent of the theory that the Estado da India should be purely a seaborne empire, with its only commitments on land a handful of strategic forts. So the Portuguese remained perplexed by what little they knew about the inland kingdoms of India; the closest they came to forging an alliance with Vijayanagara was to make friends with Timoja, a powerful pirate-cum-mercenary who transported horses across the ocean for the rajah's cavalry.[2]

Almeida now gave his son Lourenco, who had performed like a true *conquistador* at Kilwa and Mombasa, the captaincy of several ships from the Portuguese fleet and encouraged him to act independently. Lourenco learned from an agent in the friendly port of Cannanore, north of Calicut, that the Zamorin was seriously preparing for war: two deserters from Vasco da Gama's second expedition, Piero Antonio and João Maria, had set up a foundry in Calicut and made 500 small cannons.

Having collected this information, Lourenco seemed literally to lose his bearings. While looking for the Maldive islands, lying 500 miles from the south-west tip of India, he found himself instead in Ceylon, well to the south-east.[3] Eventually, Ceylon would become a Portuguese colony, but there was little time to spare for its subjection at this moment.

An error of a more deliberate kind was committed by one of Lourenco's subordinates, Gonçalo Vaz, when he intercepted a ship belonging to one of the leading merchants in Cannanore. It had a Portuguese *cartaz*, permitting it to be on the high seas, but Vaz claimed this was a forgery. He plundered the cargo, then ordered that the crew should be killed, their bodies sewn up in their own sail, then sent to the bottom with their ship. When the sail burst open the bodies were washed up on the shore. The ruler of Cannanore was so horrified that he changed from being a friend of the Christians into a resolute enemy.

Their atrocities had already made the Portuguese detested throughout the Indian Ocean, but it seemed as though retribution might be at hand. Early in 1507 the Turks had completed the building of their fleet at the head of the Red Sea. The admiral in charge, Amir Husayn, set off immediately, for there was no lack of news from India and Arabia about the damage being inflicted upon unarmed shipping and undefended ports. Despite starting swiftly, Husayn made slow progress. His twelve ships were heavily laden with 1,500 men and their weapons, as well as the best cannons the Turks could assemble.

It took eight months for the Muslim fleet to make its way, with several stops, down the Red Sea, eastwards along the coasts of Yemen and Oman, then across the entrance of the Persian Gulf to North India. No Portuguese were met en route. Husayn turned southwards beyond the Indus river delta, then anchored off the prosperous island of Diu. This presented itself as an ideal base, since Diu was at the southern end of the Kathiawar peninsula, a part of the Muslim-ruled Gujarat kingdom. The strategic significance of Diu was so plain that the Portuguese had already decided to make the island (when they could seize it) into one of their Indian Ocean strongpoints.

Waiting to welcome Husayn's fleet was Malik Ayyaz, the Russian-born governor of Diu. He was a man with a remarkable history. Enslaved and converted to Islam by the Turks after being captured as a child, Ayyaz had reached India in the retinue of a merchant. There he won his freedom by impressing the Muslim king of Gujarat, Mahmud I Begath, with outstanding skill in archery. He had risen to become governor of Diu, and transformed the island into one of the best-run trading ports in North India.[4] Ayyaz promised Husayn full support, even though his mentor, the Gujarati king, showed scant interest in the whole matter (his successor, Bahadur Shah, was to deride wars at sea as 'merchants' affairs'). Left to his own devices, Ayyaz was destined to play a devious role in the conflict ahead.

The Zamorin of Calicut was meanwhile preparing 100 light vessels armed with the cannons made by the two Christian renegades. These were to be sent 700 miles up the Indian coast carrying food for the Muslim warships. They would also give support when battle was joined. Increasingly confident, Husayn ventured south from Diu, while coming north was that part of the Portuguese fleet commanded by Lourenco de Almeida.

Dom Lourenco had heard rumours of large ships in the vicinity and imagined them to be Portuguese. He put into the port of Chaul, and was unprepared when Husayn set upon him there. The Portuguese were outnumbered and the battle was going against them as dusk fell. Lourenco's captains urged an escape under cover of darkness, for this seemed a moment when valour could best be served by discretion. The young Almeida, fearful that his father would accuse him of cowardice, refused to listen to their pleadings, and the Muslim ships renewed their attack with daylight. Lourenco was first hit in the thigh by a cannonball, but ordered his men to lash him to the mast of his flagship, so that he could go on directing the battle. Then a second cannonball broke his back. The flagship sank and the remains of the Portuguese force retreated southwards, having lost 140 men dead and many more taken prisoner. (The commander of the ships sent from Calicut also died in the battle; a magnificent tomb was built on the shore for his remains and he was worshipped for having fought against the Christians.)

When the news of his son's death reached the viceroy he swore that he would never trim his beard until he was revenged. 'They have eaten the cockerel,' he said, 'now they must eat the cock.'

It took Francisco de Almeida a year to come within cannonball range of the Muslim fleet, but during that time he had discreetly made contact with Malik Ayyaz, governor of Diu, and urged him to change sides. The governor was faced with a delicate choice: open treachery towards his fellow-Muslims would serve as a death-warrant if they won, but open support for them if they lost would make him a marked man should the Portuguese one day mount an attack on Diu. Since the likelihood was that the Portuguese, with eighteen ships, were going to overcome the ten which Husayn had remaining to him, Ayyaz went as far as he dared in reneging on his promise to the Turks a year before.

On 2 February 1509, Almeida reached Diu and found the Muslim fleet lined up at anchor, awaiting him together with a horde of smaller vessels. Both sides knew that the battle must decide who controlled the Indian Ocean for many years to come. Defeat would bring upon Almeida the shame of being not only the first viceroy of the Estado da India, but probably the last; at best, the Portuguese would be able in future to trade in the Malabar ports only by the consent of every petty rajah – and even that prospect was unlikely, since they were already so loathed.

For the Muslims, victory would bring the prospect of a return to the era of free, untroubled trade between India and the Red Sea ports. It would also destroy the aura of invincibility that had grown up around the Christians and give time in which to prepare for any attempt they might make to return to the Indian Ocean.

However, the outcome of the attack mounted by Almeida the following morning was hardly ever in doubt: his fleet ran repeatedly down both sides of Husayn's defensive line, firing broadsides as it went, and the answering fire never matched this onslaught.[5] The Portuguese ships, some carrying as many as forty guns, stood higher out of the water, so that their cannonballs hurtled down upon the foe.

Within hours, Husayn's defensive line was shattered. On Diu island, Malik Ayyaz was a passive onlooker, never firing a shot against the Christian attack. His own ships were keeping well out of range. In victory, the Portuguese displayed their customary blood-lust: whenever a Muslim ship was sunk they lowered small boats to kill their enemies struggling in the water. After all was clearly lost, the Turks capitulated; the remnants of their fleet raised anchor and fled. When Husayn told the sultan in Constantinople how the battle had been lost, he said he was betrayed at the crucial hour by the governor of Diu, who had been born a Christian.

Almeida trimmed his beard, the death of the 'cockerel' having been avenged. The Portuguese had won what was, in its time and place, a naval battle as significant as the victory of the Roman fleet over the Carthaginians in the first Punic war. This triumph now had to be driven home to people along the Indian coast; they must be shown that it did not pay to defy the guns of Portugal. It took the viceroy little time to resolve how this should be done. Despite many killings in the water, some prisoners had been taken at Diu; so whenever the fleet came to a port, Almeida called a halt and a batch of the prisoners were executed. The bodies were dismembered, then from close range the heads, arms and legs were fired into the centre of the town.

TWENTY-FIVE

The Great
Afonso de Albuquerque

> Here commences a new Dominion, acquired with a title by Divine
> Right. Ships are sent with the first opportunity; the natives driven
> out or destroyed; their princes tortured to discover their gold; a
> free licence given to all acts of inhumanity and lust, the earth
> reeking with the blood of its inhabitants; and this execrable crew
> of butchers employed in so pious an expedition is a modern
> colony, sent to convert and civilize an idolatrous and barbarous
> people.
>
> —Jonathan Swift, *Gulliver's Travels* (Voyage to the Houyhnhnms)

THE IMPACT upon the East of the Portuguese victory at Diu was as
great as Mehmet II's capture of Constantinople had been upon the West
half a century earlier. Yet the Estado da India remained insubstantial,
its captains roaming the seas like nomads, unable to step ashore on any
territory held in the name of King Manuel. So while the great plans
for the empire must still be made in Lisbon, a secure enclave was needed
in the Indian Ocean, where lesser matters could be settled without
waiting eighteen months or more for replies to requests for instructions.
It could also be the place to repair ships and store munitions, where
the crews could escape for a while from their cramped and stinking
quarters below decks, and where the sick or wounded could convalesce
and the dead be buried. It was not just a fortress that was needed, but
a colony.

Eastern Africa and western India were the obvious places where a
good harbour and some surrounding land might be seized then declared
a Portuguese possession. Africa, however, had already proved to be
infested with deadly fevers: the Kilwa fort, about which Almeida wrote
so enthusiastically to Manuel when it was built, had to be abandoned
after only seven years. On the mainland further south, small trading
stations set up at Sofala and Mozambique were intended to give succour

to ships which had just rounded the Cape, but these ships often discovered more dead and dying on shore than they were themselves carrying.

So the Portuguese quickly decided that a colony in western India would be far more agreeable. It was in India, moreover, that the spices grew, and where the coast had to be patrolled to hunt down 'Mecca ships' daring to defy the *cartaz* decree. But the difficulties with India were its wealth and population. Although the Portuguese were contemptuous of any fighting prowess but their own, they knew that Indian rulers could defend their territory with almost limitless numbers of men, as well as being rich enough to equip them with arquebuses, horses and elephants.

Some of Manuel's close advisers continued to argue that it was wrong for Portugal to think of creating any colony beyond the Cape. Merely building and garrisoning fortresses weakened the nation's seapower. The hot, brooding fortresses were unpopular with those detailed to man them, since there was no chance to take part in the raiding and looting which were the main appeal of life in the Indies: apart from guarding against a surprise attack on a fort from land or sea, many tedious months were spent on nothing better than scanning the horizons for sight of a relieving Portuguese sail.

Yet Manuel scorned those who advised against the cost and dangers of establishing a colony; for one thing, since the Spanish already had colonies in the New World, it was a matter of prestige. So less than a year after Almeida's departure from the Indian Ocean, and his death, the island of Goa was captured on Manuel's direct orders. The man responsible was Almeida's successor, Afonso de Albuquerque, the real founder of the Estado da India. He is often known as 'The Great Afonso de Albuquerque', a title bestowed on him by his devoted son who, in later years, would edit his voluminous despatches to the king.

Part-Portuguese, part-Spanish and of royal blood, Albuquerque was by upbringing moulded for a life of crusading valour. One contemporary describes him as a magnificent figure, dressed entirely in black, 'with a dagger of gold and precious stones on his hip'. In later years he had a grey beard reaching almost to his waist. Albuquerque was fervent in his desire to kill Muslims and had spent a lifetime of fighting in North Africa before making his first visit, at the age of fifty, to the Indian Ocean. He stayed for a few months then, overseeing the building of the fort at Cochin, and was back in Lisbon by the middle of 1504.

In the spring of 1505 Almeida had set sail from Portugal to become the first viceroy, and a only year later Albuquerque followed with his own fleet. The two men were to become intense enemies: Albuquerque behaved from the start with a self-confidence which suggests he already knew the king had secretly chosen him to succeed Almeida. He also had his own ideas on how the Estado da India should be ruled.

Rigid in his religious convictions, Albuquerque clung to a fond hope which most of his contemporaries had by now abandoned: that Prester John was ready and able to unite with Portugal for the overthrow of Islam. He dreamed of using Ethiopia as a base for destroying Mecca, and talked of bringing engineers from Madeira to work on the absurd scheme for diverting the Nile into the Red Sea and so starving Egypt into submission.[1]

One of his first acts on reaching the East African coast in 1506 had been to land two of his men, together with a Tunisian interpreter, with orders to take greetings to the Ethiopian ruler from King Manuel. Unlike other Portuguese sent on similar missions, they seem to have found a way there, probably by sea. In due course Manuel had a reply from the elderly Queen Helen, acting as regent for the heir to the Ethiopian throne. It addressed him, in Arabic and Persian, as 'Rider of the Seas, Subjugator and Oppressor of Infidels and Muslim Unbelievers', then went on extravagantly to promise an all-conquering military alliance with the Christians of Europe.

Albuquerque was in no way deterred by the truth which was by now emerging about Ethiopia. Writing to Manuel he declared that Prester John 'had a great number of horses and many elephants'. His kingdom stretched 'as far as Sofala and the coasts of Mogadishu and Mombasa and Malindi'. On the other side of Africa it reached the Atlantic. It had many gold-mines and the gold that reached the Indian Ocean at Sofala came from land subject to Prester John. All this was a farrago of wishful thinking, drawn from Brother Mauro's mappa mundi, in sharp contrast to the harsh practicality which Albuquerque demonstrated in normal affairs.

He had been able to show his ruthlessness while sailing along the East African coast in the first half of 1507 with his relation Tristan da Cunha (discoverer of the South Atlantic island still bearing his name). There were more than a dozen ships in their two heavily-armed fleets, and when they called in at the friendly port of Malindi its sultan suggested that they might care to chastize one of his enemies, the sheikh of Hoja, a town further up the coast. Albuquerque and Cunha needed little encouragement: they dropped anchor off Hoja and demanded submission in the name of the king of Portugal.

The sheikh, a kinsman of the sultan of Mombasa, sent back a message that his only overlord was the caliph in Cairo. He wanted nothing to do with Christians who harassed and murdered peaceful merchants going about their lawful business on the Indian Ocean. The two commanders had one answer to such defiance: the next morning they stormed ashore, each at the head of a contingent of fighting men. The townspeople could not contend with such ferocity. They fled into the bush, while the sheikh and his closest companions made a desperate, futile stand in a palm grove. Albuquerque had the satisfaction of personally killing the sheikh. The town was looted, then torched; several soldiers were so busy looting that they were consumed in the flames.

At Lamu the Portuguese met no resistance. The frightened ruler promised to pay tribute every year if his town was spared. Having no African gold on hand, he made the first instalment in Venetian ducats, an accepted currency at the time throughout the Indian Ocean. The next stopping-place on the voyage towards the Red Sea was Brava, a stone-built city dominating the arid Somali shoreline. This time the populace, numbering several thousand, marched along the beach in a show of strength, but sent emissaries out to the fleet in reply to Portuguese demands for 'peace talks'. When the talks dragged on it was decided to threaten the emissaries with drowning, to find out if they were acting on secret instructions. This threat revealed that the sultan of Brava hoped to spin out the talks, because the south-west monsoon was due to start blowing any day, and this would make it impossible for the Portuguese ships to stay off the port.

At this, some officers urged the two commanders to shrug their shoulders and sail on. But Albuquerque insisted that Brava must be punished, and his confidence in the Portuguese fighting spirit was quickly vindicated. The town was overwhelmed by frontal assault and more than a thousand inhabitants were killed for little loss among the attackers. For three days the houses were looted. Hundreds of valuable rings, bracelets and earrings were collected by cutting off the fingers, arms and ears of Muslim women. The only misfortune was the loss of a boat carrying loot out to the fleet; among those drowned was the senior chaplain.

After a few more sorties, including an attack on the island of Socotra near the mouth of the Red Sea, the two commanders parted.[2] Tristan da Cunha went south to Malabar to load up with spices, while Albuquerque chose to keep well out of the way of Almeida, still in the Indian Ocean as viceroy. He spent the rest of 1507 sailing along the coast of Arabia, using the cannons on his seven ships to devastating effect at every port he reached. In a letter to Almeida he boasted of how he occupied and looted Muscat, setting fire to all the ships in the harbour and then to the town itself: 'The town burned very slowly because all the houses in these places were made of stone and mortar, and some of stone and mud, whitewashed and very beautiful and very strong.'

His greatest success had been at Hormuz, the ancient trading city at the mouth of the Persian Gulf visited two centuries earlier by Marco Polo. His fleet was completely outnumbered (even allowing for Albuquerque's penchant for exaggeration, chances of victory must have seemed slim) but used its cannons to such effect that the enemy panicked. Hundreds of men jumped into the water; 'it was an amazing sight.' As usual, the Portuguese lowered their boats and used their lances: 'We killed countless of them in the water, and the rest, weighed down by their arms, were drowned. I am telling Your Lordship the truth when I say that there was one man that day who killed eighty men in the sea.'

After this triumph, Albuquerque extracted a promise that Saif-ud-Din, the twelve-year-old ruler of Hormuz, for whom a eunuch was acting as regent, would regard himself henceforth as a vassal of Portugal. The city also agreed to pay a large yearly tribute in gold. Albuquerque lacked the force to take Hormuz, as he intended, so the most he could do was to terrorize nearby towns. Women had their ears and noses cut off, and the men their noses and right hands. Finally, Hormuz itself was bombarded until gunpowder was running short.

Albuquerque had wanted to build a fort near the city, but the captains in his fleet grew mutinous at the very idea, for the site was barren and unbearably hot. They preferred to sail on, to attack and loot other towns. Soon five found excuses for abandoning him, so that he was left with only his own ship and one other as he sailed on to join Almeida.

Destined to become the most renowned of the Estado da India's governors, Albuquerque would never hold the title of viceroy, despite his royal blood. King Manuel was to keep his promise that in his own lifetime only Almeida would possess it. However, the awareness of his own unique status did not stop Almeida becoming incensed when his successor confronted him and said the time had come for a transfer of authority. He had Albuquerque arrested and despatched to a fortress in South India, to be closely guarded until convincing proof came from Lisbon that his claim was genuine.

This incarceration lasted for several months, until a ship arrived bearing Fernando Coutinho. He held the grand title of Marshal of Portugal and happened, moreover, to be related to Albuquerque. The documents Coutinho produced from the king left Almeida in no doubt that his time as viceroy was over.

Almeida left at once for Europe, but at Saldanha bay near the Cape his ships paused to take on water and supplies. During this stop his personal servant went ashore and so insulted two Khoi villagers that they knocked out his teeth. Almeida decided to lead a punitive raid, during which his men seized a group of children. On the way back to the beach the raiding party was ambushed by the villagers, incensed at the loss of their children.

A hail of rocks, sticks and arrows killed fifty Portuguese. The victor of Diu died on his knees, a dart through his throat.

Meanwhile, Albuquerque's liberator had handed him instructions from Lisbon to capture Goa. This port, on an island at the centre of India's west coast, had been shrewdly chosen by the royal council as an ideal setting for the Estado da India's main bastion. Coutinho himself had separate orders: to attack Calicut and achieve its total surrender, using the fifteen ships and 3,000 men under his command. This was the biggest single military force Portugal had sent to the Indian Ocean. Coutinho was nothing if not a man of action, so despite Albuquerque's reservations it was decided to attack Calicut first and leave Goa for a little later.

The landing at Calicut was made without difficulty and the marshal was so confident that he took off his helmet, put a cap on his head and handed his sword and lance to his page. 'With a cane in my hand I shall lead my men to capture the Zamorin's palace,' he said. Then he would go home to Lisbon and let the king know 'how falsely they had misled him with the fear of this famous Calicut, which has but little naked niggers, with whom it is a disgrace for armed men to fight'. This rhetoric delivered, the marshal led 400 of his force towards the palace, with Albuquerque bringing up the rear.

The contemporary chronicler Gaspar Correa sets the scene: 'The streets through which the marshal went were very narrow, like country lanes, and on either side were stone walls of the height of half a lance, and on solid foundations above them the houses and palm-trees, and from the street people go up to the houses by means of projecting stones, like steps in a well.'

Fighting hard all the way, the Portuguese reached the city's main square. In the centre of the square were large houses, made of ornately carved wood, occupied by foreign ambassadors to Calicut. The defenders fought desperately to hold the square, killing many Portuguese; whenever they could get possession of the bodies they cut off the heads and instantly sent them to the Zamorin. But finally the square was overrun by the attackers, then set alight.

At last the palace was reached. Its heavy copper and gilt doors were hacked down with axes, for the marshal had sworn to take them back as trophies to King Manuel. But as soon as they were inside the palace most of the Portuguese soldiers, sailors and slaves began plundering uncontrollably – 'cases full of costly white linen, of silk and gold and velvets and brocades of Mecca' – then they turned all their energies to dragging their loot back to the beach.

The marshal struggled forward, resolved to reach an inner room said to contain the Zamorin's treasure, his retinue smashing down gleaming copper doors barring the way. Many of the Portuguese were ambushed and killed while dragging loot through the streets, but inside the palace the marshal seemed unaware that he was about to be completely cut off from any line of retreat to the ships in the harbour.

Albuquerque arrived and cried: 'I bid you in the name of our lord the king to come away, and let us not remain here another minute, for if we do we are all dead men!' The marshal paused only to set fire to the palace, but was killed before he got back to the beach. Albuquerque was twice wounded and carried unconscious to his ship. So for all the chaos the Portuguese had caused, this first attempt to stage a land attack on Indian territory had proved a costly setback. Memory of the retreat was a stone lodged in Albuquerque's heart and he was determined to be avenged on the Zamorin for the loss of his kinsman. For the moment, however, he had to hasten to attend to his personal orders from the king.

Like Mombasa on the opposite side of the ocean, Goa was an island almost entirely encompassed by the mainland, and its waterways offered safe anchorages during the roughest monsoon weather. Turkish survivors from the fleet beaten at Diu by Almeida had taken refuge in Goa with several ships, and Albuquerque saw it as crucial to capture the island before reinforcements arrived from Egypt. Most of the population were Hindu, but Goa was part of the powerful Muslim sultanate of Bijapur, whose new ruler was Ismail Adil Shah. Fortunately for Albuquerque, almost all the troops defending the island had been withdrawn by Adil Shah to help fight a war on the far side of his domain, and during the voyage to Goa the governor fell in with the friendly pirate Timoja, who said this was the ideal moment to attack.

Indeed, it proved an easy conquest, but when the city was at his mercy Albuquerque showed all the fondness for atrocities which a lifetime of fighting in Morocco had taught him. He wrote to Manuel, three days before Christmas:

> Then I burnt the city and put everyone to the sword and for four days your men shed blood continuously. No matter where we found them, we did not spare the life of a single Muslim; we filled the mosques with them and set them on fire . . .
>
> We found that 6,000 Muslim souls, male and female, were dead, and many of their foot-soldiers and archers had died. It was a very great deed, Sire, well fought and well accomplished. Apart from Goa being so great and important a place, until then no revenge had been taken for the treachery and wickedness of the Muslims towards Your Highness and your people.

(It may be that Albuquerque exaggerated his deeds, to assert his crusading fervour, for there is evidence that many of Goa's younger women were left alive regardless of their religion; but killing certainly came easily to him.)

The governor swore that only Christians and Hindus would be allowed to live in the new Goa which he set about building.[3] His vision was of a Portuguese city in the tropics, with its own cathedral, law courts, administrative buildings, fountains and elegant homes for officials and prosperous merchants. The prime obstacle, however, was a complete lack of Christian families because no women were allowed to travel in the fleets leaving Lisbon for the Indies in these early years. So at that moment, Albuquerque took a decision that would leave its stamp for all time on the Portuguese empire: Goa would become populated by the Catholic progeny of Portuguese men married to Indian women.

The governor found no shortage of men ready to enrol for his experiment. Although he wrote to the king that the first volunteers were 'well-born and gentlemanlike', they could only have been reprieved convicts, minor artisans and sailors no longer fit for active service. Since conditions were so harsh and hopes of survival so low, men who went to sea had always been the sweepings of Portuguese society; for them, a new life in Goa with the blessing and support of its governor was a chance to be seized upon. Each was to be given a horse, a house, some land and farm animals.

The true feelings of the women chosen for this historic innovation are not recorded. However, Albuquerque was particular about those selected: they had to be good-looking and 'of white colour'. He rejected out of hand any potential brides from southern India, because they were much darker and 'dissolute' (one characteristic of Calicut, always dwelt upon by Portuguese writers, was the reputed lustfulness of its women who, as Nicolo de' Conti had observed, were prone to polyandry).

Apart from planning the new Goa and creating the nucleus of its Christian community – 'All together there will be about 450 souls' – Albuquerque was active in more warlike matters. He led a fleet eastwards across the Indian Ocean to Malacca (a port in what is now Malaysia), to attack the Muslim ruler there and ensure that Portugal would monopolize all trade from Indonesia and China. He met bitter resistance, but in the end the power of his cannons and the fearlessness of his men carried the day. One of the advantages of taking control of the narrow straits between Malacca and Sumatra was that ports within the Indian Ocean which still resisted Portuguese domination could now be denied any products from China.

More fighting was at once in prospect when Albuquerque sailed back to India, for Goa was under attack by 3,000 men sent to the island by the aggrieved ruler of Bijapur. After assembling an equal force, the governor ordered that all the bells in the town should be rung. Then he marched out to do battle. As he stood in front of a rock to survey the actions of his men, he was urged by an aide to move at once behind the rock. As he did so, a man close to him was killed by a cannonball, covering him with blood. (Albuquerque kept the cannonball and left instructions that when he was dead it should be sheathed with silver, made into a lamp covered in precious stones, and presented to a church in Goa.)

After trapping their enemies in a fort and relentlessly bombarding it, the Portuguese offered them safe-conduct out of the island if they would surrender all their guns and horses. Albuquerque imposed one condition on Rassul Khan, the opposing commander: he must hand over a group of 'renegade' Christians who had joined the Muslim side. Rassul Khan said that he could not do so, since it was against his religion, but in the end agreed to hand them over if Albuquerque promised not to kill them. Albuquerque gave his word. When he had the renegades in his power they were not killed, but mutilated in grotesque ways.

Even by the standards of the time such cruelty was extreme. In his epic poem, *The Lusiads*, Camöens condemns the governor for his treatment of Rodriguez Dias, a young officer caught taking his pleasure with Muslim women captured in the fighting at Goa. As Camöens said of Dias, 'his only crime, the amorous frailty of the youthful prime'. Brushing aside appeals from other officers who admired the courage Dias had shown in battle, Albuquerque sentenced him to be hanged. At the moment of execution his impassioned supporters cut the rope by which Dias was hanging, and again pleaded for his life. Albuquerque speedily quelled this defiance, had several officers put in irons, then saw to it that the execution was carried through.

Amid all these preoccupations in India, Albuquerque never lost his enthusiasm for seeking an alliance with 'Prester John' in Ethiopia; together they would ravage Mecca. This desire was stimulated when a man named Matthew arrived in India with two wives and a large entourage, saying that he was an ambassador from the Ethiopian emperor. He also had with him a sliver of wood which he claimed was from the 'True Cross' in Jerusalem (only the cutting down of a small forest would have supplied enough wood for the pieces of the 'True Cross' then in circulation). Many of those who met Matthew suspected he was an impostor, but Albuquerque decided he was genuine and sent him to Lisbon in the first available ship. Apart from having his wives seduced by the ship's officers, Matthew reached Lisbon in good order. King Manuel was also convinced, and wept when the piece of the Cross was produced.

Back in Goa, Albuquerque was ready by 1513 to venture into the Red Sea, with more than twenty ships and 3,000 men. It was a perilous mission, since the Red Sea was like a bottle with a tiny neck (the aptly-named Bab el Mandeb, 'Gate of Lamentation'), and there was always the risk of becoming trapped if enemies could control that southern strait. On account of contrary winds, there were only a few weeks of the year when ships could readily enter and make a safe exit. Albuquerque's first move was to mount an attack on the powerful fortress of Aden, standing at the Red Sea's entrance. It had always been Portugal's ambition to take Aden, for then there could be a virtual blockade against any Muslim ship trying to carry spices on to Egypt.

The attack was a fiasco, because the only way into the fort was by using scaling-ladders, and these repeatedly broke under the weight of the men. After several attempts, in intense heat, the Portuguese had to retreat. They suffered heavy losses and the only satisfaction they had was in setting fire to all Arab merchant ships in the harbour.

Albuquerque ventured 200 miles beyond Aden along the eastern side of the Red Sea, then ordered his ships to drop anchor close to the Yemeni shore. There was little wind and only a caravel was able to cross to the Ethiopian coastline. Men began dying from fever and some dramatic event was badly needed to raise the fleet's morale. Fortunately, a miracle happened:

> Then, as we lay at anchor, there appeared a sign in the heavens over Prester John's country, a cross, looking like this [Albuquerque sent a drawing to the king] shining very brightly and with a cloud above it. When the cloud reached the cross it split up, without touching it or dimming its brilliant light. It was visible from several ships, and many of the men knelt and adored it, while others in their devotion were moved to tears.
>
> I concluded from this that Our Lord was pleased with our voyage and had sent us that sign to show us where we could best do him service. However, like men of little faith we did not dare sail there, though I think our ships could have made the journey by tacking. Things also went wrong because I am an old man, overcome by men's natures and inclinations.

The fleet's drinking water was running low and Albuquerque had to retreat from the Red Sea and Aden with nothing achieved, apart from collecting reports that the Turks had not yet started building another fleet at Suez. However, he wrote extravagantly to his king: 'I feel that by our expedition to the Red Sea, Your Highness has given the Muslims the worst beating they have had in a hundred years.' If only the Portuguese could establish themselves in Ethiopia they would have access to all Prester John's gold: 'a sum so large that I dare not speak of it.'[4]

On his way back to Goa the governor diverted along the Arabian coast to Hormuz and enjoyed one last triumph, a consolation for the failure at Aden. He found on arriving in Hormuz that the young king, Saif-ud-Din, was now heavily under the influence of a Persian minister, Reis Hamed, who showed signs of hostility. Albuquerque was even more determined to complete the building of a fortress at Hormuz, a project he had been forced to abandon several years earlier. He was also resolved to collect two years' unpaid tribute from the city.

While his fleet lay at anchor off the port, Albuquerque threw himself into a battle of wits. Reis Hamed was a formidable enemy, always at the king's elbow, urging him to resist Portuguese demands, and it became obvious there was only one answer: to kill him. Frustratingly, the young Persian refused to put himself within the governor's grasp; days went by, yet he eluded every trap. At last, Albuquerque persuaded the king to visit the unfinished fortress, bringing Reis Hamed with him.

Albuquerque told his men to be armed and ready; in particular, Pêro de Albuquerque, his second cousin. So when the king and his small, unarmed, entourage entered the fortress the gates were quietly shut behind them. Reis Hamed realized the danger. He turned to leave, and warned the king to do so, but now there was no way out.

Reis Hamed was led to Albuquerque's presence. Quickly, the governor pushed the young Persian minister away from him and called out, 'Kill him! Kill him!' Knife in hand, Pêro de Albuquerque rushed forward to lead the onslaught on Reis Hamed, 'and in an instant he received so many dagger thrusts that he was dead before he had time to call out'. Superstitiously, the governor turned his back to avoid the dead man's eyes. As he walked away he called to his captains, 'It is nothing, it is all over.'

When the young king saw the body he agreed to all of Albuquerque's demands. Not only could the fortress be completed, but the Portuguese were allowed to take over the entire city. No Arabs living there would be allowed to carry arms. To make it plain how any opposition would be treated, Albuquerque meted out punishment in the city centre to six of his own men who had been caught trying to desert: they were burned alive in the boat they had used in their attempt to escape.

The winning of Hormuz, in April 1515, was to be Albuquerque's last great contribution to the founding of the Portuguese empire in the East. His decision to stay there for five months, overseeing the building of the fortress, was too much for his exhausted physique. After handing the keys of the fortress to Pêro de Albuquerque, and telling him to hold the king's two small sons as hostages, he sailed for Goa. His life was ebbing away and the final blow came when he heard that the king had sent out a new governor to replace him, to take over the empire he knew was his own creation. According to his son, he cried out to himself: 'Old man, Oh, for your grave! You have incurred the king's displeasure for the sake of his subjects, and the subjects' for the sake of the king!'

As his ship reached the entrance to Goa harbour, on 15 December 1515, Albuquerque died just before dawn, aged sixty-three. His mark on the history of the Indian Ocean was indelible, and he had had the satisfaction of knowing that his foremost enemy, the Zamorin of Calicut, Mana Vikrama, had gone before him. He had done his best to arrange that. As he wrote in the previous year to King Manuel: 'I hold it as certain that the Nampiadiri [the heir to the throne] slew the Zamorin with poison, because in all my letters I bid him kill the Zamorin with poison, and that in a peace treaty I will come to an agreement with him.'

TWENTY-SIX

Ventures into
the African Interior

The coast from Mozambique to Kilwa is for the most part so
mountainous, with high peaks so strangely and marvellously
shaped, and so beautiful, that it makes one imagine that here lies
the terrestrial paradise ... but the country and the climate are
among the worst in the world and fit only for such barbarous
inhabitants as the Kaffirs.
— Father Francisco de Monclaro, SJ. *Account of the Expedition under
Francisco Barreto* (1569)

VIEWED FROM LISBON, Africa was as much a part of the new empire
as India itself. The two continents were bound together by the monsoons, which the navigators of King Manuel's annual convoys relied
upon to cross the ocean. Yet the harsh differences between the continents were epitomized by the contrast in the fortunes of the places upon
which the Portuguese king had placed his highest hopes. Goa quickly
began living up to Albuquerque's faith that it would become a prosperous enclave, with many reminders of life in Europe, whereas the slow
progress of Sofala, the vaunted 'gold port', gave an early hint of Africa's
hostile nature.

To the superstitious, the auguries for Sofala were bad. Bartolomeu Dias, chosen as the first governor, had been lost at sea before he
arrived to take up his post. Five years later a ship loaded with granite
blocks as ballast sank to the bottom of the Tagus as it was about to
sail. The blocks were to have been used for the walls of the Sofala
fort.

This second misfortune was, however, just a brief setback. A Spanish-
born mercenary, Pedro de Añaya, was sent out in command of a small
flotilla whose sole purpose was to take control of Sofala. Although Añaya
had been given precise orders on how best to capture the local Muslim
merchants and seize their gold – by sailing close to the beach in a

peaceful manner with guns hidden, then rushing the town – he chose different tactics.

Bearing gifts, he stepped ashore without any show of force and asked for a meeting with the local ruler. The ruler, old and blind, was Sheikh Yusuf, a vassal of the sultan of Kilwa. During the meeting Añaya soon realized that the younger 'Moors' advising the sheikh were hostile to the idea of a Christian fort being erected beside their town.

However, Yusuf already knew about the looting of Kilwa and the destruction of Mombasa, so he felt it wiser to appear hospitable. The Portuguese were allowed to start their building work the next day: among the supplies they quickly ferried ashore were eight cannons and other weapons. A former Ethiopian slave, Akoti, was appointed by the sheikh to act as a go-between for the two communities.

A Castilian nobleman, Martin Fernandez de Figueroa, had accompanied the expedition and his memoirs give a vivid account of life in Sofala.[1] The land was immensely fertile, growing all kind of fruit and vegetables, including figs which 'turned to butter in your mouth'. The palm-trees supplied many needs, their leaves even being used as clothing by the poorest inhabitants. Sofala's wealth and power was in the grip of a small minority of pale-skinned Arabs, although they clearly had friendly ties with African societies living inland along the upper reaches of a river which ran through the town.

The newcomers could not have known for how long Arab merchants had been buying gold at Sofala: almost a thousand years, since well before the days of al-Mas'udi and Captain Buzurg. Yet it was obvious how firmly Islam was established in this southerly region of Africa, 3,000 miles from Arabia. In the words of Friar João dos Santos, an early chronicler of the Estado da India: 'In speaking of this kingdom of Sofala it must be known that formerly upon the shore along that coast, especially at the mouths of the rivers and on the islands, there were large settlements inhabited by Moors, full of palm-groves and merchandise, and each of these cities had a king . . . and they had commerce and were at peace with the Kaffir kings who were lords of the interior.' This was, in effect, the southern frontier of the great seaborne empire of Islam.

Unfortunately, there were ominous signs that Sofala might not live up to the grandiose claims Manuel had originally made for it in his letters to Ferdinand and Isabella. Although the reasons were hard to discover, the amount of gold being brought down from the interior was far less than the Portuguese had been led to expect.[2] Naturally enough, Pedro de Añaya and his subordinates soon started to suspect that plots were being hatched to frustrate their commerce.

Matters drifted along for several months, the two communities existing uneasily side by side, with the Portuguese intent upon squeezing the life out of the Muslim trade by land and sea. Emissaries were sent into the interior, bearing presents for tribal rulers and offering to buy their gold, while Añaya's ships roamed the coastline to prey on small Swahili merchant vessels bringing Indian goods from the 'emporia' ports further north. By early in the new year a different confrontation was at hand – with malarial fever; the rains had begun and the 100-strong Portuguese garrison was succumbing to violent agues. Many men could not stand and others walked only with the help of sticks. For Sheikh Yusuf this was the ideal moment to rid himself of the detestable Franks.

A nearby chief volunteered to supply the sheikh with 1,000 warriors, and plans were laid for an assault on the stockaded fort. But Akoti, the former slave from the land of Prester John, saved the Portuguese by warning them that they were about to be attacked. With his wives and servants he then took refuge in the fort, while Añaya ordered everyone able to fight to man the defences.

Howling their war-cries and waving assegais, the African warriors rushed towards the fort to be met by a thunderous cannonade and a deadly rain of fire from crossbows. They had never faced such weapons before, and they were no match for them. Their flight left Sofala at the mercy of the Portuguese, who instantly took their revenge. At midnight Añaya led the strongest of his men to the sheikh's house, setting fire to buildings on the way. Any Muslims they met were cut down.

Once inside the darkened house, the Portuguese began hunting for its blind owner. The Castilian, Figueroa, takes up the story and tells how Añaya finally found the old sheikh (referred to as 'the King') at the entrance to the kitchen.

> The King with great fury hit Pedro de Añaya in the neck with an assegai, but only managed to break the skin. Nevertheless, Pedro de Añaya, knowing he had been wounded, called for his men to bring a light, if only to see who had struck him. Arriving with a torch, they saw the Moorish King of Sofala standing there. They struck him blow upon blow, taking from him his kingdom and his life. Cutting off his head and

placing it upon a lance, they carried it back to the fort, where
it remained in memory of their signal victory: that of having
pillaged all the land and city where the King of Sofala had
his palaces.

(Although Sofala was an ancient town, known throughout the western
half of the Indian Ocean, to speak of 'palaces' was hyperbole typical of
the age, designed to inflate the scale of the Portuguese triumph.)

Sheikh Yusuf had been decapitated by Manuel Fernandez, the senior
trading agent in Sofala. In recognition, Fernandez was awarded a coat
of arms by King Manuel, bearing a Moor's head. This was a common
insignia, some crests even being adorned with a mailed fist holding a
Moor's head by the hair, with blood dripping from the neck.[3] For Añaya
the pleasure of victory was brief; he died of fever a few days later. Many
of his subordinates followed suit, and by the middle of June there were
scarcely twenty men still alive within the fort. However, the message
of its firepower had been so devastating that nobody dared attack the
fort again; when the local merchants selected one of their number to
replace Yusuf as sheikh they did so only after the Christians had given
their consent.

Having asserted their supremacy over the Muslim merchants, the
Portuguese now expected that gold in plenty would flow unimpeded
into Sofala. When that failed to happen they grew ever more perplexed
about the kingdoms of the African interior. Messengers arrived from
chiefs living close at hand, in the coastal strip behind Sofala, bringing
ivory and a little gold to be bartered for cloth and other trade goods.
But it became clear to the captains who succeeded Añaya that real
power lay further away in the higher lands where most gold was mined.
In fact, gold-bearing veins in many of the mines in Manica territory,
nearest the coast, had long been exhausted.

Attempts to learn more about the interior began with the despatch
of two black Christians towards the lands of the great Karanga monarch
known by the traditional title of Monomotapa, the 'Master Pillager'.
The two emissaries were probably West Africans, who would have found
themselves almost as much at a loss in such unfamiliar surroundings as
the Portuguese themselves. However, they penetrated right to the
borders of the Monomotapa empire (in what is now Zimbabwe) and
struck up a friendship with a chief's wife, who reputedly swore allegiance
to King Manuel on her husband's behalf as well as her own. In return

she was given strings of beads and 'one barber's basin and one piss-pot'.

Accounts of the devastation caused by the Portuguese guns had spread far, exciting the more ambitious African warlords. The most persistent of these was Nyamunda, grandson of a former Monomotapa; he promised much gold, in return for a cannon and a white man to fire it, but when he was given one cannon he immediately asked for another three. The Portuguese never quite knew whether Nyamunda would let their traders pass through his lands, or merely kill them.

It soon became obvious that a great deal of fighting was in progress in the interior, between the Monomotapa and lesser rulers whom he regarded as his vassals (but who were frequently rebellious). The vassals were also at war among themselves. This fighting was a further reason for the drying up of gold supplies to Sofala, but others were more complex. Foremost was the migration of the Karanga people from their old capital at Great Zimbabwe, due west of Sofala. They still controlled most of the gold production on the high plateau, but their new capital – 200 miles further north – overlooked the valley of the great river the Africans called Zambezi. It was now proving far easier for the Mono-motapa to sell his gold to traders coming up the river than to send it south to Sofala along overland routes dominated by enemies.

In their efforts to unlock the mysteries of the Monomotapa empire the Portuguese gave a free hand to a convicted felon, a *degredado*: Antonio Fernandes. The details of whatever crimes Fernandes had committed to warrant banishment have long been lost, and about his background it is known only that he was born in Santarem, a prosperous olive-growing district not far from Lisbon. But the man regarded as the first explorer of southern Africa was certainly both daring and quick to make friends. He was to travel thousands of miles across the interior of Africa, through warring kingdoms, sometimes staying away from Sofala for a year or more. As one of his superiors would later put it in a report to King Manuel, the *degredado* Fernandes 'has so much credit in those lands that they worship him like God, so that wherever he goes if there are wars, for love of him these are stopped at once'.

He was a survivor, able to withstand the African climate when many others round him were dying. The flimsy evidence suggests that his original banishment had been to the Congo, where the Portuguese began planting their flag and their religion even before they rounded the Cape. The first mention of him in East Africa is at the time of Cabral's voyage to the Indies in 1500. Cabral left behind several *degredados*, one being Antonio Fernandes, who was later picked up in Kilwa by another captain and perhaps taken home to Portugal. By 1506, Fernandes was back in Africa as part of the Sofala garrison.[4]

He is often referred to as a carpenter in the Sofala records, although there is no telling whether this had been his trade in Portugal or a skill he had picked up as a prisoner.[5] Later he is listed as the fort's interpreter; during his travels through the interior he would have learned to make himself understood in several distinct African languages.

His greatest explorations seem to have begun in 1511, with the encouragement of a new Sofala captain, Antonio de Saldanha. After two long journeys across what is now Zimbabwe, he sat down in the fort with the trading clerk Gaspar Veloso and told of all he had seen. Although there is a hint that he recorded his travels in a notebook, Fernandes may have been largely illiterate, but Veloso captures the flavour of his narrative. One petty chief is described as 'little better than a highwayman', whereas the emperor Monomotapa is always talked of with respect. As he had been ordered, Fernandes made a careful study of the gold production in various parts of the country, and mentions in passing how the Africans prospected for deposits by searching the bush for signs of a plant rather like clover.

Fernandes also discovered that Muslim traders were already active far inland; they had stolen a march on the Portuguese. This was a great contribution towards understanding the challenge to be faced in East Africa, and went some way to explaining why Sofala was such a disappointment as a source of gold. The Muslims were travelling up the Zambezi valley, partly on land and at other times in small boats. Fernandes had met them at the markets, or fairs, held in villages throughout the domain of the Monomotapa. (One such fair he likened to a similar event held near his birthplace in distant Portugal.) The traders, and Africans from distant places, gathered at these fairs, which were always held on the same day of the week. Gold-dust was the currency used, but Fernandes was also intrigued by the trading in copper ingots, made in the shape of a St Andrew's cross, and resembling those he had seen on the Atlantic coast. They looked, he said, like the arms of windmills in Europe.

It was clear to Fernandes that if the Portuguese wanted to control a main source of inner Africa's wealth they would, like the Muslims, have to penetrate the Zambezi valley. This assessment, which his superiors passed back to Lisbon, was to dictate policy. It stimulated the creation of the first European settlements in the interior of Africa. However, his own proposal was modest: that a trading station should be built on a small island, which he said was the size of a 'horse-race track', on a tributary of the Zambezi. From this islet, ten days' march from the Monomotapa's capital, the Portuguese could master all the gold and ivory trade of the region, if the trading station were supported by a small armed boat on the river.

His precise idea was never followed up, but during the next two decades some Portuguese traders did begin finding their way inland, beyond the sandbanks and marshes of the Zambezi delta to the point where the river took on the appearance of a wide highway leading to the heart of the continent. These pioneers were called *sertanejos* (backwoodsmen). Larger groups roamed inland behind Sofala, hunting for gold, but most found only an early grave.

In later years, the felon turned explorer was so trusted that he was given command of caravels journeying along the coast to buy food, and he had clearly accumulated a degree of wealth since one document mentions 'irregularities' in his estate. Fernandes died in Sofala sometime after 1520. Perhaps malaria brought him down at last. There had been at least a dozen captains of the Sofala fort in the years when it was the base for his journeys, and the fever had killed most of them. It is more than likely that Fernandes left behind an African wife and children, but nothing survives about them.

TWENTY-SEVEN

From Massawa to the Mountains

> There, the sacred waters of the Erythraean Sea break upon a bright red strand, and at no great distance from the ocean lies a copper-tinted lake – the lake that is the jewel of Ethiopia, where the all-pervading Sun returns again and again to plunge his immortal form, and finds a solace for his weary round in gentle ripples that are but a warm caress.
>
> —Aeschylus (572–456 B.C.), Fragment 67

ABOUT THE YEAR WHEN the explorer Antonio Fernandes died in Sofala, another Portuguese venture into the African interior was beginning from Massawa, a port far to the north on the Red Sea. Those taking part were not seeking gold (although legend said it might be all around them). Instead, they were searching for the man who had so much inspired their country's triumphs in the East: Prester John, emperor of Ethiopia.

The fourteen-strong mission, bearing letters and costly presents, was led by an ambassador, Rodrigo de Lima. His entourage included a barber-surgeon, an artist, a typographer and a musician equipped with a harpsichord and an organ. There was also a middle-aged priest, Francisco Alvares, who would eventually write a perceptive, and often humorous, account of the six years the mission was destined to spend in Ethiopia.

Alvares takes care to avoid directly challenging the Prester John legend, for he was a chaplain to the Portuguese king, who believed in it fervently. Although the Ethiopians scorned it themselves, he always refers to their ruler by the make-believe title, calling his book *A true relation of the lands of Prester John*. He decided that it was not for him to offer controversial opinions: at the very start of his narrative, which runs to 142 chapters, Alvares explains how he is simply writing down everything that he has seen while living with the Ethiopians, 'not censuring or approving their customs and usages, but leaving everything to my readers.'

The mission had been created to escort home from Lisbon the self-proclaimed ambassador known as Matthew. Always an object of curiosity and doubt, Matthew had been sent to Portugal from India by Albuquerque. Some around King Manuel accused him of being nothing but a Turkish spy, since he looked too light-skinned for an Ethiopian (and was probably an Armenian born in Cairo). For two years the king had treated Matthew with honour, but there was general relief when the moment came to be rid of this dubious guest.

In April 1515 the mission accompanying Matthew set sail from Lisbon in the fleet of Lopo Soares, newly-appointed governor of the Estado da India. Had all gone well, Father Alvares and his colleagues might have expected to be away for about five years, allowing for sailing times between Portugal and India, and a year or two in Ethiopia. All did not go well. More than twelve years were to pass before they saw Lisbon again. At moments Alvares felt convinced he would never return home.

Ethiopia was a difficult country to enter, for despite fanciful hopes of reaching it by traversing the African interior from Malindi, the only practical way was to sail 350 miles up the Red Sea to Massawa, a port over which the Ethiopians claimed sovereignty, but which was actually controlled by Arab merchants and slave-traders. The town thrived on the trade passing through it, but any Christian vessel dropping anchor in the narrow harbour between Massawa island and the mainland risked being trapped and destroyed if Turkish ships suddenly came over the horizon from Suez.

As Albuquerque had found, the Red Sea climate was pestilential, the winds fickle and the channels dangerous. It was vital for any ship from the Indian Ocean venturing up to Massawa to stay only briefly, leaving during the brief time when north winds blew down as far as the Bab el-Mandeb, the narrow outlet of the Red Sea. Then there would be time to catch the summer monsoon for India.

All these factors took their toll when the fleet commanded by Lopo Soares sailed past Aden to land the Portuguese mission. The new governor did not dare go into Massawa. Moreover, he was an enemy of Albuquerque, who had sent Matthew to Lisbon in the first place. So he tried to deposit the entire mission on some offshore islands. Matthew refused to land: he insisted that as a former Muslim, converted to Christianity, he was sure the people of the islands would kill him. So the fleet sailed off to another group of islands on the Arabian side of the Red Sea, where Albuquerque had anchored three years before and many of his men had died of fever. The results now were the same, and among those who succumbed was Duarte Galvão, the king's first appointee as Portugal's ambassador to Ethiopia (this sad end is hardly to be wondered at, since Galvão was well into his seventies). The fleet retreated from the Red Sea, paused only to set ablaze the ancient port of Zeila, then crossed the Indian Ocean to Goa.

The survivors of the mission, with the omnipresent Matthew, spent several years loitering in India until the arrival of a new governor, Diogo Lopes, who had the will to take them to Massawa. Although the mission leader was now Rodrigo de Lima, an imposing aristocrat, Father Alvares clearly felt he also enjoyed a special status as the only priest on the expedition. In a rare display of pride he relates how the governor 'in the presence of all', had told de Lima as they parted in Massawa in April 1520: 'I do not send the father Francisco Alvares with you, but I send you with him, and do not do anything without his advice.'

As the party began making its way inland towards the Ethiopian highlands, the hostility of the Portuguese towards Matthew swiftly intensified. He had insisted that they should leave the main road for fear of robbers, then climb to a mountain-top monastery where he had business to conduct. Alvares soon regretted having persuaded the entire party to accept Matthew's idea, for the path proved so steep and rough that 'the camels squealed as though sin was laying hold of them'.

There was a general suspicion that Matthew was now about to prove himself a villain by having the Portuguese ambushed, robbed and murdered. This fear was not realized, but when the exhausted expedition did struggle into the monastery, Matthew declared that it must now wait there for three months, until the weather was better for travelling. Alvares and his companions felt themselves trapped, but before they could react to this predicament their 'captor' suddenly fell ill and died. The career of Matthew had ended as enigmatically as it began.[1]

After sending messengers to a local Ethiopian governor, the Portuguese were helped on their way again. They abandoned their cannons and barrels of gunpowder because the mountain tracks were so steep, but the rest of their equipment was borne on the backs of animals and slaves. After many delays and frustrations the expedition pushed 400 miles southwards from the coast into the mountainous heart of Ethiopia, always hoping that beyond the next horizon they would come to the camp of Prester John. They had been told that he was constantly on the move, but wherever he stopped, that became his capital.

Alvares had little grasp of geography and complains of being hindered in recording his routes through the country because the Ethiopians measured distances only by the number of days a journey should take, from dawn until when the cows were shut up for the night. His narrative is often confused about where the expedition happens to be at any given moment.[2]

It is the vividness with which Alvares writes about particular incidents that brings his book to life. While the mission is still on its way to a first meeting with the emperor, villagers near the famous rock churches of Lalibela rain stones down from hills along the route (a fairly common hazard). The expedition scatters, and in a night so dark that it 'was like having no eyes', Alvares finds himself alone, riding a mule led by a slave. Fearing another bombardment of stones he dismounts, so that the mule's steps will not be heard, but at that moment is rescued by an 'honourable man'.

> This man was very tall, and I say honourable, because he treated me well; and he took my head under his arm, for I did not reach any higher, and so he conducted me like the bellows of a bagpipe player, saying *Atefra, Atefra*, which means 'Do not be afraid, do not be afraid'. He took me with the mule and the slave, until he brought me into a vegetable garden which surrounded his house.

Alvares is then given a meal of chicken, bread and wine.

The next morning the stranger reveals himself as a guardian of the mountain on which all the royal Ethiopian princes are held captive. When a ruler dies one son is immediately chosen to replace him on the throne and his other sons are imprisoned on the 'Princes' Mountain' for the rest of their lives. Those who try to escape have their eyes put out. His rescuer of the previous night leads Alvares to a locked door in front of a sheer hillside and says: 'Look here: if any of you were to pass inside this door there would be nothing for it but to cut off his feet and his hands, and put out his eyes, and leave him lying there.' The mountain above them is an *amba*, one of the unique granite formations of the Ethiopian highlands with almost vertical sides and flat summits, often the sites of fortresses and monasteries.

Much later in his book, Alvares mentions how years afterwards he sees one of the king's brothers being brought back to captivity after trying to escape: 'and he and his mule were covered with black cloths, so that nothing of him was seen, and the mule showed only its eyes and ears. The men on foot said that this man had run away a second time in the habit of a monk and in the company of a monk.' Just as he was about to escape across the border of Ethiopia, the runaway prince had been betrayed by the monk. 'Everybody said he would die, or that they would put out his eyes. I do not know what became of him.'[3]

As the expedition drew nearer to where the emperor was encamped, beside the historic monastery of Debra-Libanos, a white stranger appeared. He was Pêro de Covilham, who had left Portugal more than thirty years before to spy out the way to the Indies for Vasco da Gama, and had never returned. Although the members of the expedition perhaps knew that he was still alive, Covilham was to them like a ghost from another century and another age, before Dias had rounded the Cape and Columbus had discovered the New World. Now he possessed large estates in Ethiopia, and had several grown-up sons (whom Alvares described as 'grey' in colour).

In his diligent search for local knowledge, Alvares became Covilham's close companion. He was soon an unstinting admirer of the former spy, devoting a whole chapter to details of his career (although leaving tantalizing gaps). Alvares delights in the wit and intelligence of his new friend, 'an honourable person of merit and credit'; there is nobody to rival him in the Ethiopian court. He proudly describes Covilham (for all that the exile was a much older man) as his 'spiritual son', since he had not made confession for thirty-three years until Alvares arrived.

The narrative refers repeatedly to the role of Covilham as the interpreter and guide. He was completely trusted by the Ethiopians and his home in Shoa province was close to the caves where the royal treasure was stored. But Covilham's attitude to the Portuguese mission is soon revealed to contain more than disinterested good-will towards his compatriots. Whatever his feelings might have been during his earlier years in Ethiopia, he now wants to go home, to die in Portugal. The mission offers the best chance of escape he will ever have.

Any decision to let him go had to come from 'Prester John' – Lebna Dengel, the Negus (supreme ruler) – but the Portuguese were soon to discover that the Negus was fickle, devious and arrogant. He was still only twenty-three, despite having been on the throne for almost twelve years, and had strengthened his hold on power when only eighteen by ambushing a Muslim army as it tried to launch an attack on his kingdom; as a result, according to the Ethiopian court chronicle, 'tranquillity and peace reigned everywhere'.

When the Portuguese mission arrived at the encampment of the Negus, the ambassador, Rodrigo de Lima, asked for an audience, to hand over the letters and presents from his king. He was answered by messengers, who put seemingly pointless questions again and again. Sometimes Lebna Dengel (whose name meant 'Incense of the Virgin') would send petulant demands for gifts, at others he would shower the Portuguese with more food and wine than they could consume. The patience of the high-born Rodrigo de Lima was tested when he was told that 'he could start trading if he wished'. He responded angrily that neither he nor his father and mother, nor any of his ancestors, had been traders; he had come to Ethiopia as ambassador from the king of Portugal. De Lima's mood hardened further when most of his clothes were stolen from his tent as he slept.

Apart from Covilham, there was almost a score of Europeans attached to Lebna Dengel's court. Most were Genoese, but there were also several Castilians and a German.[4] They had all been captives of the Turks, but had managed to escape and take refuge in Ethiopia. Now they feared being kept in the country until they died; two brought secret tidings that some 'great men of the court' were urging the Negus to stop the Portuguese mission from ever leaving, because 'it was speaking ill of the country and would speak more ill if it were let out'.

The Portuguese were tantalized by the unseen Lebna Dengel for several weeks, until they were summoned to the court after nightfall. They walked between rows of men holding candles, past warriors with drawn swords, to a dais draped with heavy brocades. Lebna Dengel remained invisible behind a curtain and through his officials told his visitors to put on a display of swordsmanship. Two soldiers performed as well as they could, then the ambassador took the floor with his deputy, Jorge d'Abreu. As Alvares drily remarks, 'they did it very well, as was to be expected from such men who had been brought up and trained in war and arms.'

The Negus questioned the Portuguese on the best ways of fighting the Turks. His greatest ambition was to force open a route to the south-east, through the territory of his Muslim neighbours, until he reached the sea near Zeila; that would give him direct access to the Indian Ocean.[5] Such a venture would, however, call for many muskets.

The emperor demanded to know why the Portuguese had brought so few with them. The ambassador explained that they had come on a peaceful mission and did not wish to appear warlike, but that more guns could be sent next year by the ship from India. Repeatedly Lebna Dengel demanded to know how the Turks knew the way to make muskets and bombards. The ambassador replied that 'the Turks were men and had the skill and knowledge of men'. They were perfect in all respects, except that they lacked the Christian faith.

Several nights later, Alvares was called to Lebna Dengel's tent, where he was told to dress up in his religious vestments, then undress, then dress again, explaining the purpose and meaning of each garment as he did so. This was followed by a long religious debate. Alvares was repeatedly pressed to justify the celibacy of priests in the Catholic Church, because the Byzantine beliefs which Ethiopia had followed for more than 1,000 years had no such rule. Christianity had been the religion of the ancient capital of Aksum long before it reached Portugal, and the young ruler behind the curtain made it plain that he was unimpressed by Catholic dogma on this matter.

After a month of prevarication, the delegation set eyes for the first time on the man so long known only as 'Prester John'. With a tall gold and silver crown on his head Lebna Dengel sat high on a dais in the royal tent. He wore a mantle of gold brocade and across his knees was another golden cloth, reaching to the ground. Stretched in front of his face was a curtain of blue taffeta, which his attendants raised and lowered; sometimes only his eyes could be seen, and at others his whole face. 'His complexion might be chestnut or bay, not very dark in colour,' notes Alvares. 'He is very much a man of breeding, of middling stature; they said he was twenty-three years of age, and he looks like that.'

The Portuguese knelt in a row beneath him, wearing the silken Ethiopian clothes they had been ordered to put on before they entered. When they were told to rise, the ambassador took out of their crimson wrappings the letters from King Manuel, kissed them twice and placed them in a silver bowl. Covilham was standing by as interpreter and Lebna Dengel told him he should translate the letters into Ethiopic. The delegation was then dismissed.

Contacts grew more frequent, now that some suspicions on the Ethiopian side had been removed. Interviews ranged repeatedly over religious matters, then turned to the best way to capture Zeila. One day the visitors were invited to pit one of their number against Lebna

Dengel's favourite wrestler, Gabra Maryam ('servant of Mary'). The artist, Lazaro d'Andrade, accepted the challenge and almost at once had his leg broken. The next morning Lebna Dengel asked if his guests had any more wrestlers, and the two best candidates were sent forward. When the arm of one was instantly broken, the Portuguese decided that they had had enough of Ethiopian wrestling. The Negus was delighted with his champion's performance, and even happier when news arrived in the afternoon that one of his generals had triumphed over a Muslim army, and was sending him the heads of the defeated leaders, together with much gold and many slaves.

In the dying days of 1520 the Portuguese were feeling optimistic. As soon as they received Lebna Dengel's letters responding to King Manuel's offer of an alliance they could hurry back northwards to Massawa, where a ship from India might still be waiting. But letter-writing proved to be a lengthy affair in Ethiopia. As Alvares remarked, it was customary for all business to be done by word of mouth.

The mission did not leave in 1521; fate decreed quite otherwise. Six more years were to pass. Sometimes the Portuguese went to Massawa when a ship might be expected, but none arrived, and in other years they were stopped by the machinations of Lebna Dengel. They played into his hands by quarrelling among themselves and travelling in two antagonistic groups, one headed by the ambassador, Rodrigo de Lima, and the other by his deputy, Jorge d'Abreu. Messengers came to them from the emperor insisting that they could not leave before they had settled their differences; the ambassador refused, claiming that d'Abreu, who had insinuated himself into Lebna Dengel's favour, was plotting murder.

In 1523, a packet of letters got through to the Portuguese telling them that King Manuel was dead. Although the news was two years old, they all shaved their heads as a sign of mourning. Such a display of devotion to their monarch was admired by Lebna Dengel, but he was far less impressed with a map of the world presented by his guests, because their country, and Spain, looked paltry in area compared with his own. His awe of the 'Franks' diminished accordingly.

Alvares spent years wandering through Ethiopia. His enthusiasms ranged from hunting game to studying the circular churches which dotted the countryside. Often he was in the company of Covilham, and at other times with Coptic dignitaries. Much energy was spent in arguing over the rituals of Catholicism, occasionally in the company of the aged

Abuna Marcos, the patriarch of the Ethiopian Church. Circumcision was a topic keenly discussed: when one priest maintained that he had gone to sleep 'when already twenty years old', and had woken up to find himself 'cut smaller', Alvares retorted that it must have been done by the devil, since God would not have performed a miracle on somebody so unworthy. 'The Abuna, with as many as were in the house, laughed very much . . . and this priest from that day forward became my great friend, and came every day to our mass and was very friendly with the Portuguese.'

The moment finally came when the mission felt confident of extricating itself from Lebna Dengel's clutches, and as Covilham saw his compatriots about to depart 'a passionate desire to return to his own country came upon him'. He went to Lebna Dengel, appealing to be allowed to leave as well. Alvares and others accompanied him, pleading and begging. It was in vain.

After a sad parting from Covilham[6] the mission travelled to Barua, a few days inland from Massawa, to await news of any ship coming from India on the monsoon. Two men were sent down to the port to find out anything they could. But Arab vessels, from which came the sound of music and festivity, were the first to arrive. The two Portuguese returned from the coast 'fainting and senseless', saying: 'There are no Portuguese there to come for us, nor are there in India, for all are routed and India is lost.' It could only mean that the Turks had finally been victorious in the Indian Ocean. There could never be an escape from Ethiopia after all.

Alvares walked alone along a riverbank, until he reached a large rock, 'and I wept all the way, and with tears and sighs I laid myself down in that shade for more than an hour'. Then he steeled himself to accept that it was God's will for him to spend the rest of his days in Ethiopia. He knew the country well, and he would make the best of it.

> I shall go off near some water, and have a strong bush fence made to keep off the wild beasts, and I shall pitch my tent in which I can shelter with my attendants, and I will make a hermitage within, and each day I will say mass, and commend myself to God, since the Lord is pleased that I should be here. I will order the bushes to be cut so I can make gardens, and I will sow grain of all sorts: and with my crops and game I will support myself and attendants and servants.

Comforted by this resolve, Alvares walked back to his companions, who had been striving to set aside their woes. They all rode out hunting, trapped many hares and bustards, then made themselves an Easter supper. As they went off to their quarters for the night a servant unexpectedly appeared, 'running so fast that he could not speak for fatigue'. Finally he managed to make himself understood. There were tidings of Portuguese ships sailing up the Red Sea to Massawa. The sound of their cannons had been heard in the distance. The stories spread by the Arabs of a Portuguese defeat in India were utterly false.

As Alvares and his companions hurried to the harbour and prepared to go on board a ship, four messengers arrived. They had been sent at utmost speed by the Negus, to say that the Portuguese should return to his court, 'where he would give us much gold and clothes and would send us joyful and contented to the King of Portugal his brother'. But nobody cared to obey, least of all Zagazabo, a monk chosen by Lebna Dengel to be his ambassador to the king of Portugal. As Zagazabo explained, if he returned alone he would certainly be thrown to the four chained lions who accompanied the Negus wherever he went. A journey through unknown oceans to Europe was a far less threatening prospect.

TWENTY-EIGHT

At War with
the Left-handed Invader

> I will not give her to you because you are an unbeliever; it is
> better to fall into the power of the Lord, whose majesty is as great
> as his mercy, than into yours.
> —Lebna Dengel, Ethiopian emperor, when asked to give his daughter
> in marriage to the Muslim imam, Grañ (1538)

THIRTEEN YEARS after the first expedition to Ethiopia had returned
safely to Lisbon, the book by Father Francisco Alvares was finally published. It had a fanciful frontispiece, showing a medieval 'Prester John'
in a plumed hat and riding a caparisoned horse, with a knight in armour
in attendance. Alvares was already dead and many liberties were taken
with his manuscript, for there was strict control over writings about the
Estado da India.

For all that, the work aroused wide interest among Renaissance academics. They recognized it as the first detailed account of a land that
had been cloaked in mystery for more than a thousand years. A Venetian
collector of travellers' records, Giovanni Battista Ramusio, hastened to
include it in his volume on Africa, printed in 1550. He praises Alvares
for bringing back so much information: 'until now there has been
nothing to read about the country of Ethiopia by the Greeks or Latins
or any other kind of writer that is worth consideration.' But he goes
on to belabour the 'rough and difficult' nature of the work. Ramusio
looked upon Portugal as being a backward, provincial place where
people wrote in a 'confused and tiresome style, for such a way of writing
is very natural to men of that country'. How much better pleased the
readers would have been if Alvares had 'taken the trouble to see the
sources of the Nile', or had used an astrolabe to measure the altitudes
of the Pole star. However, one had to be grateful for 'this man's writings',
since they might encourage some great prince of Italy to send out a

more worthy person 'to the court of this prince of the negroes'.

Such condescension was typical of a general attitude towards Portugal – often envy in disguise – adopted throughout the Mediterranean countries during the sixteenth and seventeenth centuries. It shows itself equally in Baldassare Castiglione's *Book of the Courtier*. One of Castiglione's elegant characters tells how a monkey brought back from the 'Republic of Indian Monkeys' plays chess better than his Portuguese owner and checkmates him. 'As a result the gentleman flew into a rage (as people who lose at chess invariably do), took up the King (which, being of Portuguese make was very big) and gave the monkey a great blow on the head.'

This jibe was published after King Manuel had sent a menagerie of exotic animals to Rome for Pope Leo X. His gifts included panthers, leopards, parrots, monkeys and Persian horses, led in procession by a white Indian elephant which bowed three times to Leo at the bridge of St Angelo and sprayed onlookers with water from its trunk. The elephant, ridden by a richly-attired Indian *mahout*, bore on its back a chest filled with treasures. The Pope was also given several African slaves. Eighteen months later, in 1516, Manuel sent Leo a rhinoceros, but the ship carrying it sank off Italy with the loss of all aboard. The corpse of the rhinoceros was hurriedly stuffed after being washed ashore, then carted on to Rome. By such efforts to flaunt the trophies of his eastern empire Manuel had invited mockery.

Despite the ridicule heaped on the Portuguese, there was one characteristic for which they could not be faulted: courage in battle. Their readiness to rush headlong at enemies on land or sea, regardless of the odds, became widely admired, and the name of Dom Christofe da Gama was to resound throughout Europe as an embodiment of this spirit. He was the fourth son of Vasco, the great explorer, who had died in India in 1524, a few months after being appointed viceroy in his old age. Christofe had shown his qualities while still a youth, on his first visit to the East, by saving a large ship, the *Espirito Sancto*. He was aboard her when she was blown out to sea from moorings off Arabia, and had taken command of the few men on board. Together they had sailed the vessel safely all the way down the African coast until able to put into a harbour in Mozambique.

The fortunes of the da Gama family were always closely linked to India, and another of Vasco's sons, Estevão, had become the viceroy in 1540. In the following year Estevão invited Christofe to accompany

him when he led a fleet to Massawa in reply to desperate appeals for
help from Lebna Dengel, the Ethiopian emperor. It was clear that the
fortunes of the once-proud Negus had perilously declined. This was a
direct result of the mission of which Francisco Alvares had been a
member, although the Portuguese may not have realized it.

The Muslims of the region had been alarmed by the mission, because
they saw Ethiopia as Christianity's likely base for the oft-threatened
attack on Mecca. They had decided the country must be conquered
without delay. Attempts had been made in the past (usually during Lent,
when the Ethiopians fasted so stringently that they were too weak to
fight),[1] but the onslaught launched in 1528 was altogether more menac-
ing. The commander of the Muslim force was Ahmad al-Ghazi, both
an emir and an imam, a leader of men and a spiritual guide. Ethiopians
knew him simply as Grän, the 'Left-handed'. To equip him for his
invasion of the mountainous Christian redoubt, the Turks gave him
muskets and cannon; the sharif of Mecca sent a contingent of Arab
mercenaries.

There had been no way of resisting Grän and his guns. Attacking
from the southern lowlands, across which Lebna Dengel once fondly
hoped to force a passage to the Indian Ocean, he campaigned through
the mountains, destroying monasteries, burning ancient books, wiping
out Ethiopian armies, turning the emperor into a fugitive. As he neared
the church of Makana-Selassie (Holy Trinity) in Wollo, its golden tower
glittered in the sun; when standing in the nave he was dazzled by gold
and silver plaques, set with pearls, which lined the walls. While he rested
in a captured palace close by, his men plundered the church and burned
it down. He remarked contentedly as they did so: 'Is there anywhere,
in the Byzantine empire, in India, or in any other land, a building such
as this, containing such figures and works of art?'

First news of the tribulations of the 'Prester' had reached the outside
world in 1535, brought by João Bermudes, the barber-surgeon who had
been one of Alvares' companions. He had stayed on in Ethiopia and
contrived to make himself head of the Church there. On his way to
Lisbon, seeking help, he was caught by the Turks, who merely cut off
part of his tongue then let him go.

Given the distances, and the difficulty of entering Ethiopia, there was
little chance of speedy help for Lebna Dengel. Yet he had been defiant
until the end, although the armies of Grän destroyed almost every church
in his kingdom, as well as massacring or forcibly converting most of his

Muslim merchants sail to India. In this stylized painting from a thirteenth-century Iraqi manuscript the passengers gaze out from their cabins as the ship is borne along by the monsoon. The crew, from the look-out boy to the men emptying the bilges, appear entirely African or Indian

Cultural interchange across the Indian Ocean in classical times. The ivory statuette of the Indian goddess Lakshmi (*right*) was found in the ruins of Pompeii, Italy. The statuette of the Greek god Poseidon (*far right*) was uncovered at the site of a 2,000-year-old trading centre in western India

Still used in Madagascar today are small craft similar to those from which the island's first human inhabitants stepped ashore, early in the first millenium, after voyaging more than 3,000 miles from Indonesia. Outriggers fixed at right angles to the hull, for stability in strong winds, are typically Indonesian

(*Above*) Marco Polo sets out from Venice for Cathay, with his father and uncle. This medieval miniature shows the Polos (right) entering a rowing boat, to be taken to the ship (centre) for the first stage of their journey to the East

(*Left*) Fantastic creatures, half-human, half-animal, were long imagined by Europe to exist in Africa and India. These are depicted in a sixteenth-century Spanish version of Mandeville's Travels

(*Top left*) The name of Kubilai Khan, mightiest emperor in Asia, became famous in Europe. But the West knew nothing of the Chinese admiral Zheng He, the 'Three Jewel Eunuch,' who led seven great fleets into the Indian Ocean (1405-1433); he is seen studying a nautical progress report (*centre left*). One of his junks transported a giraffe to the Ming emperor from Malindi, East Africa (*top right*). According to oriental myth the gigantic peng or rukh, portrayed carrying elephants to its lair in this copy of a Persian original, lived in remote parts of the Indian Ocean (*left*)

℄Lagran Magnificentia del Prete Ianni Signore dellindia Maggiore e della Ethiopia

IOANES·PRESBR·MAX·DE·IDIA·ET·ETHIOPIA·

·FVGE·SVPERBIAN·TER·
· FVGE·LVXVRIA·DELIGNO ·
· FVGE·GVLAM·DEPLVMBO·
· FVGE·IRAM·DE·FERRO ·
· FVGE·INVIDIAM·DECVPRO·
· FVGE·ACIDIAM·DEARGENTO ·
· FVGE·AVARITIAM·DEAVRO ·

PRESTO·GIOVANNI·DE·INDIA·ET·ETHIO

The fictitious Christian emperor Prester John, ruling somewhere in 'Greater India,' warns his followers against the seven deadly sins in this illustration to a poem by a fifteenth-century Italian bishop, Guiliano Duti. The legend acquired new life when a Christian kingdom was found to exist in Ethiopia

Great Zimbabwe is the name given today to the ruins of a stone-built capital which flourished more than five hundred years ago in Southern Africa. Gold from hundreds of mines was sent three hundred miles to the coast by the rulers of Great Zimbabwe, to be traded for cloth from India and porcelain from China

Hindu civilization reached its apogee in southern India with the founding in the fourteenth century of Vijayanagara, the 'City of Victory'. The focal point of resistance by the Vijayanagara empire to Islam's onslaught from the north, it was also an aesthetic wonder, typified by the stone chariot of the Vitthala Temple complex

Symbols of rival religions: a colossal monolith of Narasingha, image of the Hindu god Vishnu, at Vijayanagara (*left*); and an heroic representation of Henry the Navigator, whose militant Christianity inspired his compatriots as they rounded Africa and made themselves masters of the Indian Ocean (*right*). Caravels and carracks sailing in the East were reputed to have miraculous experiences, when flying fish sought refuge aboard (*below*)

The great 'pepper port' of Calicut, on the Malabar coast of southern India, was Vasco da Gama's goal (*top*). The Zamorin, the Hindu ruler, soon found himself at war with the Portuguese. By the end of the sixteenth century Calicut's wealth and power was destroyed. Equally a victim of the European thrust into the Indian Ocean was Kilwa, a city-state on the East African coast; after almost five hundred years the ruins of one of its mosques still stand. Alfonso de Albuquerque, founder of Goa, was the brilliant and ruthless architect of Portuguese imperialism (*right*)

AFOSO·DALBOQVERQVE

subjects. The emperor died almost alone in a mountain-top monastery, brooding on his defeats in battle.[2]

There was a real prospect at this moment of Christianity being destroyed for ever in Ethiopia, as recently it had been in Nubia, along the Upper Nile valley. The Coptic Christianity of the Nubians, like that of the Ethiopians, had also been established since well before the birth of Islam, and likewise received its patriarchs from Egypt. However, relations between these two beleaguered Christian kingdoms were never close, and Francisco Alvares had seen six emissaries vainly plead with Lebna Dengel to lend them priests to sustain the faith in Nubia. It was only Ethiopia's precipitous geography which had, so far, allowed it to avoid the fate of Nubia.[3]

When the Portuguese arrived in Massawa in 1541 they heard about Lebna Dengel's death and learned that his son Claudius, the new Negus, was in extreme straits; yet Estevão da Gama decided to make a sortie towards Suez, taking his brother Christofe with him. They left another relation, Manuel da Gama, in charge of the rest of the fleet. The soldiery in the ships lying offshore were so keen to do some fighting on land that they became mutinous and five had to be hanged to restore discipline. A hundred nevertheless reached the shore, were ambushed by Turkish defenders and all but two slaughtered.

When the viceroy reappeared at Massawa he was undeterred by this news and decided that 400 volunteers should be sent to the Ethiopian highlands, under the command of Christofe, 'whom he would sacrifice for the king, rather than some other's son', since it seemed most unlikely that any member of the expedition would escape death. Yet there was no lack of volunteers to march with Christofe, because at the age of twenty-five he was vigorous and renowned for his bravery. Impassioned by the prospect of martyrdom in Christianity's name, the 400 men set off inland on 9 July 1541. They had with them ten cannon, swivel guns, 1,000 muskets and large supplies of powder and shot, loaded on mules. Accompanying the fighting men were blacksmiths, carpenters, armourers, shoemakers, trumpeters and drummers. There were also 150 slaves.

The journey proved laborious. On the hot coastal plain it was possible to march only at night. When higher ground was reached, Christofe and his officers helped to drag the cannon and stores up steep tracks. The countryside was so devastated by war that farms were abandoned and food scarce. Only wild animals were plentiful. The remaining

Ethiopian forces, commanded by the eighteen-year-old Claudius, were several hundred miles away to the south in Shoa; but since it was now the height of the rainy season there was no chance of joining up with them for several months.

The Portuguese used this delay to liberate the widow of Lebna Dengel from an *amba* on the northern edge of the highlands. This mountain-top had been the prison of queen mother Sabla-Wangel and one of her sons for several years (she had been put there partly to save her from the clutches of Grän, who had besieged the mountain for a year, but also to remove her and her son from the Ethiopian hierarchy). The sides of the mountain were so sheer – 'they seemed to have been cut with a pick-axe', according to a Portuguese account – that two officers sent ahead by Christofe had to be hauled singly up the last part of the rock-face in a basket.

The scene when the queen descended from the mountain to greet her liberator is romantically described by Miguel de Castanhoso, one of da Gama's captains:

> She was received by him and his troops very nobly, for by his order all were in full dress and in ranks, the captains with their soldiers, all matchlock men, with their banners of blue and white damask with red crosses, and the royal standard of crimson and white damask, with the cross of Christ heading the rest of the troops. The commander, a great gentleman, was clothed in hose and vest of red satin and gold brocade of many plaits, and a French cape of fine black cloth all quilted with gold, and a black cap with very rich decoration.

Soon it was time to march on, to do battle with Grän and his Turkish mercenaries. Stores were loaded on mules and cannon dragged by oxen on sledge carts. Da Gama travelled on foot, alongside his men. At the start of February 1542 came the first skirmish, in which the Portuguese drove away a Muslim force trying to bar their route. In the course of this fighting they captured a mosque, which Christofe ordered should be consecrated as a church, naming it Our Lady of Victory. Next the Portuguese bombarded and stormed a mountain fastness defended by 1,500 archers; all captives were slaughtered by 200 Ethiopian spearmen who had thrown in their lot with the white newcomers.

As the Portuguese neared the centre of Ethiopia, the main Muslim force led by Grãn advanced to meet them from Laka Tana, the source of the Blue Nile. Messengers went to and fro, conveying taunts and threats. Grãn said he had heard that the Christian commander was a 'mere boy . . . innocent without experience', so out of pity he would let him leave the country unharmed. Christofe sent back a large mirror and a pair of tweezers used for plucking eyebrows; this implied his enemy was only fit for womanly pursuits.

Several encounters followed, the first land battles between Muslims and European Christians on the eastern flank of Africa. At first the Portuguese did well: not only was Grãn wounded and forced to retreat, but his army had to abandon large supplies of food, which were eagerly seized. Muslim women were also left behind: 'Among the many noble ladies remaining there was a wife of the Emir who was of great beauty, whom Dom Christofe took for himself.'

The ordnance of the small Portuguese force was weighting the scales. Moreover, the Ethiopians were being taught how to make and use gunpowder. This forced Grãn to retire eastwards towards the Red Sea, but he was quickly reinforced from Arabia with almost a thousand musketeers and ten cannon. The Muslims wasted no time in seeking revenge on the Franks, advancing through the rainy season to take them unawares. In the final battle the Portuguese, totally outnumbered, were overwhelmed; almost half were killed and the rest fled as night fell. Christofe da Gama, badly wounded, was borne away on a mule (it was later killed, to use its fat for dressing wounds).

The Muslims soon rounded up the wounded fugitives, including Christofe, and paraded them before their leader. Grãn sat contentedly among the severed heads of the 160 Portuguese killed in the battle. Before being beheaded and quartered, Christofe da Gama was stripped, whipped, then had his eyebrows and eyelashes pulled out with the tweezers he had mockingly sent to the emir before their first battle. It had taken just over a year for him to achieve the martyrdom his brother had promised when they parted at Massawa.[4]

The Portuguese survivors linked up with the main Ethiopian forces and helped to turn the tide of military fortune. Grãn had been so confident after his latest victory that he sent home the Turkish musketeers; within two months he was caught in a surprise attack by Claudius and shot dead by da Gama's former valet.[5] Discipline collapsed among the Muslims, who fled in disorder towards the coast. After fifteen years of ruinous war Ethiopia once again enjoyed peace, and Claudius began trying to restore the country to the prosperity it had enjoyed in the early years of Lebna Dengel's reign.

The first news of Christofe da Gama's triumphs and death was brought to the outside world by Miguel de Castanhoso, who had struggled to Massawa with fifty other survivors in the hope of finding a Portuguese ship there. (The rest of the expedition had been prevented by the emperor from travelling to the coast.) A ship did arrive, but was so small and overcrowded that only one man could go aboard. Castanhoso was a captain, and also wounded, so the place went to him. Before he left them his companions won a promise that he would press tirelessly in India – and, if need be, before the king in Lisbon – for bigger ships to come to Massawa and take them out. They knew they faced being trapped in Ethiopia for the rest of their lives, because the Ottoman Turks were increasingly taking command of the Red Sea and could seize Massawa at any moment.

As the ship raised its anchor, Castanhoso saw the men on the shore kneel to pray to the crucifix on their banner, then mount their horses and mules. From the open sea he watched them ride slowly back inland.

TWENTY-NINE

Taking Bible and Sword
to Monomotapa

> He wages great wars against Prester John, Emperor of the Abys-
> sinians. He holds his court at Zimboaé, where he maintains as his
> ordinary guard, women and 200 large and fearsome dogs.
>
> —inscription on an imaginary portrait of 'Monomotapa, Emperor of
> Gold', by P. Bertrand, Paris (1631)

DURING THEIR FIRST DECADES in East Africa the Portuguese had given little thought to converting the heathen. This was in marked contrast to events on the Atlantic side of the continent, where the winning of souls was in progress even before Vasco da Gama's triumphant voyage to India. The king of the Congo had been baptized, and youthful Christians had been transported to Lisbon for training in the seminaries; only the slave trade marred this holy work.

However, the task of conversion was quite different beyond the Cape, because Islam dominated the African coastline and the Portuguese at first had little contact with black rulers who might be persuaded to accept the true faith. The East African climate was also a deterrent, so the missionary labours of Franciscan and Dominican friars accompanying the *conquistadores* were first directed towards the Hindus of Malabar and Goa.

A striking change of pace was apparent after the Society of Jesus, stimulated by the Counter-Reformation, was proclaimed in 1540 through a papal bull, *Regimini militantis ecclesiae*. Less than a year later, one of the founders of the Jesuits, Francis Xavier, had set out from Lisbon for the East Indies, fired by a zeal that would carry him to sainthood.[1] He was also sustained by the highest authorities, temporal and spiritual: King John III, who had come to the throne in 1521, gave him letters ordering Portuguese officials everywhere to render assistance to his Christian labours, and Pope Paul III appointed him as his vicar for all the shores of the Indian Ocean.

The ship in which Xavier travelled made a slow progress up the East African coast, giving him ample time to understand how strong was the Muslim hold on the Swahili population. In Malindi he had his first serious dialogue with an unbeliever, and his account of this contains a fine example of Jesuitical logic:

> A Moor from this city of Milinde, one of the most esteemed among them, asked me to tell him whether the churches in which we are accustomed to pray are much frequented by us ... telling me that among his people piety was losing ground ... because in that city there were 17 mosques and the people were not going to more than three of them, and to those only a handful of people. He was greatly troubled ... for he was not convinced by what I told him, namely, that the Lord God, who is utterly faithful in all things, is never satisfied with infidels, still less with their prayers; and this was why God wanted prayer among them to fail, since theirs did not serve Him ... It is proper that heathens and great sinners would live in doubt and anxiety, and it is a mercy that Our Lord causes them to live so without their knowing the reason.

Before continuing his journey, Xavier prayed at Malindi's small Christian chapel, built thirty years earlier; several Portuguese graves surrounded it. He also met the sultan, Fath bin Ali. Then by way of Socotra island (where he studied its heretical Christian community, soon to be obliterated by Islam), Xavier went on to Goa, and from there began his tireless journeys through the East, even as far as Japan.

By the time Xavier died, near the Portuguese colony of Macao in 1552, the Jesuits had brought a new religious force to the Indian Ocean through their sense of intellectual superiority. They were not a begging order, like the Franciscans, although they sometimes begged for reasons of self-mortification. Most were of aristocratic background, thus feeling an affinity with the senior officials of the Estado da India and believing that Christianity must be enforced by imperial power. They converted the poor and humble, but cultivated the rich and mighty. In the first wave of Jesuit fervour, Hindu temples were destroyed and in Goa a ban was imposed on the public calling of Muslims to prayers.[2]

In part, these acts echoed the religious convulsions going on throughout Europe. The horizons of Catholicism were constantly widening, so clearly it would not be long before the call came to the Jesuits to proselytize in other parts of the Indian Ocean. As far as Xavier had been concerned, the souls of the black Africans were no different from those of the Hindus, whom he also called 'los negros'; but once converted they would become the equal of white men.

His successors soon saw where their first missionary efforts should be directed in Africa: beyond the coastal barrier created by Islam there was one heathen king whose name was becoming famous, even in Europe – the holder of the title of Monomotapa. His empire was reputed to stretch far into the interior from the southern bank of the Zambezi river, and since the Jesuits always liked to start from the top in every society, so that a ruler's acceptance of baptism would send the true faith cascading down to the common people, Monomotapa looked to be the perfect target. When a message reached Goa in 1559 from the captain of Sofala, Sebastiano de Sá, that there were stirrings of interest in Christianity among some tribes, and when a Dominican friar claimed that Monomotapa himself might be won over, the Jesuits began paying close attention.

Within a few months Father Gonçalo da Silveira had been selected for the task of converting the most powerful monarch in Africa south of the equator. He was the ideal choice for this Christian assault on unknown territory: a nobleman with iron-willed courage, and a product of the first Jesuit seminary in Portugal, he had already distinguished himself as the administrator of all Jesuit missionary work in India.

At the start of 1560 Silveira took passage from Goa to Africa with two fellow-Jesuits. They disembarked at Mozambique island, port-of-call for many homeward-bound Portuguese ships, then transferred to a small trading boat, a *sambuq*. Despite the qualms of his companions, Silveira insisted upon sailing southwards to Sofala, which took almost a month, then on again for eight days more to the town of Inhambane. A local ruler, chief Gamba, living a short distance inland from Inhambane, was seen as a likely candidate for conversion, since one of his sons had already been baptized in the church on Mozambique island, then sent home dressed in the best available finery. This venture would be Silveira's preparation for winning the greatest prize: the emperor Monomotapa himself.

The wretchedness of their long coastal voyage during the rainy season increased when the Jesuits contracted malaria in Sofala. Moreover, they were fasting for Lent and one of the trio, a lay brother, was so close to death that Silveira was constrained to grant him a dispensation to eat meat. During the journey inland matters grew worse and Silveira had to be borne on a *machila* (a hammock on poles); he was too weak to walk. But within a few weeks he had converted chief Gamba and his senior wife, who were given the Christian names Constantino and Isabella.

With the lower orders the process of conversion was simple. A bell was rung to collect a crowd, then the priest would declaim the commandments, the Lord's Prayer and the creed, using an interpreter to urge his audience to recite these unfamiliar sounds as best they were able. Hail Marys completed the initiation. When the priest believed his message was sufficiently absorbed (a recitation session might last for half a day), these new believers were lined up for baptism. By such means, Silveira and his aides quickly brought 400 Africans to salvation. The Jesuit penetration of eastern Africa seemed well founded, and before returning to Mozambique Silveira bade a warm farewell to his host, deciding that he was 'a very good man for a *kafir*'.

Unfortunately, Dom Constantino did not quite live up to his new name, and soon regressed into heathendom. One Jesuit father, André Fernandes, had been left behind to keep the new converts up to the mark and make more whenever possible. He stayed for two years, growing ever less popular as he railed against witchcraft, polygamy and traditional customs which in Christian terms counted as incest. When a drought occurred and Dom Constantino invoked his spiritual rain-making powers, as was his duty, Father Fernandes condemned him openly. At this, the chief angrily decided to rid himself of his white wizard. The priest was starved, then isolated. He fled to the coast, and took the first ship to India. But in his report he put a brave face on matters: 'All these people receive baptism very willingly . . . The women show great devotion to images of Our Lady . . . I baptized nearly 450 Christians on the way to my vessel.'

The fate of Father Silveira was to be far more lurid. In Mozambique he made final plans for his encounter with the black emperor, then boarded another boat which was heading up the Zambezi to the trading post of Sena. This was a cluster of straw-thatched and mud-walled houses beside a small stone fort, at the site of a traditional African fair. A community of several dozen Portuguese was settled here: adventurers, refugees from the disciplines of European life, buyers of gold, ivory and slaves.[3] Although the Christians were supposed to be in competition with the Muslim merchants who had so effectively drawn trade away from Sofala, religious and racial attitudes were easy-going in Sena. Most of the Portuguese had African concubines, as had the Muslims. The community also included Indian Christians from Goa and, to judge from Silveira's remarks, other groups as well. He complained that the Portuguese of Sena were 'corrupted by the infernal sect of Mohamed, and even mixed with the pestilential Jews'.

Before Silveira left Sena he did his best to impose some religious propriety by holding marriage ceremonies for the white traders and their mulatto or African mistresses. He baptized hundreds of children and slaves. Then he moved on to Tete, the furthest Portuguese outpost, some 250 miles up the river. Among the traders operating from Tete, the most able and educated was Antonio Caiado. He spoke the Karanga language and declared himself ready to escort the Jesuit to Monomotapa's capital.

They set off across country, fording flooded rivers, and on New Year's Day 1561 Silveira reached the court of the youthful Monomotapa, Negomo Mupunzagutu. The priest was wearing his religious robes, and combined with his aristocratic bearing these made an immediate impression on Negomo, as had Silveira's polite refusal to accept presents of cattle, gold and women. 'It is not possible,' said the great African monarch, 'that a man does not want any of these things I have offered, it being so natural in all of us to desire them; surely he is not like other men.' Muslim religious teachers had already visited Negomo, so he called Silveira the *Kasisi*, derived from the Arabic *qassis* (preacher). However, this white man was clearly of different mettle.

Accompanied by his mother, the king began talks with the missionary. The three sat together on a Persian rug, with the trader Caiado acting as interpreter from the door of the room. The Jesuit was even excused the usual ritual for approaching a Karanga monarch: crawling on the stomach like a crocodile, over ground spread with fresh cow-dung, and clapping his hands while doing so. This was a promising start, and Silveira was allocated a hut close at hand and servants to care for all his needs. But soon it was rumoured that the *Kasisi* had a beautiful woman in his room: perhaps he was not, after all, so totally unlike other men. Asked by Negomo to produce his secret companion, Silveira reverently displayed a painting of the Virgin Mary; she was, he explained, God's mother, and he handed over the picture so that the Monomotapa could gaze upon it in his house.

Gently encouraged, the impressionable young monarch became obsessed with this image. Night after night, he said, God's mother was speaking to him, but in a tongue he could not understand. Silveira was ready with an explanation: her holy words could be understood only by Christians.

At this, Negomo made up his mind to embrace the white man's religion. Patiently he listened, with his mother beside him, as Silveira taught them all that was needed for baptism. After three weeks they were judged to be ready. The ceremony took place in a mood of almost hypnotic exaltation, with hundreds of subjects following the example of their ruler. The name of Portugal's young king, Sebastian, was bestowed upon Negomo; his mother became Dona Maria, because that was the name of God's mother. Afterwards, Silveira did accept a gift of cattle from his royal convert, and passed these over to the merchant Caiado, who pragmatically had them slaughtered at once, then dried the meat.

Muslims at the emperor's court saw how this Christian interloper had snatched power from them in less than the time of one full moon to the next. He was already calling for their expulsion. In three or four months, what else might happen? They began spreading the story that Silveira was a wizard, using his baptism water to cast spells. He was also a spy sent from India to learn about the land so that a vast army could come and conquer it; moreover, this treacherous white man was in league with Monomotapa's African enemies. Only death could break his spells. These rumours created hysteria in the royal circle and a witch doctor was called in to throw the bones. Since his traditional power was also under threat he declared all the charges to be true.

Almost at once, Caiado knew that his compatriot was in peril, for the king advised him to remove any of his property from Silveira's hut. The trader scribbled a note to the priest, urging him to escape while he still had time. But Silveira already knew his fate: he confessed Caiado and said: 'I am certain that I am better prepared to die than the Moors who have to kill me. I forgive the king, for he is but a youth, and his mother, for the Moors have deceived them.' He went on baptizing African converts and gave away his last few possessions.

On the evening of 15 March 1561, Caiado sent two of his servants to watch over the priest, who walked up and down in the dark until midnight. As soon as Silveira went into his hut a group of men followed after. They strangled him and dragged his body to a river, where it was thrown to the crocodiles.[4] Writing later to a friend, Caiado blamed the Muslims for putting 'wrong notions' into the head of the king.

Inevitably, the martyrdom of a man so renowned as Silveira bought threats of revenge from Lisbon. The young King Sebastian had been educated by Jesuits and his religious guardian was a Jesuit. On a more mundane level, the event was a direct challenge to Portuguese authority. Indeed, this had instantly been realized by Monomotapa Negomo himself. In an attempt to fend off retribution he had ordered four leading Muslims at his court to be executed; two were, two others escaped.

In the event it took nearly ten years to organize a punitive expedition, and the aim by then was as much to win control of the gold-mines on the Zimbabwe plateau as to exact vengeance in the name of God. The chosen leader was Francisco Barreto, given the title of 'Captain-major of the conquest of Mutapa' and captain of the Mozambique fortress. His qualifications were impressive: he was a former governor of India and had been a close friend of the murdered priest. The expedition turned into a *cause célèbre* in Lisbon, having been declared a 'just war' against heathens to extract compensation for past wrongs. Several dozen noblemen volunteered to serve under Barreto, and the 600-strong contingent included 100 Moroccan grooms to look after the Arab steeds on which the Portuguese knights would advance into battle.

Setting off for Africa, Barreto interpreted the task ahead in the *Morte d'Arthur* tradition beloved of the Portuguese. His bombastic enthusiasm was so compelling that many stowaways were discovered in the three ships under his command after they had set sail from Portugal in the spring of 1569. All legitimately on board would nonetheless have obeyed the sombre rule that everyone sailing to the East must deposit a last will and testament with the India House. It was a wise precaution.

The Jesuits were granted a major role in the conduct of the expedition, and it was to prove calamitous. Four priests, led by Father Francisco de Monclaro, were insistent that the route taken into the interior should be up the Zambezi to Sena, then along the south bank of the river to Tete, before striking off to attack Monomotapa's capital. By thus following in the footsteps of the martyr they would be paying homage to his memory. If Barreto refused to yield to this demand the Jesuits might feel obliged to withdraw from the expedition; there was no need to stress what would be the reaction of King Sebastian if such an event were to occur.

The contrary advice of local Portuguese traders had been for Barreto to advance inland by way of Sofala, where the distance to the healthier high ground was shorter, and where help might be expected from a powerful Manica warlord who was fighting against Monomotapa. They pointed out that the Zambezi valley route was fever-ridden: it would surely prove fatal to men unused to African conditions. Moreover, there were hostile tribes along the route.

Monclaro was not just a Jesuit, but also Barreto's confessor. He easily won the argument. After a desultory voyage northwards as far as Malindi and Lamu, the captain-general finally turned his thoughts towards the Zambezi. His force had now grown to 1,000 men, including soldiers from coastal forts and 200 withdrawn from a contingent en route to India. The equipment included light cannon, arquebuses and crossbows; in the baggage-train were camels and donkeys. At the start of November 1571, Barreto donned his armour and gave the order to start.

At first, all seemingly went well. By Christmas the whole force was in camp along the river bank at Sena, where supplies could be bought from local traders – Portuguese, Muslim and Indian. A messenger was sent off to Monomotapa, demanding that an ambassador should come to Sena to negotiate. All too soon, the soldiers began dying from fever and the horses from tsetse fly. Not understanding such afflictions, the Portuguese suspected that the local Muslims were poisoning them, even though the community had been friendly all along, one merchant even lending Barreto a large sum of money to pay his troops.

After a trader had been so severely tortured that he made the desired 'confession', vengeance began. With seeming equanimity, Father Monclaro records the 'strange inventions' used to kill the Muslims: 'Some were impaled alive, other tied to trees in the extreme branches thereof, the branches being forcibly brought together then released, the victim being thus rent asunder. Others were cut up with axes from the back, others with bombards.'

This massacre seemed to spread a doom-laden cloud above the expedition. When Barreto decided to advance overland from Sena he soon found himself engaged in guerrilla warfare with the Mongas people, whose king was an unruly vassal of Monomotapa. Although the Portuguese had 2,000 African slaves carrying their supplies, food began to run out, wells were found to be stopped up, and Barreto had an uneasy feeling that his every move was being watched. His anxiety was made worse because men kept dying of fever and others were too weak to hold their weapons. Eventually, the Mongas attacked in force, using a traditional African half-moon formation with extended flanks. They shouted their war-cries and were answered with the names of Christian saints. Although gunfire proved enough to drive off 10,000 warriors, the Portuguese were repeatedly engaged; each time they suffered casualties and their spirits ebbed.

Before one battle an elderly sorceress walked towards the Portuguese and threw handfuls of dust at them from a gourd, swearing that this would make them blind and powerless to resist. The Africans had such trust in her powers that they were carrying cords to bind up the white men and lead them away. The Dominican friar, Dos Santos, relates how Barreto turned to his chief gunner and told him to aim his light cannon, firing a ball weighing several pounds, towards the old woman 'so insolent and confident in her diabolical arts'. The gunner did so, and 'by God's will his aim was so sure that he hit the sorceress between the breasts and she was blown to pieces before her men'. The warriors seemed 'most amazed', although they recovered enough to fling themselves into battle.

The Portuguese finally had to retreat to the Sena camp beside the river. A negotiating team sent by Monomotapa arrived there, backed up by 200 well-armed men. The emissaries said blandly that their king could send down 100,000 warriors like them to help Barreto if he wanted to pursue his war with the Mongas. The implicit threat was plain enough. There was nothing for it but to admit defeat.

By this time, only 180 men were left of the proud Portuguese force which had set out to conquer the African interior. Most had fallen victim to fever or been killed in battle; some had deserted. Barreto returned to Sena after a fruitless journey to the coast for reinforcements, and there he died at the end of May 1573.

The remnants of the expeditionary force were taken over by Barreto's second-in-command, Vasco Homem. He managed to recruit more men, then led an exploration inland from Sofala, the starting-point rejected by the Jesuits two years before. After visiting the gold-mines of Manica, setting fire to a town and fighting several battles, the force returned to the coast with little achieved. Once more an attempt was made to penetrate the Zambezi valley, this time in search of rumoured silver-mines. Homem finally gave up in frustration and handed over command to a Captain Cardoso. Many of the expedition's last 200 survivors were killed in an ambush. The final forty died defending a mud-walled fort.

So there was little to show for this flamboyant attempt to impose

Portuguese power along the Zambezi river. Thousands of people had been killed, the cost to the hard-pressed treasury in Lisbon was severe, and the Jesuits decided they would rather leave the winning of souls in East Africa to other religious orders. The kingdoms of the interior were, on the surface, unscathed, although they had been stirred to take a keener interest in guns and other European goods. However, the receding tide of Portugal's military ambition had left behind a flotsam of white deserters, some of whom joined the scattered trading community in the Zambezi valley, while others attached themselves to African rulers as mercenaries. Acting beyond the control of Lisbon, since they were almost literally off the map, these freebooters would gradually undermine the power of the Monomotapa and other rulers on both sides of the Zambezi valley.

One Monomotapa, Mavura, agreed to be baptized by a black Dominican friar, after being restored to power by the Portuguese. Within eighteen months there was an uprising on a scale never seen before. Some Africans fought with muskets which they had been buying from the traders with gold and ivory. At the end more than 300 Portuguese and mulattoes were killed, along with several thousand of their slaves and servants. The Dominican who had performed the baptism was cut to pieces with assegais and another friar thrown over a precipice.

Fewer than fifty Portuguese survived in the whole Zambezi interior. Retribution was swift: the captain of the Mozambique coast, Diogo de Sousa de Meneses, swept inland with 300 musketeers and ravaged the Monomotapa empire. He later claimed to have killed 12,000 warriors, capturing women and cattle; priests accompanying his men said they were inspired in battle by a heavenly figure 'resplendent as the sun'. But even this miracle did little for Meneses, because his superiors were so jealous. Ordered to present himself in Goa, he was stripped of his captaincy and his possessions, then cast into solitary confinement for eighteen months.

Such irrationality had become typical of the way the Portuguese empire was being run, and served to speed its decline.[5] Refuge was taken from reality in the drawing up of elaborate but impossible schemes; one was for sending out 2,000 families from Portugal to colonize the Zambezi region. These loyal subjects would exploit the fabulously wealthy mines of gold and silver; they would grow wheat; they would defy any other European power to set foot in this hard-won land.[6] The colonists were mere phantoms of a parchment dream. Moreover, the unruly white pioneers of Zambezia wanted no part of such schemes: when a judge, Dr Pero Coelho, appeared at the riverside settlement of Sena to administer justice and also find out whether any silver-mines existed, he was shot and mortally wounded. Some forty years later a small group of immigrants, men, women and children, was despatched from Lisbon, but the death-toll was high and most of the women were erstwhile prostitutes who quickly returned to their old trade.

The best that could be achieved in the end was for the crown to lease out vast estates, known as *prazos*, for peppercorn rents; some were bestowed upon the orphaned daughters of noblemen. These slave plantations would in time become the core of the Mozambique colony. Elsewhere on the high plateau, runaway soldiers and the survivors of shipwrecks were welcomed as status symbols in the entourages of African chiefs, and became the founders of powerful mulatto clans.

What strength the Portuguese retained in East Africa after the Barreto débâcle was used to control the coast, with the commerce of the once-prosperous Arab and Swahili towns more and more drawn into their hands. A Dominican friar, João dos Santos, describes in his *Ethiopia Oriental* the condition of the once-proud 'Moors of Sofala', barely a century after the first fort was built there by Pedro de Añaya: 'They are all poor and miserable, and generally live by serving the Portuguese in their journeys and trading and also as sailors. The Moorish women, as well as the Christians, employ themselves in cultivation, and pay tithes of all their harvests to our church.'

Dos Santos was sorry for them, up to a point. He proudly relates how he set fire to a mosque on an island near Sofala, after being told of its whereabouts by three young Muslims. The mosque, with wooden walls and a thatched roof, had been built to honour the tomb of a Mwinyi (Lord) Muhammad, a Swahili merchant:

> This mosque was all hung with painted calico, the stones of the sepulchre were anointed with fragrant sandal, and around it were many braziers in which they threw incense to perfume the mosque . . . After examining it well, I set fire to it with a piece of gun-match, which I bade one of the young men to bring with him alight, not telling him for what purpose it was required, for had I done so, or had they imagined what I was about, they would not have accompanied me, as

they have a great fear of offending the dead, and much more
such a one as this, whom the Moors regard as a saint.

After the mosque had been reduced to glowing embers – 'a good
picture of the fire in which Muhammad was burning' – the local Muslims
wanted to take revenge on dos Santos. But he recalls complacently that
their fear of the Portuguese, and 'respect for Christian priests', saved
him from any harm.

THIRTY

Turkish Adventurers,
Hungry Cannibals

You will make preparations in Suez for a holy war, and having
equipped and supplied a fleet . . . you will avert the evil deeds of
the Portuguese infidels and remove their flags from the sea.
—Sultan Suleyman, to Suleyman Pasha (1538)

FROM THEIR HANDFUL of strongpoints in East Africa, the Portuguese
continued to look nervously northwards towards the entrance of the
Red Sea. Although the Ottoman Turks had been driven out of
the Indian Ocean for several decades by Almeida's victory off Diu, the
control they later won in Egypt gave them far greater influence over
Aden and Somalia. If they did send a fleet southwards along the Africa
coast, their most likely aim would be to capture Mombasa, with its fine
natural harbours. Moreover, ever since the first visit by Vasco da Gama
its inhabitants had shown unremitting hostility towards the Portuguese.
If ever the Turks held Mombasa, every ship sailing between Goa and
the Cape of Good Hope could be in peril.

Yet the Portuguese were reluctant to occupy Mombasa themselves.
They simply lacked the men to hold it. There were several other ports
serving as outlets for Africa's principal exports – gold, ivory and slaves
– and since Mozambique and Malindi were the accepted stopping-places
for ships needing water and supplies, one tempting solution was to wipe
Mombasa out of existence, to treat it as Rome had treated Carthage.

This had been tried by Nuño da Cunha, a newly-appointed governor-
general of India, when he was forced to spend six months in East Africa
in 1528–29. Violent weather in the Atlantic had caused his fleet to
round the Cape too late to catch the south-west monsoon, which would
carry it on to Goa. Having lost their flagship and several other vessels,
da Cunha and his men were demoralized and bitter at the thought of
loitering in African waters until the end of the north-east monsoon early

in the following year. Several months of buffeting outside Malindi's coral reef was an intolerable prospect, so da Cunha decided to force the issue with Mombasa. He sent messengers ahead to say that his ships were about to sail right into the main harbour and drop their anchors.

The sultan was displeased and alarmed. Memories in the city were still sharp of the havoc and destruction caused by Almeida's fleet, twenty-three years before. Looking for a compromise, the sultan offered to supply food and water, but insisted that only those men sent to collect these supplies could step ashore.

It was not good enough for the Portuguese. After six months at sea in foul and crowded ships the 1,500 sailors and soldiers under du Cunha's command were desperate to feel solid ground beneath their feet and to eat fresh food. Many were ill from scurvy and other diseases. So without more ado the fleet went into Mombasa to impose the Portuguese will.

It was met by a furious cannonade from the fort at the harbour entrance. Guns the Swahili had salvaged from various shipwrecked caravels and carracks were being put to use. The fort was much stronger than the one which had confronted Almeida, and now there were four Portuguese renegades manning the cannons. These gunners caused many casualties among their compatriots, but they could not stop the fleet from entering the harbour. The sultan was invited to capitulate, and when he refused da Cunha ordered a bombardment. It went on throughout the night, the 3,000 defenders replying with volleys of arrows. As the sun rose, several hundred men stormed ashore, led by a force of musketeers. Once more, the fearlessness of the Portuguese soldiery proved irresistible.

The population of the city fled to the mainland and the victors occupied the entire city. It had been an easy conquest, with few casualties on the Portuguese side. But the satisfaction da Cunha felt as he surveyed the scene of his success from the palace roof was to be short-lived.[1] Skirmishes with the Muslim guerrillas were frequent, and as the rains dragged on to the end of the year the death-rate among his men from malaria began to soar. The Portuguese were already in a weak physical state, and the ship's surgeons relied upon blood-letting as the one treatment for fever. When the time at last came for the fleet to renew its journey to India, the Portuguese dead from fighting and disease numbered 370.

As a parting gesture, da Cunha wanted to appoint an obedient sheikh from Malindi to become the new ruler of Mombasa. However, it was a risky honour to accept and the man first chosen declined, asserting that since his mother had been a slave he could not aspire to such a post.[2] An alternative candidate demanded that 150 Portuguese soldiers must stay behind to protect him – an impossible demand, given the losses already suffered.

At this, da Cunha decided to destroy Mombasa completely. He ordered the pulling down of all the stone houses, and the setting alight of everything that would burn. According to one Portuguese chronicler, 'the roaring of the flames, the pillars of smoke and the crashing of stone walls were reminiscent of a scene from hell'. For good measure, the plantations of palm-trees on which the commercial life of the city relied heavily were methodically hacked down.

Da Cunha was able to report proudly to Lisbon that the Mombasa fort was now demolished and the city reduced to ashes. It had been a costly triumph, however, and the inhabitants remained defiant. As the sultan returned to survey the smouldering ruins he at least had the satisfaction of knowing that his people lived to fight another day, and would have good reason to do so.

The wider conflict in the Indian Ocean ensured that they would not fight alone. Less than ten years later the first Turkish ships began to venture towards East Africa.[3] From then on, Portuguese anxieties mounted. Several small forts along the coast were strengthened, punitive raids were made on pro-Turkish towns, and yet another attack on Mombasa was mounted in 1551. This the populace repelled from behind even bigger defences and the Portuguese force had to retreat to Zanzibar, its commander wounded in the neck by a poisoned arrow.

Yet the Turks themselves had repeatedly proved incapable of scoring a decisive naval victory in the Indian Ocean. The resolve of the sultans faltered after 1554 when the renowned Muslim map-maker, Piri Reis, was executed because his carefully planned expedition had ended in failure. Then, in the 1580s, the Turkish challenge displayed a new panache with the appearance of Amir Ali Bey, a daring buccaneer. He was already experienced in fighting the Portuguese, having made a surprise attack in 1581 on Muscat, their Omani stronghold; he sacked the town, then swiftly withdrew. Four years later he set off from the Red Sea again in two galleys, one of which was so old and waterlogged that it had to give up even before rounding the Horn of Africa.

Ali Bey reached Mogadishu in the second vessel, and there persuaded the citizens to throw in their lot with him and declare their loyalty to the Ottoman empire. He was given more ships and hundreds of auxiliaries, then set off for Lamu and Pate, at the northern end of the Swahili coast. It was a triumph of bravado. Local rulers from as far south as Mombasa sent ambassadors to tell Ali Bey how much they wanted to be rid of the Franks.

The Turks captured more than forty Portuguese, including a senior captain, and sailed back to the Red Sea with them and sufficient booty to pay for the building of some bigger and better ships. Ali Bey did not reach Mombasa on this occasion, but its sultan sent a message asking him to build a fortress and supply a permanent Turkish garrison.

When news of the Turkish triumph reached Goa, it was agreed that the maximum revenge should be meted out to the cities which had helped Ali Bey. A fleet of eighteen ships was despatched and the port of Faza was the first to receive its due. After a short, sharp battle, during which the Portuguese hacked holes in the flat roofs of houses and threw grenades down to wipe out defenders, the town was overrun. The sultan, Estambadur, was killed and his head stuck on a lance.[4] The Portuguese then massacred every person in the town. In the words of the Dominican friar and chronicler João dos Santos, who was in East Africa at the time: 'The Portuguese would not pardon any living thing; they killed women and children, monkeys and parrots, and other innocent animals, with as much rage as if they had been responsible for the sins of the city.' Then the town was set on fire and 10,000 palm-trees hacked down.

The armada sailed to Mombasa and the city was ravaged once more, this time for having invited Ali Bey to build a fort. After much of the city and its surrounding orchards had been destroyed, the Portuguese were brought off with a payment in gold.

The expedition seemed like a job well done, but eighteen months later Ali Bey was back in East Africa, commanding a far more credible fleet than before, loaded with well-armed soldiers.[5] He was enthusiastically welcomed by most of the coastal rulers and made straight for Mombasa to begin building defences strong enough to deter the Portuguese from ever thinking they would be able to storm it. This time his fellow-Muslims felt sure that Ali had come to stay.

It was a moment when the entire East African coast, as far south as Mozambique, might have fallen under permanent Turkish suzerainty but for the appearance on the outskirts of Mombasa of a terrifying third force, a horde of cannibals. They were the insatiable Zimba, a tribe whose true identity and origins have been much debated, since cannibalism is unknown today in East Africa.[6] They were perhaps people who had lost their land in the upheavals following the Portuguese invasion of the Zambezi valley, a desperate and hungry horde united under the *nom de guerre* (or *nom de goût*) Simba, meaning 'lion' in many African languages; the lion, after all, is a man-eater.

Before reaching Mombasa the Zimba had literally been eating their way up the continent. Their greatest feast was in the ancient city of Kilwa, which they overran in the middle of the night after a traitor had guided them across a causeway linking the island with the mainland. More than 3,000 people were killed or captured; the captives were stored in pens, then taken out as required. The traitor was also eaten as a punishment for his lack of moral principles.

The coming of the Zimbas to Mombasa terrorized both the Swahili inhabitants and the newly-installed Turks. The attentions of Ali Bey had to be divided between building up his fortress, in readiness for the inevitable Portuguese attack from the sea, and making sure that the cannibals could not cross over from the mainland. He must have been hoping that before the Portuguese arrived the Zimba would abandon their siege and turn elsewhere for sustenance. It was not to be, because the news of his reappearance in the Indian Ocean had reached Goa with unusual speed, and the viceroy, Manuel de Sousa Coutinho, hurriedly despatched his brother, Tomé, to Africa with a fleet of nineteen vessels, led by two heavily-armed galleons, and carrying a force of almost 1,000 troops.

With the north-east monsoon in its sails the armada sighted the African coast just south of Mogadishu in less than three weeks, then turned south to do battle at Mombasa. It reached there at first light on 5 March 1589, and a flaming meteor spotted as the darkness lifted was taken as a good omen. When the Turks saw the fleet, silhouetted against the rising sun, they opened fire with heavy cannons and unfurled silken flags to declare their readiness to fight, but events would show that their confidence was already undermined by the prospect of defending themselves on two fronts.

The accuracy of the Portuguese naval gunners was quickly displayed when they began landing balls right in the fort. One of these killed the Turkish artillery captain, at which his colleagues began to retreat into the town. When Ali Bey himself was seen fleeing on horseback, a Portuguese nobleman was sent ashore with three companions to take possession of the fort. They found only four Turks inside, two dead and two alive. The latter were put to the sword and the Portuguese standard was raised in place of the flags of Islam.

If the Portuguese were astounded at the weakness of the seaward defence they soon discovered why: Ali Bey had placed his best men, in two of his ships, at the rear of Mombasa island, where it was separated from the mainland only by a narrow channel. Across the channel were massed the hungry, spear-waving hordes of the Zimba. Unaware of the cannibals, a section of the Portuguese fleet set about the two Turkish ships, whose crews fought desperately against these new enemies, but in vain. For the loss of only four of their own men, the Portuguese slaughtered 100 Turks and took another seventy prisoner. Scores of black and mulatto Christians, chained to stakes near the scene of the fighting, were freed, and more than a score of bronze cannons were captured. On the far side of the island, the remainder of Ali Bey's ships were being stormed. When it came to exuberance in battle the Turks were no match for the Portuguese, who leapt over the sides of their ships with swords between their teeth and swam ashore to join in the rout.

His hopes in tatters, the Mombasa sultan, Shah ibn Msham, sent a messenger pleading for peace. Tomé de Sousa Coutinho replied that he would consider it, but only after all the Turks in the city had been handed over to him. A day passed without reply. The Zimba were poised expectantly outside the town, and the Portuguese fleet lay at anchor in the harbour. De Sousa Coutinho ordered his men ashore, and they marched unopposed into the town behind a flag adorned with a picture of Christ on the cross. There was the usual plundering, houses were set alight, and defensive walls reduced to rubble.

As the Portuguese rejoined their ships it was the turn of the Zimba chief to send a message to de Sousa Coutinho, saying that since the Portuguese 'had honourably ended their enterprise', he asked permission to start his: 'namely to kill and eat every living thing on the island.' The Christian commander raised no objection, so the cannibals immediately swarmed across the ford and fanned out through the town, driving before them the Swahili who had been hiding in gardens and coconut plantations.

As the massacre began, Ali Bey and thirty of his officers fled into the sea, together with 200 Swahili who had escaped the Zimbas' clutches. They howled for mercy, for protection from the man-eaters. Taking pity, the Portuguese hauled the beaten enemies from the water, and fired cannons to frighten off the pursuers. Then the fleet sailed away, leaving Mombasa to its fate.

After beheading various sheikhs and sultans along the coast for displaying Turkish sympathies, de Sousa Coutinho went triumphantly back to India, with Ali Bey as his prize trophy. Brought before the viceroy, the defeated Turk conducted himself with a mixture of humility and bravado. The viceroy put him aboard a ship for Lisbon. Soon after landing, Ali Bey skilfully declared himself a convert to Christianity.

Tantalizingly, the records say nothing of his later career, and the Zimba were likewise soon to disappear from history. After doing their worst in Mombasa they set off north again and attacked the city of Malindi. The local inhabitants and a handful of Portuguese stationed there managed to hold them off – then 3,000 warriors from a tribe named the Segeju joined the fray. The Zimba had met their match at last, and only 100 survived; the chief and a few followers vanished into the African interior.

THIRTY-ONE

The Renegade Sultan

> Never have I had redress. No respect was paid to my person, and
> my treatment did not accord with my station. A royal heart is
> greatly affected by insults and affronts, and by injustice . . . Necess-
> ity recognizes no law, and this is more especially the case since
> my subjects are mere Kaffirs.
>
> —Sultan Yusuf of Mombasa, writing to Goa (1637)

THE STRUGGLES for control of Mombasa had left it with few traces
of its former prosperity. The power vacuum was made complete by the
deaths in obscure circumstances of the sultan and his three sons. The
Portuguese, who had now taken a firm decision to occupy the island,
moved in to fill the vacuum, bringing with them Sultan Ahmad of
'loyal' Malindi to become the new ruler. The possibility of a far more
formidable Turkish incursion was the main stimulus, because there were
now reports of plans being drawn up in Egypt to link the northern end
of the Red Sea with the Nile by a canal, through which Ottoman
war-galleys would sail directly from the Mediterranean to the Indian
Ocean.

In 1586 a despatch had been sent to Paris by Savary de Lanscosme, the
French ambassador to Constantinople, reporting that 100,000 workers,
40,000 asses and 12,000 camels would be used in making the canal.
When it was dug, 200 armed ships would sail through, to drive the
Portuguese back round the Cape of Good Hope. At about the same
time the anonymous author of the Turkish *Tarik-i Hindi-i Garbi* (The
Western Route to India) had written optimistically about what would
happen after the canal was built and the 'evil unbelievers' had been
expelled from the Bahr al-Zenj (Sea of Zanj): it would then become
far easier for Constantinople to enjoy 'the exquisite things of Sind and
Hind and the rarities of Ethiopia [Africa]'.[1]

A few years after reports reached Lisbon of these Turkish plans, the
Portuguese at last started work on the building of a fortress at Mombasa.

It was to be a bastion strong enough to dominate the East African coast and able to defy any force that an enemy could bring to bear. It would be called Fort Jesus. A customs duty of 6 per cent to be paid at Mombasa by all ships trading in East Africa would meet the cost of the fort and its upkeep.

Fort Jesus was destined to become an indestructible monument to Portugal's brief age of imperial splendour. Yet the order to build it was given by a Spaniard, and the architect was an Italian. The Spaniard was Philip II, who in 1580 had acquired the Portuguese throne when the Aviz dynasty petered out.

Philip had many favourites, and one was Giovanni Batista Cairati, a Milanese who as a young man had directed the building of fortifications in Malta in preparation for a siege by the Turks. The reputation of Cairati as a military architect was to spread throughout southern Europe, and by the 1570s he was working for Philip in Spain.

Soon after the ill-starred union of the Iberian states, Cairati was sent by his royal patron to be the architect-in-chief for all Portuguese fortifications in the East. After taking up his post in Goa, at the age of about fifty, Cairati diplomatically changed his name to the Portuguese equivalent: João Batista Cairato. In the last thirteen years of his life he was to design forts in various parts of the Indian Ocean, as far east as the Malacca straits. Fort Jesus was his last and greatest achievement, in which he looked back to his Italian origins. It is a remarkable example of High Renaissance theories on the way architecture should draw inspiration from the 'perfect form' of the human body. The ground plan of Fort Jesus makes this very plain: the four bastions are the arms and legs, the outworks facing the sea form the head, and the central area of the whole structure is the torso.[2] The gateway, placed to be well covered by fire from one of the bastions, is, in effect, beneath an armpit.

It was not only out of a nostalgia for the philosophical notions which had been bandied around in the Italy of his youth that Cairati used this 'human form'. The Fort Jesus plan was ideally suited to the terrain and the human resources that could be marshalled locally during a siege. During his visits to Mombasa from Goa before building began, Cairati would have realized that the effective garrison would be small (rarely more than a hundred) because of the perpetual shortage of manpower in the Estado da India. So the layout needed to be simple, with only a few defensive points, revealing as little as possible to attackers about the strength inside the fort.

Fort Jesus was none the less designed on a scale large enough to make living conditions tolerable during a long siege. It is approximately 150 yards long, and 130 yards wide to the ends of the bastion arms. The central courtyard, nearly 75 yards across, was designed to be flanked by the barracks, storerooms and a chapel, well protected by the curtain walls. A deep well gave drinkable water. A house for the fort's captain, who would be dignified with the title 'Governor of Mombasa', was sited above the gateway.

Rising from a platform of coral rock, the blank seaward-facing walls of Fort Jesus were well calculated to dismay potential enemies. Faced with coral blocks and filled with rubble, the walls were more than 12 feet thick sufficient to resist any naval guns which might be envisaged at the end of the sixteenth century. Below were the outer defences (known in Portuguese as the *couraça*), close to the sea and reached from the inner courtyard by a low arched doorway and a narrow passageway.

Cairato must have instantly recognized the western end of Fort Jesus, facing towards the centre of the island, as the place where a determined assault might most easily break through. His solution was in the best traditions of Italian military architecture. The two stubby 'legs' of the fort concealed gun emplacements in their flanks. Each of these emplacements could rake the approaches to the back wall of the bastion opposite. The plans also allowed for the building of a dry moat around the landward sides of the fort.

For several years, progress on the building of Fort Jesus was swift. Under the first captain of Mombasa, the forceful Matheus Mendes de Vasconcellos, teams of Indian masons, quarrymen and carpenters were brought from Goa. Everyone available joined in the labour, including the crews of several ships stationed in the harbour to guard against any renewed visitation by the Turks. The officers worked alongside their men. Even the new sultan made a token gesture, coming down to the waterside with his courtiers to help carry stones.

Cairato would have been happy to see so much activity. Perhaps he was hoping to visit Mombasa on his way home to Europe, for after more than ten years in the East he had told Philip II that his keenest wish was to retire to Milan. (His native city still held his affections, and he intended to leave most of his life savings to the expansion of a local hospital.) The king told him to wait until a replacement could be found. Cairato died in 1596 in Goa, still waiting.

As so often happened elsewhere in the tropical Portuguese empire, the energy and money in Mombasa soon began to peter out. Work on Fort Jesus came almost to a halt, while a succession of governors squandered or stole the funds. Almost twenty years after the fort was begun, the pioneer Portuguese traders in Mombasa were complaining to anyone who would listen that its defensive walls were not high enough. Much remained to be done. Even so, the settlement grew steadily, and there was even what passed for a main street, derisively nicknamed the *Raposeira* (Foxhole). Eventually Mombasa drew together about seventy families, plus their slaves and hangers-on. Although there is no record of them, some Indian shopkeepers and artisans must also have migrated across the ocean from Goa. Houses were built with the stone blocks from the ruined buildings of Arab merchants, as were an Augustinian church and convent.

However, the Portuguese did not trust the Swahili with whom they shared the island, because the early friendship with Sultan Ahmad soon ebbed away. He had believed that moving from Malindi to Mombasa would make him the overlord of the whole Swahili coast, whereas real power lay within the slowly rising walls of Fort Jesus; the Portuguese captains held the power and the sultan was in Mombasa on sufferance.[3] In vain did the sultan write to the king in Lisbon, saying that the fort was not needed, that his own status was being whittled away, that in matters of trade the Portuguese residents were being given unfair advantages, and that successive captains treated him with contempt.

The last complaint would have been well understood by João Robeiro, a Portuguese captain with many years of experience in the East during the seventeenth century: 'I do not doubt that among those who went out to govern those fortresses there were some who behaved kindly, but they could not set matters right; for the wrongs done by one bad man remain deeper impressed than the kindnesses done by a hundred good men.'

Sultan Ahmad's pride received another jolt when he asked permission to send merchant ships to China. He is unlikely to have owned vessels large enough to make the round journey of some 15,000 miles, but he could easily hire them in India. The cargoes for China would, as ever, be ivory, ambergris, African gold and the skins of rare animals; the ships would return laden with porcelain and silks. Perhaps there were still legends in Malindi of the visit by Zheng He's junks, almost 200 years earlier, and of the giraffe which had been sent by the city to the Chinese emperor.

The sultan knew he must ask permission of the Portuguese, because any ship caught sailing the Indian Ocean without a *cartaz* could expect to be plundered and sunk. He must also have thought that the permission would be given because of the loyalty he and his forebears had shown to the Portuguese; but it was brusquely refused.

By 1610 a new sultan, Hasan, had come to the throne, and a new captain, Manuel de Mello Pereira, was in the fort. The enmity between the two soon grew so intense that Hasan fled from Mombasa to live with an African community on the mainland. The hand of Manuel de Mello reached out, and the sultan was murdered in an ambush. The Portuguese had paid 2,000 lengths of cloth to have the deed done. When the body was brought back to Mombasa the head was cut off and sent to the viceroy in Goa, with a report saying that the sultan had only suffered what he deserved, because he was guilty of high treason.

The heir to the throne was Yusuf, a boy of seven, so the Mombasa captain installed a regent from a faction which had opposed the murdered sultan. Yusuf was shipped off to India where he was converted to Christianity, placed with the Augustinians in Goa to be educated, then sent to sea in Portuguese ships to learn the arts of seamanship and war. By the time he was in his late teens, and his name had been changed from Yusuf to Dom Jerónimo, he was judged by his mentors as fit to occupy the throne from which his father had been hounded. Dignified with the title of 'King of Mombasa, Malindi and Pemba', he was crowned in Goa, made a Knight of the Order of Christ, and sent home in 1626 in some pomp; with him went an Augustinian confessor. Moreover, he had a wife from Goa, named Isabel.

Unfortunately, Jerónimo was now too Portuguese for his own good. In his wide-brimmed hat instead of a turban, in doublet and hose instead of a long white gown, he was not the leader the local Swahili wanted to see. He even ate pork like an infidel. A preface by an anonymous priest, accompanying Jerónimo's message of loyalty to the Pope, describes him as a 'Christian king obeyed by his Moorish vassals', then rather ominously quotes Psalm 110: *Dominare in medio inimicorum tuorum* (Rule in the midst of thy foes).[4]

Torn between two cultures, Jerónimo behaved in a way which scarcely hid his inner desperation. If his own people did not trust him, neither did the Franks in Fort Jesus. In 1629 a new captain was appointed, the nobleman Pedro Leitão de Gamboa. It fell to him to make a fateful discovery: in the middle of the night the king was in the habit of going secretly to the tomb wherein lay the headless body of his father, and there he would pray, 'in the Moorish manner'. In the captain's view, this made Dom Jerónimo a traitor, fit only to be deposed and sent to Goa for trial.

Leitão de Gamboa took this decision in early August 1631, but before he could act on it some hint must have reached the king. In the late afternoon of Saturday 16 August, as the captain was lying ill in his house. Jerónimo arrived at the gate of Fort Jesus and asked to visit him. It was an odd request, because the two men were so hostile to one another that they rarely met. But the king was admitted and shown into the captain's bedroom. There was a short conversation, then the king and one of his entourage seized the captain by the arms and stabbed him to death.

Orders were then shouted to a force of African archers and Arab soldiers waiting outside the fort. They rushed the entrance, firing arrows and brandishing swords. Once in the main courtyard they began to kill indiscriminately: the captain's wife and children were the first victims. Those of the fifty or so Portuguese soldiers who were not cut down at once seem to have panicked, fleeing to the nearby church run by the Augustinian priests. By nightfall it was all over. Fort Jesus had fallen and the Portuguese houses in Mombasa town were ablaze.[5]

The victor was no longer Dom Jerónimo. Back in his palace he cast away his Portuguese clothes, donned Swahili attire with a curved dagger at his waist, and declared himself to be Sultan Yusuf bin Hasan, a true Muslim. Then he returned to Fort Jesus. He declared that for the Christians in Mombasa there was only one way to avoid the fate of those who had already died in the fort: they must embrace Islam – this in an age when death was preferable to apostasy. Even Yusuf's wife defied him; despite many humiliations it would be a long time before she accepted Islam.

The first to die for his faith was a hermit, Father Diogo. When he told the sultan of his resolve he was speared to death by the African attendants. For several days, nothing else happened. About 150 Christians were still crowded inside the church in the Augustinian convent. They included women and children who had been rescued from blazing houses, and several men who were wounded. With the Portuguese was a scattering of black and half-Arab Christian converts; among the wounded was a close relation of the sultan, a man known as Dom António, who had been carried to the fort to make a vain plea for mercy. Next to plead was the prior of the convent, formerly Yusuf's confessor. When he was asked if he would become a Muslim, and refused, he was hanged on the fortress wall.

On 20 August the sultan ordered that all the men in the church, numbering about sixty, should come out, and march to the fort. They were going to be 'sent to Christian countries'. After making confessions, receiving communion and saying farewell to their wives and children, the men emerged. They were led by priests carrying crucifixes. The sultan leaned out of a window of the fort and called to his cousin Dom António, urging him to take one last chance to abandon Christianity. When Dom António refused, the sultan gave a signal and a large force of warriors rushed forward to attack the procession. All the men were killed, except for a clerk named Silvestro Pereira. The sultan came out on horseback to the scene of the massacre, and finding Pereira still alive and protesting his Christianity, ordered him to be killed as well. In high spirits, Yusuf bent down from his saddle to jab the bodies with his lance; then they were all roped together and thrown into the sea.

Ten days passed, while the women and children waited in the church. They had little food or water, the weather was hot, and they had seen their husbands and fathers die. The sultan finally sent a messenger saying that all those who abandoned Christianity could return to their homes. Those who would not must leave Mombasa and be taken by sea to Pate, a town at the northern end of the Swahili coast. The women came out of the church, carrying their children and declaring their faith. They made their way to the waiting boats, chanting as they went.

The final act is described by an Augustinian friar who later compiled a report on the uprising:[6]

> When they had all embarked with certain slaves who had followed their mistresses in this conflict, there was a rumour that the tyrant's intention had been to make a hole amidships, so that they should all perish by drowning. But the sailors, barbarian Cafres, without waiting for this, as soon as they reached midstream and came in view of the fort where the tyrant was, began to cut the throats of these innocent sheep, tearing their children from their arms so that they might see them cut to pieces.
>
> Here was to be seen a daughter clinging to the half-living body of her mother, there a mother holding the mutilated

body of her daughter; here was to be seen a headless body with the hands holding a crucifix; whilst elsewhere there were some wounded, some half alive, whom they were throwing into the sea to increase their sufferings, and others whom they were striking with clubs and oars as they breathed out their lives. Those who were killed numbered as many as thirty-nine white women and fifty-nine children of both sexes. I could not ascertain the number of local people.

Another account told how the executioners had taken off the rings, necklaces and earrings of the women before throwing the bodies in the sea. (A year later, an ecclesiastical court in Goa heard evidence to decide whether the victims of the massacre should be honoured as martyrs who had died for refusing to abandon their Christian faith. Documents were sent to Rome to present the case for beatification, but for reasons unknown nothing further happened.)

When reports of the loss of Fort Jesus had reached Portuguese India there was disagreement as to whether the rebel sultan should be publicly beheaded in Mombasa or executed in Goa. However, the first task was to catch him. Early in 1632 a fleet of twenty ships, carrying 1,000 troops commanded by a nobleman, Francisco de Moura, appeared off Mombasa. Inside the fort were 400 men, a mixture of local Swahili and mercenaries from the mainland. Yusuf also had several hundred African warriors in hiding at key points around the island.

As the ships began firing salvoes at Fort Jesus, they revealed a bad miscalculation: their guns were not powerful enough to breach the walls. Cairato had designed the fort so well to deter the Turks that the Portuguese, unexpectedly finding themselves on the outside, could not batter a way in. What was worse, Yusuf's men were taking good advantage of the Portuguese cannons mounted in the bastions of the fort, using them against soldiers trying to seize Arab dhows anchored in the harbour, then to harass other boats in the narrow channel across which food supplies were brought to Mombasa island.

When 400 troops were put ashore near the fort, they were attacked by hundreds of African spearmen and archers. Urging on his men, Francisco de Moura was hit by thirty arrows. Some of the arrows had poisoned tips and he was saved from death only when a youth volunteered to suck out the poison; reputedly, the youth died.

Plans of attack were several times given away by deserters, and as the weeks went past the dispirited Portuguese commanders began to quarrel among themselves about what should be done next. Presents were sent to Mwana Chambe Chande, an African ruler on the mainland, with the aim of enticing him to join in on the Portuguese side. He made a token effort, then said his way was barred by the sultan's supporters. In March the rains began, making it more difficult for the arquebusiers to use their matchlocks. Finally, two guns were set up on the nearest point of the mainland to the fort and they started firing regular salvoes across the water. This achieved little, and Yusuf responded by putting one of the cannon from the fort on the flat roof of a mosque, to bombard the landing-place where the Portuguese took on water. After four months food was also running short. Moreover, some of the besiegers began devoting their energies to what one account darkly calls 'lewd and even horrible vices'. The siege was called off and the costly armada sailed back to Goa. Recriminations about the débâcle were intense, but since Francisco de Moura was well connected in Lisbon he escaped unscathed.

Two ships had been left behind to maintain the pretence of a blockade of Mombasa, but they swiftly fell into the hands of Sultan Yusuf. How this happened is uncertain; perhaps the crews were bribed, or they merely lost their nerve and fled in small craft to less turbulent Portuguese settlements along the East African coast.

Yusuf needed the two captured ships. He realized that when the next expedition arrived to regain Fort Jesus his luck might not hold. It was time to go. Everything moveable was loaded into the two ships, including the guns from the fort, and with the south-west monsoon in his newly-acquired sails the last sultan of Mombasa vanished into the Indian Ocean. His years in the Portuguese navy were to stand Yusuf in good stead, because he had decided to launch himself into a new career as a pirate.

For seven years he sailed the tropical seas from Madagascar to Arabia, sometimes in company with English and Dutch pirates. There were rumours that Yusuf was appealing to the Dutch to help him regain Mombasa, and the viceroy in Goa, Pero da Silva, grew alarmed at the possibility that Fort Jesus might fall to European buccaneers with the renegade sultan as their figurehead. He was in no doubt as to where the sympathy of the coastal Swahili lay: it was not with the Portuguese.

The viceroy swore to capture Yusuf – once even setting a thief to catch a thief, by hiring a Portuguese pirate for the task – but he never did. Sometimes Yusuf slipped into the East African ports, where he was welcomed as a hero. In the end he was killed during a skirmish in the Red Sea. Shortly before that happened he had sent one of his captives, a Dominican friar, to Goa with a letter, asking for pardon. He claimed that only the heartlessness of successive Fort Jesus captains had driven him to rebellion.

THIRTY-TWO

The Lost Pride
of Lusitania

> It is one of the results of the ingenuity and fury of men that the
> ravages of our wars are not confined to Europe. We drain ourselves
> of manpower and money so as to go to the far reaches of Africa
> and America for our own destruction.
> —Voltaire, *Le Siècle de Louis XIV* (1751)

WHEN COMPARED WITH the Spanish empire in the Americas, the
Estado da India was always a fragile creation. It defied logic for the
smallest of the western European nations, with hardly more than a
million people, to control sixteen million square miles of tropical ocean,
to make its writ run from Mombasa to Malacca, from Hormuz to Macau
on the China coast and Nagasaki in Japan. The papal bull awarding
Portugal half the world must soon prove to be only fine Latin phrases
on old parchment.

The drain on human resources was unbearable, because every year
hundreds of young men set sail from the Tagus estuary, and less than a
third ever came back. Their lack of manpower meant that the Portuguese
could never hope to colonize the interiors of the continents round
which their fortresses had been perched. Even Goa island, capital of the
eastern empire, controlled an area of the mainland only one twenty-fifth
of the size of tiny Portugal. The occupation of large swathes of territory,
after the manner of Spain in the Americas, was impossible. There was
no thought of conquering even the smaller states of India.

Although the Turks had never managed to win a strategic victory,
they and their co-religionists proved a constant irritation. The viceroy
Nuño da Cunha was driven away from the island port of Diu in 1531
by Mustafa bin Bahram, who had landed with a force of Ethiopian
slaves. (Mustafa believed in going to war in style: he brought his harem
in one ship and his treasure in another.) It was only the Mughal onslaught

on the kingdom of Gujarat, to which Diu belonged, that allowed Portugal to gain a foothold on the island several years later. Then they were twice besieged in the fortress and took full control of Diu only after 1555.

Set against this one success, which had allowed them to tighten their grip on trade through the Persian Gulf, was a steady erosion of their efforts to blockade the entry to the Red Sea. The failure of Albuquerque to capture Aden in those early years when any feat seemed possible would come to haunt the Portuguese. By 1570, when the first shock of white ferocity had worn off, oriental spices and manufactures were once more on sale in Alexandria. It was likewise possible for the Muslim rulers in Indonesia to buy large bronze cannons from the Ottoman Turks and have them transported across the Indian Ocean under the noses of the Portuguese, for use in besieging their fortresses.

The *cartaz* system still operated none the less; ships caught on the high seas without a Portuguese permit remained liable to be sunk, or at least looted; and for their self-preservation traders of all nationalities learned to speak a 'pidgin Portuguese'. Some devout Muslims felt that such humiliations at the hands of the Franks could be explained only as an act of God, a punishment for evil deeds. This was how Sheikh Zain al-Din, writing in about 1570, interpreted what had happened to people of his own faith on the Malabar coast. They were suffering for having 'gone astray' and becoming divided into schisms:

> On this account, therefore, did God bring down upon them the people of Europe, the Franks, Christians by religion (whom may Almighty God confound!) who began to oppress the Mohamedans and to bring ruin among them; being guilty of actions the most diabolical and infamous, such indeed are beyond the power of description; they having made the Mohomedans to be a jest and a laughing-stock; displaying towards them the greatest contempt; employing them to draw water from the wells, and in other menial employments; spitting in their faces and upon their persons; hindering them in their journeys, particularly when proceeding on pilgrimages to Mecca; destroying their property; burning their dwellings and mosques; seizing their ships; defacing and treading underfoot their archives and writings; burning their records; profaning the sanctuaries of their mosques.

What was more, they had captured Muslim women, then bound,
shackled and violated them, 'in this manner causing Christian children
to be brought into being'. Even allowing for an enemy's exaggerations,
it is a displeasing record.

Animosity towards Muslims being a sacred duty, the Portuguese were
always acutely short of friends. The Hindus might have become
Brothers-in-arms, but there was never any lasting rapport with them.
At first there had seemed some likelihood of an alliance with Vijayanagara, in the overtures made by Alfonso de Albuquerque. A Franciscan
monk, Father Luis, was sent to Krishna Deva, newly enthroned as the
rajah of the City of Victory, appealing to him to join the Portuguese
in their war against Calicut and the 'Moors' who lived there. In return,
promised Albuquerque, he would help Krishna Deva attack his Muslim
enemies in the north. Unsurprisingly, the rajah did not reply; the Zamorin might be an uncertain satrap, but he was also a Hindu. Later there
were more negotiations, and at the time of his death Albuquerque was
close to agreeing that the Hindus should have first call upon all war
horses imported into India through Goa.

The Portuguese were soon to realize the potential for trade with
Vijayanagara, for the city was reaching its greatest splendour under
Krishna Deva, who ruled for more than twenty years. He was helped
in his improvements to the city, including the construction of an artificial
lake, by João de la Ponte, a Portuguese engineer. Portuguese soldiers
using arquebuses also took part in several battles on the side of the
Hindus. Two merchants, Domingo Paez and Fernando Nuniz, were
living in Vijayanagara during the 1530s, and both sent chronicles back
to Lisbon. How Paez portrayed the Hindu capital might well have made
the Portuguese see the chance to acquire a mighty ally:

> The size of this city I do not write here, because it cannot
> all be seen from any one spot, but I climbed a hill from
> whence I could see a great part of it ... What I saw from
> thence seemed to me as large as Rome, and very beautiful
> to the sight; there are many groves of trees within it, in the
> gardens of the houses, and many conduits of water which
> flow into the midst of it, and in places there are lakes ...
> The people in this city are countless in number, so much so
> that I do not wish to write it down for fear it should be
> thought fabulous; but I declare that no troops, horse or foot,

could break their way through any street or lane, so great are the numbers of the people and elephants. This is the best provided city in the world.[1]

In 1547 the Portuguese finally made a treaty with Vijayanagara, but it did nothing to help the increasingly fragmented Hindu empire. The downfall of the City of Victory was already in sight, and in 1564 all the Muslim sultans of the Deccan formed a military alliance. In January 1565 they overran Vijayanagara, destroying it almost totally, slaughtering everyone who could not escape, tearing down temples, demolishing statues, setting fire to houses.[2] The Portuguese had been mere onlookers. The city was never occupied again, and when an Italian traveller, Caesaro Frederici, saw it two years later the only occupants of the houses still standing were 'tigers and other wild beasts'.

The end of Vijayanagara proved a calamity for the Estado da India, because Goa had become heavily dependent upon its trade. The historian de Couto admitted that the Portuguese were 'much shaken' by losing their profits from 'horses, velvets, satins and other sorts of merchandise'. The loss of revenue was so great that the population of Goa was permanently the poorer. The Portuguese also felt more isolated.

While remnants of the Vijayanagara empire retreated further south, a new power destined to control almost all of India was rising in the north. The Mughals quickly took the measure of the 'Franks', speaking of them with casual derision. Jahangir, the third emperor, who ruled 1605–27, makes only one passing reference in his long memoirs, while recounting the tale by an Arab sailor about Portuguese magic, how a man's head was cut off by them, then replaced. Jahangir likened the Portuguese to Bengali jugglers. The emperor Shah Jahan (1628–58), was even more dismissive: 'In truth, the Franks would be a great people but for their having three most evil characteristics: firstly, they are infidels; secondly, they eat pork; and thirdly, they do not wash that part from which nature expels the superfluities of their corporal bellies.'[3]

Such contempt might have been somewhat tempered had the Mughals better understood that more formidable infidels were already starting to oust the Franks from their seaborne empire. The Portuguese themselves knew by 1600 that there were ships in the Indian Ocean which could match or better theirs in gunnery and seamanship. Just as they had snatched the spice trade away from Venice, others were now intent on taking it from them.

As well as it could, and for as long as it could, Portugal had tried to
keep the secrets of the East hidden from potential interlopers: the ocean
routes, monsoon winds and currents, navigational dangers, the main
sources of spices, exotic fabrics and fine porcelain. For a Portuguese to
sell maps and sea-charts of the Indian Ocean, or pass on information
about the workings of the Estado da India, long remained a capital
crime. Such prohibitions had some success in maintaining a general
vagueness in Europe about the geography of the Indian Ocean: a Italian
map of the mid-sixteenth century shows Calicut as a separate peninsula,
dangling from the landmass of Asia between Arabia and India, while an
English map of the same period recording Sir Francis Drake's world
voyage depicts 'Melinde' as occupying most of eastern Africa as far as
the Cape.

This did not mean that the Portuguese had ever been able to
keep out all intruders. Within twenty-five years of Vasco da Gama's
voyage of discovery, several small French ships owned by Jean
Ango, a shipowner-cum-pirate from Dieppe, had rounded the
Cape to search for ports in Sumatra where they might buy spices.
This venture ended badly because of disease and bad weather, but it
was a portent. In 1527 another French ship, *La Marie de Bon Secours*,
sailed all the way to the Indian coast before the Portuguese arrested
her. The thirty-six sailors on board sent a petition for their freedom
to the viceroy in Goa, swearing that their voyage, financed by the
merchants of Rouen, had the approval of their king and the high
admiral of France. The ship had been captained by a Portuguese,
Estavao Dias, whose fate, although unrecorded, could scarcely have
been agreeable.

There were many other gaps in the barricades of secrecy, mainly
because Portugal was so often forced to employ foreigners to make up
for its own shortage of manpower. Most were simple sailors, often
Catalans or Genoese, illiterate and unaware of much beyond the wooden
walls of the ships they sailed in, rarely going ashore except to fornicate
or plunder.

It was far more damaging for the Portuguese when they unsuspect-
ingly transported to India somebody able to write down what he had
seen. Such a one was Father Thomas Stevens, an English Jesuit who
sailed from Lisbon to Goa in 1579 and sent home to his father in
Wiltshire a long account of the voyage. Despite a few absurdities, the
letter was greatly revealing for those English merchants and mariners

into whose hands it fell.[4] His ship was almost wrecked by drifting on
to rocks near the Cape:

> 'the shore so evill ... and the land itself so full of Tigers,
> and the people that are savage, and killers of all strangers,
> that we had no hope of life nor comfort.' Then the wind
> got up and they were saved. 'And you shall understand that,
> the Cape passed, there be two wayes to India: one within the
> Ile of S. Laurence [Madagascar], which they take willingly,
> because they refresh themselves at Mosambique a fortnight
> or a moneth, not without great need, and thence in a moneth
> or more land in Goa. The other is without the Ile of S.
> Laurence which they take when they set foorth so late, and
> come so late to the point [the Cape], that they have no time
> to take the foresaid Mosambique, and then they goe heavily,
> because in this way they take no port, and by reason of the
> long navigation, and want of food and water, they fall into
> sundry diseases, their gummes waxe great and swell, and they
> are faine to cut them away, their legges swell, and all the
> body becommeth sore, and so benummed, that they cannot
> stirre hand nor foot, and so they die for weaknesse, others
> fall into fluxes and agues, and die thereby.
>
> And this way was it our chance to make; yet though we
> had more than one hundred and fifty sick, there died not
> past seven and twenty; which loss they esteemed not much
> in respect of other times ... this way is full of privy rockes
> and quicksands, so that sometimes we durst not sail by night,
> but by the providence of God we saw nothing, nor never
> found bottome untill we came to the coast of India.

Stevens then exposes the frailty of Portuguese navigation. The 'running seas' drove the ship far off course: 'And we that thought we had
been neere India, were in the same latitude neere Zocotoro [Socotra],
an Ile in the mouth of the Red Sea.'[5] Having gone a thousand miles
out of its way, the ship turned east towards its goal: 'The first signe of
land were certaine fowles which they knew to be of India: the second,
boughes of palmes and sedges: the third, snakes swimming in the water.'

In 1586 a merchantman captained by Thomas Cavendish appeared
off Natal. Three years later the first English ship to sail right into East
African waters, the *Edward Bonaventure*, dropped anchor at Zanzibar and

stayed for three months, waiting for the monsoon to change before
sailing on to India. The crew thought highly of the food the Zanzibaris
had for sale. This visit was branded by Lisbon as sheer piracy, since the
vessel had entered the Indian Ocean without their permission. Such
complaints counted for nothing with the English, whose buccaneering
heroes, Drake and Hawkins, had shown how to pillage the Spanish
claimants to the other half of the world. Moreover, Portugal was by
now under Spanish rule, and after 1588 the English felt free to sail where
they pleased in the world, given their victory over the Great Armada.[6]

The English interlopers soon found themselves sailing the same routes
around Africa as another northern European nation, the Dutch. These
newcomers were able to profit from the insights supplied by a compatriot
with a unique knowledge of the Portuguese empire: Jan van Linschoten
had spent five years in India, working as a clerk for the archbishop of
Goa. Since the archbishop belonged to the highest councils of the state,
Linschoten was ideally placed to learn how the system operated. By
1590, immediately on his return to Europe, he was hard at work detailing
everything he had discovered about the Cape. The captains of the first
Netherlands fleet to venture to the East were able to read Linschoten's
Itinerario before they sailed in 1596. It was speedily recognized as an
invaluable handbook for all challengers to the 'Portingales'; by 1598 an
English version was in print.

The English would doubtless have relished the complaint of a Portuguese captain in whose ship Linschoten had sailed home. While trying
to round the Cape in a storm the captain 'marvelled at nothing so much
as why our Lord God suffered them [the Portuguese], being so good
Christians and Catholics as they were, to pass the Cape with so great
torments and dangerous weather, having so great and strong ships, and
the Englishmen, being heretics and blasphemers of God with so small
and weak vessels, passed the Cape so easily.'

Linschoten had kept his eyes well open even on the journey out to
Goa, when his ship stopped at Mozambique. He noted that the fort
there had 'but small store of ordinance or munition, as also not any
soldiers more than the Captain and his men that dwell therein'. (When
Netherlands ships later arrived off East Africa they found this account
of Portuguese ill-preparedness entirely true, and were quick to exploit
it.)

Linschoten's minor post in the religious hierarchy was an ideal shield
for his genteel espionage. He wrote about the best months for voyages

according to the monsoon seasons, the times when trade goods reached Goa from every part of the Indian Ocean, and how they were auctioned. But he also had an eye for social customs, and collected many anecdotes of geographical interest. One of his more intriguing snippets of information was that 'certain Moors' were in the habit of crossing Africa between Angola and Sofala. Two centuries were to pass before any written evidence confirmed such journeys.

Accounts by Linschoten and other early travellers had stimulated Dutch financiers to send their first fleets into the Indian Ocean. The cargoes brought back to Amsterdam earned such immense profits that the burghers rang their church bells with delight when homecoming ships hove into sight. Nevertheless, little had been learned in a hundred years about how ordinary seamen could survive scurvy and other diseases during many months at sea, or how fleets should best cope with violent weather. Cornelis de Houtman's four ships returned from Java in 1597 with little more than a third of their 249 sailors still alive – much the same proportion as Vasco da Gama had brought back. Even Jacob van Neck, a brilliant captain, lost a third of his vessels in the South Atlantic and the Indian Ocean.

These teething troubles had to be borne, for just as the economy of Portugal was transformed at the beginning of the sixteenth century after the costly explorations by Vasco da Gama and his successors, so was the Dutch republic's economy at the start of the seventeenth century by de Houtman and those who sailed in his wake. Resolutely, the shipowners of Amsterdam applied themselves to reducing the hazards of long-distance voyages. The disciplines of the republic were duplicated at sea, Dutch ships becoming renowned for their cleanliness. All vessels obeyed codes of conduct, prayers were read and psalms sung twice daily, and any man who absented himself was fined.

The probings by Dutch and English ships had quickly led to historic actions in Amsterdam and London. Rival East India companies were set up (the Dutch committed eight times the capital and four times as many ships as the English). Both were awarded charters bestowing thinly-disguised governmental status, and were granted national monopoly rights for trading anywhere between the Cape of Good Hope and the Pacific. Although the directors of these two companies were far more interested in profits than power, they well knew that an all-out trial of strength with Portugal and its Spanish overlord was only a short distance over the horizon. The Portuguese were equally aware of it: they hanged two Dutch captains who had been caught and sent to Goa by the rajah of Cochin after coming ashore on the Malabar coast to buy pepper.

The Dutch Vereenigde Oost-Indische Compagnie (VOC) had been given a provocative list of rights and duties, including the building of 'fortresses and strongholds', the enlisting of military and naval staff, the signing of treaties, and the fighting of defensive wars. Although the Portuguese were, quite literally, going to be first in the firing line, the English and the Dutch were aware that in time even the Indian Ocean might not be big enough to accommodate the burgeoning ambitions of both of them. It was a sign of this incipient competition that the charters were granted within two years of one another.

However, the Anglo-Dutch rivalry was for the future. First, Lisbon's puny grip on the eastern markets must be loosened. By 1605 the VOC had ranged as far as the Moluccas, on the same line of longitude as Japan, to capture the Portuguese fort at Amboina. The gauntlet had been thrown down, and any illusion harboured in the East that the appearance of these blustering blond-haired newcomers might bring relief from the cruelties of the Portuguese was soon swept away. The northern Europeans proved far more efficient but no less brutal. The equivalent of Afonso de Albuquerque, one hundred years on, was the Dutch governor-general, Jan Pietersz Coen. Even some of his countrymen complained that his sadistic atrocities were not merely unchristian, but bad for business.

Within twenty years the Portuguese were under pressure on every side. Scores of their ships had been sunk or captured and their forts were under siege. As early as 1607 and 1608 the Mozambique fortress, whose vulnerability had been so precisely noted by Linschoten, was attacked by Dutch fleets carrying regiments of troops. The town surrounding the fortress was razed, but the heavily outnumbered defenders withstood two sieges. The desire of the Dutch had been to destroy the vital 'refreshment station' between Lisbon and Goa. Thwarted, they contented themselves with trying to intercept Portuguese convoys as they emerged from the Mozambique channel.

Six thousand miles further east, Dutch freebooters attacked the prosperous Macau settlement on the China coast in 1622, but were driven off, mainly by a contingent of African slaves the Portuguese kept in the fort.[7] In the same year a brazenly-entitled 'Defence Fleet', led by the Dutchman Jacob Dedel in the *Good Fortune*, with the Englishman Michael Green in the *Royal Exchange* as second-in-command, hurried westwards from a foray in Indonesia to intercept the annual convoy from Lisbon to Goa. The Anglo-Dutch force caught the Portuguese carracks unawares off Mozambique, attacked without mercy and caused havoc.

Aboard one of the carracks was a Jesuit priest, Jerónimo Lobo, and he gives an eye-witness account of how the marauders were sighted in the moonlight and mistaken at first for Arab trading ships. When dawn broke there was a day-long battle. Casualties were heavy, and Lobo relates how he tore up his shirt to staunch the wounds of a sailor whose leg had been blown off. Three Portuguese carracks were lost, two through running aground while giving battle close inshore. But Dutch attempts to capture the Mozambique fortress by land assaults were once more unavailing.

The year 1622 also saw an action of far greater consequence than these bloody skirmishes. At the mouth of the Persian Gulf the English played a decisive part in driving the Portuguese from the port of Hormuz, the scene of Albuquerque's last great triumph in 1515. Their ally in this battle was the Persian ruler Shah Abbas, and the victory broke a vital link in the chain of Portuguese strongpoints in the Indian Ocean, opening the Gulf to agents of the East India Company. The loss of Hormuz was a wounding blow to Lisbon, since the port had been the richest source of customs revenue in the Estado da India.

On the winning side, this aggressive pursuit of commercial advantage had its human price. One casualty was the renowned English seafarer William Baffin, who a few years before had vainly searched for a route to China round the north of America, and in the process discovered the Arctic island which still bears his name. Baffin, a captain in the English fleet, died in the preliminary attack on the fortress of Kishm, on the opposite side of the straits from Hormuz. The fleet's doctor later related how it happened: 'Master Baffin went ashore with his geomentricall instruments for the taking of the height and distance of the Castle wall, for the better levelling of his peece to make his shot; but as he was about the same he received a small shot from the castle into his belly, wherewith he gave three leapes, by report, and died immediately.'[8] It was one incident in a long war of attrition.

Even Goa was threatened; the Portuguese ships in its harbour had repeatedly to come out and fight, even though severely outnumbered. They were driven to this by an Anglo-Dutch blockade – perhaps the first time any port had been subjected, year after year, to a deliberate tactic of commercially starving it to death. When the monsoon was blowing from the north-east, the time of year when the Portuguese ships were fully laden and due to start their voyage in Europe, powerful fleets would appear off Goa. There they hovered menacingly, ready for battle, until the monsoon reversed and the Portuguese were no longer able to sail out of harbour. The English and the Dutch then departed, to harass the Portuguese in Ceylon, only to return six months later.[9]

Desperate at what was happening so rapidly to their empire, some Portuguese commanders resorted to savage retaliation. The most ruthless was the aristocratic Ruy Freyre Andrade, a knight of the Order of Christ. At one time the English had Andrade in their hands, and a description of him survives: 'A proper tall gentleman, swarthie of colour, sterne of countenance, few of words, and of excellent spirit.' His custom was to put all prisoners to the sword, 'without mercy to age or sex . . . not leaving anything with life . . . nor one stone upon another'. After capturing Lima, a Persian fort near Hormuz, he 'laid waste with fire and sword, destroying people, goods and houses'. On his orders the town of Bramim was sacked: 2,000 Persians, many of them only children, were beheaded.

After their loss of Hormuz the Portuguese devoted themselves to hunting down English and Dutch merchant ships in the Gulf. Their base was a powerful fortress in Bahrain. During one battle, in 1625, an English ship, the *Lion*, caught fire and burned down to the water. Her eighty survivors were paraded before Ruy Freyre Andrade and he ordered the beheading of them all. The only man to be reprieved was the ship's cook, one Thomas Winterbourne, whom Andrade recalled as having fed him well during the time he was a prisoner of the English. The heads of the rest were wrapped up in silk cloths and sent to the nearest agent of the East India Company, 'as a present'.

Truces were negotiated in Europe from time to time by the three contending powers, but these were only grudgingly observed by the chartered companies in the Indian Ocean. For the Portuguese there could be but one outcome. In little over fifty years their commercial monopoly beyond the Cape was in tatters. The ultimate blow was the loss to the Dutch in 1658 of Ceylon, coveted both for its cinnamon and its strategic position.

At the same time, English traders were setting themselves up at various points on the Indian coast. This process was little heeded by the mighty inland rulers, although the East India Company would soon start extending its tentacles into their courts. One easy English acquisition was an undeveloped island and harbour north of Goa, called Bombay. It was part of the dowry of the Portuguese princess, Catherine of Braganza, when she became the bride of Charles II, and the king sent out 400 troops to occupy it. By the time they had done so, only ninety-seven were still alive. Soon finding he had no use for it, Charles sold Bombay to the East India Company for £10 in 1668.

Also bestowed by Catherine upon her new *milieu* was the fashion among the Portuguese aristocracy for drinking tea, until then a beverage of which the English knew little. It inspired the poet Edmund Waller to compose some couplets entitled 'Of Tea, Commended by Her Majesty':

> Venus has her myrtle, Phoebus has her bays;
> Tea both excels, which she vouchsafes to praise.
> The best of queens, and best of herbs we owe
> To that bold nation which the way did show
> To the far regions where the sun does rise,
> Whose rich productions we so justly prize.
> The Muse's friend, tea doth our fancy aid,
> Repress those vapours which the head invade,
> And keeps that palace of the soul serene
> Fit on her birthday to salute the Queen.

However, such amiable sentiments were far from the mind of Antonio de Mello de Castro, viceroy of Goa, when he wrote about Bombay to the king of Portugal: 'I confess at the feet of your Majesty that only the obedience I owe to your Majesty, as a vassal, could have forced me to this deed [the cession of Bombay], because I foresee the great troubles that for this neighbourhood will result to the Portuguese; and that India will be lost, on the same day as the English nation is settled in Bombay.' So it would prove. The Portuguese may have done the English a service by introducing them to tea. They had certainly done themselves a disservice by so casually giving up Bombay.

The relentless encroachment of the Estado da India by its rivals was watched with glum dismay by Lisbon's bankers and merchants. Early in the seventeenth century large fleets had been assembled in the Tagus each spring for the momentous round voyage, usually taking thirty-six months to Goa and back; but as the century wore on the annual fleets diminished to a few overloaded ships. These were equally laden on the way home, with boxes strewn across the decks and baskets lashed to planks projecting over the sides.

There was also an inclination to build vessels which were too large and unwieldy for their crews to handle in rough weather. Shipwrecks became more frequent, most of them happening on the Natal coast between the Cape and the Mozambique channel, through the failure of ill-prepared, under-crewed ships to cope with contrary winds and currents. Harrowing tales published in Lisbon, under the title *The Tragic History of the Sea*, were read with horrified fascination by generations of Portuguese. They told of the tribulations of survivors from these disasters, how they struggled along the rocky African shore, trying to reach Sofala and other settlements. Few managed to do so.

One of those shipwrecked near the Cape was the much-travelled Jesuit, Jerónimo Lobo. It happened in 1635, while he was on the way home to Lisbon. On reaching the safety of the shore he surveyed the wreckage: 'The beach we were traversing was all strewn with the riches of the Orient – spices, clothing, gilded objects, and quantities of chests and boxes.' Lobo found himself a hut to live in, and filled it up with fine inlaid furniture dragged from the water's edge. Eventually he and the other survivors were picked up, leaving all this treasure behind.[10]

It is a scene which epitomizes the failure of the Portuguese. They had seemed for a moment to have the wealth of half the world in their grasp, but could not hold it. Partly this was due to failures of confidence at crucial moments, in particular when Portugal fell under the bitterly resented Spanish rule, and lost many of its finest ships in Philip II's disastrous war with England.

Even without that setback, however, Portugal could never have hoped for long to fend off both the British and the Dutch. Their combined strength was several times that of Portugal. Above all, this was a contest between an archaic regime which all too often confused rhetoric and panoply with power, and emerging capitalist systems pursuing commercial objectives. Portuguese energies were still split between spice-trading and winning converts for Catholicism. The Dutch and English were concerned with making profits.

For Vasco da Gama and his immediate successors everything had seemed possible. Within 150 years, their hopes were strewn along the strand of history, the shipwreck of an empire.

THIRTY-THREE

Calvinists,
Colonists and Pirates

> They know that the inordinate desire of riches is the Root of all
> mischief, a Raging famisht Beast, that will not be satisfied, a
> bottomless Gulf that cannot be filled, a very Dropsie, wherein by
> desire of drinke a man may sooner break his Bowels than quench
> his Thirst.'
>
> — Walter Hamond. *A paradox proving that the inhabitants of Madagascar,*
> *or St Laurence (in temporal things) are the happiest people*
> *in the world . . . (1640)*

ULTIMATELY, European ambition in the entire Indian Ocean region
was governed by the relationships with India itself. The sub-continent
was always the crux, the keystone of power. As Lord Curzon would later
put it: 'The possession of India is the inalienable badge of sovereignty in
the eastern hemisphere.' However, acquiring that badge was long
beyond European abilities. Even had the Iberian roles been reversed in
the age of discovery, with the Pope giving the eastern half of the world
to mighty Spain, it would never have been able to conquer and colonize
India as it did the Americas. The Mughals and the Hindu monarchs
would have proved far less overawed and far more obdurate than Monte-
zuma of Mexico or Atahualpa of Peru.

Much later, after the industrial revolution, European power was
asserted over India and some other parts of Asia, as well as nearly all of
Africa: the crucial difference from what had happened in the Americas
was that instead of permanent colonization and the overlaying of one
culture upon another, this domination would in general take the form
of a transient colonialism.

Nevertheless, Europeans had earlier installed themselves – permanently, it might have seemed – at several vantage points around the
Indian Ocean area. Apart from the Goa enclave, the earliest settlement
of any size was the cluster of *prazo* plantations along the Zambezi valley.[1]

However, its links with white culture were tenuous; although Tete, the biggest town in the interior, did have a Christian church designated as a cathedral, 'Zambezia' was essentially an Afro-*mestico* culture, leavened by Hindu traders who had emigrated from Goa. It survived through symbiotic relationships with the surrounding indigenous kingdoms. In contrast, a far more distinctively European settlement was soon to be established further south, on the tip of the African continent.

Although some Portuguese had noted the likeness of the climate and scenery of the Cape to that of Europe, the spring departure from Lisbon always brought them in sight of Table Mountain's 3,500-feet summit during mid-winter in the southern hemisphere. The next 1,000 miles were along an exposed coast with contrary currents and a rocky shoreline upon which many carracks met their doom. So they were always glad to push beyond the Cape, to reach Mozambique in time to catch the *kaws* monsoon to India. On the return journey, their only desire was to be back in the Atlantic, sailing northwards on the last lap home. Now and then a Portuguese ship would anchor in Table Bay harbour, and a few huts were built on the shore, but Lisbon never seriously laid claim to the place.

By the early seventeenth century, ships had begun passing the Cape at most seasons of the year. The Dutch, in particular, were less dependent upon the Indian Ocean monsoons, since the region where their trading company made most profits was in south-eastern Asia. To reach it their East Indiamen sailed straight across the ocean, taking advantage of the trade winds south of the equator. So the Dutch captains began to make a habit of calling in at Table Bay. They left letters in glass bottles tied to posts for their compatriots. The place was uninhabited, apart from the pale-skinned Khoikhoi pastoralists (derisively nicknamed 'Hottentots' by the Dutch in imitation of their click-language).[2]

By the start of the seventeenth century, more interest was being taken in the possibilities of the Cape. Captain Joris van Spilbergen wrote that it was 'healthy and temperate'. All kinds of crops could be grown and deer grazed in the beautiful valleys. In 1611 an English merchant, Thomas Aldworth, on his way to India, decided that he had 'never seen a better land in his life'. He urged the founding of a settlement: 100 convicts should be put ashore there every year, with guns to man a fort. The East India Company paid no attention to this idea.

In 1647 a storm wrecked the Dutch ship *Haerlem* in Table Bay and the sixty survivors were stranded for almost a year. By the time another company ship picked them up they had built defendable quarters and had grown to like the place: the 'Hottentots' seemed friendly, crops grew easily, the climate was good. The directors of the VOC in Amsterdam listened thoughtfully to the sailors' descriptions, since they were also coming to see the Cape as a strategic point which their enemies, the Portuguese and Spanish, might occupy to harass passing Dutch vessels. In effect, it could hold the keys to the Indian Ocean.

The company acted swiftly, by the standards of the time. In April 1652 a party of ninety artisans, led by Jan van Riebeeck, was put ashore with orders to build a strong fort and start growing crops. Six thousand acres were marked off with an almond hedge to keep out inquisitive locals. The one disagreeable aspect of the long Cape peninsula was its attachment to the mainland, to the threatening vastness of Africa. As the Portuguese knew well, islands were safer. So there was even thought of turning the peninsula into an island by digging an eight-mile canal from Table Bay to the more southerly False Bay. The scheme was soon abandoned as too costly.

Van Riebeeck, a ship's doctor, spent ten years creating the nucleus of what was to become Kaapstad (Cape Town). A few men whose contracts with the company had expired chose to stay on as 'free burghers', and their women began coming out from the Netherlands to join them. The 'Seventeen' VOC directors had mixed feelings about all this, for they still envisaged Table Bay as no more than a station where their ships could call in for water and victuals, or where urgent repairs could be made. They never wanted the responsibility of a colony at the Cape, since it offered little prospect of trade or profit. The first governors were told to discourage settlers.

The company was influenced in its attitude by the vexing cost of the island of Mauritius. This Indian Ocean outpost had been occupied as early as 1598, because the magnificent harbour offered a refuge in the lonely seas to the east of Madagascar; moreover, sugar cane brought from Java had grown well there, and the dodo was (until exterminated in the 1680s) a good source of meat. For all that, the island was looked at askance by the cost-conscious VOC directors. It produced nothing saleable. After little more than a century, Mauritius would be abandoned.

However, there was difficulty in being too strict about the Cape at a time when the Dutch republic was at its pinnacle of prosperity, the age when Rembrandt and many lesser artists made their livings by painting the likenesses of complacent Amsterdam merchants grown rich on the sale of spices, silks and Chinese porcelain.[3] The VOC thrived and the Cape settlement expanded inexorably. Its inhabitants felt safe from attack by other nations – even by the English, against whom the Dutch fought three naval wars in the second half of the seventeenth century. The place was well defended, since one or two well-armed ships were almost always lying at anchor in the bay on their way to or from the East. There was also a castle, garrisoned by musketeers, although they were poorly paid and badly trained.

A new element was injected into the settler population in 1685, with the arrival of 180 French Huguenots fleeing from the persecution in their homeland; more soon followed. Their religious beliefs were fittingly Calvinistic. Moreover, they were industrious farmers, who planted vine-yards and were not unwilling to labour with their own hands. During the twenty-year governorship of Simon van der Stel (1679–99) the Cape settlement had taken shape as something far more than an anchorage for taking on food and water. By 1720 there was a white population of 2,000, with an equal number of black slaves.

If what was destined to become the Cape Colony had grown despite the first intentions of the VOC, the acquisition of Ceylon was always a deliberate goal. This island of cinnamon and semi-precious stones, dangling like a pearl from the sub-continent, so delighted the Seventeen that they contemplated calling it New Netherland (the original colony of that name, in the Americas, having been lost to the English in 1664).

Ceylon was won at heavy cost, for the Dutch had found themselves not only up against the Portuguese settlers, but also against the true inhabitants. The Sinhalese captured more than 300 Dutch soldiers and took them to Kandy as hostages; the commander, Adrian van der Stel, was killed and his head sent down to his compatriots at the coast. Documents reveal that the Hollanders had wanted all along to seize the whole island, even though governor Jan Maatsuyker had told Raja Sinha, the king of Kandy, in 1646: 'It was not in the expectation of much profit that we first brought our force to this island, but only with the desire to do Your Majesty service.' A despatch to governor-general Antonio van Dieman from the VOC directors seven years earlier shows that the Sinhalese were, in truth, only pawns in the struggle between two imperialist powers: 'The time has come for driving the Portuguese from their strongholds and depriving them of their supremacy in the Indies and taking their place. The present time seems most opportune to accomplish this.' Shortly before that was written, van Dieman had begun a full-scale invasion of Ceylon, with the encouragement of Raja Sinha, who then believed that ousting the Portuguese was the lesser of two evils.

Several desperate battles were fought. The Portuguese shored up their own troops with black slaves, and in one encounter at least 300 *'kafirs'* were involved. The Dutch used Sinhalese auxiliaries. A decisive contest took place at the south of the island in March 1640 for possession of Galle, the ancient port which the Chinese fleets had visited three centuries earlier. The Dutch commanders threw in 700 men; 100 were killed and 400 wounded before the Portuguese ran up the white flag on their fort. Hundreds of Portuguese, with their families and slaves, were taken prisoner. It was their fate to be transported more than 2,000 miles to Batavia, but many died on the way.

The English were already becoming alarmed by the acquisitions made by these erstwhile allies, whom they nicknamed 'the Butterboxes'. When the Dutch captured several Portuguese forts in Malabar they also cut deep into English commerce in southern India. The main trading station at Surat reported to London that 'the insolent Dutch domineere in all places, styling themselves already kings of the Indian seas'; as for the Portuguese, they were in a 'most miserable predicament'.

The end effectively came in Ceylon when Colombo fell to 2,000 Dutch troops after a siege lasting seven months. The trapped Portuguese had responded with fanatical courage to the ruthlessness of the besiegers, who committed many atrocities in the hope of breaking their will to resist. Starving women and children trying to escape from the siege were driven back, so adding to the pressures on the last food reserves in the redoubt. Finally, a few score men staggered out to surrender. The victors were implacable: when they discovered that a Hollander regarded as a traitor was already dead they sought his grave, dug up the corpse and hanged it upon a gallows.

What the Dutch inherited was an island ravaged in spirit and almost ruined economically. Ricefields had been abandoned, ancient dams and reservoirs breached, irrigation systems gone to ruin, villages emptied of their inhabitants, and the roads infested with herds of wild elephants. The Portuguese also left behind a religious legacy: many former Buddhists in the coastal districts regarded themselves as converts to a crude version of Catholicism (they knew how to make the sign of the cross and say one or two prayers). Later, attempts by the Dutch Reformed Church to assert a religious supremacy in Ceylon were constantly being thwarted by bands of *mestico* Catholic missionaries who descended on the island from Goa. Furthermore, the Dutch were to find themselves in conflict with Buddhist priests.

A succession of governors-general struggled to revive trade and agriculture. The hope was to make Ceylon a symbol of national enterprise, outshining the efforts of the English in India itself. Above all else was the need to collect and export cinnamon bark, a spice which held the promise of huge profits in Europe. Since there was much labouring to be done, Tamil slaves were imported from the Coromandel coast of South India, branded with the VOC symbol, then worked until they dropped.[4]

The Dutch combined harshness with remarkable efficiency, for within two years of taking full control of the island they were able to double the cinnamon exports to Amsterdam to 515,000 lb, and four years later raise them to more than 1,500,000 lb. Profits were enhanced because cinnamon was much in vogue with the well-to-do in Europe on account of its declared effectiveness in removing wind from the bowels. Amsterdam market prices almost doubled in the years 1654–64, from 1.9 to 3.6 guilders a pound, so the value of Ceylon's cinnamon exports rose fourfold in that brief time.

Vexingly, the Hollanders being installed as artisans and farmers soon proved of little value, so that hopes of turning Ceylon into a 'white' colony began to falter. The incoming governor-general, Ryckloff van Goen, complained in a despatch to Amsterdam in 1663: 'The bulk of our colonists were formerly soldiers or sailors, and are therefore uneducated people knowing no trade, only good for opening taverns and selling arrack ... We ought to make Ceylon self-supporting.'

It was not to be. Few of the burghers were willing to farm the land or engage in any other kind of honest toil. Moreover, by the start of the eighteenth century, they were becoming less and less Dutch, more and more influenced by the slave society in which they lived. Some popular dances, the 'Kafferina', 'Chikoti' and 'Baila', were performed to African rhythms. One dance was simply called the 'Mozambique'. The new settlers had also adapted to the Portuguese way of choosing brides from among the local Sinhalese population. Alternatively, they took *mestico* wives, who brought up their children to speak in the Portuguese patois. There was little alternative, despite the dismay of the Calvinist *predikants*. Few white women came out from Holland to this faraway tropical island.

The inter-marriage in Ceylon led to a sharp distinction between its social structure and that of the Cape, which was two-thirds of the way to India in sea miles, but generally less than half the distance in time. These two colonies were both administered under the Roman–Dutch law, but in contrasting environments. Although the VOC needed Table Bay to 'refresh' ships sailing to and from the East Indies, the Cape burghers never felt they themselves belonged to the East. Even those who had little chance, or wish, to return to Europe retained much of the culture of their home country, and Cape Town had become a fairly cosmopolitan place by the mid-eighteenth century.

In contrast, few visitors called at Colombo, the capital of Ceylon, and those who did tended to disapprove of it. The schools were poor, the churches ill-attended, and the quasi-European community seemed sunk in drink and vice. In a vain attempt to keep the races and religions apart it had been decreed that any Christian woman associating with a 'pagan' man should be flogged until the blood flowed, branded, put in chains for life and have her children enslaved.

Yet every year Ceylon was the gathering-point for the home-going fleets of Dutch East Indiamen. When the north-east monsoon set in, they assembled at Galle from distant ports with their cargoes of spices, muslins and silk. It was customary for the long voyage home to begin on Christmas Day, after the captains had prayed in Galle's Calvinist church. It was not only storms they feared. In times of war – as most times were – they faced being attacked by privateers in the waters around Madagascar, which lay directly athwart the route between Ceylon and the Cape.

The Dutch had always kept a wary eye on the activities in Madagascar of the other European powers, for the 'Great Island' had an obvious strategic value. Yet following the first assaults on the unsuspecting inhabitants by Albuquerque and other Portuguese, Madagascar had been, quite literally, by-passed. There was no gold; no elephants, so no ivory; no spices; and the island's potential as a source of slaves was only starting to show itself.

However, nine years before van Riebeeck's arrival at the Cape a settlement had been founded by the French at the southern end of Madagascar. The orders for this empire-building venture had been given in 1642, at the end of his life, by Cardinal Richelieu, chief minister to Louis XIII. Richelieu had believed fervently that France must not delay

in exerting its strength in the East, and Madagascar seemed well fitted
to be the stepping-stone to India. The settlement was named Fort
Dauphin in honour of the infant Louis XIV, who in later years would
formally annex Madagascar (larger in area than France) as part of his
empire. There were now four European powers seriously contending
east of the Cape of Good Hope: Portugal, Holland, England and France.

Richelieu's sense of urgency about the 'Great Island' had not been
misplaced, for in March 1645, just in advance of the establishment of
Fort Dauphin, a company of 140 English Puritans had landed in
St Augustine Bay, also in the south of the island. They intended to start
a colony like the one founded by the Pilgrim Fathers twenty-five years
earlier in Virginia. The idea had been encouraged by Walter Hamond,
a ship's doctor who had stopped at the island several times in the service
of the English East India Company. He claimed that its inhabitants,
the happiest people in the world 'in temporal things', would welcome
colonists. Hamond argued, in a book printed in 1640, for the 'hopeful
and fit plantation of a colony there, in respect of the fruitfulness of the
soyle, the benignity of the ayre, and the relieving of our English ships'.

Writing two years before Richelieu's initiative, Hamond argued that
'no Christian prince' could pretend to have title to Madagascar: 'And
the King of Spaine hath too many Irons in the fire already, to oppose
our people there, where they may enjoy the first fruits of a most plentiful
Harvest, which is better than the gleanings of America.' This claim
reflected a belief widely held in England at the time that the Spaniards
(still ruling Portugal) enjoyed too strong a hold on the New World to
be dislodged from there. It was also the heyday of the English merchant
adventurers who dreamed of starting colonies all over the world: men
such as Sir William Courten, who had landed 1,850 settlers on Barbados
in 1627; only his death had pre-empted a similar enterprise in Madagascar. More's *Utopia* and Sir Francis Bacon's *New Atlantis* encouraged
the dream of establishing ideal societies far from the greed and strife of
Europe.

An even more fulsome prospectus for Madagascar than Hamond's
was published by a merchant named Richard Boothby in 1646. By then
the Puritans had already arrived, but it was too soon to know how they
were faring. Boothby forecast that Madagascar would exceed 'all other
Plantations in America or elsewhere'. But the unhappy settlers had
already learned differently. The soil where they had disembarked proved
infertile and the natives were anything but friendly, having learned by

now to equate Europeans with slavery. The would-be settlers were besieged behind their palisade until they were dying of starvation.

Only twelve of the original 140 ever returned to England. A few were rescued and taken to India, and in 1647 a ship called the *Sun* carried three women and a preacher to Mauritius. One survivor, Powle Waldegrave, wrote a bitter response to the books which had advertised Madagascar as a 'true Earthly Paradise', saying that Hamond would have done better to stick to his labours as a surgeon.[5]

Fort Dauphin lasted much longer than the Puritan settlement, and was far more costly in lives. At least 4,000 French settlers and soldiers were sent out before it was finally abandoned in 1674, and few returned. Many died from disease, others in clashes with local communities. With steady support from the home country the settlement might have stood a better chance, but years could pass without the arrival of any French ship. The rump of the garrison was withdrawn to the island of Réunion (then called Bourbon), and to Pondichéry, France's main trading station in India. Twenty years later a Dutch captain visited Fort Dauphin and found it was being ruled by 'King Samuel', a pirate from Martinique in the West Indies. Commanding a gang of twenty white outlaws, 300 local militia, and a fleet of outrigger boats, Samuel lorded it over a long stretch of Madagascar's southern coastline.

The Dutch planted no colony on Madagascar but had purchased slaves there for their sugar plantations in Mauritius; the island was later to be exploited as a source of labour for the Cape. Hollanders had also been the first to recognize the ethnic link with Indonesia, from the similarity between the languages spoken in their possessions on the eastern side of the Indian Ocean and that used by the Malagasy élite. It was in the central massif, where mountains rise to more than 6,000 feet, that the distinctly Indonesian people known as the Hova were most strongly entrenched, exerting power over smaller communities.

Through the centuries, most of the island's population had been coloured by the African connections, especially along the western coastline only two days' sailing from Mozambique. In earlier times the 'Waqwaqs' had brought over slaves to work for them. Later, the Arab traders had imported Africans into their settlements at the northern end of the island. In the lowlands there were also many colonies of runaway blacks known as 'maroons'. By the late seventeenth century, Madagascar had become a recognized source of slaves for America's plantations. Some were brought across to the coastal barracoons from Mozambique in small craft, others captured during raids on the nearby Comoro islands. The slavers paid with guns, bangles, cloth, iron bars and brandy, then shipped their purchases round the Cape. English ships were so active in this trade that as many as eight of them would sometimes be anchored off the same depot, for Malagasy slaves were far cheaper than those from Guinea, where intense competition had driven up prices. A significant minority of plantation labourers in Barbados and neighbouring Caribbean islands came from Madagascar; others were shipped to Jamaica.

When the chance presented itself, in the shape of a lone merchant ship sailing past Madagascar, some slave-traders were tempted into high-seas robbery. They sought their prey in rivalry with cut-throats who had migrated to the Indian Ocean from the more crowded Caribbean. Soon Madagascar became notorious as the latest haunt of pirates. Romanticized reports of the luxurious lives of these buccaneers began to reach Europe, reviving the fallacy, originally promoted by Hamond, that the island was a subtropical Eden. The coastline, surrounded by coral reefs, certainly served as a hideout for sea-rovers of many nations, and one of the offshore islands, St Mary's, was a favourite rendezvous.

Pirates from Madagascar began venturing as far north as the Red Sea to prey on merchant shipping, although their problem was where to sell the loot without risk of arrest. Usually the best they could hope for was a visit by some bold accomplice, sailing in the guise of an honest merchantman, carrying arms, ammunition, clothes and liquor, to be exchanged for the captured treasure. A few of these covert supply-ships came from New England and were probably the first American vessels to enter the Indian Ocean.

According to the eighteenth-century chroniclers of the pirates, some were rather more than just blue-water vagabonds: an astonishing legend grew up around a Captain Misson from Provence, known for the elegance of his dress and the fervour of his language. He is reputed to have joined forces with Father Caraccioli, a renegade Dominican priest, to found the 'Republic of Libertalia' in Diego Saurez Bay at the northern tip of Madagascar. Tom Tew, an English pirate from Plymouth, threw in his lot with them.[6]

They and their followers proclaimed that it was more honourable for a man to steal from the rich with only the protection of his courage than to steal from the poor under the protection of the law, in the way legitimate power was generally used. The motto of Libertalia was 'For God and Liberty' and it even had a rudimentary parliament in which a kind of Esperanto was spoken. One of the sloops built by Misson was called *Childhood*.

Libertalia was short-lived. Although its seaward defences were so strong that it was able to repel an attack by a Portuguese fleet, there was no protection on the landward side, for Misson believed that the settlement had won the friendship of its Malagasy neighbours. One night he was proved wrong: the settlement was overrun. There were only forty-five survivors and among the dead was Caraccioli, the pirate-priest. That was the end of the pirates' republic.

Most famous of all the Madagascar corsairs was the Scotsman, Captain William Kidd, who had spent much of his life in New York before sailing to the Indian Ocean. When he returned to the Americas, escorting a rich prize, Kidd was arrested and taken to London. After a dubious trial he was hanged, still claiming to have been only an honest privateer, loyally fighting against the French. (A privateer captain carried a commission from his government, allowing him to hunt down enemy vessels, then loot their cargoes. If a captured ship was brought home as a prize, that was the real triumph; otherwise, the approved course was to sink it.)

Although English pirates, real and fictitious, were to be much celebrated by writers from Defoe to Robert Louis Stevenson, the French buccaneers were certainly more numerous. Early in the eighteenth century the Grand Mughal, through his governor in Surat, lodged a complaint with Louis XIV that these brigands were preventing his subjects from making the pilgrimage to Mecca. A French administrator in India conceded that the name of his country had indeed become synonymous with piracy.

Eventually the European powers would act in unison to 'sweep the seas clean', yet the French pirates left a lasting mark on Madagascar. They had given it a certain gallic ambience (quite apart from stimulating the violent tendencies of its people). In the wake of the pirates came French traders and adventurers, who pioneered routes into the interior. Despite its failure, Fort Dauphin had been a portent, a signpost on the road to colonialism.

THIRTY-FOUR

Ethiopia
and the Hopes of Rome

At length the sheep of Ethiopia freed
From the bad lions of the West
Securely in their pastures feed.
St Mark and Cyril's doctrines have overcome
The follies of the Church of Rome.
Rejoice, rejoice, sing Hallelujahs all
No more the western wolves
Our Ethiopia shall enthrall.
—from the Ethiopian Chronicle 1632 (trans. C. F. Rey)

AS THE INTRICATE CONFLICTS ebbed and flowed in the Indian Ocean, on the periphery lay a prize more precious, to some minds, than worldly power or wealth. Ethiopia began to offer a new and irresistible challenge, long after the illusions of the Prester John legend were swept away. The two Portuguese expeditions had revealed that the Ethiopians were brave but backward in warfare, and fervent but heretical in religion. The 'martyrdom' of Christofe da Gama, as described by his surviving companion-in-arms, Miguel de Castanhoso, made the first of these discoveries all too plain: Ethiopia's mountains were its only real defence against Islam. The second, the 'wayward' nature of Ethiopian Christianity, was exposed by the memoirs of Father Francisco Alvares, who had accompanied the first mission to the country.

This took on a new significance because of the religious convulsions shaking Europe. The Reformation, the rejection of Catholicism by the Protestants of northern Europe, led to the Counter-Reformation, and nowhere was this response more militant than in Portugal and Spain. Attention was being focused on heresy and heathenism everywhere. The fervour this generated was strong enough to bear the Catholic doctrine as far afield as Japan and Paraguay. The millions of souls in

Ethiopia, all brands to be saved from the burning of hell, were not to be ignored.

The Jesuits had failed disastrously among the heathens of the Zambezi, but they saw the Christians of the Blue Nile as heretics only through long isolation, true believers who might readily be made to abandon doctrinal errors. So a Portuguese Jesuit, João Nunes Barreto, had been consecrated in Lisbon to become the patriarch of the Ethiopian church. Two assistant bishops were appointed to support him. It typified the European assumption of superiority that the Ethiopians themselves, who had been obtaining their own patriarchs from Egypt for a thousand years, were not thought to merit a say in the matter. Dogmatism seemed to blind the Portuguese to all evidence brought back by their two earlier expeditions about the likely perils of this scheme for spiritual conquest. However, King John III did decide that an envoy, armed with suitable gifts, should go ahead to tell the Ethiopian emperor that the patriarch was on his way.

It was still possible, if hazardous, to enter Ethiopia, and the envoy, Dr Diego Diaz, reached the Red Sea safely and hurried inland from a small port south of Massawa, together with a Jesuit priest and a lay brother. The emperor, Claudius, welcomed him warmly, for the country still remembered with gratitude the help brought by Christofe da Gama's expedition in desperate times fourteen years earlier. The survivors of that expedition had been given farms, were raising families, and becoming prosperous by Ethiopian standards.

Then Claudius grew deeply vexed upon hearing that the Pope and the Franks had, without the least consultation, taken it upon themselves to send him a patriarch. According to Gonzalo Rodrigues, the priest accompanying Diaz, the emperor 'looked so much out of countenance and was so disordered that when we spoke to him he answered nothing to the purpose . . . he went away to visit a grandmother of his, eight or ten days off, leaving us in an open field wholly unprovided for'.

Relations grew even worse when Rodrigues composed a treatise on the doctrinal errors of the Ethiopians and asked for it to be translated into *Ge'ez* (Old Ethiopic). Although Claudius agreed, he speedily wrote a letter of protest to the Pope, insisting that the Ethiopians already walked 'straight and true', turning neither to the right nor left, 'in the doctrine of our Fathers, the twelve apostles and of Paul, the fountain of wisdom, and of their seventy-two disciples'. It was a ringing retort: 'Thus do I proclaim and thus do I teach, I, Claudius, King of Ethiopia.'

Before Diaz scurried away he was told that there were enough learned men in the country already. No more were needed. For good measure, Claudius then asked the Coptic Church in Egypt to send him a new *abuna* (who ordered, as soon as he arrived, that anyone reading the Jesuit treatise should be excommunicated). When the extent of this 'obstinacy' became known, the authorities in Goa felt it wiser to delay the voyage from India to Massawa of the Pope's chosen patriarch, Barreto. Instead, as assistant bishop, Andrew de Oviedo, was despatched to Ethiopia with five more Jesuits. (As matters turned out, Barreto never did make the crossing, but died, still in Goa, six years later, still awaiting the right moment.)

Only a matter of weeks after Oviedo and his determined Jesuit companions arrived in Massawa, the Turkish trap was shut behind them: the port became closed to all non-Muslims, and it would be five years before any messages filtered out. It then became known that matters had gone badly. Although the Jesuits were received with a wary politeness, Oviedo chose to boycott the royal court, then told all the Portuguese in the country that they need no longer obey the emperor's edicts. It was a provocative show of arrogance. Even so, Claudius was willing to debate points of doctrine with his uninvited guests, often winning the argument. The Ethiopians also showed a talent for mockery, presenting the celibate Jesuits with a book called *The Adultery of the Franks*.

Relations had already reached a low point when Claudius was killed on the Ethiopian border in renewed fighting with the Muslims. This was a disaster for Ethiopia (the skull of the emperor was exhibited triumphantly on a pillar for three years), and also a calamity for the Jesuits. The new emperor, Minas, wasted no time in showing his vexation with Oviedo by publicly beating him and threatening to run him through with a sword. For six months the defiant bishop was held prisoner, then had to live for a while in a cave, eating roots and herbs. Finally, the Jesuits were banished to a mountain-top in the north-east of the country, close to the ancient capital of Axum. There they scratched a poor existence and looked for ways to send messages to Goa. One of the priests tried to escape through Massawa, but was caught and killed by the Turks.

A few plaintive letters from Oviedo, written on pages torn from his prayerbook, did reach Europe. These made it plain that he regarded the doctrinal errors of the Ethiopians as far more important than the enmity of the Turks. One message appealed for a strong contingent of

Portuguese troops, 'who might easily make themselves masters of the seaports, rescue the other Portuguese, and compel the Ethiopians to submit to the See of Rome'. However, this proposal was looked at askance, as reflecting the Portuguese love of war rather than the true Christian spirit. Out of sight and largely out of mind, Oviedo died in 1577 and the mission began withering away.

Seven years later Pope Gregory XIII despatched three priests to sustain it, but none reached Ethiopia and one was killed by pirates. In 1595 another Jesuit was caught and beheaded by the Muslims after landing at Massawa in disguise. Finally, an Indian Christian – a Brahmin by birth and not a Jesuit – reached the lonely mission station by passing himself off as an Arab. There was nothing for him to do but lie low, hoping for the day when a new wave of Catholics might somehow enter the country.

One of the attempts to find a route had been made by two Spanish priests, Antonio Monserrate and Pedro Paez. It went awry almost instantly, for they were captured at sea by Muslims, shipped as prisoners to southern Arabia, and taken across the desert by camel and on foot to San'a in the Yemen. After three years in captivity there, they were moved on to the Red Sea port of Mocha and put to work as galley-slaves, rowing in a ship with three banks of oars.

Paez wrote later to a friend in Spain:

> Right through the night to dawn we were forced to remain sitting up, trying all the time to rid ourselves of the lice. As they fell on us from above we threw them into the sea; if when we were overcome by fatigue or sleep we lay down and covered our face, the lice forced us to get up and went on torturing us until morning . . . we had nothing to wear except some rags and a shirt. Our food was a handful of seeds like millet and nothing more.

Paez was only thirty-two, but Monserrate, by now almost sixty, was recognized by his captors as likely to die, so the two Franks were put instead to working in a quarry. At last, a young Syrian managed to take a message to Goa on their behalf. An Indian merchant was sent at once to Mocha to ransom them at any price, because Philip II had taken a personal interest in the fate of the missing Jesuits. After seven fruitless years, Monserrate and Paez arrived back in Goa, emaciated and disconsolate.

Five years later Paez was ready to try again. By now he was speaking perfect Arabic and was able to travel dressed as an Armenian, using the name Abdallah. After making friends with a Turk who was travelling up the Red Sea, and telling him he wanted to go inland at Massawa to collect the possessions of a friend who had died, Paez slipped past barriers where other Christians had come to grief. The friendly Turk waited at the port in vain for his return, but religious zeal overlaid any compunction Paez might have felt.

He reached the Ethiopian court in 1604, and found it in the throes of a dynastic conflict. A thirteen-year-old emperor named Jakob had just been overthrown by his uncle, Za-Dengel, who was twenty-six. There was little a European priest could do in such a crisis, and in any case Pedro Paez saw it as his first duty to visit Lake Tana, the source of the Blue Nile, having heard that the descendants of Christofe da Gama's soldiers were living there. After ministering to their spiritual needs he returned to the court and was welcomed with the startling news that Za-Dengel had decided to become a Catholic and intended to ask Europe to supply him with soldiers, artisans and more missionaries.[1] Paez was alarmed, foreseeing that this would only bring disaster, but his pleas for caution went unheeded. Within four months Za-Dengel had been killed in a rebellion sparked by this impetuous decision.

More years of confusion followed, until the throne was seized in 1608 by Susenyos, the son of a royal prince and a slave woman. Paez quickly made friends with the new emperor, who he said 'smiled very amiably on all' with his hazel eyes. The new emperor had a 'long but finely-proportioned face . . . his lips were thin, his beard black, his shoulders broad and brawny'.

In the years that followed, Paez strove to make himself indispensable to the emperor. The smouldering religious fires were damped down and the Spaniard devoted himself to practical work, calculated to show the benefit of following European ways. With a flair for architecture he offered to build the emperor a two-storey palace in white stone. Nothing like it had been done before in Ethiopia, so Paez recruited a team of artisans and taught them how to make stone-cutting tools. He also took on carpenters and trained them to copy European woodwork.

The palace in Gondar had a banqueting hall fifty feet long and its roof arches were supported on intricately carved columns. From a roof-top terrace, seventy feet above the ground, the emperor could enjoy a distant view of Lake Tana and see mountain peaks rising to 14,000 feet.

The overall design was like the country house of a Spanish aristocrat and the subjects of Susenyos came from every province to see this wonder. Paez went on to put up many more buildings, including a large church in the Italian style. He also interested himself in Ethiopian literature and encouraged the use of written Amharic in teaching. In nine years he wrought changes which would leave a lasting imprint on Ethiopian life.[2]

The more the emperor came to admire Paez, the more insistent he grew that Ethiopia must fulfil a debt of honour for the help given by Christofe da Gama seventy years before. That meant bringing the Ethiopian empire and its church into communion with Rome. Blindly devout, Susenyos declared that he would give the lead, by openly committing himself to Catholicism and rejecting the ancient rituals of his own church.

Although sensing that this was fated to unleash a murderous civil war, Paez could not forswear his Jesuit duty. He had done his best to win over the leading members of the court, and to isolate the Coptic *abuna*; even some prominent monks had opted for conversion. So, on 31 January 1613, he helped to compile letters to the Pope, to the Spanish king (now Philip III) and to the Portuguese viceroy in Goa. The emperor told the Pope that he was determined to 'render obedience to your Holiness' and asked to be sent a Catholic patriarch without delay.

Susenyos foresaw the peril he must soon be in, so he appealed for 1,500 European troops: 500 would occupy Massawa and patrol the coast, and 1,000 would help him in his war with the Muslims. What Susenyos really wanted was a praetorian guard, to defend him against the anger of his own people when he made his declaration for Catholicism. This was an impossible hope, and Paez must have known it.

Since secrecy was crucial, the letters to Europe would have to be sent by a route promising the least risk of interception. In the course of a decade, at least four other Jesuits had managed to slip through Massawa to help Paez, but getting out would be far harder. Susenyos insisted that the best chance for the two selected envoys – a Jesuit and an Ethiopian convert – lay in going overland to Malindi, the Indian Ocean port where Portuguese ships called regularly. It meant travelling for more than a thousand miles southwards across uncharted terrain occupied by predatory tribes, including the warlike Galla.[3] There is no evidence that such a journey had ever been made before.

The idea proved disastrous. Only a small distance beyond the southern boundaries of Ethiopia, while heading towards Lake Rudolph, the envoys were captured by a local ruler. When it became obvious that he was toying with the idea of killing them, the Jesuit priest managed to burn all the emperor's letters. The envoys were forced back northwards into Ethiopia; before they returned, after wasted months, the emperor had sent out a second batch of letters, this time northwards. These eventually reached the French consul in Cairo, and from there were sent to Rome. The Pope, Paul V, was eager to see military action in Ethiopia, arguing that 'almost innumerable souls' were at stake. However, nothing happened. The thunderclouds of his own folly were now gathering over Susenyos, who had even taken to dressing in the Portuguese style.

In May 1622, Paez died of malaria, after nineteen years in Ethiopia. He had lived to see the emperor, for better or worse, profess the Roman faith and receive the sacraments. A religious holocaust was now inevitable, and three years later the Roman patriarch for whom Susenyos had so long been waiting arrived in the country. He had come ashore in disguise at Beilur, a small harbour just inside the entrance to the Red Sea, and from there made a dangerous, exhausting trek across the Danakil desert to the highlands.

The patriarch was Afonso Mendes, a Portuguese savant whose learning was matched only by his fearlessness. He was also vain, fond of dressing with papal pomp, and utterly inflexible. As soon as he and his companion, Jerónimo Lobo, made contact with their fellow Jesuits, Mendes donned his religious robes and began a stately progress across the country with an entourage of servants, musicians and priests. The emperor was by now in a fervour of anticipation and as Mendes neared the court, on 7 February 1626, he was sent an escort of 15,000 cavalry. Crescendos of Ethiopian drumming were rivalled by the sound of guns fired in salute.

Before entering the church where Susenyos was to welcome him, Mendes halted at a tent. There he put on his mitre and patriarchal robes, then went forward on horseback at the head of a noisy procession. Inside the church he was met and embraced by the emperor, wearing a gold crown. Wasting no time, Mendes launched into an oration on the history of Christianity, up to this historic moment when Ethiopia was destined to bow the knee to Rome. Speaking in Latin and quoting liberally from Greek and Roman philosophers, Mendes was entirely

Emperor Susenyos welcomes the Patriarch Mendes, sent by the Pope to convert Ethiopia to Roman Catholicism. This event, in 1626, was swiftly to end in disaster. It was fancifully recreated by a French artist for the 1728 edition of Jerónimo Lobo's *Voyage Historique d'Abissine*

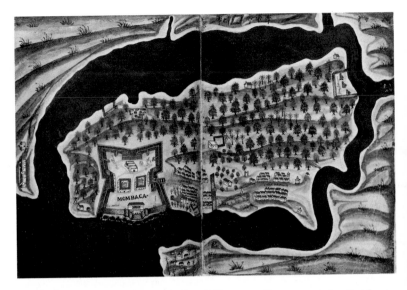

Bastion of Portuguese power on the East African coast for two centuries, Fort Jesus on Mombasa Island was lost after a three-year siege. The victors were from Oman, 2,500 miles to the north-east. The fort, now a tourist attraction, looks out over the harbour from which it was so often bombarded

Tipu Sultan, 'Tiger of Mysore,' (*right*) was an unrelenting foe of the East India Company and died fighting the British, sword in hand, in 1799. One of his proudest possessions (now in the Victoria and Albert Museum, London) was a life-size model of a tiger devouring a British soldier. A French-made mechanism emits the growls of the tiger and the screams of its victim. It had been Napoleon's dream to invade India; if he could have done so, Tipu would have been his strongest ally

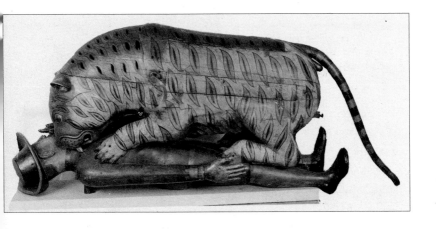

Table Bay settlement, founded by the Dutch East India Company in 1652 as a 'refreshment station' for its ships, was painted twenty-one years later by Aernaut Smit. Within half a century Cape Town was famed as the 'Tavern of the Two Seas,' and by the end of the eighteenth century the Cape Colony had 20,000 white settlers. Britain seized it during the Napoleonic wars

Hugh Cleghorn (*right*), Scottish professor and resolute spy, played a role in helping Britain acquire Ceylon. He inveigled a Swiss count, 'proprietor' of a mercenary regiment on the island, into helping him overcome Dutch resistance

German missionary Ludwig Krapf (*above left*) made the first successful European venture inland from the African coast. He sighted Mount Kenya in 1849. John Hanning Speke (*above right*) was foremost among the British army officers, mainly from India, who penetrated to the great lakes of the interior and 'discovered' the source of the Nile. Speke and James Grant, his companion on his second African journey (1860–63) made friends as they travelled; in an engraving based on one of his own sketches, Grant 'dances with an African queen' (*below*)

OPPOSITE Empire-builders: the German, Dr Carl Peters (*top left*), who in 1885 out-witted the British in East Africa with the connivance of Bismarck; Captain Frederick (later Lord) Lugard (*top right*), whose greatest assets in winning Uganda were his sang-froid and his Maxim machine-gun. The freebooter Tipu Tip (*inset*) abandoned his territories beyond Lake Tanganyika to retire in Zanzibar. There he was visited in 1903 by Richard Meinertzhagen (*bottom left*), a British officer who helped to 'pacify' the future Kenya and kept a brutally frank record of his actions

Lords of the coast and the interior: the Sultan of Zanzibar, Seyyid Said, and the Nyamwezi leader Mirambo, dubbed the 'black Napoleon' by journalist-explorer Henry Stanley. The East African dominion created by Seyyid Said was carved up in the Scramble for Africa, and Mirambo's empire collapsed after his death in 1884

The monsoon conquered. The age of steam ended two thousand years of Indian Ocean travel dictated by the seasonal winds. Ships of the P & O, such as the *SS Bentinck* illustrated here, and rival lines, sailing to precise schedules between the Red Sea and India, and then on to Singapore and Hong Kong, helped to bind the British Empire together unintelligible to almost all his congregation. That did not concern him, such was his self-esteem.[4]

Two days later the metaphor about bowing the knee to Rome became reality: the emperor publicly knelt before Mendes and took an oath of allegiance to the Pope. Whatever might have been in their hearts, his nobles and court priests followed suit. The patriarch immediately ruled that all churches must be reconsecrated, all clergy re-ordained, all believers re-baptized, all festivals fixed according to the Roman calendar. He meant to see Ethiopian Christianity riven to its foundations.

Although his arrival had coincided with a terrible plague of locusts, which the Coptic monks swore to be a sign of divine displeasure, it seemed at first as though Mendes was carrying all before him. His letters to Rome were triumphal. More Jesuits slipped into Ethiopia, energetically expanding mission stations, baptizing the peasants *en masse*, starting schools and writing manuals of religious instruction. With financial support from the emperor, a printing press was set up to help spread the Catholic message in Amharic. For the first time in the eastern half of Africa, Europeans had introduced the Latin alphabet to create a written form of an indigenous spoken language.

There was a more sombre side. Defiance was punished by hanging or burning at the stake. The more fortunate dissenters merely had their tongues cut out, and some Ethiopian monks threw themselves over precipices, rather than abandon their ancient beliefs.

Susenyos did his best to clear the path for the dedicated, celibate Jesuits by publicly condemning the Coptic archbishops for their fondness for corruption, keeping harems, deflowering virgins, and 'the foulest possible crimes, unmentionable in polite society'. But human failings could not nullify ancient beliefs. By 1628, rebellions against imposed Catholicism were breaking out in different parts of Ethiopia. The emperor's son-in-law was hanged, a leading general pushed off a cliff, battles were fought almost ceaselessly; in one, 8,000 men died. Protests were ringing out against Rome for having made the country 'drive its sword into its own bowels'.

In 1632 Susenyos was forced to abdicate and died three months later, heartbroken and exhausted; a Jesuit priest gave him the last rites. The new emperor, his son Fasiladas, had one overriding purpose: to drive out all Europeans and their alien dogma. The patriarch Mendes was quickly banished to the same mountain-top in the north-east of the country where half a century earlier his predecessor Oviedo had spent his last years. As the Jesuit missions were shut down, the whole country sang and danced with relief. Yet Mendes could not grasp how utterly Rome had been rejected. He began appealing to Goa for troops, hoping to use them to start an insurrection.

When Fasiladas realized that the Jesuits were calling for an invasion of his country, he told Mendes and all the European priests to leave Ethiopia at once if they valued their lives. After some fruitless intriguing on the coast, the patriarch and nine priests found themselves being forcibly sent to Suakin, further up the Red Sea. The local Turkish pasha at first fancied killing them, but finally decided to demand large ransoms from Portuguese India. The money was paid, as a cheaper option than sending a punitive expedition. Having been brought to safety, Mendes settled down in Goa, for ever asking, without real hope, to be sent back to his see at the head of a conquering army. He never returned to Europe, but died in India twenty years later.[5]

Seven Jesuits and an assistant bishop, Apollinaris de Almeida, had refused to leave Ethiopia. They were hunted down and two were beheaded. The rest were hanged in front of festive crowds attending a country fair. The Portuguese communities descended from the survivors of Christofe da Gama's expedition a century before were also expelled, although by now most of them were more African than European. They were forced westwards, down from the highlands into the Sennar regions between the Blue and White Niles, to vanish without trace.

Fasiladas banned all Europeans from entering Ethiopia, and even sought the help of the Muslim rulers in Aden and the Red Sea ports to make sure they were kept out. So when a party of Italian and French Capuchin fathers stepped ashore in Massawa they were killed at once. Their heads and skins, stuffed with straw, were sent to the emperor by the Turks, to assure him that his wishes were being followed.

More than a half a century after the final rejection of the Jesuits, a French doctor, Charles Poncet, was admitted by the emperor Yasu in 1698 as the envoy of Louis XIV. He noted in his diary that Ethiopians hated white grapes, because their colour reminded them of the Portuguese.

Another seventy years passed before the arrival of an adventurous Scotsman, James Bruce. He found that the Jesuits were still a bad memory, more than a century after the last of them had been expelled by Fasiladas. He made extravagant play with his own Protestant beliefs in discussions with Ethiopians, to distance himself from Catholicism:

'You have, in the first place,' said I, 'publickly called me Frank, the most odious name in this country, and sufficient to occasion me to be stoned to death without further ceremony, by any set of men, wherever I may present myself. By Frank, you mean one of the Romish religion, to which my nation is as adverse as yours.'

THIRTY-FIVE

The Great Siege
of Fort Jesus

🎔

How much of that abundant gold of Sofala, Mozambique, Kilwa and Mombasa came to our kings? How many of our people did not those islands of Querimba, Zanzibar, Mafia and Madagascar consume?

—Captain João Ribeiro (1685)

FOR FIFTY YEARS after the flight of Yusuf, the renegade sultan, Mombasa had dozed in the sun. The power of Portugal was ebbing away throughout the Indian Ocean and trade was meagre. Successive captains of Fort Jesus were indolent, or corrupt, or brutal, and sometimes all three. The rare foreign visitors to Mombasa commented upon the poverty of its citizens – a medley of Portuguese, mulattoes and Indians – in the rebuilt 'Foxhole'. The death-rate from fever and other tropical diseases was high, even among the captains.

There had been an ominous hint in 1661 of a harsh awakening to come with the appearance off Mombasa of a hostile fleet. It was commanded not by Turks, but by the ruler of Oman, Sultan Saif bin Khalifa, who eleven years earlier had shattered the myth that the Portuguese were invincible by driving them out of Muscat, their Arabian stronghold for almost 150 years. After that triumph the Muslims of East Africa had felt that their time of liberation was near and sent appeals to the sultan for help. Some rebellious Swahili in Mombasa even dared to send a delegation secretly. Now 800 of the sultan's men came ashore to plunder the Christian part of the town. They made no attempt to attack the fort, whose captain, Joseph Botelho da Silva, impotently watched them come and go, for he had only a handful of men under his command. The spoils taken back on the monsoon to Muscat, 2,500 miles to the north-east, included three Portuguese ships, captured at anchor in the harbour.

This was an omen. The Omanis were steadily growing in power, using warships of European design, and by 1669 sailed as far south as Mozambique island and almost captured it. North of Mombasa, ports such as Pate and Lamu were in open revolt, while Malindi, once the prized ally of Portugal, lay in ruins, its houses and mosques occupied by nomads.

A force from Goa led by the viceroy, Pedro d'Almeida, exacted harsh vengeance up and down the coast after the Omanis were gone, beheading the rulers of several towns and carrying off shiploads of booty. These raids and reprisals continued. The sultan of Pate and twelve of his sheikhs were transported to Goa and executed there on Christmas Day, 1688. Yet Portuguese power in the Indian Ocean was so reduced that there was no manpower to occupy the towns which had been punished.

All along the coast formerly known as the Land of Zanj[1] there were preparations for a holy war as the seventeenth century ebbed away. The scene was being set for one of the longest and most bizarre sieges in the history of warfare.

It began on 11 March 1696, when the Omanis arrived once more off Mombasa. There were seven ships carrying 3,000 men, mostly mercenaries from Baluchistan and other parts of North India. For two days, strong winds stopped the fleet entering the harbour, and after it had done so the Arab flagship grounded on a sandbank facing a small mainland fort guarding the harbour entrance. The flagship opened fire on the fort, at which the occupants – four Portuguese and 300 Swahili – abandoned it and fled. When the flagship had been floated off the sandbank the Omanis moved closer in, and put their troops ashore to occupy Mombasa town.

Some Portuguese civilians escaped by sea, but the rest fled into Fort Jesus. The veteran commander, João Roiz Leão, had a garrison of only fifty men, so he decided on bold action. In defiance of the standing order that in the event of an attack only Christians should be admitted to the fort, he invited in all the Swahili who could carry arms and had reason to be loyal to the Portuguese; these included refugees from towns along the coast which had refused to accept Omani leadership. By this means he mustered a force 2,500 strong inside the fort. The women and children of his Swahili militia installed themselves in the dry moat surrounding the walls. Warriors from a mainland people, the Segeju, also entered Fort Jesus. When the captain of the gate was rebuked for letting them in they went into Mombasa town, killed thirty Omani troops, and brought back their heads as a proof of loyalty.

Having marshalled his forces, the commander despatched a small ship to raise the alarm. It called first at Zanzibar, whose Swahili queen offered to supply food to Fort Jesus – a promise she would honour until the siege ended, despite punitive raids by the Omanis and their allies. After three months the ship returned, bringing food and twenty-eight Portuguese soldiers from the fort at Mozambique.

By this time the besieging Muslims had begun dying of smallpox. 'Big Ali', the Baluchi emir in charge of the Omani forces, left for Muscat with most of his men and all the ivory plundered from the town. About 900 soldiers, a mixture of Arabs, Baluchis and black mercenaries and slaves, were left behind. At this moment the defenders of Fort Jesus might have overwhelmed their foes, but Leão was too weak from fever to organize an attack. He died on 23 October. The siege was in its eighth month.

News of the Omani attack had now reached Goa. A realization that if Mombasa were lost, Mozambique could fall next, and the route from Lisbon to India be in peril, led to the hasty despatch of five vessels. They reached Mombasa on Christmas Day under the command of a nobleman, Luis de Melo de Sampaio.[2] There were fears that Fort Jesus might already have fallen, so a rowing boat was sent in to investigate. The first news it brought back was reassuring: the stronghold was still in Portuguese hands.

Another boat, sent out from the shore after midnight two days later, told a more alarming story. Only twenty Portuguese men, including three priests, remained alive inside the fort. Its defence now depended on the loyalty of the Swahili, who still numbered 1,500. The death-toll among the Portuguese had been caused less by combat than by fever and malnutrition. Many were weakened by venereal maladies, because their new commander, António Mogo de Mello, had allowed them to make visits to the moat, where some of the women refugees eked out a living by prostitution. Powder and shot were running low and the Omanis were keeping up a steady bombardment from earthworks they had thrown up close to the fort. The enemy had, moreover, been reinforced by 400 more black slaves from Arabia.

The appeal from the fort for reinforcements was desperate, although the prospect was scarcely inviting for those chosen to be sent ashore. Moreover, the first attempt, two days after Christmas, was a calamity.

A longboat with twenty soldiers was sent in to the harbour, followed by a small galley with twenty more. When the longboat came ashore, under heavy fire, right below one of the Arab entrenchments, the fort commander told some of his Swahili soldiers to run down to the water's edge and help the men in the boat to reach safety. But the Portuguese soldiers mistook their would-be rescuers for the enemy; they jumped into the water, others swam to parts of the shore controlled by the enemy, a few probably drowned. Only ten men reached the fort. The galley also suffered losses, but managed to unload most of its soldiers and a cargo of rice.

What the defenders most wanted was for the fleet to come right into the harbour, 'soften up' the besieging force with a bombardment from close range, then put several hundred soldiers ashore to regain control of the entire island. There was a council of war in the flagship to discuss this idea, but Sampaio lacked the courage to live up to his grandiose title, 'General of the Mombasa Relief Force'. Instead, the ships stayed outside at anchor, while food and ammunition were ferried in under fire.

The defenders did not control enough of the fort's perimeter to bring supplies in through the main gate, so these had to be unloaded on the exposed beach in front of the outworks. Unfortunately, the door from the outworks into the passage leading to the interior of the fort was too small for barrels to be pushed through. The barrels had to be opened on the beach and the contents carried in piecemeal; sometimes they were hit by enemy fire, so that the losses during the operation, of both manpower and supplies, were severe.

By mid-January 1697, the 'General of the Relief Force' decided he had done enough. He told the defenders in the fort that he was leaving for Mozambique, but would return. The news was received with horror: two Augustinian friars made the hazardous trip to the flagship to put a last plea for a full-scale assault on the island. Their appeals were brushed aside. On 25 January the flagship, the frigate *San António de Taná*, raised its anchors and disappeared. Another ship was left with orders to blockade the entrance to the harbour, but its captain waited only until the flagship was over the horizon. Then he left, heading for Zanzibar. The defenders of Fort Jesus were once more on their own.

The siege was now in its eleventh month. After only a few days had passed it was realized that something else had arrived with the extra manpower and supplies: there were the first cases of a deadly sickness, which became known as the 'swelling disease'. Probably it was bubonic plague, brought over from India. As the death-toll rose there were further blows. A Portuguese gunner deserted to the Arabs and his value to them was soon apparent: the heavy guns bombarding the fort each day grew significantly more accurate.

The 'swelling disease' began killing the Portuguese soldiers at a terrifying rate. By the start of February only twenty were still alive, including the hard-pressed commander, António Mogo de Mello. Many of the Swahili inside the fort began to desert, fearing both the plague and the imminent prospect of being on the losing side. Staring down from the forward bastions of his desperate citadel, Mogo de Mello watched helplessly as the Arabs seized control of his last point of access to the outside world: the beach in front of the outworks.

Weeks went by, then months. Somehow an effort by the attackers to scale the walls of the fort with ladders was beaten off. But Omani ships were bringing more men and supplies into Mombasa at will. Still no Portuguese vessels appeared. The siege had now lasted for more than a year.

At the end of June only six Portuguese were left alive: the commander, the Augustinian prior, two soldiers and two small mulatto children. The rest of the survivors were a few dozen Swahili, some African men and about fifty African women who had been taught how to use muskets. Among the Swahili there was one man remarkable for his loyalty to the Portuguese and his steadiness under fire: a young sheikh named Dawud, generally known as 'Bwana Daud', from the small port of Faza. Although he was a Muslim and his home town had been brutally ravaged by the Portuguese in times past, Bwana Daud had thrown in his lot with the Christians. His brother was among the besiegers and his mother a hostage, but Bwana Daud responded with 'short, dry and resolute words' to urgings from outside the walls that he should change sides. His seventeen-year-old cousin had already died fighting with the defenders.

August arrived, and by now the last of the priests was dead. The commander, Mogo de Mello, knew his own time was near. He ordered that his grave should be dug in the chapel inside the fort; then he called Bwana Daud, urging him to fight to the end and care for the two children. On 28 August the commander died and Bwana Daud took over; an aged sheikh, 'very shrewd and intelligent', became his close adviser. The siege had lasted for a year and five months.

On 16 September the flagship of the relief force, the *San António de*

Taná, reappeared outside Mombasa, together with a supply vessel. The reluctant General Sampaio had been cajoled into action by his deputy, Joseph Pereira de Brito, a man of humble origins who had begun his career as a deckhand. It did not take long for the former deckhand to show his mettle. At his instigation the frigate went right into the harbour, anchored there, and began a close-range bombardment of the Arab shore batteries and the entrenchment on the beach below the fort. Return fire, directed by the renegade gunner, was intense. Two small boats, each with twenty soldiers, were sent ashore, and although one was lost with all hands, the other got through.

At midnight a letter was sent out from the fort and the messenger brought it safely to the flagship. It made remarkable reading for the Portuguese. Bwana Daud described how he, together with a few Swahili and the fifty African women, had been holding out in Fort Jesus, defending it for His Majesty the King of Portugal. Everyone else, including the two mulatto children, was dead.

The siege had so far cost the lives of 2,500 men and 500 women and children. Bwana Daud wrote later to the king: 'Loyalty counted for more with me than ambition or maternal love.'

When the contents of the letter had been accepted as genuine and not a trap, Pereira de Brito went ashore with seventy men and fought his way into the fort. Despite the prevarications by Sampaio, he later made a series of successful attacks on Arab positions. For several weeks supplies and more soldiers were landed by night; by day the frigate maintained its cannonades against Arab positions, until the anchor cables snapped and it was wrecked after twice running ashore.[3] All the ship's 200 officers and men battled their way into Fort Jesus. Then in November came the death of General Sampaio, who had taken over command of the Fort Jesus garrison from Bwana Daud. By acclamation, Pereira de Brito was proclaimed 'Captain and Governor of the Portuguese' and Bwana Daud became 'Captain and Governor of the Fort'.

In December, when the siege had lasted for a year and nine months, the defenders had been enterprising enough to demolish many of the enemy entrenchments round the fort. One of the bravest fighters during these sorties was the young Chinese servant of Pereira de Brito. Yet there was constant activity in the harbour, with Omani ships bringing in reinforcements and supplies. Furthermore, the 'swelling disease' was still taking its toll inside the fort.

On 28 December 1697 the Portuguese sentinels on the walls cried out cheering news. Another fleet was on the horizon. When it had anchored outside the harbour a small boat was sent in and a battle plan was immediately proposed by the dual Fort Jesus commanders: the three frigates in the new relief force should come straight into the Kilindini side of Mombasa harbour and sink all Arab shipping there, while a strong force from the fort would simultaneously make a supporting sortie. However, the latest relief force commander, Francisco Pereira da Silva, would have none of this. He claimed that his mission was to unload supplies and nothing more. As had happened before, the defenders pleaded in vain for courageous action. An anonymous chronicler of these events asserts that 'although the ardour of these pleas might have set fire to the Alps in January, they could not inflame our sluggish General'.[4]

The Arabs captured one of the relief boats, and found in it a bundle of official orders from Goa about the way Fort Jesus should be relieved. The orders were read out close to the fort within the hearing of the defenders 'in good Portuguese', and in mocking tones: 'and in part they were quite right, for some of them were indeed laughable.'

After the supplies had been unloaded the mood inside the fort was declining disastrously. A new garrison commander had been brought to Mombasa with the relief force, a dour and uncomradely officer named Leandro Barbosa Soutomaior. He proceeded to insult Bwana Daud and the rest of the loyal Swahili defenders. Another source of dissension was the return to Fort Jesus of Leonardo Nunes, the renegade gunner. Believing that the Portuguese might win after all, he had decided to desert once more, this time from the Arabs. Those inside the fort who had been on the receiving end of his artillery voted to hang him at once, but the priests who had been brought in by the relief force said that he must be taken back to Goa for trial by the Inquisition. After being sent out to the flagship, Nunes told da Silva, the faint-hearted force commander, a series of lies which were calculated to destroy any resolve he had.

By 19 January 1698 the relief ships were ready to depart. On board were Bwana Daud and the best of his Swahili fighting men, for they would not stay in Fort Jesus under the new regime. Below decks were 400 women, the residue of the inhabitants of the moat, to be dropped off in Zanzibar. Also leaving Mombasa was Joseph Pereira de Brito, curtly relieved of his command. When the fleet reached Goa the viceroy ordered that Pereira de Brito should be cast in prison for taking command of the fort without authority. By some quirk of Portuguese justice the renegade gunner, Leonardo Nunes, was declared blameless.

Back at Mombasa, the siege went on. Somehow, totally cut off from the outside world, Fort Jesus survived. In September a new viceroy arrived in Goa and began to prepare yet another relief force. He assembled four frigates and 1,200 men embarked. With them was Bwana Daud, still loyal and ready for more fighting. By now, under the title given him by the Portuguese, Prince of Faza, his fame was widespread.

The viceroy, Gonsalves da Camara Coutinho, told his captains that if they found the fort still being defended, an all-out attack must instantly be launched to drive the Arabs from Mombasa island and the surrounding mainland. Portuguese power was to be restored, whatever the cost. But when Mombasa was reached, on 13 December 1698, there was a terrible sight. The blood-red flag of Oman was hanging over Fort Jesus. The siege had ended after thirty-three months.

Without trying to discover anything more, the fleet turned away and sailed to Zanzibar. Despite appeals by Bwana Daud and the Queen of Zanzibar, no attempt was made to attack Mombasa or to discover how the fort had fallen.

Almost three years later, in September 1701, an Indian servant named Braz Fialho arrived in Goa with a story to tell. He had been captured at the fall of Fort Jesus, had been taken to Arabia, and after escaping had found his way back to India, travelling first to Persia and from there to Bombay. Fialho recounted how the diminishing band of defenders had clung on until the start of December 1698. By that time there were only nine Portuguese soldiers left alive, together with the commander, Leandro Barbosa, who was dying. There were also three Indians (one of them being Braz Fialho), two African women, and the commander's young African slave. The besiegers were close up to the walls of Fort Jesus, but hesitated to attack because they had no idea that the force within was so pitifully weak.

On 12 December the commander told his little slave to go outside the walls to collect some herbs for his illness. The boy protested that he would be caught, at which Leonardo Barbosa answered: 'If they take you, tell them I am waiting for them and I am not frightened of them. If they are coming tomorrow, they may as well come today.' The boy was captured, and under questioning revealed how few the defenders were.

At night the final attack began. The battered walls were scaled and the defenders retreated into one of the bastions. There they fought until shortly after dawn on 13 December. As a last defiant gesture the dying commander advanced from the bastion with a blunderbuss. He was shot down, then killed and beheaded where he lay.[5] The flag of the victors was raised over the fort, just hours before the relief force arrived off the harbour. Probably the only people who had been in Fort Jesus when the siege began and were still there at the finish were one or two African women. Total losses among the defenders from fighting and disease were put at 6,500, including almost a thousand Portuguese and 2,500 Swahili; the rest were the non-combatants in the moat. There is no estimate of losses on the Omani side.

The fall of Fort Jesus wiped Portuguese power off the map between the Red Sea and the mouth of the Zambezi, almost exactly two centuries after Vasco da Gama had sailed along the coast on his voyage of discovery to India. Nothing was left now of the Estado da India in East Africa, except for a few small, half-forgotten ports in Mozambique and the *prazos*, the slave plantations of the unmapped interior flanking the Zambezi.[6]

THIRTY-SIX

Western Aims,
Eastern Influences

The sword of the Lord and of Gideon had served the Portuguese
very well as a motto for acquisition; but in the contemptuous
neglect by them of the arts of peace, and in the absence of any
genius for colonization, it did not facilitate retention. The Portuguese were fanatical, oppressive, and destitute of the true commercial spirit.

—Lord Curzon, *Persia and the Persian Question* (1892)

MOURNING THE DISMEMBERMENT of their empire in the East – a
process in which the English, Dutch and Arabs had all shared – the
Portuguese could comfort themselves with one noble thought. They
had, as the argument went, saved Europe by thwarting the ambitions
of another empire, that of the Ottoman Turks. They had done so by
occupying the Indian Ocean at a critical moment in history, and by
defeating the Turks in the sea battle of Diu. In retrospect they could
see themselves as the instruments of divine will: only Portuguese firepower and seamanship had held up the eastwards advance of the Turks
into Asia after the fall of Constantinople. With the wealth and manpower
of Persia and India to call upon, the Turks could have become irresistible,
their armies capable of sweeping westwards to the Atlantic from the
territories they had already conquered in the Balkans.

A belief that Christendom had only narrowly escaped such a fate was
widely held throughout Europe until well into the eighteenth century,
when the second siege of Vienna by 150,000 Ottoman troops was still
within living memory.[1] One of its proponents was Dr William
Robertson, an influential Edinburgh historian. He admired the achievements of the Spanish and Portuguese and argued that Europe owed an
immeasurable debt to Vasco da Gama for opening the route to India
when he did. 'Happily for the human race', said Robertson, the 'despotic

government' of the Ottoman empire was, as a direct result, 'prevented from extending its dominion over Europe, and from suppressing liberty, learning and taste'.[2]

However, such philosophizing counted for little at the close of the seventeenth century, when the loss of Mombasa had tolled the knell of Portuguese power in the western half of the Indian Ocean. Built to stand as a symbol of everlasting Christian supremacy, the Fort Jesus citadel had joined the list of once-prized possessions now in the hands of rivals: Hormuz, Muscat, Cochin, Malacca, Ceylon – even Bombay, tossed away in a dowry.

The collapse of the Estado da India can be blamed largely upon the stubbornly medieval form of government in Lisbon, for every high office – and with it, the chance to grow rich – was bestowed at the royal whim. In theory the Portuguese kings monopolized the East Indies trade, but they were constantly robbed by the noblemen to whom they gave patronage. Since every aristocrat in the East was assumed to be amassing wealth by means of his position, he could expect little except envy from his underlings. The cumbersome imperial system was also ill-equipped to keep control of men and events beyond the Cape. At first, all important decisions were referred back to Lisbon, but since an exchange of messages might take eighteen months, by the end of which time there could be an entirely altered state of affairs, the viceroys and their subordinates were left more and more to their own dubious devices.[3]

On top of that, the economy of Portugal had been drained during the sixty years of its 'captivity' by Spain, after Philip II assumed the throne in 1580 when the Aviz dynasty guttered out. This had happened just as the inevitable challenge to the Estado da India began appearing at the start of the seventeenth century; and the challengers, England and Holland, were furthermore the sworn foes of Spain. The Portuguese were drawn into Philip's disastrous wars against the English and Dutch, with many of its finest ships and seamen lost in the Great Armada. Portugal was taxed into penury and the people's morale paralysed. Small and backward, Portugal had earlier been sustained against all the odds by patriotism. Few of its subjects in the East now wanted to fight and die for the hated Philip II, ruling half a world away; self-interest became their main incentive.

Remoteness also encouraged a loss of social constraints. The journey to India was so long and hazardous that many Portuguese decided to forget old ties and abandon themselves for ever to the indulgence of the tropics. This tendency, the despair of Goa's clergy, had been noticed with dismay as early as the 1550s: 'for there are some who are so careless of their consciences and so steeped in vice that they let twenty to thirty years go by without remembering that they are married, or without providing for, or writing to, their wives.'[4] Even the most ascetic of societies would have been hard pressed, as enemies multiplied, to defend Portugal's vast seaborne empire. Indolence, despair and moral decay merely hastened its downfall. The idealism of the conquerors in the East had been glorified in the verses of Camoëns, but a curtain tends to be drawn across the sombre scenes of later times.

Perhaps the most telling description of the Portuguese East in its precipitous decline is given by a widely travelled Frenchman, Jean Mocquet. Dignified by the title 'Keeper of the Cabinet of Rarities to the King of France', Mocquet combined scientific pretensions – he was a botanist of some note – with a fondness for gossip. He went out to Goa in the first half of the seventeenth century, taking passage in the thirteen-strong fleet of a new viceroy, Count de la Fera.

From the start the voyage was disastrous. The picture Mocquet paints of conditions in stormy Atlantic weather well explains why the departure from Lisbon was often equated with a death sentence: 'Amongst us was the greatest disorder and confusion imaginable, because of the people vomiting up and down, and making dung upon one another; there was nothing to be heard but lamentations and groans ... the passengers were cursing the time of their embarkment, their fathers and mothers, and themselves.'

The viceroy himself quickly succumbs, and he is not alone, for others are dying in corners of the middle deck, behind chests, 'having their eyes and the soles of their feet eaten up with rats'. Mocquet soon finds himself afflicted with scurvy, 'which the Portuguese call Berber', every day going to the side of the ship to lance his rotting gums, 'holding by the cordage, with a little looking-glass in my hand to see where to cut'. When he has cut away the dead flesh 'and drawn away abundance of black blood', Mocquet washes out his mouth with urine. The best remedy for scurvy, he decides, is the syrup of gilly-flowers (cloves) 'and good red wine'.

Eventually the fleet reaches Mozambique, and is immobilized there for five months through having missed the monsoon which would have taken it on to India. People die at the rate of ten to fifteen a day, the total eventually reaching 725. Mocquet recovers from his scurvy, but his woes are far from over, because the captain of the fleet decides he is a spy, secretly compiling a sea-chart for France, and has him thrown into a jail ashore with an iron collar round his neck. The Frenchman is robbed of his money and half starved, but after three weeks he is freed and allowed back onboard. 'The Portugals,' he writes with bitter prejudice, 'being mainly of the race of the Jews, are by nature cruel and ungrateful.'

He ventures ashore again on a botanical expedition, finding 'a thousand sorts of plants and fruit to me unknown', but looking in particular for a creeping plant held to be a cure for the sickness 'gotten by having to do with the Ethiopian [African] women'. During the months of waiting for the monsoon, Mocquet collects all the gossip he can about the Africans, including a tale about the soldiers of Monomotapa, who 'cut off the privy-members of their enemies, and having dried them, give them to their wives to wear about their neck, of which they are not a little proud'.[5] He jots down every anecdote he hears, however gruesome or improbable, including one about the fate of Dutch prisoners handed over to the Africans. A soldier claims that he has seen a cannibal 'cut the throat of a Hollander . . . and swallow the blood down hot'.

When Goa is reached at last, Mocquet turns to examining the behaviour and attitudes of the Portuguese settlers: 'As soon as they arrive in the Indies they make themselves gallants, calling themselves *fidalgos* or gentlemen, though they be but peasants and tradesmen.' They refuse to pay their bills in the shops, and torment the Hindus by threatening to kill captive birds or other animals, until the Hindus find money to buy them and set them free. 'The Portugals do this on purpose to have their money.'

Mocquet is shocked by the treatment of slaves: 'As I was in my lodging in Goa I heard nothing but blows all night long, and some weak voice, which breathed a little, for they stop their mouth with a linen cloth, to stop them from crying out.' He lists various tortures practised on slaves, one with boiling lard, another with razors to make cuts which are rubbed with salt and vinegar.

Not all slaves were Africans; many were Indians and some had been brought from Japan and China. In Mocquet's lodgings the girl who served at table was Japanese, and the man of the house commented one evening on the whiteness of her teeth. His wife hid her jealousy, 'but having watched her opportunity when her husband was abroad, she caused this poor slave to be taken and bound, and pluck'd all her teeth out without compassion'.

If Mocquet's account of life in Portuguese India stood alone it could be brushed aside as a crude exaggeration, yet several other contemporary reports echo his descriptions of idleness, cruelty and lust. A seventeenth-century Neapolitan traveller, Giovanni Careri, notes in his diary how most men in Goa kept entourages of female slaves, known as 'mosses'. These women were kept busy all day 'caressing and massaging' the bodies of their masters.[6]

The name 'mosses' referred not only to the duties of the slaves. It was also a geographical term, because so many of them had been transported from Mozambique. At an earlier date the archbishop's clerk, Linschoten, had written: 'From Mozambique great numbers of these kaffirs are carried into India, and many times they sell a man or a woman that is grown to their full strength for two or three ducats.' Careri was more precise, saying that the slaves came from Mombasa, Sofala, Mozambique and 'other parts along the coast of Africa'. Some were captives in African wars, sold to visiting Portuguese ships, but others sold themselves 'in despair' during famines. They were still so cheap – 'fifteen or twenty crowns of Naples a head' – that Careri thought there would be even more in Goa, but for the superstition among Africans that the Portuguese only bought them to turn their bodies into gunpowder. He went on: 'But these Blacks we speak of, though of an ill aspect, have some of them such a noble and genteel disposition, that it were a blessing that every European gentleman were like them.'

The Portuguese were not alone in yielding to the climate and cultures of the East. The Dutch and English had quickly discovered how vain were their dreams of reproducing in the tropics the Protestant ethics and well-scrubbed behaviour of northern Europe. Almost every merchant ship sailing the Indian Ocean carried a 'seraglio' of courtesans for the pleasure of the officers. The American consul in Canton in the late eighteenth century, Major Samuel Shaw, declared himself outraged to discover that the 'filles-de-joie of Captains of ships from India' were lodging with respectable families. These 'creatures', as Shaw called them, were part-Malay or Goanese. Bombay was long notorious for its vice. Likewise, many of the British ships heading east from Calcutta relied entirely upon contraband opium for China to make their profits.

On the other hand, the chartered companies were never burdened with the exalted principles on which the Estado da India was founded. Their responsibility was not to God, but the shareholders (so when the French company went bankrupt it simply ceased to exist). The Inquisition in Goa had burnt Indian heretics at the stake, whereas the chartered companies would not even grant missionaries passage aboard their ships.

The words of Queen Elizabeth, giving her blessing to the English company, were well remembered: the promoters were to 'adventure after merchandise, gold, pearl, jewels and other commodities, which are to be bought, bartered, procured, exchanged, or otherwise obtained'. 'Otherwise obtained' could be taken to cover almost any sort of skulduggery.

Inevitably, the English in India became dishonest on a scale which astounded compatriots who visited them. Robert Clive told the court of directors of the East India Company in 1765 of the conditions he found:

> The sudden and among many the unwarrantable acquisition of riches had introduced luxury in every shape, and its most pernicious aspect . . . everyone thought he had the right to enrich himself, at all events, with as much expedition as possible . . . The sources of tyranny and oppression, which have been opened by the European agents acting under the authority of the Company's servants, and the numberless black agents and sub-agents, acting also under them, will I fear be a lasting reproach to the English name in this country; it is impossible to enumerate the complaints that have been laid before me by the unfortunate inhabitants.

Such had been the disarray that by the 1770s the company was forced to borrow £1,000,000 from the government and in return yielded up some of its independence.

One defence put forward to excuse the corruption and debaucheries was that most of 'John Company's' employees were ill-paid and likely to die early. That was true: young clerks shipped out from England sometimes succumbed to blackwater fever or malaria within a few weeks of reaching Calcutta, Bombay or Madras. A clergyman, James Ovington, arrived in Bombay from England in 1690 at the start of the monsoon rains; by the end of the rains only four of his twenty-four fellow passengers were still alive, and fifteen sailors in the ship which had brought them were dead. Ovington wrote that September and October were 'very pernicious', for an excess of vapour 'fermented the Air', raising 'a sultry Heat, that scarce any is able to withstand the Feverish Effect it has upon their Spirits'.[7] In one year in Calcutta a third of the white population died during the rains, and it became customary to hold dinners at which thanks were offered up by those who had come through.

Yet the excesses of high officials, nicknamed the 'nabobs', provoked outrage. The poet William Cowper expressed it with passion in 1781:

> Hast thou, though suckled at fair freedom's breast,
> Exported slav'ry to the conquer'd East,
> Pull'd down the tyrants India serv'd with dread,
> And rais'd thyself, a greater, in their stead?
> Gone thither arm'd and hungry, return'd full,
> Fed from the richest veins of the Mogul.
> A despot big with pow'r obtain'd by wealth,
> And that obtain'd by rapine and by stealth?
> With Asiatic vices stor'd thy mind,
> But left their virtues and thine own behind . . . [8]

At the time of the demise of the East India Company, after the 1856 Mutiny, its qualities in the second half of the eighteenth century would be summed up in the British parliament by a former chancellor of the exchequer, Sir George Cornewall Lewis: 'I do must confidently maintain that no civilized government ever existed on the face of this earth which was more corrupt, more perfidious and more capricious.'

However dire the moral record, it was none the less undeniable that commerce with India had done wonders for England's comfort and well-being. As with the ownership of slave plantations in the West Indies, the eastern trade was hugely rewarding. It helped London become a financial centre and funded the building of many stately homes. Occasionally men of quite humble origins who had the physique to survive the monsoon fevers and the wit to strike good bargains could make fortunes in India. One 'interloper' (unlicensed trader) was Thomas Pitt, who rose to be governor of the Madras presidency and founded a political dynasty: his son and grandson were both prime ministers of England. Another was Elihu Yale, an American from Boston. He also became governor of Madras, married two of his daughters into the English aristocracy, and founded Yale University. His career was far from exemplary and the verses put on his tomb in London in 1721 end with an anxious couplet:

> Much good, some ill, he did, so hope's all even
> And that his soul through mercie's gone to heaven.[9]

By virtue of their financial success the chartered companies became archetypes for capitalist enterprise in Europe. Their influence went still further, as the exports of the East were increasingly paid for with coinage made from silver mined in the Americas. Then, in the first stirrings of Europe's industrial revolution, came an augury of the never-ending conflict between free trade and national self-interest, when English manufacturers stifled the imports of muslins from Bengal by contriving a 75 per cent import duty on all Indian cotton goods. The next step was the duty-free admission of English cottons, mass-produced on power looms, into all the territories controlled by the East India Company. In thirty years an ancient industry on which millions of Indian handloom weavers depended had been wiped out.

The desolation which struck Dacca and other Indian cities where the muslin had been made was 'sad and humiliating', remarked Sir George Birdwood, a senior company official. He could hardly have foreseen that within a century the English cotton industry would itself be ruined, largely by production in the East on machinery which Britain had sold there.

PART THREE

An Enforced Tutelage

THIRTY-SEVEN

Settlers on India's Southern Approaches

My friends, out of every hundred men – especially if they be soldiers – who go to the East, seldom more than thirty live to return . . . Remember these things, my friends, and do not go to the East.

—Otto Mentzel, *Life at the Cape in the Mid-Eighteenth Century* (1784)

BY THE 1750s the white settlers in the Cape of Good Hope numbered six thousand. The reluctance of the VOC directors in Holland to allow a 'refreshment station' to turn into a colony had yielded to the enthusiasm of successive governors. The Cape was increasingly self-sufficient, even growing wheat for export to the East Indies. Some of the *boers* (literally, farmers) were now settled far inland. There they had hacked away forests, cultivated land, and begun rearing sheep and cattle. If they encountered bushmen they shot them. They generally enslaved the Khoikhoi ('Hottentots') but sometimes took their younger women as wives. These trekboers were also making their first contacts, near the Fish river, with more formidable opponents, the Xhosa, spearhead of the Bantu occupants of the vast interior.

These portents of an historic conflict went largely unnoticed in the Cape peninsula. There the inhabitants looked out to sea, and rarely towards Africa. Their numbers were still small, yet outside of the Americas this was the world's most prosperous overseas colony of Europeans consciously maintaining a transplanted culture. Van Reibeeck's wish, 100 years earlier, that the free burghers should 'come in time to regard this country as their fatherland', was unquestionably being fulfilled.

By now Cape Town was a popular port of call for ships of all nations doing business in the Indian Ocean. It had acquired a nickname: 'Tavern of the Two Seas'. The citizens of Cape Town's well-ordered streets made a good livelihood by letting rooms to sailors whose ships were in harbour. There were also brothels, staffed by Hottentot and mixed-race women. A Dutch rear-admiral, Jan Splinter Stavorinus, noting down his impressions of the Cape, commented on the unbridled eagerness of its people to extract money from foreigners. The English were always popular, because their sailors seemed to have the most to spend.[1]

One distinguished English visitor, in the autumn of 1744, was Commodore George Anson, 'Father of the Royal Navy'. He was nearing the end of an arduous voyage round the world. His chaplain, Richard Walter, recorded that the commodore was 'highly delighted' with the Cape and its 'civilized colony'. The fruits and other foodstuffs were the most delicious that could be found anywhere, the air was healthy, the water excellent; in short, 'this settlement is the best provided of any in the known world for the refreshment of seamen after long voyages'. A Mrs Jemima Kindersley, stopping in Cape Town on her way to Calcutta in 1765, wrote home with equal enthusiasm: 'I never was in a place where people seemed to enjoy so much comfort; few are very rich, none miserably poor.'

A woman of her times, Jemima Kindersley naturally did not encompass all the people of the Cape in this judgement. She came from a land whose seaports, large and small, had grown rich by sending slave ships to West Africa since Elizabethan times, a land whose North American colonies relied upon black labour. Since the English enjoyed supremacy in the Atlantic trade, few of them would have been critical of circumstances at the Cape, where the Dutch population was easily outnumbered by its slaves, for without their labour the colony could scarcely have prospered.[2] Only the diversity of the slaves was remarkable. Some came from West Africa, some from Java and China, and others from Madagascar, so conveniently close at hand. A minority were Khoikhoi, although many of these had died in 1713 of smallpox, caught from laundry sent ashore by visiting ships; the 'Hotnot' survivors were now inter-marrying into the larger slave communities. In a stratum between the burghers and their serfs were freed slaves – children of white–black liaisons, or baptized black Christians. Others had been granted liberty for performing an act of bravery or informing upon fellow-slaves planning to escape. It was easy to identify the freed slaves, since they wore hats and shoes.

Within the rigidities of their masters' Calvinism, the Cape slaves were generally treated well, and many were closely integrated into the families who owned them. However, the response to any hint of rebelliousness was draconian. In earlier years slaves had often got away, and it was well remembered how their fires had glowed threateningly at night on the slopes of Table Mountain. The treatment now meted out depended upon the example set by the company's governors; few displayed qualities of mercy. Punishments imposed on erring slaves revealed an urge to terrorize, through fear of having to report to the 'Seventeen', the VOC directors in Amsterdam, that disorder had been allowed to surface.

Moreover, reports of the frequent uprisings in the West Indies were alarming: in 1760 in Jamaica 1,000 slaves had revolted, vainly hoping to kill all the whites and turn the island into a negro republic; rioting lasted for six months and a woman slave, later executed, had been crowned queen. If any similar rebellion occurred at the Cape and ran out of control, it would threaten the colony's very existence. Europe was too distant to be called upon for speedy reinforcements in a time of trouble. So one precaution, rigidly enforced, was that the slaves must never have access to arms.

While Mrs Kindersley was in Cape Town a demented slave, found guilty of stabbings, was executed on the rack. As he died he was tormented 'with the application of burning instruments in a manner too shocking to repeat'. Some years earlier, eighteen runaway slaves had set fire to several houses, but were swiftly captured and put in the castle dungeons. Three managed to cut their own throats, knowing what lay in store, and the rest were either impaled or hanged, or bound living on the wheel after having their legs and arms smashed with iron clubs. The women were slowly strangled, while the hangman's assistant waved burning bundles of reeds before their eyes. Otto Mentzel, tutor to the children of a senior officer, noted in his diary: 'In warm weather it is usual for slaves impaled and broken on the wheel to live between two or three days and nights, but on this occasion it was cold and they were all dead by midnight.' Such punishment was deemed essential to maintain that serene atmosphere which so delighted visitors to the Cape after their long sea voyages.

Slaves bought from Madagascar to the Cape proved the most rebellious. Moreover, buying them was hazardous, because many petty potentates on the island's west coast were the feared Zana-Malata, mixed-blood descendants of pirates. The Malagasy slaves were also expensive, costing as much as 35 'Mexicans' – silver dollars, sometimes known as Spanish reals (Maria Theresa thalers, also called dollars or piastres, were another popular Indian Ocean currency).[3] However, new consignments were always needed because the slaves did not live long at the Cape, since they could not adapt to its sharp winters. Half died within a year.

In the early 1770s the VOC officials at the Cape decided to send some of their ships more than 2,000 miles to Zanzibar on slave-buying expeditions. Accounts of two of these voyages survive, written by company clerks Friedrich Holtzappel and Constant van Nuld Onkruidjt. Neither had any idea of what to expect when they reached Zanzibar, since they lived in an outpost isolated from the rest of Africa. The voyages up the African coast were uneventful, and on arrival in Zanzibar the two clerks were startled by the riches in the island's markets, where silks, Chinese porcelain, fine carpets and gold jewellery were all on offer. Their own trade goods aroused no interest among the local traders, only 'Mexicans' were in demand.

The clerks also learned about the far-reaching power of the Omani sultan in Muscat. His chosen governor ruled Zanzibar, and another appointee, from the powerful Mazrui family, was occupying Fort Jesus in Mombasa. (The capture of the fort from the Portuguese eighty years earlier was a legend celebrated in verse all along the coast.) The Zanzibar governor told the Dutchmen that he had received stringent orders never to sell slaves to Christians, as the 'entire trade along the coast must be in Arab hands'. The sultan's motives were religious as well as commercial: slaves owned by Muslims were assumed to be sure converts to the true religion.

The Zanzibar governor hinted, nevertheless, that he might be able to supply some slaves, if assisted with a loan of 500 'Mexicans'. The Dutch naively handed over the money, but received nothing in return. Then a young man oddly described as a 'priest' offered to supply some slaves secretly, and in the middle of the night ferried out nineteen men, women and children by canoe. 'The moonlight does much hinder slaves coming on board,' wrote one of the clerks morosely.

It was a slow, tortuous business. The first groups of Africans purchased had to be sequestered in hot and stinking conditions below decks until a sufficient load was collected, and they soon began falling ill. Some were mere babies, listed on the record as 'sucking girls'. Van Nuld Onkruidjt complained that the slaves bought in Zanzibar were already weak, blaming this on a famine on the mainland made worse by plagues of locusts. The slave-buyers had to travel 'far inland', according to

Holtzappel, taking trade goods with them to make their purchases. He had heard it said that 200 people at a time would come out of the bush and offer to sell themselves, because they were starving.

Hoping to find cheaper and stronger slaves elsewhere, one of the ships sailed north, past historic Malindi – now in the hands of 'unfriendly natives' – to call at the port of Brava: 'We chose a male and a female slave, but refused two elderly slave women and three small boys because the merchant would not reduce the price.' Naturally enough, the two clerks were much preoccupied with prices: the current rate for a healthy African male was 25 dollars, or 120lb of gunpowder (a cow cost 30lb). But after a year's effort, during which several crew members died, one ship had collected only sixty-eight slaves; the other was more successful, with a tally of 328.

Scattered through the two narratives are vignettes of East Africa in the late eighteenth century, as seen through rather jaundiced European eyes. The Arabs were imperious: 'As they generally have many slaves they are too haughty and lazy to work and would rather die of hunger than bring themselves to work the land.' In the evenings the Arabs would 'get as drunk as pigs' (coming from a Dutchman, this comment counted for something). Van Nuld Onkruidjt tried to classify the various types of Muslims on the coast, putting the Swahili at the bottom, the 'Moors' in the middle as 'subalterns', and the Arabs at the top: 'However, all are most afraid of the government of Muscat.'

For the African slaves, as human beings, their captors cared nothing. The only interest was in getting them back alive to Cape Town. The voyage of the second ship, with more than three hundred men, women and children below decks, proved to be a financial calamity. The death-toll was relentless. Bodies had to be thrown overboard every day as the ship sailed southwards through the Mozambique channel. The narrative is reduced to a terse daily log: 'two male, one female,' 'one male', 'two females, one boy'. Only rarely is there a more detailed entry: 'Friday, 14 November. Towards the evening two adult men died. They were about the best we had on board ... We could not understand why they died so suddenly, therefore the surgeon proposed opening the bodies, which was allowed him, but after the post mortem and careful examination he reported that he had found nothing unnatural.'

At last, Table Bay was reached, but the winds were contrary and the ship had to wait at Robben Island until it could sail into harbour.[4] The crew were delighted when the superintendent of the island's prison supplied them with ten sheep, since they had long been without fresh meat. But of the 328 slaves so laboriously acquired in East Africa, almost a third had died on the return voyage.

While the Dutch were blundering up and down the African coast, a far more astute slave-trader was striving to influence the course of Indian Ocean history. On 14 December 1776, the sultan of Kilwa signed a treaty drawn up by a certain Jean-Vincent Morice. It read:

> We, King of Kilwa, Sultan Hasan, son of Sultan Ibrahim and son of Sultan Yusuf the Shirazi, Kilwa, give our word to Monsieur Morice, a French national, that we will provide him with 1,000 slaves a year for twenty piastres each and that he will give the king a tribute of two piastres per head of slaves. No other than he shall be able to trade for slaves, be he French, English, Dutch, Portuguese, etcetera, unless and until he has received his slaves and requires no more. This contract is made for 100 years between him and us. To guarantee our word we give him the fortress in which he can place the number of cannons he requires and his flag. The French, the Moors and the King of Kilwa will henceforward be one.
>
> Whosoever attacks one of us we two together will attack him.
>
> Made on 14 December under our signs and seals.

The document was counter-signed by three of Morice's officers, Pichard, Pigne and Broüard, from his ship *L'Abyssinie*, which lay at anchor in Kilwa harbour, for it was seen as the forerunner of a far more ambitious scheme. Morice dreamed of making Kilwa the hub of the first French settlement along the East African coast, for it was strategically well situated to give France a lasting influence on the mainland.

Little is known about Morice, except that he was probably born and educated in the port of Brest, then travelled the world for twenty years as a ship's surgeon in the Compagnie des Indes Orientales. After the company collapsed in 1769 he turned to slave-trading, with such success that he soon owned a small fleet of ships, with such names as *L'Espérance*, *Le Gracieux* and *L'Etoile du Matin*. At first he bought slaves on the Mozambique coast for sale in Martinique, stopping at Cape Town to give treatment to those who were ill before making the Atlantic crossing.

Although many captains of slave ships were uncouth tyrants, as brutal to their crews as to their cargoes, there was no obloquy in the traffic itself, and there is never a hint in Morice's correspondence that he felt his adopted trade to be unsavoury: although his medical background made him careful to give vaccinations when smallpox threatened, that was no more than commercial prudence.

The surgeon-turned-slaver had support for his plans from a respected scientist and man of letters, Joseph-François Charpentier de Cossigny, a settler in the Ile de France, the former Mauritius. (Abandoned by the Dutch, the island had been reoccupied and renamed by the French.) Together, Morice and Charpentier urged upon the French navy minister in Versailles the logic and desirability of their empire-building plan. Charpentier argued that Kilwa could be used to spread Christianity: 'the most powerful, most prompt and most efficacious means of civilizing these people, that is to say, to submit them to the yoke of law, to change their ideas, to accustom them to work and instruct them in the arts of agriculture.'

The pair drew up a long document[5] about the African coastline and the interior, in which Morice sets out his considerable knowledge in reply to questions from Charpentier. The slaves, he says, come to the coast from as much as 600 miles inland, changing owners on the way. Every year, traders assemble a caravan to traverse the continent to Angola, spending two months on the journey. They go by way of a large lake, taking two days to paddle across it in canoes: 'What a curious experience it would be to make a similar journey.' Morice's belief that Angola could be reached in only two months from Kilwa was fanciful, but in general his statement rings true; there is ample evidence that half-caste Portuguese traders from both sides of Africa were already meeting at markets near the headwaters of the Zambezi.

The Ile de France was only fourteen days from Kilwa, sailing round the northern tip of Madagascar, then south-easterly. During the past forty years the former habitat of the dodo had grown into a symbol of French ambition in the Indian Ocean, compensating for the earlier failure of the Fort Dauphin settlement. In its orderliness and sense of purpose, the Ile de France was the French counterpart, on the southern approaches to India, of the Hollanders' foothold at the Cape.

The foundations of the island's prosperity had been laid in the decade after 1735 by a brilliant governor, Bertrand-François Mahé de La Bourdonnais, and by Morice's time the white élite, sugar-planters and administrators numbered more than 4,000. There was a smaller community to 'freed men' and creoles, and almost 40,000 African slaves, bought to labour in the sugar plantations. On the sister island of Réunion there was a similar society, growing coffee and spices.

Apart from the achievements of his governorship, La Bourdonnais had kept alive France's hopes of driving the English out of India, where mercenaries from both European powers were fighting in the sub-continent's wars between rival princes. With a fleet of merchant ships converted for naval warfare, he had won control of the Bay of Bengal in 1745-7, captured Madras and handed it back only in return for an immense ransom. Early in the second half of the eighteenth century the two European powers were continuing to vie for the friendship of India's princes, with troops of the respective East India companies fighting as mercenaries in the sub-continent's wars.

In diplomatic contests for the affections of the princes, the French had generally proved more adroit. Their officers were equally successful in training the armies of the Indian kingdoms. However, when England emerged triumphant from the Seven Years' War (1756-63), the French were stripped of their colonies in America and left almost powerless in India following Robert Clive's momentous victory at Plassey.[6] Their only remaining possession of any importance was the port of Pondichéry in the south-east, but all its fortifications had been demolished by the English.

The literary-inclined Jemima Kindersley, who was touring India after her visit to the Cape, regretted the way Pondichéry had been devastated, but was proud to see how the English garrisons were being strengthened in Allahabad and other cities. Despite the horror of the 'Black Hole of Calcutta', twenty years before, she feels ecstatic: 'If it was always the cold season, who would dislike India? It is really delightful! The rains are over, and not a cloud to be seen in the sky.' Her tone captures the national belief that after Clive's great victory, England has the measure of its European rivals in the East, and has already put down permanent imperial roots in India.

It is in the context of this wider struggle that Morice had made his treaty with Kilwa. His slave-trading was only one side of the coin. In a document sent to senior figures in the French government, entitled 'Plan for a Trading Centre on the East Coast of Africa', he stressed how the mainland could supply enough millet to feed the slaves in the Ile de France and become a market for the island's sugar. The Kilwa harbour was better than any he had seen throughout the world; only Rio de Janeiro could equal it. Kilwa was perfectly placed to intercept enemy ships emerging from the Mozambique channel and heading towards India. As for the post of official Resident in Kilwa, he was ready to take that on. However, the response from Paris in February 1779 was wary, telling the Ile de France administration to give Morice every support and stay on friendly terms with Kilwa's sultan, but to go no further.

Keeping on friendly terms with Sultan Hasan was not difficult, for he was flattered that the treaty called him a king and quoted his noble ancestry from Shiraz in Persia. In reality, once-mighty Kilwa was just a ruin, its houses and handsome mosques long overgrown with tropical vegetation, unrecognizable as the thriving city-state visited by Ibn Battuta four centuries earlier and later marvelled at by the first Portuguese visitors. The sultan had little left to boast about except the extravagant claim of descent from those who had founded the town a thousand years in the past. Once Kilwa had controlled the gold exports of Sofala, but now was simply East Africa's best depot for slaves from the interior. This trade was all that kept the sultan and his entourage from total penury.

Apart from its promise of a regular income, the Morice treaty gave Sultan Hasan some hope of maintaining his independence from the Sultan of Oman, who since 1750 had claimed authority over the entire East African coast and was even looking beyond to the Comoro islands and Madagascar. An Omani governor, like the one appointed to Zanzibar, had arrived in Kilwa seven years before Morice's appearance, but the sultan had managed to get rid of him. The Frenchman with his cannons might deter the Omanis when they tried to return; this explains the treaty's bravado about standing together against attackers. The sultan also had to think about possible threats from two of his brothers whom he had ousted to gain power: one for being a drunkard, the other for being a fool.

The fortress offered to Morice was the long-derelict palace of Husuni Kubwa, towards the northern end of Kilwa island; it was here that he hoped France would found a settlement, complete with a military garrison. He was reputed to have paid the sultan 4,000 Spanish dollars for the palace, on whose walls he set up eight cannons to defend the harbour.

Morice proudly flew the French *fleur-de-lys* pennant on the palace, as he did on the masts of his ships. His countrymen were popular in this part of the Indian Ocean, so much so that English slaving ships often sailed under the colours of France to make themselves more acceptable. In contrast to the clumsy efforts of the Dutch, Morice had managed to buy 925 slaves in Zanzibar at the start of 1776 (all but seventy surviving the voyage to Ile de France) and it had only been a quarrel provoked by another French captain that had made him turn from Zanzibar to Kilwa later in that year.

The stream of proposals handed to the captains of home-going ships for forwarding to Versailles suddenly came to a stop. Monsieur Morice, slave-trader and patriot, had died in the ruins of Husuni Kubwa, shortly after the loss of one of his ships, the *St Pierre*. Most probably he was killed by malaria. His treaty died with him, although the sultan of Kilwa soon found new customers for his slaves, rival French captains sailing to Rio and other Brazilian ports, as well as to the Ile de France. One of them, Joseph Crassons de Medeuil, lists more than a dozen ships which had recently loaded up in Kilwa with slaves; they included a vessel called *La Samaritaine*.

Walking amid Kilwa's overgrown ruins, Crassons noticed the finely-constructed arches of the great mosque, and speculated that 'this was once a very important town'. However, Kilwa's splendour was a thing of the past, and even the last vestiges of its independence were soon to be snatched away. In 1785 a new and more determined Omani governor arrived on the island. The sultan was deprived of all power, allowed only to cling to his title, the last reminder of a noble lineage.[7]

THIRTY-EIGHT

The Seas beyond
Napoleon's Reach

❦

Attaquons dans ses eaux la perfide Albion!
—Augustin, Marquis de Ximénèz, *L'Ère des Français* (1793)

IT WAS SCARCELY SURPRISING that France had shown little desire
to become involved in colonial adventures on the East African coast,
as urged by Monsieur Morice, because war with England was once
more consuming its energies. In March 1778 it had allied itself with
the American colonies fighting for independence, not so much out of
sympathy for them but because it seemed a good chance to seek revenge
for humiliating losses in India fifteen years earlier through the peace
terms of the Seven Years' War. The French felt bitter that many of
their most talented administrators and soldiers had given their lives in
India, only to have that great prize snatched away.

At first the renewed conflict stayed close to home, but when Spain
and Holland also declared war on England, the French felt bold enough
to despatch a fleet to the Indian Ocean once again, to help a confederation of Indian princes fighting to drive the English into the sea. The
most resolute and able of these was Tipu Sultan, ruler of Mysore.
Devoted to the arts and fascinated by scientific inventions, Tipu was
also a zealous Muslim: when he captured any of the English infidels he
saw to it that they were forcibly circumcized, just as 70,000 Hindu
captives were circumcized, then enslaved, after Mysore's victory over
the neighbouring state of Coorg. Feared and hated by the East India
Company, Tipu had sent ambassadors to France, asking Louis XVI for
military support. But Louis procrastinated, and this was to prove fatal
for Tipu.

Finally, France decided to despatch three separate convoys, carrying
thousands of troops, to fight alongside the armies of the Indian princes.

Had the warships arrived a year sooner, or had all three convoys safely rounded the Cape, the sub-continent's history might have taken a different course. But two convoys were intercepted by English warships before clearing European waters and in India the princes' confederation crumbled after a series of defeats at the hands of the British musketeers, artillerymen and cavalry.

At sea the French had better fortune. In a series of bloody battles off India the brilliant French admiral Pierre-André de Suffren Saint-Tropez trounced the English, whose sailors were enfeebled by outbreaks of scurvy; even on land the English began to fall into disarray. Then news reached India in June 1783 that peace had been negotiated in Paris five months earlier. Suffren's fleet sailed home, its triumphs all to no avail. By signing away its American colonies, to end hostilities, England had, for the time being, neutralized any French threat in the Indian Ocean.

In the following year, William Pitt the Younger steered a 'dual control' Act through the British parliament, giving the Crown ultimate power over the East India Company's rule. The Raj was born and the thrust of British imperialism was turning away from the Americas and towards the East. At the same time, the resources of the industrial revolution were making possible a more total, and more commercially rewarding, mastery of the Indian sub-continent than any previous power, oriental or European, had ever achieved.

Despite all their quarrels at home, the Britons (English, Scots, Welsh, and even Irish) now shared the common purpose of ruling other races who were far more numerous, but darker, heathen and – by an easy extension – inferior. Thus, the term 'the British Empire' acquired a new connotation. So did the word 'England'; it came to stand not so much for the place, but for a state of mind, for an innate confidence and patriotic pride, which Nelson was to invoke before joining battle with the French at Trafalgar: 'England expects that every man will do his duty.'[2]

This chauvinistic spirit was consolidated in a final round of fighting with France. War had become predictable after the French Revolution in 1789, and once again it started in Europe, but the effects were soon felt in distant places. When Holland was occupied and became a vassal of France under the name of the 'Batavian Republic' (the Batavi had been an ancient tribe living beside the Rhine), this was an ideal pretext for Britain to occupy the Cape. Moreover, the Dutch settlers there felt little rapport with revolutionary France, which had decreed that all slaves were to be freed forthwith.

Lord Macartney, appointed to be military governor at the Cape two years after its capture in 1795, warned that if a resolute enemy, such as France, held the 'Gibraltar of the Indian Ocean' it might 'shake to the foundation, perhaps overturn and destroy, the whole fabrick of our oriental opulence and dominion'. Many politicians in London agreed; indeed, the Cape would have been taken some years earlier, if the French admiral Suffren had not intervened to deflect British plans.

The emergence of Napoleon and his occupation of Egypt in 1798 with 35,000 troops once again raised the spectre of a French onslaught in the East. Without doubt, Napoleon intended his venture across the Mediterranean to be a first step towards the conquest of India: three years earlier the French consul in Cairo had written enthusiastically to Paris that ships built at Suez could carry an army to the Malabar coast in little over six weeks. 'Only in the East can one do great things,' said Napoleon, always yearning to emulate Alexander the Great.

Fittingly enough, Napoleon landed at Alexandria, founded by his hero, and his sense of destiny was conveyed in a despatch to his men: 'Soldiers, – You are about to undertake a conquest the effects of which on civilization and commerce are incalculable. The blow you are about to give to England will be the best aimed, and the most sensibly felt, she can receive until the time arrives when you can give her her death-blow.' He spread maps on the floor of his Cairo headquarters, studying how he would lead an army of 30,000 Frenchmen to the Euphrates, then on to Persia and India, while his ships sailed down the Red Sea from Suez and across the Indian Ocean.

Far out in the ocean was that indomitable redoubt, fittingly called the Ile de France, awaiting the moment of glory. The island was especially precious to Napoleon, since it was the setting for *Paul et Virginie*, a novel of romance and tragedy then beloved above all others by his countrymen. He had decorated its author, Jacques-Henri Bernardin de Saint-Pierre, and awarded him a pension, declaring that the work spoke 'the language of the soul'. Now the Ile de France would play its part in the grand design.

Bonaparte had great hopes of forming alliances with rulers in India and Arabia. On 25 January 1799 he made an overture to the Sultan of Oman: 'I write you this letter to inform you of the arrival of the French army in Egypt. As you have always been friendly, you must be convinced

of our desire to protect all the merchant vessels you may send to Suez.
I also beg you will forward the enclosed letter to Tippoo Sahib by the
first opportunity.' The letter to Tipu (addressed as 'Citizen-Sultan') was
more explicit:

> You are, of course, already informed of my arrival on the
> banks of the Red Sea, with a numerous and invincible army.
> Eager to deliver you from the iron yoke of England, I hasten
> to request that you will send me, by way of Mascate or
> Mocha, an account of the political situation in which you
> are. I also wish that you could send to Suez, or Grand Cairo,
> some able man, in your confidence, with whom I may confer.

There should have been every reason to expect co-operation from
Tipu, and some chance of support from Oman; a French doctor had
become the sultan's confidential adviser after the setting up of a consulate
in Muscat in 1795. But these overtures were little more than bravado,
because Napoleon had been forced on to the defensive six months
earlier when Nelson destroyed his fleet at the battle of the Nile. A
fortnight after sending the two letters Napoleon left for Syria; he visited
Egypt briefly in mid-1799, then slipped off to France.

The frailty of his lines of communication was also revealed when the
letters quickly fell into the hands of the enemy: they were intercepted
by the British agent at Mocha, the Arabian 'coffee port' at the southern
end of the Red Sea, and speedily sent on to India. Even had the package
reached Oman safely, it is uncertain that the sultan would have forwarded the letter to Tipu in South India, because he had recently signed
a treaty aligning himself with the East India Company against France.

In India itself no chances were being taken by its new governor-
general, Lord Wellesley, elder brother of the future Duke of Wellington.
When it became known that '*citoyen Tippoo*' had sent two ambassadors
disguised as merchants to the Ile de France, to forge an alliance with
Napoleon, the East India Company made plans at once for the total
conquest of Mysore. The capital, Seringapatam, would eventually be
taken in May 1799, and Tipu was to die in the fighting. His treasures
were looted and sent to England, including a mechanical tiger which
growled as it mauled a groaning model of a British soldier.[3]

The French had themselves partly to blame for this loss of a crucial
ally for, whereas Tipu had wished for secrecy, the Ile de France governor

had welcomed his emissaries with a cannonade and fêted them during their stay. News of their visit had soon filtered back to India.

All the rumours about Napoleon nevertheless spurred on the British to cement their bastions of power all around the Indian Ocean. They were an ideal pretext for seizing Ceylon, an island long coveted. Its motley non-Sinhalese population also accepted that their destiny was to be absorbed into the British empire, for the shadow of events in India had lain across the island. The moribund Dutch East India Company (VOC) was running Ceylon at a loss and regarded it as the last resort of 'block-heads, libertines and bankrupts'.[4]

For several decades the British East India Company had been eyeing Ceylon's exports of cinnamon and semi-precious stones, and as early as 1760 sent an emissary to the king of Kandy, suggesting an alliance against the Dutch. In 1782 the company's Madras government had tried to seize the Sinhalese trading ports and take away the cinnamon monopoly, but was frustrated by a French naval intervention.

During the last years of their rule in Ceylon the Dutch had seen hopes of a revival in the economy, for cotton and sugar were being grown successfully. However, the British noose was tightening, and in desperation the VOC accepted the proposal of a Swiss nobleman, Charles the Comte de Meuron, that he should, for a handsome fee, recruit a regiment of mercenaries and transport them to Ceylon. Earlier the count had supplied mercenaries for the Cape, and true to his word he duly arrived in Colombo at the head of almost a thousand hired troopers. Having settled them in he put his brother, Pierre, in charge, then returned home to Switzerland. A more modest detachment was sent to Colombo by the Duke of Wurttemberg, another self-styled 'proprietor' of mercenary forces; the German mercenaries were also under the command of Pierre de Meuron.

When this information reached the British in Madras there was much displeasure. It was known that previously the Dutch governor of Ceylon, Van Angelbeek, had scarcely more than 800 white soldiers at his command, plus a horde of unreliable Sinhalese auxiliaries. The mercenaries decidedly changed the balance, making the capture of the heavily forti-fied Colombo far more problematical. Even if the assault succeeded, the cost in lives was sure to be high. So despatches were sent to London, asking if there might be a chance of suborning the Comte de Meuron. At this point a Scottish professor of civil history, Hugh Cleghorn, steps into Indian Ocean history, to play a brief, spectacular and long-forgotten role. Cleghorn had held his teaching post at the university of St Andrews since he was twenty-two, and was now in his forties. But since the French Revolution he had rarely been at his desk. Instead he travelled on the continent, either as an academic, or in the guise of a merchant, but constantly sending back reports to London. In a word, Cleghorn was a spy, and all the complaints from his academic superiors at St Andrews about his longer and longer absences were brushed aside. His portrait radiates energy; he was handsome, with a cool self-assurance.

Cleghorn already knew the Count de Meuron, and in February 1795 he received a letter marked 'Secret' from the British secretary of state for war, Henry Dundas, telling him to go with all possible haste to Neuchâtel, where the elderly count lived. Negotiations 'should, if possible, be brought to a conclusion immediately', then Cleghorn must accompany the count to India to ensure that the mercenaries changed sides without delay. If the count showed reluctance to fall in with this plan he should be offered a 'handsome Douceur' of up to £2,000 (later the maximum was raised to £5,000)[5] 'to induce his acquiescence', and the mercenaries should be guaranteed 'seven years certain' in the service of Britain.

Of course, de Meuron might protest that his personal honour was at stake, but Cleghorn was ready for that: he could argue that the Prince of Orange, ousted by the revolutionary Batavia government and now living in exile at Kew, was the one to whom the count truly owed loyalty, so the question of 'desertion' did not arise. The prince had already sent a message to all Dutch governors, urging them to co-operate with Britain. Moreover, the professor had been empowered to offer the count a further inducement, one which would add grandeur to the glint of sovereigns.

The correspondence from Dundas reveals a total confidence in Cleghorn's talents. He was given virtually unlimited expenses, and told that a Royal Navy ship would be waiting at Leghorn to take him and the count across the Mediterranean to 'such port as you may think most convenient to facilitate your journey to India'. (It was judged quicker to travel by way of Egypt and the Red Sea, a journey not without hazards, yet less likely to end in disaster than going round the Cape and risking capture by the enemy.) Cleghorn was promised that if he came to grief during the enterprise his wife and seven children would be looked after.

Within hours of receiving his instructions he left London for Yar-
mouth, where he boarded a boat for Germany. He was travelling under
the name Andrew Johnston and had arranged to send coded letters back
through a friend, Andrew Stuart, a Scottish member of parliament. The
Elbe was frozen over, but the ice was thawing: Cleghorn managed to
cross with two German guides; later he heard they were drowned
on the return journey – 'probably drank too much brandywine', he
records.

Primed by a letter eloquently hinting at 'arrangements which will at
the same time advance your personal interests and harmonize with your
passion for military service', the Count de Meuron welcomed Cleghorn
heartily. He was nursing a grudge against the Dutch, who were far in
arrears with payments to him for the mercenaries. So within a few days,
in a gentlemanly fashion, the terms were settled: the count is instantly
to be appointed a major-general in the British army, and his brother a
brigadier-general (in the service of the Dutch they were mere colonels).
The mercenaries themselves are to be employed on favourable terms
when they switch their allegiance to Britain. All outstanding payments
from the Dutch are to be made good and the count is to be advanced
£4,000 immediately against his future army salary, so that he can settle
his affairs before starting off for India. During the journey he will be
'maintained in a manner befitting his rank'.

Cleghorn is gleeful when he reports to London by secret letter that
these terms have been accepted. Doubtless, it is the sudden prospect of
becoming a British general in the autumn of his days which proves
irresistible to the count. Yet there were fraught moments before the
departure from Neuchâtel. Although as a young man he had three times
been wounded while fighting for the French in the West Indies, de
Meuron now seems to lose his nerve, saying in a letter to Cleghorn
that it was 'foolish at his age, after establishing a delightful little retreat',
to set out from Switzerland on such a venture. Then the count unexpectedly hears from the Dutch that they have promoted him to brigadier-
general, arousing fears that the secret of his deal with the British may
have been compromised.

Cleghorn writes again to London, saying how urgently he needs the
count's £4,000 advance, and further funds to cover the coming voyage.
He arranges to collect these in Venice, their first destination after leaving
Neuchâtel. Eventually, the journey is discreetly under way. The count
travels with his black valet Julius and insists upon bringing a Captain

Bolle as his military aide. The professor has only his personal servant, Michael Mirowsky.

Sometimes Cleghorn's letters and diary entries hint at exasperation with his ponderous and pompous companion, but all that matters is to transport him to Ceylon alive, there to persuade his brother to defect. As the professor tells Sir Richard Worsley, the British ambassador in Venice, and Admiral William Hotham: 'The business in which I am employed is of the utmost consequence to the interests of our country.' On 8 May, a few days before leaving Venice, he receives a letter of congratulation from Dundas promising that as soon as he is back in London he will be 'liberally compensated'. Cleghorn replies loyally: 'I shall probably have no active part in the arrangement for Ceylon, but there is one satisfaction of which I cannot now be deprived – I shall share the difficulties and I shall be the companion of every danger until that Island is ours.' In a letter to his MP friend Andrew Stuart he confesses to have left without writing to his wife and family about the journey: 'I was afraid of the post, and, to speak fairly, I had not the courage.'

In Alexandria he had time to devise a plot for obtaining despatches sent from Amsterdam to the Dutch consul, for forwarding to Ceylon. He tells the British consul to arrange for the messenger to be attacked ('but not killed') and his letters seized, 'which you will forward to me by the speediest opportunity you can find'. Cleghorn then hurried the count through Cairo and across the desert to the Red Sea, always fearful of discovery by the enemy.

At Suez they boarded a filthy, overcrowded ship. Cleghorn describes the scene: 'The women were scolding, the children crying, and of the men some were supping, some singing hymns, many praying and striking their foreheads on the deck. The smell was suffocating and disagreeable and I found myself soon obliged to retire to my hole below.' The ship bore them with agonizing slowness down the Red Sea, and Cleghorn was dismayed in Jeddah to learn that British ships making the annual round trip from India had already departed, to return on the south-west monsoon. His anxieties grew worse when officials in Jeddah imprisoned him for eight days to extort his money and possessions; he even lost a prized watch, which was taken, returned, then taken again. But such losses mattered little to him when 'the interests of the state will admit of no calculation but that of time and of the means by which my mission can most surely and speedily brought into execution.'

The count added to the anxieties. He had trouble passing water and his strength started to fail in the relentless heat ('He eats too freely', Cleghorn notes in his diary), so it was a relief when they reached the port of Mocha and encountered two English coffee-buyers, agents of the East India Company. Cleghorn confided his mission to them and made good use of their generosity, which later he praised in a letter to Lord Hobart, governor of the Madras Presidency. But there was no time to dally. In a hired dhow the party bade a relieved farewell to the Red Sea, sailed past Aden, and began the last lap, the voyage across the Indian Ocean.

By now the count was preening himself, elated at the thought of how he and his brother Pierre would soon be British generals. As they sailed towards Ceylon he declared a wish to go ashore to reconnoitre. After an argument, Cleghorn vetoed the idea: 'This subject therefore for the present has dropt, and I hope the sight of Ceylon will not revive it.' At last, after the six-month journey from Switzerland, they reached South India, disembarking at a small British-controlled port where Cleghorn decided they were least likely to attract attention.

The party learned that the Dutch, sustained by the presence of the Swiss mercenaries, were still entrenched in Colombo. Although the British already held most of the island's coastline, the governor, Van Angelbeek, was swearing to fight to the last. Cleghorn wasted no time. After meeting Lord Hobart he hastened down to Ceylon, bearing a letter from the count. It tells his brother how he has come to India, and urges him to desert with all his men; the generalship awaits. However, arranging for the letter to be conveyed safely into the hands of Colonel Pierre de Meuron presented a challenge, since Van Angelbeek was naturally suspicious of any contact between the mercenaries and the outside world. Cleghorn was not to be thwarted: he hid the letter inside a Dutch cheese which was sent across the lines into Colombo as a personal gift for the colonel from a wellwisher.

As entranced as his brother at the thought of becoming a British general, Colonel de Meuron marched his men out of Colombo, after brushing aside a threat from Van Angelbeek to have them imprisoned. The mercenaries made one proviso: if there were an assault on the town they should not be asked to take part, since they had left their families and friends inside the walls. But it was now all up with the Dutch. They were demoralized by the loss of de Meuron's regiment, so that when East India Company troops from Madras landed at Colombo late in 1795 there was almost no resistance.

Cleghorn returned triumphantly to London by the same route as he had travelled out and a grateful government gave him a reward of £5,000. However, he was not done with Ceylon. In 1798 the island was declared a British crown colony, because the brutality and corruption of the East India Company's administration had provoked a rebellion. Cleghorn travelled out to take up the high post of colonial secretary. He made a good start, then fell out with the capricious governor, Sir Frederic North (later Lord Guildford). In 1800 he resigned, and returned to his native Fife.

Cleghorn's tombstone in the Stravithie graveyard proclaims him, with forgivable exaggeration, as 'the agent through whose instrumentality the island of Ceylon was annexed to the British Empire'.[6] As for Charles and Pierre de Meuron, they revelled for a while in soldiering for their new masters, then retired to Switzerland, more comfortably off than they might have hoped. Both commissioned portraits of themselves in their uniforms as British generals. The mercenaries of the 'Regiment de Meuron' served with distinction in India, many dying in the siege of Seringapatam; on their gravestones they are simply described as 'Swichter Troops'.[7]

THIRTY-NINE

The French Redoubt
and the Isle of Slaves

As long as the French have the Ile de France, the English will not
be masters of India.

—William Pitt the Elder (Lord Chatham) (1761)

In 1801, during an interlude in the Napoleonic wars, the Cape colony
was abandoned by Britain, on grounds of expense. Nelson had argued
in the House of Lords that warships, their hulls now sheathed in copper,
no longer needed to stop for careening and repairs on the way to India.
He felt well able to pronounce on such matters, having served as a
midshipman, twenty-five years before, in the Indian Ocean. But a year
after Nelson's death at Trafalgar in October 1805, the Cape was captured
again for good, amid rumours that Napoleon intended to use it as a
staging post for a seaborne assault upon India.

The youthful Lord Palmerston, just starting a political career which
would carry him to the highest office, took a typically apocalyptic view
of how events might turn out: Europe was much too confined a sphere
for Napoleon's ambition, 'and we alone prevent him from reducing
India, America and Africa under his power'. (The value Britain now
put on its eastern empire is demonstrated by the way Palmerston placed
it first; moreover, he was writing to Laurence Sulivan, a friend from
his undergraduate days at Cambridge, who had been born in Calcutta
of an East India Company family.)[1]

In reality, the envisaged threat was a chimera, for French naval power
had been ravaged at Trafalgar, and after Tipu's death there were no
significant allies left for France to liaise with in the sub-continent.
Wellesley wrote jovially to Pitt: 'If Bonaparte should choose to visit
Malabar, I trust he will find supper prepared for him before he has
reached Calcutta.' The Anglo-Indian cuisine was never put to the test.

353

For the commanders on the spot, only one irritant remained for Britain in the Indian Ocean: the Ile de France. This was the base for French privateers, who were causing such havoc that in 1808 the Calcutta merchants protested at the lack of protection given by the Royal Navy. At least forty ships had been sunk, and there was indignation at reports that United States gun-runners were supplying equipment to fit out the privateers, then sharing in the proceeds of their raids.[2] The commander-in-chief of the East Indies station ordered that the Ile de France must be 'given a wide berth', and that gold bullion being taken to England should be divided up among the fastest vessels, which should make straight for Portsmouth. It became a punishable offence to sail the Indian Ocean, and likewise the Atlantic, other than in a protected convoy. The damage inflicted on British shipping by the privateers during the Napoleonic wars was later put at ten million pounds.

How to occupy the French redoubt was a matter long debated, for its magnificent harbour was guarded by dangerous coral reefs. Moreover, the population seemed resolved to fight, despite having endured a long blockade by the Royal Navy which had effectively cut all links with the mother country. Only in 1810 was the Ile de France, together with neighbouring Réunion, finally attacked by a massive force of British grenadiers and marines, backed up by Indian sepoys. In the event it soon capitulated. Seven French warships and almost thirty merchant ships were captured. Two thousand British prisoners were set free.

Having seized the island, the victors were determined never to let go of it. For obvious reasons the island was once again to be named Mauritius, as it had been a hundred years before. The French were allowed to keep Réunion, since it lacked any harbour of use in time of war and could, moreover, be kept under surveillance from its sister isle.

The Indian Ocean could now fairly be regarded as an 'English lake'. In the words of the patriotic song, Britannia ruled the waves. The merchant ships of other nations might trade there, but Britain held all the strategic ports: Cape Town and Port Louis in Mauritius dominated access from the Atlantic; Bombay, where the Indian navy was stationed, controlled the Arabian Sea and the entrance to the Persian Gulf; from Ceylon and Calcutta, the administrative capital of the East India Company, the Royal Navy could patrol the Bay of Bengal and routes to China. Possession of Malacca port, taken from the Dutch, gave Britain mastery over all ships using the narrow artery of trade flanked by Malaya and Sumatra.

For the moment there was only one remaining seapower of any consequence in the entire region: Oman. Its new ruler, Sultan Seyyid Said, had come to power in 1806, at the age of fifteen, after stabbing to death his cousin, a rival for the throne. Said's subjects owned hundreds of dhows plying the routs to India, Persia, Bengal, Indonesia and the Red Sea; his personal fleet included several ships of European design, and he possessed a large ragtag army which was constantly fighting his various foes in Arabia.

Although the Oman capital, Muscat, stood near the entrance to the Persian Gulf and was only a few days' sailing from India, the fame of the sultan resounded for 3,000 miles down the coast of East Africa. He was intent, like previous Omani rulers, upon restoring Arabia's ancient hegemony over Zanzibar and the string of Swahili settlements on the mainland.

Some of Said's vessels had traded as far south as Mauritius, while it was still the Ile de France, taking horses and mules there to exchange for sacks of sugar. In 1807 he had signed a commercial treaty with the island, and French privateers had occasionally taken on water and food at Muscat. However, his respect for the British, so pressingly close by in Bombay, had inevitably grown stronger as they mastered the French.

Britain was likewise keen to keep on good terms with this ambitious young sultan, so that his policies might be discreetly guided. There was anxiety that he might be ousted by the rival Arab warlords living along the rocky shores at the mouth of the Persian Gulf. Many of these owned pirate fleets which preyed upon merchant ships sailing between Bombay and the Gulf ports. Some pirate dhows were so well armed that they were willing to do battle with Royal Navy warships, and at times they won. If Said fell victim to some violent domestic intrigue similar to the one which had brought him to power, the almost impregnable Muscat fortress might fall into less friendly hands. That could present a threat to the commerce of the Raj.

So Seyyid Said and the British soon grew to share a common interest in asserting control over the 'Pirate Coast'. Moreover, Said had a motive for revenge, since his father had been killed by the pirates. In 1809 a joint attack was mounted on a pirate stronghold at Ras al Khaimah, just inside the entrance to the Persian Gulf. From Bombay came eleven warships and transports carrying 1,600 British soldiers and 1,000 *sepoys*. Said assembled six warships and 20,000 levies from friendly desert tribes. The pirates were bombarded and fifty armed dhows destroyed by fire.

Unfortunately, the British force retired to Bombay too soon, leaving Said to fight it out. He was beaten, and retreated in humiliation to Muscat.

At that time the British still had their minds on the French, and this in part explains why they were such inconsistent allies. Although Said suffered repeated setbacks at the hands of a plethora of enemies, both inside and outside Omani territory, his appeals to Bombay for help went unanswered. He was still in his teens and there were around him few he could trust, except an indomitable aunt, Bibi Musa. She had supported him when he stabbed his cousin to death, and now her shrewd advice was playing a large part in his survival.

Apart from the unreliable British, Seyyid Said had a last resort: his bags of Maria Theresa dollars. He always had sufficient wealth to buy off his foes, for he held Muscat, and the struggles for control of Oman never disturbed the port's role as one of the busiest markets in the Indian Ocean. Whoever held Muscat was rich. Merchants of many races bargained in its narrow, dusty streets, and Indians were numerous there, part of the *banian* network of trade and finance now expanding throughout the ocean under the aegis of British power.

Said and his confidants turned at times to the Indians for finance, but one business was kept tightly in Omani hands: slavery. It originated in Zanzibar, the East African fulcrum of his empire. At least 100,000 African slaves, most destined to be sold in the Arab world and Persia, were shipped every year to Muscat. They were Said's main source of income, for he collected a head tax on each one, and the trade was estimated to earn him 70,000 dollars a year.[3]

The first European eye-witness to describe what was happening at the Zanzibar end of the slave route was a Captain Thomas Smee, who made a voyage down the East African coast in 1811 on the orders of the Bombay government. He found that African captives 'of all sexes and ages from six to sixty' were daily being marched through the town, the youngest at the front, and being physically examined by prospective buyers with a minuteness 'unequalled in any cattle market in Europe'. The duty on slaves exported from Zanzibar was collected by Said's chief customs officer in Zanzibar, an Ethiopian eunuch named Yakut ibn Ambar. Arab traders paid a dollar in duty for each slave put aboard their dhows. There were also European vessels in Zanzibar harbour, waiting to collect cargoes of slaves. The Christians were charged at least ten times more duty, but the trade was still profitable for them, because most of their human cargoes were taken directly to Mauritius to work in the island's sugar plantations. Apart from Arabic and Swahili, the language most widely understood in Zanzibar was French.

Captain Smee's account came as little surprise to his superiors in Bombay. They were already all too aware that Said was the Indian Ocean's panjandrum of slavery, and they did not question the estimate that three-quarters of the population of Zanzibar were Africans brought forcibly from the mainland. The sultan himself had hundreds of slaves in his retinue.

Nevertheless, there was a diplomatic dilemma here, given the wish to maintain friendship with Said, for in 1807 the parliament at Westminster had passed into law what many British people proudly regarded as Britain's moral rejoinder to the French Revolution: the Abolition Act, which outlawed trading in slaves. The Act was primarily aimed at halting the export to the Americas in British ships of negroes from West Africa, and it gave no mandate for interfering in the affairs of other nations. However, the abolitionists were already eager for new fields to conquer, and Said would in due course be vulnerable to pressure.

Anticipating trouble from home, the Bombay government began discreetly warning Said that laws were being passed in India to prohibit all slave-trading. Omani vessels were still taking cargoes of Africans to Bombay, Calcutta and other ports in the Raj, so the sultan was urged to make his subjects aware of the penalties this might incur. More generally, was it not time for him to 'align himself with civilized opinion'?[4]

Said made no response – understandably enough, seeing how his coffers were kept full by the duties levied in Zanzibar by the loyal Yakut, and by the taxes in Muscat itself. Any pressures to conform with the British law would certainly infuriate his subjects, to whom the buying and selling of *kafirs* provided a livelihood hallowed by tradition. The Bombay authorities knew that, at worst, Britain might risk contributing to the sultan's overthrow, at best it would encourage him to seek less prescriptive allies.

This awkward poser was soon to direct the gaze of the Foreign Office staff in London towards a part of the world about which they knew little and cared nothing: East Africa. None could then have foreseen how continuing revelations about the slave trade in Zanzibar would arouse passions in Britain for more than half a century, and have a significant role in shaping imperial policy towards Africa as a whole.

FORTY

'Literally a Blank
in Geography'

The new possessors of Table Bay require careful watching, or our want of energy will enable them to extend themselves northwards. Who will prevent these new colonists from selling the slaves of our southern interior, thus palpably injuring our trade, which has already lost one-third of its value.

— Dr Francisco de Lacerda, in a despatch to Lisbon (1798)

THROUGHOUT the sixty-year struggle between Britain and France for mastery in the Indian Ocean there was an uneasy bystander. Wrapped in tattered pride, Portugal waited to see how the outcome might affect its rights. It regarded the contestants as *parvenus*, usurpers of what had been won by the courage of the great Lusitanian heroes of the past. This indignity was made worse by the indifference, close to contempt, which was commonly shown towards it.

Yet Portugal still counted for something. In Africa it had clung on to Angola and Mozambique, whose value was more than symbolic, since they were an unfailing source of slaves for its plantations in Brazil. These three Portuguese colonies in the southern hemisphere were still run directly from Lisbon, like royal fiefdoms. Their lethargic administrations were mainly staffed by sycophantic courtiers, risking a few years in the tropics to grasp the chance of wealth.

Occasionally the system did throw up men of a different calibre, and one such was Francisco José Maria de Lacerda, born in Sao Paulo, Brazil, in the mid-eighteenth century.[1] He was sent to the mother country to study mathematics and there gained a doctorate in astronomy. On returning to Brazil he began travelling to remote parts of the South American interior and kept meticulous records of his adventures and discoveries. This rare energy was noted in Lisbon, and Lacerda was ordered to cross the Atlantic to Angola. In March 1797 the Portuguese regent (later John VII) gave Lacerda the task of mounting an expedition for discovering a route all the way across Africa.

It was a novel idea for reinvigorating both Mozambique and Angola. In the earliest days of the Portuguese conquest the *degredado*, Antonio Fernandes, had explored inland from Sofala to beyond Great Zimbabwe, and in following centuries the African markets of the interior were visited regularly by mulatto traders. Prospectors for gold and silver had roamed far and wide, with scant success, from the *prazo* estates of Zambezia. Now Lacerda had been given a clear challenge: to open up a trans-African highway which would be of value for commerce, 'an easy line of communication between the two coasts', and also symbolize the historic rights of Portugal.

The timing of his appointment to Angola was highly significant, since it came only two years after the British seizure of the Cape from the Dutch. Whereas the Dutch, in their decline, had been no real threat, the British were another matter, as shown by their determined empire-building in India. They even possessed an 'Association for Promoting the Discovery of the Interior Parts of Africa', founded in 1788; its interests were first centred upon West Africa, where a Scotsman named Mungo Park had been sent in 1795 with orders to explore the course of the Niger river.[2] Now that Britain had a hold on the southern end of the continent, the Portuguese feared that the association might well start busying itself there.

Lacerda hoped to forestall these new rivals – as he put it, by 'throwing an obstacle in the way of the English' – and so stop them from stealing the markets of the Portuguese traders in Angola and Mozambique. In particular, it was important to protect the trade in slaves, so vital to his birthplace, Brazil, for at the end of the eighteenth century the British had still been active in this traffic. Here was a moment for action. Lacerda was a great patriot, and quoted Camoëns, the poetic chronicler of an heroic age: 'Enough of glory 'tis for me to boast, I loved my native land and nation most.' As well as determination he possessed some novel ideas: when the trans-continental route was mapped out, camel caravans should be used to transport goods along it, instead of relying on African porters.

Lacerda did not launch into the task from Angola, but busied himself collecting information there. The Portuguese settlers, who numbered about a thousand, mostly clung to the coast; powerful peoples inland, such as the Chokwe and Mbundu, had come to dislike the sight of anyone in European clothes. Three centuries of the slave trade had devastated the region, and most trading away from the coast was carried out by half-caste bondsmen (*pombeiros*). Nevertheless, a few years earlier a white trader had managed to reach the headwaters of the Zambezi where the great river began its uncharted journey to the Indian Ocean.

The heart of the continent remained a mystery: between the furthest penetration from Angola and the Mozambique outpost of Zumbo lay a gap of hundreds of miles, where all trade was in African hands. Some 600 miles inland from the Atlantic there were busy markets in the kingdom of a monarch known as Mwata Yamvo, 'Lord of Death', who wore round his neck a chain of office made from human testicles.[3] Lesser rulers, further to the east, paid allegiance to Mwata Yamvo, so that European manufactures such as clothing, mirrors, cutlery, crockery and weapons easily filtered through to their villages. Items which had begun their journey on the west coast occasionally found their way right across the continent to Mozambique. Some items were less utilitarian: treasured for generations among the relics of one paramountcy were a pair of Virgin Mary statuettes.

His inquiries in Angola convinced Lacerda that he should begin his trans-continental journey in the east. As he boarded a ship in Benguela bound for Mozambique, he would have passed on the quayside a marble chair in which a bishop would sit to bless the slaves as they were carried in longboats to ships waiting in the harbour. During the voyage round the foot of Africa there was invariably a call at Cape Town for water and supplies, and this would have given Lacerda the chance to survey his adversaries.

Lacerda had been appointed governor of Sena, on the Zambezi, in March 1798, but wasted no time on these duties. His only desire was to start on the way to the capital of Mwata Kazembe, a powerful ruler who paid tribute to the even more powerful 'Lord of Death', Mwata Yamvo.[4] The route to the capital of the man the Portuguese called 'king' Kazembe was almost due north from the closest starting-point on the Zambezi, a distance of nearly 500 miles. The king regularly sent large amounts of ivory and copper to the Mozambique coast to barter for manufactured goods, so it was thought likely that he would welcome a visit by European emissaries.

According to the maps of the time, although they were hardly more than guesswork, Lacerda's expedition would be marching towards the legendary 'Lake Zembre', from which all the great rivers of Africa, including the Nile and the Zambezi, reputedly flowed. If a westward course was taken after reaching Kazembe's territory, the Atlantic coast could be reached, so it was rumoured, in three months.

Lacerda's ambition overcame his common sense. In the backwoods town of Tete he assembled a force so large that it resembled an army: 400 Africans hired as porters; fifty soldiers led by a Lieutenant-Colonel Pedro Nolasco; a chaplain, Father Francisco Pinto; a horde of personal servants and several guides. There were also the inevitable camp-followers, who trailed behind this great cavalcade as it left Tete at the start of July 1798.[5]

His countrymen's notoriety was to prove Lacerda's greatest disadvantage. Their tactic for survival in the interior of Mozambique had been to set one African community against another. Moreover, the continuing efforts by priests and friars to spread Christianity were resented among African rulers, who saw this as a challenge to their own spiritual authority. One rare exception had been a Jesuit, Father Pedro da Trinidade. He had built up the settlement at Zumbo, from where Lacerda's expedition would launch itself into the unknown. During a great famine earlier in the century, Father Pedro had saved many people from starvation.

Unfortunately for Lacerda, he had no guide like Father Pedro, but had to rely upon a *mestico*, Gonçalo Caetano Pereira, who claimed to have visited Kazembe two years earlier. The Africans gave everyone a nickname, and Caetano was called Dumbo-dumbo, meaning 'The terror'. He took pride in it, but with every step away from the Zambezi the expedition found itself less and less able to impose its will on the local people. Along the winding track it followed through the dense bush – which Lacerda calls in his diary the 'high road' – there were many other travellers, carrying goods in each direction; these were African traders, mostly from the Bisa community, and they clearly disliked this European intrusion. The expedition also had to face a warlike people, the Bemba: 'mortal enemies to, never sparing, the Kazembe's people.'

There were even more immediate problems: the porters carrying loads of cloth, beads and other trade goods quickly tired of the work and fled into the bush; their white superiors responded by forcing the remainder to march in chains, and by flogging any who tried to desert. During the march Lacerda recruited 200 women porters, since they were reputed to be more obedient. He writes: 'My sleep is lost and my days and nights spent in thinking how to obviate the delays, the slow marches and the Kafirs' insolence . . . When I send a command to be executed, all cry out and do nothing.' Travelling in South America had been a pleasure by comparison.

Floggings became a daily event. Lacerda describes the porters as 'barbarians', but adds that they expect 'truth, good faith and honesty' from the white man. He knew that such qualities were scarce among his subordinates.

At last, after more than three months of fighting its way through forest and swamps, the expedition staggered into Kazembe's capital beside Lake Mweru. It was welcomed with dancing and drumming. One of the ruler's aides held out his arms, pointing to the two roads across the continent, to Angola and Mozambique, to the Atlantic and the Indian Ocean; but the man whose dream it had been to open up this route was past caring. Wracked by malaria and despair, Lacerda had been borne by slaves for many weeks on a palanquin. A fortnight later, on 18 October 1798, he died.

Leaderless, the expedition at once fell to pieces, its members anxious to be back in the relative safety of the Zambezi settlements of Tete and Sena. The chaplain, Father Pinto, was nominally in charge, but few paid attention to him. Small groups began to slip away, to run the gauntlet of the hostile villages along the route southwards. The rains began, making travel near to impossible and causing even more malaria. Months went by as the quarrelsome remnants of the expedition lingered on the outskirts of Kazembe's muddy capital, whittling away the stocks of cloth and beads to buy their food. Any thought of pushing on to Angola, as Lacerda had so much wanted, was utterly abandoned.

Not until the July 1799, long after the rains had ended, did Father Pinto summon up the will to begin the hazardous journey back. It started with a bad omen, for the digging up of Lacerda's remains for bearing home was interrupted by fighting, and pieces of the body were strewn in all directions. On the march Pinto was carried in the palanquin, but his own 'wild Kafirs' refused to do the work, and the dead leader's slaves were pressed into service. Some sick slaves could not keep up with the hurried pace set by the soldiers, so they were summarily beheaded. Since they were the property of the Crown, Pinto was greatly distressed.

As recorded in his diary, the return march becomes a disorderly retreat, a saga of desperation. Pinto realizes, when the villagers agree to sell food only at 'blackmail' prices, that the Bisa traders have given instructions for the expedition to be starved and robbed. Poisoned arrows are fired from the trees and supplies are jettisoned. Even Caetano the guide, 'the Terror', becomes so bereft that he has to hand over a small slave-girl for food. Father Pinto also owns a 'little negress', and exchanges her for some millet and a handful of groundnuts.

In the final weeks of 1799 the survivors approach the outskirts of Tete, from which Lacerda had set forth eighteen months before with such great hopes. The priest is filthy and his clothes are in shreds; while carrying his palanquin, the bearers have dropped him into a river, quite deliberately, he is sure. Unwilling to lay bare the extent of the disaster in broad daylight, he decides to wait outside the town until night has fallen.

In 1808, ten years after Lacerda had warned that the 'new occupants of Table Bay' might soon start pushing northwards, an assistant surgeon named Andrew Cowan obtained an interview with Lord Caledon, governor-general of the Cape. Cowan had arrived in South Africa in 1806 with the 72nd Regiment of Foot, but treating the ailments of British infantrymen was becoming tedious work. Moreover, as a man of humble birth he was unlikely to rise much higher in the medical service, so he now made a daring request: that he be allowed to lead an expedition from the Cape to explore the interior of the continent.[6]

Impressed by such an adventurous spirit, Caledon granted permission, and Cowan chose a fellow-Irishman, Lieutenant Donovan of the 83rd Foot, as his companion. Twenty-two Khoikhoi were hired to go with them, as well as a *trekboer* named Kruger who had experience of travel in unmapped territory.

Cowan led his party across the Orange river and was joined by a Scottish missionary, William Anderson, who was stationed at one of the advance outposts of his calling. The party marched forward, then halted on Christmas Eve 1808 in country well to the north of where any Europeans had been before. Cowan wrote a letter, explaining how he would continue until he emerged on the Mozambique coast, to make contact there with one of the Portuguese settlements; the halfway point was almost reached. Armed with the letter, Anderson turned back, and reached Cape Town safely. Delighted with the news, Lord Caledon ordered that a sloop should be sent to Mozambique to collect Cowan, Donovan and their escort.

They never appeared and there was never to be any further word of them. The expedition's fate became an unsolved mystery, the only tantalizing clues being the discovery, many years later, of a few regimental buttons. For years there were rumours that the explorers were still alive but being held hostage. According to another theory, fever had suddenly wiped out the entire party. For long afterwards every British ship sailing to Mozambique was told to make careful inquiries for any news of Cowan and his companions.

Searching for the expedition was one of the duties given to the Royal Navy frigate _Nisus_ before she headed out of Table Bay in 1812 on a voyage to East Africa. Her crew would also be on the lookout for enemy ships, since the seemingly endless war with Napoleon still dragged on; however, chances of encountering them were slight, because since the capture of Mauritius the French had been swept right out of the Indian Ocean. So the frigate's formal task was to undertake a diplomatic mission to the Comoro islands, lying between Mozambique and Madagascar.

An emissary from the sultan of Anjouan, the best-known of the Comoros, had lately arrived in Cape Town to appeal for British protection against raiders from Madagascar. The emissary claimed that the raiders, using sea-going canoes, 'came in their thousands' to carry the island people away into slavery. (The Muslims of Anjouan had many domestic slaves themselves, but seeing their own free people borne off into captivity was quite another matter.)

It was a sign of the changing horizons in the Indian Ocean that the sultan – grandly referred to as 'King of the Comoro Islands' – should have looked for help to the Cape, some 2,000 miles to the south of Anjouan. Arab dhows never ventured to the Cape, so the emissary must have taken passage on a homeward-bound Indiaman. The sultan's appeal was warmly received, because the new governor-general of the Cape, Sir John Cradock, was well aware of the 'civilities and refreshments afforded by these simple and harmless islanders to the English Indiamen'. That was true enough; Anjouan was commonly known to sailors as 'Johanna', and the inhabitants were fond of taking British names. It had long been a convenient calling-place on the way to Bombay or Calcutta, and in the 1770s a ship belonging to the East India Company had helped the sultan put down a revolt by slaves and peasants. The company had also sent costly presents to the ruler for rescuing the crew of a ship which had gone down off Anjouan, reportedly while transporting slaves, all of whom had drowned.

The dignified emissary, in Arab turban and robes, was discovered to speak 'tolerable' English, acquired while living in India. As a sign of their approval for this ability his hosts called him Bombay Jack. (His proper name was indecipherably recorded as Barra Comba.) It was decided that he should be returned to Anjouan in a British man-of-war, with presents and words of warm support. On the way there would be a visit to Madagascar, to warn the populace 'by threats or negociation' that in future they must leave the friends of Britain in peace. This decision to send a gunboat to Anjouan was an early manifestation in the Indian Ocean of the British urge to become 'mankind's policeman'.

A lively record of the voyage of the *Nisus* (named by some Royal Navy classicist after a minor Trojan hero) was kept by James Prior, the ship's doctor. He tells how he quickly strikes up a friendship with Bombay Jack, whom he describes as being 'about fifty years of age, lively and good-humoured, has a penetrating eye, and expressive countenance'. What is more, notes the youthful Prior loftily, 'he understands something of our character'. Indeed, the account unwittingly leaves no doubt that the sultan's emissary understood a great deal.

Repeatedly invited during the voyage to dine with the ship's officers, Bombay Jack occasionally drinks coffee with them, but otherwise keeps himself apart, and 'frequently says we are much too good, too kind, to an "old useless black man"'. Quite apart from the dictates of religion about the preparation of food, the sheikh is perhaps making his excuses because he finds the young officers rather tedious company.

One main object of the voyage, the threatening of the Malagasy slave-raiders, is not achieved, because bad weather stops the *Nisus* from coming near the island's shoreline. Instead, the frigate sails along the Mozambique coast, making contact where possible with the Portuguese. Prior is far from complimentary about them: 'The atmosphere of the place is anything but heroic, for though first founded by heroes, their spirit has long ceased to actuate the present inhabitants.' He discovers that little remains of Sofala, once so renowned. Now there is only a lone Portuguese resident 'protected by a few black troops and a small fort'.

When the frigate reaches Mozambique island there is more to exercise Prior's literary talents.[7] The Portuguese governor is based here: 'The name of His Excellency is Don Antonio Manuel de Mello Castro e

Mendoza, and, according to report, is a person of no less consequence than the length of his name might seem to imply.'

When the British officers go ashore their first sight of the governor is at the guardhouse to his palace, where 'he received the usual honours stretched full length on his palanquin'. They discover that the governor has rarely travelled anywhere, or been exposed to the sun, 'lest he should endanger his invaluable health', and has done nothing for agriculture or trade. However, by exploiting the advantages of his office he has built up an immense fortune. His greatest pride is a billiards table, and he amuses himself by playing on it for hours each day.

Having made sufficient mock of the governor (who for his part is distinctly cool towards the British visitors), Prior puts down all he can discover about the African interior. He learns that two mulattoes, Pedro João Battista and Amaro José, have only recently made a double journey across the continent, from Angola to the Zambezi river and back. A journey one way would take only 200 days; but this would need constant speed, 'which is an improbable circumstance in any part of Africa'. Although Prior does not mention Lacerda by name, he records that several Mozambique governors, more energetic than the present incumbent, have tried in vain to lead expeditions inland: '. . . it is generally believed here that attempts made to penetrate the interior from this coast will not be successful. This, however, is a merely gratuitous supposition.'

As for Cowan and Donovan, there is no encouraging news. The general belief, based upon vague tales from the interior, is that they were massacred to a man, somewhere south of Sofala and about 'forty leagues' inland. Prior asks about the Zambezi, and is told that it rises from a lake some 700 to 800 miles from the coast. Certain 'bold and ferocious' tribes are constantly on the move behind Mozambique, attacking in force with spears, bows and arrows, and muskets.

It seems to Prior that most of Africa is lost in obscurity, 'literally a blank in geography.' The people are generally 'hideous in habits and barbarous in disposition'; however, 'to know them might be to civilize them.' He records that among Bombay Jack's entourage is a slave (typically awarded the nickname Moses) whose native language cannot be understood by any of the other Africans in the ship; clearly, there is much diversity in these hidden lands, many riddles to be solved. For all his prejudice, the young naval doctor shows himself to be a man of the new age, keen to assemble facts and draw logical conclusions.

The voyage from Mozambique to Anjouan proves uneventful, except that one of the frigate's British seamen tells the slave Moses that he is to be cooked and eaten the next day. In terror the man hides himself in the hold. Bombay Jack spends much time undoing the damage, explaining to Moses that this is only the white man's humour. There is no suggestion that the sailor has deserved, or is likely to receive, any reprimand.

In Anjouan a supply of arms and ammunition is put ashore for fending off slave-raiders, and Prior is called upon to treat various ailments afflicting the households of the sultan and his sheikhs. He boasts of his flirtation with the wives: 'During the momentary absence of the master of the mansion, one of the prettiest took my hand to examine it, and I could do no less than kiss hers in return. Far from being offended, the lady seemed as if she would not dislike a still warmer repetition of the salute, but just at that moment the trust guardian of the castle returned.'

Having done its best for Anjouan's sultan, whose coral-stone palace has been well stocked with muskets, the frigate sails on to Kilwa, her last African port of call. There Prior learns of the treaty drawn up by Monsieur Morice, thirty-five years before. In the Kilwa harbour there is even a Morice Islet, 'named after the first adventurer from Mauritius'. The ruler of Kilwa, Yusufu, claims to control a portion of the coast, and some of the frigate's crew go ashore in a dangerous and abortive search for timber suitable for spars. They find the mainland largely depopulated by the slave trade.

Earlier, Prior had remarked that the Portuguese were once exporting 10,000 slaves a year from Mozambique to America and the Indian Ocean islands; now he claims that the figure is down to 3,000, through the 'exertions of England'. This exaggeration, calculated to please armchair abolitionists, gives way in Kilwa to Prior's heavy jocularity. He tells how the French formerly bought slaves here for thirty-two dollars, equal to eight pounds sterling: 'A most compendious method of raising men, which, I am surprised, none of the promoters of war in Europe have thought of.' He goes on: 'I marvel that Napoleon has not hit upon such a cheap scheme for raising an army to attack, or at least frighten, us in India.' It is the swaggering humour of a nation confident of having got the better of its arch-enemy.[8]

FORTY-ONE

Two Ways with
the Spoils of War

> When Britain sought the eastern world
>   And her victorious flag unfurl'd,
> She came to heal and not to bruise,
>   The captive's fetters to unloose,
>   And 'tis her brightest boast and fame
>   That naught is left beyond the name,
>   Yet here the African remains,
>   Though broken are his slavish chains,
> Prepar'd to conquer or to die,
>   For her who made his fetters fly.
> —Thomas Ajax Anderson, *Wanderings in Ceylon* (1817)

IT WAS FITTING that *Wanderings in Ceylon*, by the poetically-inclined Captain Anderson of the 19th Foot, should have included some stirring couplets on slavery. The captain's vision of Africans prepared to die out of gratitude to their liberators perfectly captures the British mood just after the Napoleonic wars: pride infused with righteousness. Moreover, inspiration close at hand made Anderson turn his muse towards this topic, for the Third Ceylon Regiment was entirely made up of former slaves. The island's British rulers were proud of their African infantry, and like the Dutch before them were making good use of the musical talents of these 'unfettered' recruits by training some up to be army bandsmen.

The origin of the black soldiers of the Third Regiment is a curious illustration of the inter-relationships within the Indian Ocean. However, by the time Captain Anderson was writing his verses, this was a sliver of history which his superiors did not care to have inspected in too close detail, for it dated back to the early 1800s when the slave trade was still legal. It was also a moment when the British were painfully short of soldiers in Ceylon and still harboured acute fears of Napoleon.

The island's governor at the time, Sir Frederick North, had appealed for a regiment of West Indian negroes to be sent to Ceylon, since they would be well suited to the climate, but nothing came of that. His discreet solution was to buy African slaves and train them up to fight for Britain.

At first Sir Frederick thought of putting together no more than a 'Caffre Corps', but then his ambitions widened to buying up enough slaves for a full regiment, 1,000 strong. The obvious sources, near at hand, were Goa and other Portuguese trading centres along the Indian coast, and North was soon corresponding on the topic with Sir William Clarke, the British ambassador in Goa.[1] In July 1804 the ambassador writes to say he has already collected fifty blacks to send down to Colombo, and found a Captain Scott who is willing to transport 'any number that may be ready' in his ship *Hercules* for a price of 2,000 rupees. However, the price of the slaves themselves becomes a matter of keen debate, for Clarke points out to North that a buying agent named Colonel Taylor has been paying forty pounds a head, whereas 'the caffres I have collected will not stand you more than thirty guineas a head'.

Eventually, buying from Goa becomes tiresomely slow, because the Catholic priests there threaten to refuse the sacrament to any Portuguese who sell slaves to a Protestant. Clarke boasts that he has 'employed a little stratagem' to outwit the priests, but Sir Frederick has already decided to take the logical next step and buy blacks at the source. He sends a ship to Mozambique to load up with a complete consignment of slaves, mainly men for the regiment but also a leavening of young women.

Almost five hundred Africans are purchased on the governor's behalf, but their voyage to Ceylon becomes a nightmare. As the ship sets out from Mozambique to cross the Indian Ocean the slaves begin fighting with Indian soldiers who are on board to keep order, and twenty-three are killed. Many others die from disease before Colombo is reached.

Despite these losses, North musters enough slaves for his regiment, by the addition of Africans taken from captured French ships. He is proud of his achievement, for he is sure they will be better for the task than any similar force raised among 'natives of the Continent of India'. However, he tells his commanding officer that there must not be any more slave-buying, 'more especially as the extent to which I have purchased Caffres for the military establishment was not known to His Royal Highness the Commander in Chief, nor to His Majesty's other Ministers'. Sir Frederick's enterprise had been just in time, because two years after the Third Ceylon Regiment was established the British parliament passed the act outlawing slave-trading by all His Majesty's subjects.

The black regiment saw nothing of Napoleon, but proved useful at the start of 1815 in a brisk little war against the last king of Kandy, Sri Wickrama Rajasinha. The author of *Wanderings in Ceylon* also took part, leading a section of the 19th Foot, one of seven columns which advanced boldly into the mountains from various points on Ceylon's coastal plain.

This attack on Kandy was made in defiance of warnings from the colonial secretary in London, Lord Bathurst. More importantly than the risk of bloodshed, he frowned at the likely cost of acquiring and holding yet more acres of tropical territory with little prospect of commercial benefit. There had also been mutterings from the British troops, who did not relish struggling uphill from Colombo for more than a hundred miles over steep tracks and through thick forest. Although Kandy itself was at less than 2,000 feet, the mountains further inland, including Adam's Peak, rose to around 8,000 feet, threatening the prospect of an exhausting hide-and-seek campaign.

However, the Governor of Ceylon, Lieutenant-General Sir Robert Brownrigg, had never wavered and the army's only cause for regret was that there was scarcely any fighting, all of the handful of casualties being on the defending side. Wickrama was not a monarch like Tipu Sultan, the 'Tiger of Mysore', who had succumbed sword in hand. He simply capitulated, surrounded by his womenfolk. For Anderson and his fellow-officers, for whom 'pluck' was the highest virtue, such behaviour seemed to typify the Sinhalese. They needed firm leadership, and Britain would give it to them.

Brownrigg had played upon the rivalries within the Sinhalese nobility and was soon able to bring the captive king triumphantly down to Colombo. Meanwhile, the British troops looked in wonder at Kandy's palaces, its ornamental lake and royal gardens. There was plenty to loot in the temples, although the royal throne was saved intact by Brownrigg and sent in due course to Windsor Castle. It was covered in gold, studded with precious stones, and the arms were in the form of couchant lions, with eyes of amethysts 'each rather larger than a musket ball'.

Determined to forestall any criticism of this personal piece of empire-building, Brownrigg arranged for a justification to be written at speed in Colombo and sent to London. It was published as a seventy-three page pamphlet entitled 'A Narrative of Events which have recently occurred in the Island of Ceylon, written by a Gentleman who was on the Spot'.[2] The account was at pains to portray the king as a 'sanguinary and remorseless tyrant' and a 'monster', and Brownrigg as a benign administrator only concerned to 'deliver an innocent and helpless people' from oppression and 'receive them under the Parental Protection and permanent Dominion' of the British government. This interpretation was not an entire travesty, because Wikrama had certainly shown extreme cruelty to his enemies; moreover, the Kandyan royal family had become through marriage more Indian than Sinhalese, so seeming almost as foreign to most of Ceylon's people as the British themselves. The anonymous author of the pamphlet described the deposed king as 'above the middle size, of a corpulent yet muscular appearance, and with a physiognomy which is at all times handsome and frequently not unpleasing'.

The king was exiled with his family for the rest of his life (almost twenty years) to Vellore, a town on the east coast of India. He left Colombo with dignity, wearing all his finery and jewels as he was taken to the quayside in Brownrigg's personal carriage. While he boarded the British warship he addressed the Sinhalese who helped him as his 'children'. On Brownrigg's orders Wikrama was treated in exile like a prisoner of war 'without splendour or honours', but in comfort.

The deed having been done, the governor's apologist stressed its benefits: 'Thus, without the loss of a single life on our part, has been added to the British crown the entire and peaceable possession of the beautiful, extensive and fertile island of Ceylon . . . the advantages from this conquest are incalculable. The position of Ceylon, its fine harbours, and rich and peculiar productions, must render it a place of the utmost importance in our Eastern dominions.' Lord Bathurst's doubts were not assuaged. In the following year he ordered that all military works in Ceylon should be suspended and the administration cut back.

Brownrigg's triumph was a milestone on the forward march of the British empire, in some aspects more decisive than the much vaster acquisition of territory which was starting to take place in India. There many maharajahs and other traditional princes were left on their thrones, but guided by British 'political officers'. In contrast, throughout Ceylon there was to be direct rule by colonial administrators, without serious pretence that the inhabitants had any say in policy. A fresh pattern was being created, and this would throw its shadow ahead in the later decades of the nineteenth century. Britain now felt confident to proclaim what was best for native peoples, to 'receive them under Parental Protection', to raise the Union Jack over them and extend the blessings of progress, as that was interpreted in Europe.

Sir Thomas Munro, one of the more liberal-minded administrators in the East, crystallized his ideas on India: it was to be looked on 'not as a temporary possession, but one which is to be maintained permanently, until the natives shall have abandoned most of their prejudices, and become sufficiently enlightened to maintain a regular government for themselves, and to conduct and preserve it'.

Such theories took an exceedingly long view of the empire. Another sign of fresh thinking was the promotion of Ceylon as ideal for white settlers: its salubrious highlands were now entirely opened up for them. On the coast there was a residue of the Dutch community, and several thousand mixed-race people with Portuguese names, but a British colony needed Britons. The first newcomers arrived within a decade of Wikrama's overthrow, to grow coffee, and by 1840 there was even a 'land rush'. The island's game, especially the elephant herds, added to its charms and attracted wealthy sportsmen.[3] Ceylon had taken its place as one of the lesser jewels in the British imperial crown, and a main street in Colombo was renamed in Brownrigg's honour.

In practical terms the takeover of their island made little difference to the lives of the bulk of the people. Only the nobles had resisted: the corpse of one who committed suicide before he could be hanged was publicly beheaded. Most Sinhalese took refuge in Buddhism, the main faith of Ceylon for more than two thousand years. It had been decreed that all established religions might still be practised, and there was no lack of them: apart from Buddhism, the Tamils followed Hinduism, the 'Moors' were Muslims and people of mixed race were generally Catholics. When British missionaries began arriving they found it hard to make many converts. Only a minority of Sinhalese came into direct contact with the British settlers, through either working in their homes or on their land; but for the language barrier they would have discovered that their new masters were prone to call them savages.

Bringing Ceylon into the Pax Britannica had been a simple matter, but absorbing the other Indian Ocean island captured during the Napoleonic wars was far more taxing. Mauritius already had its white settlers, a hostile community of several thousand Frenchmen, together with their 60,000 slaves. Neither Frenchmen nor slaves were welcome additions to the empire. The task of solving this conundrum fell to Robert Farquhar, who although only thirty-five was chosen as governor for the skill he had shown as an East India Company administrator in the Moluccas, and for his interest in the problems of slavery. Writing to the Calcutta officials in 1805 he had been emphatic: 'Slavery is the greatest of all evils, and the attempt to regulate such an evil is in itself almost absurd.'

He had published, in 1807, at his own expense, a long treatise entitled 'Suggestions, arising from the abolition of the African slave trade, for supplying the demands of the West India colonies'. Farquhar's ideas were novel: he proposed a mass emigration of Chinese labourers across the world to the Caribbean. Since China was reputedly suffering from over-population, he fancied that its government would probably co-operate, despite a general tendency to be obstructive. Even if Chinese women were stopped from emigrating, that would not matter, since the men were 'indifferent about the colour or conditions of the females they cohabit with'. Farquhar argued that the Chinese were much more industrious than the poor in Europe, and more 'adroit' than Africans. They should be transported in reasonable comfort: the ships should carry a supply of live hogs, since the Chinese liked nothing better than pork.

Farquhar's plan was never implemented, but it did enhance his standing and helped to win him the Mauritius governorship, which called for firmness and diplomacy. He had found the island near to starvation after the long British blockade, so unsurprisingly his attempts to extract genuine pledges of loyalty to their new masters from the French *colons* proved futile. As for the hordes of slaves on the island, Farquhar's main anxiety was to import enough grain to keep them fit to cut the sugar cane.

On Christmas Day 1810, he had been able to send a despatch assuring the British foreign secretary, Lord Liverpool, that the island was in good order. But less than two months later he was urging that Mauritius should be allowed to import more slaves, to save it, and the sister island of Réunion, from becoming 'deserts', unable to continue producing crops. There was, moreover, no lack of French merchant ships – despite the continuing war – ready to fetch these familiar cargoes from East Africa or Madagascar. His anti-slavery ideals having been dented by the pressures of the moment, Farquhar offers a neat way of circumventing

the Abolition Act of 1807: 'I believe . . . that an Act made previously
to the acquisition of a colony . . . will not, generally speaking, bind that
colony acquired subsequently.'[4]

Lord Liverpool, soon to become prime minister, was a Tory but
high-minded, and Farquhar's proposition shocked him. 'I cannot sufficiently express my surprise that you should have supposed it possible',
he responded, 'that when the Parliament of the United Kingdom had
thought it proper upon general Principles to abolish the Slave Trade
with respect to all the ancient colonies . . . it could have been in their
contemplation that this Trade should be suffered to exist with respect
to those Islands or Foreign Possessions which the fortunes of War might
place under his Majesty's Dominion.' There was no mistaking such a
thunderbolt, and a Slave Trade Felony Act, passed in the same month
as Liverpool's despatch was sent off, stipulated 'effectual abolition of the
slave trade wheresoever it may be attempted to practise it'.

On reading Lord Liverpool's rebuff the ambitious Farquhar could see
the way he must go. He declared it was his aim to ban all shipments
of slaves to Mauritius from then on. Yet the ban was breached immediately by his agreement with the French planters of Tamatave, on the
eastern side of Madagascar. When they had capitulated to Britain they
were promised in return that they could transport their private property,
including slaves, across to Mauritius. The list of these slaves accepted
by Farquhar totalled 863, but soon the number rose to well above a
thousand. When three more French ships arrived from Tamatave their
holds were found to be crammed with slaves. The ships were sent under
escort to the Cape, but it was decided there that all the slaves should
be shared out among the French claimants, on the grounds that the
inhabitants of Mauritius had not been given time to understand British
law.

Attempts to impose an anti-slavery blockade against Mauritius were
futile, since there were few Royal Navy ships to spare for such work.
At night risky games of hide-and-seek took place among the coral reefs.
Only rarely was a slave ship caught. Even then the captains generally
went free, because Farquhar was obliged to hand them for trial to the
island's French magistrates, who refused to convict. When he tried
to send one blatantly guilty captain to the Cape, the prisoner dived
overboard in Port Louis harbour, swam ashore, and was never seen
again.

The French planters were running rings round Farquhar. In 1819 the number of slaves in Mauritius reached 80,000, from 60,000 at the time of the island's acquisition through the 'Fortunes of War'. Unsurprisingly, this came to the notice of the abolitionists in London, fervent campaigners such as Thomas Fowell Buxton. What was happening in this distant crown colony? Was the governor too weak, or even conniving with the slave-owners? Such questions were soon to echo through the House of Commons. The unease about Farquhar's performance grew keener when a Major-General Hall, running affairs while the governor was on leave, sent three French seamen to Britain for trial at the Old Bailey in 1819. They belonged to the crew of a pinnace and had been caught landing ninety-two slaves in Mauritius. Their sentence was three years' hard labour.[5]

In Farquhar's defence it was argued that he had done his utmost to cut off the flow of slaves from Madagascar, through his 1817 treaty with the Hova ruler Radama, extravagantly called 'His Majesty the King of Madagascar'. In return for swearing to prohibit any further exports of slaves from his domain, Radama was to be given each year 1,000 gold dollars, 1,000 silver dollars, 100 barrels of gunpowder, 100 muskets, a full-dress uniform, and clothes for his soldiers. Farquhar assured Radama that the king of England would be happy when he heard that the king of Madagascar had 'followed the example of the wise kings of the whites' to abolish the 'sale of black men'.

All this achieved little. There were many parts of Madagascar where Radama's writ did not run. Slaves could still be bought there, as they could from Mozambique and other parts of the mainland. (There existed, admittedly, keen rivalry from Brazil, which every year was now importing 20,000 or more Mozambican slaves.)

A further complicating factor in Mauritius was the desire to win over the defeated French whose hero, Napoleon, was living out his days on another British island, St Helena. The planters looked enviously across to their sister island, Réunion, where the *tricolor* still flew and the governor showed a quite relaxed attitude to the importation of slaves. (Réunion had been handed back to the French at the Congress of Vienna.)

A yearning to cast off British rule, to become the Ile de France once again, was being covertly encouraged from Paris. The loss of the island was felt bitterly there, especially among senior naval officers, and they were emphatic that the old enemy must never get its clutches on Madagascar, where British missionaries were already at work. As Admiral

Duperré, the navy minister, was to warn in the 1830s, it would be 'the subject of eternal reproach' to any French government which might let Madagascar slip into becoming a British possession.[6]

When Farquhar retired, knighted and appointed to the board of the East India Company, he entered Parliament. There he confronted his accusers. He was still concerned to win the planters' good-will, and managed to have the duty on Mauritian sugar, landed in Britain, lowered to the level of imports from the West Indies. However, the island was now becoming notorious as the slave-pit of the empire, a topic for constant agitation by the Anti-Slavery Society. One assertion which sent a *frisson* through British audiences was that female slaves were whipped in public.

The report of a parliamentary commission appointed in 1828 contained enough horrors to make Wilberforce turn in his grave. Even now slaves were being transported to Mauritius; although kept in chains, they made frantic efforts to escape before the ships left Africa. When disembarked they were lined up in warehouses, with prices hanging from their necks. The commission, headed by a Major Colebrooke, urged a speedy end to slave-owning in Mauritius.

The planters reacted furiously and sent one of their number, Adrien D'Epinay, to London to plead their case. Without slaves or full compensation, he argued, his compatriots would be ruined. At the start of 1832 the news reached Mauritius that D'Epinay's pleas had been in vain and the slaves were indeed about to be emancipated. A general strike was called, thousands of guns were distributed, and vigilantes marched threateningly through Port Louis. In the harbour, British warships waited for orders to send marines ashore.

The English-speaking residents were comforted by the thought that if fighting did break out they would surely have the slaves on their side. Eventually this mood of rebellion ebbed away; the planters knew their moment had passed when Major-General Sir William Nicolay arrived at the new governor. He was uncompromising, proclaiming that troops would be brought in from India if there were any further signs of trouble.

One result of the 1828 commission of inquiry had been the appointment to Mauritius of a Mr R. M. Thomas as 'protector of slaves'. He was kept busy dealing with complaints of brutality, but often tended to side with the masters. Typically, he ordered a boy named Hypolite, aged 'between nine and ten years', to be 'well whipped with a birch rod' for claiming that his owner, a Monsieur Regnault, had forced him to drink a mixture of arrack and excrement. Regnault had denied it, saying that the mixture was only arrack and ipecacuanha, to discourage the boy's fondness of alchohol. Protector Thomas duly submitted a record of his actions. Unsurprisingly, he found himself under criticism from Lord Goderich, secretary for war and colonies.[7]

When the time came to free the 70,000 slaves in Mauritius, after the passing of the Act of 1833 ending slave-*owning* throughout all lands within British jurisdiction, the French planters were placated by a two million pound recompense from the British taxpayer. The rate per head was 50 per cent higher than that awarded to slave-owners in the West Indies. Even so, there was an urgent question: who was going to cut the sugar cane in future? The blacks were obliged to serve as 'apprentices' to their masters for three years; after that, revelling in their freedom, they began making demands which the planters regarded as intolerable.

The island had to look elsewhere for cheap labour, and it quickly found an answer from within the Indian Ocean. As early as 1830 a merchant in Réunion had imported 130 artisans from Calcutta, and soon boatloads of Indian contract labourers were arriving in Mauritius. A thousand were brought in, with a few dozen women, in 1835. Convicts banished for life from India were also used to build roads. Charles Darwin visited the island in 1836 and wrote: 'These men are generally quiet and well-conducted', remarkable for their 'cleanliness and faithful observance of their strange religious rites'. He decided that it was impossible to look at them 'with the same eyes as our own wretched convicts in New South Wales'.

The 'hill-coolies', recruited in the impoverished Bihar countryside to work in the plantations, were given monthly wages of five rupees (equal to ten English shillings) plus rations of rice, spices and ghee. By 1837 there were 20,000 of them, and by 1860 more than 60,000. Sugar production had risen in parallel, from 35,580 tonnes in 1843 to 129,210 tonnes twenty years later. Few of the 'hill-coolies' ever found their way home again, despite being brought to Mauritius on five-year contracts. Some abolitionists, writing in British newspapers, protested that the life of these immigrants was scarcely better than slavery. Nevertheless, the time was not far distant when they would need less pity, when they had climbed up from their abject state to make Mauritius a prosperous 'Little India beyond the Sea'.[8]

FORTY-TWO

The Sultan and
the King's Navy

※

He is a tall, stout and noble-looking man, with a benevolent
countenance . . . and appears to wish to be considered as an Englishman in everything. The English, he says, he looks upon as his
brothers, and will willingly give them his country.
—Captain Henry Hart, RN, on Seyyid Said, Sultan of Oman

IN THE EARLY DECADES of the nineteenth century the East India
Company had the satisfaction of administering the showpiece of the
British empire. Never in history had there been such a huge capitalist
entity, enjoying unparalleled power and responsibility, yet retaining
most of the trappings of independence. When the company's charter
came up for renewal every twenty years, the court of directors were
obliged to submit to a parliamentary review of their activities. They took
this with the best possible grace; or, more exactly, with an unconscious
arrogance, for they correctly felt that their three presidencies in Calcutta,
Bombay and Madras knew a lot more about India than any parliamen-
tarians.

Sometimes the directors were forced to make concessions, as when
the 1813 review granted Christian missionaries the long-denied right to
evangelize in India. The company's former policy was to avoid any
interference with Hindu beliefs and customs – even with *suttee*, the
wife-burning ritual – but an irresistible challenge had come from William
Wilberforce, hero of the anti-slavery movement. After the Abolition
Act of 1807 he was prone to see himself as the guardian of Britain's
moral duty in every quarter of the globe, and on India he proclaimed:
'The Hindu divinities are absolute monsters of lust, injustice, wickedness
and cruelty. In short, their religious system is one grand abomination.'
His followers, the advance guard of the Victorian missionary legions,
soon conjured up a heady vision: they would win all India for Christ.

A side-effect of this crass and totally ineffectual evangelism would be to exacerbate prejudice among the 40,000 Europeans in India against the religions and cultures of the 150 million people they ruled and traded with, thereby creating a racial gulf which had scarcely existed before.

However, the Honourable Company viewed missionaries and similar busybodies with irritation rather than fear, for in the last analysis it felt impregnable. As the Raj grew the vast internal market of India became a mainstay of imperial prosperity. The fortunes of the factory-owners of Manchester, Birmingham and other British cities relied heavily upon it. The masters of India were the keepers of a golden goose.

The full extent of the company's freedom was none the less somewhat vague. Most importantly, what were its boundaries beyond India? In the east there was an effective monopoly over European exports to China (including the profitable opium trade).[1] In the west the company maintained a presence on the shores of the Red Sea. To the south the two crown colonies in the Indian Ocean, Ceylon and Mauritius, lay outside its direct control but certainly within its sphere of influence. So did the East African coastline as far south as Mozambique. However, the ill-defined empire of Seyyid Said, the sultan of Oman, bordering the Arabian Sea, was more of a puzzle. When the company had dealings with him, how far could its aims coincide with those of Britain?

The question was far from being of merely diplomatic interest, since the port of Muscat, the sultan's capital, was seen by the East India Company as crucial to its trade in the Persian Gulf. Any disorder in the Omani territories which endangered his survival must be of commercial concern to the company. But Said's empire mattered equally to the Foreign Office in London, as it monitored the constantly shifting balance of power in the Muslim world. By the 1820s there was a new obsession: that Russia might overrun Persia and break through to the Indian Ocean, so threatening Britain's dominance there. Gratifyingly, Said was hinting that he was ready to fight alongside Britain against the Russians, if it came to that.

So, in the main, the British government's policies and those of the East India Company did coincide here. Both saw the Russian intrusion into Persia as a bad omen and looked askance at any foreign sails on the Indian Ocean. Both wanted to see the end of Arab piracy and feuding in the Gulf. Yet such unity of purpose was at times undermined by the company's original *raison d'être*: trade. One instance was the response to the Gulf pirates. They were constantly in need of timber for repairing their ships, and since Arabia was almost treeless the wood was bought from Bombay. Putting a ban on timber exports to the Gulf would have been a simple way of curbing the pirates, but the government of India refused to impose one, for fear of hurting the pockets of the Bombay merchants.

There was even less inclination to take issue with Seyyid Said about a main source of his wealth: the duties levied on slaves transported from East Africa by his subjects, including members of his own family. His total revenue had risen to 250,000 dollars a year, and at least a quarter of that came from slavery. The Omani navy acted as a shield for this trade and, in the words of an American merchant, Said had 'a more efficient naval force than all the native Princes combined from the Cape of Good Hope to Japan'. Most of these ships were ordered from Bombay's thriving dockyards. The sultan was an excellent customer and his money reinforced his unctuous declarations of good-will and friendship. The time would shortly come, however, when he must be tackled on the slavery issue. Among the Wilberforce warriors, already turning their gaze from the Atlantic to the Indian Ocean, it was taken for granted in London that Said would quickly yield to the tide of history. In 1822, the colonial secretary, Lord Bathurst, had optimistically prophesied in a despatch to Robert Farquhar, governor of Mauritius, that when the sultan had 'maturely weighed the solid advantages' of ending the slave trade he would 'no longer delay fulfilling the earnest Wishes of Great Britain to which he is principally indebted for his political existence'.

The African Institution (which later became the Anti-Slavery Society) was even more sanguine. Its committee regarded Said as an 'old and steady' ally of the East India Company. Indeed, such was the intimacy between him and the governor in Bombay, and the 'confidence of the Mohammedan in Christian benevolence so great', that the sultan sent his sister to Bombay with a large entourage every year for the good of her health. The committee felt confident that the British government had 'only to express the desire' for the slave trade to cease and the sultan would make a treaty 'and as readily agree that the East India Company's vessels of war should enforce its execution'. The abolitionists could not grasp that the company, and for that matter some foreign office staff, were little bothered about oriental slavery.

Curing Seyyid Said of his bad habits was going to be harder than

Lord Bathurst and his well-wishers could have imagined, even though a promising start was made when the sultan reluctantly signed a treaty in September 1822 prohibiting the sale of slaves from his dominions to any Christian country.[2] Said also agreed that Omani ships carrying slaves to Muslim countries could only sail within an area starting just south of Kilwa, through waters close to East Africa, along the Arabian coast, and as far as Diu in northern India and the shores of Persia. His subjects were furious when the news filtered out about what he had done. They knew that the British had been allowed to throw a noose over their heads. One day it would be tightened.

This ranging shot, the 1822 agreement, became known as the Moresby Treaty, after the emissary who had steered Said into signing it. Fairfax Moresby was a young Royal Navy captain, in command of the flotilla based at Mauritius, who in later life would become an admiral. He had acted on the orders of Robert Farquhar, the long-serving governor, who in turn was obeying orders from Lord Bathurst. One of the clauses of the treaty gave Royal Navy warships the right to seize any Omani vessels found carrying slaves outside the designated coastal waters. However, contrary to the expectations of the African Institution, the treaty withheld any such powers from ships of the Bombay Marine, the naval arm of the East India Company.

This proviso was likewise the opposite of what Said might have wished, since he knew he had more friends in the company than in the British government. Moreover, the clause underlined a distinction between the status of the two British navies simultaneously cruising in the Indian Ocean. Under an edict of 1798 the Bombay Marine's first duty remained 'the protection of trade', whereas the Royal Navy was committed to protecting the wide interests of the empire; the Moresby Treaty epitomized that higher role. There was also a class distinction between the two navies: a Royal Navy officer always took precedence over a Bombay Marine officer of the same rank.

It is easy to see how the despatch of Captain Moresby from Mauritius to make a treaty with a sultan whose domain was on the other side of the equator must have rankled in Bombay. There was a schism, however well concealed, and the likelihood of a disagreement erupting was increased by the months taken for messages to travel between Britain and India. This was quickly demonstrated when another Royal Navy captain defied the company and played into its hands by entangling Britain in the intrigues of Seyyid Said's empire.

Captain William Fitzwilliam Wentworth Owen was the son of a captain killed fighting the French; his elder brother was an admiral, and he was recognized as the foremost navigator and hydrographer in the Royal Navy. Owen had joined the service at fourteen, seen action as a midshipman, and later been captured in the Indian Ocean by the French, who had held him prisoner in Mauritius for two years. When it came to taking decisions he was, by all accounts, quick to make up his mind and impossible to deflect.

By 1822 Owen was back in the Indian Ocean, commanding an Admiralty expedition to survey the coastline of East Africa.[3] This commission was a tribute to Owen's talents, since almost no accurate maps existed from which to start work. However, the survey began disastrously, because Owen's crews were ravaged by malaria as they made their way northwards from Cape Town. Almost the entire company in one ship was wiped out while surveying the south of Sofala. Between leaving the Cape and returning there seven months later, the expedition lost two-thirds of the officers and half the seamen. Personal tragedies are summed up in a sentence or two: 'The carpenter's mate had his wife on board; both were taken ill. In a paroxysm of fever he jumped overboard and was never more seen: she died a few hours afterwards.'

Although so heavy, such losses were taken stoically, for fever was still the greatest killer in the tropics. (British soldiers in India at that time were reckoned to have little more than a one-fifth chance of surviving for five years.) On the other hand, Owen's scientific mind was exercised by the possibility that mosquitoes were the true cause of the fever, and not 'marsh miasma', as universally believed. He noted the remarks of one of his officers: 'In the course of our experience, the first attacked with the fever were always those who had suffered most from the mosquitoes.' The captain displayed his independent turn of mind by ridiculing Royal Navy surgeons for their relentless bleeding of patients suffering from fever; he thought they were 'quite as much in the dark as to the nature of the disease as if they had never studied medicine at all'.[4]

The expedition set out once more from the Cape, where several slaves had been recruited to act as interpreters. They all 'turned out most orderly and useful people, and were, after some time, discharged in their respective countries, enriched by a considerable accumulation of wages'. As with most other matters, Owen held trenchant views on slavery and wrote passionately about its evils.

While his ships were making their way northwards to Zanzibar he encountered a large slave ship heading for Rio. Since it was flying the Portuguese flag and was commanded by a Senhor Alvarez it could not be apprehended. But Owen patriotically observed that because Alvarez had worked in India among the English he took better than usual care of his 'miserable cargo' and expected to have four-fifths still alive by the time he reached Brazil. On average, half the slaves died *en route*: 'To bring two-thirds to market is considered a profitable voyage.' From everything Owen had seen in Zanzibar and along the African coast, the treaty negotiated by his fellow-captain, Fairfax Moresby, was not doing anything like enough to halt this 'hell-borne traffic'. Some Portuguese slavers were simply using the Omani flag as a camouflage. Owen's outrage at what he regarded as a conspiracy to outwit Britain was to have a direct bearing on impending events.

At the end of 1823, the captain sailed into Bombay harbour in his main survey vessel. HMS *Leven*, to take on supplies. There were two incidents of significance during his stay. In the lesser of them an officer of the East India Company's Bombay army found his way aboard uninvited, and became so drunk and disorderly that he was put under guard. Owen later received a written protest from the army command about the way the officer had been detained, but 'did not think it proper to make any reply'.

That incident well demonstrated the captain's mettle and his attitude towards the 'Honourable Company'. Of greater moment was his encounter ashore with a delegation of Arabs from Mombasa, who had come to petition the Bombay government to grant them protection under the British crown; they wanted to hand Mombasa to Britain. It was an astonishing proposition and one which Mountstuart Elphinstone, the Bombay governor, had not the slightest intention of accepting. His masters, the East India Company, could not have taken such a step without the British government's approval, and in any case Elphinstone knew that it would give mortal offence to his 'close and steady friend', Seyyid Said.

The delegation in Bombay spoke for the Mazrui clan, which had been trying to assert its independence from successive dynasties in Oman for a century. Despite intermittent wars with the Omani sultans, the Mazruis had held Fort Jesus almost continuously since 1728. A party of assassins sent from Oman in 1746 had stabbed to death the Mazrui sheikh who was the current governor, but an unnamed European captain whose ship happened to be in Mombasa harbour helped the clan to regain control. The Mazruis enjoyed support along the coast and more than once had come close to capturing Zanzibar. They laid particular claim to Pemba, Zanzibar's fertile sister island, which once belonged to them and still supplied Mombasa with much of its food.

Now, in the 1820s, they faced defeat, for they lacked anything to resist the heavily armed warships which their enemy, Seyyid Said, was sending against them. All they possessed, apart from their muskets, were the massive walls of Fort Jesus. There had been times when all the coast and all the islands of East Africa were virtually in their hands. Now their power was ebbing away. What was more, they knew what to expect, after such a long defiance, if they should fall into Said's power.

That was why the Mazruis kept appealing to Bombay. There seemed nowhere else to turn. They pleaded for a flag, to show that Mombasa was 'subject to the king of England'. They even offered Britain half of their port's revenue. But Mountstuart Elphinstone was having none of it: 'It is contrary to our policy to enter on such intimate connections in Africa as those proposed by you,' he told the desperate Mazruis. Then he added: 'and, moreover, fidelity to our engagements with His Highness the Imam of Muscat [Seyyid Said] would prevent our acceding to your proposal.'

When Owen heard how the Mombasa delegation was being cold-shouldered by Elphinstone his gorge rose. Here was a heaven-sent chance to establish a British presence on the East African coast to stifle the slave trade, which he had seen for himself was being sustained by the devious Said. The political expediency of the 'Honourable Company' was clearly triumphing over principles. The Mazruis were against the wall: in exchange for British protection they could easily be persuaded to end the 'hell-borne trade' from Mombasa and all the other ports they controlled. He wrote to Elphinstone, urging him to change his mind. The governor paid no heed.

Owen now knew what he was going to do. In the last weeks of 1823 he sailed for Muscat, with letters from the Bombay authorities asking Said to give the expedition passports which would ensure a good welcome in East Africa. Although Elphinstone was probably glad to see the back of his argumentative visitor, he could only have been uneasy about what was likely to happen next.

It was Christmas Day when the *Leven* sailed into the harbour below Said's palace. On going ashore, Owen did not like what he saw: 'Muscat must be the filthiest town in the world.' But he was impressed by the number of dhows in the harbour, and the five Omani frigates swinging at anchor. The sultan himself was the chief merchant, Owen decided, and used his frigates for trade. Muscat itself was a 'sort of emporium' serving Africa, India, Madagascar and other markets.

Said displayed his usual feline charm when Owen came to see him, but soon discovered that this Royal Navy captain was far less diplomatic than Fairfax Moresby had been a year earlier. The conversation had hardly begun when Owen castigated the East African slave trade, told Said that he should ban it within three years, and announced that his ship would shortly be calling at Mombasa. He expected its people to ask for British protection: 'I should feel it my duty to my King to grant it to them, in which my principal motive would be the suppression of that hellish traffic.' From other accounts of his manner there is no doubt that Owen was prone to peppery turns of phrase. He was also close on fifty, and the sultan nearly twenty years younger, so the captain was perhaps misled by what he called his host's 'mild and gentlemanly manners' into thinking he had got him under his thumb.

Said was infuriated by this onslaught, but did not show it. Of course, he replied, he looked forward to the day when the British ruled the world from 'the rising to the setting sun'. Of course, he would be happy for them to have Mombasa. This was rather more than the captain could quite credit; there might have been, he reflected later, some 'symptoms of insincerity'. That was an understatement.

Civilities were maintained, none the less, and before Owen set sail on New Year's Day 1824, he presented Said with a New Testament translated into Arabic, receiving in return a golden-hilted sword of Damascus steel. When Said made a farewell visit to the *Leven* she was dressed overall with flags and the crew manned the yardarms. There was even a touch of hilarity, caused by the live pigs the ship carried to provide fresh meat during the voyage. To respect the Muslim suscepti-bilities of his host Owen had ordered that the pigs should be removed from the ship, but they squealed so loudly that the 'echoes reverberated from the surrounding hills'. Everyone seemed amused.

However, the moment Said was back in his palace he sat down and dictated a letter of protest to his friend Mountstuart Elphinstone in Bombay. He said it was intolerable that little more than a year after he had signed an anti-slavery treaty with the British which had put his very survival in jeopardy, they were about to lend succour to the Mazruis, his sworn foes. This complaint was soon to become the subject of a heated correspondence between the government of India, the East India Company in London, the India Board,[6] and the Admiralty.

The sultan had also sent a message by fast dhow to three of his ships occupied in blockading Fort Jesus: they should stop any bombardment and avoid trouble with the Royal Navy. If Captain Owen gave them orders, they must obey. As a result, when the *Leven* reached Mombasa and fired a shot to announce her presence the largest of the three Omani ships quickly offered a pilot to guide her into the harbour. Owen was gratified to hear the commander say he had orders to give him all help; it was also intriguing, when the *Leven* dropped anchor opposite Fort Jesus to see that the Omanis directing the blockade were on quite friendly terms with their counterparts ashore. Even more remarkable was the flag floating above the battlements of the ancient redoubt: it resembled a British ensign.

Owen looked round the harbour, decided that it was perhaps as perfect as any in the world, then told one of his lieutenants, John Reitz, to land and enter the fort, with the aim of contacting the sheikh, Sulaiman bin Ali al-Mazrui. The lieutenant soon returned, escorting a nephew of the sheikh who recited to Owen the familiar plea for a British protectorate. He also produced a letter from Bombay addressed to the sheikh but written in English. Owen discovered that nobody in Mombasa had been able to read the letter, but the sheikh and his advisers had persuaded themselves that it granted protection, so that was why they went ahead with making a rudimentary British ensign and running it up the flagpole. In reality, the letter was only a request that visiting British ships should be supplied with bullocks.

The captain decided to go ashore himself the next morning. He was already firm in his mind about what he was going to do, for he had a prophetic vision of Britain's greater role in this part of Africa. He would later expound it in a letter to the Admiralty: 'It is as clear to me as the sun that God has prepared the dominion of East Africa for the only nation on earth [the British] that has public virtue enough to govern it for its own benefit, and the only nation on earth that takes the revealed word as their moral law.'

He advocated that Britain should without delay buy from Seyyid Said all his East African possessions, paying him in perpetuity as much as he had been deriving from them in revenue. It was a 'glorious duty' to grant protection to 'these poor creatures', for without difficulty 'every foot of the coast' could be brought under British rule. Thus, at a stroke, the slave trade would be exterminated.

Never one to delay, Owen drew up his terms for bestowing British protection on Mombasa. These boldly guaranteed the Mazrui ruler that he would be 'reinstated in his former possessions', with a British agent stationed at Fort Jesus. In return Mombasa island and all the coast from Malindi south to the Pangani river – more than 150 miles – were to be ceded to Great Britain. There were clauses promising that British merchants could trade with the African interior and that all slave exports from Mombasa would be abolished with immediate effect. There would be a fixed customs tariff of 5 per cent by value on all imports and exports, to be divided equally between the protectors and the protected. (The *sine qua non* clause from Owen's standpoint was the one concerned with slave-trading, and it reflects the Mazruis' desperation that they accepted it, even feignedly.)

The treaty was, the captain told a council of Mombasa sheikhs meeting on 10 February 1824, subject to confirmation by Britain; but within himself he felt assured that history was being made, that this was a precursor of greater advances into the African continent. The hand-made British flag was hauled down and in its place an authentic version was formally raised above the ramparts of Fort Jesus.

John Reitz, the lieutenant who had first gone ashore, was appointed by Owen to be governor of the Mombasa protectorate. He would be supported by Midshipman George Phillips, plus a marine corporal and three lower-deck sailors. Sheikh Suleiman donated a house close to the fort to be the contingent's headquarters. Three days later the *Leven* sailed away, with the farewell shouts of the first British residents on East Africa's mainland echoing across the water from the ramparts of Fort Jesus. Another remarkable chapter was being added to the saga, spanning more than two centuries, of the one-time Portuguese citadel.

FORTY-THREE

Stepping Back from East Africa

First, the king of Mombasa, and all his wazirs, and all the chiefs
in the territory of Mombasa have voluntarily affirmed to become
subjects of the king of England, and that all their country is to be
under the king of England, and he is to have half the income.

— A response to questions put in 1824 by Sir Lowry Cole, governor
of Mauritius, to a delegation from Mombasa

JOHN REITZ, first governor of the Mombasa protectorate, was twenty-two. His good humour, wit and varied talents had already marked him out as someone likely to rise high in the Royal Navy. He had been born in Cape Town, the son of a Dutch navy captain who in his day had fought against the British. Yet the loyalty of John Reitz to his adopted country was unbounded.[1] Although lacking any precise instructions, the young lieutenant was determined to do his duty in Mombasa as the representative of King George IV. Making the best of his puny contingent, he at once tried to assert some authority in dealings with the medley of Arab and Swahili functionaries within Fort Jesus. In putting his views to them he was aided by his second-in-command, Midshipman Phillips, who had taught himself Arabic since arriving in the Indian Ocean.

Even so, the chain of command among their hosts was hard for the two young officers to fathom. The Mazruis had taken the lead in pressing for British protection, but they paid great deference to Ahmed bin Sheikh, leader of the local Swahili community. He was descended from the former ruling family of Malindi, and spoke some Portuguese; it seemed that nothing could be decided without him. The Arabs were a ruling oligarchy, the darker-skinned Swahili were more numerous, and both groups were quite distinct from the mainland Africans living in Mombasa, mostly as slaves.

Traders from the mainland came across to the island to exchange ivory, rhinoceros horn and gum copal for blue cloth, brass bangles, beads and other manufactures brought by dhow from India. There were also the *banians* – Indian merchants, the counterparts of similar communities in Muscat, Zanzibar, Aden and many other ports of the Arabian Sea. Reitz felt a particular responsibility for the *banians*, since they were subjects of the British empire.[2] He learned that they were often swindled by Arabs, who took goods on credit then never paid for them.

From the outset the youthfulness of Reitz and Phillips must have counted against them. Owen had been promised that Reitz would be given twelve black soldiers for police duties, but they were not forthcoming. The anger this caused was compounded for the British by the conditions inside Fort Jesus. Their flag was flying over what had once clearly been a splendid military bastion, but was now a shambles. When another Royal Navy warship called at Mombasa a few weeks after the protectorate was declared, its captain, Constantine Moorsom, noted that the fort was 'in a state of thorough dilapidation – hardly a gun fit for service – and within the walls filled with thatched huts, the habitation of the chief and his numerous family and slaves'.

The realization soon grew on Reitz that his hosts had no genuine wish to become British subjects: they merely wanted the Union Jack to scare away Seyyid Said and the Royal Navy warships to help them regain Pemba island. In despatches to Owen the lieutenant spelled out these suspicions, confirming what the captain was already discovering – that his idealistic empire-building was fraught with trouble. When the captain left Mombasa he had taken on board the *Leven* a leading member of the Mazrui family, hoping to install him on Pemba, then sail on. But the sultan's governor on the island refused to give way, despite a lecture from Owen. In Zanzibar there were more quarrels. News soon reached Said in Muscat that the obstreperous British captain had used 'threatening language' and 'certain expressions which it is not becoming to repeat'. Naturally enough, he wasted no time in conveying this news to his friend Elphinstone in Bombay.

The list of tasks given to Reitz by his captain was cursory, but a tour of inspection south of Mombasa stood high among them: after all, the coastline down to the Pangani river had been ceded to Britain under the treaty. Since life in the environs of Fort Jesus was so full of frustration Reitz was keen to set off, even though it meant heading into wind and rain, for the south-west monsoon was still blowing hard. One of the Mazrui leaders agreed to accompany him, providing a large escort and donkeys for riding, but the tropical storms made progress slow.

The party struggled through bedraggled and impoverished towns whose sheikhs paid allegiance to the Mazrui. Every place along the coast showed the marks of retribution by Said's forces. The port of Tanga was typical: once 'a greater mart for ivory than Mombasa or any other place in the vicinity', it now had a population of only 300, subsisting on fish and a little grain from inland.

To round off this first British exploration of the East African mainland, Reitz was hoping to sail up the Pangani, a main route into the interior. To reach the river's mouth he set off with a few oarsmen in a small open boat, but rain-squalls buffeted them continuously and by nightfall the boat had to drop anchor near a rocky shoreline. In the morning, on 21 May, Reitz was convulsed with malarial fever. His companions decided that they must hurry him back to Mombasa.

The return journey took only eight days, but Reitz died within sight of the town, a victim of the African malaise which had already killed so many of his fellow-officers. He was buried amid the ruins of the Portuguese church where almost two centuries earlier the Christian inhabitants of Mombasa had awaited their fate at the hands of Yusuf, the renegade sultan. In the months ahead, Midshipman Phillips would be buried there, as well as William Smith, the corporal of marines.[3]

Reitz's governorship had lasted less than four months. It could be said that impetuosity, his refusal to wait until the rains had ended, was to blame for his death. Nevertheless, the news of his death would add to the apprehension felt in Bombay and London about establishing a British presence on the east coast of Africa. Such a step was not to be taken lightly.

The remoteness of Mombasa and the slow pace of communications ensured that reactions to Captain Owen's venture were on a long fuse. Months passed before despatches began to flow between London and Bombay. When they did the tone was urgent, for there was no ignoring a situation so likely to cause a diplomatic furore. The Indian government warned that Oman might be alienated, so opening the way for Persia or Russia to control the entrance to the Gulf. Then there were hints that the Mazrui, angered by Britain's failure to satisfy their ambitions, were planning to hand over control of Mombasa to the French, whose ships were once more starting to prowl the Indian Ocean. It was even suggested that the Portuguese would be offended by the idea of a British flag flying above Fort Jesus, which they still claimed as their own.

The need for converts to his cause forced Owen to take further time away from his surveying duties in the Indian Ocean. He still had on board the delegation from Mombasa, so his first stop was Mauritius, where he tried to persuade the newly-appointed governor, Sir Lowry Cole, to confirm the protectorate formally in the name of Britain. But Cole did not dare go so far; instead, he wrote to Lord Bathurst, the colonial secretary, saying he was not entirely convinced that the Mazrui were sincere, but if they were 'His Majesty's Government could possibly find their advantage in it'. He was not disposed to be more positive than that about an outpost on the African mainland almost 2,000 miles from his own island niche.

As for Owen's plea that a military garrison should be sent to Fort Jesus, the governor was not sure if the Mombasans would even accept one, despite all the fulsome answers their delegation had made to series of questions put by him. The governor was influenced by Captain Moorsom, newly-arrived at Mauritius after calling at Mombasa; he thought that without a garrison in place the British flag was at risk of being 'prostituted'.

The East India Company's position was then sent to London from Bombay by Elphinstone. He admitted that the claim to Mombasa of 'our faithful and cordial ally', Seyyid Said, was dubious, but it was important not to upset him. If Britain did want to go ahead with the protectorate, at least he should be offered compensation. From the opposite camp, Owen went much further with the idea of buying out Said: 'I would recommend our Government to treat with the Iman [Sultan] of Muscat for all his dominions in East Africa, offering him in perpetuity precisely the exact revenue he now derives from it.' This proposal was made in one of his string of emotional letters sent to the lords of the Admiralty.

However positive the despatches from the Indian Ocean might have been, the British government would still have shied away from Mombasa. The time for colonialism in Africa was not yet. Even before Elphinstone made his views known, Bathurst had ruled that the protectorate should be abandoned. Only a rearguard action by Owen and his sympathizers was to keep it in existence for another eighteen months.

During this time the British governorship rested in the hands of another lieutenant, James Emery, who had been put ashore by the Royal Navy soon after the death of Reitz. The tenacious Emery, ten years older than his predecessor, kept a daily record of his life with the Mazrui. It shows that he never knew what to expect: sometimes his hosts were ingratiatingly friendly, at others they proclaimed their disgust with the British for failing to win them back Pemba. The intrigues were endless and Emery now and then feared for his life. Yet he managed, despite the inevitable attacks of fever, to organize the building of a wharf and the sinking of a well. For these tasks he used slaves freed from a dhow in the harbour.

Emery also found time to collect information about the interior of Africa. His best informant was Fumoluti, a minor sultan who had created an independent enclave on the coast between Malindi and Lamu. When he visited Mombasa, to seek help in fending off attacks by Seyyid Said's forces, he was happy to spend a few hours telling the Englishman about his own journeys inland.

Among Emery's gleanings from Fumoluti were details of an immense lake 'lying nearly due west of Mombasa'. Many people lived along its shores. This brief reference, unheeded at the time, is the first recorded by any European about one of the world's greatest inland stretches of water, which no outsider would see for another thirty years. The sparse facts he had collected stirred Emery's imagination, and he resolved that as soon as he was relieved of his tedious duties in Mombasa he would lead an expedition across Africa, accompanied by Fumoluti's son.

It was not to be. Despite impassioned letters from Owen and a last delaying attempt by Commodore Hood Christian, senior naval officer at the Cape, the British government stood firmly by its disavowal of the protectorate.[4] What was more, relations in Mombasa were ever-more ominous, with the Mazrui declaring in July 1826 that they no longer recognized Emery as the civil governor. At this moment another Royal Navy warship arrived in the harbour and her captain, Charles Acland, decided that his duty was to extricate the Britons before they were murdered. Emery and his subordinates were helped by Acland's crew to bring aboard all their stores, including arms and ammunition. Little was abandoned, except for two cannons on the Fort Jesus ramparts.

So on 26 July the British flag was hauled down. The Arabs, their bluff called, watched silently as Emery and his staff departed from Mombasa, together with sixteen freed slaves and the crew of a small British trading schooner from Ceylon which had sunk off the coast a month earlier.[5]

The Mombasa débâcle was to strengthen a belief in London – most particularly within the grandiose offices of the East India Company in

Leadenhall Street – that all dealings with Oman and East Africa were best left in the hands of the Bombay authorities. The disadvantage was that this must inevitably add to the pressures on the company to adopt a firmer stance against slavery, a topic most of the directors preferred to ignore. The company could fairly claim never to have been directly reliant upon slavery in India (indeed, there was little need, since cheap labour was so abundant there). Nor was there any inclination to apologize for having in the past made profits outside India in lands sustained by slavery; the directors felt few qualms about that, for they were businessmen, not missionaries.

Although it now acted in the name of victorious Britain, the world's greatest power, the company still shied away from challenging slavery in territories within its sphere of influence yet outside its direct control, such as Oman or the Portuguese enclave of Goa. A Captain Henry Bevan of the 27th Madras Native Infantry scandalized a parliamentary committee in London in 1831 by recounting his experience while in charge of a corps of pioneers working near the border with Goa. He was approached by some 'African slaves or Caffres', who offered themselves as recruits, and were accepted. The governor of Goa instantly demanded that the slaves be returned by the British to their owners. Bevan's commanding officer refused to obey, but was overruled by the 'interference of the [East India Company] government of Madras'. Bevan related the outcome: 'I witnessed, some months afterwards, the marks of harsh treatment endured by these unfortunate beings, who had been most cruelly lashed at intervals, and their wounds rubbed each time with red pepper and salt.'[6]

In response to outrage at such incidents the company could fall back on the argument that international law must be observed. However, it was more vulnerable in the face of reports by inquisitive missionaries that slave-traders were still active in the main Indian ports. The missionaries complained about a steady flow of young African eunuchs into Calcutta; they arrived, manacled, in Omani dhows, to be sold 'like the beasts of the field'. (In exchange, young Indian girls were being shipped back for service in the harems of Arabia.) The directors had their reasons for turning a blind eye none the less; they were loath to alienate India's princes, who were accustomed to maintaining stocks of slaves – in some cases, running into many thousands – by imports from traditional Indian Ocean sources. Moreover, despite the efforts and wishful thinking of the missionaries, Hinduism ruled the lives of four out of five Indians, and was said to recognize fifteen different kinds of domestic slavery. Drawing a line between those which were tolerable and those which were not could drag the company on to dangerous ground.

Such arguments served as delaying tactics, but early in the 1830s came renewed calls from abolitionists for the Raj to put its house in order. These demands were intensified by a judicial *cause célèbre* in which the central figure was a Commander Charles Hawkins, captain of the *Clive*, a Bombay Marine sloop-of-war. The commander's offence turned out to be remarkably similar to the recruiting initiative earlier in the century by Sir Frederick North, governor of Ceylon; the difference was that Sir Frederick's slave-trading had occurred just before the 1807 abolition Act was passed.

Hawkins's troubles had begun when his superiors, worried by a shortage of sailors to man their ships (even lascars were refusing to serve for the wages offered), despatched him across the Indian Ocean to look for recruits. At the start of this discreet voyage, Hawkins called at Muscat, where bags of Indian rupees were exchanged for Maria Theresa dollars, the most popular currency among slave-traders. The *Clive* then took the monsoon route to Africa and reconnoitred southwards along the Swahili coast. At Lindi, two days' sailing on from Mombasa, the commander found what he wanted: a trader willing, in return for 2,000 dollars, to sell him thirty boys. Sixty dollars a head was a fair price in 1830, so the boys were duly brought aboard and Hawkins left Lindi in high spirits. He was made even happier during a stop at Zanzibar, for Said's governor on the island sent four more boys out to the ship. Suitably British names, such as Walter Scott or Charles Fox, were jovially bestowed on them as they were lined up on deck; they were being inducted into another world.

During the voyage back to Bombay a few of the young Africans died and one fell overboard, but in general the expedition could be regarded as a great success. It was true that many of the recruits were rather young, some being less than twelve years old, but according to Hawkins these had 'cried to join their brothers'. In any case, the younger the better if they were to be moulded in the navy's ways.

Unfortunately, twenty-four hours after Hawkins's return, he was arrested, under the Indian piracy laws, for transporting slaves: his voyage to Africa had not passed unnoticed. The charge outraged his fellow-officers, who took the view that, all else apart, he had merely obeyed orders. They also knew that the motive for this move lay in a conflict between the administration and the judiciary in India. As the legal process moved irresistibly towards a trial in the Bombay supreme court, British opinion in India was divided: many people argued that life in the Marine would be far better for the boy sailors than anything they might hope for in the 'barbarism' of their homeland. Charles Malcolm, the superintendent of the Marine, stressed how well the 'Seedees' (an Indian term for African slaves)[7] fitted into shipboard life: they 'assimilated well with the Europeans, who liked them'. They were hard-working, docile, and 'next to Europeans for courage'.

While under guard awaiting trial, Hawkins was daily comforted by his friends. One was Captain Robert Cogan, assistant superintendent of the Marine, who acted as go-between with the administration. But all Cogan's help was to no avail: in March 1831, in a hot and crowded Bombay courtroom, Hawkins was found guilty, and sentenced to be transported to New South Wales for seven years' penal servitude.

Five months later a report of the trial reached London and was printed at some length in *The Times*.[8] Hawkins's junior officers had put a good gloss on the events of the voyage, but decisive evidence came from the boys themselves. One, with the name of Mitchell, told through an interpreter how he went to the ship: 'I thought in my heart I was purchased . . . I was a slave, and being helpless I went'. Later he tried to run away, but was caught, brought back and flogged while Hawkins looked on. One of the boys was so small, said the report in *The Times*, that he could hardly be seen in the witness box and 'appeared no more than six.'

As preparations were made to ship Hawkins to Australia a campaign was mounted to have the sentence overturned. Appeals from the East India Company's naval and army officers were sent to London, urging the monarch, now William IV, to grant a pardon. Before any response could arrive Hawkins was on the way to start his sentence; the ship carrying him stopped at various ports on the Indian coast and in each he was fêted.

When the Dutch East Indies were reached a further pause was made in the unhurried voyage to penal servitude. There the hoped-for reply was received from England: Hawkins had indeed been given a royal pardon. Instead of landing in disgrace at Botany Bay, he made his way to London to attend a levee in St James's Palace. William IV greeted him warmly, adding assurances that all would be well on his return to India. So it turned out: back in court the commander was told there was not a stain on his character. Reimbursed for all the discomfiture, he was restored in triumph to the command of the *Clive*. However, he did not venture to East Africa again, nor did he have the satisfaction of seeing his boy sailors scrub the decks and climb the rigging. They had been removed to a school for freed slaves.

As for the quixotic Captain Owen, who thought he had found the way to end the 'hell-borne traffic' a few years before Commander Hawkins sought to take advantage of it, he soon learned that the collapse of the Mombasa protectorate would herald the collapse of his own naval career. The promotion he most wanted, as hydrographer to the Admiralty, was denied him in 1833. His abilities were beyond question, but his temperament was beyond bearing. Owen saw it differently: 'At fifty-nine my worldly ambition was barred by corruption in high places.'

He made one despairing attempt to map out a new career by writing a year later to Palmerston, the foreign secretary, offering himself as 'Consul General for Eastern Africa and for Southern Arabia'. His somewhat incoherent letter claimed that this appointment would be welcomed by Seyyid Said, whom he praised as 'amiable, liberal and just'; it was a pathetic about-face. When the inevitable rejection arrived, Owen retired to the obscurity of a family estate in Nova Scotia and died there at the age of eighty-three.[9]

FORTY-FOUR

The Americans
Discover Zanzibar

꙰

From September 1832 to May 1835, forty-one vessels visited
Zanzibar. Of these, thirty-two were American (5,497 tons) and
seven were English (1,403 tons).
— Edmund Roberts, US Special Agent, reporting to Washington
(September 1835)

EDMUND ROBERTS, born into a New England seafaring family, had
been a prosperous merchant until his early forties. Then his luck ran
out, and he decided upon bold action to restore his finances. Roberts
chartered a merchant ship, the *Mary Anne*, in Portsmouth, New Hampshire, loaded her with trade goods, and set sail for Zanzibar. He arrived
early in 1828 without mishap and was astounded by the activity in the
island's main harbour: there were 'upwards of two hundred and fifty
sail of dhows, bagalas and other craft with pilgrims, drugs, coffee, fish,
water, &c &c.' These vessels had come from various Red Sea ports,
from Bombay, the Persian Gulf, and the African coast as far south as
Mozambique.

While the American was selling his goods, the harbour became even
more crowded. The Omani fleet arrived, led in by its seventy-four-gun
flagship, the *Liverpool* (obsequiously named in honour of Lord Liverpool,
the long-serving British prime minister). Following the flagship were
five smaller warships and 100 dhows carrying 6,000 troops. Aboard the
flagship was the sultan himself, Seyyid Said, fresh from his latest effort
(now that Captain Owen's contingent had withdrawn) to subdue the
Mombasa rebels. A typical mixture of cannon-fire and chicanery had
brought some success, for a party of Omani soldiers were now occupying
Fort Jesus, although surrounded by their enemies.

Roberts happened to be witnessing a decisive moment in Indian
Ocean history, for Said was making his first visit to East Africa. Until

now the sultan had been so preoccupied in defending Muscat against his many foes that he had never dared to venture far from the Arabian coast, but relied upon trusted *wazirs* to govern his more distant territories and collect the customs dues. At last he was able to inspect Zanzibar, and was entranced at once by its lush fertility, contrasting with the harsh terrain of Oman, more than two thousand miles to the north-east.

Said soon came to realize that Zanzibar was not only more agreeable than Oman, but as a potential capital it would be safer and closer to his sources of wealth: the exports of African slaves, ivory and gum copal. The island itself was earning money from a promising new crop, cloves. Moreover, the governors appointed to Zanzibar recently had proved either less energetic or less honest that Yaqut, the loyal Ethiopian eunuch who had died some ten years earlier. Said felt sure that if he were there in person to supervise matters the revenue would soon increase.

He was in a confident and combative mood. On seeing the *Mary Anne* in harbour he sent for Edmund Roberts, took a liking to him, and after several meetings began revealing his ambitions. The American, possessor of graphic descriptive powers, wrote later:

> He declares the Portuguese shall not own an inch of territory on the East Coast of Africa. 'Have I forgotten,' said he, 'the treatment my ancestors received from the vile Portuguese three hundred years ago – from these vile hogs? . . . By the beard of Mahomet,' said he, at the same time stroking down the noble beard which reached to his girdle, and the fire flashing from his eyes, as though he would annihilate the whole race with a look, 'I will overwhelm them like the sand of the desert.'

Roberts gives this theatrical picture of Said in a letter written later to Levi Woodbury, a New Hampshire senator (later secretary of the US navy). He goes on to explain how the sultan asked him to supply shells and other heavy ammunition for the assault on Mozambique, 'and he is anxious the English government should not know of his designs'. It was entirely understandable that Said wanted to keep his plan secret from the British, the self-proclaimed overlords of the Indian Ocean, the guardians of the peace.[1] In contrast, America had no political involvement in the region and its merchants were renowned as suppliers of guns and ammunition, especially flint-lock muskets sold by the crate.

Early in his meetings with the sultan Robert started to air a string of complaints about trading conditions for American ships visiting Zanzibar: they were allowed to sell only through Said's agents and were charged heavier duties than English vessels, which were free to trade with anyone. In his forceful way Roberts warned that if Americans were not treated better, they would stop coming to Zanzibar. This was no empty threat, for more than a score of Yankee vessels had been trading in and around Zanzibar over the past few years, far outnumbering the British (or the French, who were mainly after slaves). Said responded by saying he wanted a commercial treaty with America, although, notes Roberts, 'he showed an almost entire ignorance of the country'. Seeking to explain away the preferences enjoyed by the British, the sultan explained that he had signed a treaty with them and they granted him a subsidy; in this he was telling lies, with his natural charm.

These exchanges show how far Said's horizons were widening, and how he dreamed of ruling a vast Indian Ocean empire after repeated failures to extend his power in the Persian Gulf. Not only Mozambique, but Madagascar and the Comoro islands lay within the frontiers of his ambition. He was also quick to see the benefit of stimulating rivalry between Britain and the thrusting Americans.

Roberts sailed back to New England, to lobby for the right to negotiate with Said on his country's behalf. He also urged the appointment of a consul in Zanzibar; after all, there had been one in Cape Town since 1799. But the process of persuasion was tediously slow, for few officials in Washington had any idea where Zanzibar was. In the meanwhile, more and more American ships were appearing in East African waters.[2] Some were whalers, which called at Zanzibar for rest and refreshment. Their crews were troublesome, often mutinying or deserting because of the brutal conditions they endured while at sea.

Most American visitors were trading ships from Salem in Massachusetts. One was the *Virginia*, whose master, Henry Leavitt, decided to call in at Mombasa, where the Mazrui were still in charge. Leavitt asked the 'King of Mombaz', Salim bin Ahmed al-Mazrui, to let him take on water. When the 'King refused, claiming a shortage, Leavitt's rage glows incandescent on the pages of his log: 'Not water enough. I am astonished. I am struck dumb with amazement. Why, there is water enough to drown . . . Pugh, there is water enough to float fifty *Virginias*. It's all a plain gig to keep us here. I know I can read you, you black, squint-eyed ghost of a King.'

It took years for Edmund Roberts to win the authority he sought from Washington. He might never have succeeded but for a series of letters handed to various homeward-bound American captains by Said, appealing for the commercial treaty. At last, in 1832, Roberts was appointed by President Andrew Jackson as a 'special agent' of his government and handed a silver and gilt box with the American eagle on its lid; within was the US great seal. Also part of the official equipment was a bundle of parchment on which treaties were to be inscribed (Roberts later complained that the officials were too mean with the parchment). The special agent was told that he should not only reach a commercial agreement with Seyyid Said, but also with the king of Siam, by taking passage on the US navy sloop *Peacock*, which as to make a round-the-world voyage by way of Cape Horn and the Cape of Good Hope.

Afraid that the British would scupper his plans, Roberts travelled incognito. He was listed as the captain's clerk, only a few senior officers knowing the true role of their burly colleague. A treaty was duly signed in Siam, then the *Peacock* sailed to Bombay. While the usual courtesies were exchanged with the unsuspecting British authorities, the 'clerk' stayed discreetly out of sight. Then the Americans sailed on to Muscat, where Said happened to be mustering his forces for yet another assault on Mombasa. The *Peacock* fired a twenty-one-gun salute and Roberts invited the sultan aboard for a 'sumptuous repast in the Cabin'.

Agreeing the commercial treaty, giving American ships preferential treatment in all the Omani territory including Zanzibar and the Swahili coast, took only three days. It was written out in English and Arabic, then signed on 21 September 1833, the first such agreement between Said and any foreign power. Roberts deployed his great seal and Said described himself, in conventional terminology, as 'the unworthy, the needy'.[3] Triumphantly, Roberts sailed home with his parchment, and gave secretary of state Louis McLane his assessment of Said's 'more than adequate resources'. They were 'derived from commerce, running himself a great number of merchant vessels, from duty on foreign merchandise, and from tribute'. Discreetly, there is no mention at all of the slave trade; nor is slavery mentioned when Roberts turns to describing the exports of Africa: these are listed as including 'ivory, tortoise shell, rhinoceros horn, hides, Bees Wax, rice, etc., etc.'

Soon after Roberts's departure from Muscat, rumours of his visit began reaching India from Oman. This prompted the Royal Navy's commander-in-chief in the Indian Ocean, Vice-Admiral Sir John Gore, to send one of his ships to discover what the US navy might be up to in waters where Britain's writ was supreme. The task of finding this out fell to Captain Henry Hart, who arrived at Zanzibar in HMS *Imogene* at the end of January 1834. Hart was energetic, intensely patriotic and somewhat grand in demeanour.

Gratified to learn that Seyyid Said was also in Zanzibar, staying in his recently-built palace, Hart went ashore to make a courtesy call. The sultan at once sent two bullocks and a large supply of fruit for the *Imogene*'s crew; one of the bullocks was served up for dinner that night, with the fruit as dessert. The next morning a twenty-one-gun salute was fired by the Royal Navy and answered by one of the sultan's warships at anchor in the harbour.[4]

During a series of meetings in the palace Hart found himself discussing his host's latest ambitions and anxieties. Most intriguing of the first was Said's overture to the capricious Ranavolana, queen of Madagascar.[5] He had sent emissaries to her in one of his frigates, asking for the loan of 2,000 troops to help him capture Mombasa ('Arabs will not fight', he told Hart gloomily). He had gone further by proposing marriage, since she was a widow, yet still in her prime. Ranavolana declined his hand, saying it was contrary to her country's law for a queen to remarry; however, there was a princess available who might suit him. She was vague about the troops, saying he could have 'as many as he pleased', but more specific in her request for a necklace worth a thousand dollars. The troops would be despatched as soon as the necklace arrived.

Hart soon sensed that the sultan's advances to this difficult queen were unlikely to make much headway. He turned to the real reason for the *Imogene*'s visit: the American treaty, about which rumours were flying. At once, Said began speaking in whispers, so that his entourage might not hear, and the captain suggested that they ought to meet alone the next day; in the meantime, he took away the sultan's copy of the American treaty to read overnight. The following morning, when the captain declared himself shocked at the concessions he discovered had been made to the Americans, and forecast that Britain would see the treaty as a 'breach of faith', Said pleaded for sympathy.

Edmund Roberts was 'an old, fat, blustering man', said Said. 'I was glad to sign the treaty to get rid of him, as I did not think it of any importance.' But if the 'English government of India wished it and would support him', he would immediately cancel the treaty: 'I also promise that in future I will never make any treaty without the advice and consent of my ancient allies and good friends the English.' Clearly, Captain Hart had managed to fill the sultan with alarm. A grovelling letter was composed to the Bombay governor, in which Said apologized for not mentioning the 'trifling affair' of the treaty, and pledged that everything 'whether of the most important or most trifling import' would be reported to the governor 'in order that all suspicion be removed from the breast of such an old friend'.

Next, Said went further than Hart could have imagined: as a show of his regret, and to convince the English of his feelings towards them, he said he was resolved to present the *Liverpool*, his seventy-four-gun flagship, to King William IV. The vessel was at anchor in Zanzibar harbour, and was obviously the sultan's *folie de grandeur*, far too big for Oman's needs. Hart was unsure how the Admiralty would react to such an unusual offer, but assured the sultan that he would pass it on as a matter of urgency.

On the voyage back to India the captain had time to write down for Admiral Gore a detailed account of all that had gone on in Zanzibar, with many personal details about Said, describing the economic prospects for the island, and mentioning how he had agreed to take 8,000 silver dollars to Bombay on the sultan's behalf. He also notes: 'Of the thirteen ships which touched here last year . . . only four were English and all the rest American.'

Hart felt well pleased with his firm stance on the Yankee treaty, and in his forthright way left nothing out of his main despatch. He recounts Said's bitter complaints about the failure of the East India Company to answer his letters: the company's indifference was partly the reason why Edmund Roberts had been welcomed. What was more, Said had fallen out with the king of Persia, to whose grand-daughter he was married, because the British had warned him that he should not help the Persians attack the Bushire people if he wanted to retain British friendship; as a result he had alienated the Persian king by refusing to help him. Even so, he was still kept waiting for six months for a reply from Bombay to any of his letters.

Clearly, Hart had caught Said when his fortunes and confidence were at a low ebb, as reflected by the desperate idea of using mercenaries from Madagascar to fight for control of Mombasa. The sultan was also trying to regain his standing after attempting some ill-judged treachery towards one of his relations, Seyyid Hillal, whom he suspected of harbouring designs on power in Oman. Lured to Muscat under solemn promises of safe conduct, Hillal had been jailed, but his sister had in fury raised a rebellion and forced Said to release him.

These diverse events had allowed Hart not merely to fulfil his orders, but to go some considerable way further. He even carried from Zanzibar, like a trophy, the sultan's original copy of the US treaty, for Vice-Admiral Gore to cast his eye over. Gore was well pleased and sent copies of the captain's despatch to the Admiralty and Lord Clare, the now Bombay governor. He also wrote to Said, returning the treaty and regretting that he could not accept the *Liverpool* on behalf of his monarch until he had higher authority. At first, reaction in India was muted, the view being that if Said wanted to offer trading concessions to a foreign power, that was his right. As for his complaints about the Indian government's slow response to letters, it was decided to compose a conciliatory reply, listing dates when answers had been sent.

In contrast, when the copies of Hart's despatch reached the East India Company's offices in London in August 1834, the reaction was volcanic. Hart had interfered in political matters in an area where the company was the supreme authority. The three-man secret committee of the India Board was ordered to report at once on how 'an officer was deputed by the Vice-Admiral to hold communication with a foreign state'. The company was clearly far more possessive about its perceived rights than it had been twelve years earlier, when Captain Moresby had made his anti-slavery treaty with Said. In addition, memories were still acute of how Captain Owen had declared his protectorate over Mombasa. Here, it seemed, was yet another Royal Navy officer making mischief by exceeding his functions and playing at diplomacy.

A key figure in the furore was Henry St George Tucker, chairman of the East India Company's court of directors.[6] Arrogance came naturally to Tucker, even though his past was somewhat unsavoury; he had served six months for attempted rape in India in his younger days. Tucker was being consulted at this time by Lord Palmerston, the foreign secretary, about a report that Said wanted to send one of his relatives to London. Should this emissary be presented to the king? 'I can well imagine,' replied Tucker, 'that you will soon have many visitors, of the same description, from all parts of India.' This was deliberately caustic, for in the previous year the renewal of the company's charter had been accompanied by warnings from parliament that the 'natives' must be treated with greater sympathy, and even that nobody should be debarred from any company post on grounds of religion, descent or colour. In

Tucker's view, if Palmerston and his political friends were so eager to be kind to Asiatics, they had to be ready to entertain them in London.

The company was, at this moment, adjusting to its new role, under the renewed charter: to govern, rather than to trade. The directors, led by Tucker, now saw the chance to assert their political authority throughout the Indian Ocean, once and for all. The report of the secret committee was grand in tone: 'With respect to the treaty which appears to Captain Hart a matter of so much importance, it may very possibly prove to be no treaty at all.' If it were, that mattered little: 'The Americans are not objects of political jealousy to us in India: and [as for] the trifling trade which they may carry on in their small vessels with the territory of the Imaum of Muscat, it is not likely to interfere with our own.' Even in June of the following year the India Board remained unruffled, its despatch to the Bombay government speaking of 'a person named Roberts, said to be captain of an American ship of war . . .' The board had found no evidence that this individual possessed 'the commission which he professed to have'[7] (in fact, the US senate had approved the treaty twelve months earlier).

At home, the board 'strongly recommended' to the Admiralty that Vice-Admiral Gore and his officers should be told to 'abstain from any communication with the States in the East on points of the nature referred to, except in concert with the Government of India'.[8] The Admiralty meekly sent the correspondence to Gore, with an order that he and his officers must stop 'mixing themselves up with politics'. Gore showed Hart the despatch, including the secret committee's remarks, which implied that the captain was a naive blunderer.

Hart was not so much humiliated as enraged. He sent home two blazing letters to Tucker, pointing out that he had only gone to Zanzibar under orders. He expressed his disgust that the court of directors should hold 'so much jealousy of their powers'. By this Hart was making it all too plain that he had been shown the secret committee's report, so the India Board once more turned its fire on the Admiralty: for Hart to have seen the report was 'quite contrary to usage and equally to propriety'; how had it happened? Of course, everyone knew how it had happened, but the Admiralty was unwilling to let a flag officer take the blame. So, as a diversion, Hart was forced to apologize to Tucker, making the 'fullest reparation'. It turned out that Hart, like Owen before him, was to suffer irretrievable damage to his naval career by 'mixing himself up in politics'; although knighted he was never to advance on the active list beyond the rank of captain.

With remarkable obstinacy, the East India Company still clung to its opinion that the American treaty might well not exist. However, in September 1835, the USS *Peacock* reappeared, for the US government had given final approval to the treaty in the previous January. Edmund Roberts sought in vain for Said in Zanzibar, then the sloop headed for Muscat. She ran aground on the coast of Arabia and was attacked by pirates, but was pulled off the rocks by one of the sultan's ships. Finally the ratifications were exchanged on the last day of September 1835, and Roberts sailed on. He held high hopes of returning to the Indian Ocean, to become the first American consul in Zanzibar, but died a few months later in Macão.

In the event the Zanzibar post went to Richard P. Waters, a business-man and evangelical Christian. Although born in Salem in the Pilgrim Fathers settlement, and belonging to a family of mariners, he had never travelled to the East; what he knew of Zanzibar was picked up from his elder brother John, who skippered merchant ships trading between New England and the Indian Ocean. Active in the anti-slavery move-ment, Richard Waters was recommended for the consulship by a clergy-man whose brother was Levi Woodbury, navy secretary and old friend of Edmund Roberts. The name of Waters was acceptable to the Salem captains, who felt they could trust a man from their home port to keep the bulk of Zanzibar trade in their hands.

There was little money attached to the post, but Waters set off in the autumn of 1836 with a dual resolve: to prosper as a shipping agent and win converts to Christ. While still at sea he writes: 'I have desired to be made useful for the souls of these pagans among whom I am called to reside, that my going to dwell with them for a season may be the means of introducing the Gospel.' On the way up the East African coast his ship called at the port of Mozambique, where he saw the Portuguese slavers being loaded up with Africans destined for Brazil: 'mostly with children from 10 to 14 years of age.' He reflects: 'What can I say to those engaged in this trade, when I remember the millions of slaves which exist in my own country.' But he also has a strictly practical side, for he is 'ready to work hard for a few years . . . if I can acquire a necessary portion of riches'.

Waters reached Zanzibar in March 1837, as the first representative from any foreign power bearing diplomatic credentials to Said. He received a thirteen-gun salute from a US merchant ship in the harbour, and the sultan gave Waters an enthusiastic welcome, offering him a house and a horse.

Said's benign and generous mood was perhaps partly attributable to the success he had enjoyed at last in his struggle with his oldest foes, the Mazrui. Only a month before Waters's arrival the last Mazrui ruler of Mombasa, Rashid bin Salim, had capitulated, promising to recognize Said as his overlord and hand him full control of Fort Jesus. In return, Said agreed to let Rashid stay on in Mombasa as governor; then he changed his mind and tried to bribe Rashid to leave and come to live in Zanzibar. Suspecting treachery afoot, as well he might, Rashid refused.

Said then devised a plot, disguised as a further stage of reconciliation. He sent his second son Khalid, aged nineteen, to Mombasa in one of his corvettes with a trusted adviser, Sulaiman bin Ahmad. The Mazrui, headed by Rashid, were invited to meet Khalid in an audience room erected just outside the fort. In twos and threes they then went within the walls to exchange courtesies with Sulaiman. Only after thirty had entered was it realized that none was emerging; all had been taken prisoner.

Khalid shipped them back triumphantly to his father in Zanzibar. They were held there for a month, then forced into the hold of a vessel bound for the Persian Gulf. Most were thrown overboard, far out to sea. A few were spared and taken on to a fortress in the Persian Gulf. There they were slowly starved to death.[9]

FORTY-FIVE

Looking Westwards
from the Raj

> Captain Hamerton should take every opportunity of impressing
> on these Arabs that the nations of Europe are destined to put an
> end to the African slave trade and that Great Britain is the main
> instrument in the Hands of Providence for the accomplishment
> of this purpose. That it is in vain for these Arabs to endeavour to
> resist the consummation of that which is written in the Book of
> Fate, and that they ought to bow to superior power.
> —Memorandum from Lord Palmerston to the Bombay government,
>   for forwarding to Her Majesty's consul in Zanzibar (1846)

THE EARLY MONTHS of the American diplomatic presence in Zanzibar
did not go easily, for Richard Waters let his Christianity get the better
of his discretion. Not only did he expound his religious views to the
sultan, but soon he began handing out Bibles and tracts to the ordinary
Zanzibaris. Some fervent Muslims took umbrage; stones were showered
on the consulate roof and Waters was obliged to move to another part
of the town. By the end of 1837 the sultan had decided on drastic
action: he would ask the President of the United States to replace the
consul with somebody willing to concentrate on commerce rather than
on provoking religious strife.

A Salem brig, the *Cherokee*, was in Zanzibar harbour, so Said decided
to hand her captain a letter for President van Buren. An account of
what happened next is to be found in a letter written three years later
by Edward Brown, the *Cherokee*'s clerk, to the US secretary of state,
Daniel Webster, who had belatedly got wind of the affair. The sultan's
secretary, Ahmad bin Amir, had come to the consulate to ask how a
letter to the US President should be addressed and Brown, who was
staying there, wrote the correct form on a slip of paper. After the sultan's
letter arrived the clerk saw it on a table and noticed that the 'e' had
been left out of Buren. The next morning, as the *Cherokee* was about

to sail, consul Waters was seen with an open letter in his hand. He then ordered everyone out of the room. Brown tells secretary of state Webster: 'What then took place I cannot of my own knowledge say, not having been present, but I do know that the above-described letter for the President did not go on the *Cherokee*.'[1]

By destroying the letter Waters was able to serve out his term as consul, from then on striving less for the Lord and doing more to 'acquire a necessary portion of riches'. Seyyid Said appears to have taken the lack of any answer from President van Buren philosophically and become reconciled to Waters when his behaviour changed. As far as the outside world was concerned, the Americans had achieved a minor diplomatic coup in the Indian Ocean: the British were forestalled. The warnings given by the unfortunate Captain Hart had been vindicated, although the East India Company would never admit that.

From a British viewpoint, the most vexing aspect of Richard Waters's presence in Zanzibar was the way his government allowed him to combine diplomatic duties with private business. He had wasted little time in teaming up with Jairam Sewji, a Hindu trader with a rewarding contract from the sultan for running the island's customs. Between them, the two soon had a stranglehold on Zanzibari commerce, much to the disadvantage of a London firm which had established an agency on the island. The fact that Jairam, being an Indian, was a British subject, made this even more exasperating. The American consul was also energetically promoting his own country with Seyyid Said, to whom he gave two framed pictures for hanging in the audience room of the palace; they showed American ships beating the British in a battle during the war of 1812.

Another event directing British attention towards Said's island realm was the sudden arrival in the Thames of the 74-gun *Liverpool*. She had been brought to London by Captain Robert Cogan, the senior Bombay Marine officer who had acted for Commander Hawkins when he was charged with buying slave-boys in Africa. Cogan had now retired from the service after twenty years in India, and taken employment with Said, who called him 'Kojim Khan'. The captain declared that he had orders to sell his unwieldy charge for scrap if William IV would not take her as a gift. Caught between the prospect of grievously offending the sultan and the risk of compromising Britain's freedom of action in dealing with him, the government finally accepted, with a show of gratitude, a ship it could well have done without in a time of peace.

The *Liverpool* was renamed the *Imaum*, in honour of Said's religious title, then Britain matched the gift by sending a yacht, the *Prince Regent*, to Zanzibar. The sultan swiftly passed this on to the governor-general of India, saying it was unfit for him as a Muslim on account of its Christian luxuries. Nobody had noticed before sending the *Prince Regent* to the Indian Ocean that the upholstery in the cabins was covered in pigskin. (In any case, it was a rather tawdry vessel.)[2]

Despite some difficult moments, and the presence of the US consul in Zanzibar, British ties with Said were now strengthening. Shortly after Victoria came to the throne 'Kojim Khan' was back in London, escorting Sheikh Ali bin Nasser, who had come to pay his respects on behalf of his ruler. Palmerston treated this as something of a diplomatic challenge, and decided that the sheikh must be entertained 'within bounds' at the public expense, since he was one of Said's most trusted *wazirs*. Cogan was given an advance of £200 for the purpose, but warned to account for it fully.[3]

A visit to Windsor was organized in August 1838: the sheikh, escorted by Cogan, had dinner with the young queen and stayed for the night in the castle. He enjoyed the occasion so much that he asked to be taken there again, to say farewell. Palmerston replied firmly that it was out of the question: Her Majesty felt that she had already said farewell. The foreign secretary was equally emphatic when Cogan sought to have himself accredited as the sultan's representative in Britain: that was also out of the question, because the captain was a British subject. Palmerston turned the idea on its head, by suggesting that Cogan might like to become the British consul in Muscat. The wily captain declined, saying it would be 'fatal to his health', then vainly proposed one of his relations for the post. His true ambition was to set up trade in Zanzibar, so it suited his plans well when Palmerston accepted his offer, some weeks after the visit to Windsor, to negotiate a commercial treaty with Said. According to Cogan it was not merely the Americans who were threatening British commerce; the Russians wanted to 'establish an understanding with His Highness'. Before returning to the Indian Ocean the captain addressed the newly-formed Royal Geographical Society and persuaded it to grant Said honorary membership. That was not the only proof of Britain's esteem: Sheikh Ali bin Nasser carried home to his master a portrait of Queen Victoria which she had donated.

Some of Palmerston's colleagues hoped that Cogan might simultaneously negotiate an ending of the East African slave trade. The theory was that 'legitimate commerce' could replace slave-dealing as a source of revenue for Said and lesser rulers in the region. Cogan hinted that his new master might be willing to end the trade if he could be given a 'pecuniary equivalent' by Britain for the revenue he earned from it.[4] There could be, said Cogan, as many as 50,000 Africans a year going through Zanzibar market alone. This was certainly an exaggeration, but much to the sultan's advantage if Britain believed it and took up the idea of paying compensation. Palmerston hurriedly side-stepped the idea. Later an East India Company official did win minor changes to the original 1822 Moresby Treaty on slave-trading, but in effect the export of captive Africans to Arabia and the Persian Gulf was free to continue unabated. Said promised Britain that he wanted to end it, but had to move gradually since 'a public declaration of his sentiments would create suspicion in the minds of his subjects'. Seeing Said held the strategic port of Muscat, it was of more immediate benefit for Palmerston to keep him as an ally in the volatile politics of the Gulf.

Cogan limited himself to drawing up, in May 1839, a simple commercial treaty, giving the sultan's vessels preferential rights in Indian ports and putting Britain broadly on a par with the Americans trading in Zanzibar. In principle the Roberts treaty had allowed US ships a unique freedom to trade directly with the African mainland, but in practice they went on buying their ivory, gum copal and cloves in Zanzibar like everyone else. The Arabs and their Indian financiers made sure of keeping a tight grip on the East African trade.

Amid all the problems of the globe, the petty vexations of Zanzibar kept landing on Palmerston's desk. Said had promised to send Queen Victoria a gift of Arab horses, but they were slow in arriving. So the foreign secretary, pressed by Buckingham Palace, had to write to the India Board to demand where they were, and insist that they be shipped to England without delay. Quite apart from the horses, Palmerston was bothered by a scheme devised by Sir Thomas Fowell Buxton, the anti-slavery campaigner who in 1821 had inherited Wilberforce's mantle. Buxton was much preoccupied with West Africa, but still found time to argue that a British settlement on the eastern side of Africa would serve to stifle the Arab slave trade and spread Christian civilization among the natives.

Undeterred by the fact that Mombasa was already notorious for a failed British initiative, Buxton selected it as the ideal site for his new venture. He visualized the port and its environs as a tropical arcadia for hard-working evangelists. They could grow crops for export – such as cotton, coffee and nutmegs – as well as winning souls. It was noteworthy, moreover, that British missionaries had already enjoyed some success in that part of the world, where they had penetrated Madagascar in the 1820s, starting schools, translating the Bible into local languages and distributing many thousands of tracts. Their work had been halted only in 1835 by Queen Ranavolana, who passed a law that any of her subjects using 'new arts introduced by the Europeans' should be put to death.

Buxton's faith that Mombasa would provide more rewarding soil than Madagascar for the 'holy enterprise' was encouraged by a certain Montgomery Martin who, Buxton claimed, knew as much about Mombasa 'as any man living'. Martin had been a surgeon in one of Captain Owen's ships during the surveying of the African coastline; it is not clear that he ever set foot in Mombasa.

To solicit government backing for his scheme, Buxton first lobbied Lord Glenelg, the colonial secretary. Glenelg was an Evangelical and he listened sympathetically to his friend, whose efforts had played such a large part in ending slavery in the West Indies.[5] The colonial secretary then took the idea to Palmerston, whose response was bleak. Although the foreign secretary yielded to no man in his distaste for slavery, he was eminently practical; and while always game to invoke the Almighty to embellish his rhetoric, he found the relentless piety of Buxton tiresome.

Palmerston's letter to Glenelg sums up his mercantilist ideas on the matter:

> No doubt the extension of commerce in Africa is an object to be aimed at, but I am inclined to think that such an extension will be the effect rather than the cause of the extinction of the slave trade ... We want to sell our own commodities in Africa and we send them thither. The Africans who want to buy will pay us in whatever way we like. If we insist on having slaves, slaves they will produce; if we prefer being paid in elephants teeth, those articles will be collected, and will be got ready for our merchants.

He ridicules Buxton's ideas as 'wild and crude', adding for good measure that Lord Melbourne, the prime minister, thought likewise. So the Mombasa scheme came to naught. However, Buxton did have his uses: in the following year Palmerston sent him to Rome as Victoria's secret emissary, to invite Pope Gregory XVI to join a 'Christian League' against the slave trade. The Pope was won over, and issued an encyclical on the matter.

By now it was obvious that Britain had to take the decisive step of putting a consul on Zanzibar. Even Said took an interest, telling Palmerston in a letter what kind of person he wanted: 'a steady wise man, and a genuine English.' He added that any other people who came to live in Zanzibar or Muscat should also be 'all true, pure, English'. There was a coded message here, since Robert Norsworthy, the first Englishman sent to live on the island as a trader, had left in disgrace two years earlier after swindling his employers.

The eventual choice for the consular post was scarcely a 'true, pure English'. Captain Atkins Hamerton was an Irishman serving in the 15th regiment of the Bombay Light Infantry. The captain, aged thirty-six, was a burly bachelor from County Dublin, a Catholic, fond of liquor, with little respect for non-Europeans, and a temperament veering swiftly from jollity to rage; but his military background gave him a tenacity in negotiations and he would prove to be a tireless writer of reports to his superiors.

His appointment met the insistence of the East India Company that East Africa lay within its area of political control and the consul must be 'an officer of the Government of India'. Hamerton was first appointed in 1840 as the company's agent in Muscat and only later told that he was to become Her Britannic Majesty's consul at the court of His Highness Seyyid Said, wherever that might be.

It happened that Hamerton was taking up his duties just as Said permanently abandoned his Arabian birthplace. Muscat was in a constant state of rebellion and most of its populace intensely hated the sultan, so he handed its care to his eldest son, Thuwain, as regent. (In time, Thuwain was to prove himself as treacherous as his father, one of his more bloodthirsty deeds being castigated by a British administrator in the Gulf as 'a breach of faith rarely equalled, I believe, in Arab history'.)[6]

Hamerton and Said were an oddly-assorted pair, whose destinies were to be interwoven for the next fifteen years. The captain privately disliked Arabs – 'There are no people in the world from whom it is so difficult to get information' – but was always circumspect in referring to Said as 'His Highness' or 'the Imaum'. When he came to learn more of Said's personal life he characterized him as a voluptuary, excessively given to the pleasures of the harem and exhausting his powers upon a horde of concubines, with whom he fathered more than a hundred children. (Hamerton's condemnation was typical of the ritual disapproval voiced by Victorian administrators about the indulgences of oriental rulers.)

For his part, Said relied upon charm and an ability to hide his innermost thoughts; in dealings with his compatriots he was ruthless, with Europeans his manner was courtly and generous. One interest the sultan and the consul shared was in horses; Said had a favourite witticism: 'Preachers, women and horses never can be called good till death.' As their friendship grew they would sometime gallop together along the beach in the early mornings, since these outings gave them a chance to discuss matters of moment without being overheard.

However, the first encounters between sultan and consul, in May and June 1841, had been unpromising. Hamerton was irritated when Said began taxing him about his own loyalties, hinting that the consul was only a servant of the East India Company, not a genuine emissary from Queen Victoria.

'I now tell you what I have told you before,' Hamerton declared to Said, 'that the interests of the Malika [Queen] and the company are not two but one, and in no way different, but one and indivisible.' He dismissed the idea that the hundreds of Indian merchants and artisans living in Zanzibar and along the mainland coast were not British subjects – they were, and would always have the protection of the Malaika; since many of them were making money by financing the slave-traders they would also have to beware of Her Majesty's laws. Adopting what he called 'a high tone' with the sultan on such topics seemed to Hamerton to work wonders.

Hamerton realized that the stories against him were being spread by the American consul, Richard Waters, who naturally saw him as a threat. However, it would be a while before he could establish a superiority over Waters, partly because one of Said's ships, the *Sultanee*, had recently crossed the Atlantic, and even though some crew members resented having their beards pulled by unruly New Yorkers, others swore that America must be the finest place on earth.

In time, well-staged calls at Zanzibar by Royal Navy warships did raise Hamerton's status. Before the end of 1841 Said was proclaiming 'by the soul of the Prophet' that he fully trusted Victoria's representative and was happy to place himself 'under the protection of the English'. The consul also boasted to his superiors that he had arranged for the removal of the two paintings from behind Said's chair, showing Yankee ships vanquishing the British. These had been replaced, he claimed, by one he gave the sultan showing the defeat of the Turkish fleet by the Royal Navy at the battle of Navarino in 1827. (In fact, an American missionary, Ebenezer Burgess, had seen two paintings of the battle of Navarino hanging in the sultan's audience hall in 1839, a year before Hamerton arrived in Zanzibar.)

The Arab advisers who surrounded Said were far from ready to be won over to the British. They knew that one part of Hamerton's duties was to tighten the anti-slavery noose round their necks. Yet they made no effort to remove from his gaze the evidence of the trade's brutalities, and within a few weeks of his arrival the consul had begun writing passionately to his superiors. Slaves were 'in such a wretched state from starvation and disease' when they reached Zanzibar that some were not worth putting up for auction; to save the import duty of a dollar a head they were thrown on the beach to die, and there their bodies were eaten by dogs. Nowhere in the world could be found such 'misery and human suffering'. Yet Hamerton always tried to excuse 'His Highness', saying that if Said were a free agent the problem would soon be solved.

Stirred by these despatches the governments in Britain and India started bombarding the sultan with demands for the extinction of slavery throughout his empire. In one way the propriety was questionable, since the appointment of a consul to Said's court gave him formal recognition by Britain as the ruler of a sovereign state. On the other hand, the ending of slavery was a Christian duty for which the British saw themselves as uniquely qualified. Their messages to Said left him in no doubt of that.

He also realized that he remained in thrall to the Indian government, whose moral authority was greatly strengthened by the formal ending of slavery throughout its territories in 1843. (The abolition laws were drawn up, despite resistance from fellow-administrators in Calcutta, by Thomas Macaulay, celebrated in later years for his five-volume *History of England*.)[7] The law would be for decades 'more honor'd in the breach than the observance'; however, the fact that Indian slave-owners received no compensation, on the grounds that slavery lacked legal status in the sub-continent, was making it even less likely that Said could expect Britain to make good his lost income if he agreed to ban the trade.

With Palmerston in opposition in the early 1840s, Said found himself caught up in a tortuous correspondence with Lord Aberdeen, the foreign secretary under Sir Robert Peel. There was, just once, a hint that Britain might console Said with some money, for a brief time. However, Aberdeen repeatedly brought out the familiar argument that profits from 'legitimate commerce' would soon fill the gap created by the loss of duty on slaves. This had a splendid resonance in Westminster, but the realities were very different in Zanzibar, where legitimate commerce meant – apart from the ivory trade – the growing of cloves, maize and sorghum, as well as the harvesting of coconuts (for copra, used to make cooking oil) and gum copal for varnishes. Prosperous Arab immigrants who had come to East Africa with Said were needing evermore labour for their plantations, and knew of only one way to acquire it.

Hamerton was given striking proof of the slave economy when approached by Captain Cogan, who had negotiated Britain's commercial treaty with Said. 'Kojim Khan' was now running a trading company in Zanzibar, and had started a joint venture with the sultan to develop a sugar plantation. His problem, as a Briton, was that using slaves to cut the cane would be a crime under British law; on the other hand, there was virtually no 'free' labour on the island. Cogan put a proposition to the consul: he would buy slaves, employ them as slaves, but guarantee to free them after a set number of years. Hamerton condemned the idea outright, saying it would merely 'aid and abet the slave trade.'

There was little love lost between the two men. Hamerton complained to the Foreign Office about the 'European adventurers' who came to Zanzibar, and clearly placed Cogan in this category: 'It is truly distressing to see a prince with the endowments the Almighty has given him so easily cajoled and imposed upon.' For his part, Cogan argued persuasively that Hamerton was damaging British interests, and these opinions reached London. The India Board even advised the Bombay government to install a new consul. (A powerful case might also have been made against Hamerton for his drinking. Once in the early morning he clambered aboard a French ship in Zanzibar harbour in the fuddled belief that it was British; the French captain none the less treated him to a good breakfast.) Eventually the consul survived, whereas Cogan decided to shut his company and leave the island.

In October 1845 a new treaty was imposed on Said by Britain. It conceded that slaves could still be shipped freely within his African dominions – anywhere along the 500-mile Swahili coast between Lamu and Kilwa, or from the Swahili coast to Zanzibar and the other offshore islands – but for the first time Said promised to suppress the export of slaves from his dominions to Arabia and other parts of Asia. He also agreed that Royal Navy and, significantly, East India Company ships, would have the right to seize any vessels owned by him or his subjects found carrying slaves outside his African waters.[8]

Said fought hard for various concessions, such as the right to keep importing eunuchs and concubines from Ethiopia. Although these were not specifically granted, some clauses of the treaty were left carefully vague. Moreover, there was no attempt at all to restrict slave-*owning* by Said and his subjects, for Hamerton knew how far he could safely push his friend, who possessed more slaves than anyone else in Zanzibar.

The limitations of the new treaty were soon revealed. The Bombay government told Hamerton that slave ships from Zanzibar were still arriving continuously in Arabian and Persian Gulf ports; one was identified as owned by Said himself. Yet the sultan was quick to express horror about others active in like enterprises: when the Royal Navy demolished several large slave barracoons on the mainland south of Kilwa he called the Indian owners 'brute animals'. Public floggings were from time to time administered to slave-dealers who for other reasons had fallen out of favour.

At some moments Hamerton's despatches show him keeping up an optimistic front: the trade was being curtailed, the sincerity of Said was never in doubt. At others he is glum, admitting that little has been achieved, that the sultan's own children were defying him, that none of his officers will genuinely obey his orders.

Britain's desire was to suppress the East African slave trade at its source, yet there was always a curious illogicality about this, for where precisely was the source? It was patently not in Zanzibar itself, the site of the great market by now becoming infamous among all of Europe's abolitionist societies. Nor was it at ports such as Bagamoyo (the 'place to lay down your burden'), on the coast facing Zanzibar. The ports were merely assembly points for the caravans which returned after many months in the interior with lines of manacled prisoners bearing loads of elephant tusks. So where did the slaves come from? When interrogated they talked about faraway mountains, rivers and lakes, but were unable to describe the routes along which they had been marched to the sea. The Arabs and Swahili who controlled the caravans chose to reveal little. It was only apparent that the death-rate of slaves on these long inland journeys was as great as on the slave ships at sea.

Although curiosity about the interior of East Africa was growing in

Europe, especially among the exploration committees of the august geographical societies, Hamerton and the handful of other Europeans living on Zanzibar were not inclined to venture on to the mainland. They insisted that they would be unwelcome there and preferred to rely upon such gossip about it as they might collect close at hand.

However, a distinctly more positive attitude had been taken by the American missionary, Ebenezer Burgess, whose ship stopped in Zanzibar in September 1839.[9] He was on his way to preach the gospel in India, but was inquisitive about the 'dark continent'. He spent some days interrogating traders from the Nyamwezi people whose home country was near a 'great inland lake' far from the coast. He called them the 'Manomoisies'; Captain Thomas Smee had also met them twenty-eight years earlier and called them the 'Meeanhmaizees'. Burgess decided that the Nyamwezi were the 'richest and most enterprising tribe in that part of Africa', and he talked to a group of them who had come to the coast to make a treaty with the sultan about safety along the trade routes. Some of the men had eighty wives and 400 slaves: 'The females do the work; men work till they obtain wherewith to buy a wife, then work no more, only trade and fight.' Shortly before his ship set sail again for Bombay, the missionary had a chance to interview another party of Nyamwezi. He wrote down a basic vocabulary of their language, and numerals up to twenty, then they grew impatient: 'I amused them a short time by measuring their height, examining their ornaments, etc., but they soon left me.'

Burgess also questioned Arabs from two trading caravans recently sent into the interior by Seyyid Said. One caravan, after marching for forty-five days, had gone halfway to the 'great inland lake', and the sultan hinted that he might allow white travellers who wanted to learn about the African interior to attach themselves to these expeditions. Burgess was enthusiastic about the idea, and regretted that a caravan had set out just before he and his fellow-missionaries arrived: 'Had we been in season, perhaps the question would have merited considering whether one of our number should not accompany it, as it would have been attended by next to no expense, except the loss of time.'

Zanzibar impressed Burgess as the 'point from which to approach the eastern part of Africa'. The climate did not frighten him at all: 'Though it has been very fatal to Frenchmen, Englishmen and Americans have enjoyed good health. Of course, greater care would be necessary than in New England.' However, the insouciant Bostonian had to sail on to

Bombay without putting his optimism to the test. It would be left to a young French naval officer to make the first attempts to penetrate the mysteries of East Africa.

FORTY-SIX

Portents of Change
in the 'English Lake'

We consider the steam communication with India as at this
moment existing to afford one of the most extraordinary illustrations of the greatness of Great Britain.
—Leitch Ritchie, *The British World in the East* (1847)

ENSIGN EUGENE MAIZAN was in his early twenties when he became
seized by a desire to win glory for France. As a junior officer in the
corvette *Dordogne*, he had come to know something of the Indian Ocean
through visits to Madagascar, Réunion and Arabia; but it was East Africa
which stirred his imagination. Maizan's ambition was as remarkable as his
background. He had been born illegitimate in Montauban in southwest
France, but won his way to the Ecole Polytechnique in Paris. There
he was called frivolous and scatterbrained, his character 'bizarre', but he
gained a first-class pass and entered the French navy.

When he conceived the idea of becoming an explorer, Maizan boldly
wrote to the Prince de Jointville, third son of the king, Louis Philippe.
The prince, a naval officer himself, was impressed, and forwarded
Maizan's letter to the ministry of marine and colonies. With this royal
endorsement the lowly ensign was unstoppable. On 23 April 1844 the
ministry's political and commercial section called the project 'très-
opportune'. With the English established at the mouth of the Red Sea
and the Cape, here was a chance for France to assert itself, and exploit
East Africa's riches.

Maizan's letters from the Brest naval base were equally persuasive,
forecasting that his journey into the heart of Africa would take him two
years and bring immeasurable rewards. He successfully demanded all
manner of scientific instruments, as well as lavish funding; by the June
of 1844 he was on his way.

The commander of the *Dordogne*, Captain Charles Guillain, had described the ensign, a graduate of a distinguished academy in Paris, as 'intelligent, well-educated, courageous'.[1] For such a man there was the stirring example of the lone French explorer René Caillié, who in the 1820s had travelled in disguise across the Sahara to Timbuktu. His feat had made him a national hero.

So in November 1844 Maizan arrived in Zanzibar aboard one of three French warships from Réunion. The flotilla was under Captain Romain Desfossés, empowered to sign a commercial treaty with Seyyid Said and install a consul on the island. It was just the latest example of how the French, much to the disapproval of the British, were thrusting their way back into the Indian Ocean after a thirty-year absence. The treaty was speedily agreed, and Consul Broquant set himself up in residence, with the *tricolor* hanging limply from his balcony. Cannons were ceremonially fired, then the flotilla departed. Maizan began making his plans; from a consulate window he could gaze out across the sea towards the mainland.

When news of the treaty reached France the Paris geographical society extolled its advantages both commercially and in the field of discovery. The flimsiest scrap of information from East Africa was a great prize, and the first explorer 'able to carry the flame of European science into this barbarous country' would find a vast new field of observation.

Perhaps Maizan had begun to feel weighed down with responsibility, the burden of his duty to France; possibly he was over-meticulous in his arrangements; it is also certain that he must have heard lurid accounts from the few white residents in Zanzibar about the dangers ahead of him. Whatever the reasons, he lingered until the middle of 1845 without making a move to the mainland, giving ample time for news to spread to chiefs along the coast that a white man was coming, to pass through their lands.

Uneasy at the prospect of a calamity in territory over which he claimed sovereignty, Said offered the Frenchman an armed escort; out of 'suspicion or recklessness' (as his former captain, Guillain, wrote later), Maizan refused. For a while it seemed that he was 'undecided whether to go ahead with his project, or abandon it'. He could have accompanied an Arab caravan heading for the interior, but missed the chance. Then news arrived that a French navy vessel was nearing Zanzibar, and Maizan suddenly grew afraid that his delay might seem to reflect on his courage and honour. He hurriedly left by boat for the mainland, leaving orders that his baggage should be brought over in his wake.

With his Malagasy servant and a few Swahili porters, Maizan set off
inland. For some days he travelled with an Indian trader, Musa, then
they parted company, the Frenchman declaring that he could look after
himself. He took a meandering route for twenty days until he reached
a village in a thick forest nicknamed *Ndege la mhulo* (bird in the bush)
and halted to await his baggage. In a direct line he was still only three
marches from the coast. Maizan wrote a letter, '*pleine de découragement*',
and sent it back to consul Broquant. That night, amid a crescendo of
drumming, a sub-chief named Hembe attacked the Frenchman, garotted
him and cut his body into pieces.[2] Long afterwards Hembe said that
the murder was not his idea: he was ordered to do it by his father, one
of Said's officials on the coast.

When reports of Maizan's fate reached Zanzibar the consul sent an
urgent despatch with the first ship sailing to Réunion. The French
applied great pressure to Said to catch and punish the culprits, and when
he claimed that the place where the ensign had died was outside his
control they threatened to put a naval party ashore to do the job. With
his well-practised dissembling, Said declared that this would delight him,
but later began wondering if the French meant what they said. He knew
he could not accept such a humiliation, and sent a twenty-strong force
of his own to the mainland. This wiped out some villages and killed
everyone it could lay hands on, but Hembe escaped into the forest.
Only the man who had played the war drum on the fatal night was
captured and brought to Zanzibar. For two years he was chained up in
the open close to the French consulate, then manacled to an old cannon
in the sultan's jail for eight years; at the end of which time he died.

Maizan's death was a setback for French ambitions in East Africa, not
least since it had humiliated Said through exposing the limitations of
his power on the mainland. The truth was that the rulers directly on
the coastal strip were ready to take their orders from Said (they well
remembered the fate of the Mazrui in Mombasa), but at their backs,
inland, the traditional forces held sway. The Zanzibari ruler lacked the
will to create an effective administration which could bring any part of
the mainland under his control. In this he was merely behaving towards
East Africa as the Arabs had done for a thousand years: never seeking
to acquire territory, and interested only in trade. It was an attitude for
which his dynasty would eventually pay the highest price.

Captain Guillain, who had been Maizan's commanding officer, wrote
about Said with distaste, describing the treachery through which he had

won and retained his position: 'Everyone knows the habits of the East, where murder and duplicity are integral parts of ruling. Where palace intrigues are generally solved by poison and the dagger, where one may abase oneself without degradation, perjure oneself without dishonour.'

Zanzibar was still just a remote speck beside an unexplored continent, so only fragmentary accounts of Maizan's death ever reached Europe, and the memories soon faded. Nevertheless, it helped to prod the governments in Bombay and London towards a more 'forward policy' in East Africa. Francophobia being as strong as ever they were anxious to keep the traditional foe in check, for French interest was displaying itself in some remarkable ways, even suggesting that the continent was a place for depositing unwanted populations. Shortly after the revolutionary uprising of 1848 a French *savant*, Fulgence Fresnel, demanded of the Paris geographical society: 'Why, while England exploits the entire world, do the French only think of quarrelling over the exploitation of France? They don't know that Africa can offer a kingdom to every proletarian!'[3]

There were other strands to the rope of interwoven interests pulling the British towards their 'forward policy': they acknowledged a need to hasten the end of slavery, and there was a desire to expand British commercial showing in Africa generally. Britain lived and prospered by selling its manufactures to the empire and the rest of the world, as the six million visitors to the Great Exhibition of 1851 were to be made well aware. Palmerston, whose attitudes in many ways characterized the age, urged the view that Africa could offer new markets for the products of British mills and factories.

There were, of course, many who were sceptical of having much to do with the continent. Its climate was lethal, and West Africa in particular was considered intolerably hostile to Europeans. As the popular couplet put it,

> Beware and take care of the Bight of Benin,
> As for one that comes out, forty went in.

The most trenchant view was held by Sir James Stephen, permanent under-secretary at the Colonial Office, who had written: 'If we could acquire the Dominion of the whole of that Continent it would be but a worthless possession.' He warned how it would be impossible to colonize Africa 'without coming into contact with numerous warlike tribes, and involving ourselves in their disputes, wars and relations with one another'.[4]

However, the authorities in India had not yet the slightest interest in colonizing tropical Africa. They merely wanted to see Britain take a tighter grip on its commerce. By the middle of the nineteenth century Zanzibar's exports were worth about a million silver dollars a year, with America taking a quarter of them, Britain slightly less, France 12 per cent and Germany 10 per cent. The profits to be made, especially on ivory, were conspicuously high. The Americans had also driven Indian cottons almost completely out of the East African market with a coarse, durable calico, made in New England, known as *merikani*.

For their part, the Americans could see the looming threat. They were deeply suspicious of the hold the long-serving British consul, Atkins Hamerton, was acquiring over Seyyid Said. In July 1850 the US secretary of state, Daniel Webster, was sent a laborious despatch by Charles Ward, successor to Richard Waters as consul, about the position of the Hindu merchants in East Africa:

> Now this large number of people, who are doing nearly all the business of Zanzibar and on the coast, are virtually acknowledged as British subjects, not of conviction, but of constraint ... The American merchants feel that the time has come when they should know the pretensions of the British Consul − [He] is claiming these people as subjects of Great Britain correct and lawful, they doubt it. If it must be so, then the British consul with all the [Hindu] merchants in his hands will be suspected of more power than the Sultan himself.

Although analysing these issues in writing did not come easily to him, Ward kept returning to them in his despatches, and reached the nub of the matter in a letter sent to Washington while he was on leave in Kennebunkport in March 1851: 'The Sultan's fears are very easily operated upon by the British Consul, and the Sultan knowing the power of England, their grasping policy in India, is constantly apprehensive about the designs upon his continental possessions. The British consul is not a favorite of the sultan but he is so afraid of the injury he may do him that he is more subservient than he would otherwise be.'

Ward went on to describe the anxieties of the Arabs in Zanzibar; that when the ailing sultan died the British would decide who should succeed him, and from then on there would be a protectorate: 'From what I've heard and the many conversations I have had with the British

Consul it appears to me that it is the policy of the British Government
to take possession of the East Coast of Africa at no distant day.' If that
happened, England would gain a 'valuable and lucrative trade' and the
'immense resources of the interior of Africa'.[5]

Ward's assessment was prophetic. It was also true that Seyyid Said
was being turned into little more than a British puppet, running what
had become, in the language of the Raj, a 'subordinate state'. The
Zanzibari Arabs had grounds for fearing what would happen when Said
died, in view of Britain's 'grasping policy' now apparent in India. The
expansionist governor-general, Lord Dalhousie, was giving free rein to
his doctrine of 'annexation by lapse'; if there was dispute over the heir
in a subordinate state, the British would simply fill the vacuum by
annexation.[6]

It was Dalhousie who had put in his pocket the great Koh-I-Noor
diamond, symbol of Sikh nationalism, after the annexation of the Punjab,
and sent it to Queen Victoria as an adornment to her imperial crown.
The mood of triumphalism, that Britain could do anything, was at its
apogee, and was summed up by the popular author Leitch Ritchie in
1847: 'At the head of the Western Nations stands Great Britain, with
the proudest sceptre the world ever saw, held more easily in the gentle
hands of a woman than Alexander wielded that of the Greeks. The
subjects of this Island Queen include one seventh part of mankind, and
her territories extend over more than one seventh part of the globe.'

This pride was being generated by achievements in and beyond the
Indian Ocean, such as the colonization of Australia, the ceding of New
Zealand by the Maoris in 1840, and the growth of Singapore. Equally
significant, by tightening the bonds of empire in the East, was Britain's
conquest of the monsoon. Just as the firepower of Portugal had transformed the Indian Ocean world in the sixteenth century, now in the
nineteenth the steam-power of Britain was about to sweep away patterns
of travel dating back more than two thousand years. Sails would not
vanish from the ocean overnight, but the thumping rhythm of steam-
engines, tackling the monsoons head on, was becoming the sound of
the new age.

In 1829 a tiny steamer named the *Hugh Lindsay* had made a pioneering
Suez–Bombay voyage. Ten years later the East India Company introduced several larger vessels, 50 per cent paid for by the British Treasury;
operated by the Bombay Marine, they could also serve as warships in
the Gulf. Although most commercial freight was still carried under sail

round the Cape – a voyage taking six months – the introduction of steamers between Suez and Bombay now meant that India could be reached from London throughout the year in little more than forty days. The once slow and dusty desert trip between Alexandria and Suez had been smoothed out by British enterprise, while the rest of the journey – by Channel steamer, train across France, and fast ship to Egypt – was run to strict schedules.

This transformation had come swiftly, in response to urgings by British merchants in the Raj, although the supporters of the Cape route did not give way easily. In 1839 an engineer named Henry Wise, an admirer of 'Melville's Patent Propellors', wrote a book arguing that the Suez route could never be trusted because of the 'caprice of the Egyptian rulers'. It was best, said Wise, to stick to the Cape, using sailing ships assisted by steam engines and the vaunted patent propellors. Mastering the problem 'was an object worthy of our best exertions, and the employment of those great resources which the British nation, by the blessings of Divine Providence, enjoys'.[7]

However, by the late 1840s the debate was quite over. The passage to India was now taking only a month. The outward passage with the Peninsular and Oriental Steam Navigation Company from Suez to Calcutta was timed at precisely 523 hours, and the return voyage at 543 hours; the company was liable to fines for 'all unnecessary delays'. The sole concession to the monsoon was the adding of 120 hours to the return voyage in May, June and July. Fortnightly services from Suez carried passengers and mail to India and Singapore, then onwards to Hong Kong, which had been acquired by Britain after the 'Opium Wars'.

Above all, Britain became intent on maintaining its authority in the Red Sea, now the vital artery of communication. This resolve had been displayed as early as 1839, when Aden was bombarded into accepting East India Company rule. At that date there were suggestions of putting Aden under the formal control of Seyyid Said, but Palmerston vetoed the idea. He wanted Aden to be exclusively British, to make sure that no other power could seize it and threaten the new route. The port was also ideally placed to be a coaling station for the steamships, midway between Suez and Bombay.

This new communication with the East was seen as a proof of Victoria ingenuity. The governor of Bombay, Sir Robert Grant, believed that the steamers would allow Britain to maintain a steady influence over places formerly out of reach during the monsoons. Through the conquest of geography, life in India had been 'civilized' for British administrators, army officers and memsahibs; home was suddenly quite close. It seemed that nothing could mar this serene triumph, until the shadow of a European rival fell starkly across it.

All the old British antagonism towards France gained fresh impetus in November 1854 when Sa'id Pasha of Egypt granted Ferdinand de Lesseps a concession to build a canal across the Suez isthmus from the Mediterranean to the Red Sea. A spectre from the not-so-distant past raised its head, for Napoleon himself had toyed with that very idea. Now Cairo was again reputed to be swarming with Frenchmen and others were said to be making furtive surveys of ports in the Red Sea. France was rumoured to be scheming to capture the port of Berbera, facing Aden. One fierce opponent of the canal scheme was Palmerston; he branded it 'subtle and ingenious'.

Ernst Ravenstein, a German-born fellow of the Royal Geographical Society, summed up the perceived peril melodramatically:

> It is the avowed design of France to found in the eastern sea an empire to rival, if not to eclipse, British India, of which empire Madagascar is to be the centre. Across the isthmus of Suez leads the shortest route from southern France to Madagascar (and India); its possession by a power desirous to extend her dominions in that quarter, and capable of availing herself of its advantages, would therefore be of the utmost consequence. The mere fact of the isthmus being part of the Turkish empire, or of Egypt, would not deter France from occupying it: for scruples of conscience are not allowed by that nation to interfere with political 'ideas'.[8]

For conspiracy theorists such as Ravenstein, the proposed canal, the growing French domination of Madagascar, even the unfortunate Maizan's attempt to penetrate East Africa, were all part of a masterplan conceived in Paris. The time was at hand for a fresh display of British authority.

FORTY-SEVEN

In the Footsteps of
a Missionary

※

To the courage, enterprise and missionary zeal of that gentleman
the world is indebted for opening up the almost hermetically
sealed coast of East Africa . . . to Dr Krapf must remain the honour
of having pioneered the way.
—Charles New, *Life, Wanderings and Labours in Eastern Africa* (1874)

DR LUDWIG KRAPF was quite unlike the kind of person with whom
the raffish young Indian army officer, Richard Burton, normally chose
to associate. But on hearing that the German missionary-explorer was
also in Cairo, he determinedly sought him out. Although Burton had
just returned from a daring journey to Mecca and Medina, after entering
Arabia disguised as a Muslim pilgrim, Krapf's fame was much more
firmly established. During his last visit to London in 1850, three years
before his encounter with Burton, the missionary had met the Prince
Consort, the Archbishop of Canterbury, and Lord Palmerston. The
British took a proprietary pleasure in Krapf's explorations, for although
he had been born in Württemberg and trained in Basle, his work in
Africa had been done under the auspices of the Church Missionary
Society. In his own land he was also much respected, having been
invited to discuss geographical matters with the venerable Baron von
Humboldt, Germany's greatest scientist, and to dine with King William
Frederick of Prussia.[1]

Yet Krapf never sought worldly renown. The true driving force of
his life was a belief that the Second Coming was at hand. His Christian
duty was to save souls while there was time, to 'irrigate the arid wastes'
of heathendom. Fame pursued him simply because he had chanced to
carry out this mission in East Africa, a part of the world which was
increasingly an arena for political rivalry. Closely linked to such competition were efforts by European academics to resolve the mysteries of

the region, to 'fill in the blanks on the map'. Since Krapf had boldly ventured in the African interior, searching for potential converts untouched by Islam, he could hardly escape being a focus of attention.

What greatly excited the theorists, the 'armchair geographers' – and provoked derision from some – were the claims by Krapf to have sighted snow on the peak of a mountain, 300 miles inland on the latitude of the equator; the Africans called the mountain Kenia. A second snow-covered mountain, named Kilimanjaro, was reported to have been glimpsed further south by Johann Rebmann, one of Krapf's subordinates. Even Sir Roderick Murchison, usually keen during his presidential addresses to the Royal Geographical Society (RGS) in London to applaud any discovery which might catch the public imagination, had cast doubt on these tales of equatorial snow. But the missionaries insisted upon trusting their own eyes. Rebmann was so overwhelmed by the sight of Kilimanjaro that he sat down in the bush to read his Bible, and his gaze at once fell upon the 111th Psalm: 'He hath shown the people the power of his works, that he may give them the heritage of the heathen.'

Such pious attitudes to exploration had no appeal to Burton, but he was quick to see his opportunity, even before talking to Krapf. He would take up in East Africa where the missionaries were being forced, through a lack of new recruits, to leave off. Krapf once talked of planting a line of settlements right across the continent to the Atlantic, a necklace of Christianity, but now he was giving up the idea. When Burton met him in Cairo he was well into his forties, physically tired and on his way to Europe for medical treatment.

Krapf was also disillusioned with his younger colleagues, who seemed to have lost the will to venture far from the mission headquarters he had founded eight years earlier near Mombasa. All too often they lay prostrate with fever, which had killed some of their number and forced others to retreat to Europe. The survivors were generally content to spread the word of God by preaching from the flat roof of their house to any African who happened to come by. So the coast-to-coast journey across Africa remained a tempting fruit, ripe for plucking.

A string of letters was sent home from Cairo by Burton to his friend Norton Shaw, the RGS secretary, telling how he would 'pump' Krapf to see 'what really has been done and what remains to be done'. He ventures: 'If time only be allowed me [by the Bombay army] I will pass on to the Atlantic.' Always ready to mock a 'mish', Burton claims that when Krapf talked of 'the sources of the White Nile, Kilamanjaro and the Mts of the Moon', it reminded him of 'a de Lunatico' (the snow-covered Nile sources on Ptolemaic maps were the *Lunae Montes*). For all that, he argues in his letter to Shaw, the East African region possesses 'vast resources undeveloped', whereas further exploring in Arabia would bring him no practical results apart from the discovery of 'deserts, valleys and tribes'.

In contrast to this hard-headedness, Krapf had always been quite unworldly, yet his discoveries can be seen as having blazed the trail for imperial intervention. They stimulated a hope that from the coast opposite Zanzibar a route could at last be opened towards the unknown heart of the continent, towards the legendary lakes and mountains which fascinated romantic adventurers such as Burton. Indeed, had their religious leanings, class backgrounds and personal conduct not been so at odds, Krapf and Burton might have become partners in this next stage of exploration. Both enjoyed travel for its own sake and wrote fluently about their experiences.

Like Burton, the German missionary was a remarkable linguist: on first visiting Zanzibar in 1844 he gave Seyyid Said an account in Arabic of his previous six years in Ethiopia. The sultan was so impressed that he told Krapf he was free to start a Christian mission on the mainland, the first since the Portuguese were ousted almost 150 years earlier. It may be that Said was disposed to give this permission because Krapf said his aim was to open a 'back door' route from East Africa to southern Ethiopia. However, that idea was swiftly abandoned: despite the deaths soon after their arrival of his wife and baby daughter, Krapf settled down in Mombasa to begin producing the first written vocabularies and teaching manuals for Swahili and various mainland languages, as well as making translations of the Gospels.

One of the unbridgeable gulfs between Krapf and Burton lay in their behaviour towards strangers. The missionary felt happy strolling through the African interior with nothing to defend himself but his umbrella, whereas the other trusted in violence and had already sought to advance himself in the army by publishing a manual entitled *A Complete System of Bayonet Exercise*. Burton believed in instilling fear by a 'just, wholesome and unsparing severity'.[2]

Krapf thought Africans were sunk in 'moral misery and degradation', although his journal shows that he could sympathize with their sufferings born of the slave trade, famine and warfare. For his part, Burton felt only contempt. Like most of his fellow-officers in India he referred indiscriminately to Arabs and Indians as 'niggers', but Africans were in his opinion scarcely better than animals. Whereas Krapf never enjoyed much success in winning black converts to 'Christianity and civilization', Burton would have regarded it as perverse even to try.

By chance, in the very week when Burton's 'pumping' was taking place in Cairo, a traveller with beliefs much like those of Krapf was starting a journey which would make him the most famous explorer of the nineteenth century. Quite possibly, Burton had never even heard of David Livingstone, but Krapf was certainly aware of him. In the previous year, when the Paris geographical society awarded silver medals to Krapf and Rebmann, the same honour had been given to David Livingstone and his companion William Cotton Oswell for discoveries south of the Zambezi.

Now Livingstone was setting off from a village called Linyanti, on the middle reaches of the Zambezi river, with a bold plan to go first westwards to the Atlantic then back eastwards to the Indian Ocean. His completion of the first stage, from the Zambezi to the Atlantic, was to be hailed at the RGS by a fellow-Scot, Sir Roderick Murchison, as 'the greatest triumph in geographical research which has been effected in our times'. There were many more panegyrics to come.

Thus it was that another 'mish' was about to forestall Burton in the race for the laurels of African exploration, but there was nothing to be done about it. After parting from Krapf he had to return from Cairo to Bombay, to beg support for a new expedition and lobby for more leave from his infantry regiment. In both he was successful, for at the time the East India Company viewed him with favour: the daring trip to Mecca had proved his resourcefulness, and his most successful book to date, *Sindh, and the Races that Inhabit the Valley of the Indus*, had been obsequiously dedicated to the court of directors as an 'attempt to delineate a province of the Empire owning their extended rule'.

By the middle of 1854 he was back at Aden, so tantalizingly close to Africa. Here he had to wait for several months for a letter from the London directors granting approval for his travel plans. At first Burton was extravagantly proposing to sail from Aden to Somalia, march south towards Zanzibar, turn westwards and keep on until he reached Africa's west coast. Supporting him in this venture would be three more serving officers from India. As late as February in the following year, just before leaving Aden, he was assuring his friend Shaw: 'and *entre nous* I want to settle the question of Krapf and the "eternal snows". There is little doubt that there is an open route through Africa to the Atlantic.'

In reality, his expedition was equipped for only a limited sortie into the Horn of Africa, and even that went badly awry. Although Burton performed a solo journey – once more in disguise – to the walled city of Harar, he and his companions were ambushed by Somalis when on the point of returning to Aden. An Indian navy lieutenant, William Stroyan, was killed, an army lieutenant, John Speke, suffered eleven wounds, and Burton was speared through the face.

The spear left a permanent scar on Burton's cheek, and investigations into the disaster would likewise leave a lifelong scar on his reputation. He had been the one in charge, and it was not merely that a life was lost and much government property abandoned to the Somali attackers; British dignity had been affronted. Papers on the affair reached the desk of Lord Dalhousie, who had stern words for the expedition's members: 'In such a country, and among such a people, their negligence and disregard for all common prudence and ordinary precaution cannot be extenuated, far less excused.'

Since he had clearly lost some ground with the East India Company, Burton carefully fostered his relationships with the Royal Geographical Society while he was convalescing in England during 1855. By this time Murchison and his council members were buoyed up with David Livingstone's achievement in reaching Luanda, and were agog for news of when and where he might re-emerge from his renewed wanderings in the wilds. In his absence, Livingstone had already been awarded the coveted Patron's Medal.

The RGS, so financially frail in its earlier years, was now thriving through being in the forefront of the race to uncover the secrets of 'Inner Africa'. A fresh impetus for African exploration came in late 1855 with the publication of a map purporting to show a gigantic and grotesque lake lying across the middle of the continent. This had been drawn by Jacob Erhardt, one of Krapf's fellow-missionaries in East Africa, on the basis of stories he had collected in a coastal town south of Mombasa. Although several armchair geographers still refused to credit the eye-witness accounts of the 'eternal snows', they were willing to take seriously what soon became nicknamed the 'slug map', because it fitted so well with their own theories.

A senior figure in the RGS declaring himself impressed was James MacQueen, who some years earlier had interrogated Laith bin Sa'id, a Zanzibar Arab who was then making a visit to Britain.[3] In the heart of

Africa, according to Lief bin Said, lay a great lake, which he had twice
visited to barter for ivory. To reach the lake from Zanzibar a caravan
must travel for four and a half months, 'exactly in the direction of the
setting sun'. Everyone who lived by the lake knew it was the 'source
of the river which goes through Egypt'. So Erhardt's 'slug map' seemed
finally to confirm such stories; for the classicists there was the satisfaction
of knowing that it seemed to vindicate Ptolemy.

Burton made a visit to Constantinople in the second half of 1855, in
a vain attempt to see some action in the final months of the Crimean
War. On his return to Britain all the talk among the geographers was
about the huge African lake. Once more he gauged the opportunity
shrewdly. No longer did he talk of crossing the African continent, since
it was plain that David Livingstone, if he were still alive, must be near
to claiming that prize. What now mattered was finding the source of
the Nile.

So during the first half of 1856 Burton applied himself to marshalling
support for an expedition to the great lake, which Erhardt's map called
the Sea of Tanganyika. Some money was put up by John Speke, who
was eager to return to Africa despite having so narrowly escaped death in
Somalia. Although Speke had awkward character traits, he was physically
powerful (as Burton remarked, his ability to survive eleven wounds was
a 'lesson in how difficult it is to kill a man in sound health') and his
wealth now confirmed his place as Burton's partner.

Despite Murchison's distrust of 'Devil Dick', the senior ranks of the
RGS included enough admirers of his three-volume account of the
'pilgrimage' to Mecca to carry the day. Crucial backing came from the
Foreign Office, which put up £1,000, ostensibly for scientific research.
A further display of interest came from the East India Company, even
though it had withdrawn the offer of a donation because of Burton's
hectoring rejoinders to criticism of the way he had run the Somali
venture. Colonel William Sykes, chairman of the court of directors, was
also chairman of the RGS explorations committee, and had put a resol-
ution to it calling on the society to 'invite the co-operation of Her
Majesty's Government and the East India Company' for the expedition.
He said it deserved to be supported 'not less on the grounds of geographical discovery than for the probable commercial and, it may be, political
advantages'. The aims would include 'determining the exportable
products of the countries and the ethnography of the tribes'.

The surge of resounding phrases which sped Burton and Speke on their way was in part dictated by a wish to let everyone know who was master in the Indian Ocean, especially now that de Lesseps was scheming to build a canal across the Suez isthmus. Zanzibar was rising higher in the geo-political reckoning for, as Krapf was to observe in his memoirs, 'the possessor of East Africa will have gained a first step towards the dominion of India'. Without saying so openly, the government – in which Palmerston was now prime minister – wanted to use the expedition to tell France and other powers that Britain regarded Zanzibar as its own gateway to Africa.[4]

For the same reasons the emissaries Seyyid Said regularly sent to London were welcomed with elaborate deference and messages of good-will were despatched to him at frequent intervals. Reassuringly, the ailing sultan had named his favourite frigate *Queen Victoria*, and he treated Consul Hamerton, now a lieutenant-colonel, as though he was his grand vizier. Whenever Said left Zanzibar he insisted that Hamerton should stay on the island to watch over affairs and be ready to snuff out any signs of rebellion. These precautions sprang from the sultan's fears that one or other of his many sons might be plotting against him; it was, after all, a family trait. The banishment and death of Hilal, his eldest son, meant that the next in line became Khalid. He was disliked at first by Hamerton for holding pro-French views – he even named his Zanzi-bar estate 'Marseilles' – but later came to heel. The consul then declared Khalid to be 'of excellent character . . . in no way addicted to the vices usual with Asiatic princes' and 'exceedingly courteous to Europeans'.[5]

Even so, Hamerton lived in dread of the inevitable, the death of Said, the mainspring of his world. It finally happened in October 1856, two months before the arrival of Burton and Speke in Zanzibar. At the age of sixty-seven the sultan had succumbed to dysentery in the *Queen Victoria*, on a voyage back to Zanzibar from Muscat, where he had spent more than two years trying to smother the fires of rebellion.

To complicate matters further, the approved heir, Khalid, had earlier died in Zanzibar of consumption, and after his death there was ominous rioting by groups of Swahili and slaves from the clove plantations.[6] Hamerton had imposed a curfew and told the Baluchi mercenaries on the island to kill anyone moving around after dark. The rioting died down. On hearing of Khalid's death the old sultan had sent a message from Muscat saying that his new heir was now to be one of his youngest sons, the sickly, lacklustre Majid. That had gratified Hamerton, who saw Majid as being easy to control.

However, the death of Said himself sparked off more disorder in the island, so that when Burton and Speke came ashore they realized at once that this would delay the organizing of their expedition. On the other hand, it meant that there would be no need to beg permission before crossing to the mainland and starting their march. The newly-installed Majid had more urgent preoccupations, notably his several elder brothers, one in Zanzibar and others in Muscat, who were eager to kill him and take his place.

So the two explorers had only to contend with Hamerton's voluble warnings about the horrors of East Africa. These seemed vindicated when they both returned half-dead with fever from a preliminary exploration along the coast. While they were convalescing, Burton kept himself busy with collecting material on the history of Zanzibar. He quickly realized that the Swahili language was another proof of the links across the Indian Ocean, for he had previously encountered it among the black slaves in north-west India, while writing his book on Sindh. They had told him how they had been sold in Africa as children, for grain or cloth. He was so intrigued that he had compiled a long word-list of their language, which was unintelligible to other people in India. Now he discovered it was Swahili, spoken by everyone in Zanzibar and on the coast.

Although Burton was busy making notes for future literary use, Speke fretted far more at the delays. News about David Livingstone was like a goad, for with his return to Britain after his triumphant journey from the Atlantic to the Indian Ocean the Scottish doctor was being fêted as the man of the hour. He was receiving honorary degrees and the freedoms of cities, taking tea with Queen Victoria and putting the finishing touches to *Missionary Travels and Researches in South Africa*, a book destined to be the bestseller of the decade. Cheering crowds gathered wherever he went and every word he uttered was seized upon by the newspapers and weekly magazines. African exploration was clearly about to enter its heyday, and kicking one's heels in Zanzibar was no way to occupy the limelight.

At last, in the middle of 1857, when the weather was right, Burton and Speke took a boat to Bagamoyo, where the caravans which traded with the people of the lakes began and ended their journeys. In the six months of waiting the two officers had assembled a force modelled on these caravans. It had guides, porters and a heavily-armed escort. If they had to fight their way through, they were ready, though neither

Livingstone nor Krapf had chosen to travel in this manner. Scant advice was forthcoming from the Europeans in Zanzibar: as Burton sardonically put it, they were 'mostly ignorant of everything beyond the island'.

Hamerton crossed to Bagamoyo to see them off. Bugles were blown, muskets fired, orders shouted. There was great confusion and a last-minute shortage of porters meant that some equipment had to be left behind. Even so, if Said had still been alive and there to watch the scene when 200 men, most of them armed, set off under white control, he might have felt a certain unease about the future of his ill-defined East African empire. As Burton had already realized, the Arabs were 'adverse to, and fearful of' white travellers.

Crossing to Bagamoyo to bid the expedition farewell was one of Hamerton's last official duties. Three weeks later he was dead, at the age of fifty-three. Whisky, quinine and a dogged tenacity had sustained him for fifteen years in Zanzibar. His value to Britain had been incalculable. However, the news of his death attracted less notice than it deserved, for the Indian Mutiny had begun.[7]

The East India Company, so long the symbol of British power in the East, would be swept into oblivion by the 'sepoy rebellion' almost overnight, and for all its defiant panoply the Raj was to be driven along a course whose outcome was inescapable. However, as if in compensation a new imperial vista would at this moment be brought into view, on the long-neglected western flank of the Indian Ocean.

FORTY-EIGHT

Warriors, Hunters and Traders

> The Arab system extended to great distances, and octopus-like,
> grasped every small unprotected village community, making the
> whole country a vast battlefield wherein no one was safe outside
> the stockades.
>
> —A. J. Swann, *Fighting the Slave Hunters in Central Africa* (1910)

THE WORD 'EXPLORATION' was justifiably used to describe the journeys
of Burton, Speke and the rush of European travellers who came after
them, because they transformed knowledge outside Africa about the
vast hidden regions of the continent. However, it also implied that the
peoples of the African interior had been existing in a geographical limbo,
timeless and unchanging. They, and the mountains, rivers and lakes
beside which they lived, were not on any maps. So it was taken for
granted that they waited, inert, to be 'discovered', and could only be
grateful when it happened.

Naturally enough, many later empire-builders chose to foster the
illusion that they had struggled through trackless forests and wildernesses
to reach their goals. But Speke, in his artless way, had revealed the
reality at the very outset, in a despatch sent on ahead to the coast as he
and Burton were returning from Lake Tanganyika: 'This is a shocking
country for sport; there appears to be literally nothing but elephants,
and they, from constant hunting, are driven from the highways.' The
word 'highways' was absurd, as was Speke's assumption that the Royal
Geographical Society needed to know that the shooting in the heart of
Africa did not come up to his expectations.

Even so, he and Burton were, if not on a highway, at least on a
well-beaten track which trading caravans had used for at least forty years.
The scarlet flag of the ruler of Zanzibar was carried at the head of the
expedition, and was recognized and feared everywhere. So although
they often skirted round the fact, most white newcomers to Africa made
their way through the bush by following well-trodden routes, even

though these often seemed maddeningly circuitous. Whenever there was a chance, many self-styled explorers would also attach themselves to a caravan if it were heading in the right direction.

In East Africa by the 1850s the caravans were generally controlled by Arabs, and they were Muslims, so it was a strain on their good-will to help white men who were Christians. However, as subjects of the Zanzibar sultan they took care to hide any resentment when Britons, in particular, sought favours along the way, because they knew how powerful the British were. Some white men, such as 'Bwana Dawud', the missionary David Livingstone, would travel for many months with the Arabs, accept food from them and live in their protected encampments.

Burton had made full use of his encounters with traders on the march to question them about the lands beyond Lake Tanganyika. He was able to confirm that some Arabs had already travelled all the way to the Atlantic. So Burton knew for sure that 'the road was open' beyond the point where he and Speke turned back, and it gave him the chance to proclaim a grievance in his own despatch: 'We deeply regret that the arrangements for the expedition were not upon a more liberal scale. With £5,000, we might, I believe, without difficulty, have spanned Africa from east to west.' He made it sound easy, although books written later by both men laid stress on the unpredictable horrors they endured, among the more outlandish being Speke's efforts to dig a burrowing beetle out of his inner ear with a penknife. In truth, Burton had probably been glad enough to turn back after reaching Lake Tanganyika, rather than push further into the unknown.

This journey, with its clear geographical goal, was markedly different in style from the travels of the missionaries, yet was never seen as a reconnaissance for conquest. That did not stop Speke, in particular, from speculating. He later wrote:

> How the negro has lived so many ages without advancing, seems marvellous, when all the countries surrounding Africa are so forward in comparison ... Could a government be formed for them like ours in India, they would be saved; but without it, I fear there is very little chance; for at present the African neither can help himself nor will he be helped by others, because his country is in such a constant state of turmoil he has too much anxiety on hand looking out for his food to think of anything else.[1]

The idea that the whole of Africa could be ruled by one government, just like the Raj, seemed perfectly feasible to Speke, who had spent all his adult life in India. There was no reason, at that moment, to imagine that Africa was fated to be divided up into completely artificial colonial entities. Nor could Speke have understood, from his scanty knowledge of the continent's history, that the 'constant state of turmoil' he witnessed sprang from an accelerating process of change during the previous five decades. Life in the interior of Africa had altered more during the first half of the nineteenth century than in the previous 1,500 years.

In the past the Africans had lived in virtual isolation, in balance with their environment. The communities varied greatly in size: some were tiny villages separated from their nearest neighbours by long journeys through uninhabited bush, while others, especially near the great lakes, were highly structured nation-states to which weaker societies paid tribute in ivory, cattle and slaves. There were hundreds of distinct languages throughout the interior, and many kinds of social structures. What all these societies shared was a constant spiritual bond with their ancestors, who gave guidance through mediums in times of decision. This meant that African life was conservative, but not unchanging. Each community had evolved its separate answers to problems of survival – how crops should be irrigated or cattle protected against wild beasts – and everyone knew the duties and prohibitions to be respected from childhood to death.

Now that world was in flux. One cause was the adoption of new crops brought from the Americas, such as maize and cassava. They yielded more food from the same area of ground than traditional grains, such as millet, leading to a surge in population (by 1850, Africa south of the equator contained about thirty million people). This sharpened the rivalry for fertile land near rivers and lakes.

Another stimulus for change was the torrent of manufactured goods being brought to Africa from Europe and America: cloth, plates, cups, cutlery and all the other smaller products of the industrial revolution which men could carry inland on their heads.[2] In West Africa some powerful kingdoms, once geared almost entirely to slave exporting, were acquiring new imperatives, and although European contacts with other parts of the continent were less direct they were none the less decisive.

A starker reason for the changes taking place was the introduction of cheap muskets which, among other results, were helping to satisfy the outside world's insatiable demand for ivory; the export of tusks from Zanzibar was to grow tenfold during the nineteenth century.

The sound of gunfire, the sound of European supremacy, had echoed round the coasts of Africa since the age of Vasco da Gama. So it might be imagined that Africans of the interior would have taken to firearms as early as the sixteenth century, to put them on terms with the Europeans or to give themselves an advantage over neighbours equipped only with spears. Yet apart from those used by slave-trading chieftains in West Africa or mercenaries serving the Portuguese in Angola and Mozambique, there were few functional guns in African hands until after the Napoleonic wars.

It had always been the custom, of course, to present a few guns to African rulers upon whom Europeans were eager to make an impression, and the custom persisted. As late as the 1840s an East India Company mission gave Sahle Selassie, the Ethiopian king in Shoa, a three-pounder cannon and some muskets, together with a musical clock and musical boxes.[3] But such novelties were usually treated as palace playthings, rather than being put to practical use.

The firearm that transformed Africa was the flintlock muzzle-loader, Europe's basic weapon for almost two centuries. Its acceptance had been slow because guns were costly and, when they broke, most local blacksmiths lacked the skills to mend them; moreover, a musket might fail to work at the crucial moment – especially during the rainy season – in which case a man with a spear was far better off. Finally, there was the difficulty of obtaining gunpowder.

Only in the 1820s did cheap firearms start arriving in black Africa. Many were the detritus of the Napoleonic wars. The manufacturing city of Birmingham had a million muskets in stock after 1815, and Africa was one of the most ready markets. When this surplus had been sold off, Birmingham began turning out a low-grade musket especially for Africa; by the middle of the century half of Birmingham's output of 100,000 guns a year was being sold to the continent. There was also plenty of gunpowder to go with them.[4]

Often known as 'gas pipes', of 'sham damn iron', the low-grade muskets cost about five shillings to make (a reliable weapon cost sixteen shillings) and were prone to explode when fired. Factories in Liège were producing as many 'trade muskets' as their Birmingham rivals, and the quality was regarded as even worse. Nevertheless, Africa kept importing them.

In return, white traders always demanded ivory, so the elephant-hunters became a new élite. The Chokwe of Angola, whose blacksmiths were highly skilled, became one of the first societies to adopt muskets for hunting, with the encouragement of the Portuguese. In a pattern which would be repeated elsewhere, they effectively wiped out all the elephant herds in their own area, then ranged further afield, to the headwaters of the Congo and Zambezi rivers. In such ways, peoples once remote from one another were coming into regular contact.

In East Africa, from Somalia to Mozambique, the pursuit of ivory was also intensifying. Although elephants could no longer be found roaming almost on the seashore, as in medieval times, the herds inland seemed inexhaustible. Yet there was a unique factor in the regions which Burton and Speke had penetrated, for there the ivory trade was controlled by non-Africans: the Arab-run caravans were financed by the Hindu *banians* of Zanzibar and the tusks were bought and exported by European traders (*wazungu*) based on the island.

The payment for tusks to Africans in the interior in cloth or beads was only a tiny fraction of the price paid in Zanzibar, yet going to fetch ivory from some parts could be perilous work, as Ludwig Krapf had noted in the 1840s. He saw caravans 'from 600 to 1,000 men strong, and mostly armed with muskets' venturing into Masai country, but being 'often nearly all slain'. The vast profits from the sale of a consignment of fine tusks to the European traders made such losses worthwhile; men were cheap and so were their guns.

However, the Arabs kept muskets away from Africans as far as they could, apart from those they handed out to trusted freedmen and slaves. As Burton expressed it: 'In the interior firearms are still fortunately rare – the Arabs are too wise to arm the barbarians against themselves.'[5]

Despite this general lust for guns, the spear as a weapon of war was winning a new respect in East Africa with the arrival of warrior bands from a distant part of the continent. The invaders fought with unprecedented ferocity and their presence was adding to the 'state of turmoil' remarked upon by Speke, because they were stimulating the growth of piratical empires able to challenge the traditional structures.

The black warlords who led the black regiments towards East Africa had no set goals. They were drawn onwards by the hope of plunder in what is called the Mfecane (literally, the 'Crushing'). The origins of the Mfecane lay in the south of Africa, near the borders of modern Natal, but the effects were to be felt as far as the shores of Lake Victoria.

When the armed migration moved forward, then paused to re-create itself after each battle, new regiments were formed from the conquered; often, fresh leaders emerged. Yet in specific ways the methods of the Mfecane never changed: the warriors attacked in crescent formation, used their massive oxhide shields to deflect spears thrown by the enemy, then engaged in close combat with their short stabbing spears. These tactics were to be widely imitated.

The crucible of the Mfecane was the confined coastal lands between the Drakensberg mountains and the Indian Ocean. Peoples speaking the Nguni languages lived here, as they had done for several centuries, farming and keeping cattle. There was no contact with Europeans, apart from the occasional survivors from shipwrecks along the Natal coast and some Portuguese traders to the north in Delagoa Bay.

What had suddenly changed the way of life of the pastoral Nguni early in the nineteenth century, turning them into a constellation of rival military states, is still debated.[6] It could have been land hunger, or competition for trade with the Portuguese. Whatever the reason, it can scarcely be a coincidence that this violent diaspora happened just as the *trekboers* of South Africa were also moving northwards.

Around 1820, after bloody struggles for power, the Zulu nation had emerged in Natal as the supreme force, led by the tyrant Shaka and disciplined in a manner unknown before anywhere in Africa. It was Shaka who perfected the distinctive way of fighting with the stabbing spear. The plundering and killing by his regiments were to turn parts of Natal into empty wastelands. Pioneer white traders from the Cape regarded Shaka with a mixture of admiration and fear; some used their guns to help him in his wars, others returned to the Cape to denounce him as a bloodthirsty monster.[7]

In 1828 the havoc Shaka caused among the Zulus themselves drove two of his brothers, helped by one of his closest aides, to kill him. But the Mfecane had by now gained an unstoppable momentum. Armies rampaged across southern Africa, some going north into Mozambique, where Sofala and other Portuguese settlements were overwhelmed, and others west across the Drakensbergs. One group, the Ndebele led by Mzilikazi, came to a halt at Bulawayo. There they founded a kingdom spreading out over the high plateau, which the rulers of Great Zimbabwe had dominated five centuries earlier; this was also where early Portuguese missionaries had struggled to implant their Catholic faith, although no trace of it survived.

At least three other nomadic armies moved up to the Zambezi. The most powerful, known as the Ngoní, was led by the warlord Zwangend-aba. His force crossed the great river, near the Portuguese settlement of Zumbo, on a day when there was an eclipse of the sun; this can be pinpointed as 19 November 1835. Zwangendaba pushed northwards towards Lake Tanganyika, crushing local groups and incorporating their surviving warriors into his regiments. To the east of the lake he settled at a place he called Mapupo ('Dreams'), and died there in 1848. A grove of trees was planted round his grave.

The Ngoni then split up into five segments after quarrels over the succession to Zwangendaba. By this time only the 'officer corps' in the marauding regiments could claim to have started out a generation earlier with the original Mfecane, from the homeland 1,500 miles to the south. But the rules by which they lived and fought were unchanged. All wore the distinctive feathered headdress of the Ngoni, chanted the same battle-cries, and hanged any man showing fear in combat.

One group swung back to occupy fertile territory near Lake Malawi. The scattered villages of the area were soon overrun by the *impis* with their stabbing spears, the inhabitants were enslaved and grouped close together in new villages on the Ngoni pattern. Lakeside communities within raiding distance took to building their homes on stilts well out from the shore, because of the well-known Ngoni dislike of crossing water.[8]

The area settled by this part of Zwangendaba's army was a crossroads of East Africa's long-distance trade. Routes led eastwards to Kilwa, westwards to the copper mines of Katanga, and north-west to Lake Tanganyika. Since before the start of the nineteenth century a warlike trading tribe, the Yao, had raided here for ivory and slaves to sell at Kilwa Kivinje, a mainland town which had developed as the greatest slave depot in East Africa.

Swahili caravans came later, seeking the same commodities. The demand for slaves grew so great by the 1830s that orphans, traditionally absorbed into the families of relatives, were sold off to the caravans. So were petty criminals, who in the past would have been kept in the tribe as domestic slaves. The Ngoni disapproved of this, since their policy was still to merge into their own ranks the survivors from lands they had conquered. The rivalry between them and the slave-buyers from the coast led to decades of bloodshed.

The northwards thrust of the Mfecane finally exhausted itself on the plateau east of Lake Tanganyika. There the Ngoni broke up into smaller bands, to live by banditry or by serving as mercenaries for any chief who wanted to augment the fighting strength of his own people. Until the predatory newcomers appeared from the south, the warriors of east and central Africa had been men from the villages, who took up their spears, shields and battleaxes only in times of danger. When danger was past they put aside their weapons and returned to their usual tasks: hunting, honey-collecting, cattle-herding and making tools.

In contrast, the Ngoni were a distinct warrior class. Sometimes the individual bands would amalgamate to raid for cattle, and always they continued to absorb young warriors from local tribes into their ranks. They spread terror, as was their aim. To the people on whom they preyed they were known as '*ruga-ruga*', derived from the word for a penis. This might have been because they let their hair grow long and wove it into thick, pendulous plaits, but more likely it was because they cut off the sexual organs of their foes and wore them, dried, as ornaments.

The East African *ruga-ruga* retained the Ngoni headdress, which helped them follow one another's progress through the tall elephant grass, but changed their habits in other ways. They sometimes draped strips of bright red cloth from their shoulders, pointing to these when facing an opponent and crying in mockery: 'This is your blood!' Their ornaments included caps made of human scalps, belts of entrails, and necklaces of teeth. In their determination to make themselves invincible the *ruga-ruga* drank potions made up from parts of victims' corpses. Tales of these terrible practices spread through East Africa, yet reports of the way they employed their stabbing spears evoked an even deeper fear. Even those *ruga-ruga* who acquired muskets still retained their spears.

When the Ngoni reached East Africa they quickly came into contact with the Nyamwezi, whom the American missionary Ebenezer Burgess had recognized as the 'richest and most enterprising' people in the region. They were united in a network of chieftaincies stretching between lakes Victoria and Tanganyika, and across the central plateau, three months' journey from the coast. The leaders of the Nyamwezi were always chosen for their qualities of leadership, rather than on an hereditary system.

Through the centuries many African kingdoms had risen and fallen in this region, unknown to the outside world, leaving little trace except irrigation systems and earthworks. Since the start of the nineteenth century it had been the turn of the Nyamwezi, and they felt themselves every bit as good as the Arabs and Swahili of the coast.

Like the Ngoni the Nyamwezi were great travellers, but unlike them they lived by trade rather than war. They ventured to the south, along the furthest shores of Lake Tanganyika. At the foot of the lake their caravans turned west to the capital of the powerful Chief Kazembe, which the ill-fated Portuguese traveller, Francisco de Lacerda, had reached in 1798 from the Zambezi. (Nyamwezi traders were probably already there when the Portuguese arrived; some sixty years later David Livingstone was told that Lacerda's men had started fighting with certain visitors from Lake Tanganyika, but the king had restored peace by giving both sides presents of slaves.) The land of Kazembe was renowned as a market where the 'red' copper of Katanga could be bought. This was carried back north by the Nyamwezi in the form of wire and bangles.[9]

Early in the nineteenth century the Nyamwezi began travelling down to the Indian Ocean with ivory, beeswax, and some slaves, to exchange for *merikani* cloth and Venetian beads. They were rarely able to deal directly with the merchant vessels of Europe and America in Zanzibar, because Muslim and Hindu merchants were already entrenched on the coast. Moreover, it was the fame of the Nyamwezi as inhabitants of a distant land with many elephants which had drawn some of the more daring Arabs into accompanying them on their return journeys. The oral history of the Nyamwezi tells how their first travellers, reaching the Indian Ocean at Bagamoyo, met 'long-bearded men' (the Arabs) and showed them their ivory. 'When the Arabs saw this they wanted to go to the countries where the ivory was obtained.'

The Nyamwezi were proud and courageous, and famed for their strength in carrying heavy loads over great distances. It was probably their long-range caravans which first took the manufactured goods of India and Europe from the coast to the more distant societies around the great lakes, such as the prosperous Buganda kingdom, soon to become the goal of European missionaries and empire-builders. The first Arab traders did not reach Buganda – 800 miles from the Indian Ocean – until the 1840s.

Friendship between the Nyamwezi people and Zanzibar appeared to have prospered for a while, because in 1848 their tribal chiefs sent a 2,000-strong caravan to the coast with gifts for the sultan. However, as the nineteenth century advanced the Arabs had seized more and more control of the main trade routes. The Nyamwezi were largely reduced to becoming hired porters or guides, carrying ivory bought in the interior which fetched four times as much at the coast. In any trial of strength the Arabs were likely to win, for they had access to all the guns they needed from European traders in Zanzibar; as Burton noted, one German firm was selling 13,000 muskets a year. On the other hand, the Arabs were very few in numbers and the loyalty of their slaves was always suspect. This could make them, in Burton's opinion, 'too strong to yield without fighting', yet 'not strong enough to fight with success'.

Gradually, the Arab advance from the coast in pursuit of trade took the form of a subtle, creeping colonialism. Although no maps existed of the Zanzibar sultan's dominions, nor, in the view of Hamerton, was there 'any person who could define the boundaries', Arabs were settling permanently in the interior. Many were newcomers to East Africa, merchants from Oman who had migrated to Zanzibar in Seyyid Said's wake in 1840. They lived alongside traditional African chiefs and assiduously took their daughters as wives, but retained an Arab way of life and saw themselves as the masters. If a chief displeased them they would aim to overthrow him and exert their power in the choice of a successor.

In 1861, on his second expedition, John Speke encountered the Nyamwezi leader Manua Sera 'with thirty armed followers carrying muskets'. Manua Sera ruled Unyanyembe, most important of the Nyamwezi provinces, and in the centre of his territory was the Arab settlement of Kazé (later Tabora), midway on the route to Lake Tanganyika. When the Nyamwezi tried to impose a tax on the ivory trade a war had begun. Speke was later told by the Arabs that they had an army of 400 slaves, all armed with guns, ready to hunt down Manua Sera, 'who was cutting their caravan road to pieces, and had just seized, by their latest reports, a whole convoy of their ammunition'. It would take four years for the Arabs to catch Manua Sera and kill him.

FORTY-NINE

A Proclamation
at the Custom House

❦

> God willing, our prosperity shall, in course of time, be as your
> prosperity, and our freedom like yours.
> —Sultan Barghash, on receiving the freedom of the City of London
> (12 July 1875)

THERE NEVER WAS — never could be — another Seyyid Said. 'He is
accused of grasping covetousness and treachery,' wrote Richard Burton,
'but what Arab ruler is not covetous and treacherous?' This cynicism
embodied some truth, for Said was certainly treacherous in eliminating
his Arab enemies. He possessed a flair for survival which allowed him
to hold power for half a century: towards the end Muscat was slipping
from his grasp, but he had turned Zanzibar, his adopted home, into the
hub of a vast trading empire with its tentacles deep into Africa. It might
not be an empire precisely as Europeans understood the term, but by
the middle of the century the Sultan of Zanzibar was seen as meriting
international respect.

His death had inspired messages from Queen Victoria ('the painful
news of his decease has caused us sincere regret'), the French emperor
('the Sultan Said, of honoured memory, who had always shown himself
to be a faithful and devoted friend of France'), and the President of the
United States ('a monarch obeyed with reverence'). None chose to
mention that the sultan's subjects were still responsible for enslaving as
many as 30,000 Africans a year, and that hundreds of dhows from
Zanzibar were defying Royal Navy patrols by carrying human cargoes
to Arabia and the Persian Gulf. Even less was it remarked that 12,000
slaves were labouring on the 5,000 acres of clove plantations Said personally owned.[1]

The slave trade went on as ever after his death, but much else started
to change. Fecund to the last, Said had left behind more than a score

of sons, and several saw themselves as well fitted to be installed in his place. Each had been fathered upon different members of the harem; there was scant affection between them.

The proclaimed heir-apparent, Majid, epileptic and homosexual, had the benefit of being in command of Zanzibar's army and enjoying the support of the British. His elder brother, Thuwain, ruled in Muscat and possessed a navy, but had almost two thousand miles of ocean to cross before he could hope to reunite by force the Arabian and East African sultanates. The third and youngest contender, Barghash, enjoyed the initial advantage of being with his father when he died at sea (Said had not dared to leave him behind in Zanzibar with his half-brother Majid, at just the age when he himself had murdered his uncle to win the throne). Barghash had been able to smuggle his father's body ashore and bury it at once in the Muslim fashion, then go to the fort overlooking Zanzibar harbour. His hopes for a quick *coup d'état* went awry only because a suspicious Baluchi officer refused to hand over the keys.[2]

Yet Barghash was supported by several strata of the Zanzibar population, including the al-Harthi, an Arab clan who had been living in East Africa for centuries and resented both the dominance of Said's dynasty and the overweening influence of the British. Several rich merchants in Zanzibar led the al-Harthi; they had a private army, 2,000 strong. Equally hostile to the new sultan, Majid, and thus sympathetic to anyone also against him, were many of the Hadimu ('slaves'), descendants of the island's original African population.

The storm had been slow to break. The British in particular hardly noticed its first rumblings, since the consul, Atkins Hamerton, was dead and all attention was focused on the Indian Mutiny. There was a long delay in replacing Hamerton, and when the new consul did arrive he proved to be, although also an Indian army colonel, of a very different character. Christopher Rigby was forthright and dogmatic, whereas Hamerton had relied on guile; as the French captain Guillain shrewdly remarked, his intrigues were concealed under 'light-hearted talk and jovial drinking'. But Rigby never minced words about anything or anyone: in a letter to his friend James Grant he had called Richard Burton a 'liar' and a 'cur'.[3]

Whereas Hamerton had always shunned open quarrels about the slave trade, Rigby showed himself ready for a fight. He began by insisting that since they were British subjects all the Indians living in Zanzibar must give up their slaves forthwith. Predictably, this caused uproar, but he succeeded in having 8,000 Africans set free. Rigby saw it as his mission to liberate slaves wherever he came across them, and in a letter to Grant proudly told how in India he had freed an African boy – 'a very sharp little fellow' – and was arranging for him to be taken to England. He was quite convinced, added Rigby, that Africans, when educated from an early age, 'had no natural inferiority to any other race'.[4]

In time, Majid's evasions about the suppression of the slave trade would provoke Rigby to denounce him as a 'false, vile, scoundrel', but at first he sided with him against his jealous brothers, Thuwain and Barghash. The elder of these had been the first to act against Majid, by assembling an invasion fleet in Muscat. When the news reached Zanzibar of the impending attack, Rigby was fascinated to see how widely Majid could reach out to put together a defence force. One contingent arrived from the Comoro islands, between Madagascar and Mozambique, others came from subject towns on the East African coast, and bowmen from far inland: 'wild men who had never before approached the sea'.

Their resolve was not tested. A Royal Navy warship from Bombay was put on patrol off the Arabian coast, and when Thuwain's fleet sailed out of Muscat it was quickly intercepted. A warning that force would be used if the ships did not return to harbour was enough to sustain the Pax Britannica. Thuwain had been neutralized.

The challenge now fell to Barghash, who reputedly was in league with the new French consul, Ladislas Cochet. This notion was assiduously fed to Rigby by Majid, who declared himself to be in peril from a murder plot. Several of Barghash's closest supporters were put in irons, then imprisoned on the mainland at Lamu. Afraid that he was now in line to be assassinated himself, Barghash set up defences round his palace in a clove plantation. After vainly attacking it with 5,000 men, Majid turned to the British for help. Two Royal Navy warships were in the harbour, so 100 sailors and marines, commanded by a lieutenant, mounted a two-day assault with cannons, a howitzer and rockets. About sixty of the defenders were killed and Barghash fled. He escaped the triumphant Majid's vengeance by taking refuge with his British attackers.

These two forceful interventions to aid Majid against his brothers opened a new phase in relations between the Zanzibar sultanate and its protector. The next moves were even more precise and deliberate. Barghash was told by Rigby that he was being sent into exile, in British India. Before boarding a Royal Navy ship he was made to swear publicly his submission to Majid, and promise that never in the future would he take advice from the French.[5] Also packed off to India with him was a younger brother, Abd al-Aziz, whom Rigby also saw as a likely troublemaker. However, this banishment was not unduly painful: the Indian government provided a large house in Bombay, an allowance and a carriage.

Like a housewife tidying the backyard, Britain then invited Majid and Thuwain to ask it to arbitrate on the future relationship between their domains. Having little option, they agreed, and an Indian army brigadier drew up a report. Rigby's contribution to the report was a forecast that an independent Zanzibar could – with the slave trade extinguished – become a base from which civilization might be spread into the African interior.

For Lord 'Clemency' Canning, the Indian governor-general, who had just pulled the Raj out of the morass of the mutiny, untying the knot between Muscat and Zanzibar was easy work. In April 1861 he declared each to be henceforth a separate sultanate. Since Muscat was falling into poverty, with little to offer the world but dates, Zanzibar was ordered to make it a yearly payment of 40,000 Maria Theresa dollars; this was not an intolerable burden on Zanzibar, being about a fifth of the revenues from the slave trade, but in the event it would be handed over only irregularly.

Despite the imposed separation, neither of the sultans enjoyed much domestic peace. Five years later Thuwain was murdered in his sleep by his son, and was succeeded by a cousin who was then murdered by one of Thuwain's brothers, who was in turn murdered by his son-in-law.[6]

Although Majid eluded the fatal dagger, his subjects attacked his palace to express their rage at the Royal Navy's aggressive tactics towards the slave trade. (It was undeniable that some of the dhows being apprehended on the open sea and sunk were entirely innocent.) Consul Rigby became an implacable enemy, with whom the sultan was hardly on speaking terms, in contrast with the placid amity which had existed a few years earlier between Hamerton and Seyyid Said. When Rigby left Zanzibar after three bruising years, the farewells were cursory and cold. His superiors praised him for his 'meritorious labours', and he was promoted to the rank of general, but it was scarcely by chance that the next two colonels successively chosen for the Zanzibar consulate shied away from the anti-slavery campaign.

Majid's only ground for complaint now was the reappearance of

Barghash, whom he hoped had been banished for life. But the British, with an eye to the future, decided that the younger brother was mellowing after his two years in Bombay and was destined to be the next sultan when the sickly Majid died. They wanted him on hand when that moment arrived. Barghash knew this as well: he stayed out of the limelight and waited. Even so, Majid still harboured fears – hardly to be wondered at, given the family history.

This may explain why he used part of his wealth to found a new city, Dar es Salaam (Harbour of Peace) on the mainland. After visiting the site the new American consul, Frank Webb, reported to Washington that it was 'the intention of His Highness to make that place ultimately the capital of his dominions'.[7] Fate stepped in, for in 1870, in the seclusion of his Dar es Salaam palace, Majid fell and fatally injured himself, perhaps during a fit, at the age of thirty-six. He left one child, a daughter, and the way was clear at last for Barghash to don the royal turban.

There came a time, in the mid-1870s, when the British public identified Sultan Barghash as one of 'their' foreign potentates; one of those exotic figures who came to London in a seemingly endless stream from all quarters of the globe, to pay their respects and be shown the wonders at the heart of empire.[8] Admittedly, Zanzibar was not strictly in the empire, but its name was embedded in the national consciousness as the place where the corpse of the great hero, David Livingstone, had arrived in March 1874 on its way home from the wilds of Africa. Many popular accounts of Livingstone's life and death came out during the next few years, and engravings of Barghash in his finery were frequently included in them.

When Barghash made a state visit to London in the summer of 1875 he was escorted by Sir John Kirk, who had been a member of Livingstone's second Zambezi expedition in the 1860s and was now the formidable consul in Zanzibar ('I had all the power of a despot,' he wrote later, 'but I had a despot in my hand.').[9] The sultan met Queen Victoria, the Prince of Wales and senior members of the government. At Crystal Palace there was a firework display in his honour and his name in Arabic characters blazed against the night sky. He travelled in a royal train to see the greatest factories in the north of England and was taken to the races at Doncaster and Ascot. While in Europe he also visited Paris, Berlin and Lisbon.

The sultan was so struck with all he had seen that he ordered a commemorative book to be printed in Arabic. One engraving showed him at Ascot, standing with race-glasses in hand in an open carriage, with a member of his retinue beside him. An admiring crowd of British aristocrats was gathered round the carriage.

His hosts were too polite to remind Barghash that his trip was the reward for having succumbed two years earlier to British demands, backed by force, on that most sensitive of issues: slavery. The noose cast loosely round Seyyid Said's neck fifty years before was being tightened excruciatingly on Barghash. The decision taken to impose a new treaty upon the sultan was largely a response to public outrage in Britain at the descriptions David Livingstone had sent back about the horrors of the slave trade in Africa's interior. The passion of his speeches, directed at Portuguese complicity in the trade, during his last visit home still echoed in the national consciousness. Then in the autumn of 1872 the Welsh-born American journalist Henry Morton Stanley returned from his expedition to find Livingstone and brought with him letters from the heroic doctor, giving eye-witness accounts of atrocities by Arab slavers in the unknown lands beyond Lake Tanganyika.

The man selected to confront Barghash was Sir Bartle Frere, a senior member of the Indian government.[10] He was ordered to go to Zanzibar in January 1873 with a letter from Queen Victoria, and the advance news of his mission provoked such alarm that special prayers were offered up in the island's mosques. However, the prayers failed to prevent the arrival in Zanzibar harbour of four British warships. An American warship was also in attendance.

Escorted by a muster of all the naval officers, wearing full ceremonial dress, together with Kirk and his consulate staff, Frere marched through Zanzibar's streets to deliver the royal letter to Barghash's palace. Sullen crowds watched the procession go by. The sultan's guns fired a salute. The guns of the British flagship roared back. Frere later told the Foreign Office that the sultan took the letter 'and according to the eastern custom raised it to his head as a mark of veneration'. Well aware of its contents, Barghash may have felt more disposed to fling it to the ground and stamp on it.

Months went by. Barghash refused to submit to the demands that he must order his subjects to end all seaborne traffic in slaves and close all slave markets in his dominions. He argued that the clove plantations had been devastated in the previous year by a hurricane, so that fresh labour from the mainland was vital to restore them and so revive the economy. The new treaty could be brought in, but only step by step. Otherwise there would be a rebellion. 'A spear is held to each of my eyes,' cried Barghash. 'With which shall I choose to be pierced?'

His venerable councillors urged the young sultan to keep resisting, and he made contact with Germany and France, seeking their protection. Frere departed in a rage, handing over the negotiations to Kirk, but Barghash still observed the niceties. On Queen Victoria's birthday, 24 May, he ordered the firing of a twenty-one-gun salute and sent Kirk a whole roast sheep. The next evening he went to a reception at the British consulate. The conversation was understandably lack-lustre, but before he left Barghash noticed a Bible lying on a table. It was, he said defiantly to several missionaries standing nearby, 'a good book and authorized slavery as an institution'.

He did not know that Kirk was choosing his moment to strike, having received new orders from the British cabinet ten days previously. The sultan was to be told that Royal Navy warships were on their way to Zanzibar: if the treaty was not signed, the island would be blockaded. A week later Kirk went to the palace with this ultimatum: 'I have not come to discuss,' he said, 'but to dictate.' When Barghash said he wished to go to London to put his case, he was told he would be stopped from leaving the island; this outright challenge to his sovereignty forestalled another of his plans, that he would cross to the mainland and mount a campaign of resistance from there.

Neither Germany nor France had responded to Barghash's overtures for support, and in despair he even thought of abdicating. On 5 June 1873 he gave way, signing a proclamation which was posted up on the Zanzibar custom house. It banned the movement of slaves by sea and closed the slave markets. Now everyone knew where ultimate power lay.

FIFTY

Meeting the Lords
of the Interior

There seems reason to believe that one of the finest parts of the
world's surface is lying waste under the shroud of malaria which
surrounds it, and under the barbarous anarchy with which it is
cursed. The idea dawns upon some of us that some better destiny
is yet in store for a region so blessed by nature, and the development of Africa is a step yet to come in the development of the
world.

—Editorial in *The Times* of London (9 December 1873)

BY THE 1870s the lines across the map which traced the journeys of
white travellers were starting to make Africa look like Gulliver pinioned
by Lilliputians. The pioneering expedition by Burton and Speke to the
region of the great lakes had been followed by another, more ambitious,
in which Speke was accompanied by Captain James Grant, also from
the Indian army. They opened an overland route from Zanzibar to
Cairo, by way of Lake Victoria – as Speke had loyally named it – and
the Nile.[1]

Many of those who followed them were cast in the same military
mould. One was Colonel Charles Chaillé Long, an American who
reached Lake Victoria from the Sudan and wrote a book about his
experiences entitled *Naked Truths of Naked People*.[2] Another, the 'discoverer' of Lake Albert, was the rumbustious Samuel Baker, who shot
elephants as other men swatted flies. The first European to cross Africa
from east to west was Verney Lovette Cameron, a Scottish naval officer,
who set out from Zanzibar with forty-five black riflemen equipped with
Snider breech-loaders. Uniquely bellicose was Henry Morton Stanley,
who had served on both sides in the American civil war and regarded
it as the greatest compliment to call someone a 'fighter'.

The style of these trail-blazers, their guns at the ready, contrasted
with that of more scholarly travellers, predominantly German, such as

Heinrich Barth; in the early 1850s Barth had meticulously studied the cultures of the peoples living along the southern limits of the Sahara. Nevertheless, it would be wrong to assume that even the fiercest or most philistine of the Europeans who struggled through Africa in those early years behaved like members of a master race. They were simply in no position to be arrogant, for Africa still belonged to the Africans, who treated these uninvited visitors, with their pink faces and unsuitable clothes, as great curiosities. To let the white men pass was to do them a favour.

The duty of every chief to his people was to discover, in his own time, just who the intruders were and what their intentions might be; until he knew that for sure they must wait, for there was plenty of time in Africa. The chief also had the right, embedded in tradition, to impose the tax, commonly called *hongo*. It was a defiance of all custom if one of these strangers became too impatient and chose to shoot his way through; when the next appeared some revenge must be taken.

The delaying tactics of every petty chief, and the endless demands for *hongo*, were certainly exasperating. Yet force always had to be the last resort, for if it went wrong there was no hope of succour in the vastness of the 'dark continent'. Even sending a letter to the outside world was a gamble: if the courier did reach the coast with the letter still in his possession, the journey would probably have taken him many months.

Diaries of the early travellers show that they found it wiser to adapt to the tempo of Africa and yield to the habits of their hosts, especially when they were staying with an important ruler. Indeed, there might even be compensations. As John Speke and James Grant discovered during the six months they spent with Mutesa, the young *kabaka* (king) of Buganda, life in an African society gave them ample chance to cast aside Victorian inhibitions.

When Speke's book, *Journal of the Discovery of the Source of the Nile*, appeared in late 1863, it was a sensation in more ways than one. The British government and public had met the cost of the expedition, and the 600-page narrative of its tribulations and triumph certainly proved that they had been given their money's worth. Yet there was a sharp indrawing of breath among reviewers at the exuberant descriptions – occupying almost half the book – of how Speke, in particular, had behaved in Buganda, the rich and powerful kingdom (the nucleus of modern Uganda) on the northern shores of Lake Victoria.

It was plain, for a start, that the two white officers had been very much in the hands of Mutesa, and at the mercy of his whims. More astounding were the dealings with Mutesa's womenfolk. Was it proper for a young British army officer to have told a black queen-mother that taking a new husband was the best cure for her insomnia? By Speke's own account the queen-mother had supplied him with two frolicsome virgins, who lived in his house; this must have put him in an 'awkward position', hinted one reviewer. Repeatedly, Speke describes the 'coquetry' and 'captivating' behaviour of Buganda's women. It all aroused fears that the dashing captain might not have behaved in a manner entirely fitting for a representative of the empire.

Such fears would scarcely have been allayed if readers had been able to see the original proofs of Speke's manuscript, before his publishers bowdlerized it.[3] One incident, cut out entirely, tells how he is given a third young woman and takes her home, whereupon the two already installed insist on talking to her all night: 'Instead of turning in the bed as usual, they all three slept upon the ground. My patience could stand this hen-pecking no longer . . .'

Speke relates how he carries the favourite wife of Mutesa across a stream. With an 'imploring face and naked breast she holds out both her hands in such a voluptuous, captivating manner . . . that I could not resist compliance'. He decides that she is 'anxious to feel what the white man is like'. The original proofs of the book, as well as James Grant's private diaries, reveal Speke as not only offering the queen-mother a remedy for her insomnia, but also giving advice about troubles with her periods (*muezi ya undani*).

If that were not enough, the *kabaka* decides to consult him about the size of his penis: 'Mutesa could not believe in a short stick being so good as a long stick, because . . . the short one would only knock about the doorway.' Speke reassures the youthful monarch, then gives him some thoroughly British advice on the perils of sexual excess while too young, 'instancing the lamentable condition of the French, Turks and Arabs, who in early youth have finished their days, owing to the foolish vanity their mothers and nurses entertain of having forward boys'.

Even after such vignettes had been prudently cut by his Edinburgh publisher, Speke still emerges as amiable, open-minded and unconstrained in his dealings with Africans. In contrast to Burton, he and Grant never saw them as being inherently inferior, but simply unfortunate in having been cut off from the main currents of civilization. Along with many of his contemporaries in the Indian army, Speke felt that he understood Africans better than he did Indians. (The first chapter of his illustrated *Journal* includes a caricature of a Hindu merchant in Zanzibar, contemptuously captioned 'Banyan, contemplating his Account Book.')

He was writing only four years after Charles Darwin had expounded his theory of evolution, and 'polygenists' still argued that Africans were a totally different species from the white races, Anglo-Saxons in particular.[4] For all his prejudices, Speke was having none of that. In the opening paragraph of the introduction to his *Journal* he writes:

> To say a negro is incapable of instruction, is a mere absurdity;
> for those few boys who have been educated in our schools
> have proved themselves even quicker than our own in learn-
> ing; whilst, among themselves, the deepness of their cunning
> and their power of repartee are quite surprising, and are
> especially shown in their proficiency for telling lies most
> appropriately in preference to truth, and with an off-handed
> manner that makes them most amusing.

Speke genuinely cared about the welfare of the people he had encountered during the epic journey. After his book appeared he urged Europe to 'stretch out a hand' to central Africa. There was such a meagre response in Britain that he grew depressed and turned elsewhere. On 25 August 1864 he had an audience with the French emperor, and wrote home elatedly from the Grand Hotel, Paris: 'He was quite delighted at the prospect I held out to him of forming a new empire, and said that whilst I worked up the Nile to develop those regions, he would work from the Gabon eastwards "till he made both seas meet".' The emperor's extravagant promise was never put to the test. Three weeks later Speke shot himself, only hours before he was due to hold a public debate with Richard Burton about the source of the Nile. The shooting was declared to have been an accident.[5]

More than ten years went by before another European-led expedition managed to reach Buganda from the East African coast. The new arrival was Henry Stanley, whose successful search for Livingstone in 1871 was still resented by the mandarins of the Royal Geographical Society, because the feat had been contrived to boost a New York newspaper. Stanley was now set upon winning respectability through achieving so much – out-distancing any previous travels in tropical Africa – that his denigrators would be silenced for good. One of his self-imposed tasks was to circumnavigate Lake Victoria, and he did so, making the first accurate survey of it.

On reaching Buganda he was taken aback by its roads, well-built houses and prosperous farmlands. From the very start, the manners and 'semi-civilization' of its people astounded him. He describes his arrival in Mutesa's country from the lake: 'Half a mile off I saw that the people on the shore had formed themselves into two dense lines, at the ends of which stood several finely-dressed men, arrayed in crimson and black and snowy white. As we neared the beach volleys of musketry burst out . . . Numerous kettle and bass drums sounded a noisy welcome, and flags, banners and bannerets waved, and the people gave a great shout.' From then on, one astonishment followed another.

Least expected was the impression made by Mtesa (as Stanley preferred to spell his name). When Speke had been in Buganda the *kabaka* was only an impetuous youth, often capricious and cruel. Now he seemed maturely confident: 'Mtesa had impressed me as being an intelligent and distinguished prince, who, if aided in time by virtuous philanthropists, will do more for Central Africa than fifty years of Gospel teaching, unaided by such authority, can do. I think I see in him the light that shall lighten the darkness of this benighted region.' Coming from someone whose writing generally displayed all the abrasiveness of American journalism, this was prodigious praise.

Stanley now decided that he had a moral mission, and was far too hard-headed to give ammunition to his critics by appearing to fall like Speke into the trap of amorous dalliance. One of Stanley's few mentions of feminine charms in Buganda comes when he visits Mutesa and finds him surrounded by some of his wives 'who, as soon as I appeared, focused about two hundred pairs of lustrous, humid eyes on my person'. Much of Stanley's eight chapters on Buganda is given over to telling how he helps Mutesa to fight a war and improve his shooting, as well as exhorting him to abandon his leanings towards Islam and turn to Christianity.[6] In the decade since Speke's visit, Arab traders had been installing themselves in the Bugandan capital and spreading their religion. Stanley felt they should be given credit for many of the improvements in Mutesa's behaviour, yet took it for granted that Christian missionaries would do better.

The prose of Stanley's *Through the Dark Continent* cracks like a whip in scenes of action, but has a strong whiff of humbug whenever he writes about religion. This makes it the more remarkable that one letter he despatched from Buganda was destined to set off an unparalleled surge of missionary effort in East Africa, and hasten the coming of colonialism.

His letter, printed in the London *Daily Telegraph* and the *New York Herald* in November 1875, was a masterpiece of bombast:

> But, O that some pious, practical missionary would come here! What a field and a harvest ripe for the sickle of the Gospel! Mtesa would give him anything he desired – houses, lands, cattle, ivory, &c. He might call a province his own in one day . . . It is the practical Christian tutor, who can teach people how to become Christians, cure their diseases, construct dwellings, understands agriculture, and can turn his hand to anything, like a sailor – this is the man who is wanted here. Such a man, if he could be found, would become the saviour of Africa.

There was much more along the same lines. Stanley estimated that the *kabaka* had two million subjects, all waiting to be saved: 'Here, gentlemen, is your opportunity – embrace it!' Had Mutesa known that he and his country were the subject of so much rhetoric he would have been delighted. He badly wanted a European presence in Buganda because he thought it might help fend off the Egyptians, who were threatening to invade the region of the great lakes from the Sudan and the Upper Nile (the route earlier taken by Chaillé Long). If Stanley was anything to go by, Europeans had lots of guns – and guns, along with his 700 wives, were Mutesa's main interest in life. Religion was not one of his deepest concerns: he never fully accepted Islam because he could not bear the thought of being circumcised, and in professing a desire for Christianity he was just leading on the all-too-willing Stanley. However, the outside world was not to know that.

In Germany the elderly Ludwig Krapf read a translation of the letter, and wrote to the Church Missionary Society in London, urging them to act without delay so that battle could be joined with Islam in the heart of the continent. This happened to be a moment when a succession of deaths from malaria had again brought missionary work in tropical Africa to a low ebb: the latest to die, early in 1875, had been Charles New, a working-class Methodist with socialist ideals, who had lived among the people near Kilimanjaro, and was celebrated for being the first European to climb the mountain to its snow-line.[7]

The enthusiasm for responding to Stanley's challenge was so great that Robert Arthington, a millionaire hermit in Leeds, offered to finance a Christian expedition to Buganda if Krapf would lead it. Krapf declined – he knew his travelling days were long past – but others were game. Within six months the vanguard had reached Zanzibar. However, reaching Buganda was another matter, and the first Protestant to arrive there, fully three years after the publication of Stanley's clarion-call, was an obdurate Scot, Alexander Mackay. Several of his companions had been killed or died of fever, others had been invalided back to Britain, and many more would pay the ultimate price within a decade.

The Church Missionary Society had a further woe to contend with. Roman Catholicism was also suddenly intent on winning the heart of Central Africa, and in June 1878 a party of ten White Fathers began marching towards Buganda from the coast facing Zanzibar. They were a bold sight in their clerical gowns, with crucifixes hanging from the rosaries round their necks. Their caravan, made up of 500 porters and musketeers, showed the scale of their resolve. The White Fathers were mostly French, which was likewise calculated to make British hackles rise. The religious scramble for Africa had begun.

Long before Europe had had a chance to react to his letter, Stanley moved onwards from Buganda. As he marched south-west towards Lake Tanganyika his path crossed the territory of Mirambo, the second of the three historic leaders he was destined to meet on this trans-African journey.[8] Stanley had almost encountered the great Nyamwezi warlord five years earlier, on his journey to Lake Tanganyika to find Livingstone. Then he had been lured by the Arabs of Tabora into helping them in their war against Mirambo. Stanley only joined in a preliminary skirmish, because his main concern was to push on to find Livingstone. Nevertheless, he collected enough information about the man – at that time almost unknown – to dub him 'the African Bonaparte'; he portrayed Mirambo as a clever young chief with a tendency to banditry and a flair for bush warfare.

In 1871, Mirambo had nearly captured Tabora, the main Arab settlement in the interior burning down most of its houses and seizing large stores of ivory. He also ambushed and killed Tabora's most distinguished resident, an Omani merchant named Khamis bin Abdallah. It was Khamis who had earlier sworn to kill Mirambo, just as he had killed and beheaded the 'rebel' Nyamwezi ruler Manua Sera some years earlier.

Stanley's account of Mirambo in *How I Found Livingstone* gave an early hint that an African leader of unusual calibre was dominating an expanse of territory to the north-east of Lake Tanganyika and trying – like the ill-fated Manua Sera before him – to break the Arabs' trading monopoly. Part of his forces included what Stanley had called 'the terrible *Ruga-ruga*', heirs of the Ngoni warrior tradition.

A few more facts about Mirambo later filtered down to Zanzibar and were dissected there by the foreign consulates: his real name was Mtyela Kasanda, and he came from a chiefly background; at the age of twenty he had begun calling himself by the *nom de guerre* Mirambo, meaning 'Corpses', as a grim warning to his enemies. In appearance he was tall and imposing. Realizing early on that he would never oust the Arabs with spears alone, he had armed his warriors with muskets, buying vast stocks of these with ivory or capturing them during raids on Arab caravans.

Anxious to protect his mainland domain against this energetic pagan rival, the sultan of Zanzibar had despatched an army of 3,000 troops, mainly mercenaries from Baluchistan, to Tabora. Lack of food and poor leadership brought the sultan's campaign to nothing; it had cost 100,000 dollars, and duties on ivory and cloves in Zanzibar had to be increased to pay for it.

Since Mirambo's clear vulnerability was in gunpowder, the sultan imposed a strict blockade at the coast. At the start of 1874 the British consulate, which was dictating the sultan's tactics, reported complacently to the Foreign Office that Mirambo was 'entirely destitute of ammunition'. There was no longer anything to be feared 'from him or his adherents'. Yet Mirambo survived. His loose-knit empire stretched now from the shores of Lake Victoria to the southern extremity of Lake Tanganyika. At times he declared a truce with the Arabs but, when he wished, he could assemble an army of 7,000 men, drawn from his own Nyamwezi people and their vassals.

When Stanley met him in 1876 Mirambo was nearing the height of his power. His capital was Urambo, a town with several thousand inhabitants. The news of his march out from Urambo had terrorized the countryside through which Stanley was travelling, but the 'African Bonaparte' was not bent on war. He was merely keen to size up this white man who was passing through his territory. Mirambo sent three emissaries ahead, members of his bodyguard dressed in blue and red coats and white turbans, to ask if the white traveller would care to meet him. Stanley replied that he would 'rejoice to make strong friendship' with the chief.

After their first handshake, Stanley felt himself 'quite captivated' with this 'thorough African *gentleman*', who was so totally unlike the impression he had gained from the Arabs. He wrote in his diary:

> This day will be memorable for me for the visit of the famous Mirambo . . . A man about 5 feet 11 inches in height, about 35 years old, well-made but with not an ounce of superfluous flesh about him; handsome, regular featured, mild, soft-spoken . . . this unpresuming quiet-eyed man of inoffensive meek exterior, whose language was so mild without a single gesture, indicated nothing of the Napoleonic genius which he has for five years displayed in the heart of Africa.

That evening they pledged blood brotherhood. Each had an incision made in his right leg above the knee, blood was extracted and rubbed into the cut in the other's leg. A curse was declared if the brotherhood should be broken: 'May the lion devour you, the serpent poison you, bitterness be your food, your friends desert you, your gun wound yourself, and everything bad worry you until death.' The next day both went on their ways, and Mirambo gave his new brother an escort of five men who would make sure he was not delayed by demands for *hongo*. Typically, Stanley's farewell present was a pistol and ammunition.

He was only the second white man to see Mirambo, for whom greater fame (and ultimate tragedy) lay in store. The first was a young Swiss ivory trader, Philippe Broyon, who had ventured inland some months earlier. Mirambo gave him a house and a wife, and invited him to settle in Urambo. Stanley heard about Broyon while on the march and sent him a message asking for, among other items, castor oil and Epsom salts. Broyon sent back the castor oil, together with two bars of Castile soap and some six-month-old copies of *Le Figaro*.

Six months later Stanley was in the Manyema country, west of Lake Tanganyika. The worst part of his journey lay ahead. He knew that if he could reach the main channel of Africa's last great uncharted river, the Congo, and trace its course to the sea, he would make history. But he might well die in the attempt, together with the 150 survivors of his expedition, who included several wives and children, and Frank

Pocock, the only white assistant still surviving out of the three who had started the journey. The expedition was now entering a dense forest, to follow a dark, muddy river which might eventually prove to be a tributary of the Congo.

Stanley's immediate fear was that almost all his men would desert rather than face this completely unknown land. There were several slave-hunting and ivory-gathering settlements run by Arabs and Swahili in the hinterland they had now reached. Deserters could easily hide in these settlements before starting the long journey back to Zanzibar. His one chance was to find a way to keep the expedition together as he pushed forward, until the settlements were so distant that any deserter who turned back would almost certainly be killed by the hostile inhabitants of the forest.

The answer to his predicament lay in the hands of Tippu Tip, whose real name was Hamid bin Muhammad.[9] This potentate of the ivory trade completed the trio of the most powerful figures in the central African interior during the second half of the nineteenth century. In his youth he had been a typical slave-hunter, as one incident among many, recalled in his memoirs, makes plain: 'I went into every part of Zaramu country and in the space of five days had seized 800 men. They called me Kingugwa – the leopard – because the leopard attacks indiscriminately, here and there. I yoked the whole lot of them together and went back with them to Mkamba.' By the time he met Stanley, his wealth and fame made him almost a sultan in his own right. More than two thousand porters were recruited for his caravans to the coast, and each man carried an elephant tusk.

Tippu Tip, whose nickname derived from the sound of his guns, would in some ways prove more significant than either Mutesa or Mirambo. He survived longer, vainly struggling to retain his vast territory in the face of an irresistible European advance. Until there was no hope left he declared himself a true subject of the distant sultan of Zanzibar, and insisted that his own lands were a part of the sultan's empire.

Stanley came across Tippu Tip at one of the remoter Arab settlements: 'He was a tall, black-bearded man, of negroid complexion, in the prime of life, straight, and quick in his movements, a picture of energy and strength. He had a fine intelligent face, with a nervous twitching of the eyes.' Meeting Europeans was no novelty for Tippu Tip. He had largely grown up in Zanzibar and during his travels in the interior had come across Livingstone and given him food; on returning to the coast he carried a letter from Livingstone to Sir John Kirk, the British consul. More recently he had helped the naval officer, Verney Lovett Cameron, to find a safe route towards Angola.

Although Tippu Tip possessed all the manners and attitudes of an Arab, his roots were deep in Africa. His ancestors had lived on the Swahili coast for several generations (quite distinct from the Omani Arabs who grasped the chance to follow Seyyid Said to Zanzibar in the 1840s) and his grandmother had been a slave. His father's second wife was the daughter of an African chief. He regarded Mirambo as his friend, despite Arab intrigues to provoke a rift between them. There was a mutual respect, an agreement never to fight one another, since both were monarchs of vast swathes of territory bordering the opposite shores of Lake Tanganyika.

At the time when Stanley met him, in October 1876, Tippu Tip had not been back to Zanzibar for nine years, but he regularly sent caravans down to the coast with ivory and slaves. His wealth was being accumulated for him there by Taria Topan, doyen of the Indian Muslim merchants on the island. It was hard to impress Tippu Tip, but Stanley succeeded on the day after their first meeting. In his memoirs Tippu Tip recalls:

> The following morning we went to see him and he showed us a gun, telling us, 'From this gun fifteen bullets come out!' Now we knew of no such gun firing fifteen rounds, neither knew of one nor had seen such. I asked him, 'From a single barrel?' He said they came from a single barrel, so I asked him to fire it so that we could see. But he said we should produce a fee of 20–30 dollars for firing it once. In my heart I thought he was lying . . . I said to him, 'Over in Rumami there's a bow that takes twenty arrows. When you fire, all twenty fly together. And each one kills a man.' At that he went outside and fired twelve rounds. Then he took a pistol and fired six rounds. He came back and sat down on the verandah. We were amazed.

After this incident Stanley quickly strikes a deal with Tippu Tip, offering him the massive sum of 5,000 Maria Theresa dollars if he will accompany the expedition with his own men for two months. The temptation, both the money and the challenge to his courage, proves too much for Tippu Tip to resist. Members of his family try to dissuade him: 'What, going with a European, have you lost your senses? You have your stock of ivory, why then follow an Unbeliever?' Tippu Tip tells them to mind their own business and signs the contract with Stanley. Within a few days the advance begins, partly in canoes on the sullen river darkened by overhanging trees, and partly along the banks. There is a series of fights with hostile villagers, who fire poisoned arrows from the dense forest, but the expedition pushes on.

The parting, the critical moment, arrives. Tippu Tip warns the men of Stanley's expedition that if any of them tries to follow him on his return journey to Lake Tanganyika, he will 'certainly kill them'. This appears in Tippu Tip's memoirs, although the threat is not mentioned in Stanley's account. Instead, he paints a sentimental picture of festivities in a forest clearing, rounded off by a meal of rice and roasted sheep, on the eve of the departure. The next morning, 28 December 1876, as his men paddle their canoes into the 'gleaming portal of the Unknown', Stanley faintly hears through the trees a farewell song, chanted by Tippu Tip's people.

Within ten years of this journey the entire course of African history would be transformed.

FIFTY-ONE

The Failure of
a Philanthropic Scotsman

The Wanyamwezi are doubtless an energetic race. Under their chief, Mirambo, they have successfully protested against the tyranny of the Arab colonists, and bid fair, under his effectual leadership, to become a prosperous and peaceful, if not a civilised nation. A mission station has been successfully conducted in the immediate neighbourhood of Mirambo's town for the last two years. Wonderful influence for good has been gained over this chief, who is determined, he says, that his country and people shall learn to take their place among civilised races.
— Edward Hore of the London Missionary Society (1883)

As MORE AND MORE MUSKETS came into the possession of warriors owing allegiance to Mirambo and lesser African warlords, the balance of power on the mainland was altering. Unreliable as these weapons might often be, they made a mockery of an old saying that when you played the flute in Zanzibar, people as far as the great lakes would dance to its tune. The Arab traders on Zanzibar lacked the numbers, or the will, to engage in wars of conquest in the African bush against men with guns. If slaves were sent to fight on the mainland it would mean denuding the island's plantations of labour; in any case, they might desert and turn against their former masters.

So Sultan Barghash's claim to a vast expanse of East Africa relied upon the activities of freebooters such as Tippu Tip, who kept their fortunes and families in Zanzibar. When they emerged every few years from their fiefdoms in the interior, they would cross to the island from Bagamoyo to bow before Barghash and assure him of their loyalty. Since nobody else was asserting sovereignty over the mainland – except, of course, its indigenous rulers – he rested content, secure in the knowledge that all the mainland's exports of ivory, wild rubber and gum copal were routed through Zanzibar.

465

The customs duties he was collecting were enough for him to start paying off his debts to the Indian financiers, for exports from the island had risen in value from 765,000 dollars in 1843 to well over four million dollars by 1879. On the coast, large plantations were being run by Arabs with black slave labour; the town of Malindi, an empty ruin for more than two centuries, was alive again, surrounded by maize and sesame farms.

East Africa's trade was prospering so well largely because of that long-awaited event, the opening of the Suez Canal. Although Britain had feared the canal before it was built, seeing it as an instrument of French imperialism which might threaten the Raj, the reality proved quite different. The prime minister, Benjamin Disraeli, had in 1875 secretly acquired for Britain a 43 per cent stake in the canal company, by borrowing four million pounds from the Rothschild dynasty to buy all the shares of the bankrupt Khedive Ismail. The Royal Navy dominated the Mediterranean and the Red Sea from bases in Gibraltar, Malta and Aden. So the canal strengthened British links with India, and the entire Indian Ocean.[1]

All this meant that Zanzibar was no longer in a backwater of the Indian Ocean, tucked away on the long flank of Africa. For almost four centuries, since the age of Vasco da Gama, the only sea route to the island from Europe had been by way of the Cape, but now the canal was drawing East Africa closer to the industrialized regions of the northern hemisphere. (One incidental result was a sharp decline in American trade with Zanzibar; geography began to weigh too heavily against the merchants from New England.)

Thus it was that the outlook seemed agreeable in the mid-1870s for both the sultan and the consul, Sir John Kirk. Barghash had managed to put aside the humiliation of the anti-slavery treaty in 1873, after his heart-warming visit to Europe, and he now possessed the wealth to buy for his people some of the improvements which befitted a self-respecting monarch. Coins bearing his name were minted. Clean water was piped to Zanzibar town from springs in the interior of the island, to replace the desperately polluted supplies drawn from wells. The European community also took it as another proof of progress that the sultan was reluctant to have condemned prisoners publicly beheaded, in the traditional fashion; instead, the miscreants were left to sweat in the Zanzibari jail.

Every sunset Barghash would stand on the verandah of his palace with his courtiers, looking out over the sea to the mainland, until a cannon was fired, the national anthem was played and the blood-red flag was hauled down. What was more, despite the 1873 treaty, his subjects had not abandoned the slave trade. Far from it: Kirk estimated that 35,000 black captives were still being brought annually to the East African coast from the hinterland.[2]

Barghash had produced no heirs until after returning to Zanzibar from Europe; then his wife (his only wife) bore him two sons.[3] When the sons were still infants Barghash meekly asked if Britain would guarantee their succession and care for them if he died while they were minors. Britain declined, using the arcane argument that this might be construed as interference, violating an Anglo-French treaty on Zanzibar's independence. In reality, Britain wanted to avoid any commitment as to whom the next sultan might be – if indeed there were to be one. The time would come, for the son who survived Barghash, when British interference would be experienced in a most devastating form.

Consul Kirk was quite content to make an elaborate show of deference to Barghash, having brought him to heel over the 1873 anti-slavery treaty. Privately he hinted to friends that he could run Zanzibar better on his own, without wasting a lot of time on 'big palavers' with the 'ignorant' sultan.[4] Kirk was a person of considerable pride, lightly disguised behind a veneer of piety, and he traded constantly upon having worked with the great hero Livingstone on the Zambezi. Henry Stanley described his first introduction to Kirk: 'I fancied at that moment that he lifted his eyelids perceptibly, disclosing the full circle of his eyes. If I were to define such a look, I would call it a broad stare.' Kirk fawned brazenly upon people he felt important, but a reporter from an American newspaper had not fallen into that category. When Stanley's pen-portrait appeared in *How I Found Livingstone*, Kirk never forgave him.

However incensed the consul may have been, he had no need to worry that journalistic invective would harm his standing with officialdom in London. His government felt content that Kirk was well looking after British interests in a part of the 'informal empire'. The fiction that his first concern was to uphold the rights of the sultan was conveniently enhanced when the Egyptian government made a sudden *putsch*, by way of the Red Sea, to establish a base in the Indian Ocean. The Khedive Ismail of Egypt had been encouraged in this venture by General Charles 'Chinese' Gordon, who was working for him in the Sudan; the idea was to open an overland route to Buganda, which Gordon hoped to absorb into Egypt's Upper Nile empire. One of the force commanders was the former confederate officer, Charles Chaillé Long, who had previously reached Buganda from the Sudan.

Egypt's 500-strong contingent had landed at the Somali ports of Brava and Kismayu, northern outposts of Barghash's dominions. The Zanzibari flags were hauled down; in their place the Egyptian standard was raised. News of this affront set off a flurry of diplomatic despatches between London, Cairo and Zanzibar. The first reaction by Barghash was to place a big order for British rifles. Kirk sailed for Brava to investigate, but even before he arrived, at the start of 1876, the Egyptian force had gone; the khedive had bowed to pressure from London. Chaillé Long wrote sourly that the expedition's purposes were 'scientific and commercial', for bringing civilization to the countries of the African interior: 'The expedition, however, was recalled before its legitimate object had been accomplished.'[5]

Egypt's 'invasion', however brief, had been a portent, for Gordon went on to annex the Upper Nile for his master in Cairo. Another development swiftly followed (although its true meaning was not immediately apparent): King Leopold II of the Belgians convened an international conference in the autumn of 1876, ostensibly to discuss ways in which civilization could be taken to the heart of Africa. At that moment Stanley was still struggling to reach the Atlantic in his epic journey down the Congo river. Businessmen, explorers and missionaries came together in Brussels, all marvelling at the benign spirit of Belgium's monarch.[6] One of the proposals recalled Krapf's scheme of more than twenty years earlier: that a line of settlements should be created right across the continent. Everyone agreed that the place to start from was East Africa.

It would soon become clear that Leopold's motives went far beyond the philanthropic. He was secretly jealous of his cousin, Queen Victoria, for being monarch of an empire covering a seventh of the world's land surface. Long before the creation of his International African Association he had written: 'The Belgians do not exploit the world. They must be taught to acquire that taste.' The Scramble for Africa was about to start.

By the start of 1879 the first of Leopold's 'scientific' expeditions was setting out from Zanzibar for the interior, and although its members fared badly through fever, the king did not admit defeat. A second attempt was made with supplies carried by trained Ceylonese elephants rather than African porters, who had seemed infuriatingly prone to desert. Four elephants, two male and two female, were unloaded on the beach near Dar es Salaam and began the long march to Lake Tanganyika. Each carried the equivalent of fifteen porters' loads. The two males died of apoplexy early on, one of the females succumbed near the end of the journey, but the survivor, named Pulmalla, reached the association's base at Karema, near the southern end of the lake.

By this time Stanley had completed his great trans-African journey. Leopold quickly hired him to stake out the future Congo Free State, starting from the Atlantic coast of Africa. The idea of penetrating the continent from the west, up the course of the Congo, was novel and daring; but it meant that Leopold would have fewer rivals. He thought of also employing Gordon, who had resigned his post in the Sudan, but the general was in one of his most manic phases, possessed with religious hysteria and writing long, frenzied letters to his sister Augusta. He was not the man to occupy the heart of a continent without asking awkward questions. So Leopold stuck with Stanley, who would in time advance to the headwaters of the Congo, where Tippu Tip was still holding sway and claiming the region as part of Sultan Barghash's insubstantial empire.

By the end of the 1870s more and more missionaries were putting down roots in East Africa, each hoping they had found the most hopeful fields for evangelism. A fearful death-rate from fever did not deter them, nor the slaughtering of an advance party trying to reach the lush meadows of Buganda. Some missionaries established themselves beside Lake Tanganyika and others settled with African chiefs near Kilimanjaro. The Nyamwezi leader Mirambo, in particular, had earned admiration from the missionaries by welcoming them to his territory and urging them to stay in his capital, Urambo. It seemed that here was a powerful African king who was ready to receive the Word of God.[7]

These developments began to worry the Arab settlers in the interior. They could see that these white newcomers were not interested in trying to spread their alien religion among Muslims like themselves, but only wanted to make friends with the *ushenzi*, the pagans. They tried to persuade Mirambo that the missionaries were only white slaves, running away from the 'Sultan of Europe'. He was not deceived, and soon saw a political opportunity in his blossoming friendship with the white men. If the sultan of Zanzibar could have an official British resident, speaking for Queen Victoria, he wanted one too.

Kirk was aware of Mirambo's power and sympathized with his appeal for a consul, but he knew there was no chance of satisfying it. Luckily, the London Missionary Society had decided to send out to the 'African Bonaparte' the nearest person they had to a consul. Ebenezer Southon was, like Kirk, a medical doctor – even if the source of his qualifications was vague. Although British, he had spent part of his life in Texas. He settled down happily in Urambo, treating the local ailments, trying to run a school, and growing crops. A Belgian traveller, Jèrome Becker, called his home 'a little Eden'. Southon had laid out his garden in the European manner, with its orchard bisected by a handsome avenue of tall banana plants. Becker praised the doctor for his Texan ways: 'that quickness of execution which characterises the pioneers of the New World.'

Southon became Mirambo's amanuensis, sending a steady flow of letters to Kirk and complaining when the replies were too slow in arriving. Mirambo began to feel strong enough to demand the removal of Barghash's Arab governor in Tabora. He warned the sultan: 'I will lead my people to fight, and tell him that I won't be responsible for any caravans being attacked, the road will be closed and if white men or Arabs get killed, don't blame me.' As he explained to European visitors, he hated the Arabs because they looked down on him as a *mshenzi* (barbarian). Even so, if he could reach an honourable peace he would take it. For a time it looked as though Kirk and Barghash might yield to Mirambo's demands, and let him become the acknowledged ruler of a vast stretch of the interior, in return for a promise of free movement for the trading caravans. It was a prospect, if events had turned out well, which might have materially influenced the nature of the looming colonialism. Mirambo continued to extend his power, while patiently waiting for Queen Victoria to send him a consul.

The pace of events on the mainland was visibly quickening, so Kirk suggested to Barghash that his surest way of protecting Zanzibari interests was to put himself still further under the British wing. Moreover, the island's army needed a commander able to impose strict discipline and keep it always on the alert; in short, a British officer. The sultan agreed, and Kirk picked his man, a Royal Navy lieutenant, Lloyd Mathews, who had fought in the war to conquer the Gold Coast (Ghana), and could be granted indefinite leave from the Indian Ocean fleet for this new task on shore. Mathews started with 300 African recruits and within three years the number had quadrupled.[8] It was Barghash's army, but obeying British commands.

At this moment came yet another development that might have changed the destiny of Zanzibar and influenced the future of East Africa. The impetus came from a Scots millionaire, Sir William Mackinnon, who had started life as a grocer's clerk in the Mull of Kintyre, emigrated to India, made a fortune there in trade, and founded an Indian Ocean shipping line. Mackinnon's first contact with East Africa came in the early 1870s, when he started a regular steamer service from Aden to Zanzibar.[9] As fellow-Scots, he and Kirk quickly struck up a friendship; the consul always warmed to the wealthy, and showered praise on the shipowner for his initiative, for his work in aiding the spread of Christianity and civilization. Such compliments, from one of Livingstone's old companions, was music to Sir William's ears. Now in his fifties, he felt the time was right for good works.

When Leopold had earlier convened his Brussels conference, Mackinnon was among the British delegates. To be joined in philanthropic labours with one of Europe's crowned heads was naturally pleasing for a self-made man. Yet after a flirtation with Leopold's association, Mackinnon went his own way. He now decided that he wanted nothing less than to obtain a vast concession from Sultan Barghash, to embrace all of Zanzibar's mainland empire. It would last for seventy years.

Kirk gave him every encouragement, even making a reconnaissance of the harbours between Dar es Salaam and Kilwa, to see where Mackinnon might best start building a wagon road to Lake Malawi, which was selected as the most promising vantage-point for trade and evangelizing. The consul wrote enthusiastically to Lord Derby, the foreign secretary, in April 1877, forecasting that the entire project would end the slave trade, spread order and justice, bring wealth to Barghash and lift from the sultan's shoulders the burden of trying to control the mainland. Mackinnon's brainchild, a latterday East India Company, would do it all.

Barghash at first seemed to favour the idea, perhaps because he thought it would halt the southwards advance of the greatly feared Egyptians. Kirk, supposedly his mentor, fancied that the sultan did not really understand the 'gigantic nature' of the concession. Lord Derby held the same view: 'I cannot think the Sultan knows what he is doing. He is thinking of signing over nearly all his power.'

In time Barghash did understand better. He raised objections, put up counter-proposals, irritated Kirk. A revised draft of the concession was presented, but nothing was settled. Meanwhile, Mackinnon showed his faith in the concession by sending a team of labourers from Britain to start building the road to Lake Malawi. They began work, despite Kirk's advice, near Dar es Salaam. Nothing more tangible happened, because everyone was waiting for the British government to signal its approval.

The response was slow in coming; months drifted by. Mackinnon's courage, seemingly so high at the start of 1877, ebbed away by the middle of the following year. Perhaps fatal to the scheme was the replacement at the Foreign Office of Lord Derby by Lord Salisbury, for whom Africa was then not of the faintest interest: he suspected that open support for this outlandish venture might draw Britain into a costly imbroglio with 'savage races'.

By the end of 1878, the scheme that might have put all of East Africa under British protection was dead. The road, which stretched inland for little more than seventy miles, was abandoned. The bush soon grew back over it. Kirk made certain that if anyone was to be blamed it would not be him. Writing to Horace Waller, an influential friend in London, he says: 'I am sick and tired of the cant everyone tells me about Mackinnon [sic] disinterested views. Bosh! First I don't believe it, and if I did I don't think he would do good to Africa.' His final words in November 1878 are even more jaundiced: 'The chance has been lost, and Mackinnon never was hot enough on it to have made it a success.'[10]

FIFTY-TWO

Imperialism Abhors a Vacuum

※

Hamed, be not angry with me; I want to have no more to do
with the mainland. The Europeans want to take Zanzibar here
from me: how should I be able to keep the mainland? Those who
are dead, who see nothing of this, are at peace.
— Sultan Barghash to Hamed bin Muhammed (Tippu Tip)
(November 1886)

BY THE TIME the Mackinnon road had been abandoned, the colonial
ambitions of King Leopold were naked for all to see, although his hopes
of grasping the entire Congo basin were soon to be foiled by the
treaty-making of a French naval officer, Pierre Savorgnan de Brazza.
Events were moving fast elsewhere. In West Africa the British were
occupying the Gold Coast and dominating trade on the Niger river. In
Madagascar the step-by-step advance of France was belatedly making
real the seventeenth-century annexation by Louis XIII. Italy was starting
to stake a claim in the Horn of Africa.[1]

Even Portugal's moribund outposts in Mozambique and Angola were
being prodded back to life. A former foreign minister, João de Andrade
Corvo, told the Lisbon parliament: 'In my opinion, our country's interest urgently demands the development of our colonies. Only through
these colonies will Portugal be able to take the place she deserves in
the concert of nations; only on their preservation and prosperity does
her future greatness depend.'

Curiously, the one European power without any foothold in Africa,
and lacking an apparent interest in acquiring any, was Germany. Appear-
ances were deceiving: in 1878 an association was formed for Commercial
Geography and the Promotion of German Interests Abroad. In the
following year a pamphlet entitled 'Does Germany Need Colonies?' by
a leading missionary, Friedrich Fabri, aroused public interest. Fabri
pointed enthusiastically to the opportunities to be found in Africa. The
impetus grew: the historian Heinrich von Treitsche said that 'every

virile nation' developed colonies. By the end of 1882 a German Colonial Association was in being.

Coincidentally, demands were coming from manufacturers all over Europe for new markets, because an economic recession was in train. All were agreed that Africa seemed the best place to sell off excess production. As the journal of the London Chamber of Commerce put it, colonialism could be the answer: 'a repetition in Central Africa of the action which founded our Indian Empire.'

Lording it in Zanzibar, consul Kirk remained serenely sure that Britain could set the pace. He gave Lord Salisbury his opinion that Leopold's 'artificial' scheme in the Congo would probably fail, and Belgium was too weak to rescue it. 'On the East coast our countrymen have a better footing and one we are not likely to lose.' Yet Kirk had suggested to London in 1881 that it might be worthwhile to define the limits of Barghash's territory on the mainland. One of the quandaries about the 'gigantic nature' of Mackinnon's stillborn concession had been that nobody was able to say just how gigantic it was; as consul Hamerton had observed, long ago, there was no map of the sultan's dominions.

Kirk's suggestion fell on deaf ears, for if Britain defined the boundaries, it might one day be called upon to defend them. Lord Ripon, the new viceroy of India, who had been appointed by Gladstone and shared his anti-imperialist views, put it succinctly: Britain might risk involving itself in matters over which it could have no real influence 'without an expenditure of money and a display of strength out of all proportion to the advantages to be gained'. Ripon's views carried weight, for he had given much thought to the folly of imperial ventures in wild places. He was in the throes of extricating Britain from a futile war in Afghanistan.

While Britain trusted to the *status quo*, life in the East African interior grew more volatile as the numbers of white travellers grew. Christian missionaries of divers kinds travelled towards the lakes alongside naturalists, geographers and nondescript opportunists. The lay missionaries, often artisans escaping from poverty at home, were prone to jettison God's work and turn to ivory-trading. The motives of some intruders were harder to discern. In 1880 a German expedition seemed to be studying the commercial possibilities near Karema, the Lake Tanganyika settlement which had welcomed the last of the Ceylonese elephants.

Little notice was taken of what such expeditions were doing, for nobody was charged with the responsibility of finding out. The harassed Barghash could only urge merchant adventurers such as Tippu Tip, who had made one of his rare visits to Zanzibar in 1882, to go back to the interior and keep as much trade as possible in Arab hands.

All authority was in limbo. African villagers and groups of marauding bandits watched enviously as the lavishly-equipped white men went by. Sometimes the temptation was too strong. In 1878 the caravan of a British technician, William Penrose, taking an engine to Lake Victoria for the Church Missionary Society, was overrun by four hundred *ruga-ruga*. Penrose was killed and his stores were looted. His attackers, wearing their red cloaks and tall feathered headgear, were commanded by a one-eyed warlord called Nyungu-ya-Mawe ('the Pot of Stone that cannot break'), whose territory bordered that of the great Mirambo.[2]

Then in 1880 came a calamitous event. Mirambo's own *ruga-ruga* killed two other Britons, after a desperate fight. An Indian army captain, Frederick Carter, and a young Scotsman, Thomas Cadenhead, were members of the team which had tried to introduce baggage elephants into East Africa. The news of their deaths outraged Kirk. This was the end of acceptability for Mirambo, despite his pleas for forgiveness and assertions that he now rejected the *ruga-ruga* and regarded them as no better than 'highway robbers'. Kirk refused to receive his emissaries or listen to conciliatory messages brought by the white missionaries, some of whom had come to see Mirambo as a black statesman. When the Nyamwezi leader was visited by Tippu Tip, then on his way to the coast, he asked him to help mend relations with the consul. Kirk sent back a polite letter, but would never alter his opinion that Mirambo was little more than an unruly warlord.[3]

By now Mirambo was also in failing health, although he ate little, shunned alcohol and was still in his early forties. The advice of his doctor friend Ebenezer Southon might have helped him, but Southon was dead. Two years earlier he had been accidentally shot in the arm with his own rifle, and despite two crude amputations by fellow-missionaries he was killed by gangrene. In December 1884 Mirambo also lay dying, from an undiagnosed disease of the throat. At the very end his followers strangled him, in accordance with tradition.

The Bugandan ruler Mutesa, whose potential had provoked Stanley into sending his clarion call to Europe's missionaries, had died two months before Mirambo. These two were in a way luckier than Tippu

Tip. They were spared the humiliation of the imperialist hurricane now about to break.

The series of events which began in early 1885 overwhelmed East Africa's inhabitants so swiftly that they scarcely had time to grasp what was happening. On 27 February, after the Berlin conference whose declared aim was to maintain free trade in tropical Africa, Chancellor Bismarck released a proclamation signed by Kaiser Wilhelm, declaring a protectorate over parts of the mainland facing Zanzibar. He based this claim on twelve treaties which a young German nationalist, Karl Peters, had secretly brought home from a hasty expedition to the small communities of Usegula, Ugura, Usagara and Ukami, stretching some 150 miles inland from the coast.

With the aid of brandy and bribery, Peters had persuaded local rulers and headmen to put their marks on documents which yielded their lands to the Reich. Typical was a 'treaty of eternal friendship' made with 'Sultan Mangungo of Msovero', in which this illiterate petty ruler offered 'all his territory with its civil and public appurtenances to Dr Karl Peters as the representative of the Society for German Colonization for exclusive and universal untilization for German colonization'.

Peters, still in his twenties, had been largely driven by patriotic envy of Britain, his home for several years. Before choosing Africa he thought of trying to seize part of Brazil for the fatherland. His short-sighted eyes, staring through pince-nez, had a wild daring. With two companions, who like him had never been to Africa before, Peters had made the last stage of the journey, from Aden to Zanzibar, on a British ship. They used false names, pretending to be artisans, and travelled deck-class. One of the trio was to die during the desperate round of treaty-making. Peters staggered half-conscious into a small German mission-station on the coast at the end, before dashing back to Berlin with his dubious pieces of paper.

Reigning serenely in the British consulate, Sir John Kirk had never got wind of the Peters expedition and was shocked by the duplicity of it all.[4] He might well have been put on his guard a few months earlier by the arrival in Zanzibar of a new German consul, Gerhard Rohlfs, renowned as a traveller in Africa, who had made his name by crossing the Sahara from Tripoli to Lagos. Why was so distinguished a figure being posted to East Africa? It turned out that Bismarck had known all along what Peters was up to, for in November 1884 he sent a cable to the German consulate in Zanzibar; this was handed to Peters on his arrival, telling him that the German government took no responsibility for his actions. In the same month Bismarck was assuring the British ambassador in Berlin that Germany had no designs on Zanzibar.

The attention paid in Britain to Bismarck's bombshell was less than might have been expected, for three weeks earlier the news had come through that General Gordon was dead, cut down by the Mahdists in Khartoum. The relief expedition had arrived too late. 'Too late!' The dire words rang round Britain. But it was equally too late to help Sultan Barghash, the ever-trusting ally of the British empire.

Barghash protested, as well he might: 'These territories are ours,' he wrote to the Kaiser. 'They have belonged to us since the days of our fathers.' A bewildered Kirk sent strenuous cables to London. But Gladstone and his ministers were in no mood to take on Bismarck over a 'small colonial controversy' when they were trying to win his backing against France for their newly-established rule in Egypt. On the contrary, they quietly encouraged him, and ordered Kirk to be co-operative. Before Peters had handed over his dubious treaties, Bismarck wanted no more than to make a wide-ranging trade agreement with Barghash, but now he responded to the mood of his electorate. On 5 March 1885 he issued a proclamation putting the treaty areas – the size of Bavaria – under German law. Furthermore, he ordered five warships under Commodore Carl Paschen to head for Zanzibar.[5]

Bismarck demanded that Barghash should concede free access through his coastal territory to the newly-declared inland protectorate. The sultan refused. Kirk sent a message to London: 'Sultan if left alone must yield or else seek other protection.' There was no other protection. The consul knew it. So did Bismarck, for Lord Granville, the British foreign secretary, sent him a message on 25 May: 'The supposition that Her Majesty's Government have no intention of opposing the German scheme of colonisation in the neighbourhood of Zanzibar is absolutely correct. Her Majesty's Government, on the contrary, view with favour these schemes, the realisation of which will entail the civilisation of large tracts over which hitherto no European influence has been exercised.'

On 7 August the German fleet arrived and trained its guns on Zanzibar town. On the 11th the sultan was given twenty-four hours to yield or be bombarded. Provocatively, the German commodore had brought with him a former Zanzibar princess, a sister of the sultan. Twelve years before she had fled from the island with a German merchant who had made her pregnant. Now known as Frau Emily Ruete, the erstwhile princess strolled up and down outside the sultan's palace with an escort of German officers. If this had set off a violent incident it would have given the pretext for annexation, and Frau Ruete's half-German son could have been put on the throne.[6] The sultan resisted falling into the trap, and Kirk obtained another twenty-four-hours' grace for him. On the 13th Barghash surrendered. The Royal Navy, which so long had made the Indian Ocean an 'English lake', was nowhere to be seen.

From then on the grinding away of the sultan's power went on at a more leisurely pace. He was persuaded to give the Germans the coastal port they coveted, which was Dar es Salaam, as a point of access for the territory 'ceded' to the Peters expedition. At the end of 1885 a three-nation commission – German, French and British – was set up to decide the spheres of influence in East Africa. Lord Salisbury, the British prime minister, said blandly that he hoped its deliberations would be based on 'sound principles of law and justice'. A final deal was reached in October 1886. The sultan was allowed to keep Zanzibar and the adjoining islands, together with a strip ten miles deep along the coast. All his claims to sovereignty further inland were dismissed.

The dividing line between the German and British spheres began some fifty miles south of Mombasa, then headed north-west to the shores of Lake Victoria. It was a direct line across the map, like so many drawn during the 'scramble', taking no heed whatsoever of the wishes of the people living in its path. However, there was a curious kink in the boundary, where it curved round the north of Kilimanjaro. The Kaiser had been very keen on owning the highest mountain in Africa.

Barghash resisted the treaty until December 1886. A few weeks earlier Tippu Tip had gone to the palace and heard him say: 'Hamed, be not angry with me; I want to have no more to do with the mainland.' Tippu Tip said later: 'When I heard Seyyid's words I knew that it was all up.'[7]

Far away in London there were even some brief words of contrition from the new prime minister, Lord Salisbury: 'The Sultan of Zanzibar is being hardly treated.'

One participant in these events looked ahead and realized their relevance to British security, in particular the defence of British links with India and Australia in any future war. He was Herbert Kitchener, then a colonel and later a field-marshal, who had represented his country on the three-nation commission. In a confidential memorandum, 'Notes on British Lines of Communication with the Indian Ocean', he urged the strengthening of positions at the mouth of the Red Sea and further east, because the strategic balance was changing.

As for East Africa, he proposed that Britain should persuade the sultan to grant Britain the same rights for Mombasa as Germany was acquiring at Dar es Salaam. Casting back to Captain Owen's short-lived protectorate sixty years earlier, Kitchener wrote: 'It has not been forgotten that the British flag was once hoisted at Mombasa, and it would receive a warm welcome were it to reappear under arrangement with the Sultan. Mombasa is the most probable port from which any railway system for the opening-up of the interior would start, and its possession would give England a commercial base, without which it would be impossible to develop the trade of Central Africa.'

FIFTY-THREE

Bismarck and the *Gesellschaft*

❧

Be happy, my soul, let go all worries
soon the place of your yearnings is reached
the town of palms – Bagamoyo.
Far away, how was my heart aching
when I was thinking of you, you pearl
you place of happiness, Bagamoyo.

There the women wear their hair parted
you can drink palm wine all year round
in the garden of love, Bagamoyo.
  —traditional song of the caravan porters, returning
    to the coast (recorded by A. Leue, 1900)

WHEN THE NATIONS OF EUROPE divided Africa among themselves they were remarkably ignorant about what each was acquiring. They could, of course, measure on the map the areas bounded by Bismarck's red lines, but had only hazy ideas of how many people lived within these new possessions, whether mineral wealth awaited discovery, or if the land was fertile and fit for white settlement. It was a topsy-turvy imperialism: sovereignty was not the result of conquests, instead sovereignty was handed out first and the conquests came later.

Chauvinism and national rivalries in Europe provided much of the impetus for the occupation of Africa, but the costs were harder to justify. How could this rush of colonialism pay for itself? The finding of gold and diamonds in South Africa in the 1860s and '70s had encouraged the idea that similar riches must exist further north in the continent; but this was no more than speculation. So emphasis was laid on the untapped market for manufactured goods. Rows of figures marched like soldier-ants across the pages of books and magazines in the late nineteenth century, showing how tropical Africa could absorb huge quantities of imports from Europe. Such tables were largely specious, merely part of the effort to 'talk up' Africa's potential, and thereby soothe the doubts of European treasury ministers and taxpayers.

After all, markets needed buyers as well as sellers, and Africans had conspicuously little buying-power. Their immediate asset was ivory, but it was already becoming obvious that breech-loading rifles were fast destroying the elephant herds. Nor was there any prospect that Africans in large numbers could be turned into wage-earners with money in their pockets, like the working classes of the northern hemisphere. Livingstone had once argued that there were 'vast areas' of the continent suited to growing cotton and sugar, then warned in his quirky way: 'You must not suppose that the African will work if you do not pay him for it.'

Livingstone's vision of white plantation-owners paying black workers their due for a fair day's work was far from the minds of most of the youthful empire-builders who were being sent to East Africa from Britain and Germany. These newcomers paid lip-service to the sophistry about creating markets, as they did to the duty to 'civilize' the Africans and uproot vestiges of slavery, but they knew that the first priority was to stake out the ground and plant their flags wherever boundaries were ill-defined.

Insofar as the natives might get in the way of this urgent task they were a nuisance. Their wishes had never been seriously considered during the carve-up, on the premise that they had yet to learn what was good for them, so there was no point in seeking their approval for matters which had already been settled elsewhere. It was taken for granted that the Africans would readily accept that they must start obeying European laws, saluting European flags, and in due course paying European taxes.[1] So the extent of their defiance at being put under the protection of whichever alien power fate had decreed came as a shock to the first wave of colonial administrators. The hopes of a painless takeover, bringing quick profits, were soon abandoned. But because history is written by the victors, the true measure of African resistance – and the misery caused in subduing it – would be glossed over in official accounts.

It might be said that the first prominent victim of the colonial era in East Africa was Sultan Barghash of Zanzibar; as consul Kirk would later admit, Barghash was 'sacrificed'. As early as 1877 the sultan had declared an interest in giving Kirk's friend, Sir William Mackinnon, a seventy-

year concession over the mainland, and although the scheme petered
out it had been one more proof of the special relationship with Britain.
Yet in less than ten years the British had, as Barghash saw it, totally
betrayed him by their deal with Germany to divide up the mainland
coast between them. Kirk was not in Zanzibar to face the recriminations,
having gone on leave, never to return, a few months earlier.

When Henry Stanley reached Zanzibar in March 1887 to prepare for
his last African expedition he met Barghash, then fifty-four, and saw
that he had not long to live: 'his political anxieties are wearing him
fast.' Urged on by Stanley, the sultan signed a new version of the
Mackinnon concession, to cover the coastline of the British 'sphere of
influence'.[2] This was to give a still-unnamed British company the right,
for fifty years, to collect customs revenue at Mombasa and other ports,
in return for paying the sultan this revenue plus 50 per cent. Barghash
also promised to encourage African chiefs in the British sphere to sign
treaties with the company. The agreement was an act of desperation by
the sultan, to salvage something on the coast. It was agreed that his flag
would still fly over Fort Jesus.

Barghash clung to life for another year, afflicted by depression, consumption and elephantiasis. Some months before dying, he showed his
anger at the course of events by poisoning one of his senior advisers,
Muhammad bin Salim, for being too friendly towards the Germans.
They had begun to behave as though Zanzibar belonged to them: their
warships were constantly in the harbour, their sailors were arrogant
when ashore, and their East Africa Company (*Deutsch-Ostafrikanische
Gesellschaft*) was aggressively setting up its trading posts in Dar es Salaam
and other mainland ports.

Almost the last shreds of Zanzibari independence were buried with
Barghash in March 1888. He was succeeded, with the backing of the
new colonial overlords, by his younger brother Khalifa, who was feared
to be mentally unhinged, having been kept in an underground chamber
for six years by Barghash to stop him from attempting to seize power.
Only a month after being installed Khalifa granted the German company
a fifty-year lease – patterned on the British terms – over the entire
coastal territory in its 'sphere'; yet he still had enough pride to demand
that all tax-collection should be done in his name and under his flag.

A strong ruler, commanding respect, might have stood a chance of
making the Germans tread warily, while at the same time retaining the
loyalty of local rulers on the coast. Khalifa could do neither, and

September saw the start of the first resistance war in East Africa. The trouble had begun with the *Gesellschaft*'s decision in August to raise its own flag in Bagamoyo, the Indian Ocean terminus of the main caravan route from the interior. Since hundreds of dhows from Zanzibar were constantly arriving in Bagamoyo to land their trade goods and collect the exports of the mainland, this was a threatening move. Arab emissaries of the sultan protested that it was a violation of the agreement, but were cowed by German warships lying offshore.

Further up the coast at the small port of Pangani, a young official, Emil von Zelewsky, threatened the local Arab governor, insulted the Muslim religion and sneered at the name of the sultan. He was quickly given a hostile nickname: Nyundo (hammer). Zelewsky told the towns-people that he would call for a naval bombardment if they defied him, and as a taste of his intentions had 100 German marines landed on the beach. They smashed property and pulled down the sultan's flag.

On 4 September 1888 the first resistance leader emerged: Sheikh Abu-shiri bin Salim, the wealthy owner of a sugar plantation near Pangani. Born of an Arab father and a concubine from southern Ethiopia, he was short, fierce-eyed, and grey-bearded.[3] Abushiri dressed expensively in the Arab style and had always felt himself as good a man as the sultan – he belonged to the long-established al-Harthi community, which regarded the Omanis as *parvenus* in East Africa. It was twenty years since Abushiri had visited Zanzibar, and he claimed that if he did he risked being hanged. In his view, Khalifa had no right to hand over the coast to anyone. So, without seeking approval from the sultan, he launched an armed attack on Pangani and blockaded Zelewsky in his headquarters. The Germans were given two days to leave the coast and one of their warships was fired on as it came near the shore.

Abushiri's second-in-command, and brother-in-law, was Sheikh Jah-azi; born in the Comoro islands, whose people were renowned for their courage, Jahazi had travelled across Africa with Henry Stanley as a gunner. Although both men belonged to the Arab community, they were never short of African followers. Warriors marched down from the interior, and other contingents arrived from all parts of the coast. Soon the sheikh was leading an army, albeit one which was hard to discipline, numbering about eight thousand. When the Germans tried to land in Pangani they were driven away. Two of their officers were killed when the outpost at Kilwa was overrun. Eventually Zelewsky and his German companions were rescued by a British general, Lloyd Mathews, commander of the sultan's army in Zanzibar. Mathews did not stay long on the coast: he realized that his own men were on Abushiri's side.

By the end of the year the Germans were driven completely from the mainland, apart from holding two small trading posts in Dar es Salaam and Bagamoyo. These clung on only with the help of warships lying close to the shore: the cruiser *Leipzig* had shelled and partially destroyed Bagamoyo to drive back Abushiri's men. In Sadani, a port between Bagamoyo and Pangani, the local African ruler, Bwana Heri, had also mustered a resistance army.

Talking with a captured Austrian traveller, Oscar Baumann – later freed unharmed – Abushiri reiterated his claim to have no regard for any treaties signed by the sultan of Zanzibar. The coast was now independent. But he was reckoning without the pride of Bismarck, who saw that a successful resistance to German rule in East Africa would imperil the entire colonialist house of cards. The aura of white invincibility must be maintained.

As a curtain-raiser to military action, Bismarck ordered government newspapers in Germany to start writing about the need to 'restore order' on the coast as the spearhead of a campaign against the slave trade. This was plainly the best way to marshal public support for direct government intervention. Events played into his hands when a group of 'rebels' killed three Catholic missionaries, two of them women, in a raid near Dar es Salaam. Emotions in Germany were raised to a high pitch with the help of pro-colonialist groups and banks which had sunk money in the Deutsch-Ostafrikanische Gesellschaft (already near bankruptcy).

The first step by the 'Iron Chancellor' was to call for a sea blockade, to stop arms and ammunition reaching Abushiri. Significantly, Britain agreed to take part, and the two navies patrolled 550 miles of the East African coastline, two-thirds of which was in the German sphere. In the Reichstag almost the only critics of Bismarck's intervention were the social democrats, whose spokesman, August Bebel, condemned the company as a 'small group of rich capitalists, bankers, merchants and industrialists', whose interests had nothing to do with the interests of the German people: 'The driving force is wealth, wealth and nothing but wealth. And in order to render possible the fullest and undisturbed exploitation of the African peoples, millions of marks are to be provided from the taxpayers' pockets, from the national exchequer.'

Nevertheless, the marks were soon forthcoming. At the end of January, when it was clear that the blockade was futile, the parliament voted four million marks 'to suppress the slave trade and protect German interests'. The renowned traveller, Hermann von Wissmann, who had twice crossed central Africa, was given the task of organizing a military force. In Cairo he recruited 600 Sudanese mercenaries, and in Mozambique 350 Shangaans (described as Zulus, to make them seem more fearsome). Few local troops were hired, because their loyalty would always be in doubt. Eighty German officers and other ranks were chosen to lead the 'Wissmann unit', which trained vigorously while its commander pretended to engage Abushiri in peace talks.

When Wissmann judged himself ready, his forces were landed in two groups at Bagamoyo and Dar es Salaam. They had modern weapons, including twenty-six field pieces, and were supported by seven warships. In the words of Dr A. Becker, who had just arrived in East Africa, their duty was to 'restore German superiority' and 'liberate' the country from the 'rebels'. It was soon clear that Abushiri was doomed, because many of the warriors from the interior had drifted home, and the long wait through the rainy season had sapped the spirit of his Swahili followers. The Germans stormed his stockaded camp, inflicting heavy casualties, then fanned out along the coast. Villages were burned down, chiefs suspected of loyalty to Abushiri were hanged, and the defeated leader fled inland. Wissman then put a price of 10,000 rupees (15,000 marks) on his head.

For months Abushiri evaded capture, even returning to the coast to make a daring but unsuccessful attack on Dar es Salaam. As his prospects grew more desperate he began matching the Germans in ferocity. Harsh treatment was dealt out to local people who might betray him. Then at the end of November 1889 the defiant sheikh was reported to be building a stockaded fortress at Mwenda, only four days' march from his home town, Pangani.

This news was brought to the Germans by an African chief, Mohammed Soa, tempted by Wissmann's reward. His guides led a force of Sudanese mercenaries and their white officers to a village which was supplying Abushiri with food. After a skirmish the village was set on fire. Then the guides showed the way to Mwenda itself, and the Germans decided to mount an attack at midnight. Their soldiers crept right to the centre of the sleeping encampment before the alarm was raised. More than thirty of Abushiri's men were killed. He managed to escape in the darkness, but left behind all his possessions, including his guns, his flag and a box of documents.

A week later a headman, Magaya, betrayed Abushiri. The exhausted fugitive had come to his village, Kwamkoro, seeking food, and Magaya had taken him prisoner. The delighted Germans were led to a hut where the sheikh was lying in chains, with his neck in a forked slave-stick. He was brought down to the coast at Pangani, his home town. Abushiri bitterly told his interrogators that the men of Pangani had sworn on the Qur'ān to fight to the end to drive the Germans out: 'All the others have broken their word. I am the only one who has remained true to that oath until today.'

The sheikh and two of his lieutenants were given a summary trial, then hanged on 15 December 1889.[4] Shortly before his execution Abushiri declared that he had not, after all, been totally out of touch with the sultan of Zanzibar, that after he began his resistance war, messages from Khalifa had encouraged him in his fight. Later it was agreed by the British and the Germans that the statement should be regarded as 'most secret', to avoid casting doubt on the sultan's good faith.

By quelling the 'Arab revolt' and hanging its leaders, the Germans confirmed their grip on what was later to be named Tanganyika, a territory three times the size of the fatherland. Years of fighting lay ahead, although the end could never be in doubt. Local rulers were offered German flags and those refusing to accept them were punished by having their villages burned down. There was much flogging of recalcitrants. Unsurprisingly, the punitive expeditions were often ambushed: Captain von Zelewsky, whose behaviour had sparked off Abushiri's war, was killed while leading an attack on Chief Mkwawa, ruler of the tightly-knit Hehe people. Nine German officers and 300 African troops died with him.

In the end, firepower prevailed. One chief after another was brought to heel. Mkwawa committed suicide, rather than allow himself to be taken alive and hanged. His head was cut off and sent to Berlin. More fortunate was the Yao leader, Machemba, who had defied the Germans from the Makonde country in the extreme south of Tanganyika. An aide who had learned English with the missionaries wrote down Machemba's message to Wissmann, who had ordered him to come to Dar es Salaam: 'I have heard your words, but I do not see any reason why I should obey you. I would rather die ... If it is a matter of friendship I shall not refuse, today and always, but I shall not be your subject . . . I shall not come. If you are strong enough, come and get me.' Wissmann sent down expeditions which destroyed villages and crops. Machemba resisted for nine years, then escaped across the border into Portuguese Mozambique.

Among the Nyamwezi the independence and fighting spirit earlier shown by Mirambo was revived by Chief Isike, whose fort near the trading centre of Tabora controlled the main trading route between the coast and Lake Tanganyika. Isike refused to have any dealings with the Germans. Two attempts to capture his fort were driven back, despite the use of cannons. A third assault, led by a Lieutenant von Prince, finally broke through the fort's defences. Isike retreated with his family into a room where gunpowder was stored, and blew himself up rather than be taken prisoner. Von Prince feared that Isike had escaped his due punishment by this last act of defiance. But on learning that the paramount chief was still alive, yet dying, von Prince was in time to have him brought out and hanged.[5]

FIFTY-FOUR

Africa Hears the Maxims
of Faith and War

You are burning me, but it is as if you were pouring water over
my body. I am dying for God's religion. But be warned in time,
or God whom you insult will one day plunge you into real fire.
—Charles Lwanga, leader of the Christian martyrs in Uganda (1886)

WHILE GERMANY imposed its sullen peace on Tanganyika, the British
were hastening to exploit their own 'sphere' on the northern side of
the international boundary. Although a charter was finally granted in
September 1888 for the Imperial British East Africa Company, activities
had begun well before that. The company had painlessly raised £240,000
as a first instalment of capital, and a distinguished board of directors –
which included Sir John Kirk, the erstwhile consul in Zanzibar – was
heady with optimism, even though the government was hedging
the company round with restrictions while taking none of the financial
risk.

Sir William Mackinnon, the high-minded empire-builder, returned
to the arena, intoning a familiar refrain, that Africa's markets were
waiting for the products of British industry. He could not resist adding
that the company would also 'take its dividends in philanthropy'. The
application for the charter said the directors believed that a direct result
of European enterprise would be an advance of civilization among 'the
natives inhabiting the aforesaid territories'.

Despite their gusto, Mackinnon and his partners were still largely
ignorant of what lay behind their part of the East African coastline,
from Mombasa to Lamu. Although the missionary Ludwig Krapf had
reconnoitred as far as Mount Kenya more than thirty years earlier, the
fearsome reputation of the Masai had deterred all but a handful of
Europeans from venturing further. When the Imperial British East Africa
Company began pushing inland there was little to go on except the

diaries of a Scottish geologist, Joseph Thomson. It was only five years since Thomson had braved the Masai to reach Lake Victoria on a direct route from Mombasa.

So the 'British' interior was investigated for the company by Frederick Holmwood, formerly Kirk's deputy in the Zanzibar consulate. In the second half of 1887 he ventured some 150 miles from Mombasa towards Mount Kilimanjaro with a 100-strong escort. This was not breaking new ground – Ludwig Krapf and his colleagues had done more in the mid-century - but Holmwood was a fluent advocate.[1]

In a long memorandum sent to Lord Salisbury, the British prime minister, at the end of May 1888, Holmwood held out the familiar prospect of 'a new and vast field for emigration and an important market for our commerce such as our statesmen, capitalists, manufacturers and skilled artisans are so anxiously seeking'. All that was wanting for European enterprise to exploit this 'salubrious' region was a railway. Here Holmwood was talking the language of his times: an engraving at the beginning of Jèrome Becker's recently published memoirs, *La Vie en Afrique*, had shown a train steaming out of the dawn towards a startled pride of lions, with the caption 'L'Afrique dans l'Avenir – introduction de la vapeur'.

The most original parts of Holmwood's memorandum were his ideas on why the East African interior – its fertility 'perhaps unequalled in the world' – lay undeveloped. The long occupation of the coast by 'Mohammedan immigrants and their native converts' had cut off the 'finer and more intelligent races' from contact with the outside world, and was 'wholly inimical to the extension of European influence'. Access to the Indian Ocean had been for centuries denied to the Africans by 'half-civilized, treacherous and unscrupulous Semitic adventurers whose evil reputation everywhere preceded them'. Moreover, the Arab slave trade had depopulated some parts of the interior and made the more independent-minded populations likely to attack anyone who ventured into their territory.

From the high ground of this analysis Holmwood descended swiftly to the marketplace. The Africans living in the 'salubrious highlands', were now obliged to protect themselves from their cool climate by dressing in hides and skins, whereas what they really needed were manufactured clothes; and there were millions of them. The prospect of all these people buying English shirts, trousers, jackets and dresses was enough to enthuse even the haughty Lord Salisbury.

*   *   *

Beyond the highlands lay the 'real prize', as Kirk would later call it: Buganda and its neighbouring kingdoms on the far side of Lake Victoria. The man chosen to seize this tantalizing region was Frederick Lugard. Like so many of the earlier British travellers in East Africa, notably Burton, Speke and Grant, he was an army officer, and had served in Afghanistan and Burma. However, the tight-lipped Lugard was not an 'explorer'. He was a conqueror, with an ethos entirely different from theirs.[2]

The 'explorers' were only passers-by in lands they did not own, and this governed their behaviour. When Speke met a 'very pretty little woman' in Buganda in the 1860s he offered her his arm, 'and we walked along, to the surprise of everybody, as if we had been in Hyde Park rather than in Central Africa, flirting and coquetting all the way'. An illustration in Speke's book shows his companion, Grant, dancing with a bare-breasted queenmother.

A quarter of a century later, Lugard never felt disposed to dance or walk arm-in-arm with black women. Instead, his favourite companion in East Africa was a Maxim machine-gun, whose timely invention in 1884 by American-born Hiram Maxim was easing the path of colonialism all over the continent. Although millions of muskets had been sold to Africans (and even, during the later decades of the nineteenth century, many thousands of rifles), they counted for little against a weapon firing 330 bullets a minute over a range of a mile. The Maxim had become a great talking point, even the subject of witticisms. Sir Samuel Baker, a celebrated African traveller in his younger days, was asked by James Grant in 1890 to subscribe towards putting a missionary steamer on Lake Victoria. His letter in reply regrets he cannot spare the money, but softens the refusal with a little joke: 'I expect she will also carry a Maxim gun as well as Christian maxims.'[3]

The inventor had been so eager to have his gun tested in action that he gave one to Henry Stanley, for his trans-Africa expedition of 1887–89. Stanley thought it a 'wonderful weapon'. A single white man, ensconced behind the Maxim's protective shield, could mow down a whole horde of black warriors. The gun Stanley took across the continent had now been passed on to Lugard, and was his most precious piece of equipment when he set out from Mombasa for Buganda in the autumn of 1890 at the head of sixty-six Sudanese and Somali mercenaries, followed by the customary crocodile of African porters with sixty-pound loads on their heads. He had with him a young officer, Fenwick de Winton, as his assistant.

Lugard knew well that they were marching towards a maelstrom, for the reports from Buganda portrayed a society being torn to shreds by religion. The court of its youthful ruler, Mwanga, was a sink of intrigue, pitting Muslims against Christians. The Christians were also divided among themselves, into Protestants, known as 'Inglesa' after their English mentors, and Catholics, called 'Fransa' because they had been converted by the White Fathers, who were mainly French. These alien faiths were newly overlaid upon the traditional religion of Buganda, with its twenty-one gods.

Although Mwanga, the *kabaka* and spiritual figurehead, was crowded round by courtiers who had adopted the new religions, he needed also to show the great mass of his unconverted subjects that he still respected their beliefs and honoured the spirits of the dead. The previous *kabaka*, Mutesa, had turned back to an ancient god of the lake for help against the ailments from which he died in 1884.

Mwanga reacted violently to the pressures of the new religions, interwoven with the political rivalries among his chiefs. His behaviour typified the fear and bewilderment which was gripping Africa as the outside world burst in upon it. He inclined first towards the Muslim faction, as Mutesa had done, because it seemed to make fewer demands (apart from circumcision, which both refused). Mwanga had also learned from some Muslim merchants the pleasures of homosexuality, and he was enraged because some of his favourite young pages, who were Christian converts, refused to meet his desires. So on Ascension Day in 1886, Mwanga ordered the execution of thirty-one prominent Christians. They were taken to Namugongo, a few miles from his capital at Mengo, and killed in various ways. Some were slowly burned alive, others were chopped to pieces or eaten alive by dogs. All died crying out the word *Katondo* (God).

A year earlier Mwanga had also ordered the killing of a somewhat arrogant English cleric, James Hannington, who had arrived on the borders of Buganda from the coast to install himself as the first 'Bishop of Equatorial Africa'. Hannington was not put to death just for his Christianity, but also because of the suspicion that he was a forerunner of white domination.

Reports of the death of Hannington and the tribulations of the 'black martyrs' had produced a clamour in Europe: since the blame was being laid on Islam, the answer was to bring Buganda fully within the embrace of Christianity. The missionary societies knew they could not do it on their own, so they needed little persuading as to the virtues of imperialism. On the spot, the news of Frederick Lugard's advance from the coast with his Maxim gun was welcomed by Protestants and Catholics alike, since both realized they were in peril.

Although Lugard was the son of an army chaplain in India, religion was never his concern. His simple desire was to force Mwanga to place his mark on a treaty bringing Buganda under the 'protection' of the Imperial British East Africa Company. That would not, strictly speaking, put all of the territory between Lake Victoria and King Leopold's Congo Free State into the company's hands, but Lugard realized that once Buganda was won all else would follow. He had already been treaty-hunting in Kikuyuland, near Mount Kenya, and knew how concessions could be expanded by encouraging even the most petty chief to claim that his authority stretched to far beyond the most distant horizons. The draft treaty Lugard now had ready not only covered Buganda but embraced 'all states tributary thereto'.

The trouble with Mwanga, apart from his propensity for murder, was that he was known to be both capricious and proud. He did not want to sign over his kingdom to the Europeans. As he had written in April 1890 to Charles Euan-Smith, the British consul in Zanzibar, he would welcome foreigners to 'build and trade', but he did not want to 'give them his land'. A few weeks before writing that letter he had been visited by Karl Peters, the German adventurer who in 1884 had introduced the 'Scramble' to East Africa through his handful of questionable treaties with the chiefs near Mount Kilimanjaro. This time Peters had made a quick dash to Buganda from Witu, a short-lived German 'protectorate' on the coast north of Mombasa.

It had been Peters's hope that he could gull Mwanga into binding himself to accept German 'protection', but the nervous, giggling *kabaka* slid through his fingers, granting only a treaty of friendship and the right to trade. The Germans none the less still clung to hopes that they could outflank the British by again reaching Buganda by way of Lake Victoria's southern shoreline. When Emin Pasha (Eduard Carl Schnitzer) – earlier 'rescued' by Stanley – set out from the coast on a trans-Africa journey, he had the signing of a definitive treaty with Mwanga as one of his main goals.

Amid this fraught rivalry Lugard was suddenly given a weapon even more powerful than his Maxim gun. Lord Salisbury had proposed to

Germany that a British protectorate over Zanzibar should be recognized in exchange for Heligoland, a sandstone islet off the German coast held by Britain since the Napoleonic wars. It was an offer Berlin could not refuse: Germany's admirals felt that the possession of Heligoland by a foreign power would present a dire threat to the Kiel Canal in the event of war. So in July 1890 the deal became a key element in the settlement of territorial disputes in various parts of Africa. (The French were placated by a belated recognition of their rule in Madagascar and over huge tracts of the Sahara.)

For the Imperial British East Africa Company, and its agent Lugard, the treaty included a vital provision about the Anglo–German boundary in the interior of East Africa. Until now this boundary had ended at the eastern shore of Lake Victoria, one degree south of the equator. An extension on the map now took it horizontally across the lake, straight on until it reached the limits of the Congo Free State. So Mwanga, whether he liked it or not, or knew it or not, was put into the British sphere. He might well have become a vassal of Kaiser Wilhelm II, rather than Queen Victoria, but for those few acres of sandstone sticking up from the North Sea.

When Emin Pasha received an official letter from the coast giving news of the July settlement, he wrote sadly in his diary: 'It is certainly true that the British have taken the lion's share.' There was no longer any point in going to Buganda, so he struggled on, deeper into Africa, until he fell in with brigands and was murdered.

As for Lugard, he was marching into Buganda with a firm mandate. When he reached Mwanga's capital, on 18 December 1890, with his fifty surviving mercenaries, he was resolved only to give orders, not to negotiate.[4] Rejecting the spot where he was invited to set up camp, he chose Kampala hill as his best vantage point. The next morning he marched a mile, with twelve of his Sudanese mercenaries, through the banana plantations which separated his camp from the royal palace, a handsome thatched building surmounting a steep hill. After shaking hands with Mwanga he sat down on a chair he had shrewdly brought with him, and explained through an interpreter that he came with authority to 'make treaties and settle disputes'. Mwanga laughed nervously and stroked some of the young, white-robed courtiers gathered round him.

Lugard left quickly and went back to his own hill to work out tactics for subduing Mwanga. He had his Maxim gun and was prepared to use it, but he also had faith in his own force of personality. On the day before Christmas he went again to the palace, accompanied by Fenwick de Winton, and demanded that the king and his chiefs should sign 'if he wanted peace'. Mwanga grew evasive and Lugard rapped the table: 'I scowled and looked as fierce as I could.' The king began to tremble. Suddenly, armed men – 'rowdies' was the dismissive term Lugard later used – began putting cartridges in their guns and shouting that anyone who signed would be shot; so would the two white men. One of the 'rowdies' had his loaded gun pointed straight at Lugard, who then discreetly retreated. On Christmas Day, after dark, he tried again, hoping there would be a chance to cajole Mwanga privately; but once more the men with guns closed in, and Lugard had to flee into the darkness amid catcalls and mocking laughter.

At this threatening moment it was the White Fathers, the French missionaries, who weighted the scale for Lugard. Fearing a bloody civil war, they told their 'Fransa' converts among the chiefs round Mwanga to urge him to sign. The White Fathers knew colonialism was inevitable, accepted that the British were going to win in the end, and decided that Lugard was better than chaos, even though in the end his sympathies would surely be with the Protestant faction, the 'Inglesa'. The next day a crowd of 'Fransa' chiefs marched to Kampala hill and announced they were ready to sign the treaty. Unaware of the missionaries' 'quiet diplomacy', Lugard proudly imagined the Buganda were simply succumbing to his own threats and scowls. Seizing the moment, he strode across to the royal court, laid out the paper ceding 'suzerainty' to the British company, and handed Mwanga a pen for making his mark. 'He did it with a bad grace, just dashing the pen at the paper and making a blob; but I made him go at it again and on the second copy he behaved himself and made a proper mark.' Several of the senior courtiers had been taught to write by the missionaries, so Lugard curbed his impatience while they laboriously scrawled their names.

Mwanga and his aides had dared to add a clause saying that the treaty would be cancelled 'if another white man greater than this one shall come up afterwards'. It seemed that when Mwanga had recovered his wits he would grasp at any excuse to fight his way out of the Imperial British East Africa Company's 'protection'. Fortunately for Lugard, the next white man to appear, a few weeks later, was another company agent, Captain Williams. Best of all, he also had a Maxim gun. The British had come to stay.

One of the 'Inglesa' missionaries, R. H. Walker, admitted that

Mwanga hated the British, who had 'eaten his land' and given him nothing in return. One of the White Fathers, Père Auguste Achte, was even more blunt: 'Quelle humiliation' for the proud Mwanga 'de mettre ses milliers de sujets et de tributaires sous le protection d'une simple Compagnie commerciale!' It was only with great repugnance, said Achte, that the king had reduced himself to the status of a vassal. Lugard could scarcely have disagreed. In later years he unashamedly admitted coercing Mwanga: 'The treaty was certainly obtained against his will – I have never said the contrary.'

The tireless Captain Lugard was to spend two years fighting, signing treaties, and generally imposing his will in what was soon called Uganda (Swahili interpreters could not pronounce the initial 'B'). During this time he had an alarming moment: a letter arrived telling him to withdraw to the coast, because the Imperial British East Africa Company was on the verge of bankruptcy. This had been precipitated through the first collapse of Barings, one of the most distinguished banks in the City of London. Although the Bank of England had come to the rescue of Barings, the City was still quaking from the shock: it meant that speculative ventures in tropical Africa had no chance of raising more money.

Lugard was still in despair, in his brick-built fort on Kampala hill, when another letter arrived in January 1892. The company had been given a reprieve, because funds had been raised by the Church Missionary Society. So it was entirely fitting that when a war broke out a few days later between the Inglesa and the Fransa, the Maxim guns should be put to use for the Protestant faction, who were also issued by Lugard with 500 guns. In the first battle the two Maxims were fired from the Kampala fort towards the Catholics gathered around their church on Rubaga hill. The range was ideal using a high trajectory, and the terror they induced proved decisive.

Eventually, Mwanga fled with the Catholics to a small island in Lake Victoria, but Lugard was not prepared to tolerate such defiance. He saw it as the preparation for a flight to German territory at the southern end of the lake. Mwanga had also made a bad mistake, for the island was less than half a mile from the shore, and the range of the Maxims was a mile. About a hundred people were killed by the firing, on Lugard's estimate, plus a few who might have drowned while trying to escape in canoes. Other eye-witnesses believed that the toll was much greater. The Catholic bishop in Buganda, Monsignor Jean-Joseph Hirth, sent

his account back to Europe: 'A terrible drama has just been enacted ...
This is one of the most shameful pages in the civilization of the Dark
Continent ... What shrieks! What a fusillade! What deaths by
drowning!'

Lugard had what he wanted. Mwanga surrendered and was soon
totally in his power. When the captain left for England in June 1892,
on the way to becoming one of the great proconsuls of the British
empire, he carried an astounding letter addressed to Queen Victoria.
Purportedly written by the *kabaka*, it had this to say of Lugard: 'He is
a man of very great ability, and all the Waganda like him very much;
he is gentle; his judgements are just and true, and so I want you to send
him back to Uganda.' Mwanga dutifully bent his knee to Victoria: 'I
and my chiefs are under the English flag, as the people of India are
under your flag; we desire very, very much that the English should
arrange this country.' (Nevertheless, Mwanga's relations with the colonial masters did not end well. He and another unco-operative ruler,
Kabarega of Bunyoro, were captured in 1899 and despatched into exile
in the Seychelles.)

It had taken less than a decade for Germany and Britain to raise their
flags over more than 600,000 square miles of the East African mainland.
The last scraps of tropical Africa left unclaimed were the remote kingdoms of Rwanda and Burundi, to the north of Lake Tanganyika. These
were coveted by King Leopold, who wanted to make them part of his
already notorious Free State, and also by Cecil Rhodes, who hoped they
might become links in his visionary Cape-to-Cairo route. The two
African kingdoms were slow to give up their independence, but in
time Germany was able to exploit divisions within the ruling Tutsi
aristocracies; Rwanda was annexed in 1897, and Burundi finally subjugated in 1903.[5]

Even before these last colonial boundaries were drawn, developments
on the mainland were moving at speed, largely because of the decision
by the British government to build a railway inland from Mombasa,
precisely as Colonel Kitchener had urged several years earlier. The goal
was to lay tracks north-westwards almost to the equator, to reach Lake
Victoria and the Uganda border. Determination to embark upon such
a venture was not stimulated purely by a wish to 'open up' the territory
for British settlers, or to outdo Germany, which had a railway scheme
under way in its own part of East Africa by May 1893. What helped

to douse objections to such a costly venture were strategic factors: the line could be used to move troops swiftly inland, to protect Uganda and confront any French or Belgian moves towards the Upper Nile. The vast expanse of the Sudan was still ruled by the Mahdists, but Britain was resolved to return there, to avenge the death of Gordon in Khartoum and regain the territory for Egypt, which it now governed. (It would fall to Kitchener himself, in 1898, to smash the Mahdi's army at Omdurman.)

White railway engineers brought to Mombasa from India had been taken aback by the geographical obstacles: starting at sea level the route had to be hacked through forest and bush up to a 7,000-foot plateau, down 1,500 feet into the Rift valley, climbing again a further 3,000 feet to the Kikuyu escarpment, then finally falling 4,600 feet to Lake Victoria in 90 miles. Nevertheless, by May 1896 *The Times* was reporting that the 'Uganda railway' (not a sleeper had been laid) was going ahead at a likely cost of three million pounds: 'Eleven hundred coolies and artisans from India are now on the spot. A thousand more are expected and it has been found practicable already to use native labour.' The decision to employ Africans was gratifying to Kirk, watching events from London. He later wrote to Lugard: 'Half the earthwork is done by natives which I am glad of because Hardinge and Curzon hold that niggers will not work, while I say they will if judiciously and fairly treated.'

With less than two hundred miles of track completed the three million pounds had gone. Manpower was continually being drained away through disease, exhaustion and attacks from wild animals.[6] (In the event, 32,000 'coolies' were needed, backed up by armies of African porters and labourers, several thousand of whom died.) Yet there was no wavering: as soon as a new stretch of track was laid the locomotives snorted forwards, through terrain no white man had seen twenty years earlier. The eventual triumph of the 'Lunatic Line', at a cost of more than five million pounds, entrenched British colonialism in East Africa.

FIFTY-FIVE

From Sultan's Island
to Settlers' Highlands

> It is well, then, to realise that it is for our advantage – and not alone
> at the dictates of duty – that we have undertaken responsibilities in
> East Africa. There are some who say we have no right in Africa
> at all, that it 'belongs to the natives'. I hold that our right is the
> necessity that is upon us to provide for our ever-growing popu-
> lation – either by opening new fields of emigration, or by provid-
> ing work and employment which the development of overseas
> extension entails – and to stimulate trade by finding new markets,
> since we know what misery trade depression brings at home.
> —Colonel Frederick Lugard, *The Rise of our East African Empire* (1893)

AWAY FROM THE MAINLAND, in Zanzibar, it seemed for a time that
the artifices of another age might well survive unscathed. The sultan
was still His Highness, treated with elaborate decorum by the British
consul. It was, after all, only twenty years since Sultan Barghash had
made his state visit to Britain, amid great panoply. Salutes were still
fired and anthems played on royal birthdays, all part of the fiction that
the island's ruler was as independent as his ancestors.

Events were about to prove that the fiction might have been too
well maintained. Sultan Hamed, installed on the throne in 1893, quietly
began building up a private army at a time when British attention
was distracted by disorders along the coast northwards from Mombasa
(disorders so severe that several shiploads of troops needed to be brought
over from India).[1] The new sultan did have grounds for discontent,
because the British government had appropriated £200,000 given to
Zanzibar by Germany as the purchase price for its section of the coast.
Britain was using the money to help settle the debts of the Imperial
British East Africa Company, as a prelude to taking over Kenya and
Uganda as dependencies. Although Zanzibar would be paid £17,000 a
year compensation for the funds it no longer possessed, even British
officials viewed the arrangement as shameless.

Hamed was adroit enough to build up his army's strength to more than a thousand, and equip it with modern weapons, before the British grew alarmed. Sir Arthur Hardinge, the new consul, regarded Hamed as nothing more than a 'protected puppet prince', and was vexed by the turn of events. He blamed the main adviser in the sultan's court, Hillal bin Amari, and decided to have him deported.

By this time, June 1896, Zanzibar was linked to the outside world by an undersea telegraph cable. There was also a correspondent of *The Times* of London on the island. 'Last night the sentence of deportation was executed against Hillal bin Amari,' the report began on 22 June. It went on to describe how armed Arabs had tried to intervene, but General Sir Lloyd Mathews had shot several dead with his pistol. 'Tranquillity now prevails.'

Watching these events closely was Khalid, the only surviving son of Sultan Barghash. He was in his early twenties, clever and energetic, and enjoyed the support of most of Zanzibar's Arab élite. Khalid would have been a far more popular choice when Hamed was installed, but consul Hardinge had made sure that he was sidelined – recognizing that he might prove too headstrong to handle. What was more, he showed signs of being pro-German.

Two months after Hillal bin Amari's deportation, Hamed died unexpectedly. Khalid stormed into the palace and declared himself the new sultan, after hurriedly burying the dead ruler's body as Muslim custom demanded. His guns fired a salute and his flag was raised, while the army Hamed had created took up defensive positions. Zanzibar was gripped by a sense of grim expectation, for the British had been caught napping.

A delegation was soon on its way from the British consulate to the palace, warning Khalid that his defiance was unacceptable – it was 'open rebellion'; he must submit or face the consequences. Khalid said he would rather die than give in. His biggest guns were ranged along the palace roof.

On 27 August, under the heading 'Zanzibar: British Ultimatum', *The Times* reported that British gunboats had taken up positions in the harbour facing the palace. A late item read: '9 pm. An ultimatum has been addressed to Said Khalid, informing him that unless his flag is hauled down and he makes a complete surrender by nine o'clock tomorrow morning, the palace will be bombarded. A force of 2,000 men is with Khalid.'

By the next morning there were five Royal Navy ships in the harbour and precisely on time the bombardment began. It lasted for forty minutes. The special correspondent's report on 28 August was graphic. The warships had opened up with heavy guns and Maxims: 'At so short a range very great damage was done, but the rebels fought with pluck and determination and returned a heavy fire.' The palace was turned into 'a mass of blazing ruins', and the death-toll put at 500. 'Many leading Arabs fought on the sultan's side in yesterday's engagement. It is presumed that their property will be confiscated.'[2] An old steamer named the *Glasgow*, belonging to the sultan, had fired on the Royal Navy ships, but was quickly sunk. Except for one wounded seaman, there were no casualties on the British side.[3]

The correspondent found a place in his long account for a mention of the white women resident in Zanzibar. 'The ladies were taken on board the flagship *St George*. They behaved splendidly throughout.' There was a general opinion among the British community that the time had come to hoist the British flag and do away with 'Arab rule' for good.

As for Khalid, he survived the bombardment, slipped out of the ruins, and found his way to the German consulate. The Germans refused to hand him over without guarantees that he would be treated as a political prisoner. (He would later be spirited across to Tanganyika.) A month later *The Times* carried an item on the new, acceptable sultan, Hamoud bin Mahomed. It said that he was 'in complete accord with his English advisers'. His sympathies were so strong that he insisted that his son, Seyyid Ali, should be sent to a British public school.

All the old pretences had been blasted into oblivion by the bombardment. As Major F. B. Pearce, consul in Zanzibar some years later, succinctly put it: 'At nine o'clock on the morning of August 27th 1896, the Zanzibar Arab and Swahili learnt his lesson, and he has never forgotten it.'

By the start of the twentieth century Zanzibar was only a backwater, a place of memories of past power. A young British lieutenant, Richard Meinertzhagen, went to the island in 1903 to recuperate after a fall from his horse while subduing Africans on the mainland. A friend took him to see 'a very old man', who was Tippu Tip. Meinertzhagen wrote in his diary: 'He is not allowed to leave Zanzibar, nor does he want to. I tried to get him to talk of slave raiding days, but he clearly did not like it . . . The old man spoke very little and was clearly embarrassed by his past activities.' During the visit Meinertzhagen had admired the handsome silver pot from which coffee was served. As they parted Tippu Tip insisted on handing over the coffee pot as a gift. It was now Meinertzhagen's turn to be embarrassed, since he dared not refuse for fear of affronting his host.

Meinertzhagen went back to his duties in British East Africa. The chartered company, which had taken the first costly steps to develop the territory, was gone – financially ruined, paid off with a derisory £50,000 from the British treasury, and replaced by direct rule.

Already there could be little doubt that what was so recently a virtual 'blank on the map' would become a colonial jewel. Lugard warned that this new possession 'was not an El Dorado', but praised the 'fertility of the soil, the healthiness of the highlands, the abundance of the rainfall, and the general excellence of the climate'. Eyes were not merely on the lushness of Uganda, which the youthful Winston Churchill would famously dub the 'pearl of Africa', but the highlands round Nairobi, the embryonic capital of what would become Kenya. Although the cost of the railway had been tremendous in lives and money, by 1899 a journey of more than three hundred miles to Nairobi could be made in a day, instead of many foot-slogging weeks.

The lieutenant, Richard Meinertzhagen, kept a diary of his time in Kenya during the first decade of the century. It is vivid, shocking and unashamed, the most convincing eye-witness account of the coercion of the indigenous people so that Africa could be 'reinvented' on European terms. Meinertzhagen was no typical army officer: an Old Harrovian of Jewish stock, he was the nephew of Beatrice Webb, a socialist intellectual of great influence. He was also murderous in his treatment of Africans, as well as being keen to shoot every animal that came within rifle range.

Violence during the 'pacification' of Kenya had been inevitable, partly because the coming of the white man coincided with a series of afflictions which struck African communities during the 1890s. In succession there was drought, famine, smallpox and swarms of locusts. Worst of all was rinderpest, which ravaged cattle herds; the African animals possessed no inbuilt immunity against it. One theory was that rinderpest came from India with the draught oxen used in railway-building, but more probably it was brought from Europe by the Italians, who were carving out their colonies in Somalia and Eritrea. Later came a plague of sandflies (jiggers), imported in ships from Brazil: these attacked Africans in their feet and caused gangrene.[4] (These ecological penalties of colonialism also spread south into Tanganyika, compounding the population decline caused by intermittent fighting between the Germans and their reluctant subjects.)[5]

Meinertzhagen worked first among the Kikuyu people, for whom the death-toll from famine and other troubles had been high. Fear and hatred of the colonizers led to the murder of a white man by villagers who staked him down and urinated in his mouth until he choked. Retribution was swift:

> Though the war drums were sounding throughout the night we reached the village without incident and surrounded it ... I gave orders that every living thing except children should be killed without mercy. I hated the work and was anxious to get through with it. As soon as we could see to shoot we closed in. Several of the men tried to break out but were immediately shot. I then assaulted the place before any defence could be prepared. Every soul was either shot or bayoneted.

Meinertzhagen found it curious how easily a bayonet went into and came out of a body.

His second tour of service brought him into contact with the Nandi people, who it was decided should be confined within a 450,000-acre reserve. Vast though this area was, the Nandi were nomadic cattle-owners unacquainted with the concepts of boundaries or land owner-ship, so a great deal of force was required. The expedition sent against them was led by eighty white officers, with several thousand black soldiers, levies and porters. The force had ten machine-guns. Apart from crushing all opposition, the aim was to punish the community by expropriating its cattle. Soon Meinertzhagen was able to note in his diary (7 November 1905): 'The Nandi appear to have had a pretty good dusting during the past three weeks. They have lost some ten thousand head of cattle and about five hundred warriors killed, besides some 70,000 sheep and goats. They now profess to be suing for peace at any price.' By the end of the 'dusting' – a popular expression – the Nandi had lost more than a thousand warriors and been relieved of 16,000 head of cattle.[6]

Throughout the years of imposing white discipline, which were effectively over by 1910, only six British officers died. Losses among their African riflemen amounted to a few hundreds, but the roughly-counted toll among the conquered was many times higher. By 1911 there were already 3,000 settlers in what were designated the 'White Highlands', and confiscated cattle was sold to them. The 16,000 square miles of these fertile highlands, in which non-white ownership was prohibited, covered a quarter of the arable land in the colony. Most surrounding regions were arid, but the White Highlands had enough rain to support two crops a year. They were also healthy, invigorating and beautiful.

From the start, there was a preference for bringing in 'men of the officer class', many of whom had served in India; they were given up to a thousand acres apiece.[7] Another group favoured as settlers were the sporting upper classes, and the Uganda railway, eager for first-class passengers, directed its advertising in Britain towards them: 'The Highlands of British East Africa as a Winter Home for Aristocrats has become a Fashion. Sportsmen in search of Big Game make it a hobby.' The epitome of the well-born settlers was Hugh Cholmondeley, the third Lord Delamere, who arrived in the highlands in 1898 on a hunting trip and spent the next thirty years there, promoting the cause of white supremacy. In the informal club of settlerdom, class was all: Irishmen and Jews, except those who were exceedingly rich or well-educated, could not join. The Indians were fitted to run shops, and the Africans to labour.

Although he did not share her politics, Meinertzhagen had found that being the nephew of Beatrice Webb gave him some curiosity value among his superiors. The high commissioner for Kenya, Sir Charles Eliot, invited him to dinner: 'Eliot hopes to attract thousands of Europeans to East Africa and does not appear to accept that the natives have any "rights". I suggested that East Africa belongs to Africans and that we had no right to occupy any land which is tribal land. We should develop East Africa for the African, and not for strangers.'

It was a topic over which they had already argued during a previous encounter: 'I said that one day the Africans would be educated and armed; that would lead to a clash. Eliot thought that that day was so far distant as not to matter and by that time the European element would be strong enough to look after themselves; but I am convinced that in the end the Africans will win.'

That such a prophecy should have been made in the early years of the twentieth century is remarkable enough. Still more astonishing, with hindsight, is how quickly it was to come true.

Epilogue

> The great Imperial problem of the future is to what extent some 350 millions of British subjects, who are aliens to us in race, religion, language, manners and customs, are to govern themselves or are to be governed by us. Rome never had to face such an issue as this.
>
> — Lord Cromer (Evelyn Baring), *Ancient and Modern Imperialism* (1910)

THE OCCUPATION OF AFRICA took place when European imperialism had long been thrown off in most parts of the world, such as the Americas, or was already under threat in others, notably India. So it was natural that the rulers of the new, hurriedly-acquired colonies felt a need to justify themselves by measuring their deeds and aims against those of earlier empires. The one nearest at hand, the Portuguese Estado da India, was clearly too inefficient to be regarded as a model. Moreover, it had been founded on principles far removed from those in favour at the start of the twentieth century: when the 'Pope's line' divided the world, Spain and Portugal saw it as their duty to conquer their respective halves for Christendom. Now imperialism was secular, the declared intent was to 'civilize', and Christian missionaries were welcome to join in that task only as long as they caused no political trouble.

When the white administrators thought about their presence in Africa and the gulf between themselves and the subject peoples, it took no time at all to see where the true model was to be found. In an age when every educated European was familiar with the classics, they had only to recall the texts of their schooldays. The Iberian powers had looked to Rome for inspiration at the end of the fifteenth century, and so did the new empire-builders – but to an earlier Rome, as revealed in the writings of Caesar, Pliny and Tacitus. The British, ruling the greatest empire of their own time, had no doubt about the historic parallels, and saw in the way their own ancestors had been subjugated by the Romans a justification of their treatment of the Africans. Sir

Arthur Hardinge, first commissioner of what would become Kenya, put it pithily: 'These people must learn submission by bullets – it's the only school; after that you may begin more modern and humane methods of education.'

British officials, taking charge of the 'lion's share' of Africa, never doubted that the spreading of their own culture justified some coercion. Their thinking echoed that of the eighteenth-century historian William Robertson, whose works were much read by the Victorian middle classes. He had said of the Romans: 'As a consolation for the loss of liberty, they communicated their arts, sciences, language and manners to their new subjects.' Furthermore, 'the intercourse between the most distant corners of the earth was rendered secure and agreeable'.

The similarities with ancient Rome were expounded in an influential book, laced with quotations in Greek and Latin, by Lord Cromer, one of Britain's imperial grandees. His keenest interest was, understandably, in the destiny of India, and he maintained that to talk of self-government there was 'absurd' – 'as if we were to advocate self-government for a united Europe'. Although reforms might be needed, they must be made within a lasting framework of British supremacy. After all, the Pax Romana had lasted for centuries. Another proconsul, Lord Curzon, described the British empire as 'under Providence, the greatest instrument for good the world has seen'. Such exalted claims were rarely ventured by lesser colonial powers, even the French, but all undoubtedly felt they would be guiding Africa's evolution far into the future.

However, the peoples of Africa had scarcely been 'brought under control', and made to accept a new dispensation of taxes, land titles and centralized power, when they saw their colonial masters at one another's throats. More than that, many Africans were being recruited to fight on opposite sides in a tropical extension of the white man's war; if they were not handed guns they were made to carry ammunition and commandeered food through the bush.

Before 1914, all that was demanded of the colonial subjects was obedience. When they started being asked for loyalty, this suddenly changed the white–black relationship. By the time peace returned, some questions were taking shape in African minds. On what grounds did the rulers demand loyalty? The borders within which the colonized peoples were confined paid no heed to traditional lands, and often cut straight across them. So should Africans not rather be loyal to themselves and unite to restore their own pride? The awe in which Europeans had been held was quickly wearing thin.

As early as the beginning of the 1920s the first hints of black national-ism were showing themselves in 'welfare societies' and 'young men's associations', led mainly by mission-educated teachers and preachers. The political tempo in India had also been influenced by the war, and the effects were soon felt across the ocean in Kenya. The 'Asiatics', as they were labelled, held nine-tenths of East Africa's retail trade in their hands by 1918, and dared to demand equal political rights with the white settlers. Although they did not identify with the Africans, but rather wanted to distance themselves from them, a political debate had been opened. Reverberations were to be felt further afield – in Tangan-yika, which became a British-run mandated territory after Germany's defeat, in Uganda, and even as far south as the Rhodesias and Nyasaland.

Indian demands in East Africa led the colonial office in London to put out a White Paper in July 1923. It laid down an historic guideline: 'Primarily, Kenya is an African territory, and His Majesty's Government think it necessary definitely to record their considered opinion that the interests of the African natives must be paramount.' That echoed remarkably a declaration by the British parliament on India ninety years earlier: 'It is recognized as an indisputable principle that the interests of the native subjects are to be consulted in preference to those of Euro-peans whenever the two come in conflict.' Behind both statements there was an inescapable logic, but in Kenya the clock was already ticking after less than three decades of British rule.

In one sense there could be no going back for the rulers, in another there was no going back for the ruled. The age-old isolation was ended, the 'hermetic seal' had been torn aside, the interior was starting to dictate to the coast. (Although the flag of Zanzibar still flew above Fort Jesus this was an empty gesture, and the day was not far distant when the last sultan would be overthrown, replaced by a descendant of slaves, and given a villa on the south coast of England to live out his days.)

European education touched only a tiny minority of Africans, yet the impact was swift and startling. A photograph taken in 1934 shows the American actor Paul Robeson, naked except for a leopard-skin round his waist, during the filming of *Sanders of the River*. Alongside him, stylishly dressed in European clothes, is a black Kenyan who had worked as an extra in the film.[1] The extra, who knew neither the date of his own birth nor his real name, because he was an orphan, called himself

Jomo Kenyatta. He was later to be imprisoned by the British for political activities, then freed to become his country's first president.

While *Sanders of the River* was being shown throughout the world (and being deeply rued by Robeson, who realized too late how it glorified the white man's role in Africa) the last major act of imperialism was taking place. On the orders of Benito Mussolini the Italians invaded Ethiopia, which forty years earlier had inflicted a humiliating defeat upon them at the battle of Adowa. Although Italy had the immediate satisfaction of taking revenge, the invasion was a watershed, intensifying black resentments: Ethiopia had been a symbol, an African country which had kept its freedom during the Scramble, but the world was now standing by while the Italians conquered it with ruthless brutality.[2]

In 1955 John Gunther's monumental *Inside Africa* appeared. Gunther was a tireless researcher and his book is a period piece, firing out facts and opinions like bird-shot. Its pages are strewn with the names of colonial governors with whom Gunther had dined on his travels, but the overall message is succinct: 'About colonialism in Africa two main things should be said, without reference to various immoralities and injustices in the system. (1) It did a great deal of good. (2) It is dying.' Gunther listed some of the reasons why white rule was already doomed, scarcely half a century after being established. 'Ethics – the pervasive feeling that it is morally wrong for one nation to rule another. After all, Africa is the African's own continent. Diminishing returns – the fact that the expense of continued repressive (or even unrepressive) rule outbalances the return. Force costs money. Christianity – the missionaries taught that all men are equal under God. Woodrow Wilson – who preached the self-determination of small nations.' Gunther added to this catalogue the domino effect of India's independence and the shaking off of European control in the Middle East. However, whatever happened to colonialism, he felt sure that the bonds between Africa and Europe were unbreakable, and as an American he regarded Africa as part of the 'global frontier' of the United States: 'Europe is stuck, so to speak, with Africa, and Africa is stuck with Europe, and America is stuck with both.'

A year after Gunther's book appeared the extent to which America was stuck with Africa and Europe became clear during the Suez crisis of October 1956. Britain, still the world's foremost imperial power, had decided to strike back when the Egyptian military leader, Gamal Abdel

Nasser, nationalized the Suez Canal Company. With France and Israel in supporting roles, Britain invaded Egypt after an aerial bombardment. In Washington this piece of latter-day gunboat diplomacy was seen as an ideological catastrophe, a gift to the Soviet Union in the developing rivalry for the sympathies of anti-colonialist movements in Asia and Africa. The United States declared its opposition to the Suez venture, then turned the financial screws on Britain, forcing it and its partners to back off, greatly humbled. Vice-president Richard Nixon proclaimed it as a US victory: 'For the first time in history, we have shown independence of Anglo-French policies towards Asia and Africa which seemed to us to reflect the colonial tradition. This declaration has had an electrifying effect throughout the world.'

The outcome of the Suez crisis was also a victory for Nasser. By having twisted the British lion's tail he became a hero for scores of countries still under colonial rule, especially those with large Muslim populations who felt a religious identity with him. The end of colonialism was already looming, but Nasser's triumph surely accelerated it. Harold Macmillan, the British prime minister brought to power in the Suez aftermath, said in 1960 in Cape Town that a 'wind of change' was blowing through Africa; he might have added that it was blowing straight from Cairo.

The early 1960s saw the demise of colonialism in Africa, as suddenly and as haphazardly as it had been imposed. Many elderly Africans who could recount how startled and alarmed they once were to see the white men arrive were equally startled, not to say alarmed, to see them going.

The two Portuguese territories, Angola and Mozambique – those relics of the Pope's division of the world in the fifteenth century and the founding of the Estado da India – defied the tide of anti-colonialism for another fifteen years. As a direct consequence these countries were to be wracked by civil wars for a generation. Bloodshed and economic pressures in turn ended white resistance in Rhodesia (which became Zimbabwe), then finally in South Africa.

Forty years after the Suez crisis, the global frontiers are strikingly changed. So is the global balance of wealth. European culture still permeates Africa, and America's financial ideology is imposed on it by the International Monetary Fund and the World Bank, yet the eastern flank of the continent, from the Red Sea to the Cape, is more and more returning to its historic relationship with Asia. Links existing before the political domination by Europe are well remembered. When the Chinese built the first great railway of African independence, 1,000 miles from Dar es Salaam to Zambia, they did not fail to mention the visits to East Africa, five centuries earlier, by ships from the fleets of Admiral Zheng He.[3]

The monsoons no longer dictate when ships can travel the Indian Ocean, yet their rhythms still pervade the lives of two billion people throughout the Indian sub-continent and from East Africa to Malaysia. The Indian Ocean is renewing its status as a 'zone of encounters and contacts' and a 'crossroads of culture'. Emphasizing this structural unity, President Nelson Mandela talked at the start of 1995 of his hopes for co-operation around the 'Indian Ocean Rim'. He recalled how Mahatma Gandhi's political career had begun in South Africa and ended with the independence of India. In September 1996, an Indian Ocean Rim Association for Regional Cooperation was created, its charter beginning with the words 'Conscious of historical bonds created through millennia . . .' A secretariat was set up in Mauritius and the founding members included India, Indonesia, Malaysia, Australia and all the littoral countries of eastern Africa, from Kenya to South Africa.

Africa will have an exacting task in merging its future with that of Asia, because of the long history of underdevelopment. Just as the continent was an enigma in the past, its interior always *terra incognita*, so it is an enigma today, its evolution impossible to predict. For many centuries tropical Africa has exchanged its unprocessed exports for manu- factured imports, so that capital has never been accumulated.[4] It is still caught in that trap; the continent is seen primarily as a supplier of raw commodities for which the East's thriving industries are hungry. The challenge of the next century for the Africans will be to escape from this subservient relationship with their Indian Ocean neighbours, to find an equal place in an arena where their main contributions were for so long limited to ivory, gold-dust, leopard-skins and slaves.

ACKNOWLEDGEMENTS

This book was inspired by Harry Logan, a retired American oilman of wide-ranging interests. We discussed it during his trips to Britain to buy paintings and pursue various philanthropic ventures. Originally I had wanted to write a biography of John Speke, the nineteenth-century traveller who 'discovered' Africa's biggest lake and named it after Queen Victoria. On Logan's last visit to London we walked on a wintry day through Kensington Gardens to look at the Speke memorial there. Soon afterwards, on the first phase of my research, I was in Uganda, staying, out of loyalty to my subject, in Kampala's Speke Hotel. There I received a telephone call to say that Logan had suddenly died of a heart attack at his home in Warren, Pennsylvania.

The scope of the book has grown immeasurably since then. Partly it is because of a sense that the 'Search for the Nile' saga has been thoroughly worn out and its central characters are now rather a bore; however, Speke still finds a place in the story, as does the painfully over-explored Richard Burton. Beyond all that, I felt Logan's memory deserved some more ambitious literary effort. The task has taken, with much travelling and many diversions, far longer than I had wished, but everyone has been remarkably tolerant. This is above all true of Kay Logan, who has maintained her late husband's interest in the project. Members of my own family remained stoical during my journeys, which included sailing down the East African coast in a dhow and hitching lifts on the backs of motorbikes in Sri Lanka.

More serene were the many weeks I spent in Nairobi, in the well-stocked library of the British Institute in Eastern Africa; John Sutton and Justin Willis, director and assistant director, were constantly helpful, as was librarian Eva Ndavu. At the University of Peradeniya, Sri Lanka, I received unstinting help from Moira Tampoe and her academic colleagues, and in the Maldives was given insights into the history of the islands by Mohammed Loutfi, director of the Male research institute. Among others who encouraged me were members of the Friends of Fort Jesus in Mombasa, the late Andrew Hall in Zanzibar, three British volunteer teachers in Kilwa who let me sleep on their floor and share their precious supply of water, and that veteran politician, Ali Muhsin Barwani, who engaged me in a spirited discussion in Dubai about Swahili ethnicity.

Without the unstinting help of Rana Kabbani, author of *Europe's Myths of the Orient*, my understanding of the Muslim world would have remained painfully inadequate. Foremost among British academics to whom I am in debt is Roy C.

Bridges, professor of history at Aberdeen University. He made many perceptive remarks, on both the finer points of my text and the broader issues. Professor Andrew Roberts, at the School of Oriental and African Studies in London, gave me the benefit of his profound knowledge of pre-colonial trade. The distinguished Cambridge archaeologist, Dr David Phillipson, sought to put me right about iron-working in Africa. Such follies as remain are mine alone. Oliver Moore, at the British Museum, offered his expertise in Chinese history and language. Michael Davie generously gave me a rare eighteenth-century translation of *The Lusiads* from which the endpapers of this book have been taken (incidentally, Vasco da Gama's outward route through the Atlantic, as drawn on the map, was total guesswork, and well off the mark). That formidable scholar, Dr G. S. P. Freeman-Grenville, tireless in his pursuit of knowledge on Indian Ocean history, has patiently answered my queries and allowed me to draw upon his translations.

Marga Holness helped with translation from the Portuguese and Marc Vogl dug invaluable material out of government archives in Washington DC. For astringent observations on early drafts I am grateful to Tony Laurence, Hester Cattley, Janet and Tony Lock, Dick Hobson and Erica Schumacher. By blend-ing constructive criticism with enthusiasm Stuart Proffitt and Arabella Quin of HarperCollins have added a lot to the quality of the final narrative; they have also been astoundingly patient.

The British libraries in which I have researched include the Bodleian, Rhodes House and the Indian Institute in Oxford, the Public Record Office and the Royal Geographical Society in London, and the National Library of Scotland in Edinburgh. In all of them I have met unfailing courtesy.

RICHARD HALL
Upton, Oxfordshire

TEXTUAL ACKNOWLEDGEMENTS

The author and publishers thank the Royal Asiatic Society for permission to print extracts from the poetry of Ibn Majid translated by G. R. Tibbetts in *Arab Navigation* (London, 1971); also for permission to quote verses from *Abbasid Belles-Lettres*, edited by Julia Ashtiany *et al* (Cambridge University Press, 1990). They acknowledge permission by George Allen and Unwin to publish lines from the *Ballad of Tun Huang*, translated by Arthur Waley.

FURTHER READING

General bibliography

Despite the example set by the French historian Fernand Braudel with his much-quoted study of the relationships binding together the Mediterranean lands,* only a few books on the same lines have yet been written about the Indian Ocean. The most notable is *Trade and Civilisation in the Indian Ocean: An Economic History from the Rise of Islam to 1750* (Cambridge, 1985) by Kirti N. Chaudhuri, who acknowledges his debt to Braudel. An earlier attempt was Auguste Toussaint's *History of the Indian Ocean* (London, 1966). A wide-ranging approach is also taken by *India and the Indian Ocean, 1500–1800* (Calcutta, 1987), edited by A. das Gupta and M. N. Pearson. Of variable quality is *The Indian Ocean Explorations in History, Commerce and Politics* (Delhi, 1987), edited by Satish Chandra. The best introduction is still *The Indian Ocean*, a medley of travelogue and history by Alan Villiers (London, 1952).

Books dealing with specific topics, but recognizing the Indian Ocean world as an entity, include: *The Portuguese Seaborne Empire 1415–1825*, by C. R. Boxer (London, 1969); *East Africa and the Orient* edited by N. Chittick and R. Rotberg (New York, 1975); *Rulers of the Indian Ocean* by G. A. Ballard (London, 1927); *Great Britain in the Indian Ocean* by G. S. Graham (Oxford, 1967); and the brief but vigorous *India and the Indian Ocean* by K. M. Panikker (London, 1945). A survey ranging far wider than its title suggests is *Arab Seafaring in the Indian Ocean* by G. F. Hourani (Princeton, 1951); an expanded edition, with notes by John Carswell on recent archaeological discoveries, appeared in 1995.

Essential for the historical and religious context is the *Encyclopaedia of Islam* (new edition, Leiden, 1960 onwards, eight volumes to date). All-embracing, if somewhat dated, is the *Encyclopaedia of Religion and Ethics* (twelve volumes, Edinburgh, 1908–26). Stimulating and refreshingly free of 'eurocentricity' is *A History of the World* by John M. Roberts (London, 1976). *Asia in the Making of Europe* by Donald F. Lach (Chicago, 1964) is an impressive synthesis. Another perspective is presented in *Asia Before Europe* by K. N. Chaudhuri (Cambridge, 1990). Discursive and full of esoteric detail is the two-volume *India and World Civilisation* by D. P. Singhal (London, 1972). Philip D. Curtin's *Cross-Cultural Trade in World History* (Cambridge, 1984) takes an economic viewpoint.

---

* Braudel, F. *The Mediterranean and the Mediterranean World in the Age of Philip II*, 2 vols (London, 1972–73).

Norman Daniels offers some new insights in *The Arabs and Mediaeval Europe* (London, 1975).

The African background, viewed in a broad context, is presented in two major works of reference, both in eight volumes: *Cambridge History of Africa* (1975–86), and UNESCO's *General History of Africa* (1981–92); the latter has exhaustive bibliographies. Briefer studies ranging over the entire continent, include: *Short History of Africa* by Roland Oliver and J. D. Fage (London, 1975) and *The African Middle Ages, 1400–1800* by R. Oliver and A. Atmore (Cambridge, 1981). Useful handbooks are Colin McEvedy's *Penguin Atlas of African History* (London, 1980) and Fage's *Atlas of African History* (London, 1978). Lucid and equipped with excellent maps is the two-volume *History of Central Africa*, edited by David Birmingham and Phyllis M. Martin (London, 1983).

Basil Davidson's books on pre-colonial culture – e.g. *Africa in History* (London, 1975) – are much-needed antidotes to prejudice. Informative well beyond its religious theme is *A History of Christianity in Africa* by Elizabeth Isichei (London, 1995); more academic in manner is *The Church in Africa* by Adrian Hastings (Oxcord, 1995).

Providing a long view of history on the African perimeter of the Indian Ocean are: John Sutton's succinct and well-illustrated *A Thousand Years of East Africa* (Nairobi/London, 1990); *The East African Coast: Select Documents* by G. S. P. Freeman-Grenville (Oxford, 1975); and *African Civilisations* by Graham Connah (London, 1987). There is a wealth of material in *Documents on the Portuguese in Mozambique and Central Africa* (Lisbon, 1962 to date, ten volumes so far). Another monumental work is: *Records of South-Eastern Africa* edited by G. M. Theal (Cape Town, 1898–1903).

For exploration and travel, the many scholarly volumes published by the Hakluyt Society, London, since the middle of the nineteenth century are an invaluable source to which the author is much indebted. Outstanding among the countless 'popular' treatments of this field is Eric Newby's superbly illustrated *World Atlas of Exploration* (London, 1975).

The lists below also note key articles in academic journals devoted to historical research on Asia, the Indian Ocean and Africa. Of primary importance are the *Journal of African History* (quoted as *JAH*), the *Geographical Journal* (*GJ*), the *Journal of the Royal Asiatic Society* (*JRAS*), *Azania*, and *Journal of the Economic and Social History of the Orient* (*JESHO*).

PART ONE: A World Apart

Many works in this list are also relevant to Parts Two and Three.

Adams, W. Y., *Nubia* (London, 1984).

Ahmad, N. 'Arabs' Knowledge of Ceylon', *Islamic Culture*, vol. 19, no. 3 (1945).

Allibert, C., Argant, A. and Argant, J. 'Le Site de Dembeni', *Etudes Océan Indien*, no. 11 (Paris, 1990).

Ardika, I. W. and Bellwood, P. 'Sembiran: the Beginnings of Indian Contact with Bali', *Antiquity*, 65 (247), (1991).

Ashtiany, J., Johnstone, T. M. et al. (eds). *Abbasid Belles-Lettres* (Cambridge, 1990).

Bancroft, J. A. *Mining in Northern Rhodesia* (London, 1961).

Burnstein, F. M. *On the Erythraean Sea* (Cambridge, 1989).

Buzurg ibn Shahriyar. *Le Livre des Merveilles de l'Inde*, ed. P. A. van der Lith, trans. L. M. Devic (Leiden, 1883–86).

——, *The Book of the Wonders of India*, trans. G. S. P. Freeman-Grenville (London, 1981).

Carpenter, A. J. 'The History of Rice in Africa' in Buddenhagen, I. W. and Persley, G. J. (eds), *Rice in Africa* (London, 1979).

Casson, L. *Ships and Seamanship in the Ancient World* (Princeton, 1971).

——, trans. *The Periplus Maris Erythraei* (Princeton, 1989).

Chaudhuri, K. N. 'A Note on Chinese Ships in Aden and Jeddah', *JRAS*, no. 1 (1989).

Chittick, N. *Kilwa, an Islamic Trading City on the East African Coast*, 2 vols (Nairobi, 1974).

——, *Manda* (Nairobi, 1984).

Choksy, J. K. 'Muslims and Zoroastrians in Iran in the Mediaeval Period', in *Muslim World*, vol. 80, no. 3/4 (1990).

Clot, A. *Harun al-Rashid*, trans. J. Howe (London, 1989).

Collins, R. O. (ed.) *Problems in African History* (New York, 1968).

Crawford, O. G. S. 'Some Medieval Theories about the Nile', *GJ*, vol. 114 (London, 1949).

Cribb, R. *Historical Dictionary of Indonesia* (London, 1992).

Das, P. K. *The Monsoons* (London, 1968).

Davison, C. and Clark, J. D. 'Trade Wind Beads', *Azania*, vol. 9 (1974).

Dawood, N. J. (ed.) *Tales from the Thousand and One Nights* (London, 1973).

Deraniyagala, P. E. P. *Some Extinct Elephants, their Relatives, and Two Living Species* (Colombo, 1955).

Deschamps, H. *Histoire de Madagascar* (Paris, 1960).

Destombes, M. *Mappemondes AD1200–1500* (Amsterdam, 1964).

Dunn, R. E. *The Adventures of Ibn Battuta* (Berkeley, 1986).

During Caspers, E. C. L. 'Further Evidence for Central Asian Materials from the Persian Gulf', *JESHO*, vol. 37, no. 1 (1994).

Duyvendak, J. J. L. 'The True Dates of the Chinese Maritime Expeditions in the Early Fifteenth Century', *T'oung Pao*, no. 34 (Leiden, 1938).

——, *China's Discovery of Africa* (London, 1949).

Edis, R. *A History of Diego Garcia*, unpublished typescript (1990).

Fagan, B. M. *Southern Africa during the Iron Age* (London, 1965).

Fage, J. D. *A History of Africa* (London, 1978).

Fei Xin. *Triumphant Tour of the Star Raft* (Beijing, 1954).

Filesi, T. *China and Africa in the Middle Ages*, trans. D. Morison (London, 1972).

Fuller, E. *Extinct Birds* (London, 1987).

Garlake, P. *Early Islamic Architecture of the East African Coast* (Oxford, 1966).

———. *The Kingdoms of Africa* (London, 1978).

———. *Great Zimbabwe* (London, 1973; Harare, 1982).

Golding, A., trans. *The Excellent and Pleasant Worke of Caius Julius Solinus*, facsimile (Gainesville, Florida, 1955).

Gray, R. and Birmingham, D. eds. *Pre-Colonial African Trade* (Oxford, 1970).

Grosset-Grange, H. 'La Côte africaine dans la routiers nautique arabes au moment des grandes découvertes', *Azania*, vol. 13 (1978).

Gunawardana, R. A. L. H. 'Seaways to Sielediba', paper for Delhi seminar on the Indian Ocean (Peradeniya, Sri Lanka, 1985).

Hall, M. *The Changing Past: Farmers, Kings and Traders in Southern Africa, 200–1860* (Cape Town, 1987).

Hall, R. *Zambia* (London, 1965).

Hamada, S. and King, N. *Ibn Battuta in Black Africa* (London, 1971).

Harrison Church, R. J. *Africa and the Islands* (London, 1971).

Hart, H. H. *Venetian Adventurer* (Stanford, 1942).

Herodotus. *Histories*, trans. A. de Selincourt (London, 1984).

Hirth, F. and Rockhill, W. W., trans. *Chau Ju-kua: His Work on the Chinese and Arab Trade in the 12th and 13th Centuries* (St Petersburg, 1911).

Hitti, P. K. *A History of the Arabs* (London, 1961).

Hodges, R. and Whitehouse, D. *Mohammed, Charlemagne and the origins of Europe* (London, 1983).

Horton, M. C. and Blurton, T. R. 'Indian Metalwork in East Africa: The Bronze Lion Statuette from Shanga', *Antiquity*, 62 (234), (1988).

Horton, M. C., Brown, H. M. and Oddy, W. A. 'The Mtambwe Hoard', *Azania*, vol. 21 (1986).

Hourani, A. *A History of the Arab Peoples* (London, 1991).

Hsiang Ta. 'A Great Chinese Navigator', *China Reconstructs*, vol. 5, no. 7 (1956).

Huntingford, G. W. B. *The Periplus of the Erythraean Sea* (London, 1980).

Ibn Battuta, *The Travels of Ibn Battuta*, ed. H. A. R. Gibb and C. F. Beckingham, 4 vols (London, 1958–94).

Ibn Hauqal. *Configuration de la Terre*, trans. J. H. Kramers and G. Wiet (Beirut, 1964).

Ibn Jubayr. *Travels of Ibn Jubayr*, trans. R. J. C. Broadhurst (London, 1952).

Ibn Khurradadhbih. *Book of Itineraries and Kingdoms*, trans. Muhammed Hadj-Sadok (Algiers, 1949).

Irwin, G. *Africans Abroad* (Columbia, 1971).

July, R. W. *PreColonial Africa* (Blandford, England, 1976).

Kimble, G. T. H. *Geography in the Middle Ages* (London, 1938).

Kirk, W. 'The North-east Monsoon and Some Aspects of African History', *JAH*, vol. 3, no. 2 (1962).

Kirkman, J. *Men and Monuments on the East African Coast* (London, 1964).

———. 'The Early History of Oman in East Africa', *Journal of Oman Studies*, vol. 2 (1983).

Kuei-sheng Chang. 'Africa and the Indian Ocean in Chinese Maps of the Fourteenth and Fifteenth Centuries', *Imago Mundi*, vol. 24 (1970).

Laufer, B. *The Giraffe in History and Art* (Chicago, 1925)

Levy, R. *The Social Structure of Islam* (Cambridge, 1957).

Lewicki, T. *Arabic External Sources for the History of Africa South of the Sahara* (London, 1974).

Lo Jung-Pang. 'The Emergence of China as a Sea Power in the Late Sung and early Yuan Periods', *Far Eastern Quarterly*, vol. 14, no. 4 (1955).

Lombard, M. *The Golden Age of Islam* (Amsterdam, 1975).

Loutfi, M. I. *Male Hukuru Miskiiy* (Male, Maldives, 1986).

McCrindle, J. W. *Ancient India as Described in Classical Literature* (London, 1901).

Ma Huan, *The Overall Survey of the Ocean's Shores*, trans. J. V. G. Mills (Cambridge, 1970).

Maggs, J. and Whitelaw, G. 'A Review of Recent Archaeological Research in Food-Producing Communities in Southern Africa', *JAH* , vol. 32, no. 1 (1991).

Major, R. H. *India in the Fifteenth Century* (London, 1857).

Martin, E. B. and C. P. *Cargoes of the East* (London, 1978).

al-Mas'udi. *Les Prairies d'Or*, ed. and trans. C. B. de Meynard and P. de Courteille, 9 vols (Paris, 1861–77).

Matveyev, V. V. *Records of Early Arab Authors on Bantu Peoples* (Moscow, 1964).

Mei-ling Hsu. 'Chinese Maritime Cartography: Sea Charts of Pre-Modern China'. *Imago Mundi*, vol. 40 (1988).

Minorsky, V., trans. *The Regions of the World: A Persian Geography* (London, 1937).

Mirsky, J. *The Great Chinese Travellers* (London, 1965).

Montgomery, J. A., trans. *The History of Yaballaha III, Nestorian Patriarch, and his Vicar Bar Sauma* (New York, 1929).

Mudenge, S. I. L. *A Political History of the Munhumutapa, c 1400–1902* (London, 1988).

Needham, J. *Science and Civilisation in China*, vol. 4, part 3 (Cambridge, 1971).

Oliver, R. A. *The African Experience* (London, 1991).

Oliver, R. A. and Mathew, G. *A History of East Africa*, vol. 1 (Oxford, 1963).

Penzer, N. M. *The Most Noble and Famous Travels of Marco Polo and Nicolo Conti* (London, 1937).

Phillipson, D. W. *African Archaeology* (London, 1985).

Polo, Marco. *The Travels of Marco Polo*, trans. L. F. Benedetto and A. Ricci (London, 1931).

——. *The Travels of Marco Polo*, trans. R. E. Latham (London, 1958).

Popovic, A. *La revolte des esclaves en Iraq au III/IX siècle* (Paris, 1976).

Ptak, R. 'China and Calicut in the Early Ming Period', *JRAS*, no. 1 (1989).

Ricks, T. C. 'Persian Gulf Seafaring and East Africa', *African Historical Studies*, vol. 3, no. 2 (Boston, 1970).

Rogers, F. M. *The Vivaldi Expedition* (Cambridge, Mass., 1955).

Sastri, K. A. N. *A History of South India* (Madras, 1976).

Schafer, E. *The Golden Peaches of Samarkand* (Berkeley, 1963).

Seale, M. S. *The Desert Bible* (London, 1974).

Sealy, J. and Yates, R. 'Pastoralism in the Cape, South Africa', *Antiquity*, vol. 68 (258) (1994).

Serjeant, R. B. *Studies in Arabian History and Civilisation* (London, 1971).

Shaw, T., Sinclair, P., Andah, B. and Okpoko, A. *Archaeology in Africa* (London, 1993).

Shboul, A. *Al-Mas'udi and his World* (London, 1979).

Shepherd, G. 'The Making of the Swahili', *Paideuma*, 28 (1982).

Snow, P. *The Star Raft: China's Encounter with Africa* (London, 1988).

Spear, T. *Kenya's Past* (London, 1981).

Steel, R. W. and Prothero, R. M. (eds.) *Geographers and the Tropics* (London, 1964).

Strong, S. A. (ed.) 'The History of Kilwa', *JRAS*, vol. 20 (1895).

Summers, R. 'Was Zimbabwe Civilised?' *Conference of the History of the Central African Peoples* (Lusaka, 1963).

Sun Guangqi. 'Zheng He's expeditions to the Western Ocean and his Navigation Technology', *Journal of Navigation*, vol. 45 (1992).

Suret-Canale, J. *Essays on African History*, trans. C. Hurst (London, 1988).

al-Tabari. *The Revolt of the Zanj*, ed. David Waines (New York, 1992).

Tampoe, M. *Maritime Trade between China and the West: An Archaeological Study of the Ceramics from Siraf* (Oxford, 1989).

Tha'alibi, *The Book of Curious and Entertaining Information*, trans. C. E. Bosworth (Edinburgh, 1968).

Thorbahn, P. F. *The Pre-Colonial Ivory Trade of East Africa*, unpublished Ph.D thesis (Cambridge, Mass., 1979).

Tolmacheva, M. 'Towards a definition of the term Zanj', *Azania*, vol. 21 (1986).

Van Grunderbeek, M.-C. 'Chronologie de l'Age du Fer Ancien au Burundi, au Rwanda et dans la région des Grands Lacs', *Azania*, vol. 27 (1992).

Verin, P. 'The African Element in Madagascar', *Azania*, vol. 11 (1976).

Verlinden, C. *The Beginnings of Modern Colonialism*, trans. Y. Freccero (New York, 1970).

Waley, A. *Ballads and Stories from Tun-Huang* (London, 1960).

Wheatley, P. 'The Land of Zanj: Exegetical Notes on Chinese Knowledge of East Africa Prior to AD1500', in Steel and Prothero (eds), op. cit.

Whitehouse, D. and Williamson, A. 'Sasanian Maritime Trade', *Iran*, vol, 11 (1973).

Wilkinson, J. C. 'Oman and East Africa: New Light on Early Kilwan History from Omani Sources', *Journal of African Historical Studies*, vol. 14, no. 2 (1981).

Wolters, O. W. *Early Indonesian Commerce* (Cornell, 1967).

Wright, H. T. et al. 'Early Seafarers in the Comoro Islands: the Dembeni Phase of the IX–X Centuries', *Azania*, vol. 19 (1984).

Wright, T. (ed.) *Early Travels in Palestine* (London, 1848).

Yajima, H. 'Maritime Activities of the Arab Gulf Peoples', *Journal of Asian and African Studies*, no. 14 (Tokyo, 1977).

——. 'Islamic History of the Maldive Islands', paper for Institute for the Study of Languages and Cultures of Asia and Africa (Tokyo, n.d.).

Yamamoto, T. 'Chinese Activities in the Indian Ocean before the Coming of the Portuguese', *Diogenes*, vol. 3 (1980).

Yule, H. *Mirabilia Descripta* (London, 1863).

——, trans. *The Book of Ser Marco Polo* (London, 1903).

Zhang Jun-Yan. 'Relations between China and the Arabs from Early Times', *Journal of Oman Studies*, vol. 2, part 1 (1983).

PART TWO: The Cannons of Christendom

Albuquerque, A. *Commentaries of Afonso de Albuquerque*, trans. W. de G. Birch, 4 vols (London, 1875–84).

Allen, J. de V. 'Habash, Habshi, Sidi, Sayyid', in J. C. Stone (ed.), *Africa and the Sea* (Aberdeen, 1985).

Alpers, E. A. 'Gujarat and the Trade of East Africa', *African Historical Studies*, vol. 9 (Boston, 1976).

Alvares, F. *The Prester John of the Indies*, trans. C. F. Beckingham and G. W. B. Huntingford, 2 vols (Cambridge, 1961).

Andrade, R. F. *Commentaries*, ed. C. R. Boxer (London, 1930).

Axelson, E. *Portuguese in South-East Africa, 1488–1600 (Cape Town, 1963)*.

——, *Portuguese in South-East Africa, 1600–1700* (Johannesburg, 1960.

Ayalon, D. *Gunpowder and Firearms in the Mamluk Kingdom* (London, 1956).

Ayyar, K. V. K. *A Short History of Kerala* (Ernakulam, 1966).

Bagrow, L. 'Ibn Majid', *Studi Columbiani*, vol. 3 (Genoa, 1950).

Bannerman, D. A. *The Canary Islands* (London, 1922).

Beckingham, C. F. 'The Travels of Pero da Covilham and their Significance', *Congresso International de Historia dos Descobrimentos* (Lisbon, 1961).

Bell, A. F. G. *Gaspar Correa* (Oxford, 1924).

Bhattacharya, D. K. 'Indians of African Origin', *Cahiers d'etudes Africaines*, vol. 40 (1970).

Boxer, C. R. *Macau na Epoca da Restauracao* (Macau, 1942).

——. 'An African Eldorado: Monomotapa and Mozambique', *Journal of Historical Association of Rhodesia and Nyasaland*. (1960).

——. *From Lisbon to Goa, 1500–1750* (London, 1984).

Boxer, C. R. and De Azevedo, C. *The Portuguese in Mombasa* (London, 1960).

Budge, W. *A History of Ethiopia* (London, 1928).

Burwash, D. *English Merchant Shipping, 1450–1540* (Toronto, 1947).

Camoëns, Luis de. *The Lusiads*, trans. W. J. Mickle (Oxford, 1778).

Caraman, P. *The Lost Empire* (London, 1985).

Careri, J. F. G. *The Indian Travels of Thevenot and Careri*, trans. S. N. Sen (Delhi, 1949).

Castanheda, H. L. de. *History*, Bk. 1. trans. into English, 1582 (facsimile, Amsterdam, 1973).

Cipolla, C. M. *Guns and Sails in the Early Phase of European Expansion 1400–1700* (London, 1965).

Commissariat, M. S. *History of Gujarat* (Bombay, 1938).

Correa, G. *The Three Voyages of Vasco da Gama*, trans. H. E. J. Stanley from 'Lendas da India' (London, 1869).

Cortesano, A. *The Mystery of Vasco da Gama* (Lisbon, 1973).

Cowburn, P. *The Warship in World History* (London, 1965).

Crawford, O. G. S. *Ethiopian Itineraries, ca. 1400–1524* (Cambridge, 1958).

Crone, G. R. *The Voyages of Cadamosto* (London, 1937).

Curzon, Lord. *Persia and the Persian Question* (London, 1892).

Dames, M. L. 'The Portuguese and Turks in the Indian Ocean in the Sixteenth Century', *JRAS* (1923).

Danvers, F. C. *The Portuguese in India* (London, 1894).

Deschamps, H. *Les Pirates à Madagascar* (Paris, 1949).

Diffie, B. W. and Winius, G. D. *Foundations of the Portuguese Empire, 1415–1580* (Minneapolis, 1977).

Al-Din, Z. *Historia dos Portugueses no Malabar*, trans. D. Lopes (Lisbon, 1898).

Doresse, J. *Ethiopia*, trans. E. Coult (London, 1959).

Duffy, J. *Portugal in Africa* (London, 1962).

Earle, T. F. and Villiers, J. *Albuquerque, Caesar of the East* (Warminster, England, 1990).

Freeman-Grenville, G. S. P. (ed.) *The Mombasa Rising against the Portuguese, 1631* (Oxford, 1980).

Fritz, J. and Michell, G. 'The Perfect City', *Geographical Magazine*, vol. 71/2 (1994).

Goodrich, T. D. *The Ottoman Turks and the New World* (Wiesbaden, 1990).

Grandidier, A. et al. *Collection des Ouvrages anciens concernant Madagascar* (Paris, 1905).

Gray, J. 'Visit of a French ship to Kilwa in 1527', *Tanganyika Notes and Records*, no. 63 (1964).

Gray, R. 'Portuguese Musketeers on the Zambezi', *JAH*, vol. 12 (1971).

Greenblatt, S. *Marvellous Possessions* (Oxford, 1991).

Greenlee, W. B., trans. *The Voyage of Pedro Alvares Cabral to Brazil and India* (London, 1938).

Grey, C. *Pirates of the Eastern Seas* (London, 1934).

Hakluyt, R. (ed.) *The Principal Navigations, Voyages, Traffiques and Discoveries of the English Nation* (facsimile, Glasgow, 1906).

Hamond, W. *A Paradox, prooving that the inhabitants of Madagascar . . . are the happiest people in the world . . .* (London, 1640).

Harley, J. B. *Maps and the Columbian Encounter* (Wisconsin, 1990).

Huffman, T. N. 'The Rise and Fall of Zimbabwe', *JAH*, vol. 13 (1972).

Israel, J. I. *Dutch Primacy in World Trade, 1585–1740* (Oxford, 1989).

——. *The Dutch Republic* (Oxford, 1995).

Jahangir. *Memoirs of the Emperor Jahangir*, trans. D. Price (Calcutta, 1972).

Jayne, K. G. *Vasco da Gama and his Successors* (London, 1910).

Kimble, G. H. T. 'Portuguese Policy and its Influence on Fifteenth-century Cartography', *Geographical Review*, vol. 23 (New York, 1933).

——. 'The Ne Plus Ultra of the West African Coast', *Mariners' Mirror*, vol. 20 (1934).

Kindersley, J. *Letters from the Island of Teneriffe, Brazil, the Cape of Good Hope and the East Indies* (London, 1777).

Kirkman, J. *Fort Jesus* (Oxford, 1974).

Letts, M., trans. *Pero Tafur: Travels and Adventures* (London, 1926).

Lewis, A. 'Maritime Skills in the Indian Ocean', *JESHO*, vol. 16 (1973).

Lewis, J. P. 'Slave Traffic under the Dutch East India Company', *Ceylon Antiquary and Literary Register*, vol. 9 (1923).

Linschoten, J. van. *Voyage to the East Indies*, ed. A. C. Burnell and P. A. Tiele (London, 1885).

Livermore, H. V. *A History of Portugal* (London, 1947).

Livi-Bacci, M. *Population and Nutrition* (Cambridge, 1991).

Lobo, J. *Itinerario*, trans. D. Lockhart (Cambridge, 1983).

Lombard, D. and Aubin, J. (eds). *Marchands et hommes d'affaires asiatiques dans l'Océan Indian et la Mer de Chine, 13e–20e siècles* (Paris, 1988).

McKenna, J. B. *A Spaniard in the Portuguese Indies* (Cambridge, Mass., 1967).

McNeill, W. H. *The Rise of the West* (Chicago, 1967).

Major, R. H. *Select Letters of Christopher Columbus* (London, 1847).

Manrique, S. *Travels, 1629–1643*, trans. C. E. Luard (London, 1927).

Menon, A. S. *Social and Cultural History of Kerala* (New Delhi, 1979).

Mentzel, O. F. *Life at the Cape in the Mid-Eighteenth Century*, trans. M. Greenlees (Cape Town, 1919).

Mocquet, J. *Travels and Voyages*, trans. N. Pullen (London, 1696).

Nambier, O. K. *The Kunjalis, Admirals of Calicut* (London, 1963).

Newitt, M. D. D. *Portuguese Settlement on the Zambesi* (London, 1973).

——. 'Prince Henry and Portuguese Imperialism', *Journal of the Historical Association of Rhodesia and Nyasaland* (1963).

Nothnagle, J. 'Two Early French Voyages to Sumatra', *Sixteenth Century Journal*, vol. 19 (1988).

Nowell, C. E. *A History of Portugal* (New York, 1952).

Osbaran, S. 'The Ottoman Turks and the Portuguese in the Indian Ocean, 1534–1581', *Journal of Asian History*, vol. 6 (Wiesbaden, 1972).

Pacheco, D. *Esmeraldo in Situ Orbis*, trans. G. H. T. Kimble (London, 1937).

Pacifici, S. J. (ed.) *Copy of a Letter of the King of Portugal, sent to the King of Castile, Concerning the Voyage and Success of India* (Minneapolis, 1955).

Pack, S. W. C. (ed.) *Anson's Voyage Round the World* (London, 1947).

Padfield, P. *Guns at Sea* (London, 1973).

Panikker, K. M. *Malabar and the Portuguese* (Bombay, 1929).

——. *Asia and Western Dominance* (London, 1953).

Parry, J. H. *The Discovery of the Sea* (London, 1975).

Pearson, N. M. 'The Portuguese in India', *New Cambridge History of India*, vol. 1 (Cambridge, 1987).

——. *Merchants and Rulers in Gujarat* (Berkeley, 1976).

Pennington, L. E. *Hakluytus Posthumus: Samuel Purchas and the Promotion of English Oversea Expansion* (Emporia, Kansas, 1966).

Penrose, B. *Travel and Discovery in the Renaissance* (Cambridge, Mass., 1955).

Pescatello, A. M. 'The African Presence in Portuguese India', *Journal of Asian History*, vol. 11 (1977).

Pieris, P. E. *Some Documents Relating to the Rise of the Dutch Power in Ceylon* (Colombo, 1929).

Pitcher, D. *The Ottoman Empire* (Leiden, 1972).

Prasad, R. C. *Early English Travellers in India* (Delhi, 1980).

Prestage, E. *The Portuguese Pioneers* (London, 1933).

Purchas, S. *Hakluytus Posthumus or Purchas his Pilgrimes* (facsimile, Glasgow, 1905).

Qaisar, A. J. *The Indian Response to European Technology and Culture, 1498–1707* (Delhi, 1982).

Ramanathan, P. 'The Ethnology of the "Moors" of Ceylon', *JRAS*, vol. 10 (Sri Lanka, 1988).

Randles, W. G. L. *The Empire of Monomotapa*, trans. R. S. Roberts (Gwelo, 1981).

Ranger, T. O. (ed.) *Aspects of Central African History* (London, 1968).

Raven Hart, R. *Before Van Riebeeck* (Cape Town, 1967).

Ravenstein, E. G. (ed.) *A Journal of the First Voyage of Vasco da Gama* (London, 1899).

Read, J. *The Moors in Spain and Portugal* (London, 1974).

Rey, C. F. *The Romance of the Portuguese in Abyssinia* (London, 1929).

Reynolds, C. G. *Command of the Sea* (New York, 1974).

Roberts, A. *A History of Zambia* (London, 1976).

——. 'Pre-Colonial Trade in Zambia', *African Social Research*, vol. 10 (1970).

Robertson, W. *An Historical Disquisition Concerning the Knowledge the Ancients Had of India* (Edinburgh, 1791).

——. *Complete Works* (London, 1826).

Rogers, F. M. *The Travels of the Infante Dom Pedro of Portugal* (Minneapolis, 1961).

——. *The Quest for Eastern Christians* (Minneapolis, 1962).

Rosenthal, F. 'A Fourteenth Century Report on Ethiopia', *Ethiopian Studies* (Wiesbaden, 1983).

Rossed, R. 'The Dutch on the Swahili Coast, 1776–1778', *International Journal of African Historical Studies*, nos. 2/3 (1986).

Runciman, S. *The Fall of Constantinople 1453* (Cambridge, 1965).

Russell, P. E. *Prince Henry* (London, 1960).

——. *Prince Henry the Navigator: The Rise and Fall of a Cult Hero* (Oxford, 1984).

Sanceau, E. *Portugal in Quest of Prester John* (London, 1943).

——. *The Perfect Prince* (Lisbon, 1959).

Santos, J. dos. *A History of Eastern Ethiopia*, trans. in Pinkerton's Voyages (London, 1814).

Sassoon, C. *Chinese Porcelain in Fort Jesus* (Mombasa, 1975).

Saunders, A. C. de C. M. *A Social History of Black Slaves and Freedmen in Portugal, 1441–1555* (Cambridge, 1982).

Schoffeleers, M. 'The Zimba and the Lunda State in the late Sixteenth and Early Seventeenth Century'. *JAH*, vol. 28 (1987).

Schurhammer, G. *Francis Xavier* (Rome, 1973–82).

Serjeant, R. J. *The Portuguese off the South Arabian Coast* (Oxford, 1963).

Sewell, R. *A Forgotten Empire* (London, 1924).

Silva, C. R. de, *Portuguese in Ceylon* (Colombo, 1972).

Silva Rego, A. da. *Portuguese Colonisation in the Sixteenth Century* (Johannesburg, 1959).

Slessarev, V. *Prester John, the Letter and the Legend* (Minneapolis, 1959).

Stavorinus, J. S. *Voyages to the East Indies*, trans. S. H. Wilcocke (London, 1798).

Steensgard, N. *Carracks, Caravans and Companies* (Copenhagen, 1973).

Strandes, J. *The Portuguese Period in East Africa*, trans. J. F. Wallwork (Nairobi, 1961).

Taylor, E. G. R. 'The Early Navigators', *GJ* vol. 113 (1949).

Tibbetts, G. R. *Arab Navigation in the Indian Ocean before the Coming of the Portuguese* (London, 1971).

Trend, J. B. *Portugal* (London, 1957).

Ullendorf, E. and Beckingham, C. F. *Hebrew Letters of Prester John* (Oxford, 1982).

Ure, J. *Prince Henry the Navigator* (London, 1977).

Valentijn, F. *Description of Ceylon*, trans. Sinnappah Arasaratnam (London, 1978).

Van Duyn, J. *The Age of Sail* (New York, 1968).

Vansina, J. 'Long-distance trade routes in Central Africa', *JAH*, vol. 3 (1962).

Varthema, L. *Travels*, trans. J. W. Jones (London, 1863).

Weinstein, D. *Ambassador from Venice* (Minneapolis, 1960).

Whiteway, R. S. *The Rise of Portuguese Power in India* (London, 1899).

Wijisekera, N. D. *The People of Ceylon* (Colombo, 1949).

PART THREE: An Enforced Tutelage

Alder, G. J. 'Britain and the Defence of India – the Origins of the Problem, 1798–1815', *Journal of Asian History*, vol. 6 (1972).

Anon. *A Narrative of Events which have recently occurred in the Island of Ceylon, by a Gentleman on the Spot* (London, 1815).

Anstey, R. T. 'A Critique of "Capitalism and Slavery" by Robert Williams', *Economic History Review*, vol. 21 (1968).

Banaji, D. R. *Slavery in British India* (Bombay, 1933).

Beachey, R. W. *The Slave Trade of Eastern Africa* (London, 1976).

———. *Documents on the Slave Trade of Eastern Africa* (London, 1976).

Becker, J. *La Vie en Afrique*, 3 vols (Brussels, 1887).

Bennett, N. R. (ed.) *Stanley's Despatches to the New York Herald*. (Boston, 1970).

———. *Mirambo of Tanzania* (New York, 1971).

———. 'Phillippe Bryon', *African Affairs*, no. 62 (1963).

Bridges, R. C. 'The Historical Role of British Explorers in East Africa', *Terrae Incognitae*, no. 14 (1982).

———. 'Nineteenth-century East African Travel Records', *Paideuma*, no. 33 (1977).

———. 'James Augustus Grant's Visual Record of East Africa', Annual lecture to the Hakluyt Society (1993).

Brode, H. *Tippoo Tib* (London, 1907).

Burton, R. F. *Sindh, and the Races that Inhabit the Valley of the Indus* (London, 1851).

——. *The Lake Regions of Central Africa*, 2 vols (London, 1860).

——. *Zanzibar, City, Island and Coast* (London, 1872).

——. *The Lands of Cazembe* (London, 1873).

Clarence-Smith, W. G. *The Economics of the Indian Ocean Slave Trade in the Nineteenth Century* (London, 1989).

Cleghorn, H. *Gleghorn Papers – a Footnote to History*, ed. W. Neil (London, 1927).

Colley, L. *Britons* (London, 1992).

Coupland, R. *The Exploitation of East Africa 1856–1890* (London, 1939).

——. *East Africa and its Invaders* (Oxford, 1938).

Cunnison, I. G. 'Kazembe and the Arabs to 1870', *Conference of the History of the Central African Peoples* (Lusaka, 1963).

Davis, D. B. *Slavery and Human Progress* (Oxford, 1984).

Denham, E. B. *Ceylon Census Returns of 1911* (Colombo, 1912).

Duder, C. J. '"Men of the Officer Class": The Participants in the 1919 Soldier Settlement Scheme in Kenya', *African Affairs*, vol. 92/366 (1993).

Edwardes, S. M. *The Rise of Bombay* (Bombay, 1902).

Farrant, L. *Tippu Tip* (London, 1975).

Forrest, G. W. ed. *Travels and Journals Preserved in the Bombay Secretariat* (Bombay, 1906).

Freeman-Grenville, G. S. P. *The French at Kilwa Island* (Oxford, 1965).

Freund, B. *The Making of Contemporary Africa* (London, 1984).

Galbraith, J. S. *Mackinnon and East Africa 1878–1895* (Cambridge, 1972).

Gangulee, N. *Indians in the Empire Overseas* (London, 1947).

Gifford, P. and Louis, W. R. (eds.) *Britain and France in Africa* (New Haven, 1971).

Gillman, C. 'Dar es Salaam, 1860 to 1940', *Tanganyika Notes and Records*, no. 20 (1945).

Grant, J. A. *A Walk across Africa* (London, 1864).

Gray, J. A. *The British in Mombasa* (London, 1957).

——. *History of Zanzibar from the Middle Ages to 1856* (London, 1962).

Gregory, R. C. *India and East Africa, 1890–1939* (Oxford, 1971).

Guillain, C. *Documents sur l'histoire, la géographie et le commerce de l'Afrique orientale*, 3 vols (Paris, 1856).

Haight, M. V. J. *European Powers and South East Africa* (London, 1967).

Hall, R. *Stanley, an Adventurer Explored* (London, 1974).

Harman, N. *Bwana Stokesi and his African Conquests* (London, 1986).

Hazaresingh, K. *A History of Indians in Mauritius* (Port Louis, 1950).

Hore, E. C. *Eleven Years in Central Africa* (London, 1892).

Johnston, H. H. *The Nile Quest* (London, 1903).

Jones, M. K. *The Slave Trade at Mauritius, 1810–1829*, unpublished thesis (Oxford, 1936).

Krapf, J. L. *Travels, Researches and Missionary Labours in Eastern Africa* (London, 1860).

Langworthy, H. W. *Zambia Before 1890* (London, 1972).

Livingstone, D. *Missionary Travels and Researches in South Africa* (London, 1857).

Louis, W. R. *Ruanda-Urundi* (Oxford, 1963).

——. 'The Stokes Affair and the Origins of the Anti-Congo Campaign, 1895–1896', *Revue belge du philologie et d'histoire* (Bruxelles, 1965).

Low, C. R. *History of the Indian Navy* (London, 1877).

Lugard, F. D. *The Rise of our East African Empire*, 2 vols (Edinburgh, 1893).

——. *Diaries*, ed. M. Perham and M. Bull, 3 vols (London, 1959).

Macmillan, W. M. *Africa Emergent* (London, 1949).

Maitland, A. *Speke* (London, 1971).

Martin, E. B. and Ryan, T. C. I. 'A Quantative Assessment of the Arab Slave Trade of East Africa', *Kenya Historical Review*, vol. 5, no. 1 (1977).

Mills, L. *Ceylon under British Rule, 1795–1932* (Oxford, 1933).

Nicholls, C. S. *The Swahili Coast* (London, 1971).

Oliver, R. *The Missionary Factor in East Africa* (London, 1965).

Owen, W. F. *Narrative of Voyages to Explore the Shores of Africa, Arabia and Madagascar*, 2 vols (London, 1833).

Palmerston, Lord. 'Letters to Laurence Sulivan, 1804–1863', *Royal Historical Society* (London, 1979).

Pearce, F. B. *Zanzibar, the Island Metropolis of East Africa* (London, 1920).

Perham, M. *Lugard: the Years of Adventure, 1858–1898* (London, 1956).

——. *The Colonial Reckoning* (London, 1961).

—— and Simmons, J. *African Discovery* (London, 1961).

Pieris, P. E. *Sinhalé and the Patriots* (Colombo, 1950).

Pouwels, R. L. *Horn and Crescent* (Cambridge, 1987).

Prior, J. *Voyage along the Eastern Coast of Africa in the Nisus Frigate* (London, 1819).

Ritchie, L. *The British World in the East* (London, 1847).

Robinson, R., Gallagher, J. with Denny, A. *Africa and the Victorians* (London, 1961).

Sheriff, A. *Slaves, Spices and Ivory in Zanzibar* (London, 1987).

Smith, I. R. *The Emin Pasha Relief Expedition* (Oxford, 1972).

Speke, J. H. *Journal of the Discovery of the Source of the Nile* (Edinburgh, 1863).

Stanley, H. M. *Through the Dark Continent*, 2 vols (London, 1879).

——. *The Congo and the Founding of its Free State*, 2 vols (London, 1885).

——. *In Darkest Africa*, 2 vols (London, 1890).

Stengers, J. 'Leopold II et la fixation des frontières du Congo', *Le Flambeau*, nos. 3–4 (Bruxelles, 1963).

——. 'La première de reprise du Congo par la Belgique', *Bulletin de la Société Royal Belge de Géographie* (Bruxelles, 1949).

Stoecker, H. *German Imperialism in Africa* (London, 1986).

Swann, A. J. *Fighting the Slave Hunters in Central Africa* (London, 1910).

Thomson, J. *Through Masailand* (London, 1885).

Tippu Tip. *Maisha ya Hamed bin Muhammed el Murjebi yaani Tippu Tip*, trans. W. H. Whitely (Nairobi, 1971).

Tylden, G. 'The Gun Trade in Central and Southern Africa', *Northern Rhodesia Journal*, vol. 2, no. 1 (1953).

Wilkinson, T. *Two Monsoons* (London, 1987).

COMMENTARY

These notes provide general background to the text. Authors and books referred to without publication details will be found in the bibliography.

FOREWORD

1. An imaginary line from Cape Town to Perth in Australia may be regarded at the southern limit of the Indian Ocean, although Alan Villiers in *The Indian Ocean* would extend it to Antarctica.

2. Early contacts between Europe and the East are surveyed in *Rome and India: the Ancient Sea Trade*, ed. Vimala Begley and Richard D. De Puma (Madison, Wisconsin, 1991); also in ch. I of George Hourani's *Arab Seafaring in the Indian Ocean*. Trajan's yearning to go to India is described by Dio Cassius; *Dio's Roman History*, trans. Earnest Cary, book 68 (London, 1955).

3. The geographer Al-Biruni, writing in the eleventh century, observed that in parts of India 'it rains continuously for four months as though water-buckets were poured out'. Steve McCurry's *Monsoon* (London, 1995) depicts Indian life before and after the annual deluge.

4. John Ray wrote (1691) *The Wisdom of God manifested in the Works of the Creation*. A biography, *John Ray*, is by Charles Raven (Cambridge, 1950).

5. Hippalus, a Greek mariner of the 1st century BC, is credited with discovering how to sail on the south-west monsoon directly from the Red Sea to southern India.

6. Relics of this trade include an erotic Indian ivory statuette, of the goddess Lakshmi, unearthed at Pompeii, and a Greek statuette of (appropriately) the sea-god Poseidon, found at Kolhapur in western India. Hoards of Roman coins have been found in many parts of India.

PART ONE

CHAPTER I Wonders of India, Treasures of China

1. On the site of Siraf there is now only an Iranian fishing village. The city was shattered by an earthquake in AD977, and fell into decline soon after.

2. For 'Charlemagne's elephant' see *Mohammed, Charlemagne, and the origins of Europe*, by R. Hodges and D. Whitehouse; also *The Reign of Charlemagne*, by H. R. Loyn and J. Percival (London, 1975).

3. It was customary during stormy voyages for merchants to solicit divine mercy by pledging donations for holy places. If port were safely reached these pledges were collected by the captain.

4. The ships of the western Indian Ocean, with their triangular lateen sails, could sail 'close to the wind', but were dangerous when 'going about' (changing tack) in rough weather. The heavy yard had to be raised upright and moved to the other side of the mast. Small inshore boats used on the East African coast were called *mtepe*; their prows were said to represent Mohammed's favourite camel.

5. Muslims continued to use the name China, derived from the Chin dynasty (221BC–AD618), although it was virtually forgotten in Europe for centuries.

6. Readers of Buzurg's story of Ishaq would have known well that merchants commonly bribed local rulers to avoid customs dues.

7. Zoroastrian beliefs were 'preserved in Iran under a thin cover of Muhammadism' (A. S. Carnoy in *Encyclopaedia of Religion and Ethics*, vol XII).

CHAPTER 2   Lure of the African Shore

1. Dates from the Persian Gulf were often carried as ballast on voyages to the East African coast for sale on arrival.

2. Beyond the Zambezi delta and Sofala the monsoon wind peters out. Any ship venturing south of the Tropic of Capricorn would have to struggle back against the southward-flowing Agulhas current.

3. For the value of black slaves in the Mediterranean: *The Moors in Spain and Portugal*, by J. Read (London, 1974).

4. In the Old Testament's Song of Solomon the verse beginning 'I am black, but comely, O ye daughters of Jerusalem . . .' probably derives from the poetry of the pre-Islamic desert peoples, whose camels were tended by slaves. A renowned Arab poet, Antar ibn Shaddad, had an Ethiopian mother. Most Baghdad caliphs were the children of concubines, only three having mothers who were 'free women': *The Forgotten Queens of Islam* by Fatima Mernissi (London, 1993).

5. In a typical legend of cannibalism a Zanj queen takes a prisoner to her underground dwelling: 'If she discovers in him strength and mastery in coition, she spares him, cares for him and feeds him with the kind of fish which increases sexual power. She continues to avail herself of his services until he grows weak and tired, and when he becomes impotent she kills and eats him.' (Sharaf al-Zaman Tahir Marvizi, *China, the Turks and India*, trans. and ed. V. Minorsky. London, 1942.)

6. The fullest account of the Zanj uprisings is to be found in Alexandre Popovic's *La Révolte des Esclaves en Iraq.*

CHAPTER 3   The Mystery of the Waqwaqs

1. Some Indonesian groups may have migrated to Madagascar to escape the Indian colonization of Sumatra in the seventh century. See *Africa and the Islands*, by R. J. Harrison Church.

2. Bas-reliefs in the Borobodur temple in Java (circa AD800) show a large ocean-going vessel with tripod mast and outriggers.

3. An African rice, *Oryza glaberrima*, was being cultivated before the Waqwaqs introduced the superior Asian variety, *Oryza sativa.*

4. The identification of the original Malagasy language with Old Javanese was made by Dr C. C. Berg, professor of austronesian linguistics at Leiden university. The Indonesian connection was recognized by early European travellers: in 1603 the Dutch compiled a Malagasy–Malay dictionary, and in 1708 a dissertation on the subject was written by Adrien Reland.

5. The Waqwaqs may have introduced to Africa the coconut palm as well as various garden crops. The Malagasy use of Swahili words for domestic animals – dog, donkey, chicken, cat, goat, sheep – suggests that these were brought to the island by the first inhabitants after a halt in East Africa.

6. The theory of A. M. Jones that the widespread use in West Africa of the xylophone resulted from Indonesian voyages into the Atlantic – *Africa and Indonesia: the evidence of the xylophone and other musical and cultural factors* (Leiden, 1964) – is romantic but improbable.

CHAPTER 4   Islam Rules the Land of Zanj

1. For a thousand years, Arabs settling in East Africa had taken local wives, by agreement or force. Women captured in war were treated as booty.

2. East Africa developed closer ties with Aden and the Red Sea after the end of the first Christian millennium. By that time Egypt had replaced Iraq as the centre of Islamic power.

3. Some gold coins used by coastal traders as far south as Madagascar were the currency of the Fatimids (Ismailis), who ruled Egypt, Sicily and North Africa in the eleventh century. Despite the use of copper coins in the coastal settlements, cowries remained popular inland as currency.

4. The bronze lion statuette, 61mm high, of a type found in Indian shrines, was unearthed at Shanga, in a level dating to AD1100. It may have been cast in East Africa. (M. Horton and T. R. Blurton: 'Indian Metalwork in East Africa'.)

5. For ethnic evolution in East Africa see John Middleton's *The World of the Swahili* (Yale, 1992).

6. Al-Mas'udi describes the waves off the Zanj coast (presumably at the height of the *kaws* monsoon) as 'tall as mountains'. There were 'blind waves' and 'mad waves', with no foam on them and no crests.

7. The geographer al-Idrisi, living in Sicily and writing from hearsay, asserted that the wizards of Malindi could make the most poisonous snakes harmless to everyone 'except those for whom they wish evil, or on whom they wish to take vengeance'.

CHAPTER 5   On the Silk Route to Cathay

1. Rabbi Benjamin's memoirs were first printed in Constantinople in 1543. His warmth towards Islam illustrates the profound change in relationships between the 'prophetic' religions since his day.

2. Benjamin's account of the capture of Africans by enticing them with sweetmeats is to be found in many other sources; e.g. Sharaf al-Zaman Tahir Marvizi (*op. cit.*).

3. The accepted rendering of Marco's narrative is a synthesis of conflicting versions in several languages. A popular English printed text, published in 1527, was translated from a Spanish version of an inaccurate Venetian rendering of the Old French manuscript.

4. In 1238 the people of Friesland were so afraid of meeting Mongols that they dared not travel to England to buy herrings, according to W. Rockhill in his translation of William of Rubrouck's *Itinerarium* (London, 1900).

5. Although the Indian Ocean style of ship-building came as a surprise to Marco, the sixth-century Byzantine historian

Procopius had commented upon the sewn boats 'bound together by a kind of cording'. (*Procopius*, trans. H. B. Dewing, Cambridge, Mass. 1914.)

CHAPTER 6   A Princess for King Arghon

1. Despite occasional suggestions that Marco never went to China, his account has a strong flavour of authenticity. R. E. Latham comments: 'In no previous Western writer since Strabo, thirteen centuries before, and in none again for at least another two centuries, do we find anything remotely comparable with Polo's panorama of the nations.'

2. The trust which Marco Polo everywhere encountered among Asian merchants is confirmed by the twelfth-century traveller Ibn Jubayr, describing a journey from the Red Sea to Cairo: 'A curious circumstance . . . in the desert is that you will discover loads of pepper, cinnamon and the like thrown unguarded by the side of the road. They are left on the roads like this through the sickness of the camels that bear them . . . and they remain thus . . . secure from all risk despite the number of men of all kinds who pass beside them.'

3. Quoted in R. A. L. H. Gunawardana's 'Seaways to Sielediba'.

4. Nestorian Christianity was at the height of its power in Rabban Bar Sauma's time, with adherents throughout Asia. The sect survived with ever-declining numbers until the 1914–18 war, when about 40,000 Nestorians were hounded as refugees across northern Iraq. The survivors merged with a Christian community in Syria – where a truncated version of Sauma's story was discovered.

CHAPTER 7   The Wandering Sheikh goes South

1. For slavery on the eastern Mediterranean islands: Charles Verlinden's *The Beginnings of Modern Colonialism.*

2. Ibn Battuta's stay in Mecca was brief, by the standards of some scholars. In south India he was to meet a Somali jurist who had studied in Mecca for fourteen years,

for a similar time in Medina – and had also made a journey to China.

3. When Ibn Battuta visited the Land of Zanj there were at least a hundred Islamic settlements along the coast. Only a few, such as Malindi, Mombasa, Zanzibar and Kilwa, were ports of call for ocean-going ships. The others were served by coastal vessels.

4. Kilwa had been a thriving city for several centuries before Ibn Battuta's arrival. His failure to recall its great mosque, perhaps built by Indian craftsmen, may be attributed to his lifetime of visiting places of worship.

5. Sutton's *A Thousand Years of East Africa* has an axonometric reconstruction of the Husuni Kubwa palace; the adjoining Husuni Ndogo building was probably a barracoon for slaves.

CHAPTER 8   Adventures in India and China

1. Ibn Battuta reached Delhi overland from the Persian Gulf, but many of the places he visited before reaching India cannot now be identified.

2. From Delhi the nearest Indian Ocean port was Cambay, 300 miles to the south-west.

3. Muslim merchants from Arabia and Egypt were already becoming the power behind the Zamorin's throne.

4. The Jews of Malabar were said by Rabbi Benjamin of Tudela to be few in number, and black.

5. The Maldives' population, about 200,000 in Ibn Battuta's time, relied heavily upon the cowrie industry, controlled by the sultan. In the fourteenth century, Maldivian cowries were already reaching West Africa via the Levant. Their 'Braudelian' significance is discussed by James Heimann: 'Small Change and Ballast: Cowrie trade as an example of Indian Ocean economic history', in *South Asia*, January 1980.

6. Ibn Battuta's cursory account of China has led some commentators to imply – as with Marco Polo – that he never reached there. Yet personal incidents he

describes have the ring of truth, as when he has heart tremors after watching a Chinese conjuror and has to be given a stimulant. A friend tells him not to be afraid: 'By God, there was no climbing up or down or cutting off of limbs. It is all conjuring.'

7. The Black Death (bubonic plague) killed 40m people – more than a third of Europe's population – in the second half of the fourteenth century. It was brought to the Mediterranean when Genoese ships from the Black Sea unloaded in southern Italy.

8. Many Arabs had settled in West Africa. A famous poet from Granada, Abu Ishaq al-Sahili, was buried in Timbuktu. The walled city of Marrakesh, where Ibn Battuta died, lay on the caravan route to Mali, but also had architecture identical with that in southern Spain.

CHAPTER 9   Armadas of the Three-Jewel Eunuch

1. Apart from porcelain, used as ballast, the main trade good carried to the Indian Ocean by Zheng He's fleets was silk. Much of this found its way to Venice and other Mediterranean cities.

2. A rudder from one of Zheng He's ships was discovered in 1962 near Nanjing. It is 20ft tall and the rudder post 36ft (Joseph Needham's *Science and Civilisation in China*).

3. The average speed of the great fleets was slightly over six knots. The Chinese measurement of distance, a *li*, originally equal to a quarter of a mile, had been standardized by the fifteenth century at approximately two-fifths of a mile.

4. The writer Fei Xin, who described one of the Indian Ocean journeys, had been drafted into military service to expiate the sin of a father or grandfather. Fei Xin went to East Africa, and dismissed Somalia as 'desolation'.

5. Needham suggests that some Chinese vessels were probably sent on exploratory voyages beyond the Cape of Good Hope.

CHAPTER 10　Ma Huan and the House of God

1. Chinese legends about the *qilin* date back to 2700BC.
2. The unicorn was mentioned in 400BC by the Greek historian Ctesias as having blue eyes and a purple head. Strabo said of the 'camel-leopard' that it was not a wild beast, 'but rather a domestic animal, for it shows no sign of wildness'.
3. Beybars, founder of Mamluke rule in Egypt, reputedly sent more than a thousand Nubian giraffes as a gift to the 'Khan of the Golden Horde' in 1260. Giraffe were then the most numerous animal in Africa.
4. Zheng He's trilingual plaque was unearthed near Galle in 1910.
5. The 'Star Raft' records were destroyed in or around 1480, but the Mao Kun 'map' was preserved in the imperial archives.
6. Envoys sent to the Chinese emperor from Egypt, and possibly from Kilwa, in 1441 were perhaps the last to make the journey as a result of Zheng He's expeditions.

CHAPTER 11　The King of the African Castle

1. Many artefacts were dug up and carried away by prospectors after the ruins of Great Zimbabwe were 'discovered' by Europeans in the late nineteenth century.
2. According to some estimates there were 1,250 goldmines on the plateau controlled from Great Zimbabwe, the richest having been worked for several centuries. The gold-bearing rock was granite, and was ground up with dolorite, which is harder than granite.
3. Imported articles found by archaeologists include cutlery, crockery, copper chains, brasswork, and an iron lampstand.
4. Walls of rougher construction surrounded gold mines, as marks of ownership.
5. Roland Oliver in *The African Experience* refers to 'a small but obstinate minority of BC dates from north-western Tanzania

and Rwanda, which, despite re-testing, refuse to go away'. John Iliffe in *Africans, the History of a Continent* (Cambridge, 1995) says the debate on the source of Rwandan smelting skills is 'unresolved'.
6. A ruler's power was reinforced by religious ritual, magic and music. When mediums went into a trance they were believed to be taken over by spirits of the dead. Any courtier refusing to drink millet beer with the king was accused of conspiring to poison him and punished by death.
7. A table measuring the cultural progress of Great Zimbabwe was drawn up by Roger Summers ('*Was Great Zimbabwe Civilised?*' – history conference paper, Rhodes-Livingstone Institute, Lusaka, 1963). He concluded that aside from literacy it had all attributes of civilization by the fourteenth century.
8. Jack Goody in *Literacy in Traditional Societies* (Cambridge, 1968) stresses the importance of literacy in 'mitigating the fissive tendencies of large empires'.

PART TWO

CHAPTER 12　Prince Henry's Far Horizons

1. The capture of Ceuta (21 August 1415) placed Portugal 'on the imperial road from which there was no point of voluntary return' (Bailey W. Diffie, *Prelude to Empire*, Lincoln, Canada, 1960).
2. The River of Gold, shown on fourteenth-century maps as emptying into the Atlantic, was believed to be joined to the Nile.
3. As in Roman times, medieval Europe was being drained of gold to buy spices, silks and other luxuries from the East. It had little else acceptable to offer in exchange.
4. The Carthaginian navigator Hanno is reputed to have sailed down the Atlantic coast almost reaching the equator in about 740BC with sixty galleys and 30,000 prospective settlers, founding seven towns. The legend is suspect.
5. Ferrer, a cartographer, had set out on 10 August 1346 to search for the River of

Gold: J. B. Harley and D. Woodward, *History of Cartography*, vol. I (Chicago, 1987).

6. The Canaries were known in classical times as the Fortunate Isles. Pliny mentions an expedition to them in 40BC. Majorcan missionaries sailed to the islands in 1342, and began converting the inhabitants, the *guanches*, but were annihilated by them in 1391.

CHAPTER 13 Commanding the Guinea Coast

1. For Henry's rejection of the offer to exchange Ceuta for his brother, see M. D. D. Newitt's 'Prince Henry and Portuguese Imperialism'.

2. The pomp and extravagance encountered by Prince Pedro is vividly portrayed in *Venice, the Greatness and the Fall*, by John Julius Norwich (London, 1981).

3. Colonization of the Azores (the name derives from the Portuguese *açores*, hawks) was begun by Gonçalo Velho Cabral in 1445.

4. The theory that Africans were 'natural slaves' had first been propounded by Aristotle.

5. An assessment of Henry's character is given by J. Bensaude in *A Cruzado do Infante Dom Henrique* (Lisbon, 1946): 'There is nothing which reminds one in the smallest degree of a Renaissance prince . . .' Rather, he was 'a Percival in quest of the Holy Grail'.

6. The booty taken at Arzila was reckoned to be worth 800,000 gold doublons.

CHAPTER 14 The Shape of the Indies

1. Until the Kongo kingdom was encountered, Africa south of the equator contrasted sharply for the Portuguese with the densely-populated city-states such as Benin on the Guinea coast.

2. Venice was at pains to understand the East, the source of its wealth. Among books given to Bertrandon de la Brocquière by the consul's chaplain in the Venetian consulate in Damascus was a life of Mohammed in Latin.

3. Polyandry as a custom in barbaric societies is a theme dating back to classical times. Julius Caesar in *De Bello Gallico*, book V, writes of 'groups of ten or twelve men have wives together in common, and particularly brothers along with brothers and fathers with sons'.

4. Another informant was Josafat Barbaro, a Venetian emissary to Persia. He returned with news of China and of Calicut, 'a staple of merchants of various places' (Boise Penrose, *Travel and Discovery in the Renaissance*).

5. Brother Mauro died in 1459, the year his map was completed.

CHAPTER 15 The Lust for Pepper, the Hunt for Prester John

1. Ever since the re-discovery of the Azores, the Portuguese had navigated by the stars on the open sea, but the Pole Star could not be used when near or beyond the equator: E. G. R. Taylor, 'The Early Navigator' (*Geographical Journal*, vol. cxiii, 1949).

2. A league equalled three Portuguese miles (2,259 yards).

3. The realm of Prester John was 'the land where dreams came true', where a magic stone enabled the blind to see, or could make people invisible (Elaine Sanceau, *Portugal in Quest of Prester John*).

4. This wonderland was linked to the 'Paradise of God', as depicted by medieval theologians. It was also known as the 'Garden of Delights', and influenced artists such as Hieronymos Bosch.

5. As a depiction of the marvels of the East, the Mandeville fantasy was even more popular during the fifteenth and sixteenth centuries than Marco Polo's memoirs.

6. As used by Herodotus, 'Ethiopia' had meant no more than a boundless, unknown region inhabited by people whose faces were blackened by the sun. Medieval Europe later bestowed this name on the land also known as Middle India or Abyssinia and it was finally adopted by the inhabitants themselves.

CHAPTER 16   The Spy Who Never Came Home

1. The chart given to Covilham would have been based upon the *mappa mundi* of Brother Mauro, which the Portuguese had possessed since before 1460.
2. John II feared not merely the intrigues round his throne, but the Castilian threat to his possessions outside Europe. To assert his rights on land as well as the sea he had despatched agents across the Sahara to Timbuktu.
3. Cannanore (or Cananor) was renowned as India's 'ginger port'.
4. This Genoese merchant, Hieronomo de Santo Stephano, also reported that Calicut's people 'worshipped the sun and the ox' – a confused description of Hinduism.
5. Hormuz had a long-established Jewish trading community, which may explain the rabbi's desire to visit it.

CHAPTER 17   Kings and Gods in the City of Victory

1. The sultans of north India employed many Turks and Arabs in their armies. African slaves fought on both sides. By the fifteenth century gunpowder was being used against war-elephants.
2. Vijayanagara's ruins are spread over more than 100 square miles: numerous illustrations of the remains, including palaces, audience rooms, aqueducts, arched colonnades and sunken baths are in *Metropolis Vijayanagara* by Barkur Narasimhaiah (Delhi, 1992).
3. Before entering battle a fourteenth-century king, Kampiladeva, told all his wives and daughters that if he were defeated they should commit *suttee* to avoid falling into Muslim hands. All obeyed when the battle was lost. Kampiladeva's head was cut off, stuffed and sent to Delhi.
4. The main texts of the Ramayana epic were composed in about 500BC.
5. Merchants came to Vijayanagara from as far as Persia and Arabia. Much Chinese porcelain was imported. Despite the constant wars with Islam, the city had a large Muslim quarter.

CHAPTER 18   Da Gama Enters the Tropical Ocean

1. These details are given in A. Cortesano's *The Mystery of da Gama.*
2. John II's anxiety had been heightened in May 1493 when the Spanish-born Pope, Alexander VI, awarded Castile all the world except lands already occupied by other Christian monarchs.
3. Castilian kings often held court in Tordesillas, south-west of Valladolid.
4. Prophetically, as he was dying John told Manuel to add a globe to his coat of arms.
5. Ships of the period were tightly packed with crews, but each man had room for a small sea-chest and deck-space to make a bed.
6. The exact point of landfall was St Helen's Bay. The navigators had depended heavily on the astrolabe invented by John II's Jewish astronomers.
7. The pilots were paid with gold and a jacket apiece.
8. In the words of William Mickle's eighteen-century translation of Camöens' *The Lusiads*, this first encounter 'Gama's terrors to the East display'd'.

CHAPTER 19   A First Sight of India

1. The four Indian ships at Malindi came from Cannanore, the Malabar port where Covilham had first landed in India ten years earlier.
2. The presence in Malindi of horses, imported from Arabia, is an indication of its affluence.
3. Ptolemy had written of the 'Great Beach' where ships from India reached the African coast. *Saif al-Tawil* means Long Sword – as it might look from the sea.
4. The Zamorin was frequently engaged in putting down warlords who controlled the hilly districts inland from Calicut. In accord with local custom, he would return their lands to them after obtaining submission on the battlefield.
5. Calicut's army numbered about 60,000, including some Muslims (K. V. K. Ayyar, *A Short History of Kerala*).

6. Da Gama's reward was well over £1,000,000 at current values.

CHAPTER 20   The Fateful Pride of Ibn Majid

1. According to T. Shumovsky, in a paper to the 25th international Congress of Orientalists in Moscow (1960), Ibn Majid was a freed slave whose master was Ahmad bin al-Tamal. This is improbable: in his poems, Ibn Majid boasts of his ancestry and says that his father, a Red Sea pilot, also wrote navigational poems.

2. Arab astronomers were still far ahead of their European counterparts. Ibn Majid would have known the eleventh-century works of al-Biruni, who had considered in detail such matters as the luminosity of Mercury and Venus and their orbits in relation to the sun.

CHAPTER 21   Sounds of Europe's Rage

1. Cabral's *naus* were heavily armed. German and Flemish gunners were recruited for the expedition. All vessels encountered were to be plundered, except those of Malindi and the two Indian ports which da Gama deemed friendly – Cannanore and Cochin.

2. One ship was ordered back to Lisbon with details of Santa Cruz (the name first given to Brazil).

3. Cabral appears to have deposited several *degredados* in Malindi. Luis de Moura and João Machado were ordered to search for Prester John, but Muchado went on to India, where he took service with a Muslim ruler and re-appeared as an emissary negotiating with the Portuguese.

4. Cochin was older than Calicut, but had been out-distanced commercially – especially since the visits of Chinese fleets under Zheng He. Much foreign trade with the city of Vijayanagara was also controlled by Calicut.

5. The loss of life suffered by Cabral had initially provoked discussion in Lisbon as to whether voyages to the Indies could be borne. The immense profits on pepper resolved the debate.

CHAPTER 22   The Vengeance of da Gama

1. The extravagance of Manuel's claim to half the world can be illustrated demographically: in 1500 Portugal had little more than one per cent of Europe's estimated 84,000,000 people. Asia's population was 245,000,000 (M. Livi-Bacci, *Population and Nutrition*).

2. Correa, a prolific writer, spent much of his life in India. He describes with an almost sadistic enthusiasm the violence he witnessed or was told about.

3. Pacheco (born about 1450) had a memorable life before and after his Cochin command. The probable discoverer of Brazil, he wrote a book, *Esmeraldo de Situ Orbis*, which dared to give precise details of places known to the Portuguese south of the equator, despite King Manuel's decree that revealing such secrets was punishable by death. Retired with a pension, he re-emerged in 1520 to become commander of a Portuguese fortress in West Africa, but his career ended when he was falsely accused of malpractice and sent back to Lisbon in irons. (*Esmeraldo in Situ Orbis*, trans. and ed. G. H. T. Kimble)

4. Da Gama reached Lisbon in September 1503. His cousin, Estevan da Gama, commanding a smaller fleet, arrived separately, having sailed non-stop from Malindi.

CHAPTER 23   The Viceroy in East Africa

1. If not a Portuguese, the diarist may have been Hans Mayr, a German travelling with the fleet. Accounts of Almeida's actions were published in Lisbon by Valentim Fernandes, a German-born printer.

2. One ship was detached to make a detailed survey of the East African coast and the dangerous shoals in the Mozambique channel.

3. According to the victors, losses among the Arab defenders of Mombasa and their 500 black archers totalled 1,500 dead. The Portuguese had five killed. More

than a thousand prisoners were taken, including 'fair-skinned and beautiful women'.

4. The historian Correa says that because of the impossibility of carrying off all the loot without dangerously overloading the ships, most of the prisoners were freed and the sultan agreed to pay an annual tribute to Portugal.

CHAPTER 24   Defeating the Ottoman Turks at Diu

1. Whereas European Christians saw the Turks as little different from Arabs, since both were Muslims, the Ottoman conquests of the Levant, Egypt and North Africa had given the leadership of the Islamic world an entirely new direction.

2. Timoja was working for the Hindus against the Muslims, which made him acceptable. His piratical tendencies proved him a difficult ally and the Portuguese later put him under arrest.

3. The Portuguese did not occupy the Maldives until the second half of the sixteenth century, then built a fort, but stayed for only twenty years because of constant attacks by the islanders.

4. Ayyaz had risen to hold the title *malik*, the equivalent of king or viceroy.

5. After Diu, no Indian Ocean state dared to defy the Portuguese on water. Qaisar in *The Indian Response* underlines the impression made by European nautical skills.

CHAPTER 25   The Great Afonso de Albuquerque

1. Albuquerque's character and aims are examined in the introduction to Earle and Villiers' *Albuquerque, Caesar of the East* (although it skims lightly over his atrocities).

2. Socotra was recognized as having strategic value, but proved inhospitable, with no refuge from storms, and lacking water.

3. Goa stood on the southern edge of Muslim conquests in India. By capturing it the Portuguese were effectively allying themselves with Hinduism. The king of Vijayanagara,

Krishna Deva Rajah, was gratified, and trade quickly developed between the Hindu interior and the Portuguese in Goa. Albuquerque appointed Malhar Rao of Honawar (south of Goa) as ruler of the Portuguese mainland territory.

4. Albuquerque recognized the port of Massawa (now in Eritrea) as a possible base from which to attack Jeddah and Mecca, as well as the entry-point to the 'kingdom of Prester John'.

CHAPTER 26   Ventures into the African Interior

1. Figueroa later went to India. His book is entitled *The Conquest of the Indies, of Persia and Arabia effected by the Fleet of King Manuel. About the many lands, diverse peoples, strange riches, and great battles which took place there.*

2. As would soon become clear, the interior's gold exports had been diverted northwards, after the abandonment of Great Zimbabwe.

3. Portuguese heraldry was not alone in employing such imagery. Queen Elizabeth I of England would grant Sir John Hawkins a coat of arms embodying a bound negro, as a mark of his successes in the slave trade.

4. Since António Fernandes was the most common of Portuguese names, it is impossible to be entirely definite about the explorer's early career.

5. Not all *degredados* came from the lower orders. A contemporary of Fernandes in East Africa was Diogo Vaz, banished as a felon to Mozambique in 1507 and discharged in 1513. He had boldly written to King Manuel: 'I ask you, Sir, the favour to allow me to go by the next fleet . . . and be assured, Sir, that trade here is only for thieves and their brethren.' (*Documents on the Portuguese in Mozambique and Central Africa*, vol. II)

CHAPTER 27   From Massawa to the Mountains

1. Matthew was buried at Debra-Bizan, near Asmara, capital of modern Eritrea.

2. An early stopping-place in the Ethiopian

highlands was amid the ruins of Aksum, where Ethiopian coronations were still held. The expedition would have been still more impressed by the granite stelae and tombs, had they known that Christianity had taken root there 1,200 years earlier, when Portugal was still pagan.

3. The fate of Ethiopian princes was to be the subject of Dr Samuel Johnson's romantic novel *The History of Rasselas, Prince of Abyssinia.*

4. Most distinguished of the Europeans was an Italian painter, Brancaleone, who adorned many of Ethiopia's churches and had a lasting influence on its art.

5. In the previous century the emperor Yeshaq had briefly captured Zeila, destroying its mosques and building churches in their place.

6. Nothing is recorded about the end of Covilham's life.

CHAPTER 28 At War with the Left-handed Invader

1. Throughout Lent the only meal was of bread and vegetables, eaten after dusk. Some Ethiopians in religious orders ate only once every other day.

2. By some accounts, Lebna Dengel had led a life of debauchery, despite his devotion to religion, and was stabbed to death in his bed.

3. The last Nubian bishop was consecrated in Alexandria in 1372. After that the Christians of the Upper Nile struggled on in isolation for another 150 years: William Y. Adams, *Nubia.*

4. Christofe da Gama was in due course canonized.

5. The valet, Pêro Leam, cut off one of Grãn's ears after killing him. When an Ethiopian who claimed to have done the deed was showing the severed head to Claudius, the valet asked, 'Did the Muslim not have two ears? Whoever killed him must have the other ear.' At this he produced it from his pocket, to great applause: *Itinerário* of Jerónimo Lobo, trans. by Donald Lockhart.

CHAPTER 29 Taking Bible and Sword to Monomotapa

1. Xavier, born into an aristocratic family in Navarre in 1506, had studied for four years in Paris, where the nucleus of the Jesuits came together in 1534. The most complete account of his career is Georg Schurhammer's *Francis Xavier.*

2. The Inquisition in Goa would become infamous for the ingenuity of its tortures.

3. Portuguese 'backwoodsmen' were by now active over a wide area south of the Zambezi, often fomenting local wars for commercial advantage.

4. Fifty converts made by Silveira were massacred after his murder.

5. In 1608, Philip II (Philip III of Spain) wrote to Gatsi Rusere, emperor of Monomotapa, appointing him a 'brother in arms'. In return Gatsi Rusere was enjoined to hand over all his minerals, then send his son and ambassadors to the Portuguese viceroy in Goa 'to bow down and offer their servitude to me'. (*Documents on the Portuguese in Mozambique and Central Africa*, vol. IX)

6. A belief long existed in Lisbon that huge deposits of silver lay hidden in the lands of Monomotapa. A series of officers were granted the grandiose but empty title of 'Conquistador and Discoverer of the Mines of Silver'; nothing existed beyond small and fragmented veins.

CHAPTER 30 Turkish Adventurers, Hungry Cannibals

1. The Mombasa sultan offered 12,000 meticals of gold, about 15,000 cruzados, if the town were spared (Justus Strandes, *The Portuguese Period in East Africa*), but in vain.

2. Da Cunha's choice had been Mwinyi Muhammad, nephew of the Malindi sultan. He hurriedly put forward his younger brother, Said Abu Bakr.

3. In 1542 a Portuguese fleet of light vessels was stationed off the Somali coast to watch for Turkish ships venturing from the Red Sea. By this time the Turks were

also challenging the Portuguese in the Persian Gulf.

4. Preserved in salt, the head was shipped to Goa, where it was paraded through the streets as a warning to any other 'friend of the Turks'.

5. A map detailing Ali Bey's Indian Ocean voyages is in Donald Pitcher's *The Ottoman Empire*.

6. According to Friar João dos Santos, one of his Dominican colleagues was eaten by the Zimbas, whose chief marched about in triumph wearing the victim's religious vestments, with a chalice in one hand and an assegai in the other.

CHAPTER 31   The Renegade Sultan

1. The anonymous *Tarik-i Hindi-i Garbi* author saw the expulsion of the Portuguese from the Indian Ocean as one step towards a wider plan, for the Turks to conquer the whole world, including the Americas: Thomas D. Goodrich's *The Ottoman Turks and the New World*.

2. According to Andrea Palladio in book I of his *The Four Books of Architecture* (1570), '. . . buildings may appear as a single well-finished body within which all members agree, and all the members are necessary . . .'

3. The sultan's palace stood about a mile from Fort Jesus.

4. In August 1627, Jerónimo wrote to the Pope saying that he had personally 'converted 100 Moorish vassals'.

5. Contemporary accounts of events after the sultan's revolt are translated by G. S. P. Freeman-Grenville in *The Mombasa Rising against the Portuguese, 1631*.

6. The friar was Fr. João of Jesus, sent from Goa to investigate the massacre.

CHAPTER 32   The Lost Pride of Lusitania

1. Portuguese descriptions of Vijayanagara at its peak are translated in R. Sewell's *A Forgotten Empire*.

2. The 92-year-old ruler Ramaraja went into battle with 600,000 foot-soldiers, 100,000 cavalry and 500 elephants. But a seeming Muslim ally, Ali Adil Shah, changed sides at a crucial moment. Later, Adil Shah blew the captive Ramaraja's head off with a cannon and sent his remains to Benares to be thrown into the Ganges: *Further Sources of Vijayanagara History*, by K. A. Nilakanta Sastri and N. Venkataramanayya (Madras, 1946).

3. Shah Jahan's comment is quoted by Qaisar (*op. cit.*).

4. Stevens's accounts were seized upon by the English geographer Richard Hakluyt and published in his three-volume anthology of travel, 1598–1600.

4. This strikingly illustrated the inability, until the eighteenth century, to fix longitude at sea. Crude efforts to do so were made by dead reckoning, calculating the distance and direction sailed between latitudes: a diagram illustrating this method is in *English Merchant Shipping, 1450–1540*, by D. Burwash.

6. Portugal's power and pride had already been shattered in 1578 by the annihilation of its army in Morocco at the battle of Alcazarquivir. King Sebastian, aged 24, was killed, marking the effective end of the Aviz dynasty, which had shaped Portugal's destiny for two centuries.

7. Contingents of black slaves were used throughout the Estado da India. Most came from Mozambique, but some were transported from West Africa and others, known as 'Habshi' were acquired in India.

8. Quoted in Curzon's *Persia and the Persian Question*.

9. These tactics are described in G. A. Ballard's *Rulers of the Indian Ocean*.

10. This was Lobo's second mishap in southern Africa: 13 years earlier he had experienced the sea-battle off Mozambique against the Dutch and English.

CHAPTER 33 Calvinists, Colonists and Pirates

1. A *prazero* held his land on lease, nominally from the Portuguese crown. Often this was land previously ceded by an African chief.

2. Jacob van Enkhuisen in 1604 called the Khoikhoi 'a poor miserable folk who went quite naked ... they clucked like turkeys ...': R. Raven-Hart's *Before van Riebeeck*.

3. The economic success of Holland, at home and abroad, is detailed in Jonathan I. Israel's *The Dutch Republic*. For the conquest of Ceylon: *Some Documents Relating to the Rise of Dutch Power in Ceylon, 1602–1670*, by P. E. Pieris.

4. Slavery under the Dutch in Ceylon was highly regimented. More than 30 laws about it were introduced (*Ceylon Literary Register*, September 1935).

5. Pirates apart, no Britons set foot in Madagascar for another two centuries after this débâcle.

6. The authenticity of Libertalia, first written about in the early eighteenth century, has been questioned. It is accepted, however, by the French historian Hubert Deschamps, a foremost authority on Madagascar. Tom Tew was certainly an historical figure, and his surname is still found in his home town, Plymouth, England.

CHAPTER 34 Ethiopia and the Hopes of Rome

1. Za-Dengel had written to Europe suggesting that his son should be wedded to the Spanish monarch's daughter – precisely the proposal made by the emperor Yeshaq to Alfonso of Aragon in 1306. The idea once more fell on stony ground.

2. Paez found time in his last years to write a history of Ethiopia in Latin. It ranged from religion, morals and geography to how the rhinoceros was hunted (summary in Philip Caraman's *The Lost Empire*).

3. The Galla (more correctly, the Oromo), were by this time the

principal threat to Ethiopia. Their rulers feared that the expedition was reconnoitring a route from Malindi by which the Portuguese could attack them from the south.

4. Since the address given by Mendes was 30,000 words long, according to his own memoirs, it must have taken at least four hours to deliver, even without any translation.

5. The extent of the catastrophe which had overtaken the Jesuits in Ethiopia was little understood until Jerónimo Lobo's narrative was translated into French and published in Paris in 1728 as *Voyage Historique d'Abissinie*.

CHAPTER 35 The Great Siege of Fort Jesus

1. The East African coastline simply became known after the sixteenth century by the Swahili word *Mrima* (mainland).

2. Money to pay the ships' crews, most of whom were untrained conscripts, had to be forcibly borrowed from a religious foundation in Goa.

3. Many artefacts brought up by divers in 1977 from the wreck of the 42-gun *San António* are to be seen in the Fort Jesus museum.

4. The chronicle, which survives in the national library in Lisbon, may have been written at de Brito's instigation, or even partly by him.

5. A legend that two of the last defenders blew themselves up in the fort's powder magazine, killing 200 Arabs, was invented to salve Portuguese pride.

6. For 18 months, between March 1728 and November 1729, the Portuguese did reoccupy Fort Jesus, which had been seized from the Omanis by rebellious black slaves. Ultimately the commander surrendered to a besieging force, and was given three boats to sail back to Goa. Some of his men, in love with local women, stayed behind and became Muslims.

CHAPTER 36 Western Aims,
Eastern Influences

1. The failure of the siege, in 1683, proved a turning-point, after which Ottoman power waned in Europe and Asia.

2. Robertson's comment is in vol. 2 of his *Complete Works*.

3. Far greater interest began to be attached to Brazil, where sugar plantations flourished, gold had been discovered, and the Portuguese proved far more successful in fending off other European powers.

4. A message to the Portuguese king is quoted in vol. 7 of *Documents on the Portuguese in Mozambique and Central Africa*.

5. The wearing of dried testicles as ornaments was not unusual (see reference to Mwata Yamvo in chapter 40).

6. Careri remarked on the poor diet of the slaves in Goa, their lack of clothing and their 'mean employments': *The Indian Travels of Thevenot and Careri*, trans. and ed., S. N. Sen (New Delhi, 1949).

7. Ovington recounted his experiences of India in *A Voyage to Surat in the Year 1689*, ed. E. G. Rawlinson (Oxford, 1929). Despite the fever, Ovington found strength to castigate the debauchery he found ashore among the British in Bombay.

8. Cowper (1731–1800) was a poet of strong religious convictions, an opponent of slavery, and condemned the 'nabobs' in his satire *Expostulation*.

9. Quoted by Theon Wilkinson in *Two Monsoons*.

PART THREE

CHAPTER 37 Settlers on India's
Southern Approaches

1. Stavorinus wrote *Voyages to the East Indies*, trans. by Samuel H. Wilcocke. His curiosity ranged widely: he noted in southern India that the Jewish communities there freed their slaves, circumcised them, then treated them as 'fellow Israelites'.

2. Nevertheless, on account of the 'European climate of the Cape, the whites living there did far more physical labour than their counterparts in tropical settlements.

3. The Maria Theresa dollar, minted in Austria, was an Indian Ocean currency for 150 years, and was especially popular in Ethiopia.

4. Robben Island, where the future President Nelson Mandela and his colleagues would be incarcerated in the twentieth century, had been a jail since the early years of Dutch occupation of the Cape.

5. This document, in question and answer form, is now in Rhodes House, Oxford; it is analysed in G. S. P. Freeman-Grenville's *The French at Kilwa Island*.

6. The *nawab* (ruler) of Bengal, Siraj-ud-daulah, had opposed the East India Company's decision to fortify Calcutta against the French. A conspiracy within his own ranks led to his defeat at Plassey (1757); earlier, Clive had ousted the French from Bengal.

7. By the middle of the nineteenth century the Kilwa sultanate was extinguished, with only a scattering of Swahili villagers living on the island. The ruins have been partly excavated and are described by Neville Chittick in *Kilwa, an Islamic Trading City on the East African Coast*.

CHAPTER 38 The Seas beyond
Napoleon's Reach

1. The Anglo-French naval engagements are well described in Ballard's *Rulers of the Indian Ocean*.

2. Linda Colley in *Britons* has chronicled the welding together of the nation as a prelude to imperialism, and the continuing significance of 'Englishness'. Simultaneously, hatred of the French was whipped up to extreme heights. Nelson wrote of them in 1799 that they were 'thieves, murderers, oppressors and infidels'.

3. Tipu's Tiger, now in the Victoria and Albert museum, London, has French-made mechanical pipes emitting the growls of the animal and cries of the

victim. The tableau is based upon the real-life fate of a young Scotsman whose father, General Hector Munro, had defeated Tipu in a battle.

4. Quoted by Lennox Mills in *Ceylon under British Rule, 1795–1932*.

5. Based upon the Phelps-Brown index, £5,000 in the 1790s would be equivalent to approximately £350,000 in the 1990s (Information from the Central Statistical Office, London).

6. Cleghorn's role in Britain's acquisition of Ceylon is so little known that it is not mentioned in H. W. Codrington's *A Short History of Ceylon* (London, 1926). Codrington merely notes that de Meuron 'had arranged for the transfer of his proprietary regiment, of which five companies were in Colombo, to the British service'.

7. Almost all the surviving Swiss mercenaries were demobilized in Canada in 1816.

CHAPTER 39   The French Redoubt and the Isle of Slaves

1. The Palmerston-Sulivan letters, 1804–1863, have been published by the Royal Historical Society (London, 1979). Sulivan's father came from an East India Company family; his mother was the widow of a reputed slave trader.

2. Vice-Admiral Albemarle Bertie, in a despatch from the Cape on 30 September 1808, accused the Americans of having a contract for supplying provisions to the French in the Ile de France, with as many as fifty ships engaged in it in 1805: 'These ships delivered supplies, without which they could not exist, and how were they paid? By our captured property . . .': G. M. Theal, ed., *Records of the Cape Colony*, vol. V (London, 1900).

3. Said's income from the slave tax was certainly equal to more than £1 million a year at current values. He understandably felt his actions were hallowed by tradition, since Arab ships had been transporting Africans across the Indian Ocean for more than a millennium.

4. The chairman of the East India Company (E.I.C.) in 1805 had been Charles Grant, a supporter of the abolitionist William Wilberforce. With fervent Evangelical views, Grant believed that India's wellbeing would be advanced by the obliteration of both Islam and Hinduism. The British and Foreign Bible Society began devoting itself to translating Christian texts into all the main Indian languages.

CHAPTER 40   'Literally a Blank in Geography'

1. Lacerda was rescued from obscurity by Richard Burton's translation of Portuguese documents in *The Lands of Cazembe*.

2. The travels of Mungo Park, and subsequent expeditions to trace the route of the Niger have been the subject of many books, including Christopher Lloyd's *The Search for the Niger* (London, 1973) and *Black Nile* by Peter Brent (London, 1977).

3. Mwata Yamvo was an hereditary title. In Lacerda's time the holder was probably Yavo ya Mbanyi. An account by David Birmingham of the Lunda empire is in the *Cambridge History of Africa*, vol. 5.

4. A history of the Eastern Lunda, as related by the fourteenth Mwata Kazembe in 1942, has been translated by I. G. Cunnison: *Central Bantu Historical Texts II* (Lusaka, 1962). The Kazembe in 1798 was Ilunga, who had made himself renowned by his military conquests; he died in 1805.

5. Lacerda gave himself four months to reach Kazembe before the start of the rains, after which travelling would have been almost impossible.

6. A brief account of Andrew Cowan's career is in the *Dictionary of South African Biography*, vol. 2 (Cape Town, 1972).

7. In later years Prior wrote a life of Oliver Goldsmith and gained a modest reputation as a poet.

8. By 1812 the defeat of Napoleon in Russia had removed the lingering fear that he might attack India overland through Persia.

CHAPTER 41 Two Ways with the Spoils of War

1. Relevant correspondence between North, Clarke and others is in CO55/34 in Public Record Office, London.
2. A markedly different perspective on the removal of Vikrama and the aftermath is in *Sinhalé and the Patriots* by P. E. Pieris.
3. Samuel Baker's *The Rifle and the Hound in Ceylon* (London, 1854) celebrates the mass slaughter of elephants, deer and other game.
4. Farquhar's proposition, and the response to it, are tendentiously discussed in *The History of Slavery in Mauritius and the Seychelles, 1810–1875* by Moses D. E. Nwulia (Rutherford, New Jersey, 1981).
5. The three Frenchmen had brought the slaves from Mozambique in a schooner: *The Observer*, London, 22 February, 1819.
6. Quoted by Henri Brunschwig in *Britain and France in Africa*, ed. Prosser Gifford and William R. Louis.
7. Official 'Guardians' or 'protectors' of slaves often sided with the masters. Thomas's counterpart at the Cape, George Rogers, in a valedictory report in 1828 said: 'I am of the opinion that the present race of slaves here are far better off than millions of the lower orders in Great Britain and other parts of Europe.' He contrasted the life of 'stout and hardy' females from Mozambique with that of erring Englishwomen 'condemned to hard labour, the treadmill, and other severe and degrading penalties'. (British *Parliamentary Papers*, XV, 1830–31) The *Cape Gazette*, on 12 October 1822, gives the other side, advertising the auction of 'a female slave named Candara, of Mozambique, 54 years old, with her five children; Saphira, aged thirteen years; Eva, ten; Candara, nine; Jannetje, seven; and Carlos, five; each to be put up separately'.
8. By 1994 Mauritius had achieved an annual gross national product *per capita* of $3,180, ten times that of India.

CHAPTER 42 The Sultan and the King's Navy

1. Opium exporting to China from India was begun by the Portuguese. By 1767 it totalled 1,000 chests a year, and 1818 the trade, now largely in British hands, was 6,000 chests a year. Exports from Bengal were proscribed, but the E.I.C. enjoyed revenue from the duties levied. In 1839 the Chinese banned opium imports, and seized 20,291 chests from foreign merchants. Britain declared war, making China pay a £4.5 million indemnity and cede Hong Kong.
2. A detailed account of the dealings with Said over the slave trade, as seen through British eyes, is in Sir Reginald Coupland's *East Africa and its Invaders*.
3. The two-volume account published under Owen's name, *Narrative of Voyages to Explore the Shores of Africa, Arabia and Madagascar*, is a farrago of extracts from the diaries of the captain and his officers.
4. The combination of 'cupping' and purging was prone to speed the demise of patients already weakened by fever.
5. Owen had also been laying plans for a British presence on the Mozambique coast, to combat the Portuguese slave exports, then running at about 15,000 a year. He felt that the 'deserving Africans' were suffering under the 'wicked despotism' of the Portuguese, and marked on his chart an area called Temby, in Delagoa Bay, as 'Proposed place for an English settlement'. This came to nothing.
6. The India Board was a Privy Council committee, which dealt with policy matters in India through the Secret Committee, made up of three directors of the E.I.C.

CHAPTER 43 Stepping back from East Africa

1. Reitz's story is told in Sir John Gray's *The British in Mombasa, 1824–26*, the standard work on the short-lived protectorate.
2. The *banians*, a distinct caste, came mainly from Gujarat, north of Bombay (see

chapter 5). By the end of the nineteenth century Indians would totally dominate the retail trade in East Africa.

3. A stretch of water off Mombasa's Kilindini harbour was named Port Reitz in the lieutenant's memory. The name survives on modern maps.

4. In *Selections from the Bombay Records* (new series, XXIV, Bombay, 1856) an 'Historical Sketch of Muskat' says that as late as May 1826 the Bombay government was being vainly urged by Christians to induce Said to recognize the independence of Mombasa.

5. More than half a century later, Owen's brief protectorate would be cited by Britain in diplomatic negotiations to justify its claims to the coast of what became Kenya.

6. Bevan's evidence is in British *Parliamentary Papers*, vol. IX, 1831–32.

7. The term 'Sidi', from the Arabic *seyyid* (Lord), was used from the sixteenth century to describe the Janjira community of Africans in India; in 1668 the Janjira had captured Bombay from the British and were paid a ransom to leave: see *Bombay and the Sidis* by D. R. Banaji (Bombay, 1932). Later the expression was applied to all Africans in India, and is still used in Pakistan for people descended from black slaves.

8. Report in *The Times*, 3 September 1831. Further details are in Charles R. Low's *History of the Indian Navy* (London, 1877).

9. An account of Owen's last years, by P. G. Cornell, is in *Collections of the Nova Scotia Historical Society*, no. 32 (Halifax, 1959).

CHAPTER 44   The Americans
Discover Zanzibar

1. Some British commentators have cast doubt on Roberts's version of this meeting with Said, pointing out that the only portrait of the sultan (done from memory by an amateur artist), shows him with a short beard: frontispiece to *Said bin Sultan* by R. Said-Ruete (London, 1929). This ignores the possibility that Said might have changed his style of beard.

2. The definitive accounts of American

trade with Zanzibar in the nineteenth century are by Norman R. Bennett in *Tanganyika Notes and Records*, vols. 56, 57 and 60 (Dar es Salaam, 1959–63). Also, the same author's *New England Merchants in Africa, 1802–1865* (Boston, 1965).

3. The treaty is set out, with Arabic facsimile, in *Treaties and International Acts of the United States*, vol. 3, ed. Hunter Miller (Washington, 1933).

4. Hart's own account of his visit to Zanzibar is printed in *Selections from the Bombay Records*, 1856. The incident is put into context by G. S. Graham in *Great Britain in the Indian Ocean, 1810–1850*.

5. Ranavolana was at this time expelling British missionaries who had opened 100 schools in Madagascar and distributed 25,000 Christian tracts in local languages. She also had a number of missionaries thrown off a cliff.

6. Tucker had been born in Bermuda in 1771 of a slave-owning family, was intensively conservative, and in later years would oppose press freedom in India as likely to 'excite new ideas'.

7. These views appear in despatch no. 5 of 1835, India Board to Bombay.

8. The India Board went as far as to tell the Foreign Office that it should make no communication with Seyyid Said, 'except through the Governor-General in Council'.

9. Some members of the Mazrui clan did survive and their descendants remain influential in East Africa. Professor Ali Mazrui is an internationally recognized historian.

CHAPTER 45   Looking Westwards
from the Raj

1. This letter, sent from Salem on 31 December 1841, is in the National Archives, Washington.

2. There was another mishap with a gift from Queen Victoria. A box formally opened in front of the sultan and thought to contain a silver-gilt tea service held only a tombstone for the grave of a British sailor.

3. Correspondence on Ali bin Nasser's visit

and subsequent dealings with Said is FO54/1-3, PRO, London.

4. The idea of making good the sultan's income if he abandoned the slave trade had been aired repeatedly since the 1820s, and probably originated with him.

5. The Evangelicals were a distinct element in British Protestantism, active in the anti-slavery movement and intent upon the conversion of heathens. A typical Evangelical declaration appears in the report of a parliamentary Select Committee on Aborigines in 1837: 'He who has made Great Britain what she is will require at our hands how we have employed the influence He has lent us in our dealings with the untutored and defenceless savages.'

6. Comment by Lieut. H. F. Disbrowe, assistant resident, Persian Gulf, writing to the Bombay government in 1849.

7. Despite Macaulay's reforms he is not revered by Indians, because of his contempt for Asian cultures and his desire to produce an élite 'Indian in blood and colour, but English in taste, in opinions, in morals and in intellect'.

8. The payment of bounties to British sailors for all slave ships captured or destroyed, and for each freed slave landed alive, greatly stimulated the hunt for Arab dhows sailing between Africa and Arabia. The system was much abused.

9. Burgess wrote of his Zanzibar experiences in vol. XXXVI (1840) of the *Missionary Herald*, the organ of the Congregational Church of America, headquartered in Boston. His report was rounded off with an excerpt from Edmund Roberts' memorandum to the State Department.

CHAPTER 46 Portents of Change in the 'English Lake'

1. Guillain was generally a perceptive commentator and his three-volume *Documents sur l'histoire, la géographie et le commerce de l'Afrique orientale* is the best account of East Africa in the middle years of the nineteenth century. A dossier on Maizan (S 832/9247) is in the French naval archives in Vincennes, Paris.

2. There are conflicting accounts of how Maizan died and who killed him. In *Zanzibar: City, Island and Coast*, Richard Burton says he was murdered by a Chief Muzungera, and enigmatically blames the Christian merchants of Zanzibar 'more or less directly' for the event.

3. Fresnel's exhortation, sent from Jeddah, appeared in the Paris geographical society *Bulletin*, vol. 10, 1948.

4. Stephen's judgement, given in July 1840, is quoted in Ronald Robinson and John Gallagher's *Africa and the Victorians* as 'the official view which held good until the Eighties'.

5. Ward's consular letters to the State Department are in the Washington national archives.

6. The 'annexation by lapse' doctrine is discussed in William Lee-Warner's *Life of Lord Dalhousie* (London, 1904).

7. Henry Wise's luckless *Analysis of One Hundred Voyages to and from India, China, etc.*, advocating steam-aided sailing ships, appeared in the same year as the 660-ton *Nemesis*, an iron steamship, sailed from Birkenhead to India by way of the Cape.

8. Ravenstein's remarks are in his introduction to Ludwig Krapf's *Travels, Researches and Missionary Labours in Eastern Africa*.

CHAPTER 47 In the Footsteps of a Missionary

1. Krapf's career is recounted in the introduction by Roy Bridges to a reprint of *Travels, Researches and Missionary Labours in Eastern Africa* (London, 1968).

2. The best assessment of Burton's character remains Fawn Brodie's *The Devil Drives* (London, 1967). British army officers in India resorted to floggings as punishment for the most minor misdemeanours, so in this respect Burton was a conformist.

3. McQueen told the RGS that Lief bin Said was a Nyamwezi ('Manmoise'), but this is unlikely.

4. The manoeuvrings of the European powers for influence in Zanzibar are well

recounted in Sir John Gray's *History of Zanzibar from the Middle Ages to 1856*.

5. The intrigues within Said's vast family are seen through non-European eyes in the memoirs of one of his daughters, Emily Said-Ruete, who eloped in 1866 with a German trader: *Memoirs of an Arabian Princess*, ed. G. S. P. Freeman-Grenville (London, 1980). According to Emily (born Salme bint Said) her brother Hilal was exiled for being a drunkard, 'seduced by Christians and the then French consul'.

6. When the Omanis took power in Zanzibar they called its inhabitants *Hadimu* (the Swahili word for a slave), forcing them to pick cloves, chop wood and pay a head tax. The Arabs were viewed as oppressors, and this revolt was a futile bid to oust them.

7. Hamerton's death notice appeared in the *Bombay Gazette* only on 20 October 1857. The Mutiny had started on 10 May, when three Indian regiments murdered their officers and marched on Delhi.

CHAPTER 48 Warriors, Hunters and Traders

1. These sentiments appear in the introduction to Speke's *Journal of the Discovery of the Source of the Nile*.

2. Many insights into the effects of manufactured imports on African life are contained in *Pre-Colonial African Trade*, edited by Richard Gray and David Birmingham.

3. See 'Narrative of a Journey to Shoa' by W. C. Barker, in *Travels and Journals preserved in the Bombay Secretariat*, ed. G. W. Forrest.

4. If the proportions of ingredients of gunpowder were incorrect – especially, if there was too much saltpetre – the gun would burst. Birmingham's 'African muskets' might explode in any event: they were certainly inadequate for bringing down heavy game. In 1865, flintlocks were being sold in Africa for 6s. 9d.

5. However, guns were now entering Africa from so many directions that it

was becoming impossible for the Zanzibari Arabs to control the supply.

6. A recent contribution to the controversy is 'Has the Mfecane a Future?' by J. D. Omer-Cooper in *Journal of Southern African Studies*, vol. 19 (Johannesburg, 1993).

7. The career of the Zulu tyrant and his dealings with white traders are described by Stephen Taylor in *Shaka's Children* (London, 1994).

8. The Ngoni impact is analysed by Leroy Vail, 'The Making of the Dead North' in *Before and After Shaka*, ed. J. B. Peires (Grahamstown, 1981).

9. Livingstone's account of the fighting between Lacerda's men and another group of visitors to King Kazembe appears in his *Last Journals*, vol. 1 (London, 1874). The visitors are referred to as 'Ujijians', meaning that they were from the north-eastern shore of Lake Tanganyika. Ujiji became an Arab trading centre, but certainly not as early as 1798, when Lacerda was with Kazembe.

CHAPTER 49 A Proclamation at the Custom House

1. All the sultan's children also owned plantations – Emily Said-Ruete (*Memoirs of an Arabian Princess*) describes riding through them 'for hours' with her sister Zamzam.

2. Barghash's coup attempt is described by Coupland in *East Africa and its Invaders*. If Islamic law had been strictly followed Said's body should have been buried at sea, but this might have provoked suspicions that Barghash had murdered his father.

3. Letter Rigby-Grant, 5 January 1865, in National Library of Scotland, ms. 17910.

4. Where Indians were concerned, Rigby was typically prejudiced. Writing to Grant, 16 November, 1864, he complained that 'a fat Banian' had just been made a judge of the Bombay supreme court, with power to reverse the decisions of English judges and magistrates.

5. Rigby's diaries reveal the obsessive fears of the British about French intentions in

Zanzibar and the western Indian Ocean generally.

6. As a sign of changing times, Thuwain's son Salim had used a revolver for his parricide, rather than the traditional dagger.

7. A history of Dar es Salaam by C. Gillman is in *Tanganyika Notes and Records*, no. 20 (Dar es Salaam, 1945).

8. Barghash's visit was reported in *The Times*, *Pall Mall Gazette* and other London journals during June and July 1875. These accounts were reproduced in newspapers as far afield as Constantinople.

9. Letter Kirk-Lugard, 7 January 1902, in Lugard papers, mss. Brit. Emp. s. 69 (Rhodes House, Oxford).

10. Frere's visit is vividly recreated in Abdul Sheriff's *Slaves, Spices and Ivory in Zanzibar*.

CHAPTER 50   Meeting the Lords of the Interior

1. The best-known of many accounts of this journey (at the end of which Speke cabled the RGS that 'the Nile was settled'), is in Alan Moorehead's *The White Nile* (London, 1960).

2. In his introduction, Chaillé-Long approvingly quotes the French geographer Victor Malte-Brun, that Africa was the last portion of the world 'awaiting at the hands of Europeans the salutary yoke of legislation and culture'.

3. Speke's original material on his experiences in Buganda, and the correspondence relating to it, are in the National Library of Scotland (Blackwood mss. 4872).

4. The racial debate between 'polygenists' and 'monogenists', and the influence of Francis Galton, author of *Tropical South Africa* (1853), are discussed by Robert E. Fancher in 'Francis Galton's African ethnography and its role in the development of his psychology' (*British Journal for the History of Science*, No. 16, 1983).

5. Speke had handled guns all his life. If he were fated to die through an accident

with one (shooting himself almost straight through the heart) it was an astounding chance that this should happen on the very day of his debate with Burton.

6. Islam had a 25-year lead over Christianity in Buganda, which had been reached by a Zanzibari trader, Ahmed bin Ibrahim, in 1844.

7. A shoemaker before arriving in Africa in 1862, New had markedly different views from those of officers such as Chaillé-Long. He wrote: 'Africa for the Africans, and Africans for Africa, should be the motto of all who wish well for this country and people.'

8. Norman Bennett's biography, *Mirambo of Tanzania*, brings together material from a wide range of sources. Engravings in Jerome Becker's *La Vie en Afrique* and a photograph by a British missionary, the Reverend W. G. Willoughby, show the 'black Napoleon' as thoughtful and dignified.

9. Tippu Tip (whose familiar name is written in various forms) features in three of Stanley's books. His autobiography and Leda Farrant's biography give some picture of the man. The most wide-ranging study is *Tippo Tip* by F. Renault (Paris, 1987).

CHAPTER 51   The Failure of a Philanthropic Scotsman

1. The argument that the Suez Canal had become 'the strongest link in the chain which bound India to Britain' is forcefully put by K. M. Panikker in *India and the Indian Ocean*.

2. This is probably an over-estimate, although Arab slave exports from East Africa may have reached 30,000 a year in the 1870s. In that decade the slaves in Zanzibar numbered more than 180,000, out of a population of little more than 200,000: 'A Quantitative Assessment of the Arab Slave Trade of East Africa', by Esmond B. Martin and T. C. I. Ryan in *Kenya Historical Review*, vol. 5 (Nairobi, 1977).

3. As a young man Barghash had a large growth on his scrotum. This may have

been operated upon, to good effect, in Bombay or London.

4. 'The lives of Kirk and Barghash were intertwined for sixteen years. Kirk was the bulwark of Barghash's authority and the means of weakening it' – John S. Galbraith in *Mackinnon and East Africa, 1878–1895*.

5. On the implications for Zanzibar: 'Kirk and the Egyptian Invasion of East Africa in 1875 – a Reassessment', by E. R. Turton (*JAH*, vol. XI, 1970).

6. The character and motives of Leopold would be better understood by the start of the twentieth century, especially through the efforts of Edmund Morel. The evidence is assembled in Neal Ascherson's *The King Incorporated: Leopold the Second in the Age of Trusts* (London, 1963).

7. An expedition led by the missionary J. B. Thomson was welcomed by Mirambo in 1878. Henry Stanley had urged the London Missionary Society to settle in Urambo.

8. Mathews would in due course be knighted by Britain and given the rank of general. A biography, *An Apostle of Empire* is by Robert Lyne (London, 1936).

9. Previously, some of Mackinnon's steamers had been profitably employed in transporting supplies to the Red Sea for the British expedition to overthrow the Ethiopian emperor Theodore in 1868. This may have encouraged him to see the possibilities in Africa.

10. Kirk-Waller, 17 October 1878 (Waller Papers, Rhodes House, Oxford).

CHAPTER 52 Imperialism Abhors a Vacuum

1. As early as 1870, the Italians had gained control of the Red Sea port of Assab.

2. See 'Nyunga-ya-Mawe and the "Empire of the Rugu-Rugas" ', by A. Shorter (*JAH*, vol. IX, 1968).

3. The heart of Mirambo's empire is depopulated today because of sleeping sickness, but remains of his capital was still discernible in the bush in the 1960s: Sutton (op. cit.).

4. Kirk was directly to blame for the failure to pre-empt Peters. In July 1884 the British traveller, H. H. Johnston, had written from the Kilimanjaro area: 'Here is a land eminently suited for European colonization . . .' He warned that if Britain did not take it the French or Germans would. The foreign secretary, Lord Granville, wanted the sultan to extend his borders inland to protect the area. As Johnston left, Peters arrived. See 'Clement Hill's Memorandum and the British interest in East Africa', by Muriel Chamberlain (*English Historical Review*, vol. 87, 1972).

5. A succinct account of the German initiative in East Africa is by Helmuth Stoecker in *German Imperialism in Africa*. For a wider perspective, Thomas Pakenham's monumental *The Scramble for Africa* (London, 1991).

6. Emily Ruete's own explanation of her visit was that she wanted to claim inheritance money which Barghash refused to hand over. She disliked Barghash, and warned her readers against him, claiming that in his heart he had 'never hated anything so much as the mere name of Europeans' (*Memoirs of an Arabian Princess*).

7. Tippu Tip had met so many Europeans in the interior in the previous year that he must have sensed that events were slipping from Barghash's control. However, even after he returned to the mainland Barghash wrote to him repeatedly with appeals to hold on to his territory.

CHAPTER 53 Bismarck and the *Gesellschaft*

1. To salve moral doubts about the occupation of the continent Africans had to be temporarily 'de-humanised'. As one aspect of this process they were denied credit for building Great Zimbabwe or making the Benin treasures seized by the British in West Africa. See *Reinventing Africa* by Annie E. Coombes (New Haven, 1994).

2. Stanley describes his meeting with the ailing sultan in vol. I of *In Darkest Africa*.

3. A portrait of Abushiri and a resumé of his campaign is in vol. 7 of the Unesco *General History of Africa*. The fullest account of resistance to German occupation is by John Iliffe in *A Modern History of Tanganyika* (Cambridge, 1979).

4. The last days of Abushiri, with a picture of him just before he was hanged, are in 'The Capture and Death of the Rebel Leader Bushiri' by Dr A. Becker, trans. Iris Davies (*Tanganyika Notes and Records*, no. 60, 1964).

5. Nyamwezi resistance finally ended in 1894, the year after Isike's death (Stoecker in *German Imperialism in Africa*). But in Roland Oliver's *The African Experience* the extent of black resistance is questioned: 'Conquest was, in fact, but one aspect of a slow process of infiltration, much of which was completely bloodless.'

CHAPTER 54 Africa Hears the Maxims of Faith and War

1. Holmwood was a tireless advocate of British settlement in East Africa: in 1879 he had urged the Manchester chamber of commerce to take advantage of the opportunities there. In 1884 he had supported Johnston's call for occupation of the Kilimanjaro region. In 1886 he succeeded Kirk as consul in Zanzibar, but was removed after a year because of his anti-German opinions, which had angered Bismarck; he was then sent to report on the 'capabilities of the British zone' (FO 84/122 in PRO, London).

2. The most comprehensive account of Lugard's career is Margery Perham's *Lugard: the Years of Adventure, 1858–1898*. An African viewpoint is found in *A Political History of Uganda* by S. R. Karugire (Nairobi, 1980).

3. Baker's letter is dated 22 June 1890 (National Library of Scotland, ms 17931).

4. Kenneth Igham's colonial-era version of Lugard's actions in *The Making of Modern Uganda* (London, 1958) contrasts with Pakenham's sharper assessment in *The Scramble for Africa*, published in 1991.

5. *Ruanda-Urundi* by W. R. Louis examines the origins of the two ill-starred colonies which at independence became Rwanda and Burundi.

6. Although the losses from fever, accidents and man-eating lions were considerable in the building of the Uganda Railway, these did not compare with the human cost of the Congo-Ocean line to the Atlantic. In 1890–92, there were 900 deaths while laying only nine kilometres – one life for every ten metres: Joseph Ki Zerbo in *Présence Africaine*, no. 11, 1957).

CHAPTER 55 From Sultan's Island to Settlers' Highlands

1. Efforts to control the coast of the 'British zone' were complicated by the existence of Germany's short-lived Witu protectorate south of Lamu. This was abandoned in 1890, but in 1893 the consul in Zanzibar, Rennell Rodd, led a 250-strong punitive force to reclaim the area for the sultan from a renegade chieftain. Later, the British found themselves caught up in a guerrilla war with forces led by the Mazrui, descendants of the erstwhile rules of Mombasa. See *Children of Ham* by Fred Morton (Boulder, Colorado, 1990).

2. This was a well-informed forecast. In September the estates of 12 wealthy Arabs were expropriated.

3. Such disproportionate casualties were usual in colonial conflicts. More than a thousand Ndebele were killed for the loss of five white men in one battle in 1893 during the occupation of Rhodesia.

4. The early years of colonial rule are assessed by John Lonsdale and Tiyambe Zeleza in *A Modern History of Kenya*, ed. W. R. Ochieng (London, 1989).

5. An estimated 75,000 people died during the Maji-Maji rebellion of 1905–7 in Tanganyika.

6. Meinertzhagen's *Kenya Diary* (London, 1983) has a preface by Elspeth Huxley beginning: 'It would be useless to pretend that this is a pleasing book or that its author emerges from it as a sympathetic character.'

7. Boer farmers also settled in the White Highlands from 1905. All but a handful

returned to South Africa before independence in 1963.

EPILOGUE

1. Robeson's meeting with Kenyatta during the filming of *Sanders of the River* (on location in a re-created Congolese village in Shepperton studios, England) is described in *Paul Robeson* by Martin Bauml Duberman (New York, 1989). Kenyatta would never speak about his part in the film.

2. After an attempt was made to assassinate the Italian viceroy, Marshal Graziani, 37,000 Ethiopians were massacred in Addis Ababa in February 1937.

3. See *The Great Uhuru Railway* by Richard Hall and Hugh Peyman (London, 1976).

4. The dilemmas facing Africa in its relationship with the rest of the world are examined in *The Rise and Fall of Development Theory* by Colin Leys (London, 1996).

GENERAL INDEX

INDEX OF PERSONAL NAMES

Landscape & Memory

Simon Schama

'This is one of the most intelligent, original, stimulating, self-indulgent, perverse and irresistibly enjoyable books that I have ever had the delight of reviewing...' PHILIP ZIEGLER, *Daily Telegraph*

Landscape & Memory is a history book unlike any other. In a series of exhilarating journeys through space and time, it examines our relationship with the landscape around us – rivers, mountains, forests – the impact each of them has had on our culture and imaginations, and the way in which we, in turn, have shaped them to answer our needs. Schama does not make his argument by any conventional historical method. Instead he builds it up by a series of almost poetic stories and impressions, which cumulatively have the effect of a great novel. The forest primeval, the river of life, the sacred mount – at the end of *Landscape & Memory* we understand where these ideas have come from, why they are so compelling, what they meant to our forebears, and how they still lie all around us if only we know how to look.

'Schama long ago established himself as one of the most learned, original and provocative historians in the English-speaking world... *Landscape & Memory* is that rarest of commodities in our cultural marketplace, a work of genuine originality.'

ANTHONY GRAFTON, *New Republic*

This is a *tour de force* of vivid historical writing... It is astoundingly learned, and yet the learning is offered with verve, humour and an unflagging sense of delight.'

MICHAEL IGNATIEFF, *Independent on Sunday*

'Schama's intensely visual prose is the product of a historical imagination which is not restrained by conventional academic inhibitions...It is his ability (and willingness) to write this sort of narrative prose that makes Simon Schama the obvious modern successor to Macaulay' KEITH THOMAS, *New York Review of Books*

ISBN: 0 00 686348 5
Price: £16.99

Anthony Storr

Music and the Mind

'Anyone who feels like reflecting about the origins, the impact and the significance of music will find Dr Storr's book helpful and stimulating.'
Alfred Brendel

In this challenging book, Anthony Storr, one of Britain's leading psychiatrists, explores why music, the most mysterious and intangible of all forms of art, has such a powerful effect on our minds and bodies. He believes that music today is a deeply significant experience for a greater number of people than ever before, and argues that the patterns of music give structure and coherence to our feelings and emotions. It is because music possesses this capacity to restore our sense of personal wholeness – in a culture which requires us to separate rational thought from feelings – that many people find it so life-enhancing that it justifies existence.

'This beautifully written book, humane, intelligent and thoughtful, is a significant contribution to our understanding of those mysterious movements of the mind.' Adam Lively, *Times Educational Supplement*

'It is a stimulating inquiry aimed at discovering what it is about music that so profoundly moves so many people, in the course of which he describes the physical effects of mescaline, considers the relation of bird-song, the burbling of babies and the language of literature to music, and touches on many other fascinating topics, concluding that its most significant aspect for us is its power to create order out of chaos.' Frances Partridge, *Spectator*

'Reading Storr's work is always like being taken on a journey through a foreign country by a great enthusiast. It doesn't matter if you don't know the language because he teaches you what you need to know along the way. His knowledge is vast and his enthusiasm infectious . . . Storr is an extraordinarily gifted communicator.'
Mary Loudon, *New Statesman & Society*

ISBN 0 00 686186 5

The New Emperors

Mao and Deng: A Dual Biography

Harrison E. Salisbury

'A fascinating story . . . enlivened by personal anecdotes and packed with splendid reports of the two "New Emperors" that will make addictive reading not only for diplomats, scholars and their colleagues, but also for businessmen and tourists.'

CLARE HOLLINGWORTH, *Daily Telegraph*

Harrison Salisbury's knowledge of China and its leaders – based on twenty years of study and first-hand research – has produced an epic narrative history of the new Communist dynasty. As he surveys the convulsive events that shaped modern China – the Nationalist-Communist civil war, the Communist takeover, the mass famine following the Great Leap Forward, the Cultural Revolution – Salisbury focuses on Mao and Deng and their complex relationship.

How Deng won Mao's favour by building Mao's secret Third Line, a gigantic industrial redoubt whose crippling cost was in inverse proportion to its ultimate strategic value, and rose to power; how he was ousted and persecuted by Mao during the Cultural Revolution; how he was recalled by Mao and then toppled by Mao's wife; and how General Ye Jianying plotted to overthrow the Gang of Four and install Deng as the 'new emperor' – all are sketched in dramatic detail.

'A stunningly detailed account of two enigmatic figures'

Financial Times

ISBN: 0 586 21864 5

Younghusband

The Last Great Imperial Adventurer

Patrick French

'The soldier, mystic and explorer Francis Younghusband, who fulfilled the romantic dreams of the late British Empire, was once as legendary a figure as Marco Polo or Lawrence of Arabia. He lives again most vividly and entertainingly in Patrick French's remarkable book. Deftly interweaving his own research adventures with his subject's exploits, he ingeniously brings immediacy and historical perspective to his narrative. From its endearing Introduction to its revelatory Epilogue, this is a story full of excitement and insight, humour and curiosity'
Michael Holroyd

'Breathtakingly accomplished . . . Ranks as one of this year's most thrilling biographies'   Jonathan Keates, *Observer*

'I cannot begin to do justice to the skill and the fun of this happy work . . . *Younghusband* is a glorious biography, frank, and always interesting . . . They don't come much more enjoyable than this'   Jan Morris, *Independent*

'This is a wonderful book: beautifully written, wise, balanced, fair, funny and above all extremely original . . . In his strange and riveting tale of Younghusband's metamorphosis, Patrick French has made an altogether brilliant debut, and it seems highly unlikely that a more amusing or more innovative biography will be written this decade'
William Dalrymple, *Spectator*

'A brilliant and sensitive portrait of one of the foremost players of the Great Game. A remarkable achievement' Peter Hopkirk

`This truly is a brilliant book, and brilliantly funny as well'
John Keegan, *Daily Telegraph*

ISBN 0 00 637601 0

The Civilization of Europe in the Renaissance

John Hale

Winner of 1993 *Time-Life* Silver Pen Award

The Civilization of Europe in the Renaissance is the most ambitious achievement of Britain's leading Renaissance historian. John Hale has painted on a grand canvas an enthralling portrait of Europe and its civilization at a moment when 'Europe' first became an entity in the minds of its inhabitants. The book does not simply survey 'high' culture but with an astonishing range and subtlety of learning builds up a gigantic picture of the age, enlivened by a multiplicity of themes, people and ideas. It contains memorable descriptions of painting, sculpture, poetry, architecture and music; but Hale is not simply concerned with the arts: he examines the dramatic changes during the period in religion, politics, economics and global discoveries. At a time when we are thinking more and more about what 'Europe' and European culture mean, this is a book which shows us more than any other where we can find the roots of both of them, and how much the present and future can be illuminated by the past.

'A superb evocation of the Europe of "the long sixteenth century", wonderfully fresh and rich in its copious illustrative detail, full of innumerable incidental delights. [The book] takes its place as the summation of John Hale's career as a historian, and as the crowning achievement of a master-designer whose richly fabricated works have given so much pleasure.'   J. H. Elliott

'This study deserves to stand alongside Braudel's classic account of the Mediterranean in the time of Philip II. Hale is as generous as he is knowledgeable; his life's work has culminated in a meticulous masterpiece.'   Frederic Raphael, *Sunday Times*

'This is a magnificent book which fills a long-standing gap. It is the product of a lifetime's scholarship by someone with a quite irrepressible curiosity and prodigious breadth of reading . . . together with the enviable gift of writing clearly and beautifully.'
A. V. Antonvics, *Times Educational Supplement*

ISBN 0 00 686175 X